Dorothy Simpson worked first as a French teacher and then for many years as a marriage guidance counsellor, before turning to writing full time. She is married with three children and lives near Maidstone in Kent, the background to the Thanet novels. *Last Seen Alive*, the fifth in the series, won the Crime Writers' Association's Silver Dagger Award in 1985.

'Simpson can disinter the past with the best of them, and her portrait of a small community is matchless' *The Times*

Dorothy Simpson is a contemporary Agatha Christie, renowned for weaving murder mysteries round credible characters in very English settings' *Annabel*

'Thrillers that are both well written and crisply plotted do not come along every day, so a Dorothy Simpson novel is a welcome and engrossing treat' *The Lady*

'All the traditional home comforts of English village murder, with a final twist' *Observer*

'The creation of that most likeable policeman, Detective Inspector Luke Thanet, and his sidekick, Mike Lineham, was a stroke of genius' *Yorkshire Post*

DOROTHY SIMPSON

THE SECOND INSPECTOR THANET OMNIBUS

CLOSE HER EYES
LAST SEEN ALIVE
DEAD ON ARRIVAL

WARNER BOOKS

A *Warner* Book

This edition first published in Great Britain in 1995 by Warner Books
Reprinted 1996

Second Inspector Thanet Omnibus copyright © 1995 Dorothy Simpson

Previously published separately:
Close Her Eyes first published in Great Britain in 1984 by Michael Joseph Ltd
Published in 1986 by Sphere Books
Reprinted 1987, 1988, 1989, 1991
Published in 1994 by Warner Books
Copyright © 1984 Dorothy Simpson
Last Seen Alive first published in Great Britain in 1985 by Michael Joseph Ltd
Published in 1986 by Sphere Books
Reprinted 1987 (twice), 1988, 1989, 1990 (twice), 1991
Published in 1993 by Warner Books
Reprinted 1994, 1995
Copyright © 1985 Dorothy Simpson
Dead on Arrival first published in Great Britain in 1986 by Michael Joseph Ltd
Published in 1987 by Sphere Books
Reprinted 1988, 1990, 1991
Reprinted by Warner Books 1992, 1994
Copyright © 1984 Dorothy Simpson

A CIP catalogue record for this book
is available from the British Library.

ISBN 0 7515 1396 2

Printed in England by Clays Ltd, St Ives plc

UK companies, institutions and other organisations wishing
to make bulk purchases of this or any other book
published by Little, Brown should contact their local
bookshop or the special sales department at the address below.
Tel 0171 911 8000. Fax 0171 911 8100.

Warner Books
A Division of
Little, Brown and Company (UK)
Brettenham House
Lancaster Place
London WC2E 7EN

CLOSE HER EYES

To Anne

Stone walls do not a prison make
Nor iron bars a cage
                    Richard Lovelace
                    1618–58

1

The news that a young girl is missing is likely to penetrate the armour of the most hard-bitten policeman, and Thanet was anything but that. The telephone receiver was suddenly slippery in his hand.

'How old?'

'Fifteen.'

'And how long missing?'

'Since Friday morning.' Lineham's voice was heavy with pessimism.

'Friday morning! But that's nearly three days ago! What the hell were the parents thinking of, not to have reported it till now?'

'It's a bit complicated, sir. The father says ...'

'Save it. I'll be in as soon as I can.'

Thanet glanced down at his stained knees, grubby shorts and grimy hands. He would have to make time for a quick shower. Taking the stairs two at a time he wondered why he was bothering to hurry. If the parents hadn't reported the disappearance for three days ...

There could be a good reason, of course. They could have believed her to be spending the holiday weekend with a friend. She might even have gone off of her own free will. Fifteen was an especially vulnerable age, a peak time for traumatic rows at home ... Nevertheless he was showered and dressed in less than ten minutes, slowing his pace only to peep in at Bridget and Ben, sound asleep with the bedclothes thrown back against the stifling warmth of one of the hottest Spring Bank Holiday Mondays on record.

Over the weekend all England had sweated and sweltered in the unseasonable heat. Motorists had taken to the road in

9

record numbers, the sea exerting on them a magnetic pull which they were powerless to resist. As temperature and humidity soared hundreds of thousands of families had fretted and fumed away their precious holiday hours in traffic jams, trapped in their little metal boxes.

Thanet had had more sense. He and his mother-in-law had decided to pack the children into the car and spend the half-term holiday at her cottage in the country, trying to restore the garden to some sort of order. It wasn't the way Thanet would have chosen to spend one of his rare long weekends off, but he had felt that it was the least he could do. For the last two years, while Joan had been away at college completing her training as a Probation Officer, Mrs Bolton had been looking after the children and running the house for Thanet. Very few women, he felt, would have been prepared to give up home and freedom as she had, and he still felt grateful to her for the sacrifice. In just under three weeks Joan would be home for good, thank God, and it was time to start thinking of ways to help his mother-in-law to take up the reins of her own life again. The cottage was only ten miles away from Sturrenden, the busy country town in Kent where Thanet lived and worked, and after the weekend Mrs Bolton and the children could stay on for the remainder of the week's holiday while Thanet drove in daily to the office. But now it looked as though his time off was about to be curtailed.

He hurried out to the tiny, brick-paved terrace behind the house where the mingled scents of lilac and orange blossom, overlaid by the pungent odour of broom, hung heavy in the gathering dusk. Not a leaf stirred. The air was as suffocatingly hot and humid as if the entire garden were encased in a plastic dome.

Margaret Bolton was sitting limply in a deck chair, eyes closed, empty glass dangling from one hand. In repose she looked almost young again, the lines around eyes and mouth smoothed away, the fading light kind to the grey in the fair, curly hair so like her daughter's. For a fleeting moment it almost seemed to Thanet that he was looking at Joan herself twenty years hence, and briefly the sense of mortality ever-present in his working life spilled over into his private world, laying a cold hand upon his heart. He experienced a sudden and intense longing for Joan's warm, living presence. Then Mrs Bolton opened her eyes, blinked at the transformation in his appearance, and normality was re-established.

'Work?'

'I'm afraid so.'

She made to rise. 'I'll make you a sandwich.'

'No.' Gently, he pushed her back. 'I'll pick up something later. I'm not hungry anyway, it's too hot. Let me get you another drink before I go.'

'I don't want one, thank you. Honestly.' She smiled ruefully. 'I hope you're not too tired to feel fit for work.'

'Not at all. It's been a pleasant change, to do something physical.' And it was true, he didn't feel in the least bit tired, despite the nagging ache in that troublesome back of his. A quarter of an hour ago he'd felt as exhausted as his mother-in-law now looked, but the adrenalin coursing through his veins since Lineham's call had miraculously restored him. He was impatient to be gone.

In a few moments he was on his way, winding along through country lanes adrift with the white froth of Queen Anne's lace and heady with the sweet, green scent of early summer. Already he had relinquished the tranquillity of the cottage, the sleeping children, and was keyed up to meet the challenge ahead.

Detective Sergeant Lineham was waiting for him in the reception area and hurried forward to give him a précis of the facts.

Thanet listened intently. 'Where is he?'

'In interview room three. PC Dennison is with him.'

'What did you say his name was?'

'Pritchard.'

As they entered the room Thanet experienced a fleeting reaction of surprise at the embarrassment on the young constable's face before understanding the reason for it: Mr Pritchard was kneeling on the floor, elbows on the seat of one of the chairs, forehead resting on clenched hands.

11

He was praying.

Thanet and Lineham exchanged a quick glance of uncomfortable astonishment. Never, in all his years in the force, could Thanet remember such a situation arising before. No wonder PC Dennison had been nonplussed. Dismissing the constable with a smile and a nod Thanet advanced into the room.

Clearly, Pritchard hadn't heard them arrive. The intensity of his concentration was such that it seemed to emanate from him in waves, etching upon Thanet's mind a black and white image of near-photographic clarity: dark suit, shiny across the seat, with black mourning band stitched around one sleeve; white shirt, black hair divided by the white line of a centre parting so straight that it might have been drawn by a ruler.

Thanet hesitated. It seemed almost blasphemous to trespass upon such pious concentration. Then, telling himself that even at this late stage further delay could be a threat to the girl's safety, he laid one hand gently on Pritchard's shoulder and softly spoke his name.

Pritchard's eyelids snapped open in shock and he twisted his head to look up at Thanet. His eyes were very dark, almost as black as his hair and full of an agonised resignation. Slowly, he stood up, unfolding his long, thin body with the jerky, unco-ordinated movements of a marionette.

Thanet found himself apologising. 'Sorry to disturb you, Mr Pritchard, but we have to talk.' He introduced himself.

Pritchard hesitated. 'I've been wondering if I was too precipitate. Perhaps I shouldn't have come.'

Thanet frowned. 'What do you mean?'

'I've been thinking it over. I'm afraid I panicked. I should have had more faith.'

'Faith?'

'We are all in God's hands, Inspector. And we have to trust in Him. I can't really believe that He would have let anything bad happen to Charity ... I'm sorry to have wasted your time.' He gave a curious little half-bow and began to move towards the door.

Thanet couldn't believe what he was hearing. 'Mr Pritchard. Please ... Wait a moment.'

Pritchard paused and, with one hand on the door-knob, half-turned, eyebrows raised in polite enquiry.

Thanet moved a little closer to him. 'Let me make sure I understand you. You mean, you don't want us to make any attempt to find your daughter?'

'That's right.'

'Perhaps you've realised where she must be?'

Pritchard shook his head. 'No. But I do believe that wherever she is, she must be safe in God's care.'

It was incredible. The man really was prepared to let the matter rest there. Some might find such faith moving; Thanet, well-versed in man's inhumanity to man, thought it foolhardy to the point of insanity. Deliberately, he kept his voice low, his tone reasonable. 'Then don't you think it might be sensible to try to find her? Let's just sit down for a moment and discuss the matter.'

'There's nothing to discuss. I told you, God is sure to be watching over her.'

He was opening the door now and with a flash of combined inspiration and desperation Thanet said softly, 'Even God has to work sometimes through a human agency, Mr Pritchard. Are you perhaps in danger of overlooking the possibility that He might have sent you here, to us?'

Pritchard hesitated. The dark eyes clouded and then bored into Thanet's as if trying to test the validity of his suggestion.

Thanet waited. The little room was stifling and he was conscious of the prick of sweat down his back and under his armpits.

Pritchard closed his eyes and remained motionless. A minute passed, then two. Thanet and Lineham exchanged anxious glances. Outside in the corridor there was a brief buzz of conversation, then a door closed, cutting it off. As if this were a signal, Pritchard relaxed a little, sighed, opened his eyes.

'You could be right, I suppose.' But still he hesitated a moment longer before moving back to the table. 'Very well,' he said. And sat down.

Relieved, Thanet slipped off his jacket and hung it over the back of his chair before seating himself. He glanced

13

at Lineham. The sergeant was ready. Careful now, Thanet told himself. This one will have to be handled with kid gloves.

'Sergeant Lineham here has given me the facts, very briefly, but I'd be grateful if you could go over them again for me in a little more detail.' Then, as Pritchard hesitated, 'As I understand it, your daughter was supposed to be spending the weekend in Dorset, with a friend.'

'Yes. They were going to one of the Jerusalem Holiday Homes. They were supposed to leave on Friday morning and get back tonight. They've been there before together, at Easter, and it all went off very smoothly, so there was no reason to think it wouldn't this time.'

'Let's take it a step at a time. What time did Charity leave the house on Friday morning?'

'About nine thirty, according to my wife. I was at work by then, of course.'

Little by little the tangled tale was unravelled. Charity and her friend Veronica Hodges had planned to go to Dorset by train, catching the ten twenty-three to Victoria. Charity was to call at Veronica's house to pick her up on the way to the station. She found, however, that Veronica was unfit to travel, having woken up that morning with a high temperature.

'Didn't Mrs Hodges try to contact you, to let you know Veronica wouldn't be able to go?'

'Neither of us is on the phone.'

'I see. Go on.'

According to Mrs Hodges, Charity had taken the disappointment calmly and after spending a few minutes with her friend, had left. Knowing that the Pritchards would never have allowed Charity to travel alone and that the Holiday Home in any case insisted that girls under eighteen should travel in pairs, Mrs Hodges had assumed that Charity had returned home.

'But she didn't?'

'Not as far as we know.' Pritchard took an immaculately folded clean white handkerchief from his pocket and mopped at the sheen of sweat on his forehead.

14

'Why don't you take your jacket off, Mr Pritchard? It's like an oven in here.'

Pritchard shook his head, a sharp, involuntary movement, as if the idea offended him.

As well it might, Thanet thought. The man was so stiff, unbending, that it was difficult to imagine him ever relaxing in shirt sleeves.

Pritchard put the handkerchief back into his pocket.

'Soon after I got to work that morning, at about half past nine, I suppose, I had a phone call from my wife's sister in Birmingham. My mother-in-law had had a severe heart attack during the night and her condition was critical. I spoke to my employer and he told me to take the rest of the day off.'

Pritchard, who worked as storeman in a wholesale stationery firm, had gone home to break the news of her mother's illness to his wife. By the time they had packed and given their next-door neighbour the Birmingham address where they could be contacted in case of emergency, it was too late for them to catch the same London train as the girls and they decided to leave a note on the kitchen table for Charity, in case she arrived back before they did. She had her own key and would be able to let herself in. They had expected that one or both of them would be back in time for her return this evening, but after lingering on over the weekend the old lady had died this morning and, wanting to stay on for the funeral, Mr Pritchard had rung the Holiday Home to inform Charity of her grandmother's death and to suggest that she stay at Veronica's house for a day or two, until her parents returned home.

It had been a shock to learn that neither Charity nor Veronica had turned up, Mrs Hodges having rung the Home from a phone-box on Friday morning to tell the Principal of Veronica's illness.

'Was your daughter mentioned?'

'Only in passing, apparently. It was taken for granted that she wouldn't be going. As I said, they're very strict about girls travelling in pairs. When you book, the parents have to sign a form, saying they won't allow their daughters to travel alone. Mrs Hodges rang them quite early in the morning, and at that

15

point even my wife and I didn't know we were going to be called away.'

'Didn't you think to let Mrs Hodges know, when you decided to go to Birmingham to see your mother-in-law?'

Pritchard dropped his face into his hands, and groaned. 'If only I had. Looking back now, it was irresponsible — wickedly irresponsible, not to have been in touch with her before leaving. But it was all such a rush — so much to do, so many things to think of ... We did leave a note next door, of course, I told you ... And then we knew that Mrs Hodges was here in Sturrenden in case of emergency ... But you're right, of course you are. We should have thought ...'

'Or if Mrs Hodges had let you know that Veronica was ill ...'

Pritchard's shoulders stiffened. 'That's right.' He raised his head and stared at Thanet, eyes glittering. 'She should have, shouldn't she? If she had, Charity would simply have come with us, and we wouldn't be in this position now.'

Thanet was sorry he'd made the suggestion. Wanting to alleviate Pritchard's sense of guilt by showing him that the responsibility had not been his alone, he had merely succeeded in giving the man a grievance which could distract him from the task in hand.

'We mustn't digress,' he said firmly. 'Can we go back to this morning, and your phone call to the Home, from Birmingham? When the Principal told you that neither of the girls had been able to go because of Veronica's illness, what did you think had happened to Charity?'

'I assumed she'd gone home and found our note. We thought that, knowing how worried her mother would be about her grandmother, she'd hesitated to add to the burden by telling her that the holiday arrangements had fallen through.'

'So at that stage you weren't really too worried?'

'Well, we were very upset to think she'd been alone in the house all over the weekend, of course. She is only fifteen, after all ...'

'So what did you decide to do?'

'As there was no way of getting in touch with Charity, we thought I'd better come straight home and go up to Birmingham for the day on Friday, for the funeral.'

'You didn't think of contacting Charity through us?'

'Through you?' Pritchard looked at Thanet as though he had suggested communicating through a creature from an alien planet.

'Well, we do often help members of the public out, in that sort of situation.'

Pritchard shook his head. 'It would never have occurred to me.'

'So you came back to Sturrenden and went home, expecting to find Charity there.'

'Yes.' Pritchard wiped his forehead again, then transferred the handkerchief from his right hand to his left and began to pluck agitatedly at one corner with long, bony fingers. No doubt he was reliving the shock he had experienced upon finding the house empty.

'Was there any sign that she had been there at any time over the weekend?'

'No. The house was exactly as we'd left it, so far as I could see.'

'No indication that she'd eaten, drunk anything?'

Pritchard put his hand up to his head, began to massage one temple. 'No ... I don't know ... I didn't think to look in the larder.'

'Or in the fridge?'

'We haven't got a refrigerator.' Then, wearily, as if explaining something he had attempted to explain many times before, 'We of the Children live very simply, Inspector, in a way which you would no doubt find incomprehensible.'

'The Children?'

'The Children of Jerusalem.' Even now, in the midst of his anxiety over his daughter, the dark eyes suddenly burned with religious fervour. 'The true Church of God. We believe ...'

From what Thanet had seen of the man he guessed that once Pritchard was side-tracked on to the question of religion he would be as difficult to stop as a runaway steamroller. Quickly,

17

he intervened. 'I see.' He remembered what Lineham had told him. 'So that was when you decided to go and see if she'd spent the weekend with the Hodges?'

Pritchard blinked. It was as if a switch had been clicked off in his head and there was a pause before he said, 'Yes.'

'You said just now that before Charity left the Hodges' on Friday morning she spent a few minutes alone with Veronica. Did she give Veronica any hint of what she was going to do now that their holiday was cancelled?'

'I don't think she could have, or Mrs Hodges would have mentioned it. In any case, at that point Charity didn't know that we were going to be away. Otherwise she'd have told Mrs Hodges, I'm sure, and Mrs Hodges would probably have suggested she stay there for the weekend.'

'You didn't actually speak to Veronica herself?'

'No.'

'And then?'

'I came here. I told you, I panicked.'

'Understandably, I think.'

Pritchard frowned. 'As I said, we must trust in God at all times, Inspector. I have to believe that He is watching over her.'

Despite his words Pritchard gave Thanet a beseeching look and Thanet sensed his desperate need for reassurance. But what reassurance could he possibly give?

'Can you think of any other friends with whom Charity might have spent the weekend?'

'She didn't have any other friends.'

Thanet bit back the questions which rushed into his mind concerning the girl's classmates, clubs, leisure activities. Time for all that later, when it was certain that they were necessary.

Pritchard dropped his head into his hands and groaned. 'I just can't think where she might be.'

Thanet stood up and Pritchard raised his head as the chair scraped the floor. His face was bone-white, the skin stretched taut, his eyes tormented.

'What are you going to do, Inspector?'

'First we'll go to your house, to check that she really hasn't

18

been back at all over the weekend. Then we'll go and talk to Veronica. After that, well, we'll see.'

As they ushered Pritchard down the stairs and into the car Thanet fervently hoped that after that they wouldn't be launching into a full-scale murder hunt.

2

It took them only ten minutes or so to reach Town Road, where the Pritchards lived; had it not been for the one-way system they could have done it in five. Sturrenden lies deep in the Kent countryside. It is a busy market town of some 45,000 inhabitants, the centre of a complex web of country lanes and scattered villages. The new traffic system has alleviated day-time congestion of the town centre, but older inhabitants still find it infuriating. Thanet's attitude was ambivalent: the policeman in him appreciated its benefits but the private citizen resented having to take twice as long to reach his destination, especially on occasions like tonight, when the streets were deserted and he was in a hurry.

Town Road was a long, narrow street of yellow-brick Victorian terraced houses with square-bayed windows upstairs and down. Cars were tightly packed along the kerbs on both sides of the road and Lineham was forced to park some little distance away from number 32.

All along the street light spilled into narrow front gardens from uncurtained windows, but the Pritchards' house was in darkness and Thanet and Lineham had to wait for a few moments while Pritchard fumbled with his keys. They followed him into a narrow passage and he switched on the light, an unshaded low-wattage bulb whose sickly glare revealed worn linoleum and bare walls.

'You take upstairs,' Thanet murmured, and Lineham obediently moved towards the staircase at the far end of the passage.

Thanet asked to see the kitchen first and looked around him with disbelief. How many kitchens like this still existed? he asked himself. It was as though he had stepped back fifty years.

Mrs Pritchard still cooked at an old kitchen range. The fire was out and there was a reek of stale soot. A battered aluminium kettle stood on the hob above the side oven. There was a shallow stone sink with a single tap, an upturned white enamelled bowl inverted on the wooden draining board, a narow wooden table, its top bleached ivory with much scrubbing and a storage cupboard beside it, painted brown. There was a rag rug on the floor in front of the hearth and a wooden armchair into which Pritchard subsided with a groan.

'Go ahead, Inspector. Do whatever it is you want to do.'

It certainly didn't look as though Charity had been back here, Thanet thought as he checked. The sink, the bowl, the dishcloth and tea-towels were bone-dry, the cast-iron range stone-cold. The larder was as spotlessly clean as the kitchen, despite the faint, sour smell of stale cheese. There was no bread, no butter, no milk. They had taken all three with them, said Pritchard, when they left for Birmingham. Thanet guessed that it would have seemed sinful to throw good food away.

Pritchard seemed to have sunk into a kind of stupor and Thanet went alone to take a quick look at the front room. People's homes, Thanet believed, were highly revealing. A man's sitting room is an expression of his personality — his choice of colour and patterns, his furniture, his *objets d'art*, his books, his records, all are evidence not only of his tastes but of his attitudes and habits.

What he saw here appalled him. Apart from a three-piece suite upholstered in slippery brown rexine and a heavy upright piano standing against one wall, the room was bare of furniture. The only ornament was a wooden clock placed dead in the centre of the mantelpiece, the only concession to comfort a small beige rug in front of the empty Victorian basket grate, the only wall decoration a religious text in a narrow black frame. *Thou, God, Seest Me,* it proclaimed in curly black letters on a white ground.

Thanet shivered. It was as if he had been vouchsafed a glimpse of the poverty of Pritchard's soul, of the barren rigidity of his outlook. What could Charity be like, he wondered, raised in an atmosphere such as this. Yet there was a piano. He crossed to glance at the neat stack of sheet music on top. *The Associated Board of the Royal Schools of Music*, he read. *Grade VII (Advanced)*. So Charity at least had music to enrich her bleak existence.

He heard Lineham coming down the stairs and went out into the hall to meet him.

'Anything up there?'

'Nothing. No sign of a suitcase in her room. Everything neat and tidy.' Lineham grimaced. 'The whole place gives me the creeps.'

'I know what you mean. What about the bathroom?'

Lineham raised a quizzical eyebrow. 'What bathroom?'

'No bathroom ... Can't say I'm surprised, after what I've seen down here.'

'Nothing downstairs either?'

'No trace of her. We'd better get over to the Hodges'. I'll just have a word with Pritchard first.'

In the kitchen Pritchard was just as Thanet had left him, motionless in the armchair, hands on knees, head bowed, staring at the floor.

'We're just going over to see Mrs Hodges now, Mr Pritchard, and then we'll come back here. Are you all right?'

Pritchard raised dazed eyes and Thanet could see the effort the man made to concentrate on what Thanet was saying.

'Are you all right?' Thanet repeated.

'Yes. Yes, I'm fine, thank you.'

'I'd like you to stay here in case Charity comes home while we're gone. But there's something I want you to do, while you're waiting.'

'Yes?' A spark of interest, now.

'I'd like you to write down the names of all the people with whom Charity could conceivably have spent the weekend. Family, friends, acquaintances, school friends, church members, anyone at all who is even a remote possibility. Could you do that?'

Pritchard pressed thumb and forefinger into his eyes. 'Yes. Of course.'

22

'Have you pencil and paper?' Thanet wanted Pritchard launched on the task before they left.

'Pencil and paper,' Pritchard repeated, looking vaguely around. 'Let me see.' He heaved himself out of the chair. 'Yes. In the table drawer. Here we are.'

They left him to it.

'Doesn't look too bright, does it, sir?' said Lineham when they were in the car.

Thanet shrugged. The interview with Pritchard had alleviated some of his earlier anxiety. 'We can't tell, yet. It's quite possible that after finding out that Veronica couldn't go to Dorset with her, Charity went home, found the note, thought I'm not spending the weekend in this dump by myself — and who could blame her? — and decided to throw herself on the mercy of one of her school friends.'

'Why not go back to the Hodges' and ask if she could stay there?'

'I don't know. Perhaps she didn't like to ask, if Veronica was ill. Anyway, the point is, if she did spend the weekend with a friend, she wouldn't have felt it necessary to come back until this evening because she knew that her parents wouldn't be expecting her until then anyway. So she might well yet turn up safe and sound.'

'True.'

They slowed down to allow an ambulance to overtake them.

'How's Louise?' said Thanet, his memory jogged.

Lineham's wife was soon due to produce their first child.

'Oh, fine, thanks. The heat's getting her down at the moment, of course, and she'll be glad now when it's all over.'

'How much longer is it?'

Lineham sighed. 'Another four weeks.'

Thanet grinned. 'Cheer up, Mike. The first time's the worst. After that it gets easier every time.'

'Some consolation at this stage!' Lineham swung the steering wheel. 'Ah, here we are. Lantern Street.'

More terraced cottages, but smaller and older this time, many of them boarded up or in disrepair. It looked as though

23

the landlord had decided that the site was worth more than the rents.

Number 8, however, presented a brave face to the world. Groups of scarlet tulips glowed like clustered rubies in the dusk and the brass door-knocker shone with much polishing.

The woman who answered the door was short and plump, with fluffy fair hair.

'Mrs Hodges?' Thanet introduced himself. 'It's about Charity Pritchard.'

'Oh? What's the matter? What's wrong?'

'I thought you knew. She seems to have disappeared. Mr Pritchard told me he'd been here earlier this evening, that you hadn't seen her since Friday morning.'

'Oh yes, but she's been here herself since then. In fact, she only left about a quarter of an hour ago. She should be home any minute.'

'I see. Did she say where she'd been?'

'Staying with a friend, she said. I told her her dad had been round and she looked a bit upset — well she would, wouldn't she? I expect she'll be for it when she gets home.'

Had he imagined that there had been a hint of satisfaction in her voice?

'So,' said Lineham as they returned to the car. 'You were right. All a storm in a teacup.'

'Looks like it.'

'All that hassle for nothing,' Lineham grumbled.

'Let's just be thankful that it's turned out the way it has.'

They drove back to Town Street in silence.

Pritchard opened the door to their knock almost at once, as if he had been waiting in the hall and stood back wordlessly for them to enter. In the wan light his face was the colour of old parchment. Clearly, Charity wasn't home yet.

'It's all right, Mr Pritchard,' Thanet said gently, touching him reassuringly on the arm. 'Charity is safe.'

'She's all right?' Pritchard closed his eyes, swayed slightly and put one hand against the wall for support. 'I thought ... I was afraid ...'

'I know.' Thanet took him by the elbow and eased him along

24

the passage into the kitchen, sat him down in the wooden armchair. 'But it's all right. No harm has come to her. She'll be home any minute now.'

'God be praised.' Pritchard hunched forward, dropping his head into his hands.

'Mrs Hodges said that Charity called in this evening on her way home. She'd spent the weekend with a friend, apparently. We only missed her by fifteen minutes or so. I don't know how long it takes to walk from the Hodges' house, but she really should be here at any moment.'

Pritchard said nothing, did not look up, but Thanet could tell that he was listening. His body was tense, his breathing stilled.

'Would you like us to wait until she gets here?' Thanet offered. It wasn't really necessary for him to do so but by now he was rather curious about the girl. And they shouldn't have to wait long.

For a minute or two Pritchard did not respond. The silence stretched out and Thanet glanced at Lineham, who responded by raising his eyebrows and shrugging. Thanet was even beginning to wonder if Pritchard was so exhausted by the nervous strain of the last few hours that he had dropped off to sleep. Then the man stirred and slowly straightened up, sat back in the chair.

'Thank you,' he said. 'I'd be grateful if you would.' His lips barely moved, as if even the effort of talking was too much for him and he had scarcely finished speaking before he closed his eyes and, head lolling back against the chair rail, dozed off.

With one accord Thanet and Lineham quietly left the room and went into the sitting room. It was the first time Lineham had been in here and as he looked around Thanet could see mirrored in his face the same incredulity which Thanet had felt at his first sight of the kitchen.

'My God,' said Lineham. 'Talk about Cosy Corner!'

'Shh.' Thanet made sure the door was closed. 'Not exactly a home from home, I agree.'

They both sat down in the hard, slippery armchairs.

25

'How can they stand it?' said Lineham. 'The bedrooms are the same, you know — lumpy flock mattresses which look as though they came out of the Ark, rusty bedsprings, bare lino on the floor ... I just can't understand people being prepared to live like this.'

'Perhaps they can't afford to do otherwise?'

'Oh come on, sir! It's not just lack of money I'm talking about, and you know it. It's the sheer drabness of it all. Just look at it! Anyone can buy a tin of emulsion paint and brighten things up if he wants to.'

'Then obviously, the Pritchards don't want to. This, incredible as it may seem to us, must be how they like it.'

'Like it!' Lineham's face was a study in disbelief.

'From what we've seen of Pritchard, I'd guess it's a question of religious principle. He probably thinks comfort is sinful, an indulgence of the flesh.'

'Is that what they're like, these Children of Jerusalem?'

'I don't really know. I'm only judging by some of the things he's said, and by this place.'

'They meet in that hall in Jubilee Road, don't they? The one with the green corrugated iron roof?'

'That's right.'

'They can't exactly be thriving. The place looks as though it's about to fall down.'

'They may be going downhill now, but at one time they were a force to be reckoned with in Sturrenden, I believe.'

'How long have they been around?'

Thanet wrinkled his forehead. 'I'm not sure exactly. But quite a time. I think I once heard, since the middle of the nineteenth century.'

'As long as that! And presumably they're not just a local group, if they still have these holiday homes.'

'Quite.' Thanet shifted restlessly, aware that beneath the apparently innocuous surface of this brief conversation there had been a growing undercurrent of unease. He noticed Lineham glance surreptitiously at his watch.

'Mike, are you thinking what I'm thinking?'

'It's twenty past ten,' said Lineham flatly.

26

'And she left the Hodges' at about nine thirty-five.'
'Three-quarters of an hour.'
'For a twenty-minute walk.'
They looked at each other.
'I don't believe it,' said Thanet. 'Not with two policemen sitting in her own front room, waiting for her.'
'We're clucking like a pair of mother hens,' agreed Lineham.
'Suffering, no doubt, from residual anxiety.'
They rose in unison.

The brief rest did not appear to have done Pritchard any good. His pallid forehead glistened with sweat in the dim light and his eyes were fixed, staring. The bones of his knuckles shone white through the skin where he gripped the arms of the chair. When he saw Thanet and Lineham he moistened his lips with the tip of his tongue. 'You said she was all right.' he said, in a near-whisper. And then, with a suddenness that made them both start, he erupted from the chair. 'If she's all right,' he bellowed, raising clenched fists, 'where is she? You tell me that!'

It was an effort of will not to flinch from that archetypal figure of despairing wrath.

'We were about to ask you, Mr Pritchard,' Thanet said calmly, 'if there was anywhere she might have stopped off, on the way home.'

The reasonableness of the question and Thanet's matter-of-fact tone punctured Pritchard's fear and anger and he seemed to deflate back to normal size. He shook his head in bewilderment. 'I don't know.'

'Which way would she have come?'

Pritchard frowned, his eyes unfocused. He shook his head as if to clear it, put one hand up to his temple. 'Let me see ... She'd have turned right out of Mrs Hodges', then left at the end of Lantern Street into Victoria Road. Then, if she had any sense, she'd have gone to the end of Victoria Road, turned left into St Peter's Street and left again into Town Road.'

Thus describing a wide semi-circle, Thanet thought. 'You said, "If she had any sense ..." '

Pritchard swallowed, as if to control rising nausea. 'Half

way along Victoria Road there's a short cut. A footpath.'

A footpath. The word conjured up darkness, a narrow, confined space where shadows lurked at every corner. At this juncture the very word had a dangerous ring to it.

'Where does it come out?'

'Just along the road from here, about fifty yards away. But surely she wouldn't have ... Not at night ... in the dark ...' Fear had dried Pritchard's throat and tightened his vocal cords. His voice was little more than a gasp, a whisper.

Unless she'd been in a hurry, Thanet thought, anxious to get home quickly and minimise her father's anger and anxiety. Of course, the opposite could be true. She might have opted for delaying tactics. He repeated his earlier question.

'I suppose she could have called in at my brother's,' said Pritchard, his voice stronger now. 'He and his wife live in Gate Street. There's another footpath linking Gate Street and the short cut we were talking about. But I really can't see why she'd have gone there instead of coming straight home.'

'What number in Gate Street, sir?' asked Lineham.

'Fourteen.'

'And your brother's full name?'

'Jethro Pritchard.'

Lineham took it down.

'Could you tell us what Charity looks like?' said Thanet.

'Looks like ...' Pritchard repeated. Once again he shook his head as if to clear it, passed his hand across his eyes as if brushing cobwebs away. 'She's ... not very big. Comes up to here.' He laid his hand on his chest. 'She's got brown hair, light brown. Long. Wears it tied back. Brown eyes ...' Pritchard's lips worked and his face threatened disintegration.

'All right, sir, that's enough, I think.' It would have to do, Thanet thought. With Pritchard in his present state too much time would be wasted trying to obtain either a more detailed description or a photograph. And time might be of the essence. The beat of urgency was back in his brain now, surging through his veins and tingling down into his legs, his feet. He shifted restlessly. 'Sergeant Lineham and I will just stroll along and ... meet her. We shouldn't be ...'

28

'I'm coming too,' Pritchard interrupted. 'I can't sit about here doing nothing a minute longer.'

Thanet didn't like this idea one little bit. The man looked dangerously near to cracking up, and if anything had happened to Charity ...

'Wouldn't it be better for you to wait here, in case she comes home while we're gone?'

'No! I'll leave the lights on and the front door ajar if you like, to show I won't be long.'

Thanet looked at him and empathy raised its inconvenient head. How would he himself feel if Bridget were missing in circumstances like these? He would be frantic to be up and about doing something, anything, to find her.

'As you wish. Let's go, then, shall we?'

3

Outside it was now marginally cooler and the air, though still humid, smelt clean and fresh after the stale, almost foetid atmosphere of number 32. The street was deserted. Lineham fetched torches from the car and they set off in the direction of the entrance to the footpath.

After a few moments Pritchard stopped. 'Here it is.'

A narrow slit, barely three feet wide, flanked on either side by the blank side walls of two blocks of terraced houses. Dim light from a street lamp illuminated the first few yards. After that, darkness.

Thanet had already made up his mind. He dared not risk Pritchard stumbling across Charity's body alone. One of them would have to stay with him.

'Sergeant, you go the long way round with Mr Pritchard. I'll cut through the footpath and wait for you at the far end.'

Thanet half-expected a protest from Pritchard, but there was none. Perhaps he was by now incapable of further rebellion. He moved off obediently beside Lineham and Thanet switched on his torch and plunged into the black, yawning mouth of the alley.

Once past the houses the darkness thinned a little. The footpath now seemed to run between back gardens, and the six foot high close-boarded fence on either side was punctuated by wooden doors and gateways beyond some of which loomed the bulk of garden sheds of varying shapes and sizes. Thanet's footsteps beat out an irregular tattoo as he paused to check each entrance. Some were padlocked, others were not and if there was access he opened the gate as quietly as possible and shone his torch inside. The detritus of years seemed to have washed down the gardens and come to rest here. Wheel-less, rusting bicycle frames vied for space with broken toys, rotting card-board boxes, unrecognisable pieces of machinery, neglected tools and legless chairs. It was impossible to search thoroughly at present, he had neither time nor justification and he forced himself to keep moving on, dissatisfied.

And all the while there was growing in him a sick certainty of what he was going to find, the apprehension that this time he would have no opportunity privately to prepare himself for the one moment in his work as a detective that he dreaded more than any other, his first sight of a corpse. He had never fully managed to analyse that split second of unbearable poignancy, compounded as it was of regret, compassion, sorrow, anger, despair and a sense of having brushed, however briefly, against the mystery of life itself and he had never talked about it, even to Joan, from whom he had no other secrets. For years he had fought against this weakness, had despised himself because of it until he had eventually come to realise that to do so was pointless, that this was one battle he would never win. And so he had in the end become resigned, had even managed to persuade himself that that one moment of private hell was necessary to him, the springboard from which he could launch himself whole-heartedly into an attempt to track down the murderer.

If Charity was dead . . . if he were to find her. . . . His stomach clenched and, praying that she had chosen to go the long way around and was even now safely in the company of Lineham and her father, he softly opened yet another door and played his torch over the mounds of junk, his fearful imagination at once transforming a broken mop into a battered head, a discarded rubber glove into a severed hand . . .

Enough, he told himself severely. You're letting this get out of hand. Determined to keep his thoughts firmly under control he shut the door, turned away and began to walk more briskly.

After only a few steps his foot made contact with something that went skittering away across the path and hit the opposite wall. He focused his torch, advanced upon it frowning and bent to examine it.

It was a hairbrush.

31

He did not touch it, but quickly flashed his torch around it in ever-widening arcs. The immediate vicinity was clear but as the light probed the tunnel of darkness ahead the beam picked out a scattering of lightish splotches some ten to fifteen yards away.

Slowly, carefully, he advanced, the certainty of what he was going to find churning his stomach.

And yes, there she was.

With one comprehensive sweep of his torch Thanet took in the whole scene: the gaping suitcase in the middle of the path, a jumble of clothes spilling out of one corner; more clothes, strewn haphazardly about and, the focal point of it all, the crumpled body of the girl, lying at the foot of a door in the left-hand wall of the alley.

Thanet hurried forward, noting with relief that her clothing seemed undisturbed. Perhaps she had at least been spared the terror of a sexual assault — could even still be alive. He squatted down beside her and shone the light on her face. The brief flare of hope was at once extinguished. That blank, frozen stare left no room for doubt and the jagged gash on her right temple looked lethal. But, to be certain, he checked. There was no whisper of breath, not even the faintest flutter of a pulse. This, he was sure, was Charity. He looked at the rounded, still childish contours of brow and cheek and closed his eyes as the familiar pain swept through him. For a few seconds he remained motionless, abandoning himself to the protesting clamour in his head in the way that a patient resigns himself to the screaming whine of the dentist's drill. Then, jerkily, he stood up.

Now she was a case for Doc Mallard.

The thought reminded him of Lineham and the girl's father, waiting for him at the end of the footpath, and at once he realised his predicament. He dared not leave the body and risk someone else stumbling upon her. But if he didn't, Lineham and Pritchard would most surely become impatient and return along the footpath to meet him. And to think of Pritchard seeing his daughter lying there like that ...

If only some passer-by would come along the alley it might

be possible to despatch him with a message to Lineham, but on this Bank Holiday evening everyone seemed to be immersed in his chosen form of entertainment. Thanet hadn't seen a soul since leaving Pritchard's house. He glanced at his watch. A quarter to eleven. The pubs would soon be out. It was vital to get the footpath sealed before then. So, what to do?

His dilemma was resolved by the sound of footsteps, approaching from the far end of the alleyway. He listened carefully: yes, two pairs. Lineham and Pritchard? If so, he must warn Mike in time ...

He waited tensely until the bobbing disc of light that was probably Lineham's torch had become visible around a bend in the path some fifty yards ahead and then he called softly, 'Mike?'

There was a low answering cry and the footsteps accelerated.

Thanet switched off his own torch, hoping that Lineham would take the hint.

'Mike?' he repeated urgently, advancing to meet them. 'Wait. Stay there. Switch off your torch.'

But it was too late.

Involuntarily, Lineham had flashed his torch ahead, briefly illuminating the body of the girl and with a hoarse cry Pritchard rushed forward, shoving Thanet aside. Thanet staggered and put out a hand to hold him back and Lineham reached out, but the man's frantic impetus had already carried him to where the girl lay and before they could stop him he had fallen to his knees and with a cry of anguish had gathered her up into his arms.

Lineham made as if to pull him away but Thanet restrained him. 'Leave it, Mike. The damage is already done.'

Both men were painfully aware that forensic evidence might well have been destroyed before their eyes.

'Sorry, sir,' Lineham's voice was thick with guilt. 'I should have thought ... I shouldn't have flashed that bloody torch.'

Pritchard was weeping now, harsh, strangled gasps, his arms wrapped tightly around Charity's body.

Thanet turned to Lineham. 'Go back to the car, get things

organised as fast as you can. Stress the urgency, the pubs'll be out in a matter of minutes. I'll wait here, with him.'

Lineham nodded and was gone, his receeding footsteps soon no more than a hollow, echoing blur.

Pritchard slowly quietened down, the storm of tears gradually diminishing to irregular, sobbing breaths at ever-lengthening intervals.

Lineham was soon back.

'Everything's laid on, sir,' he whispered.

'Doc Mallard?'

'Available.'

'Good. I'd like you to get Pritchard away now, then. Fast. Stay with him till I come.' Thanet knew that it would be only a matter of minutes before the first reinforcements arrived. He stepped forward, laid a gentle hand on Pritchard's shoulder.

The man stiffened, turned his head to look up.

'I'm sorry, Mr Pritchard. Deeply sorry. But you must leave her, now.'

Pritchard gave his daughter one last, lingering look, then laid her gently down and stood up, staggering a little. Thanet steadied him with a hand under one elbow.

'Sergeant Lineham will take you home.'

Pritchard turned away without a word.

Thanet waited until they were out of sight then flashed his torch once more over the girl's body. Her sightless stare seemed to him a mute reproach, a silent protest against a life cut short.

He promised himself that the moment the photographers had finished with her he would close her eyes.

4

The bald patch on top of Doc Mallard's head gleamed in the light from the arc lamps as he knelt to examine Charity's body.

It was half past eleven and the secrets of this section of the alley were now laid bare, the harsh, merciless light probing into every crack and crevice. The last three-quarters of an hour had been packed with furious activity: the footpath had been sealed and a team of men despatched to inform the householders whose gardens backed on to it that it was temporarily out of bounds; photographs, sketches and preliminary searches had been made; Charity's pathetic belongings gathered up and borne away and various samples assembled in polythene bags by the Scenes-of-Crime Officer.

Now it was the turn of the police surgeon.

Thanet was leaning against the fence, patiently awaiting Mallard's verdict and jealously guarding a potentially vital piece of evidence. He knew better than to ask importunate questions. Ever since, some years ago, Mallard had lost his adored wife, he seemed to have lived in a state of imperfectly suppressed irritation. Thanet, who was fond of the older man and had known him since childhood, sympathised with Mallard's inability to come to terms with his grief and was tolerant of his testiness.

'Poor little beast,' murmured Mallard at last, sitting back on his heels.

Thanet waited.

'Well,' said the little doctor, heaving himself to his feet and dusting himself down, 'for what it's worth, and with the usual reservations, of course, I'd say she's been dead for between one and two hours.'

'That fits. In fact, we can narrow it down further. She was last seen alive at about 9.35 and I found her at 10.40.'

Mallard looked gratified. 'Hah! Thought you'd catch me out, did you?'

'Didn't work, though, did it?'

They grinned at each other.

'You found her yourself, you say?'

Thanet grimaced. 'Yes.' He told Mallard how this had come about. 'Can you commit yourself as to the cause of death?'

Mallard frowned at Thanet over his half-moon spectacles. 'You know I don't like committing myself at this stage.'

'We both know that,' said Thanet equably, mentally castigating himself for his careless choice of words. 'All the same, I'd appreciate ...'

'A signed statement, no less!' Mallard relented. 'Oh, all right then, if I must. You've probably worked it out for yourself anyway. I'd say it was that blow to the right temple. I'd look for something fairly sharp and jagged, possibly metal.'

'This, for example?' Thanet pointed to his bit of potential evidence, the rusted iron latch of the door at the foot of which Charity was lying. The projecting piece of metal which must be lifted to release such latches had been partially broken off and its jagged point glistened.

Mallard peered at it. 'Highly probable, I should think. Right height, too, I should say.'

'That's what I thought.' Thanet saw it all in his mind's eye: Charity walking along the dark footpath, suitcase in hand, the menacing figure of her assailant (lying in wait for her? Walking towards her? Running after her? Or even most hideous of all, accompanying her, in the guise of a friend?) He attacks her, Charity swings the suitcase at him but it bursts open, leaving her completely vulnerable; during the course of the ensuing struggle she is hurled against the door, striking her head against that wicked-looking metal spike ... Thanet sighed. The Super wasn't easily going to forgive him for allowing Pritchard to interfere with the forensic evidence.

'What did you say the father's name was?'

'Pritchard.'

'Pritchard,' repeated Mallard thoughtfully. 'Pritchard, Pritchard. Rings a bell. Can't think why, though.'

Thanet waited, but Mallard shook his head with finality. 'It's no good, I can't remember. Perhaps it'll come back to me. Anyway, her pants and sanitary towel — she was menstruating — seem undisturbed, and there's no sign of violence, so it doesn't look as though she was raped. Might be some comfort to the parents, I suppose. She was fifteen, you said?'

'Yes.'

'I'm surprised. I'd have said she was younger, even though she was physically mature. They'll be reaching puberty before they're out of their cradles soon, the way things are going.'

'She does look younger,' said Thanet thoughtfully. 'I wonder what it is ...'

Death, perhaps, he thought grimly, but no, it was more than that. The way she had done her hair, then, scraped back into a thick pigtail?

No, it was her clothes, of course. He didn't know much about young girls' fashions but Bridget had become very clothes-conscious of late and he now realised that Charity's clothes were dowdy in the extreme, strongly reminiscent of school uniform: dark skirt, plain white blouse buttoned up to the neck, plain dark cardigan, white ankle socks and Clarks' traditional-style school sandals. All in all, very odd clothing for a fifteen-year-old to be wearing on holiday these days, when cheap and pretty clothes are the rule rather than the exception. No doubt it was the religious influence. And from what he'd seen of the Pritchard household he would guess that there would be little sympathy for a desire to buy anything frivolous.

Once again he wondered what she had been like, this young girl whose future was now reduced to a dissecting table. Had she been content, satisfied to live within the limitations imposed upon her by her parents' religion? Or had she yearned for laughter, joy and beauty?

Thanet clenched his teeth. However much or however little potential Charity had possessed, she had had a right to live to fulfil it. As he stood looking down at her he could feel the determination stiffening the sinews of his body, filling him with a sense of purpose and an urgency that made him itch now to be gone, to get on with his work, take the first steps towards bringing her killer to justice.

Doc Mallard picked up his bag. 'I'll be getting along, then.'

'I'll come with you.' Thanet turned and nodded to the men who had been patiently waiting for Doc Mallard to finish. 'You can take her away now.'

As he and Mallard approached the canvas screen which had been erected across the entrance to the footpath Thanet heard a familiar sound, the hum of an expectant crowd.

'The ghouls are out in force, by the sound of it,' murmured Mallard.

Thanet scowled, grunted agreement.

The noise increased as he and the doctor came into view. The crowd was enjoying this unexpected Bank Holiday late-night entertainment. The uniformed branch had done their best, stretching tapes across the road to right and left, carefully ensuring that the Pritchards' house was included in the empty section of the street, but even so Town Road was a very different place from the quiet thoroughfare Thanet had left a couple of hours previously.

Supressing a familiar anger at the public's relish of a tragedy, Thanet escorted Doc Mallard to his car, told the ambulance driver to back right up to the footpath entrance, then dealt briefly but courteously with the reporter from the *Kent Messenger* who had been awaiting his appearance, thankful that it was as yet too early for the national press to have arrived on the scene. His relationship with the media was good and he never made the mistake of under-estimating the value of the help they could give him or of the damage they could do if the police were deliberately obstructive, even though the thought of achieving personal publicity through another human being's violent end had always nauseated him.

Then he made his way swiftly to number 32.

Lineham came along the ill-lit passage to meet him as the uniformed constable on duty at the front door let him in.

'How is he?'

38

Lineham pulled a face. 'Pretty distraught, I'd say. But I'm only guessing. He hasn't said much.'

'Doctor been?'

'Refuses to have one. Against his principles, apparently.'

Briefly, Thanet regretted having let Mallard go, but realised at once that it would have been pointless to detain him. There was a deep stubbornness in Pritchard, an inflexibility which, even in these circumstances, would prevent him from abandoning his principles.

'Have you found someone to stay with him tonight?'

'I suggested his brother, but he said no, he didn't want anyone. He was going to spend the night in the company of the Lord. Anyone else would be superfluous.'

'I presume you mean, in prayer.'

'That's right. I told him we'd arrange for someone to break the news to Mrs Pritchard.'

Thanet nodded. An unenviable task, but it had to be done. 'Where is he now?'

'In the kitchen.'

Thanet peeped in. Pritchard was kneeling on the stone floor, elbows resting on the seat of the armchair, head in hands. He did not stir. Thanet withdrew.

'How long has he been like that?'

Lineham shrugged. 'An hour or more, I'd say.'

'You've done a search?'

'Yes. The only thing that looks even remotely promising is a diary. It's in Charity's school satchel, in her bedroom. I left it there, I thought you'd probably want to take a look around yourself.'

'Right. I'll do that now.'

Upstairs there were only two bedrooms and Charity's was the smaller, at the back. Here was the same drabness, the same total lack of interest in physical surroundings as downstairs. The walls were bare and so were the floorboards, save for a postage stamp of a bedside rug. The bed looked supremely uncomfortable and the door of the wardrobe would not stay closed without a small wad of paper to hold it in position. Thanet peered inside. Here hung Charity's school raincoat and blazer, both carefully buttoned up to hold their shape. It was the distinctive navy and yellow striped blazer of Sturrenden Girls' Technical School, Thanet noted. There were two or three skirts in sober colours, a couple of drab floral dresses and three pairs of shoes: black walking shoes, plimsolls, a pair of stout brown brogues. Two long drawers beneath the hanging space revealed underclothes, handkerchieves, carefully folded blouses and sweaters, all utilitarian in the extreme.

There was no bedside table — reading in bed would perhaps be considered self-indulgent? — and the only signs of human occupation were the school satchel Lineham had mentioned hanging on a hook behind the door and, near the window, a small wooden table piled with books. Thanet glanced through these: school textbooks, with only one exception, a black, leather-bound copy of the Bible. On the flyleaf was written *To Charity, on her tenth birthday, from her loving parents. Prov. 3: 5-6.* Thanet flicked through the text, found the place: *Trust in the Lord with all thine heart; and lean not unto thine own understanding. In all thy ways acknowledge him, and he shall direct thy paths.*

Thanet winced.

The diary, it seemed, was his only hope and he plucked it out of the satchel with eager fingers, turned to the Spring Bank Holiday weekend. In Friday's space Charity had written, V. 9.50. The remainder of the weekend was blank. Thanet frowned. Strange that she hadn't noted the visit to Dorset.

He quickly leafed through the first half of the diary, to date. There were two regular entries each week, one on Tuesdays, one on Fridays. He opened the book at random to the third week in February and held it up to the dim central light in an attempt to decipher the pencilled scrawl. Tuesday's entry read: *Close next big hurdle, Gr. 7. Mr. M 'great strides'.* A music lesson, Thanet wondered, remembering the music on the piano downstairs. Friday's entry read: *Grp. v. int. tonight!* A religious group, he'd be willing to bet. Bible study, perhaps? But the exclamation mark surprised him.

So these had been the highlights of her life.

Sad, and not very promising from Thanet's point of view.

They did however prove that Charity had had some outside interests and contacts, apart from school, and that her father's claim that she had no friends other than Veronica might have been exaggerated. Thanet put the diary in his pocket. He would study it at leisure later.

Meanwhile he would have to see if Pritchard were fit to be questioned.

Thanet always hated this business of interrogating people still raw with shock and grief, but it was necessary, indeed essential, to gather together as much personal information as possible about the victim, early in the case.

This house was the still centre of the hurricane of furious activity now raging in connection with Charity's death. This was where she had lived and it was here that her character had been formed. Perhaps it was her very innocence, her ignorance of the sophistications of the modern world that had left her unprepared to cope with one of its evil manifestations when it had come upon her.

In any case, it was Thanet's responsibility and his special skill to try to understand how this had come about, his firm conviction that except in cases of random violence (and this was a possibility he always bore in mind), if he could only come to understand *why* it had happened, the *who* would eventually become apparent.

And for that he would need Pritchard's help.

He checked that there was nothing hidden under the mattress and, remembering one of his earlier cases, that there was no trapdoor in the ceiling, and then took one last, lingering look around the room. As he gazed at Charity's monastic little cell there came unbidden to his mind a brief, vivid image of Bridget's room, of the bulging bookcases, overflowing cupboards, the pretty curtains, fitted carpet and walls crammed with posters, the whole rich, disorganised clutter which fed her imagination and catered to the needs of her expanding mind and personality. Raised in this bleak atmosphere, restricted and hedged about as she surely must have been with a father like Pritchard, what had happened to those hidden aspects of Charity's character? Had they shrivelled up and died? Or,

41

starved of external stimulation, deprived of emotional satisfaction, had they turned in upon themselves, become warped and twisted and in some way led finally to Charity's death in that alley?

He was being fanciful, Thanet told himself as he closed the door softly behind him. She had probably, quite simply, channelled them into her music.

Well, time would tell.

5

When Thanet came down to breakfast next morning there was a note on the kitchen table: *Joan rang. Ask.*

He sat down, gingerly, for his back had stiffened up overnight, and waved the piece of paper at his mother-in-law, who was making toast.

'What time did she ring?'

'Ten fifteen. I told her you probably wouldn't be back till late.'

Thanet frowned. Lately, he and Joan always seemed to miss each other when they phoned and he felt as though he hadn't spoken to her properly in months.

'How did she sound?'

'A bit tired, I thought. Abstracted.'

Thanet knew what Mrs Bolton meant, and he didn't like it. Theoretically there was no reason why Joan should not be relatively free now. She had finished her final placement —in a boys' borstal—some time ago, had handed in her final essay three weeks before. So, why was she so elusive? It would be a relief to have her home again where he could see her, talk to her, touch her, reassure himself of her affection. He'd even begun to wonder, of late, if the distance between them was not merely geographical, if Joan was slipping away from him. Once again he supressed the unbearable thought that she might even have met someone on the course who was proving more interesting to her than a husband whose attraction had been eroded by familiarity. The name of Geoffrey Benson, for instance, was cropping up far too often for Thanet's liking.

'Did she say when she'd ring again?'

'She said that if you were just launching into a new case, it might be easier if you rang her. She hopes to be in all evening.'

43

'Good.' Thanet sipped at his scalding coffee, hoping that it would clear his head a little. It had been after three this morning by the time he'd finally got to bed.

Bridget came skipping into the kitchen, cheeks flushed and eyes shining. She flipped his tie. 'I thought you had one more day off, Daddy.'

He kissed her back. 'So did I, Sprig, but unfortunately it hasn't worked out like that. How's my girl, this morning?'

'Fine, thanks.'

Already, at the age of ten, Bridget was springing up. It was another hot day and in her brief shorts her tanned legs were long and shapely. Thanet looked with a mixture of pride and alarm at the smooth oval of her face, the gleaming fall of spun-gold hair; the policeman in him couldn't help feeling that these days beauty could be a mixed blessing.

'Does that mean we'll all have to go home today?' she asked with a frown.

'Do you want to?' he teased.

'Oh *no*. It's lovely here, isn't it, Ben? There's such lots to do.'

Ben, two years younger, had just hurtled into the kitchen and skidded to a stop beside his father. Already, at seven thirty in the morning, his face was streaked with dirt, his jeans smeared with mud.

'Ben!' His grandmother was outraged. 'What on earth have you been doing with yourself? Go and wash at *once*, do you hear me?'

Ben glanced sideways at his father who, unseen by Mrs Bolton, gave him a consoling pat on the back before nodding. Ben departed, scowling, followed by Bridget. Inwardly, Thanet sympathised with his son. He and Joan had never made a fuss about dirt. Why bother, when it was so easily washed away? Rudeness, destructiveness, bad manners were different. Here, the Thanets had always been firm; spoiled children, they believed, grew up into unlikeable adults.

Mrs Bolton, on the other hand, believed that children should look clean and neat at all times and it was not surprising that Bridget and Ben — particularly Ben — had found it very difficult to adjust to such different expectations.

'But it's only clean dirt, Grandma,' Ben used to protest at first.

'Don't be silly, Ben. How can dirt be clean? I never heard such nonsense. Now, go and wash, at once.'

Thanet, torn between sympathy for Ben and gratitude to his mother-in-law for stepping into Joan's shoes, had forced himself not to intervene. When Ben had complained he'd simply tried to explain that older people find it difficult to change and that as these arrangements were only temporary Ben would just have to grin and bear it.

Over the last few months there seemed to have been an increasing number of such minor conflicts. Patience was wearing thin on both sides as the time of Joan's return grew near.

Thanet finished his coffee and rose. 'Don't keep supper for me, I expect I'll be late.'

Bridget came back into the kitchen. 'I've opened the front gate for you, Daddy.'

'Thanks, poppet.' He kissed her goodbye. 'Where's Ben?'

'In the garden.'

Outside Ben was wobbling away down the sloping drive on Mrs Bolton's ancient sit-up-and-beg bicycle, which was of course much too big for him.

Thanet took in Ben's lack of control, the open gate ahead. Simultaneously he became aware of an ominous sound: out on the road, invisible because of the dense screen of trees and shrubs which fronted the cottage garden, a tractor was approaching.

The next few seconds were a blur. Thanet's shouted warning, Ben's futile attempt to stop, the flash of red as the tractor came into view, the heartstopping moment when the off-side wheel of the tractor slammed into the back wheel of the bicycle and Ben was catapulted over the handlebars ...

Thanet pounded down the drive, fear drying his mouth and thundering in his ears. Ben's crumpled body seemed infinitely far away, as if he were looking at it through the wrong end of a telescope. Then, as he drew nearer, he saw with frantic hope that Ben had landed on the grass verge at the far side of the road.

Just before Thanet reached him, Ben rolled over and stood up.

He was all right.

By that mysterious alchemy peculiar to parents Thanet's anxiety and relief exploded into anger and before he could stop himself he had given Ben a resounding whack on the bottom.

'How many times have I told you *never* to ride down that drive when the gate is open!'

'He came right out under my wheels,' said the tractor driver defensively, raising his voice to make himself heard above Ben's howls.

'I know. I saw. It wasn't your fault.'

Bridget and Mrs Bolton came running down the drive. 'What happened? Is Ben all right?'

Explanations and recriminations were soon over. Ben was sent to his room for an hour as punishment and before long Thanet was on his way, shaken but thankful. When he thought how it could have ended ...

In the office, mounds of reports awaited him. Lineham was already hard at work, sifting through them.

'Anything interesting?'

'Not so far. Reports from neighbours verify Pritchard's story. The house was deserted from the time they all left on Friday morning until Pritchard arrived back last night. They're not very popular, it seems.'

'Actively disliked?'

'Pritchard is. No, I suppose that's not strictly true. Perhaps "not liked" would be nearer the mark.'

'And Mrs Pritchard and Charity?'

'Neither has any friends amongst the neighbours. They keep themselves to themselves, don't mix, never take part in local activities. Apparently this is normal, amongst members of their sect.'

'Mmm.' Thanet was busy lighting his first pipe of the day and he waited now until it was drawing properly before saying, 'Well, we'll skim through the rest of these and then get along to Town Road. Let's hope Pritchard is feeling more co-operative this morning.'

Last night it had been impossible to get anything out of the man. In any case, Pritchard had so obviously been in a state of shock that Thanet had been unwilling to press too hard. Adamant in his refusal to see a doctor or to have anyone to keep him company through the night, Pritchard had clung stubbornly to his sole source of comfort. When they left he was still kneeling on the stone floor of the kitchen.

Thanet wondered if he was still there.

'Any news of Mrs Pritchard, Mike?'

'A Sergeant Matthews rang this morning, from Birmingham. Someone went to break the news to her last night. If she was up to it, she was going to travel down early this morning.'

'If. I shouldn't think we could count on it. Imagine what it must be like to lose both mother and daughter on the same day! Is someone coming with her?'

'I don't know. Of course, they're all tied up, up there, with the admin. to do with the death of the old lady.'

The death round, thought Thanet, that infinitely depressing ordeal of the newly bereaved: death certificate, registry office, undertaker. He couldn't see that Mrs Pritchard would be in much of a state to be questioned this morning.

Surprisingly, he was wrong. It was she who answered the door and although her face was puffy and her eyes inflamed with weeping, she was composed.

'Come in, Inspector.'

She was small and slight, her bony features and prominent nose accentuated by the way she wore her light brown hair, dragged back into a neat bun on the nape of her neck. She was wearing a shabby black dress and Thanet smelt mothballs as he and Lineham followed her down the passage and into the front room. The skimpy beige curtains were drawn and in the dim light filtering through them the room looked more depressing than ever.

'I'll fetch my husband.'

Perhaps her presence had had a calming effect upon Pritchard. Although there were traces of fluff adhering to his neck where he had cut himself shaving, he appeared to be more in

47

control of himself this morning. He looked unfamiliar in grey flannel trousers and a knitted cardigan.

Mrs Pritchard glanced nervously from Thanet to her husband. It was obvious from their faces that they were both apprehensive of what he was going to say. Perhaps they thought that he was bringing them news of their daughter's murderer. Thanet only wished he were. He decided to take the initiative.

'Perhaps we could sit down?'

The Pritchards backed away and perched side by side on the edge of the settee. Thanet and Lineham took the armchairs.

'Look, Mrs Pritchard, Mr Pritchard, I'm sorry to trouble you both at a time like this. I really mean that. But I'm afraid we're going to need your help.'

They exchanged a brief, uneasy glance and Pritchard frowned. 'What sort of help?'

'I need information — about your daughter's friends, associates, activities —'

'Activities?' Pritchard's voice was dull, lifeless.

'Meetings, hobbies, clubs ...'

'Clubs?'

Mrs Pritchard shifted restlessly on the settee. Since her husband had joined them she hadn't spoken a single word.

'Mrs Pritchard?' said Thanet.

She glanced at her husband as if for permission to speak. But he did not look at her and she sighed, bowed her head.

'You were about to say something?' Thanet persisted.

'Leave my wife alone, Inspector.' Pritchard's voice was heavy with despair. 'She knows no more than I do. Hasn't she suffered enough?'

'Mr Pritchard,' said Thanet gently, 'I know that she is suffering, that you are both suffering, but don't you see that if Charity's ... if the person who is responsible for Charity's death is to be found, I really do need your help.'

'What's the point? It won't bring her back. Nothing will bring her back ...' Pritchard's eyes filled suddenly with tears and he dashed them angrily away, jumped up and crossed to stand with his back to them at the curtained window.

Thanet was filled with compassion. But pity, emotional involvement, were luxuries he could not afford. He needed this man's co-operation, had to have it if he was to get anywhere. He gave Pritchard a moment or two to recover and then said harshly, 'Are you suggesting, then, that we should do nothing? Allow this man to go free? Perhaps to kill someone else's daughter?'

Mrs Pritchard gave an inarticulate little moan of distress and pressed the knuckles of one hand hard against her mouth as if to prevent any more sounds escaping, and Pritchard swung around to face them. Thanet's severity had had the desired effect and jolted him out of his state of inertia. The black eyes were glittering with anger as he returned to the settee and put a protective arm around his wife's shoulders.

'What sort of a man are you?' he said in a low, furious voice. 'Can't you see — ?'

'No, Nathaniel.' Mrs Pritchard suddenly straightened her shoulders and sat up, laid a placatory hand on her husband's sleeve. 'The Inspector's right, don't you see? We must help him. It would be dreadful if ... I couldn't bear it if ... It's our *duty* to do all we can to make sure this man is caught.'

His wife's unexpected revolt had obviously taken Pritchard by surprise. His eyes widened and his mouth dropped open slightly. For a long moment he stared at her, searchingly. Then, slowly, he nodded. 'Very well. I suppose you're right.'

With Pritchard's capitulation the tension in the room slackened and Thanet heaved an inward sigh of relief. 'Thank you. I'll try to be brief.'

As Thanet had already noted, Charity had been a pupil at Sturrenden Girls' Technical School. Her parents had never received any complaints about either work or behaviour and her end of term reports had always been satisfactory. The one subject in which she excelled had been music.

'She passed all her grades with distinction.' Mrs Pritchard put in shyly. It was the first time she had volunteered any information.

'That's her music on the piano?' Thanet rose and crossed to

glance at it, sensing that Mrs Pritchard might respond to an interest shown in Charity's special gift.

'Yes. She was going to take her Grade Seven at the end of this term.' Mrs Pritchard's mouth began to go out of control and she bit her lower lip, hard.

'God gave her a great talent, Inspector,' said Pritchard. 'And she used it in His service. She used to play the organ for us at Sunday Service.'

'Which day was her music lesson, Mrs Pritchard?'

'On Tuesdays, after school'

So he had been right about the Tuesday entries in the diary. Small consolation, really, for the diary had yielded nothing else of interest. He had spent some time examining it last night, to no avail. 'And was that the only day of the week she used to stay behind after school?'

'Yes.'

'And she travelled?'

'By bicycle.'

'With anyone?'

They both shook their heads. 'No one else from around here goes to the Girls' Tech,' said Pritchard.

'Could you tell me a little about out-of-school hours? What did Charity do in her spare time?'

Pritchard frowned. 'She didn't have any "spare time", as you put it. The Devil always finds work for idle hands, Inspector, and Charity was brought up to use her time properly.'

'Could you tell me what you mean by "properly"? What did she do in the evenings, for example?'

'Do her homework. Help her mother in the house. Practise the piano.'

'She always practised for at least an hour, every day, Inspector, sometimes more,' put in Mrs Pritchard.

'And she never went out in the evenings?'

'Only to Bible class on Fridays,' said Pritchard.

'And where was that held?'

'At our meeting house, in Jubilee Road.'

'Did she go alone?'

50

'In summer, yes. In winter I used to take her. And my brother, her uncle, used to walk home with her.'

'He is a member of your sect?'

'Of course. My family has always belonged, as far back as we can remember.'

'Does he work locally?'

'He's caretaker at Holly Road Primary School.'

'And he attends this Bible Class, presumably?'

'He is the leader. The group is for our younger members. It is essential these days to ensure that young people receive the correct spiritual food. There is so much evil in the world, so much temptation ...'

Pritchard was getting that fanatical light in his eyes again. Quickly, Thanet interrupted him. 'And Saturdays? What did she do on Saturdays?'

Pritchard gave a brief, angry parody of a laugh. 'Well may you ask. She usually spent it with that girl.'

'Veronica?'

'Yes. And look where it got her!'

'What do you mean?'

'It's obvious, surely. If she hadn't been friendly with that girl she wouldn't have been going to Dorset, she would have been safe with us in Birmingham, and none of this would ever have happened.'

'You can't blame Veronica, though, Nathaniel,' said Mrs Pritchard timidly. 'What happened to Charity ... Veronica had nothing to do with that.'

'Nothing to do with it! Nothing to do with it!' His solicitude for his wife apparently forgotten, Pritchard had turned on her with eyes blazing. 'How can you possibly say that? How can you be so *blind*. I told you, didn't I? I warned you. I said that girl would be a bad influence on Charity and I was right!'

'What do you mean, bad influence?' said Thanet.

'In every way! You've only got to look at the girl to see what I mean, with her painted face and skirts halfway up her thighs. Disgusting, that's what she is, disgusting!'

'Are you suggesting, then that she ... ' Thanet didn't know

51

how to put it tactfully. There *was* no way of putting it tactfully.
' ... that she contaminated Charity?'

Pritchard's face seemed to swell and a tide of bright colour ran up his neck and into his cheeks. 'How dare you! How dare you come into my home at a time like this and make insinuations about my daughter! What right have you got, to ...'

'I made no insinuations, Mr Pritchard. You said that Veronica had had a bad influence on Charity, I was merely trying to clarify what you meant.'

'You implied ...'

'I implied nothing. I repeat, I was simply seeking to clarify what you were saying, that's all. Now look, Mr Pritchard, all I'm trying to do is understand what Charity was like. You, as her parents, are best qualified to help me. I know that this must be very hard for you, but please, try to understand that I have no interest in drawing false conclusions. I merely want the truth.'

'You were twisting my words. You were implying ...'

'I repeat, I was implying — *am* implying — nothing. Simply asking for information.'

But it was no good. Pritchard would not be pacified and, cursing himself for his tactless choice of words and, perhaps, for insensitivity for broaching such a predictably sensitive area so soon, Thanet decided to give up for the moment.

Mrs Pritchard accompanied them to the door.

'Inspector,' she whispered as she let them out, glancing back over her shoulder at the sitting room door. 'If I can help, in any way ...' Her eyes filled with tears. 'You will ask, won't you?'

'Of course.' Thanet touched her shoulder and smiled encouragement at her. 'I promise.'

She hesitated and Thanet sensed her reluctance to return to her husband. And who could blame her? he thought as he turned away. And yet ... it took collusion, to establish that kind of relationship. Pritchard's domination could not have been achieved without aquiescence on the part of his wife. Did she enjoy playing the submissive role, Thanet wondered, or had she, over the years, adopted it for the sake of peace?

'Difficult customer,' said Lineham.

'Pritchard? They don't come much more prickly, that's for sure. And I had to put my foot in it, of course.'

'Bound to happen sooner or later, with someone like him. Anyway, it was obvious we weren't going to get anywhere. I shouldn't have thought they've have had much more to tell us.'

'You may be right.' Thanet paused to extract pipe and matches from his pocket.

'So, what now, sir?'

'Time for you to improve your mind, I think. Do a bit of research.' Thanet grinned as he saw Lineham's expression. 'Come on, Mike, you know you quite enjoy ferreting for facts, once you get down to it.'

'So what do I have to do?'

'Go down to the library, see if you can dig anything up on the Children of Jerusalem. They've been around quite a long time, as I told you, so you should be able to glean something.'

'And you, sir?'

'A word with Pritchard's brother, I think. Then with Veronica. I'll see you in the Hay Wain, around one, and we'll swop notes. You can take the car, I won't need it.'

'Right, sir.'

Thanet watched him drive off, then allowed himself an indulgent smile. Naturally Lineham would have preferred to accompany him; interviews were much more interesting than dusty archives. Nevertheless, he had a feeling that this particular piece of research could be important. Lineham would have to put up with the disappointment as best he could.

Thanet turned and walked briskly up the street towards the entrance to the footpath. A quick check, first, on whether a daylight search had turned up anything interesting, then he'd visit Jethro Pritchard.

He was rather looking forward to that.

6

The search was still going on, but as yet nothing of interest had turned up. Thanet stopped for a word here and there and then walked on, past the spot where Charity's body had lain. According to Pritchard there was a footpath which linked Gate Street, where his brother lived, with this one. He found the entrance to it on the right about a hundred yards further on, just beyond the bend around which Lineham and Pritchard had come into view last night. It ran between the side walls of two blocks of gardens and was only about seventy-five yards long. If he had come this way, Charity's assailant could have been well away in a matter of minutes.

The front door of number 14 was flung open with such force that it rebounded from the wall. Square in the opening stood a formidable woman; legs planted apart and arms akimbo she reminded Thanet of a picture of the Genie from Aladdin's lamp in one of Bridget's books of fairytales.

Her expression, however, was anything but benevolent.

'Mrs Pritchard?'

'We are sick and tired of being pestered like this. Persecution, that's what it is, persecution.'

'My name is . . .'

'Whatever you've got to say, I don't want to hear it. Go away, or we'll call the police.'

Thanet fished in his pocket.

She was still in full flood. 'I meant what I said. Scavengers, that's what you are, scavengers. We haven't had a minute's peace since daybreak. And there's no point in waving that thing in my face. Press cards don't cut no ice with me. I said, if you don't go away I'll call the . . .'

'POLICE,' said Thanet, holding his warrant card up in

54

front of her nose. And then, more quietly, 'I *am* the police.'

She snatched the card from him, held it away to peer at it long-sightedly, then sniffed, her mouth twitching sideways.

'Why didn't you say so?' She held the card up, comparing photograph and original. 'Why aren't you wearing uniform, then?'

For a moment Thanet could not believe that she was serious. Was it possible that anyone these days could be unaware of the existence of plain-clothes policemen? But of course, the Jethro Pritchards were also of the Children. Perhaps, if one never watched television or even, for all he knew, read a newspaper or listened to the radio, it was just conceivable ...

'I'm from the CID — the Criminal Investigation Department. We all wear plain clothes.'

She pushed his warrant card at him and reluctantly stepped back.

'I suppose you'd better come in.'

She lingered to scowl up and down the street before closing the door behind them.

'In here.' She opened the door of the front room.

Here was the same drabness, the same musty, unused odour that had characterised the sitting room of the house in Town Road. Thanet was surprised to see that there were two people in it, a middle-aged man and an old woman, and that despite the heat of the day there was a small fire burning in the hearth; in his experience such rooms were kept exclusively for occasional visitors.

The man had risen.

'My husband,' said Mrs Pritchard ungraciously. 'And my mother-in-law.'

Then Thanet understood. The three of them were wearing black. This was the official face of mourning.

What had they been doing before he arrived? he wondered. Presumably, at such a time it was considered unseemly to go about one's daily business as if nothing had happened. Yet there was no reading matter lying about, no radio, no sewing or knitting ... And looking at this ill-assorted trio he simply couldn't visualise them engaged in amiable conversation.

Jethro Pritchard was a small, stooping, sepia version of his brother. They shared the same bony facial structure, but Jethro's hair was brown and thinning, carefully combed in separated strands across his baldness, his manner timid and placatory. After shaking his clammy hand Thanet had consciously to restrain himself from wiping his palm on his trouser leg.

The old lady was sitting close to the fire, her legs swathed in a rug, her shoulders draped in a black, knitted shawl. She did not acknowledge Thanet's greeting, but simply went on gazing at him with faded, rheumy eyes in which there was no flicker of acknowledgement or response.

'You'd better sit down, I suppose.' But Mrs Pritchard remained standing, arms folded. This interview, her posture indicated, was going to be very brief.

Thanet had no intention of being browbeaten and he sat back as comfortably as possible in his armchair's inhospitable embrace and prepared for battle. An imp of mischief urged him to take out his pipe and relight it, but he resisted temptation. No point in arousing unnecessary antagonism, there was enough here already.

But why? That was the interesting question.

Mrs Pritchard was still glowering at him. 'I can't think why you need to bother us again anyway. We've been through it all once already.'

'Were you fond of your niece, Mrs Pritchard?'

The unexpectedness of the question caught her off-balance. She hesitated and, before she could suppress it, some fierce emotion glittered in her eyes. She blinked and it was gone.

'Well ... of course.'

But her initial response had betrayed her. She had disliked Charity, had felt positive hostility towards her. Now why was that? Thanet wondered.

'Then you will naturally wish to co-operate with the police to the fullest possible extent,' he said blandly.

She stared at him for a moment longer, then crossed to sit beside her husband. 'We're all very upset this morning.'

Thanet recognised self-justification when he heard it. Still, he pretended to take it at face value.

'Understandably,' he said.

Jethro Pritchard made a small, choking sound in his throat. His hands were tightly clasped in his lap, his lips clamped together as if he were afraid of what would emerge if he opened them. A thick, worm-like vein across his temple pulsated in a rapid, regular rhythm. He caught Thanet's eye.

'She was like a daughter to us,' he said.

Old Mrs Pritchard suddenly stirred. 'Jethro, what's that man doing here?' Her voice was shrill, querulous.

Jethro looked at his wife as if for guidance and licked his lips. 'He's from the police, mother. Charity's had an ... accident.'

The old woman stared at her son without comprehension.

'You remember Charity, mother? Nathaniel's girl?'

'I don't like it in here,' she said. 'I want to go back in the kitchen.'

Jethro glanced at his wife, who nodded.

'I want to go back in the kitchen,' repeated old Mrs Pritchard. 'I don't like it in here.'

'Would you mind, Inspector?' said Jethro, half-rising. 'I'm afraid once she gets an idea in her head ...'

'Carry on, by all means.'

'Come along then, mother. I'll take you back. Up we come ...'

It took several minutes for Jethro to lever his mother out of her chair, manoeuvre her out of the room and get her settled in the kitchen, all the while keeping up a flow of solicitous encouragement.

'All right then, mother?' Thanet finally heard him say, and a moment later he returned. It was at once apparent that the old lady's dependence had somehow given him strength. He was moving briskly and his facial muscles had relaxed.

Damn, thought Thanet.

'We are particularly interested in tracing Charity's movements last night and over the weekend,' he said, when Jethro was settled again.

57

'Over the weekend?' Mrs Pritchard's eyes stretched wide. 'But we know where she was over the weekend.'

'Oh? Where?'

'In Dorset. With that Veronica Hodges. At one of the Jerusalem Holiday Homes.'

'But that's the point, Mrs Pritchard. She wasn't.'

Pritchard and his wife exchanged a puzzled glance.

'Veronica was ill, and couldn't go to Dorset. Therefore Charity couldn't go, either. Because of the rule about young girls not travelling alone.'

'Quite right, too,' put in Jethro. 'But doesn't Veronica know where Charity was over the weekend?'

'Apparently not.'

'Perhaps she was at home?'

'She wasn't.'

They were both silent, staring at him with identical expressions of blank incomprehension.

'She must have stayed with a friend,' said Mrs Pritchard.

'Do you happen to know the names of any of her friends?' They shook their heads.

Thanet looked at Jethro. 'What about the Bible class?'

'What do you mean?'

For a moment Thanet could have sworn he'd seen a hint of panic there. Had he been mistaken?

'Well, I understand that you lead a Bible class on Friday evenings, and that Charity was a member. Was there anyone in it with whom she was particularly friendly?'

'Only Veronica.'

Thanet was beginning to feel that all roads led to Veronica.

'Are there any boys in the class?'

Jethro said stiffly, 'Two.'

'How old?'

'Ten and eleven.'

'I see.' Much too young to be of interest to a girl of fifteen. 'Did Charity ever speak of a boy friend, to either of you?' He knew it was a pointless question, but it had to be asked.

'Charity didn't have any boy friends.' Mrs Pritchard had sucked her lips in disapprovingly.

'Maybe not in the accepted sense of the word. But did you ever hear her refer to a boy, even in passing?'

More headshaking.

'She knew no young men at all?'

Again, negative — though there had been a flicker of some indefinable emotion in Mrs Pritchard's eyes.

'You're sure?' Thanet pressed.

They were sure.

'We know that Charity left Veronica Hodges' house at around 9.35 last night, and she wasn't found until 10.40. We were wondering if by any chance she called in here on her way home?'

Jethro turned to his wife, eyebrows raised interrogatively.

So, thought Thanet. Jethro had been out last night.

Mrs Pritchard frowned. 'Why should she have wanted to call here?'

Thanet shrugged. 'If she was like a daughter to you ...' It was difficult not to let a hint of sarcasm creep into his voice.

Mrs Pritchard's shoulders twitched impatiently. 'Well, she didn't.'

'You were here?'

'Of course I was here,' she snapped. 'Where else d'you think I'd be at that time of night? Anyway, I can't leave my mother-in-law by herself.'

'I'd have thought an old lady like that would be tucked up in bed pretty early.'

'If you knew anything at all about old people, you'd know they need very little sleep. My mother-in-law may go to bed early, but she's often still awake when we go up. There's always the danger she might start wandering around and fall down the stairs or something.'

'And you were out, I gather, Mr Pritchard?'

'There was a meeting at the school — I'm caretaker at Holly Road Primary.'

'On Bank Holiday Monday?'

Jethro flushed. 'It was a special occasion. They're supposed to be closing the school down, and the parents have been up in arms about it. They've been trying for months to get Peter

59

Hannaway to come and hear their case and in the end he said the only date he could manage was Bank Holiday Monday.'
Peter Hannaway was the local MP. Jethro gave a cynical little jerk of the head. 'Some of the parents thought he only suggested that date because he hoped most of them would be too busy off enjoying themselves to turn up, but if so he was disappointed. The hall was packed.'

'What time did the meeting end?'

Jethro hesitated fractionally. 'About 9.30.'

'And you got home at ...?'

'Quarter past ten,' said Mrs Pritchard, with a long-suffering glance at her husband.

'I didn't get away till after ten,' said Jethro defensively. 'There's always a lot to do after a meeting — tidy up, switch all the lights off, lock up ... And there're always a few people who don't seem to have homes to go to.'

So Jethro had been out and about for part of the relevant time ... Thanet had already familiarised himself with the geography of the area and was aware that at one point, just before Charity entered the footpath, Jethro's route would have touched on hers. 'On your way home, did you see Charity?'

Jethro shook his head vehemently. 'If I had, I'd have told you, wouldn't I?'

That depends, thought Thanet.

'Not even a glimpse in the distance?'

'No! And it was dark by then, remember.'

'And you're both absolutely certain that you can't think of anyone with whom she might have spent the weekend?'

They couldn't. No point in wasting any more time here at present. Thanet left.

All the same, he thought as he set off briskly for Lantern Street, the interview had been interesting, if not particularly informative. Mrs Pritchard's hostility to himself, for example. Was it because she had taken an instant dislike to him? Because that was how she treated everyone? Or — much more interestingly — because she had been on the defensive in this particular situation?

One thing was certain. Whatever Jethro had felt about his

niece, Mrs Pritchard had disliked her intensely. Thanet remembered that hint of satisfaction in Mrs Hodges' voice last night, when she had said that Charity would be in trouble at home after her weekend's absence, and he began to wonder: what was it about the girl, which had provoked dislike? It could be very important to find out. Dislike, magnified over and over, can become hatred, and in hatred may lie the seeds of murder.

Perhaps Veronica would be able to enlighten him.

7

'What a terrible thing, Inspector!' burst out Mrs Hodges as soon as she saw who was on the doorstep. She gestured to him to come in.

'Your constable called to tell me just before I heard it on Radio Medway. Veronica doesn't know yet, she left very early on a trip to Boulogne. She'll be ever so upset, when she hears. I can't bear to think about it. I mean, it must have happened when Charity was on her way home from here ... Oh, do sit down.'

By daylight, Mrs Hodges was revealed as short and plump, her ample curves inadequately corseted into a tight, pink crimplene dress. Her frizzy blonde hair haloed a round, pleasant face, a face which somehow lacked definition, like a jelly which has been poured into one mould and then, when it was almost set, transferred to a different one. She was wearing fluffy pink bedroom slippers and exuded a faint odour of fresh perspiration overlaid with cheap talcum powder.

'Would you like a cup of tea? Or coffee? I was just going to have one, the kettle's already boiled. Oh dear, it seems awful to be talking about cups of tea, when ...'

Thanet smiled. 'That's very kind of you. I'd love a cup of coffee.'

'Won't be a minute.'

One glance at this room had told Thanet that, whatever Veronica's religious convictions, Mrs Hodges did not belong to the Children. The morning sun, streaming through the gap between the frilly net curtains, reflected off the row of brass ornaments on the mantelpiece, gleamed upon the surface of small, highly-polished tables and glowed through vases of coloured glass filled with garish plastic flowers. A vivid print of a Spanish dancer with a rose between her teeth took pride of place above the fireplace.

Thanet looked thoughtfully at Mrs Hodges as she returned with the coffee. Owner and room were strangely at variance. He would have expected the creator of all this exuberance to have a natural gaiety, but now that he looked at her more closely he could see in her face a settled sadness which he felt had nothing to do with the shock of Charity's death.

'Here we are, then,' she said.

She had exchanged the slippers for high-heeled shoes which gave her a jerky, stiff-legged gait reminiscent of the pigeons in Trafalgar Square. Thanet was touched to see that she had taken trouble with the tray. There was a starched linen cloth of dazzling whiteness and a plate of homemade biscuits. He took one.

'Mmm. Delicious,' he said.

She looked gratified. 'Veronica's favourites.'

'She's gone on a day trip to Boulogne, you said?'

'Yes. With some friends from school. Four of them. Of course, as I said, she hadn't heard the news or I don't suppose she'd have gone.'

'What time will she be back?'

'I'm not sure. They're catching the four o'clock boat, that's all I know.'

'Did she happen to mention which friend Charity had been staying with, over the weekend?'

Mrs Hodges shook her head.

'Or where the friend lived?'

'No.'

'I'd very much like a word with her. Would you mind if I came back this evening? You can stay with us while we talk, of course.'

'If you think it'll be any help ...'

'Thank you ... Was Charity supposed to be going on this trip?'

'Oh no. Her father would never have let her. Anyway, I don't suppose she'd have wanted to. She never was one for a crowd.'

'Veronica was her only friend?'

Mrs Hodges shrugged. 'So far as I know. And ...'

'Yes?'

'Well, to be honest, I've never really been able to understand why Veronica took up with her in the first place. Mind, they've known each other for years, ever since they were kids. They went to Dene Road Primary together.'

'But they weren't particularly friendly at that time?'

'No. That wasn't till after....' She shook her head, looked away from him.

'After what?'

She compressed her lips. 'After Veronica's dad died.'

Thanet knew the value of silence. He waited.

Mrs Hodges sighed, shook her head again, sadly. 'I suppose it was all down to me — Veronica taking up with Charity, I mean. When Jim — my husband — was killed in a road accident two years ago ... It was such a shock. I just couldn't take it in. He went off to work one day and ... never came back.'

Lineham's father had died in similar circumstances. Thanet vividly remembered the sergeant speaking of the experience in just these tones.

Mrs Hodges gave Thanet a shame-faced glance and then looked away again, out of the window, eyes glazed with memory. 'It hit me so hard I just went to pieces. And Veronica ... poor kid, she just used to shut herself up in her room, for hours at a time. And I was so busy feeling sorry for myself I just didn't see she needed comforting just as much as I did.'

She fell silent.

'And that was when she became friendly with Charity?'

'Yes.' Mrs Hodges gave a rueful grin. 'And, would you believe it, at the time I was grateful to her for taking Veronica off my back!'

'You mean, you later regretted encouraging the friendship?'

'Did I just!'

'Why?' said Thanet softly.

She looked full at him then, a fierce, assessing stare. He could almost hear her thinking, *Will he use anything I tell him to*

64

hurt Veronica? He held her eyes steadily with what he hoped was benign reassurance and after a moment he saw her shoulders relax as she sat back a little in her chair.

'Because she had far too much influence over Veronica, that's why. You wouldn't believe how much Veronica's changed since she started going around with Charity.'

'In what way?'

'She used to be full of fun, always laughing. But now, well, you're lucky even to get a smile out of her.'

'Adolescents are often moody, I believe.'

'I know that! I'm not just talking about moods, this is *all* the time. Veronica used to have loads of friends, this place used to be full of kids in and out all day long, but now ... today's the first time she's done anything with anybody but Charity for ages, and she took an awful lot of persuading before she said she'd go, I can tell you.' Mrs Hodges was really launched now. 'Then there's that Jubilee Road lot ...'

'The Children of Jerusalem, you mean?'

'That's right. Downright peculiar they are, I can tell you. And once they get hold of you ... I'm not saying anything against religion, mind. I go to church regular myself, at Christmas and Easter, and people are entitled to their own opinions, but that lot ... No telly, no boyfriends, no make-up, no dancing, no pictures, Bible classes once a week and church all day on Sundays ... It's not natural and Veronica's heart wasn't in it, no one can tell me otherwise.'

'Then why did she go along with it, do you think?'

'Beats me. To please Charity, I suppose. And yet ...'

'Yes?'

'Well, you might think this sounds stupid, when they used to spend so much time together, but I never really felt Veronica *liked* Charity.'

'She must have, to a certain extent, surely. They've even been away on holiday together, haven' they?'

'Just a weekend at Easter, to the Jerusalem Holiday place in Dorset. And that's another thing. I didn't think Veronica had enjoyed it that much at Easter but there she was, begging to go again. Went on and on about it till I said yes ...'

'As it turned out, she couldn't go because she was ill. That's right, isn't it?'

'Had a temperature of 103 on Friday morning. I took one look at her and said, "That's it, my girl. You're not going anywhere today and that's that." And d'you know, after all that nagging to allow her to go, I could have sworn she was relieved! I ask you! It's beyond me, I can tell you.'

'She's all right again now, I gather.'

'Yes. I don't know what it was, but by Saturday she was back to normal.'

'How did Charity take it when she found that the holiday was off?'

'Didn't say much. But she wasn't very pleased, I could tell. Well, I could understand that, when she was all packed up and on her way, it was bound to be a disappointment, wasn't it? But there wasn't much she could do about it, was there? And she didn't say a word about her parents going away.'

'She didn't know herself, at that point, that they were going to.'

'Ah. I see. Well anyway, when she did find out she could easily have come back here. I'd willingly have put her up for the weekend.'

'Even though you didn't like her?' said Thanet softly.

'I didn't say that, did I?' She caught Thanet's eye, gave a rueful little smile. 'No, well, I suppose it's pretty obvious. I didn't, and that's the truth.'

'Why not?' Thanet was very gentle. This could be important.

Mrs Hodges wrinkled her nose. 'I feel terrible, talking about her like this, with the poor girl barely cold ...'

'But ...?'

'But I can't help the way I feel, can I?'

'No one can.'

Again, he waited, and once more his patience was rewarded.

Mrs Hodges twisted her hands in her lap and said, 'I don't know why it was, really, I've never tried to put my finger on it before. She was always very quiet, polite, well-behaved ...' She stopped, looked surprised.

66

'You've just remembered something?'

'Yes. I'd forgotten. It was so long ago. When they were quite little — six or seven, perhaps — Charity was forever in hot water at school. I remember now, Veronica was always coming home with tales of what Charity'd been up to. Then, suddenly, it stopped.'

'You don't know why?'

'I never thought to ask, at the time. But now, looking back, it does seem a bit odd. I mean, knowing Charity as she is now — was, I mean — I just can't imagine her as naughty as that. D'you see what I mean?'

'Yes.' Thanet was thoughtful. If true, this was interesting. But there was always the possibility that Veronica had been fantasising. At a certain age naughtiness has a fascination for many children.

'You were trying to explain what it was you didn't like about Charity.'

'Yes ... But it's so difficult to pin down. She just made me feel ... uncomfortable, that's all.'

'How do you mean, exactly?'

But try as he would, Thanet could not get her to be more specific. Finally, there was just one other question he wanted to ask. He should have put it to Charity's parents, but he'd forgotten.

'Just as a matter of interest, if the girls had gone to Dorset as planned, what time would they have got back last night?'

'Same time as Charity got here. They were going to catch the 7.20 from Victoria.'

'I see. Thank you.' Thanet arranged to return at 9 pm to see Veronica.

Lineham was already waiting for him in the car park of the Hay Wain.

'Looks as though it's under new management,' said the sergeant as they walked into the public bar.

'Very nice, too.' The place had been redecorated and recarpeted, but the old high-back oak settles had been retained and none of the atmosphere sacrificed on the altar of modernity.

67

The food looked good, too: homemade soups, pâtés, pies and quiches, interesting salads and even desserts. Thanet chose a wedge of cold game pie packed with a variety of meats, Lineham a slice of tuna and tomato quiche. Both added a baked potato, with butter.

'I'm surprised the place isn't packed out,' said Lineham, chewing appreciatively.

'I expect it soon will be, once the word gets around.'

They had found a corner table where they could talk without fear of being overheard.

'How did you get on, then, Mike?'

Lineham pulled a face. 'All right. Not exactly riveting stuff, though.'

'Well?'

Lineham took out his notebook.

'Children of Jerusalem: started in the mid-nineteenth century by one Jeremiah Jones. According to the books I found, many troubles — unspecified — were sent to test him and at the end of this time of trial he had a vision of God and the Holy City and started the Children of Jerusalem. His mission, and that of the sect after his death, was to carry the flame of Truth and pass it on to each succeeding generation.'

'And the Truth was ...?'

Lineham consulted his notebook. 'That only the Children will go to Heaven, the rest of us will be dragged straight off to the other place; that God is one person, Jesus and Jeremiah Jones his prophets, that ...'

'Wait a minute. They're not Christians, then? They do not accept that Christ was the Son of God?'

'Nope. They believe that the only way to be saved is to repent of one's sins and to strive to obey God according to the laws of the Old Testament. Sickness, according to them, is the penalty for sin. Healing is forgiveness. God is the only physician. And the Devil, Satan, is the chief of evil spirits, the personification of evil.'

'So salvation lies in ...'

'Well, repenting of one's sins, as I said, and then giving a tenth of one's income to the Church. No smoking, drinking, dancing, no cinema or television, no boy friends or sex before marriage, marriage partners to be found only within the sect ... They see life as a continual war against the power of the Devil.'

'Anything else?'

'Worship: a typical Sunday will include a morning service comprised of sermon, hymns, prayer and witness — that's a sort of extempore statement of one's experiences in relation to one's religious beliefs — followed in the afternoon by discussion groups and in the evening by a·confession service, known as The Shriving ... Doesn't leave much scope for people to enjoy themselves, does it! Enough to drive anyone off the rails, I should think, especially the youngsters.'

'Mmm.' Was that what had happened to Charity, Thanet wondered. If so, there had been no indication of it as yet. But if it had ...

'What about you, sir? What did you get from Veronica?'

'I didn't.' Thanet explained, then went on to fill Lineham in on the interview with Mrs Hodges. 'No doubt about it, there's something very odd going on there, Mike.'

'Between Charity and Veronica, you mean?'

'Yes. Mrs Hodges is far from being a perceptive woman and of course, she's very partisan. Veronica's her only chick and she's fiercely protective. Jealous of Charity, too, so we have to take everything she says with a grain of salt. All the same, there do seem to be grounds for thinking that Veronica was almost forced into agreeing to go to Dorset with Charity, against her will.'

'You mean, because she begged her mother to allow her to go and then seemed relieved when she couldn't?'

'Yes. It even occurs to me that the so-called illness might have been psychosomatic.'

'Genuine, though?'

'Oh yes, but with an emotional rather than physical origin. I should have thought it was unusual for girls of that age to throw such a high temperature one day and then be perfectly fit the next. Young kids, yes, but at fifteen ...'

'You're suggesting she was actually *afraid* to go?'

'Well, it does rather seem that way to me. I think it might be an idea for you to have a chat with the Superintendent, Principal or whatever he's called, of the Holiday Home, see if anything happened to upset Veronica when she was there at Easter. Do it this afternoon.'

'Right. But in any case, the implication of all this is that Charity had some sort of hold over Veronica, which she was using to make her do something she didn't want to do.'

'Precisely. And if so, it'll be very interesting to find out what that hold was. Even more interesting is the avenue of investigation it would open up. If Charity was capable of exerting that degree of pressure on one person, she was presumably capable of exerting it on another.'

'You don't think you're being a bit, well ...'

'Yes, Mike?' Thanet grinned. 'No, don't bother, I'll finish for you. "Fanciful" is what you were going to say, I believe?'

Lineham gave a sheepish grin, but stuck to his guns. 'Well, don't you?'

Thanet had a sudden, vivid mental image of that small crumpled body in her schoolgirlish clothes. He sighed. 'I know what you mean. And God knows, it's difficult to see where she could have found opportunities for blackmail, with the sort of life she was leading. By the way, there was another interesting point ...' Thanet told Lineham what Mrs Hodges had said about Charity's reputation for bad behaviour while at primary school. 'Come to think of it, it might be worth having a word with the Head of Dene Road School, at some point. If he or she is still there, of course. It was seven or eight years ago.'

'Yes. Though it shouldn't be too difficult to trace him, even if he's retired. Unless he's moved right out of the area and bought himself a cottage with roses around the door in the West Country.'

'Anyway, we might be able to get to the bottom of all this when we see Veronica herself. I've arranged to go back this evening. Want to come?'

'You bet,' said Lineham fervently. 'And what about the Pritchards? The Jethro Pritchards, I mean.'

'Yes, well, that was interesting too.' Again, Thanet gave a brief account of the interview.

'Are you saying you think Mrs Pritchard might be a candidate, then?'

'She certainly didn't hold any brief for Charity, that's for sure. I know she claims she was in all evening, but whatever she says, once her mother-in-law was tucked up in bed, Mrs Pritchard could easily have slipped out.'

'You mean, with the intention of waylaying Charity on her way home?'

'Perhaps.'

'But what possible motive could she have had?'

'I can't begin to guess at the moment. And the same goes for Jethro. But he was definitely out and about at the crucial time, and we must remember that they could easily have found out what time Charity was expected back. They weren't to know the arrangements for the weekend had been called off.'

'And in any case, Charity obviously planned to arrive home at the same time as she'd originally intended.'

'Quite. I wonder where she was, over the weekend.'

This was still one of the most intriguing questions of all. There had been no clue in Charity's shoulder bag — no tickets, receipts, nothing to indicate whether she had stayed locally or travelled further afield, and no word as yet from the 'friend' Charity had mentioned to Veronica.

'Come on, Mike, let's get out of here. I could do with some fresh air.'

Outside the sun was at its zenith and heat shimmered on the tarmac of the car park.

'Wonder how long this is going to last,' said Thanet.

'All summer, I hope.' Lineham, like Thanet, thrived on hot weather. 'Anyway, you think it's worth keeping the Jethro Pritchards in mind.'

'They were certainly holding something back. Though it could be quite irrelevant, of course.'

'What about Mrs Hodges?'

'Mmm, well, we can't dismiss her entirely, I feel. If she

71

thought Charity was a serious threat to her Veronica, she could be pretty fierce, I should imagine.'

'But in that case, she surely wouldn't have told you any of that stuff about their friendship being peculiar, would she?'

'I don't know ... Come on, Mike, enough speculating for the moment. We'll just have to wait and see.'

Back at the office there was a message for Lineham: *Your wife rang from the hospital. She's being kept in. Could you pick up her suitcase (ready-packed in bedroom) and bring it in?*

Lineham showed it to Thanet. 'They must have kept her in after the clinic this morning. Oh God, what if something's gone wrong?'

'Come on, Mike, no need to imagine the worst. Perhaps they're just being careful. And even if she's gone into premature labour, there's an excellent chance that the baby'll be fine. She's thirty-six weeks, you said?'

Lineham nodded. 'Yes, but ...'

'There you are, then.' Thanet could hear the heartiness in his own voice and hated himself for it. Nothing would reassure Lineham but the sight of Louise in apparent good health. Fortunately Louise, a qualified nurse herself, was a sensible girl, not liable to panic in circumstances such as these. Thanet fervently hoped that nothing was seriously wrong. He glanced at Lineham's still, set face. He could imagine how he was feeling. Becoming a father for the first time was no joke even when everything was running smoothly. And when it wasn't ...

'Well, what are you waiting for?' he said gently. 'Go on, on your way.'

8

Thanet lit his pipe, sat back in his chair and drummed his fingers thoughtfully on his desk. The last hour had not been very productive. After Lineham's departure he had worked his way through the fresh reports awaiting his attention (nothing interesting there), made an unproductive telephone call to the Holiday Home in Dorset (the Principal had been out) and had despatched DC Carson to the railway station to enquire about arrivals last night (so far without result).

So, what now?

What he really needed was to talk to someone who could give him an assessment of Charity's character which was both unbiased and perceptive. Also, someone who could provide information about possible friends. Ah, yes ... he reached for the telephone directory.

He decided to try the school first. In his experience the Heads of large secondary schools invariably spent a considerable part of any holiday catching up on paperwork.

He was in luck. Yes, Miss Bench was working today, the secretary informed him. And yes, she was free to see him if he so wished. Thanet said that he would be right along.

His spirits rose as he set off. This was the part of his work that he enjoyed most, the interviewing. No two individuals are alike and the same person may be interviewed by two different people with completely different results. The variables are infinite. This, then, is the detective's testing ground. Here he must sharpen his perceptions and develop his skills in order to coax out of his witness that one (with luck, more than one) little nugget of information which may appear irrelevant at the time but which might eventually prove crucial to his understanding of the case.

It had taken Thanet a long time to realise that it wasn't simply a matter of interviewing technique — though that was important — but something much more subtle: interaction between questioner and questioned. Slowly and painfully, through years of trial and error — especially error — he had come to understand that an interview is rather like an iceberg; only a fraction of it is visible above the surface. A significant aspect of the detective's task is therefore to watch out for and interpret the minute, unconscious signals which rise to the surface like bubbles of gas in lemonade and betray what lies beneath. Only occasionally did he have the good fortune to come across a witness who was both honest and direct.

This time he was in luck.

Miss Bench rose as he was ushered into her study. He had not met her before and his first reaction was one of surprise as his preconceived notions of a headmistress shrivelled and died an instant death. She was a little younger than he — in her early thirties, he guessed, tall and slim. Elegant, too, in a narrow dress of dark blue linen with floppy lace collar and cuffs. Her straight fair hair was cut in what has become known as the Princess Diana style. If Thanet had seen her in the street he would have guessed her to be a high-powered secretary. No, he corrected himself, not a secretary, however high-powered. There was an unmistakable authority in those calm, pale blue eyes, an assumption that the world would shape itself to her command. There'd be no problems of discipline in this school, he thought. He was disconcerted to see that her smile had more than welcome in it, there was amusement, too. She was aware of the effect her appearance was having upon him and was enjoying it.

They settled themselves in easy chairs on either side of a low coffee table. Evidently she did not need her desk and chair, props of her authority, to bolster her self-confidence.

She came straight to the point.

'It's about Charity Pritchard, I suppose.'

'Yes.' There was obviously no need to beat about the bush. 'I wanted to talk to someone who could give me an impartial opinion of her.'

74

'Oh dear.' Her mouth tucked wryly down at the corners. 'You don't consider that you qualify for that description?'

'I'm afraid not. I'm sorry to disappoint you.'

'You disliked her?'

'Yes. Oh, I can't say that it doesn't grieve me to think of the way she died. It does. I wouldn't wish that on my worst enemy.' There was pain in her eyes, in her quick, fierce frown. 'But it would be hypocritical to say that I shall mourn her.' She gave a self-deprecating little smile. 'I know that teachers are supposed to be above likes and dislikes and I would certainly hope that no personal preferences or prejudices would ever show in my behaviour or distort my judgement. But there it is. Contrary to popular belief, teachers are human, after all.'

'Like policemen.' Thanet grinned.

She smiled back. 'Exactly.'

'Tell me why you didn't like her.'

Miss Bench sighed, plucked abstractedly at a loose thread on one of the lace cuffs. 'Ah, now there's the problem. It's so difficult to say. Don't think I haven't asked myself why, I always do, when I discover an antipathy towards a pupil.'

Thanet said nothing, waited.

'Usually it's relatively simple to pinpoint the reason. But in Charity's case ... She's ... she was a model pupil, you see — conscientious, hard-working, well-behaved, I can't ever recall having to take her to task for bad behaviour. In fact, thinking about it now, I suppose she was almost unnaturally well-behaved. One expects to find even the most decorous of girls occasionally lapsing into some minor breach of discipline. But not Charity.'

She paused, lips pursed and eyes narrowed. 'Why didn't I like her ...?' She shrugged. 'It was a purely emotional reaction.'

'A gut-reaction.' But for the first time he sensed that she was being less than frank with him.

She looked amused. 'Not quite how I would encourage one of my girls to put it. But yes, that's it, exactly.'

'Hmm.' Thanet was silent for a few moments, thinking. Miss

75

Bench waited calmly, sitting back into her armchair and crossing her legs.

Temporarily distracted, Thanet forced his attention away from those shapely planes of nylon-clad flesh (her shoes were prettily feminine too, he noticed, high-heeled, strappy sandals) and tried to feel his way into understanding the qualities for which this woman would have an instinctive dislike. They would probably be character traits diametrically opposite to those which she valued in herself. Which would be ...?

He saw her blink, no doubt at the intensity of his gaze.

'I was thinking,' he said.

'So I gathered.' She gave a wry grin. 'Did you reach any conclusions?'

He had. 'Would you say that Charity was devious?'

She hesitated. 'I suspect she was,' she said reluctantly.

'Untrustworthy?'

'I suppose so. Well, yes, then. Potentially, anyway. Oh dear.' She gave a shamefaced little laugh and lifted her hands helplessly. 'I can't help feeling rather guilty, talking about her in this way.'

'Because you don't like speaking ill of the dead, you mean?'

So that was the reason for her reticence just now. He had thought her too objective to be influenced by so universal an irrationality.

She tuned in disconcertingly on what he was thinking. 'I know you'll say it's irrational to feel this way, but I'm not so sure. One is always aware that the dead have no right of reply, that they can't defend themselves and never will be able to again. And when someone has died as Charity did, a victim of violence, it almost seems as though one is compounding the crime by blackening all that is now left to her, her reputation.'

Strange that he had never thought of it in quite this way before. He was impressed by her natural delicacy, almost felt himself rebuked for insensitivity. Not that he could allow himself to be influenced by such scruples, of course — his job would become virtually impossible if he did — but he was inclined to respect hers. Ignoring the little voice which whispered that he could afford to be magnanimous because he had

76

got what he wanted and forced her to betray her true opinion of Charity, he said, 'We'll talk about something else, then. Tell me about her friendship with Veronica.'

This was easier for her. She relaxed.

'It's interesting that you should ask about that. It has always puzzled me, that friendship. On the surface they're so very different — or perhaps I should say, *were* very different. I'm not using the past tense because of Charity's death, you understand.'

'Veronica changed, you mean?'

'Yes.'

'Because of Charity's influence?'

Miss Bench considered. 'I'm just not sure.' She hesitated again. 'It's difficult to tell. Certainly the initial change was ... Perhaps I'd better explain. I took up my post here two years ago last September. It was my first Headship and of course it was a busy time for me, picking up the reins and generally establishing myself. For some months most of the girls were just a blur — we have over seven hundred pupils here and it is quite impossible to get to know them all at once. But I did notice Veronica because she was always bubbling over — a bit silly, giggly, but invariably bright, cheerful. She was always the centre of a noisy group — I suppose her high spirits were infectious. And then, towards the end of that first term, early in the December, her father was killed. It was a hit and run affair and the man was never caught. A very sad business altogether. I understand that they'd been a very close family, the Hodges, that Veronica was the only child and they'd both adored her. The suddenness of her father's death absolutely devastated her. Overnight she became quiet, withdrawn — sullen, almost. I talked to her, of course, tried to help her, but without success. I told myself that time would help, that she'd come out of it gradually, but somehow she never has.'

Miss Bench sighed. 'I'm afraid I feel somewhat responsible. With so many girls to look after, it's a question of priorities and Veronica did seem to be coping, she didn't become clinically depressed. The only excuse I have for not giving her more attention is that at that time I suddenly found myself with a whole crop of problems to deal with. One of the fifth form girls was found to be pregnant, there was a spate of petty thieving and to cap it all there was an outbreak of german measles which decimated not only pupils but staff, too. I can tell you, by that first Christmas I was beginning to wonder if I was going to survive ...

'Anyway, the point is, that when I emerged from this period of frantic activity I realised that in the interim Charity and Veronica had become friends. Frankly, I didn't think it would last. I believed that as time went on and Veronica regained her natural ebullience, she would revert to being one of the crowd again, but she never has. And I still don't understand why the friendship has lasted.'

'Has Charity any other friends?'

'Not to my knowledge, no. Before Veronica, she was always a rather solitary creature. Rather pathetic, really.'

'I wanted to ask you ... I believe Dene Road Primary School is in your catchment area.'

'That's right, it is.'

'So you know the present Head?'

'Mr Hoskins, you mean? Yes.'

'Do you happen to know how long he's been there?'

'I can easily find out.'

Miss Bench's secretary quickly came up with the information that Mr Hoskins had become Head of Dene Road five years previously, when the former Head had retired, a Miss Foskett.

'Foskett ...' said Miss Bench thoughtfully. 'I'm sure I ... Ah yes, I remember now. I met a retired Headmistress called Foskett a few months ago, at some local Department of Education function.'

With any luck it would be the same woman. Good. With a relatively unusual name she shouldn't be too difficult to trace.

Thanet's thanks were sincere. It had been a useful interview. There was one scrap of information in particular that had given him food for thought.

Outside the sun was still beating relentlessly down and the sky overhead was a very pale, unclouded blue, shading off to a whitish glare at the limits of vision. A blast of stored-up heat gushed out at him as he opened the car door. Thanet took off his jacket, which he had donned for the interview with Miss Bench, and slung it on to the passenger seat.

He wondered how Louise was, and whether Lineham was back from the hospital yet.

9

'DS Lineham back yet?'

'Came in about half an hour ago, sir.'

And the news wasn't good, by the look of it, thought Thanet, as he entered his office. Only a couple of hours had gone by since he had last seen the sergeant, but in the interval the planes of Lineham's face seemed to have sharpened and there was a taut, stretched look about his eyes.

'How is she?'

Lineham grimaced, shook his head. 'She *says* she's fine, but I think she's putting on an act for my benefit. Underneath I think she's scared to death.'

Thanet sat down, prepared to listen. Joan had had two trouble-free pregnancies, thank God, but each time she'd been in hospital there had been others less fortunate. Thanet had heard enough stories to know that the maternity wards had their own share of tragedy.

'What's the trouble, exactly?'

'High blood pressure. Therefore possible toxaemia.'

'Which means?'

'The oxygen supply to the baby diminishes, might be cut off. And of course, if that happens ...'

Oh God, thought Thanet. To carry a baby for eight months and then to lose it, at the eleventh hour ... 'So what is happening?'

'She's been put on complete bed-rest, suitable medication, to see if they can get her blood pressure down.'

'And if they don't succeed?'

'They'll induce. Fortunately, as you pointed out earlier, she's thirty-six weeks already and the baby'd have an excellent chance of survival.'

'It's a first-rate maternity unit, Mike. They'll keep a very close eye on her. They would with any patient, but with one of their own they'll give just that little edge of special care, I'm sure.'

Until four months ago Louise herself had been a ward sister at Sturrenden General.

'That's what I keep telling myself.'

'Look, would you prefer me to put you off the Pritchard case, give you something less demanding?'

'You mean, I'll be no good to you, in this state?'

'Oh come on, Mike, I hope you know me better than that. If that was what I'd meant, I'd have said so. You know perfectly well that there's no one I prefer to work with. It's just that I thought you might prefer to be relatively free for the next day or two.' But even as he spoke, Thanet knew that it had been a stupid suggestion. With nothing but his anxiety to dwell on, Lineham would be far worse off than he was now.

'I'd go round the bend. If you don't mind, I'd really prefer to stay on.'

'Good. But if at any time you change your mind ...'

As if to demonstrate his ability to set his personal worries aside, Lineham picked up some of the papers spread out before him and said, 'There've been one or two interesting developments while you were out.'

'Oh?'

'DC Carson's report ...'

'On his visit to the railway station?'

'Yes, sir, Apparently the ticket collector on duty last night says that he saw Charity get off the London train.'

'At what time?'

'Eight fifty-eight.'

'Did he, now! How sure is he?'

'Dead certain, apparently. But here's the best bit. She was with a man.'

'*With* him?'

'That's what the ticket collector says. Claims they got off the train together, walked along the platform together, left the station together. He remembers, he says, because that's a pretty dead time of the evening and there were very few passengers.'

'Let me see.'

Lineham handed the report over and Thanet read it through quickly and then again, more slowly. 'Of course, it could just have been someone she knew, someone she met by chance on the train. In which case it would have been quite natural for them to leave the station together. Still, we'll follow it up, obviously. Quite a good description, isn't it? Pretty distinctive, too ... "Mid-thirties, medium height, fair hair, pebble-lensed glasses, carrying an orange rucksack." And there's always the interesting fact that we now *know* — assuming the ticket collector is right — that she was away from Sturrenden yesterday, at least.'

'He does sound pretty positive on the identification, don't you agree, sir?'

'I do indeed. Good. There was something else, you said?'

'Yes. While I was waiting for you to get back, I rang the Holiday Home, as you asked.'

'Ah yes, I tried a couple of times earlier on, but the Principal was out.'

'Well he was back, and I managed to talk to him.'

'And?'

Lineham hesitated — deliberately. Thanet recognised that look. He'd seen it before when the sergeant had managed to unearth a particularly intriguing piece of information.

'Of course, there might be nothing in it ...'

'Mike!'

'It could just be that both families happened to forget to mention it ...'

Thanet sat back, clasped his hands and began to rotate his thumbs around each other in a gesture of mock impatience.

Lineham grinned. 'Apparently Veronica and Charity did not stay for the entire weekend at Easter. They were called home a day early, by telegram — well, a tele-message, as they're now called — addressed to Charity. One of her family was ill, apparently.'

'Is that so?' Thanet considered. Lineham could, of course,

be right. Both the Pritchards and Mrs Hodges might just have happened to forget to mention the fact, the incident having been driven out of their minds by shock, or grief, or both. Or it simply might not have occurred to them to mention it because they did not consider it to be of any significance. He said so. 'All the same, it is just possible that neither family mentioned it because neither knew about it. In which case ...'

'The girls could have sent the telegram to themselves! Look, sir, I've been thinking about it while you were out. They could have been bored stiff, wanted to get away early. Perhaps they originally intended going straight home, perhaps not, but in any case, when they found they had a whole day — and night — of freedom, to do whatever they wanted to without their families knowing ... Well, Charity's parents were pretty strict, weren't they? The temptation may have been irresistible.'

'What are you suggesting they did?'

Lineham shrugged. 'Could have been something perfectly innocuous, like going to the cinema — even that would have been living it up, by the Pritchards' standards — or, just possibly, they could have decided to be a bit more daring, pick up a couple of boys.'

Thanet remembered that still, childish figure. How attractive to the opposite sex would Charity have been? But then, some men were really turned on by young girls, the younger-seeming the better ...

'They could even,' concluded Lineham triumphantly, 'have arranged to meet them again last weekend!'

They could indeed. Thanet remembered Veronica's apparent ambivalence over returning to Dorset. If Charity had been the ring-leader in all this, if Veronica had not enjoyed the exercise, had dreaded going through it all over again ... Yes, Lineham was right. This would certainly have to be followed up.

Lineham was watching him eagerly. 'What do you think, sir?'

'You don't think, Mike, that you're being a little, well... fanciful?' Thanet teased.

'Perhaps it's catching, sir. Like measles.' Lineham gave an impish grin.

'Anyway, yes, you're right. It's definitely worth looking into. But don't raise your hopes too high. There might be a perfectly innocent explanation.'

'The man she got off the train with. He could be ...'

Thanet held up his hand. 'No, Mike. Let's take it one step at a time, wait until we've established a few more facts.'

'We'll go and check with the Pritchards?'

'Mrs Hodges, I think. I don't really want to bother the Pritchards any more today, if I can help it.'

'I'll go, if you like, sir.' Lineham was already getting up.

'Mike! Hold your horses!' Thanet could understand Lineham's need to stifle anxiety with action, but had no intention of allowing it to precipitate him into rash behaviour. 'I think we ought to discuss tactics, first.'

'I'm not sure I follow you, sir. It's a fairly straightforward enquiry, surely.'

'It's a question of timing. Consider the implications. We have here a piece of information which may be useless. The girls may quite legitimately have been called home a day early. In which case, timing wouldn't matter. But, if the parents know nothing about that telegram, if the girls were involved in some sort of deception, then that information is potentially valuable, could open up important avenues of exploration. But, and this is the point, only one person could give us access to them.'

'Veronica.'

'Exactly. And we have an appointment with her in — let me see — just under four hours from now. Now think. If, meanwhile, we went to see her mother, discovered that she knew nothing about all this ...'

'The first thing she'd do when Veronica got home would be to tackle her about it and we'd not only lose the element of surprise, she'd have time to think up a story, too ... Good grief! Did you say just under four hours from now?' Lineham consulted his watch, leapt out of his chair. 'It's a quarter past five, already, and I promised Louise I'd pick one or two things

84

up for her before the shops close this afternoon. Would you mind ...?'

Thanet waved a hand. 'Carry on. There's nothing urgent, here. You still want to come to the Hodges' this evening?'

Lineham grinned. 'Try and stop me.'

'See you there, at nine, then.'

When Lineham had gone Thanet sat back in his chair and closed his eyes. At once his mind was full of confused images and snatches of conversation from the many interviews he had conducted today. His impressions of Charity were gradually gaining substance; outwardly conformist, abiding faithfully by the rigid rules laid down by her overbearing father, she had lived a life apparently blameless in the extreme. And yet ... underneath, there was more to it, he was sure. There had, for instance, been something about her which invariably provoked dislike — antipathy, even. Aunt, Headmistress, friend's mother, all had felt it in varying degrees, and her one friend had been a friend in name only, it seemed. How had this come about? What had gone wrong in the life of this young girl, to make her incapable of forming good relationships with others?

'Charity was forever in hot water at school.'

Mrs Hodges remark returned once more to intrigue him. If this were true, what had happened to change the child so radically?

He opened his eyes and reached for the telephone directory. As he had expected, there were very few Fosketts and only two were local. One was a man, the other an E V Foskett. Address, Jasmine Cottage, Nettleton. Nettleton was on his way home ...

The voice at the other end of the telephone was brisk, businesslike. E V Foskett it seemed, was indeed the former Head of Dene Road Primary School. Yes, Charity had been one of her pupils and certainly, Inspector Thanet was welcome to call if he thought she could be of any help.

'I'll be with you in about fifteen minutes,' he said with satisfaction.

10

Jasmine Cottage was quite the tiniest cottage Thanet had ever seen. Tucked away in a little lane off the main street of Nettleton village, its minute leaded windows, timbered walls and crooked chimney would have elicited murmurs of admiration from any foreign tourist. The garden was to scale. There was a pocket-handkerchief of a lawn, surrounded by low stone walls topped with cushions of yellow alyssum and a delicately-woven tapestry of aubretia in palest pink, red, purple and mauve. Trained against the house wall was a rare Banksia rose, with its clusters of tiny golden blossoms. Thanet inhaled their scent appreciatively as he waited for the door to open.

After all this miniature beauty Miss Foskett was a surprise. Square and chunky, with iron-grey hair cut in an uncompromising bob, she almost filled the low doorway.

'Do come in,' she said with a smile. 'This is exciting. I've never had a policeman on my doorstep before. Though I deplore the circumstances which have brought you here, of course.'

The sitting room displayed the same diminutive charm: low ceiling, spindly occasional tables, a small Persian rug on the floor of polished red brick.

Miss Foskett waved him into a pretty Victorian spoonback armchair and seated herself in the only sizeable piece of furniture in the room, a large wing chair beside the inglenook fireplace. He was disconcerted to find that her eyes were twinkling with amusement.

'I know what you're thinking,' she said. 'We don't match.'

I don't believe it, thought Thanet. Two perceptive witnesses in one afternoon ... He smiled back. 'Well, to be honest ...'

'I can always tell, when someone's clever enough to spot the discrepancy. It doesn't happen often, but when it does I always feel I owe them an explanation. The truth is, I inherited it all, lock, stock and barrel, from a truly miniscule aunt who died at the ripe old age of eighty-nine, last year. I was living in a rather dreary bungalow at the time, and frankly, I couldn't resist. The whole place was so delightful I decided to keep it exactly as it was. Except for this chair,' and she patted the arm as if it were a dog, 'my nice roomy bed and a few odds and ends with sentimental associations.' She frowned and her eyes grew sombre. 'So you want to talk to me about Charity Pritchard, poor girl.'

'Yes.'

'I don't see how I can possibly help, but of course I'm willing to try.'

Thanet decided to come straight to the point.

'I've been talking to Mrs Hodges, Veronica's mother ...'

'Just a moment. Hodges ... Ah yes, I remember Veronica. A fluffy, rather silly little girl, as I recall. But I don't quite see ...'

'She and Charity have been close friends for the last couple of years, by all accounts.'

'Really? You do surprise me. Chalk and cheese, those two.'

'According to Mrs Hodges, at one time, while the two girls were pupils at Dene Road, Charity was always in hot water. Veronica was forever coming home with tales of Charity's escapades. And then, apparently, the stories suddenly stopped. Is this true?'

Miss Foskett sighed. 'I'm afraid so.'

'Would you tell me about it?'

'Certainly. Though I must confess I don't like dwelling on my failures any more than the next man.'

'What do you mean, failures? No, sorry, perhaps you could ignore that for the moment. I'd like to hear about Charity's behaviour, first.'

'Charity *was* my failure. Look, are you sure you want me to go into all this? It's all water under the bridge now, and rather a long story.'

'It's why I've come.'

She shrugged. 'If you think it will help ...'

Thanet sat back and prepared to listen.

'It's difficult to know where to begin, really ...' She caught his eyes, smiled. 'I know ... at the beginning. Very well ... Soon after she started school, it became obvious that Charity was going to be a difficult pupil — disobedient, lacking in application and concentration, rebellious, uncooperative, often downright naughty. She was bright, mind, but whatever we did we couldn't seem to harness her abilities, get her to use them constructively. We tried everything — praise, admonition, condemnation, punishment, but nothing worked. I kept on hoping she would settle down, find her feet, but to no avail.'

'You spoke to the parents about this?'

'Initially I didn't want to make an issue of it. It was the mother who used to turn up at parents' evenings, and I did try tackling her about it, but nothing happened. She was a quiet, ineffectual little woman and I guessed she simply didn't have the strength of character to get Charity to toe the line. Having met her, and having been aware all along that there must be some reason for so young a child to be so troublesome, I concluded that either the father was as ineffectual as the mother, and Charity had always been allowed to have her way unchecked, or that he must be a very powerful, repressive person who kept Charity so firmly under control at home that at school she was reacting against being over-disciplined. Ah, I can see from your face, you've already met him. Of course, you would have, in the circumstances. You'll understand what I'm going to tell you, then ...

'Well, eventually I reached the point where I decided that I must have a word with him, and the next time Charity was in trouble I told her that that was what I had decided to do. I can assure you that I've never seen that particular warning have so powerful an effect. The child was petrified. She must have been — oh, let me see — about six and a half at the time. She begged me not to send for him, promised there'd be no more misbehaviour.'

'So you didn't see him?'

'Not at that point. I thought that the threat alone might have achieved the desired outcome and indeed, for a while, Charity was much better behaved. But gradually she began to slip back into her old patterns of behaviour. Now I didn't like ruling a child by fear, and I don't like making threats which are never put into practice, because obviously they lose their efficacy. I gave her one or two gentle warnings and privately decided that if this went on, I would have to talk to Mr Pritchard, if only to satisfy my own need to know the right way to handle Charity. I thought, if we could have a sensible discussion together, we might be able to help her.'

Thanet could see what was coming.

'Well, things came to a head about six months later. Charity's form teacher came to me and told me that she'd caught the child red-handed, pouring ink over a set of brand-new text books. Those particular books had been on order for months, and the entire class knew it. I called Charity in, told her I'd definitely decided to ask her parents to come and see me. She became hysterical. She screamed, she sobbed, she swore she was sorry, that she'd never, ever put a foot wrong again ... It was so distressing. I felt in something of a dilemma. If I back-pedalled now, I would undermine my authority and destroy my credibility, make Charity think that she could always manipulate me if the need arose. On the other hand, the child was clearly so terrified at the prospect ... Anyway, I finally decided to go ahead, on the grounds that there was clearly something radically wrong in her relationship with her father, and that if I were to be able to help her, I needed to know what it was. I can see, you've guessed what's coming, haven't you?'

'Possibly. But I want to hear it all the same. In detail. So do go on.'

Miss Foskett shook her head sadly. 'The interview was a disaster, from start to finish. I talked, they listened. I'm not exaggerating when I say that Mrs Pritchard did not say a single word, from beginning to end. Any questions I asked were countered by further questions from Mr Pritchard. There was no discussion, as such, at all. I really did try very hard, but soon realised that it was pointless. The man had a completely closed mind ... You know they belong to that sect called the Children of Jerusalem?'

'Yes.'

'I've had difficulties in dealing with the children of families belonging to it before, but never in quite such an extreme form. As soon as I saw that there really was no point in continuing, I brought the interview to a close.' Miss Foskett shivered, hugged herself as if she were cold. 'And do you know what he said, as he went through the door?'

Thanet waited.

'I've never forgotten it. He turned, looked at me with those very dark, burning eyes of his and said, "Thank you, Miss Foskett, for bringing the matter to my attention. The Devil walketh about, seeking whom he may devour."'

'And then?'

'They left.'

'What did he mean, do you think?'

'Presumably, that the Devil was responsible for Charity's behaviour, that he had seduced her into evil, so to speak ...'

'And the result?'

'Disaster, to my mind. Charity was away for a week and when she came back she was a different child — really different. Apart from being painfully thin, she was polite, quiet, well-behaved, industrious ... You'll probably ask what I'm complaining about, when this was precisely the effect I'd been struggling to achieve, but to my mind ... How can I explain? After this incident she was ... lifeless. There was no vivacity, spontaneity, responsiveness ... And yet, I still don't see how else I could have handled the situation constructively. As I told you, I still think of Charity as one of my worst failures — perhaps the worst failure of all. And I would like to assure you that I'm not given to self-castigation. It's so unconstructive to brood on failure. Better, by far, to learn from it and forget it. But in Charity's case ... I suppose you might say that that child has haunted me, over the years. And now ...' Miss Foskett shook her head regretfully and then added briskly, 'Well, that's about it. I can't really see why you wanted to hear all this rigmarole, but for what it's worth, there it is.'

Thanet did not feel that this was either the time or the place to embark upon a dissertation on the importance of understanding the victim's character in a murder investigation such as this. He merely assured Miss Foskett that what she had told him was extremely helpful to him and that he was grateful to her for being so frank.

Before she closed the front door behind him she said, 'You know, I'd have given anything to know just what he did to her in that week she was away from school.'

And so should I, thought Thanet. So should I.

What was more, he was going to have a damned good try at finding out.

11

'She's in the front room.'

It was precisely nine o'clock and Mrs Hodges had clearly been waiting for their knock; the door had opened almost before the reverberations had died away. In the narrow hall she hesitated. 'She's ever so upset. You won't . . . ?'

'I do understand that, Mrs Hodges,' said Thanet. 'And I'll be as gentle as I can, I promise.'

This seemed to satisfy her and she opened the door, led the way inside.

The girl huddled in the armchair facing them raised blank, terrified blue eyes. She was very like her mother in build and colouring, with a bush of elaborately frizzed hair haloing a round face puffy with weeping. Beside her, on the arm of the chair, lay a damp, wadded face-flannel. Thanet had a brief, vivid image of Mrs Hodges kneeling on the floor beside her daughter, murmuring soothing words and sponging away the tears as if Veronica were a little girl again and had hurt herself while playing in the garden.

But the marks of this injury were not going to be so easily eradicated, he thought as they all sat down. Crouching on the edge of her chair with fixed, stricken gaze, hugging herself as if she were afraid that her body might be about to fly apart, Veronica reminded him of a wounded bird waiting for the vultures to descend upon her and tear at her vulnerable flesh with their sharp beaks.

If he was right, she was more sinned against than sinning, and had had a pretty bad time over the last two years. But her evidence was crucial, of that he was convinced, and somehow he must win her confidence sufficiently to obtain it.

He glanced approvingly at Lineham, who had positioned

himself behind the girl's line of vision, on a small upright chair. Louise's condition was apparently unchanged and the sergeant seemed marginally more cheerful this evening. He was as aware as Thanet of the importance of this interview and clearly his mind was on the job.

Mrs Hodges had seated herself protectively on the arm of Veronica's chair, with an arm around the girl's shoulders.

'I really am sorry to have to bother you at a time like this, Veronica — I may call you Veronica?'

He waited for her tight, wary nod before going on.

'I do appreciate what a terrible shock this must have been for you. But I'm sure you'll want to do all you can to help us.'

She bit her lip and he cast about for a reassuring opening. Every line of questioning seemed fraught with potential menace for the girl.

'Your mother tells me you've known Charity for a long time? Since you were at primary school together, I believe?'

'Yes.'

It was barely audible, but a beginning. For the next quarter of an hour Thanet concentrated on putting her more at ease, chatting innocuously about Dene Road School, then about the Girls' Technical School and gradually he was rewarded by seeing Veronica relax a little, speak more readily.

When he judged that the time was right, he said, 'Now I know that you might find some of the questions I have to ask you a bit upsetting, but I want you to remember that I'm not out to browbeat or frighten you — in fact, that's the very last thing I want to do, and if at any point you feel you'd really rather call it a day, you only have to say so and we'll stop. Though it's only fair to warn you that in that case we'd have to resume some other time. It'll be up to you. I'm trying to be completely frank with you, you see.'

She was listening intently. So was her mother.

'The other thing I want to say is that whatever you may have to tell me about your friendship with Charity, we're not here to judge you. We're not out to find a scape-goat, merely to try to find out a little more about her. Charity didn't seem to have many friends and we really do feel that you might be able to help us perhaps more than anyone else can. You follow me?'

A small, tight nod. She was frightened again but, Thanet judged, prepared to be co-operative, within limits. Here goes, then, he thought. He had no choice, really, he had to begin with the business of the telegram. So much of his subsequent questioning would depend on whether or not there was an innocent explanation. If there wasn't, he hoped that Mrs Hodges' reaction to the news of the girls' duplicity would not interfere with the course he wanted the interview to take. If only he could have seen Veronica alone ...

'Perhaps we could begin by going back to last Easter, when you and Charity went to Dorset.'

This was unexpected and she didn't know whether to be reassured or alarmed. Her eyes widened slightly and she glanced up at her mother, who squeezed her shoulder.

'When did you leave Sturrenden?'

'On the Friday morning.'

They had arrived at the Holiday Home soon after four. They had been in a group of twenty-four young people from all over the country. Ages ranged from fourteen to eighteen and most of them were girls. The three boys, like Charity and Veronica, were among the youngest. All of them had been expected to make their own beds in the dormitories, to follow a rota system for laying the tables and washing up, to follow the tight schedule of Bible classes and discussion groups and to participate in the organised games in the afternoons.

'You enjoyed the weekend?'

'Yes, of course.' But her voice lacked conviction.

'So why did you leave a day early?' His voice was mild and he had phrased the question very carefully, leaving the way open for a straightforward explanation of telegram and family illness, if that was the way it had been.

Her eyes told him at once that it had not. That quick, agonised upward flicker in the direction of her mother only just preceeded Mrs Hodges' reaction.

'A day early?' she said sharply. 'What do you mean, a day early?'

94

'I'm sorry, Veronica,' said Thanet. 'But I'm afraid all this really does have to come out.'

Mrs Hodges' face had gone red. 'What do you mean, sorry? What are you talking about?' And then, to Veronica, 'What'll all have to come out?'

'No!' Veronica began to shake her head wildly. 'No no no no no . . .' Then she buried her face in her hands and began to cry without restraint, rocking to and fro as if noise and motion together could block out awareness of the ordeal now facing her.

Mrs Hodges, looking shocked and bewildered, slid off the arm of the chair, knelt before her daughter and, putting both arms around her, tried to calm her.

Lineham raised his eyebrows at Thanet. *Delaying tactics?* he mouthed.

Thanet shook his head. He had been expecting just this reaction and had decided how to deal with it. He waited until the girl's sobs had begun to abate and then, raising his voice, said, 'Veronica, there's no need to be so upset. Your mother's not going to blame you, you know, when she hears the whole story.'

As he had hoped, this gave her pause. Slowly, she raised a streaming face from her mother's shoulder and looked at him.

He met her gaze squarely. 'I really mean that.'

She wanted to believe him, he could see. She looked doubtfully at her mother, who was now sitting back on her heels.

It was Mrs Hodges who clinched the matter. Levering herself up with one hand on the arm of the chair, she scrambled to her feet. Then she put her hands on her hips.

'Well, I haven't the foggiest idea what all this is about, but if you're worried about what *I* think, love, forget it. Anything's better than all this palaver. And if you do know anything that'll help the police, well, you owe it to Charity to tell it.'

'Owe it to Charity!' Veronica burst out. 'But that's just the point, Mum. I don't owe her anything, not a bloody thing!'

'Watch your mouth, girl! You know your dad couldn't stand women swearing.'

'Oh all right, Mum, I'm sorry, but honest, you just don't know what you're talking about.'

'Well how am I supposed to, if you won't explain!'

But still Veronica hesitated before taking the plunge. She glanced from Thanet to her mother and back again. Then she shrugged and said, 'It was Charity's idea. The telegram.'

'What telegram?' said Mrs Hodges.

Thanet raised his hand. 'Please, Mrs Hodges, I think Veronica would find this easier if you could just listen, for the moment. I know it won't be easy for you, but if you could wait, save your questions till later ...'

'All right.' She was reluctant, but seated herself on the arm of Veronica's chair again and prepared to do as he asked.

'You might prefer to tell us in your own way, Veronica,' said Thanet. 'If you get stuck, I'll help you out.'

Veronica shifted restlessly.

'You were bored, I suppose,' prompted Thanet.

'Out of our minds!'

'Then why ...?' Mrs Hodges caught Thanet's eye, subsided.

'Never a minute to yourself,' said Veronica as if her mother had not spoken. 'Lights out at ten o'clock, jolly hockey sticks every afternoon, washing up for thirty-odd, including the staff, who never lifted a finger to help ... And the atmosphere of the place! Long faces, everyone in dead earnest all the time ... So in the end, Charity said, come on, let's get out of here, I've had enough.'

'This was when?'

'On the Sunday afternoon. We were supposed to be staying until Wednesday morning. Well, I'd had enough too and we talked about it for a bit. I knew Mum wouldn't mind if I got home a couple of days early. But we haven't got a telephone here and we knew they'd never let us go without permission from our parents. So Charity suggested the best way would be to send ourselves a telegram, pretend there was some emergency at home. There was a pay-phone booth at the Home and we had just enough change between us, so we decided to send it right away, but when we enquired we found that although you can phone in a telemessage any time up to eight in the evening,

96

they're not actually delivered until the next first class post in the area. And there was no post next day, being a Bank holiday. So we had to wait to send it until the Monday and it came first thing Tuesday morning.'

'And it worked?'

'Oh yes, no problem. We were away by mid-morning.' Veronica paused, glanced uneasily at her mother.

Mrs Hodges opened her mouth to speak, closed it again as Thanet shook his head. *Wait,* his eyes signalled. *You'll find out soon enough.*

'Go on, Veronica,' he said gently. Then, as she still hesitated, 'Let me help you. When you were on the train you were upset to find out that Charity had no intention of going straight home. Instead, she was suggesting that you should make the most of the unexpected day's freedom, live it up a little ... Am I right?'

Thanet heard Mrs Hodges' sharp intake of breath as Veronica nodded miserably.

'How was I to know she was going to suggest anything so crazy!' Veronica burst out. 'We hardly had any money left after paying more than three pounds for the telegram and naturally I thought we'd be going straight home. But no! The minute we sat down in the train she started on me. She had it all worked out. We'd pick up some boys on the train or, failing that, in London, and get them to pay for everything ... Don't look at me like that, Mum! You needn't worry, I didn't go along with her, though believe me, you ought to give me a medal for holding out. She just went on and on and on ...'

'So what did you do, in the end?' asked Thanet gently.

'We split up. When we got to London I didn't know what to do ... In the end I looked up the YWCA in the phone book. They've got an accommodation and advisory service. I couldn't stay in one of their hostels because I was broke, but they managed to fix me up just for the night in one of their emergency hostels ... It was *awful,* having to throw myself on their mercy like that. I've never felt so humiliated in my life...' Veronica shook her head as if to erase the memory and rubbed her eyes.

Thanet could see that Mrs Hodges was again bursting to ask a question and again he knew what it was: *But why didn't you just catch a train, come straight home?* Thanet gave her a quick, fierce frown. *Later,* he mouthed. He had his own reasons for not wanting to put that particular question at this point.

'And Charity?'

'Went off with some fella she picked up on the train. She was mad with me, of course. In the end she saw I wasn't going to budge and she said if I wouldn't go along with her she'd bloody well — sorry, Mum — do it by herself. So off she went to the buffet car and that was the last I saw of her till Paddington.'

'She did pick someone up, you say?'

'You bet.'

'You saw him?'

'Yes. When we got to London. They got off the train together.'

'How far away were you?'

'About fifty yards, I suppose.'

'Did you get a good look at him?'

'Not really. Only a side view.'

'Can you give me a description?'

Veronica frowned, recalling. 'Young — early twenties, I suppose. Black hair and beard.'

'Tall? Short?'

'Medium. He had his arm around Charity's shoulders and they were laughing ... He was a few inches taller than her and she's ... she was the same height as me, five four.'

'So, five eight or nine, then?'

'Yes.'

'What sort of clothes was he wearing?'

'Jeans and a black leather jacket.'

'Anything else you can remember?'

'No. Sorry. Oh ... just a minute, yes ... He was carrying a crash helmet. Yellow, it was.'

'Was he wearing glasses?' Thanet had to ask, though he knew that the question was pointless, really. The description was quite different from that of the man who had got off the London train with Charity last night.

She shook her head.

'Did she ever tell you anything about him, later?'

'No. She liked being mysterious about him. She was always going on about how terrific he was, how crazy about her, what a marvellous time they'd had, that sort of thing ...'

'Did she spend the night with him?'

'Yes.' Veronica was studiously avoiding her mother's eye.

'Did she say where?'

'No.'

'Did she tell you where he lived?'

'Sorry, no.'

'Whether she was going to meet him again?'

Veronica hesitated.

'Was she going to meet him again?' said Thanet softly. 'Last weekend, for example.'

Veronica bit her lip. 'I'm not sure.'

'But Veronica!' burst out Mrs Hodges, unable to keep quiet any longer.

Thanet leaned across to lay a restraining hand on her arm. 'Mrs Hodges, look. I do appreciate how difficult this is for you. But I've nearly finished, now. If you could just bear with me... When we've gone, you and Veronica will be able to talk as much as you like.'

Mrs Hodges compressed her lips, scowled at him. 'It's all very well for you. It's not you sitting here listening to your daughter telling you ...'

'I know. But I won't be much ionger, I promise. This really is very important.'

He took her silence for assent, turned back to the girl. 'What were Charity's plans for the weekend?'

Veronica glanced nervously at her mother. 'To book up at the Holiday Home again, then, on the morning of the day we were due to arrive, ring to say one of us was ill. That would mean neither of us could go because of this rule they have about girls travelling in pairs. Then we'd go to London, have a good time ...'

99

'Pick up some men again, you mean?'

'That's what she said, but ...'

'But what?'

'Well, I just didn't know whether to believe her or not. You never knew, with Charity. She could tell lies and look so innocent about it that you'd believe every word she was saying. It was ages before I cottoned on to that.'

'So what made you think she wasn't telling you what her real plans for the weekend were?'

'I don't know. It was just an impression. And a letter came for her, three or four weeks ago, from London.'

'It came here, you mean?'

'Yes. Inside an envelope addressed to me. She'd even had the nerve to tell him he could write to her here!'

'The man she met at Easter, you mean? I see, so you suspected that they might have made arrangements to spend the weekend together, and that you were going to be — how shall I put it? — ditched, when you got to London.'

'That's right. But do you think I could get her to admit it? Whenever I tried, she'd just laugh, say I was imagining things.'

'But when you saw her last night, when she called in on the way back from the station ... Didn't she tell you where she'd been, over the weekend?'

'London, that's all. With a friend. As a matter of fact, I had the impression the weekend hadn't been much of a success.'

'What do you mean?'

'I thought she looked tired. And a bit ... subdued, depressed. Though I suppose that could have been because Mum had told her her father'd been round here looking for her and she knew she'd be for it when she got home. No ... I still think there was more to it than that.'

'Do you happen to know if Charity knew a man who wears pebble-lensed glasses?'

The question had taken her by surprise. Thanet glimpsed shock and recognition before she shook her head, a little too hastily.

'I'm afraid not, I'm sorry.'

100

She was lying. Should he press her? The girl was looking exhausted and he had the feeling that she couldn't take much more. No, he'd leave it for the moment. There was one other question he wanted to ask before he had to stop. He'd saved it until last because he had the feeling that it was the one Veronica would find most difficult of all to answer, especially in her mother's presence. He hesitated, wondering how to phrase it tactfully.

Mrs Hodges beat him to it. Taking his brief silence as an indication that he had finished, she leant forward and said, 'But Veronica, love, I don't understand. Why go along with all this, if you didn't want to? Why go on being friends with Charity at all, if that's what she was like?' Mrs Hodges gave a little shiver of distaste. 'Your dad would've had a thousand fits if he'd been here listening to all this.'

Veronica's gaze slid away from her mother's. Her hands, until now lying loosely in her lap, curled into fists and Thanet saw her feet move slightly as her toes bunched up inside her shoes. He had been right. This was the question she had feared most of all.

'Veronica?' said her mother sharply.

'I was sorry for her,' Veronica muttered.

'Sorry for her? *Sorry* for her? So sorry that you had to go begging for somewhere to spend the night in London, rather than come home a day early?' Mrs Hodges' pent-up bewilderment and frustration suddenly erupted into anger. She jumped off the arm of the chair and stood over her daughter, feet apart, hands on hips, eyes blazing. 'You really expect me to believe that? That you begged me to allow you to go to Dorset again knowing that you had no intention of doing so ... that you deliberately set out to deceive me — me, your own mother — just because you were *sorry for Charity*? What kind of a fool do you take me for?'

Veronica had shrunk back in her chair, desperate as a cornered animal. Poor kid, thought Thanet. She couldn't defend herself without giving herself away. Her only resort would be to react angrily, use the quarrel as a smoke-screen.

101

As if she had read his mind Veronica sprang to her feet and shouted furiously, 'So that's what you think of me, is it! I'm a liar, am I?'

'Well, what else am I to think? You knew what she was planning, yet you agreed to go along with it. You *begged* me to let you go. You'd even packed your suitcase! If you weren't going to Dorset and you didn't intend doing what she wanted you to do, what *did* you plan to do? Spend the entire weekend with tramps and drop-outs at an emergency hostel in some grubby part of London?'

'But I didn't, did I? I *didn't* bloody go! Just remember that, will you?'

And, bursting into tears, Veronica ran out of the room. They heard her pound up the stairs, then there was silence.

For a few moments Mrs Hodges stood rigid, staring blankly at the door. Then, moving very slowly, she lowered herself into the armchair Veronica had vacated and slumped back into it. 'That's done it,' she said ruefully. 'Now I'll never find out. I shouldn't have lost my temper, should I?'

'I shouldn't give up hope,' said Thanet equably. 'Give her time. She's in a pretty fragile state at the moment, remember. She's just had a very bad shock, learning about Charity's death, and then, on top of that, having to be questioned ...'

But Mrs Hodges was still shaking her head. 'Time was, I'd have agreed with you. We were so close, Veronica's dad, her and me ... If you'd told me it would ever come to this ...' Her eyes clouded, became almost opaque. 'If I'd had any idea what was going on, I'd have ...' She stopped, passed her hand across her face as if brushing cobwebs away and seemed to become aware of their presence again. 'And I don't suppose she'll ever forgive me for shouting at her like that in front of you ... I should have listened to what you said, kept my mouth shut until you'd gone ... I'm sorry, I suppose you ... Had you finished? Your questions, I mean?'

'Most of them. But there were one or two small points ...' Not to mention the delicate issue over which the interview had broken down. 'I'll have to come back tomorrow morning, I'm afraid. If that's all right by you.'

Mrs Hodges gave a resigned shrug. 'I suppose if you must, you must.'

Thanet waited until he and Lineham were in the car before asking him for his impressions of the interview.

'Looks as though we were right. Charity did have something on her. I wonder what.'

'As a matter of fact, I've got a good idea. It was something her headmistress said ...' Thanet explained his theory.

Lineham whistled. 'Could be ... That would be just the sort of thing she'd be terrified would come out. But I was thinking, while I was listening, back there ...'

'Yes?'

'Well, we haven't had the PM report yet, of course, but I think you'll agree that from what we saw of the circumstances of the murder, last night, it did look as though it could have been an unpremeditated job.'

'Possibly, yes.'

'I know he could have been lying in wait for her with the deliberate intention of attacking her — or anyone else, for that matter — but he could simply have been waiting for her for some innocent reason — he may have wanted to talk to her about something.'

'True.'

'Or, he could have been walking with her, and they had a quarrel during which he gave her a violent shove, causing her to fall against that lethal bit of iron.'

'Agreed.'

'Or,' said Lineham slowly, 'he could even have followed her, caught up with her and then ditto. I'm saying "he", but of course, it could equally have been "she". It wouldn't have taken that much strength ...'

'So what are you suggesting?'

'Well, as I said, while I was listening, I was thinking ... Supposing Veronica had had just about as much as she could take, from Charity. Suppose that after Charity left her last night she thought about it for a minute or two and then decided to follow her, tell her just that.'

Thanet didn't like it. But he had to concede that Lineham

could, just possibly, be right. Perhaps Veronica's desperation, which he had attributed to fear of her mother finding out the reason why Charity had had a hold over her, had really been terror of discovery. As Lineham had suggested, Charity's death could well have been an accident, the unfortunate result of a jagged piece of metal being in the wrong place at the wrong time. But would Veronica then have gone calmly off on a day trip to Boulogne?'

He put this to Lineham.

'How do we know it was calmly?' said Lineham. 'I think you'll agree, sir, that Mrs Hodges would do anything to protect Veronica. It could have happened like this ... After the accident Veronica rushes home to mum, in a state of shock. Mrs Hodges calms her down and they discuss what they are going to do. They decide it would be best to behave as though nothing has happened, that Veronica should go on her trip as planned. It'll give her a breathing space, a chance to get over the shock a bit ...'

'So that performance we just witnessed was just that, a performance?'

'Not entirely,' said Lineham eagerly. 'Mrs Hodges might genuinely not have known anything about the business with the telegram at Easter ... But I haven't quite finished, yet, sir. Or ...'

'You're brimming over with theories tonight, Mike. Don't tell me there's another one coming up!'

'Well, it did just occur to me ...'

'Come on, then, let's have it.'

'Well, it could equally well have been Mrs Hodges — who killed Charity, I mean. After all, we've only got her word for it that Charity left there at 9.35. All we know — if the ticket collector is right — is that Charity got off that train at 8.58. I'd guess it's about ten minutes walk to Lantern Street, so she would have got there about ten past nine. If Mrs Hodges is telling the truth, Charity must have spent about twenty-five minutes there, but for all we know it was nothing like as long as that, it could have been ten minutes, or even five. Now, say during that time Mrs Hodges overhears something between

Charity and Veronica — an argument, anything which tells her that Veronica is getting desperate about her relationship with Charity ... Mrs Hodges could have decided to have a word with Charity on her own, follow her and have it out with her. She catches up with her ... they quarrel ... we have that fatal shove ... and Mrs Hodges rushes home, just getting back in time to look innocent when we arrive on the doorstep asking where Charity is ...' Lineham paused, took his eyes off the road long enough to glance hopefully at Thanet.

'Could be ...' Again, it was possible. Mrs Hodges had obviously disliked Charity, resented her influence over Veronica. But, enough to kill her ... Though she might not have *intended* to kill her ... 'We'll do some checking on their movements tomorrow.'

They were in the car park now and Lineham reached for his notebook.

'Starting with a house to house in Lantern Street?'

'Yes. Covering the earlier period, too — say from nine o'clock onwards.'

'Right. Incidentally, Veronica was lying, when you asked about the man in glasses, wasn't she?'

'You spotted that too. Yes, I'm certain of it. I'll have to have another go at her about that, when we see her tomorrow. And we must both set our minds to working out how to trace either of the two men.'

'The one she picked up at Easter could be tricky, sir. He could be anywhere in the country by now — or abroad, for that matter.'

'Come on, Mike. Let's just regard it as a challenge to our ingenuity.'

Lineham grinned, gave a mock salute. 'Yes, sir. Right, sir. Any other homework for tonight?'

On the way home Thanet pondered the sergeant's suggestions. Could Mrs Hodges or Veronica be guilty? If so, his own antennae had let him down badly during that interview. Perhaps he had been too preoccupied with trying to ask the right questions in the right order, and with preventing Mrs Hodges from messing the whole thing up. This, after all, was one of the main reasons for having an observer: a non-participant had a much better chance of seeing what was going on beneath the surface. Had his own perceptions really been so dulled, tonight?

It was a sobering thought, but it was pointless to dwell upon it. He began instead to consider the task he had set Lineham: how to trace either of the shadowy male figures of whom they had been given such tantalising glimpses.

He tried to picture Charity with the young man Veronica had described, but somehow he couldn't do it. That virile, male image in jeans and black leather jacket simply didn't go with Charity's schoolgirlish style of dressing. And the clothes at home and in her suitcase had been much the same — dull, sober, juvenile. Perhaps Veronica had been telling a pack of lies? Perhaps it had been she who had been the prime mover in the Easter escapade and it had been Charity, not she, who had spent the night in a hostel.

Thanet shook his head unconsciously. No, he didn't believe that. It was Charity who had been murdered and besides, Veronica's story had rung true, had fitted in with the emerging picture of Charity as a girl whose rebellion against her repressive father, driven underground during her childhood years, had recently begun to manifest itself in much more devious and dangerous ways. He frowned. The trouble was, she just hadn't *looked* the part. If she had been dressed differently, now...

Inspiration came as he swung into his mother-in-law's drive. Of course!

He cut the engine and the dense, country silence enfolded him. He sat for a few minutes, thinking. If he were right, it would explain so much — how Charity had so completely hoodwinked her parents, for example, and why she had called first at Veronica's house, instead of going straight home from the station ...

Yes, it all made sense.

Why on earth hadn't he seen it before?

106

12

Thanet slammed the receiver down in frustration. He'd already tried twice to get through to Joan earlier on this evening, before leaving for Veronica's house.

'No luck?' His mother-in-law had just come into the room with two cups of tea balanced on a tray.

'Still out.' Thanet sat down heavily on the settee and essayed a smile as he accepted the tea. He didn't feel in the least like smiling. A quarter to eleven and Joan was still out, after saying she'd be in all evening. Where the hell was she?

It was above all at times like this, when he had had a demanding day and was in need of the solace which she had never failed to give, that the fear of losing her — or perhaps having already lost her — surfaced most strongly. They'd known that this time apart would be difficult, of course, and had both been aware that it would be harder for Thanet and the children than for her. She would be working towards a goal, would be expanding her knowledge and experience, breaking new ground all the time, whereas he would remain in the same situation, conscious only of his sense of loss, of the yawning gap left by her absence.

What he had not anticipated was the burgeoning crop of fears: that her taste of freedom from family ties and domesticity would give her an appetite for more; that she was drifting further and further away from them; that he might even lose her for good.

Above all, he had not anticipated this gut-twisting jealousy, the terror that she might have found a more congenial lover. In his more rational moments he knew that he was a fool even to entertain the idea. Joan, unfaithful? Never. They had always been very close, had valued their relationship, taken care to nurture it. Thanet had believed that they had been moving into that satisfying stage when marriage becomes a liberating force, when each partner, secure in the knowledge that he is fully accepted and understood, becomes free to develop in ways undreamt of earlier on in life. Not that there hadn't been disagreements, of course, but somehow they'd always managed to take them in their stride, been ready to compromise . . .

He shook his head cynically. Compromise, indeed! Look where compromise had brought him! But, if he had held out, over this? If he had refused to listen to Joan's plea to be allowed to train for a satisfying career of her own? He would have lost her anyway, or at best theirs would have been a relationship crippled by bitterness and resentment on her side, possessiveness and stubbornness on his.

No, he really didn't see how he could have acted otherwise. All the same, it was sometimes very difficult to convince himself that he had done the right thing.

'I shouldn't worry.' Margaret Bolton was watching him sympathetically. 'You know the sort of crises that are always cropping up in her sort of work . . . It's just unfortunate that yours is equally unpredictable.'

'"Never the twain shall meet," I know.' Thanet sipped at his tea, made an effort to pretend nonchalance. He had never discussed his marriage with anyone and had no intention of starting now. Joan would soon be home for good, he told himself once more. Until then, he'd grit his teeth and hang on.

Mrs Bolton sighed, leaned her head against the back of her chair and closed her eyes. She looked very tired, Thanet thought guiltily. Joan's absence was taking its toll of her mother, too.

'Children been difficult?'

She opened her eyes, smiled ruefully. 'A bit. I just don't seem to have as much energy as I used to. And it's been so hot . . .'

It still was. The French windows were wide open and the sweet scents of the garden had drifted into the room. There was another smell, too, Thanet realised: furniture polish. He looked about him and realised that his mother-in-law had been taking this opportunity to give her house a good clean;

the furniture was shining, the copper coal scuttle and brass fire-irons in the inglenook fireplace gleaming. After all that gardening over the weekend, too ...

He looked at her anxiously. 'All this is taking too much out of you, isn't it? Two houses to run, two gardens, the children to look after ...'

She shook her head. 'I don't mind. It's only for a little while longer, after all. Another couple of weeks and Joan'll be back.'

So she was counting the weeks too.

'We don't tell you often enough how much we appreciate what you're doing.'

She smiled. 'Nonsense. Joan's my daughter, after all. And at my age it's good to feel needed from time to time, believe me.'

But his words had pleased her, he could tell. He made a mental note to have a word with the children, try once more to get them to understand that their grandmother didn't have endless reserves of energy to draw upon. But they were so young, and it was a difficult time for them, too ...

'I think I'll go to bed now,' said Mrs Bolton.

'Me too. You go on. I'll lock up.'

After making the rounds Thanet made one more attempt to ring Joan. She was still out.

Just over two more weeks, he told himself as he climbed the stairs. Seventeen days.

Next morning he and Lineham arrived in the car park simultaneously.

'How's Louise?'

'The specialist is seeing her this morning. She had a reasonable night, apparently.'

Which was more than could be said of Lineham, by the look of it. The taut, stretched look was back and the skin beneath his eyes was dark with the bruises of insomnia and anxiety.

'What time are you supposed to ring again?'

'Not before twelve, they said.'

Inside they were greeted with the news that the post mortem on Charity was scheduled for this morning and that Doctor

109

Mallard had arranged to be present. The unofficial results should be through in an hour or so.

They had just settled down to work their way through the reports on the previous day's work when the phone rang.

'Mr Pritchard is here, sir. Wants to see you. It's urgent, he says.'

'Do you know what it's about?'

'No, sir. He won't say. But he's in a bit of a state.'

'Send him up. Pritchard,' Thanet explained to Lineham. 'In a state, apparently.'

'I wonder what he wants.'

They would soon find out, thought Thanet as Pritchard was shown in. The man was bursting with barely-suppressed emotion. The immaculate black hair was ruffled and his eyes blazed with a feverish light.

'I've just seen Mrs Hodges.'

'Do sit . . .'

'It's not true, is it?'

'Please, Mr Pritchard, do sit down.'

Pritchard came across the room in a rush and, leaning on Thanet's desk, bent forward and shouted into Thanet's face, 'I have a right to know!'

'Mr Pritchard, no one is . . .'

'How dare you withold information from me, her father!'

'Mr Pritchard! If you would just calm . . .'

'It's outrageous! It's . . .'

Thanet stood up so abruptly that his chair crashed over on to the floor. 'Mr Pritchard!'

Pritchard recoiled, his mouth hanging slightly open.

Thanet was sorry for the man, could understand his distress, but this sort of performance was intolerable. 'I refuse, categorically, to be bullied and harangued in my own office. If you're prepared to sit down and discuss this matter in a civilised fashion, then do so. Otherwise, I'm afraid I shall have to ask you to leave.'

For a moment Pritchard stood motionless. Then, without another word, he subsided on to the chair Lineham brought forward.

Thanet calmly righted his own, followed suit. 'Now then, perhaps we could start again.'

Pritchard ran his hand through his hair and, controlling himself with difficulty said, 'I've just seen Mrs Hodges.'

'And?'

'She told me some tale about a telegram, about Charity and Veronica leaving Dorset a day early at Easter ...' Pritchard faltered, stopped.

'Yes?'

'Is it ... is it true?'

'I'm afraid so.'

'But it can't be! It's impossible. Charity would never have ... That girl has made it all up.'

'Veronica, you mean?'

'Yes. She's evil, through and through. I told them. I knew it from the start. She's been a bad influence on Charity right from the beginning. But they wouldn't listen, they ...'

'Veronica didn't make it up,' said Lineham.

The new voice penetrated Pritchard's diatribe. His head swivelled in Lineham's direction. 'How do you know?'

'It was Sergeant Lineham who talked to the Principal of the Holiday Home,' said Thanet gently.

'Mr Harrison, you mean?'

Lineham nodded. 'That's right.'

'You know him?' Thanet asked Pritchard.

'I have met him, yes.'

'And would you say that he is the kind of man to fabricate a story like this?'

Pritchard avoided a reply by turning to Lineham. 'You spoke to Mr Harrison himself?'

'Yes.'

'What ... what did he say?'

'That on the Tuesday morning, a day before they had been due to leave, Charity received a telegram saying ...'

'It was addressed to Charity, not Veronica?'

'Yes.'

'What did it say?'

'That someone in the family was ill,' said Lineham patiently.

111

'Charity's grandmother, Mr Harrison thought. And that Charity should return home immediately.'

Pritchard ran his hand over his face, rubbed his eyes as if to erase his confusion. 'Who was it supposed to be from?'

'Mr Harrison wasn't sure. But he rather thought ... from you, sir.'

'Me!'

'You didn't send it?' interrupted Thanet.

'I did not.' Pritchard's eyes glittered like faceted jet. 'Really, Inspector, it's obvious, isn't it? Veronica sent it. And she addressed it to Charity so that if the truth ever came out, it would be Charity who got the blame. Which is precisely what has happened ...' His eyes narrowed, glazed.

'Something has occurred to you, Mr Pritchard?'

'What?'

'I wondered if you'd thought of something just then.'

Pritchard's stare was as blank as if Thanet were speaking a foreign language. Then he shook his head, made a visible effort to refocus his attention. 'I was simply explaining what must have happened.' His voice was flat.

'If something did occur to you, then it really is your duty to tell us,' persisted Thanet.

'I don't know what you're talking about, Inspector. And I think I'm entitled to an apology, don't you?'

Thanet gave up. He couldn't force the man ... 'Apology?'

'And an explanation. Why I haven't been told any of this before. Me, the girl's father! Why I had to find out myself, by accident, come around here and have to drag the information out of you ...'

Once more Pritchard seemed to be working himself into a rage. But this time, thought Thanet, it was different. For some reason the fire had suddenly gone out of him. Disillusionment, perhaps?

'I agree, it was unfortunate that you should hear of it second-hand ...'

'Unfortunate!'

'. . as we had every intention of telling you ourselves, later on today. No, Mr Pritchard, please let me finish. When we first heard about this telegram, yesterday afternoon, we didn't go around to your house to question you about it for one reason and one reason only. We thought that you and Mrs Pritchard had had just about as much as you could take, for one day. We judged it kinder to wait. Furthermore,' Thanet went on, raising his voice as Pritchard opened his mouth to interrupt again, 'furthermore, I must make it clear here and now that although we shall obviously keep you informed of the progress of our investigation, we have no *obligation* whatsoever to report to you every new development that comes along.'

'Indeed!' Now the indignation was genuine once more. 'You don't consider that we, as Charity's parents, have a right to know what is happening?'

'Not if imparting that information could prejudice the progress of the case, no, I'm sorry.'

'Don't lie!' roared Pritchard. 'Sorry, indeed! And *case* ... Yes, that's all it is to you, isn't it? A *case*.' His voice suddenly dropped and, piercing Thanet with a look of entreaty, he said, 'But she was my *daughter*, my only child ... Can't you see, I *need* to know.' His eyes filled with tears. 'Can't you understand that?'

Thanet could, only too well. The man's despair hammered at the wall of professionalism which was his only defence at such times. He shook his head, said gently, 'I'm sorry, Mr Pritchard. I truly am. All I can promise is that we'll keep you as fully informed as possible.'

Pritchard stared at him for a moment longer and then rose, blundering out of the room so clumsily that he almost knocked Doc Mallard over.

'I did knock,' said the little doctor plaintively, clutching at the doorpost to regain his balance, 'but there was so much noise ...'

'Come in, Doc. Yes, sorry about that, the poor man was in rather a state ... PM finished yet?'

Mallard ignored the question. He scowled and advanced into the room, straightening his half-moon spectacles. 'Who was that, anyway?'

'Charity's father. Nathaniel Pritchard, to be precise.

113

Doc, have you got the ...'

'*Nathaniel?* I thought that went out with the Victorians.'

'With the Old Testament, more like,' said Lineham with a grin. 'The Pritchard clan all sound as though they came out of the Ark.' He shuffled through the papers on his desk, picked one up. 'Hannah Pritchard — that's Charity's mother; Jethro Pritchard, Pritchard's brother; sister-in-law, Mercy Pritchard...'

'And that's a misnomer if ever there was one,' said Thanet, recalling Jethro's formidable wife. 'Look, could we discuss the ...'

'Jethro,' said Mallard thoughtfully. 'Now that is an unusual. name. Rings a bell ...'

Pointless to ask any more questions about the post mortem, Thanet realised. Mallard would impart the information in his own good time, was probably enjoying keeping them in suspense. 'You said that before, about "Pritchard", when you were examining the body.'

'Yes, I did, didn't I?'

'You haven't remembered why?'

'I'd have told you, if I had,' said Mallard irritably. 'What was Pritchard shouting about, anyway?'

'He thinks we ought to keep him fully informed about the progress of the case. And he was upset because he'd just discovered his daughter had been deceiving him.' Thanet told Mallard Veronica's story of the telegram and Charity's subsequent behaviour. 'You don't seem surprised,' he commented, when he had finished.

'Not really, no. Not in the least, in fact.'

'The post mortem!' said Thanet.

Mallard nodded sagely. 'If Pritchard was as upset as that about the business at Easter, I can't imagine how he'll react when he hears this.'

'Hears what?' cried Thanet, patience giving out at last.

But there had been no need to ask, really. Suddenly the knowledge was clear and cold within him and Mallard's reply, when it came, merely echoed the words in his mind.

'She'd just had an abortion.'

114

13

So that was that, Thanet thought. He had wanted proof to support his theory about Charity and now he had it. Her innocent image had finally shattered into a thousand pieces. It was true that, so far at any rate, he had not found her at all likeable, but now he was suddenly filled with pity for her. To have been in that particular situation with Pritchard as a father ... She would never have dared tell him. How desperately alone she must have felt.

'So that's where she was over the weekend,' said Lineham. His voice was tight with barely suppressed emotion and Thanet realised why: with Louise in danger of losing their baby, the thought of an abortion must at this particular moment be especially abhorrent to him.

Mallard nodded. 'Must have been.'

'But surely she couldn't have had an abortion without her parents knowing?' objected the sergeant. 'She was only fifteen, after all.'

Mallard sighed. 'I'm afraid it's only too possible. The medical profession is still divided on this issue of confidentiality. If a young girl comes to you and you confirm that she is pregnant, what do you do? Many of my colleagues feel bound to respect her confidence. They'll ...'

'I think that's positively irresponsible!' said Lineham.

Thanet glanced uneasily at Mallard. How would he react to such an attack on his profession? Would he realise the reason for Lineham's unwonted rudeness? Apparently he had. The little doctor gave the sergeant a sharp, assessing glance over his half-moons before saying testily, 'As I was about to say, they would naturally try to persuade her to confide in her parents, but if she refuses point-blank ... What can they do? And,'

Mallard raised his voice as Lineham opened his mouth to answer what had been merely a rhetorical question, 'if she does refuse to tell her parents and is determined about wanting an abortion, what then? Again, many of my colleagues would feel that she has the right to make up her own mind.'

'But how can a kid of that age possibly make up her own mind about something like that?' Lineham burst out.

'She isn't allowed to make the final decision in a hurry, believe me. First, she'd have to have counselling ...'

'Counselling!' said Lineham scornfully.

Mallard looked as though he would explode any minute now. He took a deep breath and in a voice taut with anger said, 'Look, sergeant, I've neither the time nor the inclination just now to go into the ethics of abortion. I'm simply trying to give you the facts. And the facts are that with sufficient determination, yes, Charity could have got an abortion without her parents' knowledge or consent. Either on the National Health, if she were lucky ...'

'Lucky!' muttered Lineham.

'Or,' Mallard went on, turning his back on Lineham and addressing his explanation to Thanet, 'at a clinic, if she could have afforded it. There are plenty of clinics which are prepared not to ask too many questions, provided the patient can pay.'

'Well I think ...'

'That's enough, Mike,' Thanet snapped. There was a limit to what he could allow Lineham to get away with, even in these circumstances.

Lineham frowned rebelliously, but clamped his mouth shut.

'Anyway,' Thanet went on, 'I should think it highly unlikely that Charity would have been able to pay, even if her parents had known about it, and I'm pretty certain they didn't ... If she'd had it done on the National Health, Doc, would it have been done locally?'

'Not necessarily. It would depend on who she saw initially, what he was able to arrange in the way of a second opinion and so on. Anyway, couldn't the baby's father have provided the money?'

The man she met at Easter? The timing would be right. 'It's possible, I suppose,' said Thanet doubtfully.

Mallard stood up. 'Well, I'll leave you to it. It's your problem now. Just thought you ought to hear right away. You'll get the full report later, of course, but I don't think there was anything else of much significance.'

'Cause of death?' said Thanet with a grin.

Mallard smote his forehead. 'You'll have to pension me off soon, I must be getting senile ... As a matter of fact, it was rather interesting. Contre-coup.'

'Really?' Thanet had heard of this, of course, but had never actually come across it in one of his cases.

Lineham was looking puzzled. 'It rings a bell, but ...'

Mallard loved expounding. 'Very interesting type of head injury.' He picked up an ash tray. 'Imagine this is your victim's skull. Now in the classic blow to the stationary head with a blunt instrument,' and he demonstrated by clenching his fist and hitting the side of the ashtray, 'you have a rather nasty fracture, with bits of bone being driven into the soft brain tissue lying directly below the area of impact. This is the most common type of head injury, the "coup" injury — "coup" meaning "blow", of course. But in *contre*-coup you have an injury to the *opposite* side from the point of impact, and this occurs when you have a *moving* head coming into contact with a stationary surface.' He demonstrated by striking the ashtray on Thanet's desk and putting his finger on the rim at a point directly opposite the site of impact.

Lineham was working it out. 'So you're saying that the damage to Charity's brain was on the opposite side from the injury from the latch.'

'That's right. It is believed that what actually happens in this type of injury is that you have compression of brain tissue when it strikes the inside of the skull and also a kind of tearing effect on membrane and blood vessels due to rotational forces which cause the brain to go on moving inside the skull after the head has come to rest.'

'So she must have been thrown against the latch with considerable force,' said Thanet.

'Not necessarily. If she'd been off balance, for example, with most of her weight resting on her right foot, the side of the injury ...'

'Was there any evidence of the blow, shove or whatever it was that threw her against the door?'

'Only a slight bruising across the right side of her face and neck'

'Caused by?'

'Ah, now here we enter the realm of speculation,' said Mallard, getting up. 'And that's your job, not mine. I must be off, I'm late already.'

'Just one more point,' said Thanet quickly as Mallard headed for the door.

Mallard stopped, turned to peer at Thanet over his spectacles. 'What?'

'Were there any traces of make-up on her face?'

'As a matter of fact, there were. Very slight traces, mind. Eye make-up, chiefly. Mascara and so on. Why do you ask?'

'Just wondered. Anyway, thanks for coming up, Doc.'

'Er ... Doc.' Lineham was on his feet, looking sheepish. 'Sorry I got so worked up just now.'

Mallard twinkled at him over his spectacles. 'If I apologised for every time I'd lost my temper, I'd be a rich man. Forget it.'

Thanet was glad that Lineham had saved him the trouble of a reprimand in somewhat delicate circumstances He gave the sergeant an approving nod and said, 'Now then, Mike ...'

'Just a minute, sir. Before we start talking about something else, why *did* you ask? About make-up.'

'Think, Mike. Do you recall seeing make-up of any description in her belongings? In her bag? In her suitcase? In her room at home?'

'No. So I still don't get it. What did make you ask?'

Thanet stood up. 'Come on, I'll tell you on the way to Lantern Street. We've got an appointment to see Veronica again, remember.'

'You see, Mike,' he went on, when they were in the car, 'last night on the way home, I was thinking ...'

Lineham groaned.

'What's that supposed to mean?'

'It was a groan of despair. When you say you've been thinking, I know that I'm going to hear something I should have thought of, if I'd only had the wit to do it.'

'You'd rather not hear?'

'On the contrary. I can't wait. I'm a masochist.'

'Well you did ask ...'

'So?'

'Well, as I said, on the way home last night, I was thinking. About Charity. Trying to assimilate all the stuff we learned yesterday.'

'I did that, too,' said Lineham resignedly. 'But it didn't lead me to questions about make-up.'

'Are you going to listen, or aren't you? If you want to go on beating your breast, then fine, go ahead and do it. If not, just listen and apply that brain you're forever saying you haven't got.'

Lineham's self-deprecation always irritated Thanet. He knew it ought not to, because he had long ago realised that it was a kind of barometer of the sergeant's state of mind. When Lineham was feeling good it was conspicuous by its absence. When things were going badly at home, or in his relationship with his difficult, demanding mother, the sergeant's confidence seemed to crumble away. At the moment, of course, he must be frantic about Louise.

'You see,' said Thanet, 'what puzzled me most was that if Charity had been going off the rails in the way Veronica described, why hadn't it shown in her appearance? The answer was ...'

'She wouldn't have dared let it show. Her father would have been down on her like a ton of bricks.'

'Exactly. But all the same, I somehow just couldn't picture her behaving as she was supposed to have behaved looking like a twelve-year-old schoolgirl.'

'There are plenty of men who like little girls.'

'Maybe. But the man Veronica described, the one Charity picked up on the train, just didn't sound that type.'

'That's true. Too young, for one thing. And his clothes ...

Sounded the sort to fancy himself with the girls, didn't he?'

'Quite. So then I thought, but suppose she *had* looked different. Put her in jeans, let her hair down, put some make-up on her and she'd have been transformed.'

'You're suggesting she actually did have other gear, then?'

'I am. And if she did, where would she have kept it?'

'I *see* ... Veronica's, of course!'

'Exactly.'

'Which was why she went there first on Monday, instead of going straight home from the station. She had to change.'

'Right. Of course, we didn't think to ask Carson to check how she was dressed, when he was making enquiries at the station.'

'Nor to ask Veronica, last night.'

'It hadn't occurred to me, at that point.'

'She didn't mention it herself, though — that Charity had left some stuff at her house.'

'Scarcely surprising. She was in rather a state, with one thing and another.'

'Let's hope she's calmed down a bit by now.' Lineham parked neatly in front of the Hodges' house and they both got out.

By day, Lantern Street was even more depressing than by night. It looked as though only four or five out of the forty or so houses were occupied. The minute front gardens, surrounded by crumbling brick walls, were gateless and rubbish-strewn. Broken gutters leaned crazily down over walls stained green with algae and the rows of boarded-up windows imparted a slightly sinister air to the place.

Lineham grimaced. 'Pretty grim, isn't it?'

'Infested with vermin, too, I shouldn't be surprised. I wonder why they stay here.'

'Cheap? It's not easy, being a widow, with a child to bring up.'

Lineham would know all about that particular struggle, Thanet thought. The sergeant had been only six when he had lost his father and Mrs Lineham had never remarried.

'Perhaps. Possibly the council won't re-house until the tenants are actually homeless.'

Mrs Hodges opened the door on the chain.

'I thought it might be Mr Pritchard back again,' she explained as she let them in. 'And there was no way he was going to get over my doorstep again.'

'Yes, we heard he'd been round to see you this morning.'

'According to him I'm the one who's to blame for Charity's death, because I didn't let him know Veronica was ill on Friday morning! As if it wasn't just as much his fault, going off to Birmingham like that without a word to me. And you should have heard him, ranting and raving about Veronica corrupting his precious Charity, who of course was as pure as the driven snow. Well I soon put him straight on that one, I can tell you. I really let him have it, believe me!'

'So we gathered.'

She pulled a face. 'Oh dear. Did he go round and start on you? I am sorry. Please, sit down, both of you.'

She looked exhausted, Thanet thought. Her skin was the colour of a tallow candle and her eyes were red-veined with lack of sleep. And yet, there was a lightness about her which had not been there yesterday.

'We've come to see Veronica, Mrs Hodges,' he reminded her gently. 'How is she, this morning?'

Her hands tightened in her lap. 'She's still in bed, I'm afraid.'

'I'm sorry. It really is important that we see her.'

She gave him a long, considering look. 'Perhaps you ought to know ... We had a long talk after you went, last night, Veronica and me.'

Thanet said nothing, waited.

'I couldn't just let it go like that ... She was so upset. When I went up, I could hear her crying ... I knew I wouldn't sleep. And I thought, well, she must think she's done something terrible, to be so afraid of me finding out. But she is my daughter, after all, and she's all I've got. We can't go on like this, what have I got to lose?·So I went in to her. At first she wouldn't listen, put her hands over her ears, but in the end I managed to make her see that I didn't care what she'd done, it wouldn't make any difference to the way I felt about her . . . So then she came out with it.'

Mrs Hodges hesitated. 'You may think it's a silly thing to get so worked up about, but then, you didn't know Veronica's dad. Straight as a die, he was, and honest as the day is long. I think that's why she felt so bad about it . . . She felt she'd let him down, as well as me . . .' Mrs Hodges sat up a little straighter and looked defiantly at Thanet. 'She'd been stealing, you see.'

Thanet nodded. 'At school.'

She looked astounded. 'You *knew*?'

'I guessed. I went to see Miss Bench the other day and amongst other things she mentioned that there'd been an outbreak of stealing at the school, shortly after she went there as Headmistress. And as you'd already told me about Veronica's distress and your inability to cope, at the time . . .'

'Miss Bench doesn't know, about Veronica?' said Mrs Hodges in alarm.

'Oh no. Certainly not. As I say, the matter was only mentioned in passing and not in connection with Veronica at all, I assure you.'

Mrs Hodges sagged a little, with relief. 'Thank goodness for that. Veronica couldn't have borne it coming out at school.'

'Charity found out, I suppose, and blackmailed her into going along with her?'

'Yes. She caught her at it one day. She didn't say anything at first, but gradually she started tagging along with Veronica and Veronica didn't dare say she didn't want to be friends with her . . . Veronica was terrified, all the time, that Charity might give her away, and gradually it got so that Charity was expecting her to spend all her free time with her, go around with her at school . . . It was just as I thought, Veronica didn't like her at all, she only went along with her because she was afraid of what would happen if she said she didn't want to. And all this time, the matter was never mentioned between them, not openly . . . Veronica said it was just the way Charity would look at her . . . And then the crunch came, a month or two before Easter. Charity wanted her to go on holiday with her, to

Dorset. Veronica didn't want to go. She wanted to stay here with me, she knew I'd be all on my own, otherwise, right over the holiday ... But Charity wouldn't take no for an answer. And that was when she finally threatened her. Oh, not directly, openly, "I'll tell," that sort of thing. But slyly, nastily. "What a pity it would be if your mother found out ..." Then, another time, "Wouldn't it be awful if Miss Bench found out ... if the girls found out ..." So in the end Veronica gave in. She simply could not *bear* the thought of being branded as a thief.' The muscles along Mrs Hodges' jaw tightened as she clenched her teeth. 'If I'd known what was going on ...' she said balefully.

Then what? Thanet wondered. Would Mrs Hodges have been so furious with Charity that it could have happened as Lineham had suggested? A quarrel, a blow struck in anger ...

But if so, Mrs Hodges was putting on a superb performance. He wouldn't have thought her capable of such dissimulation. Still, there was a lot at stake, for her. The most ordinary person is capable of extraordinary feats when the whole fabric of his life is threatened.

Mrs Hodges was shaking her head in bewilderment. 'I don't understand any of it. I still can't believe that Veronica could have ... But she told me herself, so I suppose I must believe it. I can't imagine what got into her. Stealing ... her dad would have turned in his grave.'

'Mrs Hodges,' said Thanet gently. 'You remember when I came to see you, yesterday?'

She nodded.

'You remember telling me how your husband's death hit you so hard that later you blamed yourself for not understanding just how badly Veronica was taking it?'

'Yes, but I don't quite see ...'

'Mrs Hodges, did you know that if a previously honest child suddenly starts stealing, it is often regarded as a cry for help?'

'What do you mean?'

'It's a bid for attention. It often begins with stealing from the parent whose affection is desired. Did you notice whether you yourself lost any sums of money around that time?'

Mrs Hodges passed a hand over her face. 'Now that you mention it ... Yes, I do remember. I just put it down to me. I mean, I was in such a state I didn't really know whether I was coming or going ...'

'Presumably, when Veronica found that that didn't work, she started stealing at school.'

He watched as understanding afflicted her. 'Are you saying ... you're saying it was my fault, then.'

Thanet shook his head with impatient compassion. 'I think that at this stage it is irrelevant — it doesn't matter — whose *fault* it is. The important thing is to understand what went wrong, and why. Then you can pick up the pieces and start again. I'm simply saying that I'm sure Veronica is not by nature a thief — the very fact that she has gone to such lengths to keep it from you shows how upset and ashamed she is of what she did — and that her behaviour at that time was the result of a particularly distressing set of circumstances. I honestly don't think anything is to be gained by dwelling on whose fault it was. From what you say it sounds as though you and Veronica have got the chance of a fresh start, and who knows, the fact that you've been through difficult times together may bring you closer than you ever were before.'

Mrs Hodges was listening intently. Oh God, he thought, just listen to me preach. Thanet the social worker again. When I start off on that tack there's no holding me. If Lineham starts grinning I swear I'll ... but a glance out of the corner of his eye told him that the sergeant was listening with apparent solemnity.

'Yes ...' said Mrs Hodges. 'Yes, I can see that ...' She was silent for a few moments and then said, 'Well, you've certainly given me something to think about, Inspector. Thank you.'

All in the day's work, said an ironic little voice in Thanet's head. But he simply smiled, said, 'Good.'

'There's just one thing, though,' said Mrs Hodges anxiously.

'What's that?'

'There won't be any need for Miss Bench to know, will there?'

'I should think it extremely unlikely. But I think I can promise you that if it did become necessary for her to know, Miss Bench wouldn't even consider making the matter public. She's a very understanding woman.'

'You really think so?'

'I do. And now, Mrs Hodges, if we could see Veronica ...'

She jumped up, her movements suddenly buoyant. 'I'll go and see if she's up. If she's not, she may take a few minutes.'

Thanet smiled. 'Don't worry. We'll wait.'

As soon as the door had closed behind her, Lineham said, 'Bull's-eye again!'

'What are you talking about?'

'The stealing. You were right, yet again. Sickening, that's what it is, sickening. First you guess about the stealing, then about the make-up ... It's enough to give anyone an inferiority complex.'

'Oh come on, Mike, aren't you laying it on a bit thick? They're both very minor matters, after all.'

'Minor! Well, OK, they might be minor in themselves, but the one put you on to the fact that Charity might be a blackmailer, the other on to where she stashed her gear ...'

'We don't *know* that yet, Mike, we're only guessing.'

'It's your guessing I'm complaining about. Some guess! I bet you a fiver you're right ... No! I take that back. I can't afford to throw fivers away like confetti, I'll bet you a pint ...'

Thanet laughed. 'Done!'

'What am I doing? I must be crazy. We both know you're right.'

'We're about to find out.'

They grinned at each other as footsteps were heard on the stairs. Thanet felt his stomach clench in anticipation. He had to be right. He needed Charity to have left her belongings here. There was no telling what he might find ...

A moment later Mrs Hodges entered the room, followed closely by Veronica. Like her mother the girl looked pale and very tired. Without the make-up she had been wearing last night she looked much younger.

'Ah, Veronica,' said Thanet with a reassuring smile. 'I hope you're feeling better, this morning?' Then, without waiting for an answer, 'We've just come to collect Charity's things.'

'Things?' said Mrs Hodges. And then, with relief in her voice, 'Oh, her jeans and so on . . . Run up and fetch them, will you, love?'

Veronica disappeared with alacrity.

Lineham, behind Mrs Hodges, rolled his eyes at Thanet in mock despair.

Thanet ignored his clowning with difficulty. 'You knew she left stuff here?'

'Well of course. Why shouldn't I? There's only one small bag . . . I felt sorry for the girl,' she added defensively. 'I may not have liked her, but I did feel sorry for her, with a father like that. She could hardly blow her nose without asking his permission first. As for doing any of the things girls usually do . . . And she did ask my permission — didn't she, love?' She turned to Veronica, who had just returned, a large nylon shoulder bag dangling from one hand.

'To do what, Mum?'

'To leave that here.' Mrs Hodges nodded at the bag.

'Yeah, sure.'

'It was only a few bits and pieces of clothes. Some jeans and that . . . and some make-up. Her father would have locked her up rather than let her wear trousers, wouldn't he, Veronica, and as for make-up . . . He'd have thought she was on the streets or something.'

'So when did she wear them?' said Thanet. 'She could hardly have gone out in them, in case it got back to her parents.'

'Indoors, mostly,' said Veronica. 'She'd come round on a Saturday, change into her jeans, put some make-up on and we'd play pop records.'

'To tell you the truth,' said Mrs Hodges, 'I encouraged it. Made me feel she was more normal. It was just a harmless bit of fun, that's all.'

Harmless? Thanet wondered. Or had it fed Charity's fantasies, encouraged her secret rebellion? Had those stolen moments been so heady, spiced as they were by the knowledge

126

that she was breaking out of the rigid guidelines laid down by her father, that she had grown to hunger for more dangerous ways of defying him?

'You said, "Indoors, mostly" ...'

'Well, she did wear them on the way home from Dorset at Easter,' said Veronica. 'She couldn't have worn them at the Holiday Home, trousers weren't allowed for girls.'

Mrs Hodges made a clicking sound of disgust. 'Ridiculous,' she muttered.

'She changed in the toilet, on the train,' Veronica added.

'And this weekend?'

'She wasn't wearing them when she left, but she was when she came back.'

'And presumably she changed back into her normal clothes when she called here on the way home from the station?'

'Yes. And washed her make-up off.'

Thanet held out his hand for the bag. 'May I see?'

She handed it over. Thanet could feel Lineham's attention riveted to the bag with the quivering anticipation of a terrier watching a rat-hole. Normally, at this point, Thanet would have left, returned to the office to examine its contents at leisure. But today he didn't. He rather thought — hoped — that he would have to question Veronica about something that was in it. He lifted it on to his knees, unzipped it and rummaged about inside. Ah yes, here it was ... His fingers closed triumphantly over the small oblong shape and withdrew it.

The other three stared at the wallet as if mesmerised.

Turning aside a little so that its contents were not visible to the two women, Thanet flicked through it, his calm, unhurried movements betraying nothing of his inward agitation. If he was right, this small leather object could hold the key to the riddle of Charity's death. He *had* to be right ... But it didn't look as though he was. The letter he had hoped to find was not there, and the wallet contained only a bundle of five-pound notes (he'd check how much, later) and, in a separate compartment, a polaroid photograph. Perhaps this would help ...

He took it across to the window, to have a look at it in better light. Charity smiled up at him. She was wearing jeans and a yellow crash helmet and was sitting astride a motor cycle. And yes ... He gave a satisfied nod. The registration number was clearly visible. He handed the photograph to Lineham, who immediately saw the point. They exchanged a gratified glance.

'Let Veronica take a look, will you, Sergeant?'

Thanet waited while Mrs Hodges and the girl studied the photograph together.

'Do you know whose motor cycle that is?'

Both women shook their heads.

'Unless ...' said Veronica.

'Yes?'

'It could belong to the chap she picked up at Easter. She told me he had one — and he was carrying a crash helmet when I saw him at Paddington, I told you.'

Thanet retrieved the photograph. No point in wasting time asking questions. It would be a simple enough matter to check. There was just one other point he wanted to bring up, though.

'I asked you last night if Charity knew anyone — a man — who wears pebble-lensed glasses.'

Even before he had finished speaking Veronica was shaking her head. 'I told you, no.'

'I wondered if, having had time to think about it over-night ...?'

But she was equally emphatic. No. And he was equally certain she was lying. It was pointless to persist at the moment, she obviously wasn't going to budge.

He thanked them both for their help and left.

'Why d'you think she's lying about the chap with glasses?' said Lineham, when they were in the car.

'Protecting him, perhaps?'

'But why should she?'

'Fellow feeling? He could be another of Charity's victims. Blackmailers rarely stop at one, once they get a taste for it. If Veronica knows him, likes him, even, and is aware that Charity had some sort of hold on him ...'

'Could be, I suppose. Bit of luck with the photograph though, sir, wasn't it?'

'Being able to read the registration number, you mean. Yes. As soon as we get back, you can ring Maidstone, get them to run it through the computer.'

'With any luck, we've got him!' Lineham exulted.

'Perhaps.' Over the years Thanet had learned that it was safer not to expect too much.

All the same, he knew the excitement in Lineham's face was reflected in his own when the sergeant put the phone down and said triumphantly, 'Got it, sir! David Williams, 10, Bryn Mawr Terrace, Cardiff.'

14

'There's the Severn Bridge, sir.'

Thanet knew that the note of satisfaction in Lineham's voice was caused not by their first glimpse of the famous suspension bridge but by what it signified: they were nearing the end of their journey.

He eyed the soaring, swooping curves appreciatively. 'Impressive, isn't it?'

As soon as the computer had come up with Williams' address, Thanet had decided to drive down to South Wales that very afternoon. Lineham had been against the idea from the start.

'What's the point, when we know he lives in London?'

'But we don't know where, do we? This seems as good a way as any, of finding out. So just get a move on and arrange clearance for us, will you? I'd like to be away between one and two, if possible.'

'But . . . two hundred miles there and two hundred back, just for an address?'

'It's not quite as simple as that.'

'But why can't we just get Cardiff to check it out for us, sir?'

'I agree, we could. But I'd prefer to go myself.'

'But . . .'

'If you say "But" just once more, I'll . . . Look, Mike, we're going, and that's that. At least, I am.' Then, more gently, 'Mike, I appreciate that this is not a good time for you to be out of Sturrenden. If you'd prefer not to come with me, I'd quite understand.'

Lineham flushed. The gynaecologist had confirmed that an induction would be necessary, but had refused to commit himself as to timing. Louise would be kept under constant observation, her case under daily review, and that was all he was prepared to say at present.

'It's not that, sir. Oh, hell, to be honest, I suppose it is. Not that they'll do anything now before tomorrow.'

'You're thinking of not being able to visit her tonight, I suppose?'

Lineham nodded miserably.

'In that case, why not stay here? I can easily get another driver.'

'But I'd like to come, sir ...'

Thanet swallowed his exasperation. 'Look, why don't you nip along to the hospital now, see if they'll let you in to see Louise for a few minutes?'

'Do you think they would?'

'You can but try. They might well, in the circumstances ...'

They did, and three-quarters of an hour later Thanet and Lineham were on their way. They shared the driving, changing over when they stopped for a quick cup of coffee at Membury Service Station, and so far the journey had gone without a hitch. The M25 had been almost deserted and although the tedious stretch along the A322 through Bisley, Bagshot and Bracknell had been slow, once they were on the M4 they'd been able to keep up a steady 70 mph and were now only half an hour from their destination.

'They say people used to queue for hours to cross on the old ferry, before the bridge was built,' murmured Thanet, gazing out across the glittering expanse of water.

'Why did you say, "it is not quite as simple as that"?' said Lineham suddenly.

'What?'

'When I said it wasn't worth driving two hundred miles there and two hundred back, just for an address ...'

'Ah, yes ... Well, if you don't mind, I'd rather tell you later. On the way back. I may be wrong ...'

Lineham frowned. He hated being kept in the dark. Thanet, equally, hated giving explanations before he was ready for them. And it was rather a long shot, after all ...

Thanet once more gave his attention to the scenery. He'd

131

never been to Wales before and now he regretted that he was approaching it at such speed and on such an errand. Road signs in Welsh began to flash by, giving him a sense of entering a foreign land, and already the character of the landscape was changing. Hills dotted with sheep loomed ahead and he began to sense the nearness of the mountains. Even the grass in the fields looked tougher, coarser, less groomed, subtly creating the impression of a greater wildness to come.

As they skirted Newport Thanet thought how much pleasanter it would have been if Joan had been with him and they had been setting off on a holiday weekend, just the two of them, and they could have made a more leisurely approach, through Chepstow, perhaps ...

'Cardiff,' said Lineham with satisfaction. 'This is where we turn off.'

'Straight through the city centre, they said. Though we haven't exactly chosen the best time of day, have we?'

It was a quarter to five and the traffic was thickening by the minute. They crawled along the Newport Road into the heart of the city, paid their courtesy call and emerged with directions to Bryn Mawr Terrace. They reached it just before six o'clock.

'Don't think much of the local architecture, do you?' Lineham said.

'Depends what you're used to, I expect.'

This, Thanet supposed, was the Welsh version of the Victorian Terrace: narrow little houses built of ugly rough stone blocks, with the window surrounds picked out in a variety of garish colours. Number ten sported a particularly virulent shade of orangey-pink. The net curtains at the downstairs window twitched as Thanet knocked at the door.

'Mrs Williams?'

The woman peered up at him like a suspicious sparrow. She was middle-aged, her sharp face and skinny body all knobs and angles. Her head was encased turban-style in a blue chiffon scarf punctuated by the ridges of plastic rollers.

'What do you want?'

'We'd like a word with Mr David Williams, please.' Thanet introduced himself, offered identification.

132

She glanced up and down the street. 'You'd better come in a minute.'

The hall was so tiny that there was barely room for the three of them to squeeze into it, but she did not offer to show them into the sitting room. She shut the front door behind her and turned to face them, folding her arms across her chest.

'What do you want with our Dai?'

Thanet had no intention of telling her in any but the vaguest terms and there followed a few minutes of sparring, each of them in his own way enjoying the contest. Eventually she capitulated.

'He works at a garridge round the corner,' she said grudgingly. 'Mechanic. He'll be home any minute now.'

Thanet carefully avoided giving Lineham a 'told you so' look.

'You'd better wait in here.' She squeezed past them to open a door, led them in.

A motor cycle roared up the street, cut off outside.

'That'll be him.' She scuttled off, closing the door behind her, and there was a murmur of voices in the hall. When she came back in, followed by her son, she was carrying a sheet of plastic which she draped over one of the armchairs.

'I'm not having you dirtying my nice clean chair with that filthy old pair of jeans.'

She was determined to stay and listen ('It's my right, he's my son, isn't he?') and it wasn't until Thanet courteously pointed out that he, too, had his rights and one of them was to take the boy away and question him at the police station that she reluctantly left them in peace.

David Williams was in his early twenties and certainly fitted the description Veronica had given them. Thanet could see why Charity would have been attracted to him. He was a well-built, good-looking boy with an air of slightly swaggering virility. He had adopted an almost aggressively nonchalant pose, sitting well back in his chair with the ankle of one leg resting on the knee of the other. He was chewing gum with the non-stop, rhythmic movements of a cow chewing the cud.

Thanet decided that he couldn't be bothered to waste a lot of time in preliminary skirmishing. He and Lineham still had a long drive ahead of them tonight. He produced the polaroid photograph.

'That your motor cycle?'

Williams' jaw stopped moving for a moment, then began again, more slowly

'What if it is?'

'Oh come on, Williams. Don't you read the newspapers?' The boy's eyes narrowed. 'What're you talking about?'

He really didn't know, Thanet was prepared to swear to it.

'That girl, in the photograph ... She's dead.' He caught the flash of relief in Williams' eyes before the boy said disbelievingly, '*Dead?*'

'To be precise ... Murdered.'

Williams stopped chewing altogether and for a moment his jaw hung down. Then he sat up and with an impatient movement took the gum from his mouth and flung it in the direction of the empty fireplace. It landed on the hearth where, thought Thanet, its presence would no doubt later earn Williams a sharp rebuke.

'You're having me on.'

Thanet shook his head. 'And as we found that photograph amongst her belongings ...'

''Ere, what you getting at?'

'... we'd like you to tell us about your relationship with her.'

'Relationship!' Williams gave a bark of sour laughter. 'Oh boy, I like that. Relationship! Look, Inspector, that bird was a good screw, that's all. A one-night stand, no more, no less.'

'People don't write letters to a one-night stand,' said Thanet. He shook his head reprovingly. 'Most unwise, to commit yourself to paper like that.'

Williams was looking frightened now. Thanet glanced at Lineham.

'Of course,' said the sergeant smoothly, 'we don't make snap judgements. We can't afford to. Especially in murder cases.'

'I didn't even know she was dead till you told me, a minute

ago! I told you, I only ever met her once, and that was months ago.'

'Once could be more than enough, in certain circumstances,' said Thanet.

'What ... circumstances?'

'Suppose you tell us?' said Lineham gently. 'Perhaps we've got it wrong.'

Little by little Lineham teased out the sorry tale. Williams had been working in London and had driven down to Dorset to deliver back to its owner a motor cycle which had been involved in an accident. Charity had picked him up on the train back to Paddington. He had taken her out for a Chinese meal and then they had gone back to his room, where they had spent the night together. The photograph had been taken "for a lark", next morning.

'Did you know she was under-age?'

Williams stared blankly at him for a moment, then groaned, put his head in his hands.

'Did you?'

Williams raised his head, eyes blazing. 'What do you think? Look, Inspector, I don't want to sound like I've got a swollen head, but I don't have no problems finding birds, see? I don't have to go risking trouble with the law running after little girls. If I'd known, I wouldn't have touched her with a bloody barge-pole!'

'Oh come on, Williams, you must have suspected, surely. After all, she was a virgin.'

'Virgin!' Williams was shaking his head in disbelief. 'I don't know what fairy-tales you've been listening to about her, but believe me, Inspector, someone's been leading you up the garden path.'

'Well of course, you would say that, wouldn't you. It lets you off the hook.'

'It's the truth!' shouted Williams. 'That little bitch knew her way around, I can tell you. That's why ...' He stopped abruptly.

'That's why what?'

Williams shook his head. 'Nothing.'

'You were going to say, that's why you didn't believe her when she told you that she was pregnant and that you were the father.'

'If you bloody well know it all, why are you going on at me like this?' snarled Williams.

'We want the details,' said Thanet. 'This is a murder case, remember.'

'OK, OK, I'll give you the bloody details, if it'll get you off my back ... Like I said, she left next morning and I didn't see her again, not once, from that day to this. There was something about her ...' He shook his head, as if to erase the memory. 'Once was enough, that's all.'

'Yet you wrote to her.'

'To try and shut her up! She was a real pain, that girl. Kept on and on writing me letters, always the same garbage ... How much she'd enjoyed herself with me, how much she was looking forward to seeing me again, blah, blah ... how difficult it was for her because her old man was so strict ... As if I cared! Far as I was concerned it was over, finito!' A complacent little smile curled the corners of his mouth. 'Had other fish to fry, didn't I?' The grin disappeared. 'Then she writes and tells me she thinks she might be able to get away over the Bank Holiday. We'd be able to have the whole weekend together, she says. She had it all worked out — what time she'd arrive, where we'd go, what we'd do... Well, that did it, I'd had it up to here. This time I did write back and told her straight, I wasn't interested, I'd found someone else, I'd be away that weekend anyway — well, you've read the bloody letter, you know what I said in it.'

Throughout this recital Thanet had once again unexpectedly been filled with compassion for Charity. He imagined her romanticising the sordid encounter at Easter until it took on the aura and intensity of a *grande passion,* transforming this shallow, callous youth into everything that was noble and desirable in a man. He saw her eager hopes dashed as the days and then weeks went by without a word in reply, pictured her last attempt to recreate reality from fantasy in her bid to join Williams for the weekend, her shattering disappointment when she at last received the longed-for letter ... And then, to cap it all, the mounting panic as she realised that her period was overdue ...

'And it was soon after that she drops her little bombshell,' said Williams.

'Told you she was pregnant, you mean?'

'Yeah. In a bloody telegram, no less. Probably afraid if she sent a letter I'd chuck it straight in the bin without reading it.'

'Claiming you were the father, I presume?'

'You bet. You could've knocked me down with a feather ... Oh no, I thought, you're not pinning that one on me, no matter how hard you try.'

'So what did you do?'

'What would you have done? I scarpered, of course, moved back home. I knew she'd never find me down here and I was pretty sure I could get my old job back.'

Thanet believed him. It was, in fact, precisely what he had expected Williams to do.

'Just one last question, then. Can you give us an account of your movements last Monday evening, between nine and eleven pm?'

'Between nine and eleven,' repeated Williams, frowning with concentration. 'Monday ...' Abruptly, his face cleared and a slow grin spread across his features. 'Is that when she ...?'

Thanet could see what was coming.

'From eight till midnight I was playing in a group at a disco, here in Cardiff.' His fingers jauntily thrummed imaginary strings. 'Guitar, Inspector. Go ahead and check.'

They would, of course, thought Thanet as Lineham took down the details, but Williams was so cocky in his relief that it would obviously be only a matter of routine. It really did look as though the Welshman was out of the running.

He said so to Lineham as they walked back to the car. 'We'll get Cardiff to check for us, in the morning.'

Lineham did not reply and Thanet looked sharply at him. The sergeant's face was closed, brooding.

'What's the matter, Mike?'

'You knew, didn't you?'

'Knew what?'

'That Williams would be here. That's why you were so determined to come.'

'Not knew. Guessed, perhaps.'

'How?'

Thanet shrugged. 'I just tried to think myself into his shoes, work out how he would react . . . It was very much a long shot.'

'But it came off,' said Lineham gloomily.

They had reached the car.

'Shall I drive for the first half?' Thanet hoped that Lineham would take the hint and drop the subject. He really didn't feel in the mood for another session of breast-beating by the sergeant.

'I don't mind.' Lineham obediently got into the passenger seat and sank into a silence which lasted until well past the Severn Bridge.

'Well, Mike,' said Thanet eventually. 'What do you think? Think he was telling the truth, about Charity being sexually experienced? Incidentally, odd about that letter, isn't it? That it never turned up. I really did expect to find it in the bag Charity left at Veronica's.'

'Hmm?' Lineham made an effort to rouse himself. 'She probably tore it up. After all, it wasn't exactly the sort of letter to cherish, was it? She was probably furious he'd given her the brush-off.'

'True. Anyway, do you think he was telling the truth?'

'About her sex life, you mean? Yes, I did. Didn't you?'

'Yes. But of course, if he was, the question is, who?'

'Difficult to see how she ever had the opportunity.'

'I agree. Mrs Hodges can't have known anything about it, or she'd have mentioned it, I'm sure.'

'Might be one of the masters at school, sir?'

'At a girls' school, Mike?'

'With respect, sir, I think you're a bit out of date. You often find masters in girls' schools these days. As a matter of fact, Louise and I met a master from Sturrenden Girls' Tech at a party recently. Teaches history.'

'You're not going to tell me he wears pebble-lensed specs?'

Lineham smote his forehead in mock self-admonition. 'Why ever didn't I think of him before? Of course he does!'

'All right, Mike, cut out the sarcasm. You're right. If there's one master at the Tech, there might be more. We'll get on to the school first thing in the morning.'

'What about the Bible classes?'

'I told you, there are only two boys, and they're much too young. There's Jethro, of course. He often saw her home, apparently — and come to think of it, he's just the type to have a yen for little girls. Inadequate, probably sexually deprived . . . And his wife's enough to make any man impotent. Yes, the more I think about it, the more likely it seems. It could explain why Mrs Jethro hated Charity so much — and why Jethro himself was so on edge, when I saw him . . .'

Thanet settled down to concentrate on his driving. At Membury they stopped again to refresh themselves with a cup of coffee and a substantial snack. Thanet, aware that it would be too late to ring Joan when he got home, tried to contact her from a phone booth in the service station complex, but without success. Once again, she was out. He gritted his teeth as he slammed the receiver down. He felt as though she was daily floating further and further away from him, like a balloon cut loose from its mooring, and he was helpless to do anything about it.

Now it was his turn to sit in brooding silence and Lineham, preoccupied no doubt with his own anxieties, made no attempt to break in upon his reverie until they were approaching Maidstone.

'Isn't that lightning ahead?'

'I didn't notice.' But a moment or two later Thanet saw the distant flicker for himself. 'You're right, Mike. Looks as though there's a storm coming up.'

Now he had something else to worry about: Bridget. She'd always hated thunderstorms and invariably woke up if there was one during the night. He began to pray that he would get home before it broke. His mother-in-law could sleep through anything.

139

He made it in the nick of time. The first really loud clap of thunder came as he was running his car into the garage and by the time he emerged the first heavy drops of rain were falling. In his hurry he had forgotten to shut the gate and, cursing, he sprinted back down the drive to do so. He wasn't going to risk a repeat of yesterday's performance, with Ben.

By the time he reached the front door the rain was hammering down and his hair was plastered to his scalp. In the hall he tilted his head, listened intently. Was that a cry? Yes, there it was again.

'Mummyyyy ...'

Peeling off his wet jacket as he went, he took the stairs two at a time as outside the lightning flashed and, a second later, there was a deafening crash of thunder. He tossed his jacket in the direction of his bedroom door and went straight into the children's room.

'MUMMYYY ...'

Bridget was sitting bolt upright in bed, hands pressed hard over her ears, eyes tight shut, face screwed up. Ben, who had inherited his grandmother's knack, slumbered on undisturbed.

'Sprig ...' Thanet plumped down on the bed beside her and gathered her into his arms. Hers at once coiled themselves around his neck and she burrowed her face into his shoulder.

'Daddy ...'

He began to stroke her hair with soothing, rhythmic movements. 'Hush darling, it's all right, Daddy's here. Don't cry, it's all right ...'

Lightning flared and, simultaneously, there was a thunderclap so loud that Thanet's eardrums rang and the house shook. Torrential rain lashed against the windows.

Bridget's body convulsed and she gave a little cry, clung to him even more tightly.

'Don't worry, darling. It's quite safe.' He fervently hoped that this was true, that his mother-in-law's house had a good earthing system.

'The house ... It *trembled.*'

'This house has stood here for hundreds of years, love, and it's going to stand for hundreds more ...'

He continued to administer comfort and murmur reassurances while the storm raged overhead and presently the intervals between lightning and thunder began to lengthen as it drifted away. Gradually Bridget quieted and, exhausted by the tensions of the last half an hour, closed her eyes and relaxed against him. When he judged that she was almost asleep, Thanet began to ease her gently down into the bed.

'Don't go 'way, Daddy,' she said sleepily.

He told her that he would stay just a little while longer but that the storm had moved away now and that yes, if it returned, he would come to her again.

Suddenly, shockingly, she opened her eyes wide and in them there was the painful honesty of someone who at last faces a long-evaded truth.

'Mummy's never coming back, is she, Daddy?'

'Sprig!' Weakness buckled his legs and he subsided on to the bed again. 'Of course she is! In just over two weeks now she'll be home for good. Whatever makes you say such a thing?' Into his weary brain sprang the question: has she heard something I haven't?

'Because she doesn't love us any more.'

'Darling, that simply isn't true! Of course she loves us.' But the statement had chimed in so exactly with his own fears that he knew he'd sounded unconvincing. For Bridget's sake he tried again. 'You *know* she does.'

But Bridget was shaking her head, her eyes solemn. 'If she did, she wouldn't have gone away ...'

'Sprig ...' Thanet put his arms around her and lifted her into a sitting position once more, conscious of a sudden spurt of anger against Joan. How dare she cause such insecurity in their beloved daughter? And how dare she put him once again into the impossible position of defending something which, in his heart of hearts, he found indefensible?

Since Joan had started work they had had to deal with many uncomfortable questions from the children and for Thanet, especially, it had been difficult to find convincing answers. For the first ten years of their marriage Joan had apparently been content to remain a housewife, and it had come as a rude shock

141

to find that inwardly she had long been hankering after a satisfying career of her own. Fortunately Thanet had seen the light in time and, having realised that if he persisted in opposing Joan he would most surely lose her, he had at last capitulated and given her his support.

But all along, deep down inside, he had known that, given the choice, he would have preferred it to be otherwise and at a time like this, when his own doubts and fears were more profound than they had ever been, it took an almost super-human effort to attempt to convince Bridget that hers were unjustified.

But for her sake he did his best, only to find that when at last he crawled into his lonely bed, his own anxieties had prolif-erated, hydra-like.

Suppose Bridget was right, and Joan wasn't coming back. This might explain why she'd been so elusive of late. Perhaps Bridget had overheard a fragment of conversation between her mother and grandmother, on the telephone.

Or — and in some ways this thought was comforting, in others it made him feel even worse — was it possible that his own anxieties over Joan were becoming so powerful that he was unwittingly communicating them to the children? He had heard of such things happening.

What a responsibility children were, he thought as he tossed and turned, a truly awesome responsibility. You embarked upon 'having a baby' without ever really considering that the baby soon becomes a toddler, a child, an adolescent, that it will make impossible demands upon your patience and tolerance, stretch your financial resources until they snap, and bring to an end for ever the twosome for which you abandoned your bachelor state.

He loved Bridget and Ben, couldn't begin to visualise life without them, but there was no doubt that bringing up child-ren was uphill work most of the way. Not just physical work, though in the early years that was demanding enough; equally wearing were the endless decisions to be made, decisions in which mundane things like food, clothes, toys and television programmes became inextricably bound with ethics and morality, so that you were constantly struggling to define your attitudes and justify your behaviour in an attempt to communicate your values to your children.

Then there was the vexed question of discipline: to punish or not to punish? And if so, how? To what degree? It was all so difficult, so complicated. It was much easier, he supposed, if you had a rigid code to follow, like Pritchard. For Pritchard everything was white or black, right or wrong, good or evil. Pritchard would never have to stop and ask himself if he were doing the right thing. Though Pritchard's religion must be cold comfort to him now, when he had lost the daughter he had alienated by it.

Once again Thanet found himself wondering exactly what had happened during that week seven or eight years ago, when Charity had been kept home from school. Whatever it was, it had changed her radically from a lively, mischievous child whose unacceptable behaviour had no doubt been an over-reaction against too strict a discipline at home, into little more than a zombie. No, not a zombie, he corrected himself, for underneath Charity's rebellion had continued. She had simply bided her time, waited until she had gathered sufficient strength to deal her father a mortal blow, sharpening prematurely the only weapon she possessed, her sexuality.

Furthermore, Thanet was convinced that whatever Pritchard had done to her during that week had not only changed her outward behaviour and steeled her antagonism towards him, but had also taught her some bitter lessons which had soured her expectations of life and destroyed her chances of enjoying good relationships with others.

He had to find out what had happened and before he finally fell asleep he determined to put it high on the list of the next day's priorities.

15

Next morning Thanet was riffling hurriedly through the reports which had piled up during yesterday's absence when Doc Mallard put his head around the door and said, 'Got it!'

Thanet glanced up abstractedly. 'Morning, Doc.' Then, as he took in Mallard's air of suppressed excitement, 'Got what?'

Mallard glanced back over his shoulder. 'Ah, morning, Sergeant.' He opened the door wider and advanced into the room, followed by Lineham. 'How's your wife?'

'Much the same, thanks, Doc.'

'I heard she'd gone into hospital early. What's the problem, exactly?'

The two men chatted about Louise for a few moments and Thanet, anxious to be off, waited with as much patience as he could muster. At last there was a suitable hiatus and he put in quickly, 'Got what, Doc?'

'Jethro Pritchard. You know I kept on saying the name rang a bell? Well, I finally remembered.' Mallard clasped his hands behind his back and gave a self-satisfied little bounce on the balls of his feet.

'Remembered what?'

'Can't recall the details, I'm afraid. Not surprising, really. Must have been all of — oh, twenty years ago, I'd say.'

'What must have been?'

'The Court case.'

With difficulty Thanet refrained from saying, 'What Court case?' The little doctor, he realised, was enjoying keeping them in suspense. But he did wish he'd get on with it ...

Mallard glanced from one attentive face to the other and said, 'Very unsavoury it was, that I do remember. Something to do with little girls ... Yes, I thought that would interest you.'

He glanced at his watch. 'Good gracious, I'm late for surgery already.'

'But ...'

Mallard flapped his hand. 'Sorry. Told you, can't remember the details. Can't do all your work for you, can I?'

'Thanks, Doc,' Thanet called after his retreating figure. He and Lineham looked at each other.

'Bible classes, indeed!' said the sergeant.

'Let's not jump to conclusions. What I don't understand is that Pritchard — Charity's father — must have known about this conviction. And in that case, why on earth did he trust his brother to see Charity home?'

'Perhaps he thought that being his brother, and her uncle ...'

'Bit naive, don't you think?'

'Perhaps Jethro convinced him he was on the straight and narrow. After all, if all this happened twenty years ago and he's not been in trouble since ...'

'But we don't know that, do we, Mike? Anyway, I think the first thing is for you to go through the files, find out exactly what happened. We can't tackle him until we're sure of our facts. You'd better get someone to give you a hand. I really must be off. I only dropped in to the office for a few minutes, just to see if anything important had cropped up ...'

'You don't call this important?'

'Yes, of course it is, but the point is, I've been wanting a chance to get hold of Charity's mother alone, and on the way in this morning I saw Pritchard in the street, heading for the town. I'd like to catch her before he gets back.'

'How do you know he wasn't on his way to work? Oh, of course, he told us he didn't have to go in for the rest of the week, didn't he. Right, then. Is there anything else you want me to do? I know I've got to check with the school, see if there are any other male teachers ...'

'Get that house to house on Lantern Street started, concentrating on the earlier times. And go through these reports, see if there's anything interesting.'

'Right, sir. Don't worry, I'll cope. See you later.'

On the way to Town Road Thanet sternly resisted the temptation to consider the implications of Mallard's news. It was a question of priorities. He would have ample time, later, to think about Jethro Pritchard. For the moment it was Mrs Pritchard he wanted to concentrate on, and he spent the short journey clarifying in his own mind precisely which points he wished to raise with her, and in which order. He only hoped that she had not taken advantage of her husband's absence and gone out.

But he was in luck. Although there was at first no answer to his knock, he thought he saw movement behind the net curtains in the front room, and tried again. A moment later Mrs Pritchard opened the door.

'Good morning, Mrs Pritchard. You said I could come and talk to you if I needed your help.'

She hesitated, then stood back. 'Come in.'

She led him into the bleak little sitting room, untying her apron as she went. She laid it over the back of a chair and sat down, folding her hands in her lap. Her meek, waiting stillness, her black dress and the severity of her hair-style combined to give her the simple dignity of Quaker women in the late seventeenth century.

Thanet seated himself opposite her. 'This has been a terrible week for you.'

His sympathy at once brought tears to her eyes, but she blinked them impatiently away, compressed her lips. 'My mother's funeral has been put off until Tuesday.'

Thanet nodded.

'What ... what about Charity?'

'I'm afraid there'll have to be an inquest first.'

'Oh.'

She hadn't realised, he could tell from her stricken, resigned look.

'When will that be?'

'On Monday ... Mrs Pritchard, I came to see you because, although I know that this must all be incredibly painful for you, I feel that as Charity's mother you can help me in a way no one else can.'

146

'How do you mean?' It was barely more than a whisper.

'First of all, there's something I must tell you, something which I know will distress you. It will have to be made public at the inquest and that is why I wanted to see you first, to tell you myself. So that you will be prepared.'

She was rigid in her chair, bracing herself against what was coming.

'When she died, your daughter had just had an abortion.'

Thanet watched with pity as her eyes snapped shut, as if to repudiate this glimpse of a too-harsh reality. He could only guess at the powerful and confused emotions she must be experiencing, but of one thing he was certain: they were all painful.

Suddenly she opened her eyes again. 'You don't mean ... Are you saying that she wasn't ... killed, after all, that she died because of ... what she'd had done to her?'

'Oh, no. No, I'm sorry if I misled you. But if it's any comfort at all, I can tell you that she didn't suffer. She died instantly.'

Mrs Pritchard flinched.

'But you must see that because of the abortion, however unlikely it might have seemed to you and your husband, Charity must have been ... ' How could he tactfully put it? '... on intimate terms with a man.'

She ducked her head to hide her embarrassment. 'Yes, I can see that,' she whispered. Then she looked up and said in a kind of gasp, as if the protest were being forced out of her, 'But I just don't see how she could have. I mean ... she would never have had the opportunity.'

'Nevertheless ...'

For a long moment they sat in silence as the indisputable implications of the word sank in.

'Yes,' she said at last, with a sigh. 'You're right, of course. Nevertheless, she must have.'

Again she was silent, thinking, and Thanet waited patiently. Finally she said, 'I'm sorry, Inspector, it's no good. I can't think of *anyone*. She just didn't know any men, not ... privately, so to speak. Not to my knowledge, anyway. She must have ...' She shook her head in sad disbelief.

147

'She must have been deceiving us for some time.'

'I know. And you must believe me when I say I'm sorry to cause you additional distress at a time like this.'

For the first time she smiled, if that brief, joyless upturning of the corners of her mouth could be called a smile. 'You're very kind, Inspector. Not a bit like what I imagined a policeman to be.'

Now it was his turn to be embarrassed and he brushed the compliment aside by hurrying on. 'So what I want you to do is talk to me about Charity, tell me what she was like, as a person. I think that somewhere along the line things must have gone badly wrong for her somehow, and I feel that if I can understand why, it would help me in investigating her death.'

'I don't see how.'

'It's difficult to explain, precisely. But I always find that the more I understand about the ... victim, of such a crime, the clearer things become.'

'I'm not sure, anyway, after what we've just been saying, that I knew her as well as I thought I did.'

'I can see that. All the same, she lived in this house with you all her life. I really would be grateful if you would just talk to me about her. Say anything you like.'

At last Mrs Pritchard relaxed a little. She sat back in her chair and gazed at the fireplace with the blank, unseeing gaze of someone focusing on a mental image. 'There's not much to tell, really. As I said before, she was quiet, considerate, used to help me with the chores ... I never had to chase her, to get on with her homework or do her piano practice.' Mrs Pritchard's eyes flickered briefly in the direction of the piano.

It was shut, Thanet noticed, and the music had been put away, out of sight.

Mrs Pritchard lifted her hands helplessly. 'I just don't know what to say. She never gave any trouble.'

This was the opportunity Thanet had been waiting for and he tried not to appear over-eager as he said, 'Never?'

Mrs Pritchard gave a puzzled frown. 'What do you mean?' But she avoided his eye, he noticed.

'Well, I understood that when Charity was around seven

148

or eight, she used to be quite a handful at school.'

She was staring at him, remembering, and plainly wishing that the conversation had not taken this particular turn. 'How did you know that?'

He shrugged. 'We pick up all sorts of snippets of information during the course of an investigation such as this. One of the people I talked to was Miss Foskett.'

She was silent, waiting, clearly apprehensive.

'I understand that you and your husband went to see her, at her request, to see if anything could be done.'

Still she said nothing.

'Miss Foskett said that after that interview, Charity was away from school for a week, and that when she came back, she was a different child ...'

Mrs Pritchard's eyes slid away from his questioning gaze. 'It's all such a long time ago,' she murmured evasively.

Thanet was sure that the whole episode was indelibly etched upon her memory. He also saw that she was now faced with a dilemma: she wanted to be co-operative, help him as much as she could, but she didn't want to be disloyal to her husband. Her next words confirmed this.

'My husband is a man of very strong religious faith, Inspector.'

'I know.'

'He ... he sees it as his duty to try to stamp out evil wherever he may come across it.'

Thanet inclined his head.

'Even when it is in his own daughter.' Her voice was no more than a murmur.

'I suppose,' said Thanet encouragingly, 'he sees any kind of unruly behaviour as the work of the devil.'

She looked up, eagerly. 'You *do* understand. That's right. That's exactly what he does feel.'

'And you agree with him?'

'Of course.' But her voice lacked conviction. 'Well ... to a large extent, yes.'

'But not, perhaps, when it came to trying to discipline Charity.'

149

'She was so small,' Mrs Pritchard cried, her sudden passion shocking in its intensity. 'She didn't understand. How could she? Oh, she'd been very naughty, I know that, but ...'

'So what did he do?'

Mrs Pritchard moved her feet restlessly as if she would like to get up and run away. Thanet regretted having to press her, but he felt that this incident, so far back in the past, might have been of profound significance in Charity's life, had perhaps shaped and directed her future behaviour to such an extent that it could even have been partly responsible for her death. But it was possible that he had misinterpreted the whole affair and if so, he had to know.

'He punished her, I presume?' he said, as gently as possible.

Mrs Pritchard pressed her lips together, looking away.

'Did he beat her?' said Thanet, even more softly.

The muscles in her jaw worked and still she refused to look at him.

'Locked her up in her bedroom perhaps? Fed her on bread and water? Told her she'd stay up there for ever if she didn't learn to behave herself ...?'

Mrs Pritchard was shaking her head now as if the movement could shut out his words. Her body was stiff with tension and Thanet hated himself for having to do this. All the same he found himself persisting, almost savagely.

'Said she'd burn in hell, no doubt, if she didn't promise to ...'

Mrs Pritchard clapped her hands over her ears and fell back in her chair.

'Don't!' she cried. She sucked in air as if she were suffocating and then expelled it in a long, slow sigh. Her hands fell away from her ears. 'I can't bear it,' she said.

What price kindness now? thought Thanet grimly, shaken by his own inhumanity. He felt thoroughly ashamed and asked himself what right he had to deplore the way her husband browbeat her if he himself then proceeded to behave in exactly the same way. Once again, he asked himself if there was some quality in the woman herself which called forth this sort of response in men. And had Charity's revolt against her father's

150

strictures partly been the result of a determination not to become like the mother whose lack of spirit she had come to despise?

So, how should he proceed? Should he leave it, or should he persist? Was his duty to the dead or to the living? Loyalty and obedience to her husband were obviously deeply engrained in Mrs Pritchard's emotional make-up. What right had he, Thanet, to attempt to break down anyone's moral code? If he were to continue, succeed in overcoming Mrs Pritchard's resistance, how would it affect her relationship with her husband? Would powerful feelings of guilt cause her even more, unnecessary suffering, or would she perhaps find it a liberating experience, the first step out of the state of resigned submission in which she had lived all her married life?

He had to risk it, he decided. If, after all these years, Mrs Pritchard still found even the memory of the experience so traumatic, how much more powerfully must Charity have been affected.

But from now on there would be no more bullying. He loathed browbeating witnesses such as this. Already, in the last half an hour, his self-respect had suffered, his image of himself become tarnished, and these things were important to him, he had to hold on to them to be able to feel right about his life, his work.

It would have to be persuasion, then.

'Look,' he said gently, 'I know how you're feeling, believe me. I can see that the memory is painful to you and that you are constrained by loyalty to your husband. All right, I accept that. I won't push you any further. But I can assure you that I wouldn't be pressing you like this if I didn't feel that it really is important for me to know.'

This, he decided, was as far as he was prepared to go. If she still refused, then that was that, he would have to desist.

He waited, and the silence stretched out, on and on. At last he made up his mind that he would give her just ten more seconds. He began to count silently. One, two, three . . .

He had reached nine when she spoke.

'All right, I'll tell you.' Her voice was barely audible.

151

She leant forward in her chair and clasped her hands in her lap, staring down at them as if they could give her strength for the ordeal. Then, taking a deep breath she began to talk in a halting monotone.

When Charity had got home from school that day, Pritchard was waiting for her. He told her to go straight up to her room, where earlier he had spent some time making his preparations. Mrs Pritchard had had no idea what those preparations were, she only knew she had dreaded Charity's return more than she had dreaded anything in her life before.

Pritchard went upstairs behind the little girl and shut the bedroom door behind them. Mrs Pritchard, terrified, had crept half-way up the stairs to listen, ready to flee at a second's notice. She knew that her husband would have been furious to think that she was eavesdropping. A few moments later Charity began to whimper.

Mrs Pritchard looked up. 'But he didn't lay a finger on her, I swear it. I'd been so afraid he would lose his temper, but he didn't. In some ways it might have been better if he had. At least it would have been over and done with, then.'

A few moments later Charity began crying out, 'No, Daddy, no, no, no,' over and over again.

Mrs Pritchard's hands were twisting, squeezing, kneading. 'I couldn't think what he was doing to her. I still hadn't heard him say a single word. And then, a few minutes later, I heard him coming to the door, and I ran downstairs, as quietly as I could.'

Thanet was imagining it all: the crying child; Mrs Pritchard on the stairs, hand pressed against her mouth, ears straining; the heavy thud of Pritchard's footsteps crossing the room and Mrs Pritchard's silent flight to the kitchen.

'He opened the door of the bedroom and called me. "Hannah?" he said. "Come up. I want you to hear this."'

Thanet swallowed. His mouth was dry, his heart-beat accelerated. He had longed to know what had happened to Charity to change her so, but now that he was about to find out he feared the knowing.

Mrs Pritchard's eyes were screwed up against the pain of the memory and her next words emerged jerkily as if forced out against her will. 'He had ... he'd tied her up. He'd attached ropes to the four corners of the bed and padded them around her wrists and ankles. She was ... she was spreadeagled. She looked so ... so helpless, and I shall never forget the look she gave me. It was so full of ... terror, and entreaty. She didn't speak — I don't think she could. She just lay there ... "Take a good look," my husband said, "because it's the last time you'll set eyes on her until she's seen the error of her ways. And as for you, my girl," he said to Charity, "there you'll stay until the Devil comes out of you." Then he pushed me out of the room and locked the door behind me, put the key in his pocket.'

Mrs Pritchard pressed her fingers against her trembling mouth, then, doggedly, she went on. 'He just left her there, day after day ... He fed her, of course, or tried to ... bread and water, that's all ... but she wouldn't take them, spat them out. He said this was a sign that the Devil was still strong in her ... But the worst thing was ... he didn't untie her, not once, not even to go to the toilet. He just let her lie there in her own filth ... She must have hated that, she was always such a clean little girl.'

Mrs Pritchard's control was slipping now and she bit her lip, took another deep breath. 'In the end, one day while he was out, I went up to the landing and called through the door. "Charity, listen," I said. "You've got to say you're sorry, do you hear me? Even if you're not sorry, pretend you are, or you'll be locked in there for ever. Tell Daddy you'll behave yourself in future ... Please, darling, do it for me, do it for Mummy ..." '

Now, at last, the tears which she had held in check brimmed over as she relived the scene outside her daughter's door. She fumbled blindly for the apron she had folded over the back of her chair and Thanet realised that she was seeking a handkerchief. Silently he took one from his pocket and pressed it into her groping hand. Then he rose, crossed to the window and stood looking out, giving her a chance to regain her self-control.

Her story had shocked and revolted him. In his work he had come across many instances of child abuse, cruelty and neglect, and the worst, for him, were always the ones in which 'punishment' was inflicted in cold blood. Pritchard's calculated approach, the prolonged nature of Charity's suffering, filled him with anger and a compassion which extended only in part to Charity's mother, for had she not stood by and let it happen?

And yet ... what did he understand of a woman like Mrs Pritchard, conditioned as she was, no doubt, by the rules of her sect to obey her husband and live cut off from society in this soul-destroying atmosphere? The Pritchards and their like inhabited a strange, harsh landscape as alien to him as a primitive tribal culture. What right had he to judge or to apportion blame?

Mrs Pritchard was calmer now, drying her eyes and blowing her nose.

'I'm sorry,' she said. 'Your handkerchief ... I'll wash it.'

Thanet smiled at her. 'Don't worry about it.'

'Inspector ...' She hesitated. 'These last few days I've wondered ... Perhaps I'm being punished for what I did. But she was so little and I was so afraid she was going to ... just waste away. Do you think I was wrong, to tell her to deceive him like that?'

'What nonsense! You behaved as any mother would, in the circumstances.'

But even as he spoke the thought slid insidiously into his mind: had Charity's mother, in an attempt to save her daughter, unwittingly set her on the path of deception which had led, ultimately, to her death?

Mrs Pritchard was shaking her head. 'I didn't know what else to do. I've thought and thought about it and I just don't know what else I could have done. I couldn't leave it to go on indefinitely, could I?'

Once again, Thanet gave her the reassurance she needed. Besides, it was true that she didn't seem to have had any alternative; loyalty would have prevented her from reporting him to the police and open defiance would have been unthinkable.

'My husband was only doing what he thought was right.' But her tone lacked conviction and suddenly she stiffened, cocked her head. For a moment there was panic in her eyes.

'There he is, now.' She pushed Thanet's handkerchief out of sight between her skirt and the side of the chair, then smoothed her hair, straightened her shoulders, and stroked her dress into neat, disciplined folds. By the time Pritchard entered the room a few moments later she was apparently quite composed, her face turned expectantly towards the door.

'Ah, there you are, Nathaniel. Inspector Thanet was just ...'

But Pritchard was less self-absorbed, more observant than Thanet would have given him credit for. He looked searchingly into his wife's face and turned to Thanet.

'Why has my wife been crying? I told you, I don't want her bothered.'

Beneath the belligerence Thanet detected the concern. Better get it over with, he thought.

'Your wife is upset because I brought some rather bad news.'

'Well?' snapped Pritchard.

'As you probably know, in cases of unnatural death, there has to be a post mortem. The results of the post mortem on your daughter will be made public at the inquest next week, and I came here this morning because I knew that the findings would be a shock to you, and I wanted you to have the opportunity of hearing them in private.' There was no way of cushioning the blow. 'She had just had an abortion.'

Pritchard seemed to stop breathing and briefly he had no more animation than a waxwork, with painted hair, painted eyes, a painted face. Then he put out a hand and groped behind him for a chair, sank into it as though his legs would no longer bear his weight.

'I don't believe it.'

'I'm afraid it's true.'

'There must be some mistake.'

Thanet shook his head. 'No mistake. I'm sorry.'

Pritchard stared at him, thinking. Eventually, 'Who was

responsible?' he said, his eyes beginning now to glitter with anger.

'The father, you mean? We don't know, yet.'

'Then shouldn't you be trying to find out?'

'That's precisely what I am trying to do,' said Thanet patiently.

'What do you mean?' Pritchard glared at him. 'You're not saying you expect us to know anything about it, I hope? You don't think we'd have tolerated any kind of ... loose behaviour, do you? Oh no, believe me, if we'd had any idea what was going on, we'd soon have put a stop to it, I assure you.'

'You are her parents,' said Thanet. 'I thought that you might perhaps have had some suggestions ...'

'Well we haven't! To our knowledge, Charity never even knew any men, let alone had any opportunity to ...' His mouth worked and his nostrils flared in disgust. And then, for so brief a moment that Thanet could almost have thought he had imagined it, Pritchard froze and a name flashed telepathically between them, each syllable as clear and precise as if it had been shouted aloud: *Jethro*.

Pritchard stood up as precipitately as if he had been propelled by some powerful, invisible force.

'I'm sorry, Inspector, we can't help you. Neither my wife nor I wish to discuss this matter any further.'

Thanet came slowly to his feet. 'Very well, Mr Pritchard. But if anything does occur to you ...'

'Then of course we'd be in touch.'

The man was hurrying him to the door now. Clearly, he couldn't wait to be rid of him.

The overnight storm had cleared the air, bringing the unseasonable heatwave to an end, and outside the air was cool, almost chill. Thanet shivered as he walked to the car, thinking. He wouldn't mind betting that Pritchard's next move would be to go steaming around to Gate Street and accuse Jethro of seducing Charity — possibly, even, of murdering her. Thanet could be wrong, of course. Perhaps Pritchard had not immediately suspected Jethro. But in case he had, the question was, should Thanet try to get to Jethro first? If he did, he could use the fact that Pritchard was probably on his way to get Jethro to talk. And of course, it was possible that Thanet was misjudging Jethro, in which case he perhaps had a moral responsibility to warn the man of a possible visit from Pritchard.

On the other hand, he didn't want to tackle Jethro until he was in possession of the facts about that earlier conviction — always assuming that Mallard was right, and there had been one.

He'd contact Lineham first, he decided, see if he'd got anywhere with records. Cursing the fact that in his haste, earlier, he had used his own car and not a radio-equipped police car, he drove to the phone box at the end of the street and, with one eye on the Pritchards' house, rang the office.

Lineham sounded pleased with himself.

'Doc Mallard was right, sir.'

'Well?' said Thanet impatiently. He wasn't in the mood for a session of Lineham's dramatic pauses.

'In 1966 Jethro Pritchard went down for eighteen months, for indecent assault on a fourteen-year-old girl.'

'What was her name?'

'Janet Barker. Address: 4, Davies Street, Sturrenden. I've got the rest of the details here, if you want to hear them.'

'Later. Look, I want to see Jethro Pritchard as soon as possible, and I want you with me. How soon can you get around to Gate Street?'

'Five minutes. I'm on my way.'

Thanet hurried back to his car. There was still no sign of Pritchard. Good. He drove to Gate Street and parked a little way up the road from number fourteen. On edge in case Pritchard beat Lineham to it, he settled down to wait with as much patience as he could muster.

He didn't have to wait long. Lineham was as good as his word, and a few minutes later his car pulled up in front of Thanet's with a flourish.

'What's the hurry, sir?'

Briefly, Thanet explained. 'So it's my guess that Pritchard will be arriving at any minute. Now, I've been thinking, while I was waiting for you. We haven't enough time to get a full confession out of Jethro, and in any case I have the feeling he's the type who'll talk more readily to one person than two. So what I want to do at the moment is soften him up for when I next see him, show him that we know what he's been up to, and then leave him to stew. So we'll look as official as possible — notebook much in evidence and so on. All right?'

'Fine.'

'You've not met either of the Jethro Pritchards yet, have you?'

Lineham shook his head.

'A pleasure in store for you, then. Come on.'

Mrs Pritchard answered the door. 'He's out,' she said in response to Thanet's request, her eyes glinting with satisfaction at being able to thwart him.

'Could you tell us where he is?'

'At the school,' she said grudgingly.

Thanet thanked her politely and they turned away.

'Imagine living with that!' said Lineham.

'Don't feel too sorry for him.'

'Sympathy could get in the way, you mean? You're a fine one to talk!'

They grinned at each other. Over the years their working relationship had become so finely tuned that there was mutual recognition of the times when it was necessary to fall back on protocol and the times when the barrier of rank simply did not exist. Both of them were aware that it was Thanet, not Lineham who had to be on his guard against emotional involvement.

'I bet he's pretty pathetic, though,' said Lineham. 'Child molesters usually are.'

'Judge for yourself. There he is.'

Jethro Pritchard was approaching. He was walking slowly, head down, shoulders hunched. He hadn't noticed them yet.

'Looks pretty preoccupied,' said Lineham.

'He's got reason to be, wouldn't you say? Good morning, Mr Pritchard.'

Jethro stopped dead and his head came up with a jerk. They

158

caught the flash of fear in his eyes before he mumbled a response.

'We wanted a word with you. This is Sergeant Lineham.'

Jethro's eyes flickered from one to the other, seeking reassurance and finding none.

'Shall we go into the house?' said Thanet. 'Or perhaps you'd prefer to sit in the car. Oh, don't worry, we're not taking you in ... yet.'

Jethro hesitated, caught between two equally unpalatable alternatives: running the risk of his wife overhearing the conversation and being seen to be 'helping the police in their enquiries'. He chose the latter as the lesser of the two evils. He and Thanet got into the front seats and Lineham scrambled into the back, ostentatiously producing his notebook and leaning it on the back of Thanet's seat, pencil at the ready.

'What's all this about?' said Jethro, with a nervous glance at the notebook.

'Janet Barker,' said Thanet. 'That's what this is all about.'

But his shock tactics hadn't worked. Jethro's watery brown eyes were merely resigned. 'I was expecting you to dig that up.'

'I suppose you must have been. After all, there is a certain obvious similarity between the two cases.'

'What two cases?' faltered Jethro.

'Oh come on, Mr Pritchard. Janet and Charity, of course.'

'I don't understand.'

'Don't you?'

'No!' cried Jethro. 'I don't. Janet was just ... well, that was different. But Charity ... Charity was killed.'

So Jethro had prepared himself for this, had decided to pretend ignorance of Charity's sexual experience. All Thanet's instincts told him that Jethro was guilty of something, but of what, that was the question. Of having seduced Charity? Of having murdered her? Or of both?

Thanet studied the man carefully. Jethro's eyes fell away from his. Sweat beaded his forehead.

'I'm not just talking about Charity's murder, and well you know it,' said Thanet fiercely. He had used the ugly word deliberately and had the satisfaction of seeing Jethro wince.

159

Jethro's ferrety features had sharpened, as if the flesh were melting away, and his sallow skin had taken on a waxy, yellowish hue. He moistened his lips with the tip of his tongue.

'I don't know what you mean,' he muttered.

'Don't you, Mr Pritchard? Oh, I think you do ... Where did you go after Bible classes, you and Charity? Did you stay at the meeting hall? Go to the school? Or perhaps you came here, when your wife was out and your mother safely in bed ...'

'I don't know what you're talking about, I tell you,' said Jethro frantically.

'I don't think your brother is too pleased, that you should so have abused his trust. He's very upset, naturally. In fact, I have the feeling he'll be along at any minute, to ... shall we say, discuss the matter with you.'

Jethro cast a desperate glance back along the street.

'Well, I think that's all for the moment, Mr Pritchard.' Thanet leaned across and released the door handle. 'Out you get.'

'I can go?' Jethro was bewildered.

'For the moment. But make no mistake about it, we'll be back.'

Thanet waited until Jethro had got out and then said quietly to Lineham, 'See you back at the office.'

They left Jethro still standing on the kerb, gazing after them.

Thanet was quite pleased with the way the interview had gone. Now, what he needed was more evidence against Jethro. He would have to run a second house to house check in Gate Street. It was surprising how often a second check paid off. And it would be worth finding out exactly what time the meeting at the school had ended, and making enquiries in the row of houses opposite. He already knew that Jethro had been out and about for part of the relevant time, but if they could find someone who had actually seen him leave the school that night, and could prove that he had lied ...

He said so to Lineham as they climbed the stairs to the office together.

'I'll get someone on to it right away, sir.'

Thanet picked up a sheet of paper which had been left in a prominent position on his desk.

'A message from Carson ... ah ...'

'He was still trying to get through to the school when I left. What does it say?'

'You were right. There are four masters at the school. One of them is in his thirties, has fair hair and wears pebble-lensed specs. What's more, guess what he teaches?'

'Music!' said Lineham, with a flash of inspiration.

Thanet gave a slow, satisfied nod.

'Music.'

16

Leslie Mathews, music master at Sturrenden Technical School for Girls, lived in a large Victorian house on the main Ashford Road. Once the home of a prosperous Sturrenden tradesman, the place now had a sad, neglected air, the row of bells a mockery of the generous life-style for which it had been designed.

Thanet twice pressed the bell marked Mathews and waited, but no one came.

'He's out, by the look of it.'

'Unless the bell's not working,' suggested Lineham.

'Better go up and see, I suppose.'

Mathews lived on the top floor. The front door was unlocked, they discovered, allowing people to come and go as they pleased, and Thanet and Lineham climbed the three long flights of stairs tutting at the lack of security. The distant throb of pop music grew louder as they rose.

Facing them at the top was a door with a china plaque. A garland of flowers surrounded the legend, *Roger lives here*. The capital R would have graced a mediaeval manuscript, thought Thanet. It was an elaborate affair of precise brushstrokes and graceful curlicues.

'Very pretty, I'm sure,' said Lineham's sarcastic voice in his ear.

A second door, a few paces to the right along the narrow landing, bore a roughly-torn scrap of paper tacked to the door with a drawing pin. DAVE, it proclaimed in sprawling capital letters. This was where the music was coming from and it was now so loud that Thanet could feel the floorboards vibrating beneath his feet.

By contrast, the card on Mathews' door was reassuringly

orthodox: a small oblong of white pasteboard with the sur-name only written in neat, italic script. Thanet wondered how Mathews got on with his neighbours.

There was no answer to their knock.

'Dave?' said Lineham.

Thanet nodded and they moved back along the landing. Lineham had to hammer on the door with the side of his fist to make himself heard above the din and when at last it was flung open a tide of sound swept out to engulf them. How could anyone bear to shut himself in a confined space with that level of noise, Thanet wondered. It would be his idea of hell.

Dave was unshaved, unwashed (by the smell of it) and undressed, save for a skimpy towel draped around his waist. Over his shoulder Thanet glimpsed a tumbled bed and a girl's face.

Dave hadn't appreciated the interruption.

'What d'yer want?'

'Mathews,' bellowed Thanet, pointing along the landing.

'How the hell do I know where he is!' And Dave made to slam the door.

Thanet put his foot in the gap and produced his ID.

Dave glowered at it, muttered something and rolled his eyes.

'Hang on.'

Leaving the door ajar he went back into the room, switched off the tape and returned a moment later with a dressing gown slung around his shoulders.

'OK,' he said resignedly. 'But make it quick. I'm otherwise engaged, as no doubt you've noticed.' And he gave a salacious wink.

'We wanted a word with Mr Mathews,' said Lineham, 'and he seems to be out.'

'So?'

'Have you any idea where he might have gone?'

'Half term, isn't it? Could be anywhere.'

'Where, for example?'

The man shrugged. 'How should I know? Now, if you don't mind ...'

'But we do,' said Lineham. 'So why not give us a suggestion or two and we'll leave you to ... get on with it.'

Dave grinned. 'How can I refuse an offer like that? OK, let's see. Tried little Miss Prim and Proper yet?'

Charity? Thanet wondered. Surely Mathews hadn't brought her here.

'His fiancée,' said Dave. 'Er ... what's her name ...' and he snapped his fingers in the air, once, twice. 'Eileen,' he said triumphantly. 'That's it. Eileen.'

'Eileen who?'

'Something to do with hunting. That's how I remember names, see. There's a word for it. Let me see now. Hunting ... hunting ... got it! Chase. Eileen Chase. That do you?' And he began to close the door.

'Where does she live?' said Lineham quickly.

'Sorry, haven't a clue.'

'And her job?'

'Teaches. Same school as him.'

Lineham thanked him and let him go. The music blared out again behind them as they clattered down the uncarpeted stairs.

'So, what now, sir?'

'Might as well go and see Eileen Chase, if we can get her address. If she and Mathews are engaged, there's a chance he might be with her. And anyway, I'm curious about her, aren't you?'

A phone call to the school produced the address and they drove to the quiet residential area on the far side of Sturrenden where, according to the secretary, Eileen Chase lived with her invalid mother. It was a nineteen-thirties development of semi-detached houses, each with its small front garden sporting a minute lawn and the ubiquitous rose-bed. Shangri-La was distinguished from its neighbours by a beautiful Nelly Moser Clematis. Thanet paused for a moment to admire the fountain of huge, pale pink flowers with their distinctive carmine bar before approaching the tiny front porch.

Once again there was no answer to the knock.

'Not our day, is it?' said Lineham, turning away in disgust.

Thanet held up his hand. 'Just a minute.' His head was cocked to one side, listening.

'I can't hear anything.'

Thanet gave a quick, admonitory shake of the head, then pointed to the ground.

Lineham looked down. The single step up into the porch had been converted to a ramp. He looked chagrined. 'Of course, the mother ... I didn't notice.'

Now he knew what they were listening for and a moment or two later they heard it: the faint, rhythmic squeak of a wheelchair approaching.

Then the door opened, on the chain.

'Yes?' The segment of face was at waist level.

'Mrs Chase?'

'That's right.'

'Nothing to be worried about, ma'am. We're just on a routine enquiry. Police officers.'

'Why aren't you wearing your uniforms?'

'Plain clothes police, ma'am.'

'I want to see your identification.'

'Certainly.' Thanet extended his card and a hand emerged through the crack, plucked it from him. Then the door closed.

Thanet caught Lineham smothering a grin. He didn't blame him. What if the old lady didn't open up again? Thanet found himself imagining the farcical scene in which he confessed to the Super that he'd been relieved of his warrant card by an old lady in a wheelchair.

The door opened again, wide, this time.

Mrs Chase was tiny, and painfully thin, the bone structure of face and hands clearly visible beneath the pale, almost transparent skin. Her shoulders were hunched and she had to twist her head sideways and back at an unnatural angle to look up at her visitors. There was a rug over her knees and her face was heavily scored with lines of pain and ill temper — scarcely surprising, Thanet thought. He had heard of people who managed to endure the most horrific lives with sweetness and good humour, had even met one or two of them, but suspected that if he himself were ever to find himself in such a

165

position he would lapse at once into peevishness and self-pity.

She held out his card. 'You can't be too careful these days, you know.'

'Quite right, ma'am. It's very sensible of you, to take precautions.'

Especially, he thought, in her position. One of the most abhorrent recent manifestations of violent crime was the upsurge of attacks on the most vulnerable members of society, the old and the handicapped, often in their own homes.

'What do you want?'

'We're trying to find Mr Leslie Mathews — your daughter's fiancé, I believe. He wasn't at home, so we thought he might be here.'

At the mention of Mathews' name she had pursed her lips and a look of intense dislike had flitted across her face. Now there was satisfaction in her voice as she said, 'What's he done?'

'As I said, ma'am, this is just a routine enquiry. We think Mr Mathews might be able to help us.'

She squinted up at him and Thanet guessed that she was trying to work out how best to turn this unusual situation to her own advantage.

'You'd better come in,' she said at last.

'If you could just tell us whether or not Mr Mathews is with your daught —'

'Come in, I said.' Her sharpness revealed that she was not accustomed to being thwarted. With astonishing deftness she swivelled the wheelchair and set off down the passage. Thanet and Lineham had no option but to follow.

The room into which she led them looked as though someone had taken a gigantic broom and swept all the furniture to the edges of the floor. This was presumably to allow Mrs Chase freedom of movement in her wheelchair, Thanet thought, but the effect was curiously disturbing, as though the stage had been cleared for some major upheaval or confrontation. A gas fire was full on and the atmosphere was suffocating.

'That's better,' she said. 'Chilly out there. Sit down.' She waved a hand at a settee against the wall and both men complied. At once she manoeuvred her chair into a position squarely in front of them and only a few feet away, thus giving herself the psychological advantage of being able to look down on them. And who could blame her, Thanet thought. He could understand such stratagems becoming second nature to someone in her position.

He decided deliberately to relinquish the initiative, see where she led them. Lineham glanced at him, obviously wondering if Thanet's continuing silence indicated that he wanted the sergeant to take over the questioning. Thanet gave an almost imperceptible shake of the head. Lineham sat back.

'I knew it!' said Mrs Chase. 'I knew there was something. As soon as I set eyes on him, I could tell there was going to be trouble. I warned Eileen, but she wouldn't listen.' Her mouth twisted. 'Mooning about like a love-sick schoolgirl. At her age!'

'How old is your daughter, Mrs Chase?'

'Thirty-seven. I ask you! She should know better, have some dignity. What's more, he's four years younger than she is. Disgusting, that's what I call it. Engaged, indeed!'

'When are they hoping to be married?'

'They haven't deigned to inform me, yet.'

'They'll live here, I suppose?' What an appalling prospect, thought Thanet. Mathews must be either a brave man or an insensitive one even to contemplate such an idea.

'So they say. Going to convert upstairs into a self-contained flat. Eileen says it won't make any difference to me, she'll be able to do for me everything she does now, but I can't see it, myself, when she's got a husband to fuss over.'

And this, Thanet thought, was no doubt the root of the trouble. Understandably. This late blossoming of her daughter's love-life must have filled Mrs Chase with terror. Thanet couldn't like the woman, but he could sympathise with her predicament.

'Why do you want to see him?' Mrs Chase's eyes were suddenly avid, alight with the hope that Thanet might be able to throw her a life-line, that her daughter's romance was about to be still-born.

167

'I'm afraid I can't tell you that ... He is out with your daughter, I presume?' He wouldn't put it past the old woman deliberately to have led him up the garden path in the hope of extracting information from him.

'Oh yes, he's out with her all right. Gallivanting, as usual.'

'Where have they gone, do you know?'

'For a walk, that's all I know. They only left about twenty minutes ago.'

Thanet glanced at his watch. A quarter to two. He suddenly realised that he was hungry. He and Lineham hadn't yet had any lunch.

'What time will they be back?'

'Half past three, they *said*. But they're usually late.'

Thanet could understand why. With Mrs Chase's hostility waiting to ambush them the moment they stepped through the front door, there could be little incentive to be punctual.

'Your daughter has been at home all over the half-term holiday?'

'If you can call it being at home, yes. Spent most of it up in her bedroom. I was looking forward to having a bit of company for a change, but no, all over the weekend she was going around looking as though the world had come to an end. To tell you the truth, I thought they might have split up. No such luck, unfortunately.'

'She didn't see Mr Mathews at all, over the weekend?'

'No. Wouldn't tell me why, either. Just said he was away and she didn't want to discuss it. And then, on Monday night he turns up, large as life, at ten o'clock at night.' Her nose wrinkled in disgust. 'He'd been drinking, too. I could smell it the minute he walked into the room. But her ... she's got no pride. When the doorbell went she couldn't get there quick enough. And when she came back in with him ... you'd have thought someone'd given her the crown jewels.'

'Did Mr Mathews say where he'd been, over the weekend?'

'I didn't wait to find out. As soon as I saw the condition he was in, I made Eileen put me to bed.'

168

Her look of gloating satisfaction told Thanet that Mrs Chase would have prolonged this process as much as possible, in order to keep the lovers apart.

'Is that what you want to know?' she said eagerly. 'What he was doing over the weekend?'

Thanet stood up. 'I'm afraid I can't tell you that, Mrs Chase.'

'You're not going?'

'We must, I'm afraid.'

Why was it that this sort of person always brought out the worst in others, Thanet wondered, as he experienced a brief and shameful sense of satisfaction at her disappointment.

'But you'll come back, at half past three?'

'Possibly.' But he had no intention of allowing himself to be manoeuvred into interviewing Mathews in the presence of this woman. He and Lineham would wait outside, catch the couple as they returned home. And if the man was innocent of any involvement in Charity's death, well, Thanet only hoped that by coming here he hadn't handed Mrs Chase another weapon with which to make her daughter's life a misery. One of the unfortunate results of a criminal investigation is that its effects spread outwards, like ripples on a pond, disrupting the lives of the innocent as well as the guilty.

He and Lineham had something to eat at a little sandwich bar on the edge of Sturrenden — it was too late, by now, to go to a pub — and by a quarter past three were in position, parked a little way up the road, where Mrs Chase would not be able to see them.

At twenty to four Lineham nudged him. 'There they are.'

Walking slowly towards them was a youngish couple, holding hands, feet dragging like children facing a particularly unpleasant day at school. They were talking, engrossed in each other, and as they drew nearer they saw that the man was wearing pebble-lensed spectacles.

Thanet and Lineham got out of the car and went to meet them.

'Mr Mathews?'

The intrusion was a shock and they stopped, startled,

surprise changing to apprehension when Thanet introduced himself.

'We'd like a word with you in private, if we may.'

Mathews and Eileen Chase edged closer to each other, as if Thanet were threatening to rip them apart by force.

'My fiancée and I have no secrets from each other.'

Mathews fitted the description: medium height, fair hair, thinning at the temples. His clothes were nondescript — fawn cords and a green sweatshirt.

Thanet shrugged. 'As you wish. Is there somewhere quiet nearby, where we can talk?'

Mathews looked questioningly at Eileen and she said quickly, 'There's the park.' She was small and slight with a high, bony forehead and slightly protruding eyes. Her shoulder-length hair was caught back in an Alice band, in a style which gave her a curiously immature, little-girl look, an impression heightened by her dress, a shirt-waister in green and white checked gingham.

She and Mathews led the way to a pair of wrought-iron gates a little distance away on the other side of the road. Apart from some children playing on the swings in the recreation area, the place was deserted.

'Over there will do,' said Thanet, indicating a small paved area backed by hedges, where two wooden benches were set at right angles to each other.

They all sat down, Mathews and his fiancée watching Thanet apprehensively.

'I won't beat about the bush, Mr Mathews,' said Thanet. 'We are investigating the murder of Charity Pritchard and we understand that you and she travelled down from London together on Monday night.'

This was no news to Eileen, Thanet noted. She merely looked calmly at Mathews, waiting for his reply.

'No! Yes ... well, not exactly.'

'Oh come, Mr Mathews. Either you did or you didn't.'

'Well, we did travel down on the same train, but it was purely a matter of chance. We just happened to get into the same compartment at Victoria.'

'You sat together?'

'Yes ... Well, it seems silly, if you see someone you know on a train, not to sit with them, doesn't it?'

'Depends on whether you *want* to sit with them, surely,' said Lineham. 'I know some people I'd run a mile to avoid.'

'I didn't have much choice about it. She came and sat opposite me, and I could hardly have moved away without being downright rude.'

'Rather awkward,' said Thanet.

'Quite.'

'I mean, I suppose you really have to be very careful, a man in your position.'

'What do you mean?'

'Well, a male teacher in an all-girls school,' said Lineham. 'And an unmarried one at that ... Bound to be the occasional schoolgirl crush to fend off, surely?'

Mathews cast a panic-stricken glance at Eileen and her grip on his hand tightened. Thanet wondered how much the girl knew, whether it would be worth trying to question her alone. It would probably be a waste of time, he decided. Her loyalty to Mathews was patent.

'Did Charity have a crush on you, Mr Mathews?' he said softly.

There was a brief silence. Mathews and Eileen did not look at each other, but Thanet was aware of the current of sympathy and strength flowing from the girl to her fiancé through those linked hands. She may not have looked a force to be reckoned with, but Thanet knew that a woman who falls in love for the first time relatively late in life will probably be prepared to fight tooth and nail to keep her lover.

Mathews leaned forward slightly, his eyes so magnified by the lenses of his spectacles that Thanet found it impossible to read their expression.

'What, exactly, are you implying, Inspector?'

It was a good try at indignation, but it lacked that note of conviction imparted by genuine innocence. Up until this moment Thanet had been uncertain of the precise nature of the relationship between Mathews and Charity. He was well aware

171

that Mathews could have been telling the truth, that he and Charity had met by chance on that train, and that Mathews' nervousness might have been based on nothing more than the knowledge that this unfortunate coincidence might appear to implicate him in the murder of a girl who had been no more to him than one pupil among many.

But now, suddenly, he was certain: Mathews and Charity had had a sexual relationship and, what was more, Eileen Chase had known about it.

'Not implying, merely asking, Mr Mathews.'

It would be best, now, if Mathews were left wondering just how much the police knew. Thanet changed tack.

'I understand that you were away for the whole weekend?'

Mathews shifted uneasily on the seat. 'That's right.'

'Would you mind telling us where you went?'

For some reason, this was the wrong question. Mathews relaxed a little. 'By all means. I was walking. In the Chilterns.'

What was the question he should have asked? Thanet was frustrated to find that he didn't know.

'Alone?'

'Yes. I was camping out. I do, from time to time. Does you good to get right away from civilisation.'

Especially with problems like yours, thought Thanet. 'Can you think of anyone who might remember seeing you — when you stopped to buy food, whatever?'

'Not offhand.'

It was pointless to waste time trying to get the man to come up with verifiable details at this point. This was clearly a no-danger area for Mathews. 'Perhaps you could think about it, give us a ring ... And now, if we could just go back to Monday evening again ...'

'I really don't see what else I can tell you. As I said, we met by accident, travelled down in the same compartment, and that's it.'

'You left the train together,' said Thanet.

'Well, naturally ...'

'*And* left the station together,' said Lineham.

Thanet leaned forward. 'Of course, what we're really interested in, is what happened then.'

'Happened?'

So far Eileen Chase had not said a single word throughout the entire interview. Now, the strain was beginning to tell. The taut muscles of her jaw betrayed the force with which her teeth were clamped together.

'What did you do, when you left the station?' Lineham took up the questioning at Thanet's signal.

'I went to see my fiancée.' Mathews glanced at Eileen for confirmation and she gave a quick, taut nod.

'Arriving at her house at what time?'

'About ...' Mathews stopped.

Would the temptation to lie, give himself a false alibi, prove irresistible, Thanet wondered.

Mathews turned to the girl. 'What time was it, darling, did you notice?'

She hesitated. Then, 'Ten o'clock,' she said, looking straight into his eyes.

The message was clear. *Tell the truth as far as possible*, she was saying. Of course, there was Mrs Chase to take into account. Would Eileen have lied, if she lived alone, Thanet wondered.

Mathews looked back at Lineham. 'If Eileen says it was ten, then it was.'

'So what were you doing in the meantime? The station is only ten minutes walk from here.'

'I stopped at a pub, had a drink or two. Any law against that?'

'None. Which pub?'

Mathews hesitated. 'I'm sorry, I don't know.'

'You don't *know*?'

'I don't make a habit of going to pubs. I've no idea what most of the pubs in Sturrenden are called. I just happened to be passing this one and felt like a drink, so I went in.'

'Where was it?'

'Somewhere between here and the station.'

'You really can't be more precise than that?'

'No ... I wasn't feeling well.'

'You were ill?'

'Not exactly. Just a bit under the weather ... Well, if you must know, I was trying to make up my mind about something.'

'What?'

'I'm sorry, I can't tell you that. It's a private matter.'

Some unspoken communication passed between him and the girl, and Thanet saw her fingers tighten on his again. She was backing up his decision not to speak. There was no point in pressing the matter.

Lineham had understood this. He raised his eyebrows at Thanet. *Shall I push him?*

No, Thanet returned.

'How long did you stay in this pub, Mr Mathews?' said Lineham.

'I'm not sure. But if I left the station about nine and didn't get here until ten. it must have been three-quarters of an hour or more.'

'Did you see anyone you know?'

'Not that I can recall.'

'And how many drinks did you have?'

'Two, three perhaps.'

'Beers?'

'Whiskies.' Mathews lifted his chin defiantly, as if defending his right to drink whatever he wanted.

Lineham glanced at Thanet, relinquishing the questioning.

Thanet allowed a long pause, leaning back in an almost leisurely manner and giving Mathews a long, assessing stare. 'You must see, Mr Mathews, that all this uncertainty about your movements does leave you in a most unfortunate position. I'm surprised that in the circumstances you haven't taken the trouble to retrace your steps and discover exactly which pub you did go into.'

'But why should he!' Eileen Chase could keep silent no longer. 'It never entered our heads that my fiancé would have to answer all these ... ridiculous questions, just because of a chance meeting on a train!'

174

'Miss Chase, your loyalty does you credit. But it shouldn't blind you to the facts. And those are that on Monday evening Charity Pritchard travelled down from London with Mr Mathews, was seen leaving the station with him and shortly afterwards was murdered. No, wait a minute,' he went on as she opened her mouth to protest. 'You really must see that in the circumstances it is no more than our duty to question Mr Mathews closely, especially as he is so vague as to his movements. But there is one way in which you might be able to help him.'

'How?'

'Do you happen to have a photograph of him?'

As he had guessed, she had one in her wallet. It was a good likeness, too.

'Thank you. We'll get someone to check the pubs and see if we can find someone who can corroborate his story.'

'Inspector,' said Mathews, 'can I ask you something?'

'Go ahead.'

'It's obvious, from all these questions, that Charity was killed some time after she left the station that evening. Do you know exactly when?'

Thanet didn't see why he shouldn't tell him. 'Not to the minute. But some time between 9.35 and 10.40.'

'I see.' Mathews' response was carefully neutral, but underneath there was suppressed excitement. 'And how was the earlier of the two times fixed?'

So that was it. 'As you have guessed, because that was the time at which she was last seen alive.'

'But in that case, I'm in the clear, surely! If she was seen alive after we parted?'

'I'm afraid we won't be able to accept that unless we can find someone who can verify that you were elsewhere between 9.35 and 10.'

'This is absolutely monstrous!' said Eileen Chase. Her pale skin was stained with pink and her prominent eyes bulged with anger. 'To suggest that Leslie could have ... He's the kindest, most gentle person imaginable.' She cast him a glance of pure adoration. 'He'd never do such a thing, never.'

'Maybe not, in normal circumstances. But murder never is committed in normal circumstances, not by ordinary people, anyway. They are driven to it by a compulsion outside their everyday experience. Oh yes, someone had a powerful reason for wishing Charity dead, Miss Chase, and believe me, I am going to find out what that reason was. And when I do ...' Thanet rose, and his tone suddenly became casually conversational, 'well, when I do, I shall have found the murderer, shan't I? Good day.'

Mathews and Eileen Chase sat as if turned to stone as the two detectives walked away across the park.

17

Thanet flexed his spine and massaged the dull, nagging ache in the small of his back. Whenever he was tired or under stress it seemed to become worse, an unwelcome distraction when he was least equipped to cope with it.

It was a quarter past six and he was alone in the office. He had dispatched Carson to check Mathews' alibi at all the pubs between the railway station and Eileen Chase's house, and had then insisted that Lineham go and visit Louise.

'You can't miss two nights in a row.'

'But what about all those?' Lineham had gestured at the piles of unread reports on Thanet's desk.

'They won't run away. Go on, hurry up, or you'll be late. I could do with a breathing space anyway.'

Which was true. Thanet felt as though his brain were so clogged with information that it had almost ceased to function. What he really needed now was to go home and have Joan thrust a drink into his hand and insist he relax for a while before supper. He closed his eyes, visualising her smile, the touch of her hand on his arm, the luxury of sinking into an armchair and knowing that she was there, moving about in the next room. How little we appreciate these simple pleasures while we have them, he thought. His longing for her presence was almost a physical pain, an ache deep inside him. Just to hear her voice again ...

He opened his eyes, stared at the telephone. Why not? It might be a good time to catch her. He found that, without making a conscious decision, he was dialling.

'Could I speak to Mrs Thanet, please?'

He braced himself for the familiar, 'I'm afraid she's out,' but it didn't come.

'Just a moment, I'll see if she's in.'

The seconds ticked away and Thanet found that he was holding his breath, hope ebbing with every moment that passed. She wasn't back yet, had already gone out, was spending the evening with a friend ... Fiercely he repudiated the threatening fantasy of a friend who was not only male but physically attractive, intelligent, sympathetic, enlightened ...

'Hullo?'

Joan's voice, as familiar to him in its every inflexion as his own face in the mirror.

'Got you at last!' As soon as the words were out of his mouth, he could have kicked himself. His attempt at light-heartedness sounded merely reproachful.

'Luke!' If Joan had noticed, she chose to ignore it. 'Darling, how lovely to hear you! We always seem to be missing each other, these days. How are you? How are the children? How's the case going?'

'Fine, fine and not so fine, in that order. What about you?'

'Exhausted! You remember the remand home where I did my last placement? Well, they've had an epidemic of mumps there, and as two of the staff had gone down with it — it's an especially virulent strain, apparently — Geoffrey and I have been going back in the evenings to help out.'

Geoffrey Benson was also on the training course. Thanet had never met him.

'I see.' Thanet tried to ignore the red light flashing in his brain. 'Sounds as though you've been having a hectic time. I should think we'll all seem as dull as ditchwater when you get back home.'

Joan must have picked up the underlying anxiety beneath his attempt to tease her, for her reply was vehement.

'Nonsense, darling. I can't tell you how I'm longing to be home again, start leading a normal life again.'

Had she meant it? To Thanet her tone was strained, as if she were trying to convince herself as well as him.

Thanet gave her the latest news of Louise and then she said,

178

'But tell me how the case is going. Properly.'

'It's going, and that's about all I can say at the moment. At least I'm not completely stuck yet.'

'Anyone definite in mind?'

'Not really. We could take our pick from about half a dozen possibilities.'

'Sounds complicated.'

'It is, a bit. Joan ... I do miss you.'

'And I miss you too, darling.'

'But ...' How to describe the immensity of his need, this hunger for her mere presence? Over the years I've got out of the habit of expressing such feelings, he thought desperately, and the words just won't come easily any more.

'Anyway, it won't be long, now, will it, Luke? Only another couple of weeks ... I suppose your back's playing up?'

How well she knew him. 'A little.'

'Where are you?'

The question surprised him. 'In the office. Why?'

'Anyone else there?'

'Not at the moment.'

'In that case, why don't you lie down on the floor for a little while, do your exercises, relax.'

'Here? What if someone came in?'

'Couldn't you say you didn't want to be disturbed for a bit? There'd be nothing unusual in that, surely?'

'I could, I suppose ...'

'Then do it. You'd feel miles better, afterwards. Promise?'

'Well ...'

'Luke!'

'Oh, all right. I suppose it might be a good idea.'

'Of course it would. Look, sorry darling, but I'm afraid I must go now. I've got to get back to the Home. I was just leaving when you caught me.'

'Well I'm glad I did.'

'So'm I.' She blew him a kiss down the line. ''Bye, darling. I love you.'

'I love you, too.'

The line went dead and Thanet replaced the reciever, sat

staring at it for a full minute before pressing the buzzer on his desk.

'I don't want to be disturbed for half an hour.'

'Right, sir.'

'Not for *any* reason, is that clear?'

Allowing himself the luxury of a slight groan, Thanet stood up, rubbing his back, then carefully lowered himself to the floor. The carpet, though thin, was at least clean. The pain flowered as taut muscles met the hard, unyielding surface, then began to ebb as the tension started to seep away.

Thanet worked conscientiously through the exercises which his physiotherapist had given him, then began the relaxation routine: tighten leg muscles ... relax. Arm muscles ... relax. Shoulder ... neck ... jaw ... He began to breathe deeply and regularly. In ... out. In ... out. Veronica ... Mrs Chase. Jethro ... his wife. Mathews ... Eileen Chase.

Which of the six could it be?

He was pretty certain that Veronica was out of the running. She was too passive, too self-pitying, a victim rather than an assailant. He couldn't see her being sufficiently devious to plan a murder in cold blood, nor sufficiently aggressive to strike out in anger with the degree of force that had hurled Charity against that unfortunately-placed piece of jagged metal. And so far there hadn't been so much as a whisper of anyone seeing her outside the house that night.

Memo: check through the files again, to be sure on that point.

Mrs Hodges, now, was a different matter. Not by nature an aggressive woman, she would certainly be capable of extremes of behaviour in defence of her one ewe lamb, Thanet was sure. Yes, she should definitely be considered a suspect — it was quite possible, as Lineham had suggested, that she had followed Charity and killed her *before* returning to the house and greeting Thanet and Lineham as though nothing had happened. After all, there was only her word for it that Charity had still been alive at that point. The house to house reports covering that earlier period should be on his desk by now. Thanet resisted the urge to get up at once and check through

180

them. He needed a little more time, first, to order his thoughts properly.

Then there was Mathews. Now here was another promising suspect. His motive was powerful. If, as Thanet suspected, he had indeed had a sexual relationship with Charity, then his whole career would have been at stake. No one was going to employ a teacher who had not only seduced a pupil — and an under-age one, at that — but had driven her to seek an abortion without her parents' knowledge or consent. If any of this had ever come out, Mathews would have been finished and so long as Charity was alive the threat of exposure would remain.

Then there was the possibility that Charity had threatened to tell Mathews' fiancée about the baby, and that he had killed her to prevent her doing so. Eileen Chase clearly adored Mathews and Thanet thought that she would probably be willing to forgive him anything, so long as she could keep him. But, would *he* have known that?

Thanet thought back over the afternoon's interviews and tried to work out exactly what had been going on between the engaged couple. Mrs Chase had said that all over the weekend Eileen had gone around 'looking as though the world had come to an end'. And Mathews had gone away on a walking trip because 'it does you good to get away from civilisation'. Everything pointed to a quarrel before the weekend, a reconciliation afterwards.

A quarrel about Charity?

Say that it had been about her. Say that Mathews had decided to confess to Eileen — or say that Eileen had found out about the relationship and had decided to confront Mathews with it . . . No, the latter was unlikely, Thanet decided. If Eileen had found out, then it would have been more in character for her to say nothing for fear of rocking the boat, and hope that the affair would die a natural death.

So, say that Mathews had decided to confess, and had told Eileen that he felt he was no longer worthy of her and that their engagement was off. She would have protested, Thanet was sure, but the outcome had nevertheless been that Mathews had gone away alone for the weekend. In his chosen solitude he had obviously thought things over and decided that he really didn't want to lose Eileen, and that if she was prepared to forgive him he would be a fool not to bow to her generosity. When he got back he would go at once to see her and ask her to take him back.

Then, on the train, he had met Charity, had found himself in the position of having to travel down with her.

This was where the scenario became blurred. After leaving the station Mathews could have left the girl and headed straight for Eileen's house, as he claimed, stopping to boost his courage with a couple of drinks on the way.

Or he could have followed Charity and killed her.

Thanet couldn't really see Mathews setting out to murder in cold blood, but say that he had been provoked into it? Say that Charity, still in a precarious emotional state after the thoroughly unpleasant experience of having had to seek and undergo an abortion without any moral support whatsoever, had told Mathews that she intended to expose him to the Education Authorities? He would have argued, begged, pleaded and, if he had not succeeded in persuading her to change her mind by the time they left the station, could have walked home with her to continue the argument. Would he have risked being seen with her in public? Only if he was desperate, Thanet decided. Which he might have been. There was no word of their having been seen together in Sturrenden that evening after they left the station, but that didn't necessarily mean that they hadn't been ...

'Sir?'

Someone was shaking him by the arm.

'Sir! Are you all right?'

Lineham's concerned face hovered over him.

'Of course I am, man.' Thanet was furious at being discovered stretched out on the floor. Careful, even in his haste, not to undo the good work, he rolled over on to his side and climbed cautiously to his feet. 'I'm still breathing, aren't I? Anyway, I thought I gave orders not to be disturbed for half an hour.'

182

'That was at six twenty-five. And it's a quarter past seven now. When I saw you on the floor I thought ...'

He must have fallen asleep. 'Never mind what you thought,' snapped Thanet. 'You were wrong, weren't you. I was simply ... meditating. Complete relaxation is highly conducive to meditation.'

'I must remember that, sir. Shall I put a directive up on the noticeboard?'

Thanet opened his mouth to make a sharp retort, caught Lineham's eye and grinned. 'All right, Mike, so you caught me out.'

'Back, sir?'

Thanet didn't know whether to be relieved or angry, that his sergeant had so immediately understood.

'You're not my nursemaid, Mike, and don't you forget it. How's Louise?'

Lineham's face sagged. 'Still putting up a good front. We're both so bloody cheerful ...'

'Did you have a word with the Sister?'

'They think it might be tomorrow — the induction, I mean. They haven't told Louise yet, thought it might send her blood pressure up even further.'

'It hasn't come down at all, then?'

Lineham shook his head gloomily. 'Slightly higher, in fact.'

'Look, are you quite sure you wouldn't prefer to be off the case at the moment? I could easily ...'

'No! Thank you, sir, but no.'

'All right. But if you change your mind....'

'Thanks. Have you ... er ... had time to go through any of those, yet?'

'No need to be so tactful. No, I haven't. I told you, I was thinking.'

'Come to any conclusions?'

'Not really.' Thanet briefly outlined the thoughts he had had before dropping off to sleep. 'That's as far as I got.'

'What about Eileen Chase? If she'd had the whole weekend to brood over Mathews chucking her because of Charity, she could have decided to have it out with the girl herself.'

'Slipped out of the house without her mother knowing, you mean? Yes, I'd thought of that.'

'Mrs Chase might well have been watching television and thought Eileen was still up in her room, moping.'

'But how would Eileen have known how to find Charity?'

Lineham shrugged. 'No idea. But it's still possible, isn't it! I should think she'd be prepared to go to almost any lengths to keep him.'

'Then there's Jethro ... No, I've had enough of speculating for the moment. Let's get down to these reports.'

They divided the pile between them and Thanet lit his pipe before settling down. He felt much refreshed by his brief dereliction of duty. Therefore it hadn't been dereliction at all, he decided.

He began with the forensic report. He had glanced through it before, but now he checked it more thoroughly. His first impression had been correct: there was nothing of any significance in the findings. Just as well, perhaps. If there had been, and Charity's father had blurred the issue by that untimely but understandable intervention, Thanet and Lineham would have been in serious trouble for not having managed to stop him. But the fact that there was no evidence of a preliminary struggle did support the theory of a blow struck in anger — and therefore an unpremeditated crime.

Thanet relit his pipe, which had gone out, and started on the Lantern Street reports.

There was nothing. No one, at any time during that evening, had seen either Veronica or Mrs Hodges outside the house. This did not of course necessarily mean that neither of them had been out — for one thing, so many of the Lantern Street houses were unoccupied that it might be quite easy to miss being seen — but it did mean that there was absolutely no evidence as yet to support Lineham's theory.

'Sir!'

The note of excitement in Lineham's voice brought Thanet's head up sharply.

'That second house to house we asked for, in Gate Street...'

'Well?'

'They haven't quite finished it yet, but some of the reports are in.'

'And?'

'As usual, they found several people who'd been out the first time they called, and one of them was the daughter of a Mrs Wells, the Jethro Pritchards' next-door neighbour, at number twelve. The girl — she's nineteen — says that just after half past nine that night there was a persistent knocking at the Pritchards' front door. She knew Mrs Pritchard must be in, because if ever Mrs Pritchard goes out in the evening, it's Mrs Wells who old-lady-sits, so when the knocking went on and on she wondered what was up and went to look out of the window.'

Thanet found Lineham's habit of giving an interesting piece of information a dramatic build-up either engaging or infuriating, according to his own mood at the time. Now, he almost expected the sergeant to say, 'And guess who it was!'

'Get on with it, man,' he snapped.

Lineham leaned back in his chair, confident of the impact of his next words. 'It was the Jethro Pritchards' son!'

'Their son!' Thanet digested this piece of news in silence for a moment and then said, 'I wonder why no one has mentioned him before.'

'According to the girl — and I quote, "Caleb's the black sheep of the family. Got himself chucked out because he couldn't stand all that boring old religious stuff."'

'Just how black, I wonder. How old is he?'

'Twenty, she says.'

'Twenty ... and Charity's cousin. What do you think, Mike?'

'Well, he was obviously in the area at the right time, wasn't he?'

'Quite. Did Mrs Jethro open the door to him eventually?'

'Yes. But he didn't go in. The girl stayed at the window, hoping for a bit of drama, I suppose. Or because she fancies him.'

'Hmm. Interesting. We'll have to find out more about him,

185

obviously. Have you come across anything else, on Jethro or his wife?'

'The same girl confirms that Jethro did arrive home at ten fifteen, sir.'

'Does she, now ... Well, we'll go around first thing in the morning, find out where this young man is living, whether he and Charity kept in touch. And I'd also like to know why they haven't told us about him before.'

'Because we didn't ask?'

'Well, we're going to ask now.'

18

When Thanet drove into the car park next day, Doctor Mallard was just getting out of his car. It was a sparkling morning. The weather seemed to have settled down again into its seasonal norm and a stiff breeze chased little puffs of cotton-wool cloud across a sky of soft, luminous blue.

'Morning, Luke. Lovely day.'

'Morning, Doc. Beautiful, isn't it.'

'Bit late, aren't you?'

'Had to transfer my family back home, after the half-term holiday. We've been trying to get things tidied up a bit, at my mother-in-law's.'

'When's Joan coming back?'

'Another fortnight, yet.'

'And she'll have completely finished her training, then?'

'Yes.'

Mallard laughed. 'Thank God, eh? By the way, did you know that young Louise is having her induction this morning?' He glanced at his watch. 'Correction, she'll have had it by now.'

'Yes, I'd heard. What are her chances?'

'Excellent, I'd say. But the baby — well, we'll just have to wait and see.'

Thanet stopped. 'You mean, there really is a chance it might not survive?'

'Unfortunately, yes. These toxaemia cases are so unpredictable, it's impossible to tell, in advance.'

'Does Lineham know this?'

'Oh, he knows, all right. And, I'm sorry to say, so does Louise, having been a nurse herself. It can't help her particular problem.'

187

No wonder Mike has been so distracted over the last few days, Thanet thought. He remembered guiltily the occasions when he had felt impatient or irritated with the sergeant. 'You think I ought to insist Lineham has the day off? I've offered him a few days leave, several times, but he's refused to take them.'

'I should leave it to him to decide. He's probably better off working, than worrying himself sick. And nothing'll happen for hours yet, anyway. Does he intend to be present at the birth, do you know?'

'I'm pretty sure he does.'

'Then I should say that as long as he keeps in touch with the hospital it would be better to keep him busy until labour is well established.'

'Right, I'll do that. Thanks, Doc.'

Pausing in the office only long enough to scoop up a gloomy-looking Lineham, Thanet set off for Gate Street. Charity's mother was just coming out of Jethro's house. She started when Thanet greeted her.

'Oh ... Good morning, Inspector. I didn't see you.'

She looked harrassed. Hair was escaping from her normally immaculate bun, and her black cardigan was buttoned up askew.

'We're just going to have a word with your sister-in-law. We didn't realise, until last night, that she has a son.'

Mrs Pritchard squinted at him, shielding her eyes from the sun. 'Caleb?'

'Yes. Why has no one mentioned him, do you know?'

'His parents have nothing to do with him, now. We've all lost touch with him, since he moved away from home.'

'Charity, too?'

'Oh, yes. They never got on, anyway, even as children ...'

She closed her eyes, swayed slightly. Thanet put out his hand to steady her.

'Mrs Pritchard, are you all right?'

'Yes ... yes. Thank you, I'm fine. It's just that I'm not sleeping too well, that's all ...' Her voice trailed away and there was an awkward silence. Then she gave him a quick, nervous glance. 'Inspector ...'

'Yes?'

She hesitated, then shook her head. 'Nothing. I must be getting home.' And she turned, set off down the street with a slightly unsteady but dogged gait.

'Think I ought to see her home, sir?'

Thanet was still watching the receding figure. She was walking rather more briskly now.

'I think she'll be all right.'

'She looked just about at the end of her tether, to me.'

'Scarcely surprising, is it?'

Thanet knocked at the door of number fourteen. He had already decided that as far as Mrs Jethro Pritchard was concerned, it was pointless to waste time on the tactful approach. Her hostility so far had been unremitting and it was a surprise, therefore, to find that he was greeted by a baring of the teeth that was clearly intended to be a smile.

'Good morning, Inspector. Come in, won't you?'

He and Lineham raised eyebrows at each other behind her back and followed her into the sitting room.

'Do sit down.' She brushed an imaginary speck of dust off the arm of one of the chairs. 'I'm afraid I haven't got around to cleaning in here yet, today.'

'It looks fine to me.'

By now Thanet had guessed the reason for this sudden change of attitude: Mrs Jethro Pritchard was afraid.

Charity's father had probably come storming around, as Thanet had expected, and had accused Jethro of seducing his niece and causing her to seek an abortion. With both brother and wife against him, Jethro had no doubt crumbled, confessed. Now, Mrs Pritchard was afraid that she and her husband were about to be plunged into a scandal far worse than the one they had weathered before, a scandal involving not only incest but, possibly, murder. Thanet couldn't like the woman, thought it very likely that a measure of the responsibility for her husband's aberrations lay at her door, but he couldn't help feeling a twinge of pity for her now. She had seated herself opposite him, solid knees clamped together, hands clasped tightly in her lap. She was waiting for the axe to fall.

Or was it possible that her fear was on her son's behalf?

'Is your husband at home, Mrs Pritchard?'

'No. He's at the school.'

'There's a question I wanted to ask you both.'

She said nothing, seemed almost to stop breathing.

'Why didn't you tell me you had a son?'

For a moment she looked at him blankly, as though she must have misheard. Then she shook her head a little, as if to clear it. 'I'm sorry ...?'

Thanet repeated the question.

Her mouth became a thin, hard line. 'Our son is dead to us, Inspector.'

Thanet said nothing, and eventually his silence forced her into a reluctant explanation.

'He has chosen to walk with the ungodly.'

'He left the Children of Jerusalem?'

'Yes.'

'How long ago was this?'

'Eighteen months or so.'

'When we asked you if Charity knew any young men, you said no.'

'I told you, Inspector. Our son is dead to us. As far as we are concerned, he doesn't exist.'

'How did Charity get on with him?'

'Not very well. They never really took to each other.'

'Did they ever meet after Caleb left home?'

'How should I know? He leads his own life, now. He has nothing to do with any of us.'

'Then why was he knocking at your door on Monday night, Mrs Pritchard?'

'Who told you that?' Her eyes sparked with anger. 'They had no right. Spying on people ...'

'They had every right, Mrs Pritchard. A duty, even. This, I would remind you, is a murder case ... What did he want?'

'How should I know?'

'But you let him in.'

'I did not! As soon as I saw who it was I told him once and for all that I didn't want him coming around here bothering us, with his long hair and greasy jeans ...'

'He must have said why he'd come.'

'I told you, I didn't ask!'

And from this evasion she would not budge.

'Could you tell us where he lives?'

'I've no idea.'

'Where he works, then?'

'Works! That's a joke! Works!' She leaned forward, her eyes hot and bitter. 'Work is sacred, Inspector, which as far as my son is concerned is a very good reason for not doing any.'

This was all Thanet could get out of her.

'Right, Mike,' he said, when they were back in the car. 'I want you to find Caleb and talk to him. You might get his address from Jethro, at the school. If not, well, you'll just have to use your initiative. If you think it necessary, bring the boy in for questioning. Use your own judgement. You can drop me off at the office, first. Oh, and Mike, you'll no doubt be giving the hospital a ring from time to time. When they say that Louise is ready for you to join her, let me know, then drop everything and go. Understood?'

'Yes, sir. Thank you.'

There were more reports on Thanet's desk. He lit his pipe and settled down to read them. Within minutes he was on his feet again. He wanted to see Jethro. At once.

On his way to the school he thought about the new information which had just come in. A woman who lived opposite Holly Road Primary School had worked late in her front garden on Monday evening. She had been keeping an eye on the time, because she wanted to watch a television programme which began at 10. People had begun to stream out of the school just before 9.30 and within ten minutes or so the place had been deserted. Last of all, just before a quarter to ten, she had seen Jethro come out, locking the school gates behind him.

It was only ten minutes walk from the school to Jethro's house, and yet he had not arrived home until 10.15. What had he been doing, during that half an hour? Charity had left the Hodges' house at 9.35. Had their routes converged?

Suppose that Jethro had somehow managed to scrape together the money to pay for Charity's abortion, and had been anxious to know that everything had gone according to plan. She might well have told him what time she hoped to arrive home. They could even have arranged to meet. Jethro would have been on tenterhooks to know that the operation had been a success, full no doubt of good resolutions never to land himself in the same mess again. But suppose Charity had seen things differently? Suppose that she had decided to keep up the pressure, demand more money for her continuing silence? Jethro might well have lashed out at her in an explosion of anger, disappointment and fear.

In any case, he certainly had some explaining to do.

Thanet ran him to earth in one of the cloakrooms, fixing a leaking lavatory cistern. His left eye was almost invisible in an area of swollen, discoloured flesh.

'I'd like a word. Where can we talk?'

Jethro groaned. 'Not again! Your sergeant only left a few minutes ago.' Reluctantly, he led the way to a little cubby-hole of a room equipped with a sagging armchair and an electric kettle. A crumpled newspaper lay on the arm of the chair. Thanet picked it up and noted with interest that it was today's, and that it was folded back at the racing page, and marked. Jethro was evidently a backslider in more ways than one.

'Your brother's been to see you, then.' Thanet nodded at the black eye.

Jethro's hand instinctively began to move towards his bruised face, then stopped. 'I don't know what you mean.'

'Oh come, Mr Pritchard. You won't convince me you got that by walking into a door.'

'A ladder, as a matter of fact.'

'Oh, a ladder, was it? Well, I'm afraid I don't believe you. In fact, I'm beginning to think I can't believe a word you say.'

'What do you mean?'

'Look, I've had enough of beating around the bush. I'll give it to you straight. We know that you had a sexual relationship with your niece, we know that she became pregnant, we know

192

you gave her money to enable her to procure an abortion and on top of all this, we now know that you lied to us about the time you left here the evening she died. We have a witness, Mr Pritchard, a nice, solid witness. In view of all this, if you were me, what would you think?'

Thanet paused for a moment. There was a sheen of sweat on Jethro's forehead and the empurpled area of flesh was vivid against skin the colour of grubby linen.

'I ...' But he couldn't continue.

'Exactly. Now, this witness states that she saw you lock the school gates behind you at around 9.45 that night, instead of after 10, as you claimed. And that quarter of an hour to twenty minutes make a lot of difference, Mr Pritchard. In fact, you could call it of paramount importance.'

Thanet paused again, but Jethro was still speechless.

'Charity, you see, left Mrs Hodges' house at 9.35 — ten minutes before you left here. It would have taken her around ten to fifteen minutes to reach the entrance to the alley ... which leaves you with about five minutes in hand to get to the place where she was killed. If you hurried, you could have done it easily. What did you do, Mr Pritchard? Hang around in that alleyway, hoping to catch her on her way home? Or had the meeting been arranged before she left?'

'No!' Jethro burst out. 'It wasn't like that, Inspector, I swear it wasn't. We hadn't arranged ... I didn't meet her, I swear I didn't. I didn't even see her.'

He was sweating profusely now, and he dragged a dirty handkerchief from his pocket, mopped at his forehead.

'I'm sorry. I don't believe you.' But it was interesting to note that Jethro had denied none of the other allegations. This, Thanet decided was the moment to set the record straight, while Jethro was still terrified of being arrested for murder.

'You don't deny the rest of what I said?'

Jethro hesitated and for a second Thanet thought that he was going to hold out after all. Then, slowly, he shook his head.

'What's the point?' he said, wearily. 'You've got it all worked out, haven't you? If I do deny it you'll only keep on and on until I give in ... But I didn't kill her! I swear I didn't!'

'You admit, then, that you seduced her, that she told you that she was pregnant, and that you gave her money to procure an abortion?' Briefly, Thanet regretted Lineham's absence, that he had no witness to Jethro's confession, but the thought did not trouble him unduly; Jethro was too weak a character to stick to a retraction, even if he chose to back-pedal when it came to the point of making an official statement. But if he knew his man, alongside Jethro's admission would run a need to justify himself. He was right.

'Maybe I did, but it wasn't my fault. It was her.' Jethro was even managing to work up some indignation against the dead girl. 'She was a real little whore ... Putting her arms around me and rubbing herself against me ... Sitting on my lap and wriggling so I thought it would drive me mad ... Believe me, she was asking for it — begging for it, even. And once we had ... she couldn't get enough of it, I can tell you. She was mad for it. She frightened the wits out of me. She'd want it anywhere — up against the wall of the alley, in the kitchen of my own house, even, with my mother sitting there with her back to us and my wife coming down the stairs ...'

Jethro was shaking as he relived the state of fear Charity had induced in him. And Thanet believed him. It was difficult to reconcile that child-like, innocent-seeming figure in the alley with the nymphomaniac Jethro was describing, but Thanet was sufficiently experienced by now not only to recognise the ring of truth when he heard it, but to know that even the most beautiful apple can be rotten at the core. Fleetingly he remembered a local murder case. A fourteen-year-old girl had helped her middle-aged lover to plan and execute the murder of his former mistress and in his summing-up the judge had said that he wished to make it clear that this was not, as many people might think, a case of an older man leading a young girl astray, that she was, in his opinion, the most truly evil person he had ever encountered in all his years on the bench.

Had Charity been another such?

Now that Jethro had started talking he couldn't seem to stop. He went on and on detailing times and places and Thanet

194

let him, knowing that with every word Jethro was making it more and more difficult to go back, later, on what he was saying. Eventually, though, the flow of sordid detail sickened Thanet and he cut through the torrent of accusation, self-pity and self-justification.

'Pretty unbearable, was it?'

Pathetically grateful that Thanet appeared to understand, Jethro agreed that yes, it had been.

'How unbearable?' said Thanet softly. 'Unbearable enough to make you want to take active measures to prevent it going on indefinitely? Unbearable enough to make you decide to kill her?' But even as he spoke he was asking himself if Jethro would have had the guts.

Too late, Jethro saw the trap into which he had fallen. His one good eye gazed at Thanet with a fixed, frantic stare. Then, with a groan, he lowered his face into his hands, shaking his head from side to side in despair.

'Well?' said Thanet sternly. 'I'm waiting.'

Still no reply.

Thanet stood up. 'Very well, Mr Pritchard, if you can't satisfy me as to your precise movements between 9.45 and 10.15 on Monday night, then I shall have to ask you to accompany me to the police station.'

Jethro lifted a face like a trapped rabbit's. 'No! Look, Inspector...If I...If I did tell you where I was, during that half an hour, can you give me your word my wife won't find out?'

What was coming now? 'That depends,' said Thanet cautiously.

'On what?'

'On whether the information has any relevance to the case.'

'Well, it hasn't ... Or at least, only for me ... Look, sit down, Inspector, and I'll tell you.'

Thanet sat.

Even now Jethro procrastinated. He blew his nose, made a show of putting his (now revolting) handkerchief away, sat up a little straighter.

Thanet folded his arms in an exaggerated gesture of patience.

195

'My wife'd kill me if she knew . . . I was in a pub,' said Jethro, with the air of someone confessing to a major crime. 'With my son.'

So that was it. If Mrs Jethro knew that her husband had not only committed the sin of imbibing alcohol — and in a public house, at that — but had also been fraternising with the son who was 'dead' to her, Jethro's life would be hell on earth.

'You'd arranged to meet?'

Jethro shook his head. 'I bumped into him soon after leaving the school. He was coming to look for me. He'd been to the house, apparently, but my wife . . . I keep on trying to patch things up between them, but it's no good, she won't listen.'

'She told him where you were?'

'Oh no. He just came along on the off-chance. Well, there aren't many other places I could be. He knows I come here sometimes, even when the school is closed . . . just to keep an eye on things.'

Jethro's eyes flickered around the tiny, shabby room with a proprietorial air. This, Thanet realised, was his sanctuary. Though it was still beyond him to understand how Jethro, with a conviction for indecent assault on an under-age girl, should have managed to get a job in a school in the first place. Perhaps he had somehow managed to suppress the information?

'Which pub did you go to?'

'The King's Head. In Denholm Street. We usually do, when we have the chance.'

Well away from this area, then — presumably to minimise the chance of Mrs Jethro finding out. Did this mean that, if Jethro was telling the truth, he was in the clear?

Thanet's brain moved into top gear, inventing and discarding one scenario after another — Jethro had met and killed Charity before meeting Caleb . . . after leaving him, later on . . . they had done it together . . .

This was the point at which Jethro dropped his bombshell. 'We had a lift.'

'A lift?' An independent witness? 'Who from?'

'Friend of my son's. Came by just after we met, gave us a lift

196

over to the King's Head. We all had a drink together. Then he ran me home. Nice young chap.'

'Name?'

'Pete.'

'Pete who?'

Jethro shrugged. 'Dunno. Never heard his last name. Caleb — my son — would know, I expect.'

'You gave your son's address to Sergeant Lineham?'

'Yes.'

Thanet left in a dispirited mood. They'd check, of course, but it really did look as though that was the end of one of his most promising suspects. And he wasn't getting very far with the others. In default of any shred of evidence against Mrs Jethro, Mrs Hodges or Veronica (whom Thanet had never really seriously considered anyway), it looked as though the list was now reduced to two. All he needed now was to find Carson's report on his desk confirming that every moment of Mathews' time was accounted for, from the moment he left the station to the time he arrived at Eileen's house, and the case would come to a grinding halt.

Thanet tried to reassure himself that this had happened before, that it did not necessarily mean defeat, that sooner or later something would turn up, some scrap of information hitherto ignored or unavailable ... Nevertheless, Thanet loathed finding himself in the position of having to rely on such stray crumbs. All the while there were leads to follow up it was possible to feel optimistic, but when there were none it was difficult not to sink into a mood when he could think only of all the unsolved murders still in the files of every police force in the country, and wonder if he himself was this time going to have to admit defeat.

But back at the office a surprise was awaiting him.

'There's a Mr Mathews and a Miss Chase to see you, sir. They've been waiting nearly an hour.'

A confession? Hope burgeoned once more.

'Where are they?'

'Interview room two.'

'I'll see them right away.'

197

19

Mathews had armoured himself in respectability: dark suit, white shirt, sober tie. Eileen, too, was formally dressed in a fawn linen suit, cream blouse with Peter Pan collar. They both stood up when Thanet came into the room.

'What can I do for you?'

They glanced at each other. Eileen gave a small, encouraging nod.

Mathews' Adam's apple moved jerkily in his throat. 'I . . . we thought we ought to clarify the position.'

'Shall we sit down, then?' Thanet checked: the policewoman who had come to take notes was ready.

'I don't know where to begin.' Mathews looked helplessly at his fiancée.

Eileen edged her chair closer to his and took his hand. 'Begin with why we decided to come,' she said softly.

Mathews clutched her hand in both of his, like a talisman. 'It's just that . . . Well, we're not exactly stupid, Inspector. We appreciate the position I'm in. We know that you're bound to be looking for a *man* in connection with Charity's death, in view of . . .' His courage failed him and once again he cast a desperate glance at Eileen.

'In view of the fact that she'd just had an abortion, Inspector,' she said calmly. 'As my fiancé said yesterday, we have no secrets from each other. It's obvious that there would have been a post mortem and that in the circumstances you would look first for the father of that child.'

Mathews had gained strength from her intervention. 'It was clear from your questions, yesterday, that I was high on your list of suspects, so we thought that if we came and told you everything, you would believe me when I said I was innocent.'

'Of the murder, Leslie means.' Eileen leaned forward in her chair, the protruberant eyes bulging earnestly. 'You must believe that.'

So they had come to confess to the lesser crime in the hope of exonerating themselves from the greater. Well, we'll see, thought Thanet.

'What do you mean by "everything"?' he said cautiously.

Mathews' face was suddenly flooded with scarlet. 'The child was mine.'

So, candidate number three for the paternity of Charity's baby. Thanet wondered what Matthews would say, if he knew about the other two.

His confession made, Mathews suddenly became voluble. 'As I said, it was obvious, yesterday, that you suspected the truth. And we thought it would only be a matter of time before you started to put pressure on me, ask for blood samples and so on. So, to be honest, we thought it would look better if I came in of my own free will and confessed — to being the baby's father, that is. But the murder ... Inspector, I swear I had absolutely nothing to do with that. When I heard ... I just couldn't believe it. And I'd travelled down from London with her, just before! I knew how bad it would look, so at first, I ... we thought it would be best if we kept quiet.'

'You helped Charity arrange for the abortion?'

'No. She fixed it up herself, said she didn't need any help from me. Only the money.' Mathews released Eileen's hand and wiped his palm on his trouser leg.

'How much?'

'Two hundred pounds.'

Charity, it seemed, had had a talent for capitalising on even the most unpromising situations. Just before Thanet left Jethro had told him that he, too, had given Charity two hundred pounds — money he had won betting and had tucked away 'for a rainy day', unknown to his wife. It was not surprising, then, that even after paying for the abortion Charity had had over a hundred and fifty pounds left — and there would have been more, Thanet reminded himself, if she had managed to squeeze money out of the young Welshman.

All in all, Thanet found that he was liking Charity less and less with every day that passed.

'You know which clinic she went to?'

Mathews shook his head. 'She wouldn't tell me. Somewhere in London, that's all.'

'You arranged to meet on the train, on Monday night?'

'No! That was pure chance, I swear. If I'd known she was catching that one ... She was the last person in the world I wanted to see, I assure you. As I said, she got on after me, came and sat opposite.'

'How did she seem?'

'Very quiet. Tired, I thought. Well, that would be understandable ...'

'What did you talk about?'

'We didn't talk, not really. I just asked her if it had gone off all right and she said yes. She dozed, most of the way. To tell you the truth, I was relieved. It was a pretty embarrassing situation.'

'I can imagine. And when you got to Sturrenden?'

'As I told you, we parted outside the station. And that was the last I saw of her.'

'Excuse me for a moment, will you?'

He left them exchanging an apprehensive look and hurried up to his room. Before proceeding he needed to find out if Carson's report was in. He shuffled through the reports he had not yet had time to read that morning and found the one he sought. His eyes skimmed the single sheet of paper, his spirits plummeting.

The landlord of the Red Lion, in Cresset Street, remembered Mathews coming in soon after nine. He was firm on the time because his daughter, who helped behind the bar, had left for a disco at nine. The landlord hadn't been too pleased to be left single-handed to cope with the Bank Holiday crowd. He'd first noticed Mathews just after she left. He remembered him partly because he was not a regular, partly because of the orange rucksack he carried, and partly because he had looked so depressed. He had spoken to no one, had consumed several whiskies and was walking unsteadily when he left at about ten to ten. At no point during the three-quarters of an hour had Mathews left the bar.

And Eileen's mother, who could have no possible reason to lie, had been quite definite about the time of Mathews's arrival that evening: ten o'clock. So Mathews simply wouldn't have had time either to have followed Charity after leaving the station or to have intercepted her on her way home.

Thanet tossed the report on to the desk with an exclamation of disgust. There was no point in questioning Mathews any further at present, he might as well let the couple go. He was at the door when the phone rang. It was Lineham.

'Any luck, Mike?'

'I found him, sir. Caleb. Got his address from Jethro, as you suggested. Jethro's got a lovely black eye, by the way.'

'Yes, I know. I've seen it. What did Caleb say?'

'No wonder Mrs Jethro Pritchard has disowned him. Guess what he does for a living?'

Thanet was in no mood for games. 'Just tell me, Mike, will you?'

'He's a one-man band! You know, blow through a comb, play an accordion, clash the cymbals with a string attached to one foot ...'

'I get the picture.'

'I rather liked him, actually.'

'And, let me guess, he spent the relevant time having an innocent drink in the King's Head with his daddy.'

'That's what Jethro says?'

'Yes.'

'So does Caleb. And I'm afraid it looks pretty cast-iron. There's a third party who bears them out.'

'The chap called Pete?'

'Peter Andrews, yes. I've been to see him, too. He's a mechanic at Potters, in Biddenden Way.'

'Reliable, you think?'

'I'd say so, yes. He says he picked them both up just along the road from the school, drove them to the King's Head, had a drink with them and then took Jethro home — the old boy was getting a bit agitated in case his wife got wind of what he'd been up to. Andrews gave him a peppermint to suck and dropped him off at the corner of Gate Street, just before 10.15.'

'When the girl next door saw him arrive home.'

'He could easily have gone out again.'

'There's been no whisper of that, from anyone. Just a moment.'

A policewoman with a slip of paper in her hand had just come into the room, looking urgent.

'A message for DS Lineham, sir. Switchboard said you were on the phone to him.'

'Well?'

'The hospital rang. His wife is asking for him.'

'Thank you.'

Thanet relayed the information to Lineham, told him to take the rest of the day off and returned to interview room two.

'Right, well I think that's all, for the moment.'

Mathews and Eileen exchanged a disbelieving glance and then looked up at Thanet in mingled astonishment and hope.

Eileen was the first to find her voice. She came slowly to her feet as she said, 'You mean, you believe us? That Leslie had nothing to do with Charity's death?'

'His alibi has been checked. That's why I left you, just now. I thought that the report was probably in, but I hadn't had time to look at it before talking to you earlier. Mr Mathews seems to be in the clear.'

Mathews stood up and he and Eileen looked at each other, transfigured by joy. Then Eileen turned back to Thanet, the radiance fading. 'We needn't have come and told you all this after all, then. I should have thought . . . we should have waited . . . how stupid of me. I panicked, I suppose.'

Thanet noted the varying pronouns with interest.

Mathews put an arm around her shoulders. 'Never mind, darling. It doesn't matter, now . . . except that . . . Inspector, may I ask . . .?'

'Go ahead.'

'Will there . . . In view of the fact that Charity is dead . . . will there be a prosecution?'

'For unlawful intercourse, you mean? Extremely unlikely, I

should think. After all, you can't have a prosecution without evidence and as the main witness — as you so rightly point out — is dead, I can't see that it would have much chance of success. And I imagine that you have learnt your lesson.'

'Oh I have,' breathed Mathews fervently. 'Believe me, I have.' And in a daze of incredulous happiness, they left.

Thanet watched them go, glad that this case had had at least one positive outcome. Mathews, he was convinced, was no pervert, had merely been too weak, too flattered, perhaps, to resist a young girl's determined advances.

For by now Thanet believed that in the case of each of her 'lovers', it had been Charity who had initiated the affair. With young Williams she had failed to shape matters as she would have wished, he had been too experienced for her, but Mathews and Jethro had, he was sure, been as clay in her manipulating fingers.

Yes, he thought as he returned to his office, there was no doubt about it, his feelings towards the girl had undergone a considerable change since the moment he had first stumbled upon that pathetic figure huddled in the alley. Then, he had seen her as innocence destroyed, now he felt that despite her tender years she had herself been a destroyer, totally lacking in compassion, loyalty or finer moral feeling. He had no idea whether or not her awakened sexual appetite had truly been as gross as both Jethro and the young Welshman had claimed it to be, but in any case, Thanet was more certain than ever that Charity had consciously used that sexuality to strike back at her father in retaliation for the long years of tyranny.

How heady must her sense of power have been, while she explored its deadly potential. But unfortunately for her it proved to be a weapon she could not control. She had become pregnant. How had she reacted? Would she have been in despair, as most girls of her age in her position would have been? Probably not, Thanet thought. She would have been much more likely to have been furious with her own body, for having dared to betray her. In any case, she had not lost her head. She had been determined to turn even this situation to her own advantage.

203

But unwittingly she had set in motion the forces which would ultimately destroy her.

To Thanet's mind, the saddest aspect of Charity's life was that she had evidently come to believe that to possess power over others was the road to fulfilment. Lacking generosity of heart she had failed to inspire it in those around her, and she had died without ever having experienced the joy of giving and receiving in love. Of all the people he had met on this case, not one, apart from her parents, had expressed any affection for her and it seemed that no one else would mourn her passing.

But it was still Thanet's task to find out who had killed her and he took a piece of paper and once more wrote down the names of his suspects. Then he sat brooding over it. Every one of these people had suffered because of Charity. The question was, which of them had decided to retaliate? And, even if he could find out, how could he prove it? It looked as though his two most likely candidates, Jethro and Mathews, were out of the running. With uninvolved third parties to support their stories, there didn't seem to be much likelihood of proving their guilt. And all four women — Veronica, her mother, Eileen Chase and Mrs Jethro — well, so far there was not a single scrap of evidence to connect them with the crime.

So, where did he go from here? Thanet sighed. The answer was all too familiar: back to the files. Past experience had taught him how easy it was mentally to dismiss something as unimportant, only to find later that it was a tiny but crucial piece of the jigsaw. Somewhere in those mounds of documented facts and statements he might find a chance remark, an innuendo, perhaps even something left *un*said, which could point him in the right direction.

At the moment, he'd be glad to be pointed in any direction.

20

Thanet closed the last of the files, sat back in his chair and massaged his temples. It was nine o'clock and after the long hours of reading his head was aching, his back stiff and his eyes gritty.

And it had all been for nothing.

No bells had rung, no new insight had rewarded his dogged determination to finish the task he had set himself.

He had missed Lineham, too. Normally they did this particular job together, pausing to comment, suggest, argue, speculate with the unconscious ease of long association. Deprived of this stimulation and of Lineham's value as a sounding-board, Thanet had gradually found himself sinking into a stupefied inertia; ideas either failed to flow or seemed too uninspired to warrant more than passing consideration.

Reminded of the sergeant, Thanet now rang the hospital. After a short delay he was informed that Louise's labour was progressing satisfactorily but that the birth was not yet imminent. No hope of Lineham returning to the office tonight, then. Thanet stood up and stretched. Time he gave up and went home.

Despite the open window the room was stuffy, stale with tobacco smoke. Thanet folded his arms on the window sill and leaned out, taking in deep breaths of fresh air. The street below was almost deserted, the shop fronts illuminated for the hours of darkness ahead, but above the roof-tops the light still lingered in an oyster-shell sky streaked with apricot and rose. It all looked very peaceful and yet, somewhere out there a murderer walked free, growing daily more confident, perhaps, that his crime would remain unsolved.

As well it might, thought Thanet despondently. Where have

I gone wrong? What have I left undone? What have I missed?
There must, surely, be something. Perhaps it was merely a
question of viewpoint. Thanet was still convinced that this had
been no casual killing. There had been no robbery, no sexual
assault, no struggle. But the blow which had sent Charity
reeling against that wicked piece of iron had caught her
unprepared. So what, exactly, had precipitated it?

Thanet stared unseeing over the chimneys of Sturrenden,
transported by his imagination back to the narrow alley where
Charity had met her death.

*Scenario one: Charity and the murderer were walking side by
side along the footpath. Tempers were rising, the killer's anger
building inexorably towards flash point.*

Thanet frowned and narrowed his eyes, as if intense concentration would reward him with a glimpse of the killer's face.

With whom would Charity have been quarrelling?

With Veronica, because Veronica was refusing to go along
with Charity's schemes, ever again?

With Mrs Hodges, because she had discovered the reason
for Charity and Veronica's 'friendship', and was making it
clear that she was not going to allow her daughter to be
blackmailed and browbeaten any longer?

With Eileen Chase, because she wanted Charity to leave
Mathews alone in future?

With Mathews, because ... No, Mathews was now in the
clear, remember. And so was Jethro.

With Mrs Jethro, then, because she had found out about her
husband's relationship with Charity and was determined that
she and her husband were not going to suffer the ignominy of
another court case?

Thanet was no nearer enlightenment and he shook his head
wearily. What was the point of going on? But he couldn't leave
it alone. Obsessively, he returned to the darkness of the alley.

*Scenario two: the murderer was lying in wait for Charity,
poised to spring as the hurried, echoing tattoo of her footsteps
came closer and closer ...*

Well, if that was how it had been, Thanet simply couldn't
visualise either Veronica or her mother crouching there in the

206

shadows with murder in her heart. Eileen Chase? Well, possibly. Thanet was by now even more convinced that Eileen would fight tooth and nail to preserve her last chance of happiness. Mrs Jethro, too, would be a determined and formidable adversary.

But, would either of them be prepared to kill?

In any case, there was no evidence against either of them, and besides, the manner of Charity's death argued against it having been a premeditated crime. If murder had been planned in advance the killer would surely have come equipped with a weapon, and none had been either used or found.

No, that blow had been struck in anger, Thanet was sure of that. So ...

Scenario three: Charity's murderer comes hurrying along the footpath, either to meet her or to catch her up. For whatever reason he is already in a precarious emotional state, keyed up to challenge her or to present her with an ultimatum, perhaps. They meet, he speaks and then ... Ah yes. Then she responds in such a way (with scorn? Contempt? Defiance?) as to cause his self-control to snap.

If indeed it had happened like that, which of his suspects was most likely to fit the bill? All of them, he decided dejectedly. So he was no further forward. But wait! Perhaps he had been too limited, too blinkered in his thinking. Perhaps this was why he hadn't got anywhere. True, there had so far been no hint of anyone else caught up in Charity's toils, but that did not necessarily mean that such a person did not exist. Perhaps Thanet had not even met him yet. Or ... perhaps the murderer was someone with a familiar face, someone they simply hadn't thought of casting in this role?

The wail of a fire engine somewhere over to his right briefly penetrated Thanet's absorption and he automatically turned his head, seeking the glow which would indicate its destination. There was nothing, but the strident signal of danger must have touched the alarm button in his subconscious, because he was suddenly remembering that incident with Ben a couple of days before.

In a kaleidoscope of recollected sound and vision he saw the

207

bicycle rolling towards the open gate, heard the roar of the approaching tractor, his own frantic shouted warning. Again, Ben somersaulted over the handlebars, lay motionless upon the green of the grass verge and, in a miracle of resurrection, scrambled unharmed to his feet. Thanet relived his own relief, anger, shame as the palm of his hand cracked against Ben's tender flesh.

'How many times have I told you never to ride down that drive when the gate is open?'

A face that was already familiar ... someone in a precarious emotional state ...

Illumination was blinding and Thanet straightened up with such a jerk that he struck his head on the lintel. The combination of physical pain and mental dazzlement disorientated him and he staggered, clutching at the windowsill to steady himself.

After a few moments, when he felt more in control, he returned to his desk and sat down, rubbing the back of his head.

Was it possible?

That unique response, familiar to every parent, of intense anxiety instantaneously transmuted into relief and then into anger when the danger is over ... Was this what had brought about Charity's death?

Had she been killed by her own father?

Thanet's mind raced as he began to test this new theory against the events of that night.

He had never seriously considered Pritchard as a suspect because Pritchard had reported Charity's disappearance before the crime was committed and because Thanet had therefore had the impression of having had the man under his own surveillance for the entire evening. But now he realised that this was not so. For twenty minutes or so, while Thanet and Lineham were visiting Mrs Hodges, Pritchard had been left at home alone, on Thanet's own suggestion.

Say that Pritchard, unable to bear the inactivity, had decided to go and look for his daughter along the footpath.

Here was a new scenario indeed: Pritchard advancing

slowly, fearful of stumbling at any moment across his daughter's body. After the long hours of slowly-mounting tension he is keyed up to an almost unbearable pitch of anxiety. Then he thinks he recognises the footsteps approaching. Hope burgeons. Can it possibly be Charity?

It is, and at once, now that he is assured of her safety, anxiety is transformed into an overwhelming rush of anger. He demands to know where she has been. And Charity?

What does Charity do?

She, too, is in a state of tension. She knows, from Mrs Hodges, that she has been found out, that there is no possibility this time of covering her tracks, of fobbing her father off with evasions or half-truths. Pritchard is going to want to have chapter and verse, corroboration of her story down to the last detail. And although her rebellion has long been in the making, she is not yet ready for open confrontation. At fifteen she is not equipped for independence and cannot hope to throw off the shackles of home in the same way as her cousin Caleb.

She really has only two options: to try to brazen it out, or to attempt to forestall him by jumping in first with profuse apologies and a plea for forgiveness. In her weakened state it was quite possible, Thanet thought, that she would have opted for the latter, but in any case he was pretty certain that all the way home she would have been bracing herself for the meeting and rehearsing the part she would play.

And then, suddenly, while she was still unprepared, there her father was. It was easy to imagine the rest. Thanet remembered the way he himself had shrunk from the power and impact of Pritchard's rage in the kitchen that night. One false word from Charity — or even no response at all — and after the long hours of fear and tension Pritchard's self-control would have snapped. One hard slap would have been enough ...

But would Pritchard have left his daughter's body lying there? Not if he had realised the extent of the damage he had done, but it was extremely unlikely that he should have known of the existence of that broken latch and it was possible that after striking Charity, unable to trust himself further, he had at once wheeled blindly away and hurried home to await her return.

Thanet now remembered that when he and Lineham had arrived back at the Pritchard's house after seeing Mrs Hodges, Pritchard had been waiting in the hall. At the time, Thanet had assumed that this was because the man was eager to hear their news, but perhaps he had only just got home and had really been waiting for Charity to turn up. And when Thanet had assured him that Charity was safe, Pritchard's relief — which Thanet had attributed to the information that Mrs Hodges had recently seen the girl — could have been because he thought that Thanet was saying that he had seen Charity *since* the scene in the alley, and that no harm had been done. And then, when Pritchard had realised that this was not so ... this must have been the point at which he had begun to be afraid that that blow had done more damage than he had intended.

Thanet mentally reviewed the remainder of the events of that evening and saw that all along Pritchard's behaviour had been entirely consistent with this new interpretation of events. It was Thanet's own assumptions as to the man's motivation, his own misinterpretations of Pritchard's behaviour, that had led him astray.

Yes, the more he thought about it, the more convinced he became that he had hit upon the truth. He had always felt that Pritchard's sanity was balanced on a knife-edge, imperilled by religious fanaticism and dangerously unrealistic expectations of those about him. Thanet still believed that in his own way Pritchard had loved his daughter and had genuinely tried to do what he believed to be best for her. In Pritchard's eyes Charity had been a brand to be plucked from the burning and it had been his duty, however unpleasant, to ensure her salvation. How shattering it must have been to find his worst fears confirmed, to see Charity lying dead in that alley and to realise that he himself had killed her. Scarcely surprising, then, that his raw, agonised exhibition of grief had been almost too painful to witness.

What effect would the realisation that he had killed his own daughter have had upon such a man? Would he be crushed by guilt, sorrow and remorse — or would he seek to justify himself?

Thanet remembered what Miss Foskett had told him, recalled Mrs Pritchard's account of Charity's harsh punishment all those years ago, and wondered: would Pritchard have tried to persuade himself of his innocence by trying to convince himself that in striking out at Charity he had really been attacking the devil that was in her?

Thanet had come across religious fanaticism before and was only too well aware of its capacity for self-deception and delusion. Nevertheless the man would have realised that the police would not be prepared to accept this excuse as justification for murder and would have been on tenterhooks in case they discovered the truth — or, for that matter, in case anyone discovered the truth.

Mrs Pritchard, for instance?

Thanet suddenly recalled Mrs Pritchard's appearance when he had seen her leaving her sister-in-law's house, this morning. She had looked distraught, on the verge of disintegration. He had attributed her distress to natural shock and grief, but what if it had had a more sinister origin? He remembered now that she had seemed to want to tell him something, but had held back. And he, intent upon his errand, had made nothing of it. Assuming that Pritchard had indeed killed his daughter, what if Mrs Pritchard had begun to suspect the truth?

Thinking back to his previous conversation with her, Thanet began to wonder if he himself could have been responsible for arousing such suspicions. He still believed that this whole tragic train of events had been set in motion when Charity had been cowed into apparent submission by her father's harsh and misguided treatment. He had not actually said so to Mrs Pritchard, but it would not have been too difficult for her to work it out for herself after he left. What if, having done so, she had finally shed her stubborn loyalty to her husband and begun to blame him for what had happened? Not for the murder, of course. Thanet was certain that at that point Mrs Pritchard would not have suspected him of that. But she could

211

have begun to hold him responsible for setting Charity on the wrong road, the road which had led her to deceit and, finally, to death.

And if so, Thanet was sure that her attitude to her husband would have changed. Mrs Pritchard had loved her daughter. Once she had begun to blame Pritchard for Charity's death her change of attitude would have filtered through into her behaviour. What if Pritchard had misinterpreted the reason for that change? What if he had assumed that his wife had begun to suspect him of Charity's murder? Thanet could envisage only too well a conversation begun at cross-purposes and ending, on Mrs Pritchard's part, in horrified enlightenment. And although she may at one time have been prepared to justify her husband's behaviour, Thanet could not believe that she would now be prepared to do so. To condone punishment was one thing, but murder, and of her own child . . . No, she would have been bound to condemn him.

And how would Pritchard have reacted to that? Here, surely, was a highly explosive situation. Had Thanet unwittingly put Mrs Pritchard herself in danger?

Thanet rose and began to pace about the room. If only he were able to discuss all this with Lineham. Perhaps the entire fabric of the case he had built up against Pritchard was no more than the product of an over-heated imagination. But he didn't think so. There was an essential rightness about it which both elated and appalled him. Because if he were right, Pritchard was not to be trusted and Mrs Pritchard must be warned, convinced of the necessity of removing herself to safety.

Was he being alarmist? Should he go and see her now, tonight? Or should he sleep on it, wait till morning?

But if he did, and harm came to her, he would never forgive himself for not having tried to prevent it. He would go. At least, then, he would be able to gauge the emotional temperature, see how things stood between them.

He hurried out to the car park.

21

Well before he reached Town Road Thanet realised that, somewhere in the quiet residential area ahead, something was amiss. An ambulance overtook him, its blue light flashing, and he began to notice small knots of pedestrians hurrying in the same direction. He was aware of the strange osmosis by which news of disaster spreads, and he began to feel as though he and all these others were being sucked into the same maleficent vortex.

He was driving with the window open and simultaneously he smelt smoke and remembered the siren he had heard shortly before leaving the office. A fire, then. Impatiently, he repudiated the idea that there could be any connection between his mission and the emergency ahead. But he failed to convince himself. If his theory was correct, Pritchard had been living on a short fuse. What more likely than that the situation had now exploded?

He turned the last corner before the entrance to Town Road and saw that ahead of him the sightseers had come to a halt against a cordon of uniformed police, like detritus washed against a sea wall. Abandoning his car he jumped out and shouldered his way through the crowd, ignoring the indignant protests from all sides. Within seconds he had been recognised and was allowed through. Noting with a sinking sense of inevitability that the furious activity ahead was indeed centred on or near the Pritchards' house, he set off at a run. All along the street the inhabitants of Town Road had come out on to the pavements to enjoy their grandstand view.

It *was* the Pritchards' house. And the fire had really got a hold. The doorway was an orange gateway to hell and long, forked tongues of flame licked hungrily at the brickwork through window spaces from which the glass had long since exploded. Arching jets of water were being directed into the house through every opening, but the firemen had no doubt been hampered in their task by the fact that these houses had no rear access. The fire could be fought on one front only, and it seemed that someone must be trapped inside, for the men were now setting ladders against the eaves.

Thanet knew better than to approach the station officer in charge of operations at this particular moment. Human life came first, curiosity could be satisfied later. Though what prospect there could possibly be of saving anyone trapped inside that inferno, Thanet could not imagine.

Out of breath, he skidded to a stop beside the two ambulancemen and showed them his warrant card.

'What's happening?'

'Some crazy bastard's trapped inside. They went in, to try and get him out, but he'd barricaded himself in the attic. Now they're going to try and break in through the skylight.'

Thanet looked up. The small black oblong of glass set into the roof was still black. The fire, then, had not yet penetrated there. Pritchard — for it must be he — still had a chance, if he chose to take it. No one can rescue a man determined not to be saved.

Thanet put the question he dreaded to ask.

'Where's his wife?'

He was scanning the faces of the watchers now, seeking Mrs Pritchard's slight, submissive figure, that distinctive, old-fashioned bun.

'Got out just in time, apparently. When she couldn't stop him splashing petrol around she ran to the phone box and rang the fire brigade. By the time she got back, the place was well alight. He's a real nut-case, if you ask me.'

Petrol. That would account for the ferocity of the blaze, the speed with which the fire had gained hold. And, now that the word had been mentioned, Thanet could smell the sharp, pungent tang of it in the air.

But Mrs Pritchard was safe, thank God, and now he spotted her, an island of immobility in the shifting, restless crowd on

214

the far pavement. She was gazing intently upwards, the knuckles of one hand pressed against her mouth. Thanet had just begun to move towards her when there was a collective groan from the crowd, audible even above the roar and crackle of the flames.

The black oblong in the roof was now illuminated by a flickering glow from within. The fire had reached the attic. The redness was increasing in intensity with terrifying speed, the fire feeding itself no doubt upon the accumulated clutter of a disused attic, tinder-dry from years of storage. And according to the ambulancemen, Pritchard himself had accelerated matters by piling it all into one place, against the door.

Thanet hoped that it would not become the man's funeral pyre.

One of the firemen had now almost reached the skylight, which was two-thirds of the way up the roof slope. Suddenly it was flung open and Pritchard heaved himself out. The fireman steadied himself and put up his hand to grasp Pritchard's, but Pritchard ignored him, turning his back and scrabbling to secure first one foothold then another on the upper edge of the window frame. Spreadeagled against the roof, his body contracted in readiness to spring and then launched itself upwards in a desperate lunge, hands clawing for the roof ridge.

Along with the crowd behind him, Thanet caught his breath, tensed himself for the inevitable fall.

But it didn't come. With an agility born surely of desperation, Pritchard had somehow managed to secure a handhold, had hauled himself up and was now attempting to stand. Slowly, arms outstretched like a tightrope walker, he managed it, teetering slightly as he straightened up. He stood for a moment steadying himself and staring down at the furious activity below, then lifted his face to the sky.

'God is my witness!' he cried.

The words floated faintly down to the silent watchers in the street below. Then something must have collapsed in upon itself in the attic, for almost at once and so swiftly that it was over almost before it had begun, a fountain of sparks erupted from the skylight opening, spraying out in all directions, and tongues of fire spread with lightning speed up Pritchard's legs and body and along his outstretched arms.

Some of the petrol, Thanet realised, must have splashed on to the man's clothing.

For a brief, appalling moment, Pritchard stood in flames against the sky, a horrific parody of the cross which he had always denied. Then, with an agonised scream, a seething, writhing mass of fire, he slid diagonally down the roof, cartwheeled over the edge and landed with a sickening thud in the street below.

Mrs Pritchard started forward with a cry as firemen rushed to put out the flames. Thanet caught her by the arm.

'I should give them a few moments.'

She stared blankly up at him for a moment, as if wondering who he was, and then she recognised him, gave a little nod. But she did not speak, simply stood watching the activity around her husband's body, hands pressed to either side of her face.

The flames were already extinguished, the ambulance men carefully transferring Pritchard to the waiting stretcher.

Thanet touched Mrs Pritchard's arm. 'I'll go and ask how he is.'

Pritchard was still alive, apparently. Just.

'Should think he'll be dead on arrival, though.'

'His wife'll want to go to the hospital with him,' said Thanet.

'OK. But hurry.'

Thanet helped Mrs Pritchard into the ambulance and then jumped in beside her. She didn't seem to register his presence. She still hadn't said a single word and throughout the brief journey sat staring into space.

Shock, thought Thanet. And who could wonder? Mother, daughter, husband, home, all lost within the space of one short week. The only way to survive such an experience must be at first to blank out reality, to curl up inside yourself like a snail in a shell and stay there until some instinct tells you that you can now begin to cope with life again.

They were almost at the hospital when the attendant who had been keeping a watchful eye on Pritchard glanced up and caught Thanet's eye. His expression of regret and slight shake of the head were enough to tell Thanet that Pritchard was dead. Mrs Pritchard had not noticed the brief exchange of glances. Better to break the news when they were no longer cooped up with her husband's body, Thanet decided.

He waited until a whispered request had produced a small, private room and a cup of tea from a sympathetic night sister.

'It's bad news, I'm afraid, Mrs Pritchard.'

His tone had forewarned her. Suddenly she was alert, her eyes wary.

'Your husband. He died, on the way to hospital.'

For a second she froze. Then her cup began to rattle in its saucer.

Thanet reached out, took it from her, set it on the table.

'There was nothing they could do. I'm sorry.'

She gave a fierce nod, pressed her shaking hands together. 'Just give me a few moments.'

Thanet waited in a sympathetic silence, admiring her effort at self-control.

At last she flung back her head, took several deep breaths. When she looked at him again he flinched from the pain in her eyes.

'He was ... unbalanced,' she said, forcing each word out with difficulty. 'Perhaps even ...'

But she could not bring herself to say it. Thanet said nothing, waited. If Mrs Pritchard needed to talk, who else was there to listen? Her sister, perhaps, but she was far away in Birmingham. And as for her brother-in-law Jethro, or his wife ... no one in a vulnerable state could possibly seek either comfort or understanding there.

'You know he ...?' Again, she could not put it into words.

He had to help her. 'Charity, you mean?'

She nodded. 'He didn't mean to ... It was an accident.' Then, fiercely, as if even now it mattered to her that her husband should be exonerated of evil intent. 'You must believe that,' she cried.

'I do.'

But his acceptance was not enough. Now that she had begun

217

she had to continue, to justify, elaborate, explain. 'It was while he was waiting for you to come back from Mrs Hodges' house ...'

It had all happened exactly as Thanet had thought: the impulsive decision to go and look for Charity along the footpath, the lashing-out in anger, the immediate return to the house, confident that Charity would soon come creeping home in a properly chastened frame of mind. And when she didn't, the growing fear that he had hit her harder than he had intended to, that she was lying unconscious, perhaps, in the alley — and, finally, the genuine grief and agony of mind when at last he saw her, dead ...

'I had a feeling there was something wrong, right from the beginning,' said Mrs Pritchard miserably. 'He was upset, of course, that was only to be expected, he really loved her, in his own way. But there was more to it than that, I was sure of it and then, when we heard that Charity had been ... carrying on with someone, it was almost as if he was glad! He began to go on and on about how bad she was, how the Devil had been in her right from the day she was born ... And in the end it dawned on me that what he was really saying was that it was a good thing she was dead, that he was talking as though whoever did it had done something ... *praiseworthy.*' Her voice cracked in disbelief.

'Looking back, now, I can see that he was trying to justify himself, but that was when I began to wonder ... when I began to be afraid ...' She pressed her knuckles hard against her mouth, in that characteristic gesture of hers, as if she were trying to batten down the horrific memory of her dawning suspicions.

'I didn't know what to do. I couldn't believe it, but the more I thought about it, the more I saw that it would make sense. I began to feel that if I couldn't talk to someone about it, I'd go out of my mind. But I couldn't think of anyone to go to, anyone who'd understand. This morning, when I saw you, I almost told you then ... But how could I? You're a policeman. I just couldn't betray my own husband. And yet ... If he had done this terrible thing ...'

She could control her distress no longer. Suddenly her face crumpled and the tears began to stream down her face.

Thanet thrust a handkerchief into her hand, patted her on the shoulder and said, 'I'll be back in a moment.' He left the room, granting her that which she had so far denied herself, the luxury of abandoning herself to grief. Quickly, he arranged that she should be kept in hospital overnight. She would, he was assured, be given a sedative that would ensure her a good night's sleep. Then he returned to her.

Her eyes were red and swollen, her face puffy, but she had stopped crying and was looking calmer. She nodded gratefully when he told her of the arrangements he had made, but protested when he said that he thought it would be best for her if they continued their conversation tomorrow.

'I'd much rather finish telling you tonight. Otherwise, I shall just lie awake, going over and over it in my mind.'

'If you're sure ...'

'I am. Truly.'

'Very well.' He sat down again.

'I was trying to explain to you how I was feeling this morning ...'

'You were in an impossible situation.'

She nodded, blew her nose. 'I'd never want to live through these last few days again.'

But you will, thought Thanet sadly, you will. In your imagination you will live them again and again. Perhaps the memory will gradually fade, the pain become less acute, but they'll be with you till the day you die.

'By this evening I felt I couldn't stand it any longer ... the doubts, the suspicions ... I felt I just had to *know*. And there was only one way of finding out, really. I knew he'd be angry, but honestly, I was past caring ...

'At first, I didn't dare ask him straight out if he'd killed her, so he didn't know what I was talking about — or perhaps he did know, and was just pretending to misunderstand. So in the end, I asked him outright. He ... he just stared at me, and for a minute I thought he was just going to walk out on me. Then he started ...

219

'He went on and on about how evil Charity had been, how the Devil had always been in her, how he thought he'd got rid of it when she was a little girl, but he hadn't, and it had been there, lurking inside her all these years, waiting for its chance to come out into the open at last ... Then he began to cry, said how much he'd loved her, that he hadn't meant to hurt her, not Charity, his little girl ... He begged me to believe that. But I must see, he said, that it was all for the best ...

'I just couldn't speak, couldn't say anything, and in the end he began to get angry with me. He said he could see I didn't believe him, but he could prove that he had been right to do what he did. If God hadn't wanted Charity to die, she wouldn't have, he said, and God would give me a sign to show me that he'd only been acting as God's instrument. If our eye offended we should pluck it out, he said, and if the evil lay in our only child, then our only course was to sacrifice that child on the altar of duty ... He went on and on and I couldn't bear it. I kept on thinking of Charity, of how much I'd loved her, how God would surely never have asked that of me ... And in the end I put my hands over my ears. He was beside himself with rage then, grabbed my arms and forced my hands down. I would listen, he said, whether I liked it or not. He'd told me he could prove that he was innocent of evil and he would do so. Then he rushed out of the house.

Thanet could guess what was coming.

'When he got back he was carrying this huge can of petrol. He wasn't shouting any more, he was quite calm. God would be his witness, he said. Like Shadrach, Meshach and Abednego he would walk through the fire unharmed and I would see at last that every word he had been saying was God's truth. All the while he was talking he was splashing the petrol about, everywhere ... in the bedrooms, down the staircase, in the sitting room ... He was cool, methodical, and now I was the one who was screaming, begging him to stop. He just shook me off and went on with what he was doing ...'

Thanet already knew the rest, but he went on listening, patiently, as Mrs Pritchard told the remainder of her tragic tale. When she had finished she closed her eyes and leaned

220

back in her chair, exhausted, as motionless as a mechanical doll that has run down.

Thanet waited for a little while and then said gently, 'He must have been in torment over the last few days.'

She opened her eyes and there was gratitude in them, for his understanding.

'He was. I think he knew, really, that there was no justification, never could be any justification for what he had done. He was desperate to convince himself otherwise — well, you saw him for yourself, tonight. In the end I don't think he could have gone on, not knowing. I think he just had to find some way of giving himself the final proof.'

Had Pritchard known, in the last, few agonising moments of his life, that he had been deluding himself, Thanet wondered. Perhaps Mrs Pritchard was right and deep down inside he had known all along that he was, and had come to feel that he could not live with the knowledge.

Mrs Pritchard had closed her eyes again. Now that she had unburdened herself, perhaps she would be able to rest. Quietly, he left the room, went to fetch the Sister.

Before she was led gently away Mrs Pritchard attempted a smile. 'Thank you for listening to me.'

Thanet touched her shoulder and left.

Outside, on the hospital steps, he paused to take in great lungfuls of fresh air. He felt as though he were sloughing off the claustrophobic, unnatural atmosphere of Pritchard's world and emerging into a universe where sanity was the norm and optimism possible again. His car, he remembered, was still parked near Town Road and he decided that the walk would do him good. For once he would break his own rule and leave writing up the day's reports until tomorrow.

In the car, the pace of his driving reflected the exhaustion that was beginning to steal over him and by the time he turned into his own driveway he could think of nothing but falling into bed and sinking into oblivion. He couldn't be bothered to put the car away, but left it in the drive. As he trudged wearily to the front door he was surprised to see a line of light around the sitting room curtains. His mother-in-law was usually in bed long before this. There must be something on television she especially wanted to see, he decided, as he let himself in. Yes, the sitting room door was ajar and he could hear the murmur of conversation.

As he shut the door behind him the sound cut out.

'Luke?'

He stood stock still. Joan's voice? Surely he had imagined it.

There was a movement within the room, a shadow across the band of light spilling into the hall, and the door opened wide.

Joan stood silhouetted in the doorway.

He wanted to believe it, but he couldn't. She wouldn't be home for two more endless weeks. This vision had been conjured up by his own tiredness, need and longing.

'Darling? Are you all right?'

The light in the hall clicked on and now he had to believe the evidence of his own eyes. Joan really was here, only a few steps away. Without a word he opened his arms and she came into them, smiling, kissing his cheek and then laying her head against his shoulder. He folded his arms around her, burying his face in the springy golden curls, breathing in the unique smell of her.

She *was* real, she *was* here.

Even in the days of their courtship, when to see and hold her had been his paramount need, Thanet could not remember feeling quite like this. It was as if the body pressed against his was truly the other half of him and only in her presence was he complete. He closed his eyes and let the joy and peace wash over him.

They stood for a moment or two longer and then she leaned back in his arms and wrinkled her nose at him. 'You smell like Bonfire night.'

If only she knew why, Thanet thought. Briefly, the horrifying image of the burning cross that had been Charity's father flashed across his mind and he was pierced by a painful shaft of pity for them all — for Pritchard, for Mrs Pritchard and for Charity, their ill-starred daughter, doomed by heredity and environment to her brief, unhappy life and untimely death.

With an effort he wrenched his thoughts back to the present and essayed a smile. 'Do I?'

She was watching his face. 'What is it, darling? What's happened?'

He shook his head and kissed the tip of her nose. 'Tell you later.'

She waited for a moment to see if he would say anything more and, when he didn't, stepped back a little. Smiling, she lifted her hands as if to display herself. 'Well ... surprised?'

'Let me pinch you, see if you're real.' Gently, he squeezed her chin between thumb and forefinger, clowned surrender. 'You're real!'

She was laughing now, tugging him into the sitting room, talking all the while.

'I decided I just couldn't last out another fortnight, so this afternoon when two of the staff at the Home were pronounced fit for duty again, I said, "That's it, I'm off to see my poor neglected family" ... Look, I've made you coffee and sandwiches.'

Thanet allowed himself to be pushed gently into a chair, fussed over.

Joan poured him some coffee, then sat back and studied him critically. 'Just as well I did come home, by the look of it. You look terrible. I don't know whether to feel gratified or horrified, that you obviously can't survive without me!'

Thanet leaned across to kiss the tip of her nose. 'Gratified, of course. What else?'

She dropped her bantering tone. 'Case going badly?'

He shook his head. 'It's over.'

'Want to talk about it?'

'Tomorrow.' Time enough, then, to plunge back into the murky depths of the Pritchards' life, relive the grim events of the last few hours. For tonight he just wanted to savour the pleasure of having Joan home again, to relish the relief of knowing how wrong he had been ever to suspect that she had been slipping away from him. He knew her too well for her to succeed in a face-to-face pretence; her joy at being home equalled his.

223

The telephone rang.

Joan groaned. 'Oh *no*. Not tonight. Here we go ... Down to earth with a bang.'

She knew that his conscience would never allow him to leave it unanswered, and she watched with resignation as he heaved himself out of his chair.

'Lineham here, sir. It's a boy!'

'Mike! Congratulations! How's Louise?'

'Fine. They've knocked her out now, as a precaution against something called — I think — eclampsia — but they say she'll be all right, there's absolutely nothing to worry about.'

'That's marvellous.'

'They say the baby's fine, too. Yelling his head off.'

'What are you going to call him?'

'Richard.'

'Nice name.'

'Well, just thought I'd let you know. Got some more phone calls to make now, of course. See you tomorrow.'

'Right. Thanks for ringing.'

Thanet turned to Joan. 'Mike, as you'll have gathered. It's a boy. And both Louise and the baby are fine.'

'Wonderful. What a relief!'

'Certainly is. Tell you what, we'll go and see Louise tomorrow, smuggle in some glasses and a bottle of champagne. I feel like celebrating.'

He held out his hands, tugged Joan to her feet and put his arms around her once more. The case was over, Louise and baby were doing well, Joan was home. What more could he want?

At moments like this he felt that life itself was a celebration.

LAST SEEN ALIVE

To Hazel

Reviens, reviens
Ma bien aimée . . .
Berlioz, *Nuits d'été*

ONE

Even before Thanet had closed the front door behind him Bridget was hurtling down the stairs, face radiant and long hair flying.

'She spoke to me, Daddy! She spoke to me!'

'She did?'

Thanet smiled indulgently as Bridget flung her arms around him. No need to ask who 'she' was. Like countless other young girls the world over, twelve-year-old Bridget was an ardent admirer of the Princess of Wales. Ever since that fairy-tale vision had floated up the aisle of St Paul's Cathedral, capturing the hearts and imagination of millions, Bridget had taken an avid interest in anything and everything to do with Princess Diana. Her bedroom was crammed with posters, books, commemoration china and bulging scrapbooks and she had been looking forward to today's royal visit for months.

When it had been suggested that the Princess should be asked to open the new children's orthopaedic unit at Sturrenden General Hospital, nobody had really expected her to say yes. But she had, and the small country town had been in a fever of anticipation ever since.

Thanet had been somewhat less enthusiastic. For the police, a royal visit means weeks of planning, a crescendo of detailed organisation culminating in a day of hectic activity and high tension, especially when the visitor is as universally popular as Princess Diana. But now it was all over and they could breathe a sigh of relief that nothing had gone wrong. The enormous crowds had dispersed without serious incident, the support groups drafted in from Canterbury had departed and traffic signs had been cleared away from the route. Most important of all, the Princess had gone and others were responsible for her safety. Thanet did not envy them their job.

'How exciting! What did she say to you?'

'She asked me how long I'd been waiting, and I said, since eight o'clock this morning.'

'And?'

'She pulled a little face and said, what a long time.'

'And that was it?'

'Yes. I was really *close* to her, Daddy. I could have put out my hand and touched her! I didn't, of course, but oh, she's so beautiful, she really is, far more beautiful than all the pictures of her . . .'

Thanet put an arm around Bridget's shoulders and they moved towards the kitchen as she chattered enthusiastically on. Thanet put his head around the living room door as they went by. 'Hullo Ben.'

'Hi, Dad.' Ben scarcely turned his head. He was deep in 'Doctor Who.'

In the kitchen Joan was shaking the water out of lettuce. She looked up, smiled and came to kiss him. 'It all went off well, I gather.'

'You weren't there? I thought you were going with Sprig.'

Joan shook her head. 'Mary took her, with Belinda. I had an emergency call.' Joan was a probation officer. 'Sprig, go and lay the table, will you?'

'Oh, but I haven't finished telling Daddy about . . .'

'Later, poppet.'

'But I wanted to . . .'

'I said, later. Go along.' Joan scooped up a handful of cutlery and pressed it into her daughter's reluctant hands. 'Go *on*.' She waited until Bridget had left the room. 'It was Tracey Lindop — you remember, the persistent shop-lifter? Well, she's pregnant, apparently, and by her stepfather. When her mother found out, she just threw her out. I had to find her somewhere to stay. She's only fourteen. Just think, Luke, that's only two years older than Sprig. And, what's more, she's saying she's not only going to have the baby, she's going to keep it.'

'She might well change her mind, as time goes on.'

Joan shook her head. 'I doubt it. She seems pretty set on the idea. Honestly, she has absolutely no idea of the difficulties involved. How on earth is she going to manage? She has no qualifications, she'll never get a job . . .'

'She'll scrape along on social security, I expect.'

'Yes, but what sort of permanent prospect is that? She says, if she keeps the baby, at least she'll have someone to love who'll love her. . . . I can just see the whole cycle starting up again. Sooner or later the baby'll begin to get on her nerves and she'll probably batter it just as her own mother battered her. . . . The whole business is so depressing.'

Thanet gave her a brief, wordless hug.

'Honestly, I sometimes wonder if I'm achieving anything, anything at all . . .'

'Are these ready, Mum?' Bridget had returned and picked up two of the plates on the table.

'Yes. Come on, we'll eat.'

Bridget, still fizzing with excitement, chattered on through most of supper. Thanet and Joan listened benevolently and it was some time before Thanet noticed that Ben was unusually subdued and was only picking at his food.

'What's the matter, Ben? Aren't you hungry?'

Ben shook his head and mumbled something about having eaten a large tea at Peter's house.

Thanet raised his eyebrows at Joan, who gave a little shrug, but said nothing. Thanet, following her cue, let the matter drop.

After supper they all settled down to watch a family quiz show. Thanet felt in the mood to spend the entire evening mindlessly in front of the television set, then have an early night. It was good to have the prospect of a free Sunday ahead tomorrow, his first for some time. He hoped that nothing would crop up at work to spoil it. He lit his pipe and relaxed into the comfortable depths of his armchair. They'd get up late, he thought contentedly, go to church together, enjoy Sunday lunch at home, and in the afternoon they'd take the children to the sea . . .

The call came while they were still at breakfast next morning. Resignedly, he replaced the receiver and returned to the kitchen. Just as well he hadn't mentioned the beach to Bridget and Ben.

'Oh, no,' said Joan, after one glance at his face.

'I'm afraid so.'

'Couldn't someone else go, just for once?'

'Not possible, love. I'm sorry.' He gave a 'not in front of the children' glance at Ben and Bridget. He needn't have bothered.

'Is it murder, Dad?' Ben, whose uncharacteristically quiet mood seemed to have lasted the night, was at last showing signs of animation.

'Could be.' Almost certainly was, by the sound of it.

'Where?' Ben was on his feet, following Thanet and Joan into the hall.

Thanet ruffled his son's hair. 'Don't be a ghoul. You'll read all about it in good time, I daresay.'

'Oh, *Dad*. What's the point of having a police inspector for a father, if you don't hear all the juicy bits before anyone else?'

'That's enough, Ben,' snapped Thanet. 'Murder is not supposed to be a source of entertainment.'

Ben returned to the kitchen, scowling, and Thanet kissed Joan goodbye. 'Not sure when I'll be back.'

'You don't have to tell me. . . . Take care.'

To add insult to injury, it looked as though it was going to be another lovely day, he thought gloomily as he drove through the deserted streets. It was now the end of July, and so far it had been a truly glorious summer, one golden day following another in a seemingly endless procession. It was really galling to have this one snatched away from him at the eleventh hour. With difficulty, he forced himself to stop dwelling on his disappointment and concentrate on the scanty information he had been given.

The dead woman's name was Alicia Parnell and she had arrived in Sturrenden the previous day. She had been a guest at the Black Swan, the oldest and most luxurious hotel in the town. For centuries it had been a coaching inn, much frequented by travellers on their way to Canterbury, but with the advent of the motor car its fortunes had declined and the beautiful old building had become more and more delapidated. Then, in the late nineteen-fifties, when the country was gradually recovering from the bleak austerity of the post-war years, it had been bought by a man called Jarman, an ex-R.A.F.

Wing-Commander who had recognised its potential and had accurately predicted the tourist boom. Now it was a thriving business, run by his son.

Thanet turned in through the arched opening in the black and white façade and parked in the cobbled yard alongside two other police cars and Detective-Sergeant Lineham's Ford Escort.

Lineham was in the foyer, talking to the proprietor. Thanet knew most of the prominent people in Sturrenden and Jarman was no exception.

'Ah, there you are, Inspector.' Jarman came hurrying across, looking harassed. He was in his early forties, his well-cut suit almost, but not quite, hiding his growing paunch. The Swan had a superb chef.

'This is terrible. I don't know what to say. It's just . . . unthinkable. I keep wondering if I'll wake up and find it's all a nightmare.' He mopped at his forehead and moved closer, lowering his voice. 'Look, do you think we could . . . The other guests . . . My office, perhaps?'

'Not just yet. I must go upstairs, first. There's no need for you to come with us, I'm sure you must have a lot to attend to down here. Sergeant, have you had time to talk to any of the staff yet?'

'Only the chambermaid who found the body, sir.'

'In that case, Mr Jarman, perhaps you could have a discreet word with your members of staff, find out if any of them saw the woman at any time since her arrival yesterday. When did she get here?'

'So far as we can tell from the register, some time between four and four-thirty yesterday afternoon.'

'She was alone?'

'Yes.'

'Right, well, if you could do that, then . . . Oh, and make sure none of the other guests checks out until we've been able to talk to them.'

Jarman closed his eyes in despair. 'If it's absolutely necessary . . .'

'Come, Mr Jarman, you must see that it is.'

Jarman gave a resigned shrug and Thanet followed

13

Lineham to the lift, trying to ignore the cramp-like sensation in his stomach. No one could have guessed from his calm, business-like demeanour just how much he was dreading the next few minutes. Even Joan, with whom he shared almost all his secret hopes, fears and aspirations, was unaware of this one most private weakness, his inability to look upon the newly-dead with equanimity. For years he had hoped that he would overcome it, that custom would dull the edge of his sensibility, but gradually he had had to accept that this wasn't going to happen. Now he tried to meet the experience with the same stoicism with which he faced the dentist's drill: endure, and the pain will soon be over. And it always was, thank God. It was just that first sight of the corpse . . .

'What did the chambermaid have to say, Mike?'

'Nothing much. She found the body when she went to make the bed this morning. She wasn't on duty last night, so she hadn't seen the woman before.'

'What do we know about this Mrs Parnell?'

'Very little. She's in her late thirties, I'd say. Pretty well-off, nicely dressed — well, you'll see for yourself. She's been strangled, manually by the look of it.'

'Dead long?'

'Late last night, I should think. Rigor is pretty well-established.'

'Is the SOCO here?'

The Scenes-of-Crime Officer is an essential part of any murder investigation. It is his job to find and preserve the forensic evidence which, however microscopic, may succeed in establishing the vital link between murderer and victim.

'Arrived shortly before you, sir. The SOCO sergeant has come along too.'

'What about Doc Mallard?'

Lineham grinned. 'On his way. Not too pleased about having his Sunday morning disturbed, though.'

'He's not the only one.' But Thanet's tone was mild. He was too preoccupied with bracing himself against the next few minutes to resurrect his sense of grievance.

'Here we are.'

The lift had stopped at the third floor. A corridor stretched right and left, with rooms on either side. The carpet was thick, the wallpaper expensive, and there were original prints on the wall.

'Stairs?'

'There's a flight at each end of the corridor, I'm afraid.'

Lineham turned left and Thanet followed him. Strangled. Sir Sydney Smith's description of a strangler's victim flitted through his mind. '. . . *Not a pretty sight . . . Bluish or purple lips and ears, change of colour of the nails, froth and possibly blood-staining about the nose or mouth, the tongue forced outwards, the hands clenched . . .*'

They had arrived. Lineham opened the door and Thanet preceded him into the room, automatically returning the greetings of the SOCOs, who were still busy taking photographs. They stood back as he approached the body. Grimly, without touching her, he silently confirmed Lineham's diagnosis, forcing himself to note the details as the roaring in his ears faded to a hum and his stomach settled. She was half-lying on the bed, her short, softly-waved dark hair framing that hideous parody of a face, the bulging brown eyes fixed in that blank, motionless stare which instantly proclaims the absence of life. Her black dress and high-heeled sandals were clearly expensive, and a heavy gold chain bracelet encircled her right wrist, a cocktail watch her left. She also wore a chased platinum wedding ring and an engagement ring, a sapphire and diamond cluster. Somebody's wife, then, probably somebody's mother. Thanet was filled with the familiar anger at the waste of a life, with all its attendant suffering for a shocked and grieving family.

'Robbery certainly wasn't the motive, anyway,' said Lineham's voice, close beside him.

'Nor a sexual assault, by the look of it.' Thanet stepped back. 'Carry on,' he said to the photographers.

He looked around. There were no signs of a struggle. The Black Swan certainly did its customers proud, he thought. It was a beautiful room, more like a room in a private house than a hotel bedroom, with leaded casement windows and sloping ceilings striped with ancient beams. The bed on which the woman was lying was an authentic four-poster, with chintz hangings and bedspread in delicate shades of cream, lilac and pink. Ruched blinds of matching chintz hung at the dormer windows and the fitted carpet was lilac. The bedside table and the chest of drawers were genuine antiques. The adjoining bathroom was equally luxurious, with an oval lilac bath, thick cream carpet and built-in dressing-table. Alicia Parnell's cosmetics — all expensive — were neatly ranged upon it.

In the bedroom a cream silk jacket was lying across an armchair. It looked as though she might have tossed it there when she came in. Had she been out, Thanet wondered, curiosity beginning to work in him like yeast. And if so, where had she gone, and with whom? What had she been like, this woman? He spotted a photograph in a silver frame on the bedside table and bent to examine it. A man and a woman — Mrs Parnell and her husband? — smiled up at him, the man seated and invisible from the chest downwards, Mrs Parnell standing behind him with her hands on his shoulders. Thanet frowned. Surely . . .

It looked as though the frame had already been dusted for prints, but he checked before picking it up and examining the picture more closely. Yes, he was sure, now. Alicia . . .

Image after long-forgotten image began to race through his mind: Alicia, hair streaming behind her in the wind as she and the others sailed past in Oliver Bassett's open-topped sports car . . . Alicia on the tennis court, her sensational legs golden beneath the flare of her brief white skirt . . . Alicia cycling past in the usual noisy, laughing group, her straw school hat pushed back at a forbidden angle, her face tilted provocatively up at the boy beside her. . . .

Thanet glanced at the body on the bed and his grip on the photograph frame tightened.

Lineham had noticed the look on his face.

'What is it, sir?'

Thanet put the photograph carefully back on the table. 'I knew her, Mike, long ago, when we were at school.'

'Well?'

Thanet shook his head. 'Oh no, not well. But she . . . she was stunning, then. She was a couple of years older than me, and I don't suppose she even noticed my existence, but half the school was in love with her, or claimed to be.'

'She was at the Girls' Grammar?'

'Yes. She and another girl — I can't remember her name, but she had red hair, that I do remember — used to go around with a group of sixth formers from the Boys' Grammar . . .' Thanet shook his head. 'I can hardly believe it.'

'You're sure it's her?'

'Certain.' Thanet picked up the photograph and held it out. 'Look at her.'

Alicia Parnell had had the sort of face which, once seen, is not easily forgotten. The chin was too pointed, the nose too tip-tilted for beauty, but combined with huge dark eyes and high, classically-rounded cheekbones, they created an individuality which had not become blurred over the years. Looking at the snapshot over Lineham's shoulder Thanet could clearly visualise the softer, more rounded adolescent Alicia beneath the mature face in the photograph.

'I see what you mean,' said Lineham.

'I'd have recognised her anywhere, though I hadn't seen her in years. Not since . . .' He stopped, remembering.

'Not since what?'

There was a knock at the door and Doctor Mallard appeared, escorted by Jarman, who took one brief, hunted glance around the room and withdrew. Thanet crossed to meet the little police surgeon.

Mallard, as usual, looked irritable, but Thanet ignored this. The loss of his dearly-loved wife, many years before, had left Mallard at odds with the world. Thanet sympathised with his inability to come to terms with his grief and tended to treat him as if he were still the good-humoured old friend Thanet remembered so well.

'What have we got this time?' said Mallard, frowning over his half-moon spectacles at the photographer who was obscuring his view of the body.

'Nearly finished, Bates?' said Thanet.

'Yes, sir. Just one or two more.'

'Hurry it up, then, will you?'

Mallard's examination of the body did not take long. When he had finished he rose stiffly to his feet, pointedly ignoring

Lineham's outstretched hand. 'No need to tell you how she died. Any dunderhead can see that for himself.'

'Manual strangulation?'

'Yes. The bruises are clearly visible, as you've no doubt noted. No scratch marks on the neck, though. Of course, her nails are very short . . .'

'What about time of death?'

Mallard hesitated, considering. 'Taking all the various factors into consideration, I'd say between ten and eleven last night. That's only a guess, mind.'

'Of course,' said Thanet, trying not to grin. Mallard was rarely wrong in such 'guesses'.

Mallard gave him a severe glance over his spectacles. 'I mean it.' He picked up his bag. 'Well, if the guardians of law and order are satisfied, perhaps I may now be allowed to return home and go to church, like a civilised human being. Don't bother to come down with me.'

'I've got to have a word with the manager anyway.'

While they waited for the lift Thanet said, 'She was a local girl, you know.'

'Local? What makes you think that?'

'I recognised her. From years back. . . . There was a photograph on the bedside table,' he explained as Mallard opened his mouth to protest that nobody could possibly have made such an indentification from that distorted face. 'She hadn't changed much — scarcely at all, in fact.'

'What was her name?'

'Her maiden name was Doyle. Alicia Doyle.'

'Doyle . . . Doyle . . . Let me see, didn't she go around with one of the Rain boys for a while?'

'Yes. Nicholas Rain. The violinist.'

'Don't treat me like an idiot! I know he's the violinist. As a matter of fact I was quite close to the Rain family at one time. His father and I were friends for years, good friends, up until the time of his death. I've followed Nicholas's career with great interest, right from the start. He was playing in Sturrenden last night, you know. I went to the concert.'

'Ah, yes, I'd forgotten. We've been so tied up with the royal visit . . .'

18

'Bach's double violin concerto. With that young girl he's just become engaged to. A fine performance they gave, too . . . though a bit too sensual for my taste.'

'I wonder if that was why she was here — Mrs Parnell, I mean. For the concert.'

'Could be.'

They had reached the ground floor and they parted. Thanet knocked on the door of Jarman's office.

'Come in.'

Jarman was sitting at his desk, head in hands.

'Sit down, Inspector. Have you finished, upstairs?'

'Not quite. In any case, I'm afraid it will be some time before the room is available to you.'

'When do you think you'll be able to get around to dealing with the guests? I've got three couples who are all packed and ready to go, and they're not too pleased at being held up, I can tell you.'

'Very soon. In most cases it'll just be a question of taking a brief statement and making sure we have their names and addresses.'

'Good. Oh, by the way, I'm afraid two couples had already left, before the . . . before the crime was discovered.'

'Which floors were they on?'

'One was on the third, two doors from Mrs Parnell. And the other was on the second.'

'How long had they been here?'

'The first couple came a week ago, the second the day before yesterday. They were all on holiday and booked some time ago.'

'And Mrs Parnell?'

'Booked a fortnight ago, just for the one night.'

'I'd like their addresses, and a quiet room where we can question the other guests.'

'There's a small lounge on the first floor. Would that do?'

'Fine. Thank you. Have you had an opportunity to question the staff yet?'

'Some of them. Of course, a number of those who were on duty last night are not here this morning. The chambermaid, for instance, and she's not on the phone. . . . There were two

19

points you might find interesting. The first is that Mrs Parnell made a local call, soon after she checked in.'

'Do you have the number she rang?'

'Sorry, no. She just asked for an outside line, around four-thirty.'

'And the other point?'

'My receptionist saw her in the foyer at about seven o'clock, talking to some local people, a Mr and Mrs Leyton.'

'Would that be Mr Richard Leyton, the fruit farmer?' Thanet hadn't seen him in years.

'That's right. There was a Rotary Club Ladies' Night here last night, in the Fletcher Hall. My receptionist recognised Mr Leyton because he'd been involved in organising it.'

Thanet groaned inwardly. The place must have been crawling with people between ten and eleven last night. 'You have the Leytons' address?'

'Their telephone number,' said Jarman unhappily. He handed Thanet a slip of paper. 'I've written it down for you. I don't like doing this, but I see that I must. Anyway, apparently this was only a brief conversation and then Mrs Parnell left the hotel. She hadn't had dinner here, we don't start serving until seven-thirty.'

'And she didn't mention where she was going, to your receptionist?'

'No.'

There was a knock on the door. The ambulance was here to remove the body. With Jarman hovering in the background, anxious to ensure that maximum discretion was observed, Alicia Parnell's mortal remains were discreetly removed via back stairs and rear entrance.

While Thanet had been talking to Jarman, Lineham had been getting on with the search.

'Found anything, Mike?'

Lineham shook his head. 'Apart from the contents of her handbag, there's nothing interesting at all. She'd brought very little with her, just a nightdress, a change of underwear and her toilet things.'

And the photograph, thought Thanet. Why had she brought it, on such a brief trip? And where was her husband — if the man in the photograph was her husband . . .

'What was in her bag?'

'Just the usual stuff — oh, and a rosary.' Lineham held it up.

'She was a Catholic then.' Thanet took it from him and ran the beads through his fingers. How often had Alicia handled them in just this way? Thousands, hundreds of thousands of times, perhaps?

'Where did she live?'

'Fulham. Runs an employment agency, by the look of it.' Lineham handed over a business card.

Alicia had a partner, it seemed, a Jessica Ross. Both their names were on the card, together with the address of the agency in the Fulham Road.

'No home address?'

'No. Perhaps she lived over the shop, so to speak.'

Thanet remembered Alicia's expensive clothes and jewellery. 'Unlikely, I would have thought. I wonder if Jarman's got a London directory.'

He had, and Lineham's guess proved correct. Alicia was listed as A. Parnell, with a different telephone number from the agency, but the same address. There was no reply, when they tried ringing.

'We'd better go and take a look,' said Thanet.

It took a little while to get clearance for the trip from the Metropolitan Police and while they were waiting Thanet organised the work to be done in their absence: the hotel staff and guests were to be questioned and the Leytons were to be interviewed.

Then he and Lineham headed for the M20 and London.

21

TWO

The Sunday morning traffic was light, and they were soon on the motorway. The London-bound carriageway was virtually empty, but on the other side of the crash barrier a steady stream of cars was speeding towards the coast, crammed with families heading for their weekly dose of sun, sea and sand. For a while both men were silent, thinking back over the events of the morning. Eventually, 'Since what?' said Lineham.

'Mmm?' It took a moment or two for Thanet to register the question, but when he did he had no problem in knowing what Lineham meant. He and the sergeant had been working together for so long that they were well-attuned to each other's thought processes.

'Oh . . . I'd been going to say, not since just after the inquest.'

Lineham, who was driving, shot Thanet a quick, interested glance: 'What inquest?'

'Odd, isn't it? You don't think about someone or some period of your life for years and then suddenly, something triggers off that particular memory chain and the images come so thick and fast, so vividly, that you wonder how on earth you could have forgotten them.'

'Inquest on who?'

'Whom,' corrected Thanet. 'A boy called Paul Leyton. It was a real tragedy. He was one of those who seemed to have everything. He was brilliant, for a start, all set to become a fine classical scholar. But he was also a first-rate sportsman — captain of cricket, of rugger, you name it, he could do it better than anyone else.'

'I can't stand people like that.'

Thanet cast an amused glance at his sergeant. Obviously, Lineham did not enjoy being reminded of his own inadequacies.

'For us younger boys he had an almost god-like quality. He looked like one, for that matter — the sort of profile you see on Greek coins, golden curls . . .'

'Ugh.'

'. . . the lot. And whatever you say, it didn't seem to stop his contemporaries liking him. I was a couple of years younger than he — he was the same age as Alicia — but I know he was immensely popular with his year. And the masters liked him too.'

'So what happened to this paragon?'

'He killed himself.'

'What?'

Lineham was genuinely shocked, a little ashamed, too, Thanet thought, of his sneering tone of a moment ago.

'But why? The way you were talking, it sounds as though he had everything to live for.'

'That's what everybody said. But at the inquest it came out that he had been very much in love with Alicia — yes, the same Alicia — that his work had been falling off because things hadn't been going too well between them, and that on the day he committed suicide she had finally broken off with him. The whole thing caused a bit of a furore at the time because Paul had been so universally popular. Alicia and her parents left the area shortly afterwards.'

'Just a minute,' said Lineham, with a note of excitement, 'did you say Paul *Leyton*? Wasn't that a Richard Leyton who was seen talking to Mrs Parnell in the foyer last night?'

'Paul's younger brother.'

'Interesting.'

'Very.'

'You don't think . . .'

'At the moment I'm not thinking anything. We've only been on the case five minutes and it would be a waste of time.'

They were both silent for a while. They had switched to the M2 at Dartford and were now coming into the outskirts of London. Lineham gestured at a For Sale sign.

'Louise and I had hoped to go and look at some more houses today.'

The Linehams were still living in the tiny terraced house they had bought when they were first married. Their son, Richard, was now eighteen months old and they were beginning to think of a second child. This was the time, they felt, to try to find somewhere with a little more space — a third bedroom, and a larger garden, perhaps. They had begun by putting their own house on the market, and had been delighted if somewhat disconcerted when it had found a buyer within a week. They had plunged at once into an intensive search for the kind of property they wanted, so far without success. Now, completion was only a matter of weeks away and the matter was becoming urgent.

'Too bad. Anything promising?'

'There was one. A Victorian semi-detached in Frittenden Road. I think Louise is going to go over it tomorrow.'

Frittenden Road would have the merit of being further away from Mrs Lineham senior, Thanet noted. The Linehams' present house was only five minutes' walk from hers. For years the sergeant's life had been complicated and bedevilled by the unreasonable demands of his possessive mother. Widowed young, she had had to bring up her son alone, and for Lineham, emerging into adulthood, life seemed to have been one major battle after another — first to enter upon his chosen career in the police force, then to marry the girl of his choice, Louise. For the first couple of years of his married life he seemed to have been perpetually caught in the cross-fire between wife and mother, constantly trying to placate both and succeeding in pleasing neither. Then, with Richard's birth, things had changed. Mrs Lineham senior, with a new focus for her attention, had begun to channel her devotion towards her grandson. This had created a whole new set of problems for Louise, but had at least had the merit of taking the pressure off Lineham. Thanet couldn't help admiring his sergeant's determination to make his own choices and fulfil his obligations as he saw them, despite the pressure of two dominating women. Many men, he felt, would have gone under long ago and it was good to see Lineham in calm waters at last, if only temporarily. Though Thanet couldn't help feeling that if the young couple did move to the other side of town, it wouldn't be long before Mrs Lineham senior followed them. In any case she certainly wasn't going to allow it to happen without giving them a bad time first.

'I'm not sure of the way from here, sir. Could you keep an eye on the map and the road signs, now?'

'I think it'll be fairly straightforward so long as we don't hit too many one-way streets.'

Alicia Parnell's employment agency was called Jobline and appeared to be thriving. The single-storey premises were freshly painted in black and cream and the shop front was full of advertisements for jobs, some on display boards, others on slowly-revolving columns. The plate glass was clean and when Thanet peered in he could see that the office was close-carpeted and attractively furnished with sleek desks, leather chairs and flourishing pot plants. In the back wall was an inner door.

'There's no upstairs.' said Lineham. 'If she does live here she wouldn't want to go through the office every time she goes in and out. This'll be her front door, don't you think?'

Alongside the entrance to the shop was a solid, panelled wooden door without a number, unobtrusively painted black to match. Cunningly concealed in a fold of the moulding was a spyhole. Alicia, then, had been security-conscious. Had she lived here alone? If so, at night she would have been pretty isolated. To the left of Jobline was a small boutique called Annie's, to the right a shoe-repair shop.

'Must be,' he agreed. 'We'd better ring, first, in case her husband's at home.'

There was no answer, but they rang twice more and waited several minutes before Thanet took Alicia's keys from his pocket. The second fitted perfectly, turning twice in the lock before the catch was released.

They found themselves in a long, wide corridor which obviously ran the depth of the shop. It was carpeted in a soft, leaf green. When Lineham found the light switch they saw that the wallpaper was cream, with a tiny, geometric scribbled design in green, and that there were green-framed abstract prints evenly spaced along the left-hand wall. The door at the far end led to a surprisingly spacious ground-floor flat.

'I should think this runs along behind the agency and both

25

the shops on either side,' said Lineham. 'Pretty plush, isn't it?'

The sitting room was large, with ceiling-height patio doors leading into a tiny walled garden with climbing plants on the walls and white, wrought-iron chairs and table. Apart from a thick creamy rug in front of the long, low settee upholstered in soft, blond leather, the floor of polished, golden wood blocks was bare. There was one matching armchair, a low coffee table and, near the hatch leading into the kitchen, a dining table of smoky glass and four cream tulip-shaped dining chairs. The long, abstract painting in creams, browns and misty blue which hung above the settee was the only decorative object in the room apart from a six-foot tree with feathery leaves which stood in a huge cream ceramic pot near the patio doors. The effect was light, airy, yet austere, the taste of a woman given more to understatement than to exaggeration.

The main bedroom displayed the same restrained elegance, this time in blue and white. On the wall above the bed hung a crucifix, further evidence of Alicia's devotion to her faith. Interestingly enough, although one half of the long, fitted wardrobe contained men's clothing, there was no other sign of Parnell's presence in the flat. The double bed had only two pillows, one on top of the other in the centre of the bed, and one of the two bedside tables was bare. In the bathroom there was no shaving cream or aftershave lotion, no male deodorant, nothing to show that anyone but Alicia had lived here.

'Perhaps he's dead,' suggested Lineham. 'He'd hardly have left all his clothes here if they were divorced or separated.'

Alongside the mirror on the built-in dressing table was a larger, studio portrait of the man in the photograph they had seen in Sturrenden. Thanet picked it up. Parnell — if it was Parnell — had been in his early thirties when this was taken. It was a thin, sensitive face with deeply-etched lines around the mouth. Lines of pain? Thanet wondered. Something had been nagging at him ever since they had entered the flat and now he suddenly realised what it was.

'Have you noticed the doors, Mike?'

'What about them?' Lineham walked across and studied the bedroom door. 'Ah, I see what you mean. Unusually wide, isn't it?'

Thanet joined him. 'At least four feet, wouldn't you say? And custom-made, without a doubt.'

'You think Parnell was in a wheel-chair?'

'Seems likely, don't you think? There's no sign of children. And all the doorways are the same. If Parnell was crippled, it would explain why they built this place on behind the agency. No stairs, convenient for the office . . . Well, come on, we'd better get down to details. We'll start with the desk in the bedroom. That looks the most promising.'

Alicia's bank statements revealed that if she hadn't been exactly a wealthy woman, she at least had had no financial worries. But apart from a bundle of letters from her father and an address book, there was little else of interest.

'No mention of her mother,' said Lineham, skimming quickly through the former. 'Looks as though she might be dead, too.' He made a quick note of Mr Doyle's address. 'I suppose we'll have to contact him, to tell him the bad news.'

'Where does he live?'

'Manchester.'

'We'll see to it as soon as we get back. We'll take the address book with us.'

'Odd that there are no legal documents, isn't it, sir?'

'She may have kept them in the office safe, as it's so close.'

'Are we going to take a look around the agency before we go back?'

'I don't think we can do that until we've talked to Miss Ross. Come to think about it, it might be an idea to try and see her while we're up here. I expect her address is in here.'

It was. Jessica Ross lived not far away, in a block of modern flats on a side street off the Fulham Road. Unfortunately, according to a neighbour, she was away for the weekend.

'Where, do you know?'

The woman squinted up at him. She was elderly, with wispy white hair and skin like tissue paper which has been scrumpled up and then smoothed out again.

'Sorry, no idea.'

'When did she go?'

She shrugged. 'I saw her go off to work on Saturday morning and I haven't seen her since. Usually, when she's at home, I can hear noises through the walls.' Her mouth twisted with disgust. 'These modern places are all the same. Blown together, that's what they are. And flimsy. . . . You can't clean your teeth without other people hearing.'

'She was carrying a suitcase?'

'No. Just one of those squashy bags.'

'But she did tell you, that she was going away?'

The old woman was becoming exasperated by Thanet's persistence. 'Not in so many words, no. But I've got my eyes and my ears and there's nothing wrong with either, and I told you, I haven't heard a sound since early Saturday morning. So it stands to reason she's away, doesn't it?'

Thanet gave up. There was nothing for them here, at present.

'Looks as though we'll have to come up to town again tomorrow,' he said, as they walked back to the car.

'What a bore.'

'I agree, but there's nothing we can do about it.'

'Been a wasted journey, really,' grumbled Lineham.

'Not quite, I think. Not quite.'

All the same, he was anxious now to get back to Sturrenden.

THREE

Thanet and Lineham went straight to the Black Swan. In their absence, much had been accomplished. Bentley and Carson had accelerated the initial questioning of the fifty-eight hotel guests by dividing them into two groups and conducting interviews simultaneously. Only five now remained to be seen, all of whom had left the hotel early to go out for the day. Nothing of interest had emerged, however. One couple, who had signed in immediately after Alicia, had fixed her time of arrival more precisely — four-twenty — and another woman remembered travelling down in the lift with her at around seven o'clock. Apart from that, nothing.

'You've taken all their names and addresses?'

'Yes, sir.' Bentley was big, burly, painstaking. 'And verified them by checking driving licences and so on.'

'Good.'

'Some of them are getting a bit restive, sir.'

'I can imagine.' Thanet sighed. 'Well, we don't want a riot on our hands. . . . So long as we can get in touch with them if necessary, I think they can be told that they're free to carry on with their plans.'

'Right, sir. I'll see to that straight away.'

'Just a moment. What about the staff?'

'Bates and Warren interviewed them, sir.'

'Have they finished?'

They had, but once again nothing of significance had surfaced.

'Is DC Sparks back yet?'

Sparks had been sent to do the outside interviews. A new recruit to Thanet's team, he was an A-level entrant, thin and dark, with a quick grasp of new disciplines and a degree of ambition which did not endear him to his more pedestrian fellows. Thanet didn't think that he would be with them long, he would be off, up and away.

'Yes. Came in about ten minutes ago, sir.'

'Find him for me, will you?'

Sparks looked pleased with himself.

'Nothing new from the receptionist who was on duty last night, sir, nor from the chambermaid. She went in to turn Mrs Parnell's bed down at about eight-thirty pm and everything was in order then.'

'So? Come on, out with it, man.'

'Well, sir, it did occur to me that Mrs Parnell might possibly have ordered a pot of tea or a drink, and no one had thought it important enough to mention, so I checked and she had. I managed to track down the waitress who took afternoon tea up to her at about five o'clock, and she told me that when Mrs Parnell let her in there was a red folder lying on the bed. She noticed it because it was a splash of colour against all those pastels. . . . Well, I hope you don't mind, sir, but I had a quick check around Mrs Parnell's room, and there's no sign of any folder, red or otherwise, so unless you took it away earlier . . .'

'I didn't,' said Thanet thoughtfully. 'Well done, Sparks. You might have another word with both the chambermaids, ask if either of them saw it.'

'I have, sir, and they didn't.'

He might have guessed. Sparks was always one jump ahead.

'Interesting . . . And what about Mr and Mrs Leyton?' Thanet had hesitated before sending Sparks to see the Leytons. As an old friend of Alicia Parnell's, Richard Leyton might well turn out to be a suspect. But Thanet knew that opportunities for conducting potentially important interviews were thin on the ground for keen young detective-constables and was well aware, too, that it is always a temptation to keep the really significant interviews for oneself. He had decided to risk it and give Sparks a chance to show what he could do. 'Did you manage to see them?'

'Yes. They were pretty shaken when I told them what had happened. Apparently they both knew Mrs Parnell years ago, when they were at school. She used to live here, and they were all in the same crowd.'

'Just a minute,' said Thanet. 'Has Mrs Leyton got red hair?'

'Yes, sir.' Sparks grinned. 'And plenty of it.'

Prompted, Thanet's unconscious came up with the name he had been trying to remember. 'Vivienne,' he said. 'Her name is Vivienne.'

'That's right, sir.' Sparks paused, to see if Thanet had anything to add.

Thanet shook his head. 'Go on.'

'Well as you know, they ran into Mrs Parnell in the foyer, but they didn't talk for long because Mr Leyton had things to do in connection with the Ladies' Night and Mrs Parnell was on her way to a concert.'

'The Nicholas Rain concert?'

'Yes, sir. Anyway, they had one of those "Fancy meeting you here after all these years" conversations — they both said they were amazed how little she'd changed, that they'd have known her anywhere. And she said how surprising it was that she'd only been in Sturrenden five minutes, so to speak, and she'd already bumped into three of her old friends.'

'Three?'

'Apparently, on the way to the hotel from the station, she'd met another man from their old crowd, a Mr Oliver Bassett. She said he was going to the concert that evening too.'

'Was he, indeed. With her?'

'That wasn't the impression I got, sir.'

'Anything else?'

'Not really.'

'But?'

Sparks hesitated, for the first time. 'It was just an impression, sir, but I had the feeling they hadn't really been pleased to see Mrs Parnell. I mean, they were full of how surprised they were to run into her and so on, but I had the impression that the surprise had been one they could well have done without. On Mrs Leyton's part, anyway.'

'Really. And they didn't see her later on, when she came back to the hotel after the concert?'

'They said not, sir.'

'But you didn't believe them?'

Again, Sparks hesitated. 'I'm not sure, sir. I think Mrs Leyton was holding back on something . . .'

'On what?'

'I couldn't make up my mind, sir. Sorry.'

'You've done well, Sparks.'

Lineham had been following all this with interest and when Sparks had gone Thanet said, 'Well, Mike, what do you think?'

'Sounds as though we ought to see the Leytons ourselves.'

'I agree. But we'll leave them to stew for a while, I think. Meanwhile . . .'

'A visit to Mr Oliver Bassett?'

'Yes. Get his address from the telephone directory, then ring, find out if he's in.'

He was, and could see them whenever they wished. Lineham arranged that they would go along right away.

'One advantage of it being a Sunday,' he said, putting the phone down. 'Most people are at home. Though I could think of better ways of spending it, myself.'

'I know. I'd hoped to take the children to the sea. It would have been a perfect day for it.'

It was now four-thirty and the sun was still hot, the sky cloudless. Bassett lived in one of the sidestreets off the far end of the High Street. It wasn't far, and they decided to walk.

Sturrenden is a busy market town in the heart of the Garden of England, as Kent is often called. It is best avoided on Tuesdays and Fridays. On the former, market traders from far and wide converge on the large open space which on Fridays become the cattle market, and on both days parking spaces in the town are virtually impossible to find. The Town Council has tried to solve the problem by introducing a one-way system and providing free parking on the edge of the town, but with little success. Today, however, it was empty of any but sightseers enjoying its picturesque High Street, admiring the higgledy-piggledy conglomeration of ancient façades and lingering in front of the antique shops which dotted its length.

Mill Street was quiet, elegant, its terraced Georgian houses raised slightly above ground level. Each front door, with semicircular fanlight above, had its own short flight of steps edged by curving wrought-iron railings. The door of number fifteen was painted a glossy purple.

'Looks prosperous,' commented Lineham as they awaited an answer to their knock.

'I should think he's fairly well-off. He's the Bassett of Wylie, Bassett and Protheroe.'

'The solicitors in the High Street?'

'That's right. What's more, he's a bachelor, so he doesn't have a wife and family to support. I knew him at school,' Thanet added hurriedly as the door began to open.

'Ah, Thanet. Do come in. And this is . . .?'

'Detective-Sergeant Lineham.'

Bassett was tall and well-built, with a beaky nose, high forehead and a small, pursed mouth which gave him a curiously prim, old-maidish look. Although he was presumably spending a quiet Sunday afternoon at home, he was formally dressed in what was obviously a tailor-made suit in fine, brown herringbone tweed, tattersall-check shirt and slub silk tie. His highly-polished brogues were the colour of ripe chestnuts.

'This way.'

He led them through a spacious hall with curving staircase into a drawing room overlooking the garden at the back of the house. The atmosphere was one of restrained opulence, a combination of deep, muted colours, genuine antique furniture, carefully-arranged bric-a-brac and richly-textured soft furnishings. The effect was as impressive and as impersonal as a photograph in a glossy magazine.

'I was having tea when you telephoned, so I made a fresh pot. Will you join me?'

It would have been churlish to refuse. Thanet sat down on a Victorian tub chair upholstered in jade-green velvet and accepted the proffered porcelain cup and saucer with a murmur of thanks.

'Well then,' said Bassett, when he had served them both. 'How can I help you?'

'I believe you ran into an old friend in the High Street yesterday afternoon?' Thanet drank off his tea, which had been only luke-warm, and carefully put his cup and saucer

33

down on a tiny mahogany table beside his chair.

'An old. . .' Briefly, Bassett had looked puzzled, then his face cleared. 'Oh, you mean Alicia Doyle — or Alicia Parnell, as she now is.' He gave a little half-laugh. 'But of what possible interest could such an encounter be to you, Inspector?'

Inspector now, not *Thanet*, Thanet noted.

'You obviously haven't heard the news.'

Bassett frowned. 'What news?'

Thanet saw no reason to cushion the blow. 'That she was found murdered this morning.'

Bassett's eyes opened wide with shock. 'Murdered? *Alicia*? Where?'

'In her room at the Black Swan.'

'My God!' Bassett heaved himself jerkily out of his chair and went to stand for a few moments with his back to them, looking out into the garden. Then he swung around. 'I can hardly believe it. But as I certainly can't think that you are playing some kind of charade, I suppose I must. Well . . . Alicia . . .' He shook his head, returned slowly to his seat. 'So how can I help you?'

'I'll be frank with you. At the moment, we have very little to go on. Mrs Parnell lived in London, where she ran a small business, and so far we haven't found anyone who knows anything about her. No one knows if she had arranged to meet anyone down here during the weekend.'

'Except that she was obviously seen talking to me,' said Bassett with a hint of displeasure.

'Not exactly. She herself told someone that she had run into you on her way to the hotel yesterday afternoon.'

'Who could possibly have been interested?'

'Some mutual friends of yours, Mr and Mrs Richard Leyton. They ran into her in the foyer of the Black Swan last night. They were arriving for a function and she was on her way to the Nicholas Rain concert.'

'Ah, I see . . . I presume she also told them that I was going to the concert, too?'

'Yes, she did.'

'And, naturally, you want to know if I saw her during the evening?'

'As you say, naturally.'

34

'Well, the answer is yes, I did. . . . More tea, Inspector? Sergeant? No? Well now, let me see . . . I first saw her in the bar, during the interval. We chatted for a few minutes about the concert — you may or may not be aware that we both knew Nicholas Rain quite well, in our younger days — and I invited her to join me for a late supper, afterwards. I thought it would be interesting to hear what she'd been doing all these years . . . . But she said she was sorry, she couldn't, as she'd already arranged to see someone else.'

'Did she say who?'

'No. Later on, though, when I was in the foyer, I saw her talking to Rain. I didn't think anything of it at the time . . .'

'Did you assume it was Rain she'd arranged to meet?'

Bassett shook his head. 'No. After all, his fiancée, Melanie Knight, was there, she'd been playing in the concert with him. He and Alicia only talked for a few minutes, then he left her to join Miss Knight.'

'And Mrs Parnell?'

'I lost sight of her. There were a lot of people milling about, of course, and I didn't see her again, after they parted.'

'Were you close to them during their conversation?'

'No, some distance away. I just kept getting glimpses of them, as people in the crowd shifted.'

'What about Mr Rain? Did you see him again?'

'I saw him moving towards the door, with Miss Knight. People kept stopping them, to congratulate them, I imagine — they gave a really superb performance, by the way — so I assume they left together.'

'What time would this have been?'

'Let me see . . . the concert ended at a quarter to ten and I suppose it would have been about five past, when I saw Alicia talking to Rain. . . . It must have been about twenty past, when he and Miss Knight left.'

'So you have no idea what time Mrs Parnell left?'

'Sorry, no.'

'And you?'

'A few minutes after Rain.'

'And what did you do afterwards?'

'Came home, of course. No, wait a moment . . . I went for a

35

stroll by the river, first. It was a lovely night, and the concert hall had been rather stuffy. I thought I'd have a breath of fresh air before turning in.'

'You hadn't taken your car?'

'It wasn't worth it. The hall's only ten minutes' walk from here, and as you've probably noticed, these houses have no garages. I rent one in Denholm Street, and by the time I'd got the car out I would have been half-way there. . . . Look, Inspector, I can quite appreciate that you need to build up a picture of Alicia's movements last night, but do you have to have quite so much information about mine?'

'Oh come, Mr Bassett. You're a man of the law, you know what a passion for detail we have . . .'

'And I'm your best bet so far,' said Bassett good-humouredly. 'Yes, I can see that. And as I'm pure as the driven snow I will demonstrate my innocence by providing you with cooperation par excellence. . . . What else would you like? Fingerprints? Shoe size? The clothes I was wearing last night?'

Thanet wasn't going to be distracted or deflected. He smiled. 'I don't think we need to go quite as far as that at present. We'd settle for your time of arrival home.'

'About ten to eleven, give or take a few minutes. I'm afraid there's no one to corroborate that, you'll just have to take my word for it.'

'Thank you,' said Thanet, rising. 'You've been most helpful.'

'Not at all. Though I can hardly call it a pleasure, in the circumstances. . . . I'll show you out.'

At the front door Thanet hesitated. 'Did Mrs Parnell tell you why she'd come to Sturrenden?'

'Not in so many words. I rather assumed, to go to the concert.'

Lineham waited until they were in the street and the door had closed behind them before commenting, 'Smooth, isn't he?'

'Oh, very. Do you think he was telling the whole truth and nothing but, Mike?'

'I think I'll reserve judgement on that one, for the moment . . . Do you think that was why she came to Sturrenden?'

'For the concert? Could be. Nicholas Rain was her boyfriend once. Perhaps she was curious about this girl he's just got engaged to?'

'Yes, I read about that in the local paper, not long ago. She's much younger than him, isn't she?'

'In her early twenties, I believe. I imagine he's been too busy buzzing all around the world on concert tours to have thought of settling down before. I understand they met about a year ago, when she stood in for someone who was due to play the Bach double violin concerto with him — the same piece that they performed last night, incidentally. . . . I saw them together in Sturrenden once, a couple of months ago,' Thanet added reflectively.

'And?' enquired Lineham, intrigued by his tone.

'They were leaning on the parapet of the bridge, looking down at the river.' Thanet was remembering the powerful waves of sensuality which had emanated from those entwined figures. They had reminded him of Joan and himself, on their honeymoon . . .'

'So?' Lineham sounded puzzled.

'They were very engrossed in each other, that's all.'

'Understandable in the circumstances, I should think . . . But to get back to Mrs Parnell, sir . . . it's a bit far-fetched, isn't it, to think she would have taken the trouble to come down here, spend the night in a hotel, just to take a look at the girlfriend of someone she hadn't seen in donkey's years?'

'What are you suggesting, Mike?'

'Well, don't you think it's a lot more likely that she and Mr Rain have kept in touch? Perhaps, if her husband is dead, she might even have been cherishing the hope that Rain might marry her. She was a very attractive woman . . .'

'And she came down hoping to put a spoke in the wheels, you mean? Possible, I suppose . . . Anyway, our next move's obvious.'

'Mr Rain?'

'Mr Rain,' repeated Thanet, nodding. 'He lives out at Barton.' He quickened his pace. 'Come on, we'll have to fetch the car.'

FOUR

The village of Barton is about three miles from Sturrenden and Thanet and Lineham wound their way along country lanes whose hedges were starred with dog-roses and festooned with the wild clematis. Through five-barred gates they caught glimpses of spreading acres of golden corn, ripe for harvesting, and once the monstrous bulk of a combine harvester loomed above a hedge on their left.

Thanet was not a countryman, but he loved the constant, unvarying rhythm of the seasons and the changing beauty of the Kent landscape with its orchards and arable land, sheep and cattle. This evening the sunlight lay upon the land like a benediction and it was with reluctance that he responded to Lineham.

'What did you say?'

'I said, I suppose you're now going to tell me you knew Rain at school, too.'

'Certainly. He was one of the same crowd. Though I don't suppose for a moment that he'll remember me.'

'How many more of them were there?'

Thanet frowned, thinking. 'Let me see. There was Alicia, of course, Paul Leyton — the one who committed suicide — Richard, his brother, Oliver Bassett, Nicholas Rain and Vivienne, the girl with red hair who's now Richard Leyton's wife. That's all, I think.'

'Six of them, then. Four boys and two girls. Bit uneven, wasn't it?'

'I suppose so, yes. But it didn't seem to matter. You'd never guess it from their behaviour now, but they were always together, during Alicia's last year at school. Wherever you went, there they were, the lot of them. You couldn't miss them because they went everywhere crammed into Oliver Bassett's car.' Thanet gave a reminiscent laugh. 'That car was the envy of the school. It wasn't like nowadays. In those days you were lucky to own a scooter, let alone a car, and a sports car at that. Bassett was an only child, his mother was a widow and it was said that she'd have gone up to the moon in a rocket if he'd wanted a piece for his supper.'

'It's all right for some,' said Lineham, with a hint of bitterness. His own mother had had a struggle to manage, after his father died. 'She couldn't have been short of a penny.'

'His father was the original Bassett in Wylie, Bassett and Protheroe. Then, later, Oliver went into the firm himself.'

'What about Mr Rain?'

'Ah, well he was something very different.'

Having known Nicholas Rain at school, Thanet had followed his career with an almost proprietorial interest. Rain's father had taught history at Sturrenden Grammar School for Boys, and being a devout Catholic he and his wife had produced a large family of four boys and a girl. Although it had quickly become obvious that Nicholas was musically gifted, his father had steadfastly refused to allow him to neglect his general education in order to concentrate on music; in his opinion it was both limiting and unwise to specialise too young. Nicholas had therefore taken his O and A levels like any other bright youngster and had then, at the age of eighteen, been allowed to devote himself exclusively to music. He had gone first to the Royal Academy in London and from there had won prize after prize, scholarship after scholarship until, at the age of twenty-three, he had at last considered himself ready to launch upon his career. After his first spectacularly successful concert in the Festival Hall his future was assured and it was confidently predicted that he would go down in musical history as one of the truly great violinists.

'When his father died seven or eight years ago,' Thanet finished, 'he bought his mother this house in Barton, and he uses it as a base whenever he's in England — which isn't very often.'

'She lives there alone, the rest of the time?'

'No, with his young sister, Penny. She's the baby of the family. She'd be, oh, about twenty now, I should think. His brothers are all married and living away.'

'Presumably he'll be looking for a house for himself, now.'

'Or a flat. His fiancée's a soloist too, remember, so I imagine she'd want something pretty easy to manage.'

'If he's that successful, he could afford permanent staff to run his home while he's away.'

'True.'

They had just come into Barton and the church bells were ringing for Evensong. They stopped to ask for directions and a few minutes later turned into the gravelled driveway of Three Chimneys. The house was beautiful, a black and white timbered yeoman's house set in a traditional cottage-style garden with mixed plantings of shrubs and perennials. A narrow brick path flanked by low bushes of purple lavender and the feathery greenish-gold flowers of Alchemilla Mollis, the Lady's Mantle, led up to the massive front door of bleached wood. Despite the warmth of the day all the windows were closed and there was no sign of occupation.

'Looks as though they're out,' said Lineham.

There was no answer to their knock.

'Let's take a look around the back, in case they're in the garden.'

But the place was deserted and they returned to the car frustrated.

'Back to the Swan, I think,' said Thanet. 'We'll try again later, but we'll ring first. I can't imagine why we didn't this time.'

'Probably because of what I said about finding most people in on Sundays.'

But luck was on their side after all. As Lineham turned cautiously out of the front gate into the narrow lane a young girl wheeling a bicycle emerged from a gateway a hundred yards further on.

'A neighbour?' said Thanet. 'We'll have a word with her. It's just possible she knows what time they'll be back.'

The girl was in her early teens, her long, fair hair tied back in a ponytail. She frowned at Thanet's question.

'I expect Mr Rain's at the hospital.'

'The hospital? Has there been an accident?'

'The day before yesterday.' The girl bit her lip and tears

filled her eyes. 'Penny was driving Mrs Rain back from Sturrenden and they collided with a lorry that was coming round a bend in the middle of the road. Mrs Rain's still unconscious and Penny's in a bad way, too.'

'I'm sorry to hear that,' said Thanet. 'You're obviously very fond of them.'

'They're lovely people.' The girl dashed her tears angrily away. 'Why should it happen to them?' she cried passionately. 'They never did anybody any harm . . .' And mounting her bicycle she pedalled furiously away down the road.

Lineham frowned after her. 'Let's hope she calms down. She doesn't look too safe, to me.'

They decided to go straight to the hospital. If Rain had been able to give a superb performance at the concert last night despite his mother's apparently critical condition, he was fit to be interviewed, Thanet thought. Little by little they were managing to build up a sketchy picture of Alicia's activities the previous evening, and although Bassett had said that Rain had left with his fiancée, not with Alicia, Thanet was anxious to find out what Rain and Alicia had talked about. If, as Bassett claimed, Alicia had been going to meet someone afterwards, she might even have mentioned this person's name to Rain.

Mrs Rain was still unconscious, and in intensive care, they were told. Her daughter had compound leg and arm fractures, broken ribs and mild concussion, but was in no danger and was making satisfactory progress. The Sister in charge of the intensive care unit told them that Mr Rain had been in to sit with his mother earlier, and had now gone to visit his sister. Thanet and Lineham duly tramped their way along seemingly endless antiseptic corridors to the women's orthopaedic ward, where a number of people carrying bunches of flowers, magazines or bulging paper bags of fruit were sitting or standing around in the corridor waiting to take their turn at the bedside of friends or relations. The two-visitors-to-a-bed rule was obviously strictly observed.

Up until the birth of their son, Lineham's wife Louise had been a Sister in Sturrenden General. The Sister in charge of this ward knew Lineham and readily agreed to take a message in to Rain, and to let them interview him in the privacy of her office.

'So long as it doesn't take too long, mind,' she said. 'Visiting time is usually fairly quiet, but I can't guarantee no interruptions.'

'Thank you, Sister,' said Thanet formally. 'It's very kind of you.'

Rain emerged from the double doors of the ward looking puzzled and slightly irritated.

Thanet stepped forward to meet him. 'Mr Rain?'

'Yes. What is it? What's happened?'

Everything about him was clearly defined — crisp, curly black hair, short, neat beard and piercing dark brown eyes. There were sharp creases in his navy-blue linen trousers and his pale blue open-necked shirt looked as though it had just emerged from its polythene wrapping.

Thanet introduced himself and ushered Rain into the office. 'I apologise for disturbing you at a time like this, but I'm afraid the matter is urgent. Won't you sit down?'

Rain shook his head impatiently. He was staring at Thanet with narrowed eyes. 'Thanet . . . haven't I . . .? Just a moment . . . weren't you at Sturrenden Grammar?'

'Yes, I was. A couple of years below you.'

. 'And now an Inspector, no less, in the CID . . .' Rain was looking more genial, 'Well, well . . . so, Thanet, how can I help you?'

'It's to do with an old friend of yours, Alicia Parnell. You were talking to her after the concert last night.'

'Oh, Alicia Doyle, you mean. Parnell . . . I didn't know that was her married name.'

'She didn't mention it?'

'No. Just said she'd been married and was now a widow.'

'What else did you talk about?'

'Look, forgive me if I appear obtuse, but I really cannot see of what possible interest that conversation could be to you. Unless . . .'

'Unless?'

Rain shook his head. 'No, you tell me, Thanet. You said this is to do with Alicia. What about her?'

'I'm afraid I have some rather unpleasant news, Mr Rain. Mrs Parnell was found dead in her hotel bedroom this morning.'

'Dead?' Rain blinked, and there was a moment's silence. 'But I was talking to her only last night — well, you know that, of course — and she seemed perfectly all right then. Oh God, how awful. What was it? A heart attack?'

Thanet shook his head. 'I'm afraid she was murdered.'

'Murd . . .' Rain groped for the nearest chair and sat down, heavily. 'This is incredible. I don't believe it. How terrible . . . How could such a thing happen here, in Sturrenden? How did it happen?'

'She was killed in her room at the Black Swan.'

'In her room . . . Was it . . .?'

Rain had been allowed to take the initiative long enough, Thanet decided. 'I'm sorry, Mr Rain, I can't tell you any more at present. The point is, we've been trying to trace her movements since she arrived in Sturrenden yesterday afternoon, and we've eventually arrived at five past ten last night, when she was seen talking to you after the concert.'

'Yes, I see . . . Well, anything I can do to help, of course . . . Though I don't really see how I can. It was a very brief conversation.'

'So we understand. Nevertheless, we'd be grateful if you could give us the gist of it.'

Rain frowned, thinking. 'Well now, let me see . . . It was in the foyer, after the concert. My fiancée had gone to look for her parents — they're staying here for a few days — and I was waiting for them. Alicia came up to me and said, "Hullo Nicky, remember me?" '

'And did you?'

'Yes, of course. It was astonishing, how little she'd changed. Anyway, she said how much she'd enjoyed the concert and congratulated me on my recent engagement, and then she enquired about my mother and sister — you're obviously aware that they were both involved in a serious accident on Friday morning.'

'You weren't with them at the time?'

'No. I didn't get back to this country until Friday afternoon — I've been on a ten-day tour of Canada. You can imagine how I felt, being greeted with news like that . . .'

'How did Mrs Parnell know about the accident?'

'She'd seen it in the newspaper, yesterday morning. Said she'd lit a candle for them both. . . . She knew my mother well at one time, our families were very friendly when the Doyles were living in Sturrenden. Anyway, that's about it. I don't think much else was said.'

'What about your end of the conversation?'

'Well, I asked her if she was married — that was when she mentioned my engagement. She told me that her husband died last year. She did most of the talking, actually, and in the end I caught sight of my fiancée and her parents coming towards us. I didn't want to get involved in introductions, explanations and any more polite chit-chat, so I said I was sorry I had to rush off, but I was anxious to get back to the hospital — which was true. I really was very concerned to find out if my mother had recovered consciousness.'

'I understand she's still in a critical condition. I'm sorry.'

'Yes. Well if that's all . . .'

'Not quite, I'm afraid. Just one or two small points . . . did Mrs Parnell say why she had come to Sturrenden?'

'No. And I didn't ask. As I said, it really was a very brief conversation.'

'Did she telephone you around four-thirty yesterday afternoon?'

'No, certainly not. Why on earth should she?'

'Or mention what she was going to do after leaving the Concert Hall?'

'Go back to the hotel, presumably.'

'She told you she was staying at the Swan?'

'No, I didn't know that until you told me, a few minutes ago.'

'So she didn't mention that she was meeting someone, afterwards?'

'No.'

'And you . . . what did you do, after you left her?'

'Put my fiancée and her parents into a taxi and came straight here. Originally we'd intended having supper together, but as I told you, I was anxious to find out if my mother had come round. They quite understood.'

'When was the last time you saw Mrs Parnell — before last night, I mean?'

Rain gave a derisory little laugh. 'Over twenty years ago. Not since she and her parents left Sturrenden, just after we'd both taken our A levels.'

'Do you happen to know if she'd been back to Sturrenden at all, during that period?'

'I don't think she had.'

'She didn't actually say so, then?'

'Not in so many words, no. But I certainly had that impression.'

'You were quite close at one time, I believe.'

'We did go around together for a while, yes. But that finished some months before she went away. Look here, Inspector, I don't want to seem unreasonable, but I really don't see the relevance of all this. And I would like to get back to my sister before visiting time ends.'

'Yes, of course.' Thanet stood up. 'Thank you for your time.'

'Well,' said Lineham as they watched him go, 'that didn't get us very far, did it?'

'She wasn't invisible, Mike. Someone must have seen her, after she and Rain parted.'

'They might have *seen* her, but would they have *noticed* her? The hotel was crawling with people that night, with the Ladies' Night going on. I enquired. The dinner finished at ten-fifteen and then the guests all drifted off to the cloakrooms while the Fletcher Hall was cleared for dancing. If Mrs Parnell did go straight back to the hotel she would have got there just about then, when everyone would have been milling around.'

'You'd have expected the Leytons to notice her, if they'd seen her. Sparks didn't seem too sure on that point, did he?'

'Are we going to see them next?'

'No. If possible I want to be armed with a little more information about Alicia, first.'

The Sister knocked on the door and put her head in. 'All finished?'

They thanked her and left.

'The trouble is,' said Thanet as they made their way back along the corridors, 'I can't help feeling that we're working in

45

a vacuum at the moment. So far we know practically nothing about her — what she was like as a person, who her friends were — or her enemies, for that matter. . . . Before we see anyone else I want to talk to her partner, Miss Ross. We'll go up to London again in the morning. Meanwhile . . .'

'Don't tell me. Meanwhile, reports.'

'Reports,' said Thanet, grinning.

Thanet had a love/hate relationship with reports. He resented the demands they made on his time, but appreciated their value. Not only did they provide a detailed record of work in progress — a record which could prove increasingly useful as interviews proliferated and the mass of facts accumulated — but the act of writing them was an excellent discipline, forcing one to think back and assess and then to present one's findings succinctly. A sloppy report, he believed, reflected sloppy thinking, and by now his men had learned that if they didn't want to do the whole thing over again, they might as well spend time getting it right in the first place.

The trouble with setting standards, he reflected as he settled down at his desk, was that you had to make sure you upheld them yourself.

He said as much to Joan, when she commented sympathetically on his lateness. It was past eleven. She was in her dressing gown, having bathed and been on the point of going to bed when she heard his car.

'I've made you some sandwiches. They're in the fridge.'

He followed her into the kitchen and sat down at the scrubbed pine table, while she made him some tea. The sandwiches were good, crammed with succulent pink lamb from the Sunday joint he should have enjoyed at home. Slowly, he felt himself revive.

Joan was sitting across the table, sipping her tea slowly, to keep him company.

'Better?' she said, when he had finished.

'Much.' He yawned, stretched, winced as the aching muscles in the small of his back protested. Always, after a long day, the spectre of his old back injury raised its hoary head.

'What's the case?'

Thanet hesitated. He trusted Joan completely and had

46

always tried to share his working life with her, believing that this was the one way to prevent the barrier of resentment so often erected by policemen's wives against the impossible demands of their husbands' work. At one time, too, he had believed that the vicarious satisfaction she gained from such discussions was sufficient to compensate for the lack of variety and excitement in her own life as a housewife. He had learned otherwise when, a few years ago, she had announced that she wished to train as a probation officer. He still preferred not to think about the separation which they had been forced to endure during the last part of her training, when Joan had had to take a residential course.

'Luke?' Joan was puzzled by his reluctance. 'What's the matter? Don't you want to talk about it?'

'No, it's not that . . .'

'What, then?'

'It's just that . . . do you remember a girl at school called Alicia Doyle?'

'Alicia?' Joan grinned. 'Asking that question of any of the girls who were at Sturrenden Grammer the same time as her is rather like asking a Catholic priest if he's heard of the Pope. Why?'

'This new case . . . Alicia was the victim.'

'Oh, *no*.' The amusement died out of Joan's eyes and the muscles of her face slackened and re-shaped themselves into lines of shock.

Thanet was dismayed at the strength of her reaction. 'She wasn't a personal friend of yours, was she, darling?' He didn't think she could have been, or Joan would surely have mentioned her at some point.

'Oh, no. No, of course not. It's just that . . . to think that something like that should have happened to Alicia, of all people. . . . She was so full of life,' Joan said, in response to Thanet's questioning glance. 'So vivacious, so . . . To us third-formers all the upper sixth seemed to be impossibly beautiful, talented and glamorous, of course, but Alicia outshone them all. And she was so *nice*, too. Most of us had a crush on her at one time or another — I did myself. It was as if she were a candle, and other people the moths. She was always

47

surrounded by a crowd, the centre of attention. And of course we were all green with envy over her ability to attract the boys . . .' Joan gave a shame-faced little laugh. 'Sorry, darling, I don't suppose you want to hear all this.'

'Oh but I do. Do you realise, you're the first person I've talked to who's made her come alive for me.'

'Is that so surprising? I don't suppose you've seen many people, yet.'

'True.'

'Tell me about it, Luke.'

'You're sure you want to hear?'

'Yes, of course. More than ever, now I've got over the initial shock.'

She listened carefully to his account of the day's work.

'And nobody has any idea why she was in Sturrenden in the first place?'

'So they say. Unless she came down for the concert.'

'Possible, I suppose. If you once had a boyfriend who later became an international celebrity, sheer curiosity would make you want to go and hear him for yourself. But what about this person she was supposed to be meeting afterwards? Perhaps he — or she — was the real reason for coming to Sturrenden, and the concert was just to fill in time?'

'Odd time to be meeting someone anyway. Unless that person simply wasn't available until then.'

'You don't suppose it was Nicholas Rain she was meeting?'

Thanet shrugged. 'I've no idea. On the face of it, no. His fiancée and her parents were there, and if he hadn't had to go back to the hospital to see how his mother was, he'd presumably have gone ahead with the original arrangement, and had supper with them.'

'Don't you think it's strange that in the short time she was here, yesterday, she should have run into so many of her old crowd?'

'Oh, I don't know. Not really, if you think about it. It was a Saturday, after all, and people tend to be out and about. I don't suppose I could walk down the High Street on a Saturday without seeing someone I'd been at school with, could you?'

'I suppose not. And the meeting with Rain wasn't exactly by chance. She knew he'd be there, and probably sought him out. As I said, I expect she was curious, to see what he was like, now . . . It really is so sad, Luke, to think she should have died like that, so young, and alone in a hotel bedroom. And it doesn't sound as if she's had much of a life, does it, with her husband dying last year. And he was crippled, you think?'

'That's only a guess, at the moment. We'll know more when we've talked to her partner, tomorrow . . . Now, tell me about you. Did you have a good day?'

'Lazy. Sat in a deckchair in the garden, all afternoon . . . Luke, have you noticed how quiet Ben is, at the moment?'

'I had, yes. Why, do you think there's something wrong?'

Joan was frowning. 'I'm not sure. He says not, but I just have this uneasy feeling that he's hiding something.'

'What sort of thing?' Thanet was becoming concerned.

'I've no idea. As I say, it's just a feeling. He isn't his usual lively self, and he's off his food . . . And that's not Ben at all.'

'What did he do today?'

'Well, that's partly what made me wonder. Usually, over the weekend, he's off to see his friends, as you know, or they come here, but today — on a glorious day like this — he stayed up in his room most of the time, playing tapes. And when I looked in, he wasn't doing anything, just lying on his bed. I asked him why he wasn't out with the others and he snapped my head off. It's all so uncharacteristic . . .'

'Perhaps he's sickening for something.'

'He says he feels fine . . . Oh, I don't know, perhaps I'm fussing about nothing. But I can't seem to get anywhere with him and I was wondering if you might manage to have a word with him some time, see if you could find out what's the matter.'

'I'll do it tomorrow.' Without fail, Thanet promised himself.

FIVE

'There's a message from Manchester,' said Lineham. 'Mrs Parnell's father, Mr Doyle, is away on holiday, apparently, and can't be contacted.'

'When's he due back?'

'Some time on Saturday. Imagine coming home to news like that.'

'Have we managed to get in touch with either of the two couples who checked out of the Swan early on Sunday morning?'

'Not yet, no. Perhaps they're touring.'

'Keep trying.'

Thanet and Lineham were going quickly through the various odds and ends of information that had come in overnight before setting off for London to see Jessica Ross.

'Perhaps Miss Ross'll be able to tell us what was in the mysterious red folder,' said Thanet.

'Was Mrs Parnell carrying it when she met the Leytons in the foyer?'

'The receptionist didn't mention it. Just a minute.' Thanet shuffled through the stack of reports on his desk. 'Knowing Sparks I shouldn't be surprised if . . . Ah, yes, here we are, I thought so. He checked. . . . No, only her handbag, apparently. The receptionist says she's certain she would have remembered if Mrs Parnell had been carrying anything as conspicuous as a red folder. It would have looked very odd with what she was wearing, she says.'

'So if the murderer took it . . .'

'It could well be important.'

'You two look very grim.' Doc Mallard had come bustling into the room. 'Just popped in to tell you the PM's scheduled for tomorrow morning. How's it going?'

'We're off to London in a minute, to see Mrs Parnell's

partner. We hope to know more then. So far we've been kept busy trying to trace her movements on Saturday. She seems to have run into a number of her old friends in the short time she was here. She did go to the concert on Saturday night, by the way.'

'Alone?'

'Apparently. She had a chat with Nicholas Rain afterwards, in the entrance hall.'

'Really? You've talked to him?'

'Yes. At the hospital.'

'Of course. The accident. I heard about that yesterday afternoon. Terrible. Mrs Rain is still in a coma, I believe, and Penny was pretty badly hurt, too — though nothing that won't mend in time. She was driving the car, I understand, and if her mother doesn't recover, she'll never forgive herself. They're really devoted to each other, those two. I always think of them as the supreme example that adoption really can work.'

'So she's not really Rain's sister?' said Lineham.

'Not by blood, perhaps, but believe me, he cares about her just as much as if she were.'

Lineham was looking puzzled. 'But they already had several other children, didn't they?'

'Four. All boys. And that was the point.' Mallard perched on the edge of Thanet's desk. 'The Rains had always wanted a girl, you see. They weren't too worried when first Charles, then Nicholas appeared, but by the time John and Peter had arrived they were beginning to give up hope. They were practising Catholics, by the way, and half-expected more tiny feet to come pattering along, but they didn't. The four boys were all born within six or seven years and then — nothing. Until Peter, the youngest, was about thirteen, when lo and behold, Mrs Rain found she was pregnant again. And this time it was a girl.'

'But I thought you said . . .'

'Patience, sergeant.' Mallard flapped his hand at Lineham. 'As I said, it was a girl, and you can imagine how delighted they were, all of them. I think the boys had been a bit embarrassed at first when their mum started to bulge, but by the time the baby was born they were reconciled to her arrival and made a great fuss of her. And then, when she was three months old, she died. One of those fiendish cot deaths that strike out of the blue. Well, as you can imagine, they were shattered, all of them, but especially Mrs Rain. For a while she blamed herself for the child's death, as so many mothers — quite wrongly, of course — do, in those particular circumstances. She was pretty depressed for some time, especially as there had been complications after the birth and she'd been told she could never have any more children. Then, about a year later, I heard they'd decided to adopt. And, as I said, it was a resounding success. Penny's twenty now and they all adore her, and vice versa. So, as I say, if Mrs Rain doesn't recover, Penny's going to be desperately upset.'

'You sound very fond of them all,' said Thanet.

'They're a very nice family. And as I told you, Derek Rain was one of my closest friends. I don't see much of them now, but I still take an interest.' Mallard slid off the desk and strolled across to the window. 'That's when you really become aware of the passage of time, when your own friends start dying.'

It was unusual for Mallard to sound so serious or so sad, or to come so close to referring to the death of his wife. Neither Thanet nor Lineham, inhibited by the presence of the other, knew quite what to say. There were a few moments of uncomfortable silence and then Mallard gave a little snuffle of laughter and turned to peer over his spectacles at them. 'On which cheerful note I will leave you. No doubt we've all got better things to do at this hour on a Monday morning than sit around telling each other stories.'

'I've never seen him in that mood before,' said Lineham, when Mallard had gone.

'Don't be fooled by his usual manner, Mike. That's just a smokescreen. Underneath he's as soft as butter. We'll just arrange for Sparks to go to the hospital and check what time Rain arrived there on Saturday night after the concert, then we'll be on our way.'

As it was a weekday, traffic would be heavy and parking in London difficult, so they decided to go by train. They reached Jobline just before twelve. Two of the three desks in the main office were occupied, one by a young woman in her early twenties, who was on the telephone, and one by an older woman who, Thanet guessed, would be around the same age as Alicia. He approached her.

'Miss Ross?'

She looked up, warily. 'Yes?'

She was a large, plain woman with unnaturally blonde hair, pale blue eyes and a heavy jaw. She was heavily made-up and was wearing a tan linen dress which looked expensive. It was rare for Thanet to take an instinctive dislike to someone but he was aware of that little shock of emotional recoil which told him that this was what was happening now. On his guard against betraying his feelings, he introduced himself and Lineham. 'It's about Mrs Parnell.'

'Ah, yes.' Miss Ross closed her eyes and clamped large, yellowing front teeth over her lower lip, then took a deep breath and held it for a moment.

Genuine grief? Thanet wondered. Or a device to gain herself a few moments' breathing space? He glanced at the other woman, who had finished her call and was watching Miss Ross. She had been crying, he noticed, and he caught a cynical gleam in her eyes before she realised that he was looking at her. She flushed and began shuffling papers about on her desk.

Miss Ross stood up abruptly, steadying her chair as it almost overturned. 'We'd better go into my office. Lock the outer door when you go to lunch, will you, Faith?'

Her office, Thanet noted, not Alicia's. The room was clean, pleasant, functional. There was a small safe in the corner.

'I gather you've heard about Mrs Parnell's death.'

'I read about it in the paper this morning. It was a terrible shock.'

Her voice was accusing and Thanet was furious to find himself saying defensively, 'We tried to contact you yesterday, but you were out.'

'Oh? What time was that?'

'Around lunchtime.'

'I'd just gone out for a breath of air.'

'Really? Your neighbour had the impression you were away for the weekend.'

'That must have been because I wasn't moving around much. I wasn't feeling very well on Saturday — I get migraine and sometimes, if I catch it in time, I can stave it off to some extent. So when I got home at lunchtime I went straight to bed and stayed there.'

'The agency is open on Saturday mornings?'

'Yes.'

'And Mrs Parnell came to work as usual?'

'Yes, she did.' Jessica Ross shifted a little in her chair and frowned.

'You've just remembered something?'

'Well, I did notice that she seemed even more on edge than usual.'

'What do you mean?' Thanet glanced at Lineham, indicating that he should take over the questioning.

Miss Ross shrugged. 'She'd been looking terrible lately. She hasn't been sleeping well, she's lost weight . . .'

'Are you saying that she was ill?' said Lineham.

'I don't know. If she was, she never said so . . . But no, I don't think it was that. It all began soon after her husband died, six months ago.'

Alicia's marriage, it seemed, had been a happy one. She and her husband had been devoted to each other, despite the accident which had threatened to ruin their lives. Alicia and Kenneth Parnell had married in 1971, when she was twenty-four. He had been the personnel manager of a large company, she his secretary. On the way back from their honeymoon in Scotland they had been involved in a multiple pile-up on the M1 and Kenneth had been left paralysed from the waist down. His firm had kept his job open for him, but even when he had made as full a recovery as could be expected, the sheer physical difficulties involved in getting to work had made it an impracticable proposition. He and Alicia had therefore decided to use the insurance money they had received after the accident to start a small business. With his skills in personnel management and her secretarial training, an employment agency had seemed the obvious choice.

By 1977, when Jessica Ross had joined the firm, Jobline was thriving. Unfortunately, internal injuries sustained during the accident had left Parnell with health problems other than the paralysis, and increasingly he had had to withdraw from taking an active part in running the agency. Initially, Alicia had handled the administration, Kenneth the interviewing and job-matching, but as his health deteriorated they had switched roles and, more and more, Jessica Ross had been called in to take over Alicia's work. When he died it had seemed natural for her to run the business during Alicia's absence and eventually Alicia, depressed and distraught by her husband's long illness and death, had invited her to become a partner.

It took Lineham some time to elicit all this information and during the long, patient, question-and-answer session Jessica Ross revealed rather more about her relationship with her former employers than she realised. Thanet perceived that she had been fond of Kenneth Parnell and jealous not only of his good relationship with his wife, but of Alicia's warm personality, her ability to inspire loyalty and affection in her staff. Above all, he learnt that Jessica Ross was ambitious, that being offered a partnership in Jobline had probably been the most important thing that had ever happened to her.

'And then, of course, three months after Kenneth died, Alicia's mother died too, and that made things even worse.'

'How, exactly, Miss Ross?'

Lineham was doing well, Thanet thought. And he was clearly enjoying the challenge of coaxing all this information out of such an unpromising witness.

She shrugged. 'In the beginning, after Kenneth's death, Alicia was very, well, fragile, I suppose you'd call it. Not surprising, really. Kenneth had been ill for a long time, it must have been an awful strain. . . . And then, losing your husband and your mother in three months . . . it's a bit much for anyone to cope with, isn't it? But I did hope that as time went on she'd start to pull herself together. Instead, she became . . . withdrawn, positively . . .' Jessica Ross hesitated.

'Positively what, Miss Ross?'

The woman compressed her lips, cast an almost defiant glance at Thanet. 'I was going to say, irresponsible. I suppose you'll think I'm unfeeling, talking about her like this when she's . . . when she . . . But I'm just trying to tell you how it was.'

'And that is precisely what we're here to find out,' said Thanet. 'So please, do go on with what you were saying. How do you mean, irresponsible?'

She shook her head impatiently, made a helpless gesture with her hands — hands quite large and powerful enough to have squeezed the life out of Alicia's slender throat, Thanet noticed. 'Her mind just wasn't on the business, that's all. She'd be late for appointments with prospective employers — or worse, not turn up for them at all. She'd go off somewhere without telling me, forget to answer important letters, or file them away in the wrong places . . .'

'And you felt that this uncharacteristic behaviour wasn't simply due to distress over the death of first her husband, then her mother?'

'Well to begin with, yes, of course I did. But then I began to think . . .'

'Yes?'

'Well, that she was preoccupied with some other matter.'

'What, for example?'

'I don't know. I've thought and thought, of course, and tried to get her to confide in me, but it was no good. She simply said she didn't know what I was talking about. Though I did wonder . . .'

'What?'

'Well, I thought she might be trying to find somewhere else to live. It would have been understandable, wouldn't it? I mean, her flat was custom-built for her and Kenneth, she might have found it too depressing to go on living there. Though if it was that, I don't see why she wouldn't have wanted to let me know. Or it did cross my mind to wonder if she was trying to find someone else to take over her share in Jobline. She obviously just wasn't interested in the business any more.'

'But in that case she would have discussed it with you, surely?'

'You'd have thought so,' said Jessica Ross bitterly.

'Tell me a little more about her behaviour.'

'Well, it's difficult to describe, it was so variable. In the beginning she was very low, very depressed. She was just beginning to pull out of it a little when her mother died, and of course that set her back again. She went up to stay with her father for a week and when she came back she was different.'

'How, different?'

'She seemed brighter. Almost, well . . .'

'Almost what?'

Jessica Ross shrugged, lifted her hands in a gesture of frustration. 'I was going to say, almost excited about something.'

'But you have no idea what?'

'No idea at all. Anyway, it didn't last. A few days, a week or so, perhaps, and she went back to being depressed. Then she became very tense, jumpy, absent-minded. That was when she started going off, without so much as a by-your-leave. No matter how busy we were, she'd just take off, without warning. One minute she'd be here, the next she was gone.'

'How long did she usually stay away?'

'It varied. Three or four hours. Once it was a whole day.'

'And how did she seem when she got back?'

'Quiet. Withdrawn.'

'And this went on for how long?'

'A couple of months, I suppose. Then one morning, a couple of weeks ago, I came in to work and she looked really terrible. Pale, shaking, as if she'd seen a ghost. I asked her if she'd like me to call her doctor, but she said no, it wasn't necessary, she'd be fine in a little while. Anyway, I persuaded her to go and lie down for an hour and later on she came back into the office and carried on as usual. But ever since, she's been even more on edge. As if . . .'

'Yes?'

'Well, it was almost as if she was waiting for something to happen.' Jessica Ross shook her head. 'And now . . . You don't think . . . I mean, it couldn't have had anything to do with . . .'

'With her death? Who knows . . .? Do you think we could go back to Saturday morning? You say that she seemed even more tense than usual?'

'Yes. She looked awful, as though she hadn't slept all night — pale, bags under her eyes . . . As soon as I arrived she asked me if I'd mind if she took the morning off. Well, I suppose she felt she had to ask, we're always so busy on Saturdays. And I said . . .'

'Yes?'

'I . . . I said I did mind.' Jessica Ross tossed her head and added defensively, 'Well, one of the girls was away sick and I was just about fed up with Alicia not pulling her weight. I thought it was about time I came right out and told her so . . . Now, of course, I feel awful about it, after what's happened.' She put her hands up and began to massage her temples with her fingertips.

'Did she argue with you?'

'No, she just shrugged, said if that was how I felt, she'd stay. She was very quiet, all morning, and at lunchtime she went off without a word.'

'Did you know she was going away for the weekend?'

'Yes, she'd mentioned it earlier in the week. I'd suggested we go to the cinema, on Saturday night. I thought it might do her good to get out for an evening . . .'

'Did she tell you where she was going?'

'No. Just that she would be away.'

For the first time Thanet sensed that if Jessica Ross wasn't exactly lying, she was holding back on something. What could it be? He could tell, by the way her lips had folded in upon themselves, that it would be pointless to try and get it out of her. Up until now she had been remarkably forthcoming and he wondered if this had been intentional, designed to persuade him that she had nothing to conceal. He decided to let it go, for the moment. Patiently, he continued the questioning. Alicia, it seemed, had led a very quiet life. Her husband had taught himself to be as independent as possible but naturally his condition had made considerable demands upon her time. They had gone out very little, seeming content with each other's company, and Alicia had therefore made no close friends outside the office.

'I suppose I was her closest friend.' Jessica Ross gave what was obviously intended to be a modest smile. 'And of course, she relied on me, especially after her husband died.'

Thanet caught Lineham's eye. He could read the sergeant's mind. *With friends like that, who needs enemies?*

'And enemies? Do you know of anyone with a grudge against her?'

'Against Alicia? Good heavens, no. She just wasn't that sort of person.'

'No one amongst your clients, who might have thought he'd been unfairly treated?'

'Certainly not! We can't afford to offend people, it wouldn't do at all. A satisfied client will tell his friends about us, and that brings more business. And Alicia was very good with people.'

'Did she ever talk of her childhood?'

'I knew she'd been brought up in Kent, that's all. She may have mentioned things she'd done, or places she'd been to.'

'But never people?'

'No.'

'Just two more points, then, Miss Ross. You've been very patient. First, I wonder if you could tell me whether or not Mrs Parnell kept any personal papers in the office safe? There seem to be very few in her flat.'

'Yes, she did.' Jessica Ross rose, smoothing down her dress as she crossed the room. She opened the safe and took out an oblong, black metal box. 'It's locked, I'm afraid.' An ugly tide of colour flooded her face as she realised what she had said. She handed it to Thanet.

'Thank you.'

'And the other point?'

'Do you use folders in the office?'

'Yes. Why?'

'What colour are they?'

'Green, yellow, blue,' she said, promptly.

'Not red?'

'No.'

'Do you recall ever having seen a red folder in Mrs Parnell's possession?'

Her eyes narrowed. 'Now that you mention it, yes, I do.'

'Have you any idea what was in it?'

'I'm afraid not. I saw it on, let me see, only two occasions. Once when Alicia was looking for something in her briefcase, and had to take everything out, and once when I went into the flat with her, and it was lying on the dining table. I noticed it because it made such a splash of colour in that room — well, you've seen the place, you'll know what I mean.'

'Yes, I do. I see. Well, thank you, Miss Ross, you've been most helpful. Is there anything else you want to tell me?'

For a fraction of a second he could have sworn he saw a spark of fear in her eyes, then she said firmly, 'No, I don't think so. You seem to have covered just about everything, Inspector. But if there's anything else I can do . . .'

'I would like to look through Mrs Parnell's desk. It's in the outer office, I gather.'

'By all means. Yes, whoever does the administration has always worked in here, it's more convenient. Everything's to hand.' The defensive note was back.

'And also, I'd like a word with the young lady we saw in the outer office as we came in.'

'Faith, you mean. I'm sorry, that won't be possible.'

'Oh?' Thanet glanced at his watch. It was half past one. 'Is she still out at lunch?'

'No. I'm afraid she won't be back this afternoon. We have a new client, the manager of a factory out at St Albans, and Faith has gone to discuss his requirements with him. Alicia was going to do it, but now . . . Faith is very reliable, and I thought that in the circumstances it would be a good idea to give her more responsibility.'

'You mentioned another girl . . .'

'Yes, Carol.' Jessica Ross suddenly looked as though she were sucking a lemon. 'She's still off sick.'

He would be interested to meet Carol, Thanet thought. 'I see.' He stood up. 'Well in that case, if I could just take a look at that desk . . .'

But the desk yielded nothing of interest, so he and Lineham carried the metal box into Alicia's flat, where they could examine it at leisure. They had found the key on Alicia's key-ring. Its contents were disappointing, however: birth and marriage certificates, Parnell's death certificate, details of insurance policies and a modest list of shareholdings.

'No will,' said Lineham.'

'The next best thing, though.' Thanet picked up a single

sheet of paper at the bottom of the box. It was a letter from Alicia's solicitor, dated four months ago, informing her that her will was ready for signing and asking her to call. 'Made soon after her husband's death, by the look of it. We'll give this Mr Thrall a ring. He might manage to fit us in, while we're up here.'

But again they were out of luck. Thrall was tied up in court and wouldn't be able to see them until Wednesday morning.

'Pity,' said Thanet as he put the phone down. 'Never mind, we'll just be in time to catch the 2.36, if we hurry.'

At this hour of the afternoon the train was almost empty and they had a compartment to themselves. Thanet's back was beginning to ache again and he eased himself into a more comfortable position before lighting his pipe and flapping his hand to dispel the inevitable clouds of smoke.

Lineham unobtrusively edged away a little.

'Well, what did you think of Miss Ross, Mike?'

Lineham pulled a face. 'Can't imagine why Mrs Parnell offered her a partnership, that's for sure.'

'Gratitude, Mike. Gratitude and guilt.

'Guilt?'

'Alicia Parnell sounds the sort of person who'd be only too willing to do others a good turn, but would find it very difficult to be on the receiving end herself. I imagine that when she began to recover, after her husband's death, and realised that it was Jessica Ross who had really been keeping the agency going, she felt so grateful and so guilty that she offered her a partnership on impulse.'

'And no doubt repented at leisure.'

'Probably. In any case, I should think she found that she'd bitten off more than she could chew. It wouldn't surprise me if Jessica Ross changed considerably, once she was in a more powerful position. She strikes me as being just the sort of person to suck up to those in authority and then, when she acquires some power herself, to treat her subordinates in a way she wouldn't have tolerated being treated herself.'

'Also, that agency means a lot to her. She wouldn't have liked it one little bit when she saw it threatened. So when Mrs Parnell didn't manage to pull herself together, began to neglect the business and even damage it . . .'

'Quite. The question is, just how far would Jessica Ross have been prepared to go, to protect her interests?'

'You really think she might have been prepared to kill for them, sir?'

'I certainly think she would be capable of being ruthless, if necessary. We'll have to find out more about her and also check that non-existent alibi of hers pretty thoroughly. I'll put Sparks on to it, it's the sort of thing he enjoys. And I think we'll check all the overnight accomodation in Sturrenden, just in case she followed Alicia down on Saturday. There are no trains back to London after 10.15.'

'She could have come by car, sir.'

'If she's got one. We'll ask Sparks to find out. But one thing's certain. There's a good deal of strong feeling boiling away beneath that not very attractive exterior, wouldn't you agree, Mike?'

'Yes, I would. And I think she was jealous as hell of Mrs Parnell, don't you?'

'Trying hard not to show it, of course.'

'But failing.'

Thanet relit his pipe, which had gone out. 'I suppose it's not surprising, if you think about it. There would have been quite a bit to be jealous about. Alicia was a very good-looking woman and a very nice person, by the sound of it. Look at the way she stuck by her husband . . . I had the impression she was liked by the two girls in the agency, too. Faith had been crying, did you notice?'

'Yes, I did.'

'I'll ask Sparks to have a word with her, and with the other girl, Carol. I expect they could give us a pretty good idea of what's been going on. I imagine the atmosphere hasn't been too pleasant, lately. Jessica Ross doesn't strike me as being the sort of person to suffer a grievance in silence. And I'm quite intrigued to know what made her pull that face when Carol was mentioned.'

'Yes, I noticed that, too. . . . I have the impression Miss Ross felt the situation was getting out of hand, slipping away from her control. She presents herself as being very patient and forbearing, but I imagine the truth is, she tackled Mrs Parnell about it more than once, but didn't manage to get anywhere . . . I wonder where Mrs Parnell used to go during those unexplained absences?'

'Intriguing, isn't it? What do you think Mike?'

'Well I certainly don't think she sounds the sort of person to sell her share of the agency without even discussing it with her partner. Anyway, that explanation doesn't really fit the pattern, does it? I think it may have been what Jessica Ross was afraid might happen, but that's a different matter.'

'I agree. Her other suggestion was marginally more likely, don't you think?'

'The house-hunting, you mean? I don't know. If so, I don't see why it would have been necessary for Mrs Parnell to be so secretive about it.'

'And what about that red folder, Mike?'

'Could have contained house agents' details, I suppose.' Lineham pulled a face. 'Scarcely a motive for murder, is it? Unless we're going to be really far-fetched and say she might have witnessed a crime while she was looking over an empty property and was killed because she could identify the criminal.' He grinned. 'How's that for a flight of fancy?'

Thanet laughed. 'We'll bear it in mind. Anyway, it certainly sounds as if she was preoccupied by some specific project.'

'Perhaps she decided to cultivate an interest, to take her mind off her unhappiness.'

'Such as?'

Lineham shrugged. 'Collecting something?'

'There's no sign of any kind of collection, in her flat.'

'But if she was only just getting started . . . She could have been going to auction sales, which would explain why the absences were irregular and for varying lengths of time. If she'd taken up French classes, or Pottery, she'd have been going at the same time each week.'

'And the mysterious folder?'

'Auction catalogues, lists of dealers, antique shops, adverts cut out of newspapers . . . No, it's pretty feeble, isn't it? Hell, sir, I'm only guessing. We've absolutely nothing to go on. Have you got any ideas?'

'Not really. I agree with you, it's pure speculation. Fascinating, but pointless, really. Maybe it's of no significance anyway. Maybe she just felt at times that she had to get out of the office, away from Miss Ross, and didn't see why she should have to give explanations.'

'Though that wouldn't explain away the red folder.'

'True. But we must remember that although it seems likely that there's a connection between the murder and the red folder, in view of the fact that it's missing, there's not necessarily any connection between the folder and those unexplained absences.'

'Yes, I see what you mean.'

Back in Sturrenden Sparks had been busy. He had spoken to the Night Sisters who had been on duty in both the intensive care unit and Penny Rain's ward on the night of the concert. Rain had arrived at the former at about ten to eleven, had spent a few minutes discussing his mother's condition with the Sister and had then gone up to enquire about Penny before leaving the hospital.

'Bending the rules a bit, weren't they, Sparks, allowing him in at that time of night?'

Sparks grinned. 'I gather he's a bit of a favourite, sir. And of course, he is a celebrity.'

'True. They're certain of these times?'

'The Sister in charge of intensive care was, because a patient died just after Mr Rain left, and the time of death is entered as eleven pm.'

'Right. Well now, I've got something else for you. A bit of digging in the Metropolis, tomorrow.' Thanet smiled as Sparks's eyes lit up. 'I thought you'd be pleased. There's a woman called Jessica Ross . . .'

Yes, he thought, as he watched Sparks depart after the briefing, the young constable wouldn't be with them long. Thanet had never yearned for the big city, but this boy would thrive on it. Not for him the parochial atmosphere of small-town crime. The faster pace, the excitement and challenge of an urban enviornment, would be more suited to his temperament and his ambition.

'Interesting,' said Lineham. 'If Rain put his fiancée and her parents into a taxi around twenty past ten, why should it have taken him half an hour to get to the hospital? It wouldn't have taken him more than a quarter of an hour even if he'd walked, and as he'd have had to come in from Barton I imagine he would have had his car with him.'

'I agree. We'll have to see him again. Give him a ring, this time. We don't want another wasted journey.'

Rain was at home and free to see them and they retraced the route they had taken the previous day. This time there were two cars parked in the drive, a silver Mercedes and a Renault 5 with the name of a Sturrenden car-hire firm printed on a notice stuck inside the back window.

'Visitors,' said Thanet.

'Very nice,' said Lineham, admiring the Mercedes. 'Oh, sorry, sir, yes. His fiancée's parents, perhaps?'

'Possibly.'

Rain himself opened the front door and led them through a wide passageway with walls of panelled wood into a spacious sitting room which extended right up to the exposed roof timbers.

It was a most attractive room. There were Persian rugs on the highly-polished floorboards, pieces of oak furniture gleaming with the unmistakable patina of the genuine antique and, predictably, a grand piano scattered with sheet music. Nearby was a music stand, and Rain's violin lay in its open case on a chair. The flower arrangements, Thanet noticed, were beginning to droop.

The three people seated before the huge ingle-nook fireplace looked up as they entered and Rain made the introductions: his fiancée, Melanie Knight, and her parents. They were having tea. A large silver tray stood on a low table near Mrs Knight's chair.

'May we offer you a cup, Inspector?'

'Thank you, no.' The sight of the dainty triangular sandwiches and mouth-watering cream sponge reminded Thanet that somehow he and Lineham seemed to have missed out on lunch today, and he hoped that his stomach would not begin to rumble. He wondered why Rain had not shown them into another room, where they could have talked in private. Because he had hoped that the presence of his fiancée and her parents might inhibit the police? If so, he was about to be.

disillusioned. Thanet had no intention of allowing himself to be manipulated into leaving without answers to his questions.

'It would be no trouble to get some more cups,' said Melanie, sliding forward to the edge of the settee, preparatory to rising.

This was the first time Thanet had had a good look at her. That glimpse in the street a couple of months ago hardly counted, as she had had her back to him. He saw at once that the newspaper photographs hadn't done her justice. She really was beautiful. Her hair was long, dark and shining, the soft, luscious waves tumbling in ordered disarray about her shoulders. Her face was a perfect oval, her features regular, her eyes large, dark and expressive, and the heart-shaped birthmark on her right cheek did not detract from her beauty but merely served in some mysterious way to underline it, in the manner of the beauty patches worn by the courtesans of old. She was wearing a pale yellow cotton shift dress which hinted at an excellent figure and revealed long, shapely legs. All this and talented too, Thanet thought. Rain was a lucky man.

'No, please don't bother. It's very kind of you, but this won't take long. And I don't want to intrude on your tea, so I'll have a word with Mr Rain in private, if I may.'

Everyone looked at Rain, who was standing in front of the enormous fireplace, hands clasped behind his back. Thanet glanced around. Melanie appeared apprehensive, her parents uncomfortable, and as he watched, Mrs Knight put her hand on her husband's arm. They were obviously a devoted couple, Thanet thought, one of those pairs who, with the passage of time, have grown to look so alike that they could almost be taken for brother and sister. They were both tall, like Melanie, with lean, angular bodies and neat, well-shaped heads. They were even alike in colouring, with short, well-cut light brown hair and clear blue eyes. They looked prosperous and well-groomed, perfectly at home in this affluent setting.

Rain laughed and rocked a little on his heels. 'That won't be necessary, Inspector. I can guess what you've come about. When I got home last night I was thinking back over our conversation yesterday and realised I'd unintentionally misled you. As I recall, I told you I went straight to the hospital after

67

putting my fiancée and her parents into a taxi on Saturday night, but in fact I didn't. I imagine you've come to interrogate me about that rather sinister gap. Is that right?'

Thanet smiled. 'I think that perhaps "interrogate" is rather too strong a word, Mr Rain. But you're right, of course. Naturally, we have to check up on any discrepancy, however slight, in anything to do with any of the people to whom Mrs Parnell spoke on Saturday night, and during the course of our investigation it did emerge that there was, as far as you were concerned, a "sinister gap", as you put it, between twenty past ten and ten to eleven that night. I gather that there is a perfectly innocent explanation for it?'

'It's very simple, really.' Rain left the hearth and went to sit beside Melanie on the settee, his movements easy and relaxed. 'Do sit down, Inspector, Sergeant.'

He certainly didn't look like a man with an uneasy conscience, Thanet thought as he and Lineham complied.

'As you know, I've been desperately worried about my mother — still am, for that matter.' Rain's face was sombre now, and Melanie put out her hand to cover his. He didn't look at her, though, Thanet noticed, or respond to her gesture. He was too preoccupied with his anxiety, perhaps, to have been aware of it.

'I expect that was why I came to mislead you. I had rather too much on my mind. What actually happened on Saturday night was that after saying goodbye to Melanie and her parents, I suddenly realised that when I left home for the concert, earlier in the evening, I had forgotten to bring with me a small bag of stuff that my sister had earlier asked me to take in to her, the next time I visited the hospital. I'd already taken in a few essentials, in the morning, but by the afternoon she was feeling well enough to make a short list of things she thought she'd need. I could have left it until Sunday morning, of course, but I'd promised and . . . I don't know if you've ever been in a similar situation, Inspector, but one of the most difficult things to cope with is a feeling of complete helplessness, the knowledge that there's absolutely nothing useful you can do. I know this was only a very small matter, but it suddenly seemed very important that I should keep that promise. There was something almost, well, superstitious about it. You know . . . if I keep my word to the letter, the gods might smile on me and mother might recover . . .' He gave a sheepish little laugh. 'Stupid, really, but there you are . . . So what I did on Saturday night was to come back here, pick up the bag, which I'd already packed, and take it in to the hospital with me. Ask the Night Sister, she'll confirm this.'

While Rain had been talking the tension in the room had gradually seeped away, like air escaping from a balloon and now the Knights looked at Thanet, their faces bright with expectation, confident of his reception of Rain's disarming confession.

And of course, he had no choice but to accept it. There was one point, though . . . He opened his mouth, but again Rain forestalled him.

'There's no one to corroborate this, I'm afraid, Inspector. We have no permanent staff here and I don't recall seeing anyone I know, on the way.' He smiled. 'I'm afraid you'll just have to take my word for it.'

'I gather that you are not staying here with Mr Rain,' said Thanet, glancing at the Knights and their daughter.

'No. We were going to,' said Knight, 'but then, when Mrs Rain and Penny had that terrible accident, we felt it would be much simpler for Nicholas if he didn't have to bother about us. We couldn't get in at the Black Swan at such short notice, it was fully booked, so we went to the George — and I must say, in view of what happened, we were glad that that was the way it had worked out.'

'Poor woman,' said Mrs Knight. 'What a terrible business. When Nicholas told us he'd known her as a child, we lit a candle for her, this morning.'

So the Knights were Catholic too, Thanet thought. Nicholas and Melanie were indeed well-suited. Her parents must have been delighted at the match — except, perhaps, for the age-gap.

The main point, though, was that Rain had no alibi for half the crucial period on Saturday night. Lineham said as much, when they were in the car.

'We'll send someone to check up on the bag he claims to

have taken in for his sister,' said Thanet. 'Though even if he did take it in — and he would be very foolish to lie about something which can so easily be checked — it wouldn't prove he's telling the truth. He could easily have put it in the car earlier, when he left for the concert.'

'And decided to use it to cover up what he was really doing during that half an hour.'

'Meeting Mrs Parnell back at the hotel, you mean? I suppose it depends on whether they've kept in touch or not, as you suggested. I mean, you don't go up to a boyfriend you haven't seen for twenty years and after a few minutes' conversation invite him back to your hotel bedroom, especially when you know he's just got engaged and his fiancée's present.'

'No. But if, after her husband died, she had been hoping they might get together again. . . . She could have threatened to make a scene there and then, if he didn't agree to meet her later. . . . He might well have given in just to shut her up.'

Thanet's bleeper went.

'Wonder what that's about. Did you notice a telephone in the village, Mike?'

'Opposite the church.'

There was a message from Joan, apparently. Would Thanet ring home, at the first opportunity?'

Thanet frowned. 'She didn't say what it was about?'

'No, sir. Sorry.'

Thanet fished out some more change. What could be wrong? Joan never rang him at work unless it was really urgent.

SEVEN

In the few seconds it took to get through, Thanet visualised
disaster after disaster. Obviously Joan herself was all right
or she wouldn't have been able to ring, so it must be one of
the children. Bridget or Ben, injured . . . maimed . . . dead,
even . . .

'Hullo?'

'Joan? I got your message. What's the matter?'

'Oh darling, I'm sorry to bother you . . .'

'Never mind that. What's wrong?'

'It's Ben. Just a minute.'

Thanet could hear the television in the background. The
noise was suddenly cut off. Joan must have gone to close the
door. What had she meant, 'It's Ben'? He ground his teeth
with impatience.

'Hullo?'

'What's the matter with Ben? Is he hurt?'

'No, no. Sorry, darling. No, they're both all right, but . . .
they brought a letter home from school, today.'

'A letter? But what . . .? Sorry, go on.'

'It's Andy. He's . . . he's dead.'

Andy was one of Ben's closest friends.

'Dead? Oh God, how awful. What happened?'

'That's the point, Luke. Glue-sniffing.'

'Oh, *no*.' Thanet was shocked and disbelieving. Until a year
ago, Andy had been a cheerful, freckled extrovert. Then his
parents' marriage had gone wrong and Thanet and Joan had
watched helplessly while week by week he had become more
withdrawn and unhappy. There had been talk of problems at
school, truancy, even. Now, this . . .

Thanet was well aware that 'solvent inhalation', as it is
officially called, is the most common drug abuse for children
aged eight upwards, and that its danger lies in the risk of

71

convulsions, brain damage or death by suffocation. He knew too that parents are often first alerted to the problem by a change in their child's behaviour, and fear twisted his stomach as his mind flashed back to the weekend.

'Ben's desperately upset,' Joan was saying. 'I think he's been bottling it up all day. The whole school was told about it at assembly this morning, Bridget says, and warned again of the serious risks involved in glue-sniffing. And, as I said, they all brought a letter home to their parents. I didn't know any of this when I picked them up from Marion's of course, and there wasn't time for her to tell me, because I didn't go in, just tooted, and the children came running out. I noticed Ben was very pale and quiet, but he wouldn't tell me what was wrong — looking back, I honestly think that by then he was literally incapable of speaking — and it was Bridget who told me what had happened. By the time we got home Ben was shaking and when we got indoors I bent to put my arms around him, but he just shoved me aside, burst into tears and raced up the stairs to his room. I left him for a little while, then went up. He'd stopped crying by then, but he's lying face down on the bed and he just won't talk to me.'

'You don't think . . .?'

'I don't *know*. Oh Luke, I am sorry to bother you like this, in the middle of an important case, but I don't want to do the wrong thing.'

Thanet could never remember Joan being at a loss like this before. Always, in the past, she could be relied upon to handle any and every crisis with the maximum skill and delicacy.

'I'll come home right away.' *And please, God, don't let Ben be involved in glue-sniffing*. He ran back to the car. 'Drive me home, will you, Mike?'

'Sure. What's wrong, sir?'

Thanet opened his mouth to tell him, then hesitated. He was so used to thinking aloud with Lineham present that it seemed unnatural to hold back when the words were waiting to tumble out in an anxious flood. But this was private, personal. It wasn't that he didn't trust Lineham to keep his mouth shut, just that to express his fear aloud would have seemed like a betrayal of his son.

72

'A problem to do with one of the children, that's all.' *All.*

'Nothing serious, I hope?'

'I hope not, too.' *Why didn't I notice that there was something wrong? Look at the way he was behaving over the weekend.*

Lineham knew better than to press the matter. 'Is there anything you want me to do, at the office?'

Thanet forced himself to concentrate. One of the next items on the agenda was a visit to the Leytons, but that wasn't urgent and would now have to wait until tomorrow. Meanwhile . . . 'One thing I'd intended to do was to look out the inquest report on Paul Leyton.'

'Paul Leyton? Oh, the boy who committed suicide, you mean?'

'Yes. It may be quite irrelevant, but let's face it, if Jessica Ross turns out to be innocent, there's nobody else we know about in Alicia's present life who could possibly have a reason for wanting to kill her. In which case, we might have to look to the past — especially as her former friends keep cropping up. And we can't get away from the fact that it was very strange that having been away from Sturrenden all these years, she was killed almost immediately after setting foot in it again.' *He was off his food for one thing. And quiet. Shut himself away in his room. It was staring me in the face. Why didn't I see?*

'You'd like me to glance through it, sir?'

'Through it? Oh, the inquest report. Yes. I'll take a look myself, tomorrow morning. And get someone to drop my car back for me some time this evening, will you, Mike?'

They had arrived. Thanet said a hasty goodbye and hurried up the path to the front door. Joan was waiting for him and they went into the kitchen, where she had been preparing supper. Even in a crisis, routine must go on.

'How is he?'

'I haven't been up since. There didn't seem to be much point.'

'What do you think?' said Thanet grimly. 'Has he been involved, in the glue-sniffing?'

'I don't know. He hasn't been showing any of the symptoms

— no smell of glue on him, no signs of drunkenness, no sores around nose or mouth . . .'

'And no hallucinations either, thank God. But he has been very quiet lately.'

'He stayed in on Sunday, remember,' said Joan optimistically. 'We thought it odd at the time. But if he has been involved it could mean he's decided to keep well out of it.'

'Oh God, I hope so. I do hope so. . . . You think I ought to have a word with him now?'

'I don't know. What do you think?'

Each saw his own anxiety mirrored in the eyes of the other while they considered what to do for the best.

'We can't just leave it,' said Thanet at last. 'We'll have to tackle him some time.'

'But when would be the best moment, that's the point. He must be desperately upset about Andy.'

'And just think how Matt and Angela must be feeling.'

Andy's parents were not amongst Thanet and Joan's closest friends, but they knew them quite well and shared a moment of mourning now on their behalf.

'Restricting the sale of glue just isn't enough,' said Joan angrily. 'They'll always get hold of it, if they really want to — like any other drug.'

'I know . . . But Ben . . . you're right. If we question him too soon, he might clam up on us.'

'On the other hand, now might be the best time, while he's still shaken . . .'

'I think I'll pop up and see him anyway,' said Thanet. He needed to see Ben, to touch him, to reassure himself that Ben was all right. And if all the boy needed at the moment was comfort, well, that was fine by him. Bracing himself for a difficult few minutes, Thanet went upstairs and let himself quietly into Ben's room.

Ben was lying face down on the bed, his head turned towards the wall.

'Ben?'

No response. Thanet sat down on the edge of the bed and laid a hand on the boy's shoulder. He felt him stiffen.

'Are you all right?'

No reply.

'We're both very, very sorry, about Andy.'

Ben said nothing, but made an inarticulate little sound somewhere between a gasp and a sob.

Thanet began to stroke his son's hair. 'We do understand how upset you are.'

Still no reply.

'We know how fond you were of him.'

In a sudden flurry of activity Ben scrambled on to his knees and hurled himself at his father, bursting into noisy floods of tears. Thanet put his arms tightly around the small body and hugged it close, rocking to and fro and murmuring softly in Ben's ear, taking the boy's pain into himself and absorbing it.

Slowly, Ben's tears abated and eventually Thanet was able to release him. With sinking heart he noted that Ben was still not able to meet his gaze. Should he question him now or not? He agonised over the decision. It was so important to get the timing right. He made up his mind. No, despite his own desperate need to know, it would be better to do it when the boy was calmer.

'Come on,' he said. 'Let's get you undressed. Then Mummy'll bring you some ice cream. Would you like that?'

Ben nodded and submitted to being fussed over. By the time Thanet left him he was looking much more settled.

'I'll come and read you a story later, if you like.'

Deliberately, he waited for an answer, determined to get Ben to say at least a few words before he left him. 'Would you like that?' he persisted.

'Yes please, Daddy.'

Satisfied, Thanet went downstairs and gave Joan an account of what had happened.

'Do you think I ought to call the doctor?'

Thanet shook his head. 'We don't want to make too much of a thing of it. He'll be all right now, I think.'

'What about school, in the morning?'

'Let's wait and see. Children are pretty resilient. He may be feeling much better by then.'

And he was. Ben appeared at breakfast looking pale and subdued but otherwise normal. Far better for him to go to school, Thanet thought, than to sit about at home feeling miserable. Besides, they weren't sure how their usual baby-sitter would cope with this rather delicate situation. They would have a further talk with Ben that evening, they decided.

It was Thanet's turn to take the children to school and he gave them both an extra hard hug before dropping them off. Watching them run towards the school gates he hoped that in their concern for Ben he and Joan hadn't completely neglected Sprig's reaction to the news. But she had seemed fine, he reassured himself. He allowed himself at last to start thinking once more about work.

Had Alicia been the sort of person to resort to emotional blackmail? he wondered, as he remembered yesterday's conversation with Lineham about Rain. He wouldn't have thought so, but then he still knew very little about her, as yet. Jessica Ross had been too self-absorbed to give him any dependable idea of what her partner had been like. Alicia had been loyal, that was clear, and must have had considerable reserves of inner strength to have stuck to her husband and helped him to rebuild his life after the accident. She must have been under severe strain for years, and it wasn't surprising that after his death she had apparently gone to pieces.

Nevertheless, she had survived. She had continued to take an interest in her appearance, had run her home efficiently and had continued to work, albeit with less enthusiasm than before. And she appeared to have found some new interest in life, a preoccupation which had been sufficiently important to her for her to ignore or shrug off Jessica Ross's displeasure at her neglect of the business.

Could that interest have been Nicholas Rain? Unconsciously, Thanet shook his head. If Alicia had been slipping out to meet a lover, she would surely have looked at least a little more cheerful upon her return, and Jessica Ross had said that she invariably seemed depressed. It really was pointless to speculate. Enlightenment could come only through finding out more about Alicia's life, her character, and as she appeared to have no close friends and her father, her only relative, was still away on holiday, there seemed to be only one possible avenue of exploration. He would have to talk to her former friends here in Sturrenden. Alicia at seventeen must of course have been very different from the mature woman of thirty-eight, but the seeds of her future development would surely already have been sown and for all he knew those links with former friends may never have been broken. She might well have kept in touch with the only other girl in the group, Vivienne Leyton, for instance.

Yes, a visit to the Leytons was long overdue, but he still thought it might be profitable to study first the report of the event which had caused that group to disintegrate, Paul Leyton's suicide.

Lineham was already at his desk.

'Anything interesting come in, Mike?'

'Oh, morning, sir. Nothing much. We've got the forensic report now, but there's nothing of any use to us. The room was plastered with different fingerprints, as you would imagine, in a hotel bedroom. Let me see. what else . . .? Ah, yes. The hospital confirms that Mr Rain did bring in a bag of stuff for his sister late on Saturday night, but as you said, that doesn't really get us any further. And that's about it. Everything all right at home, now?'

'Yes, crisis over.' If only he could be sure that were true, Thanet thought. He wasn't looking forward to this evening.

Lineham's enquiry had put him in a slightly awkward position. The sergeant had been very helpful yesterday and Thanet really owed him some sort of explanation, but he didn't want to give one yet. Not until he was sure that Ben was in the clear.

He would just have to appear ungrateful. 'Did you manage to read the inquest report on Paul Leyton?'

'Yes. I was just making some notes on it when you arrived. Here it is.'

'Thanks. What are your impressions?'

Lineham leaned back in his chair. 'Well, it seems there's no doubt that it was suicide. He took an overdose and left a note for his parents.'

'What did it say?'

' "Sorry, I just can't go on." That's all. As you told me, the precipitating factor was the split with Alicia Parnell — Alicia

Doyle, as she was then — earlier in the evening. But there was more to it than that, apparently.'

'I'd better read it through myself.'

Paul Leyton had killed himself on the night of June 4th 1964. His body had been found next morning by his mother, when he had failed to come down for breakfast and she had gone up to call him. He had apparently been withdrawn and moody for some time before that. He had been a brilliant boy and everybody had hoped that he would win a scholarship to Oxford when he sat the Oxbridge examination the following November, but for the month previous to his death his work had fallen off badly and the day he died his Latin master had taken him to task over a very poor essay he had handed in.

The master, a man called Hollister (whom Thanet remembered from his own time at the school as being an exacting but excellent teacher) had been called at the inquest and had said that he had told Paul that if he didn't very quickly pull himself together and start concentrating on his work again he could not only say goodbye to Oxford but to getting respectable grades in his A levels as well. Hollister had said that he now deeply regretted having been so forceful. He had known of Paul's association with Alicia Doyle and had assumed that the boy's preoccupation with her was affecting his work, but he hadn't mentioned the girl, had simply said that the next few months would be crucial as far as Paul's future was concerned and that he must try to let other interests sink into abeyance for the moment.

Alicia had then told the court about two conversations with Paul later that day. For some time she had felt that his feelings for her were becoming too intense. She knew that in the autumn they would both be going away to university and she hadn't wanted to become too involved with any one boy. So, when she met Paul in the coffee bar where they often used to congregate with their other friends after school, she asked him to walk home with her and told him that she had decided that it would be best if they didn't go out together again. She hoped that they would still remain friends, she told him, but she would prefer him not to think of her as his girlfriend any more.

78

Paul had argued with her, pleaded, and was still very upset when he left her. Later in the day, after supper, he had returned, begging her at least to say that she would reconsider her decision, but she had felt that if she conceded at this point, she would never find the determination to go through all this again, and she had held firm. She was terribly upset by what had happened, she said, and wished now that she had behaved differently. Perhaps it would have been better just to let the relationship peter out when they both went away. That way, Paul would gradually have become used to living without her and would have found the final break easier when it came.

Oliver Bassett had then been called. He had been on his way home at about nine o'clock that night, he said, when he had passed Paul in the street. He had pulled up and offered him a lift home. Paul had seemed very depressed, and when they arrived at the Leyton house Oliver had accepted Paul's rather half-hearted offer of a cup of coffee, thinking that perhaps Paul might find it helpful to talk. But Paul had remained sunk in gloom and after a while Bassett had left, thinking that there was nothing more he could do. He bitterly regretted not having stayed on longer, at least until one of the family arrived home.

The next witness to be called was Richard Leyton, Paul's younger brother. He told the court that he had also been out that evening and had got home at about ten-thirty. His parents had not yet returned from their bridge evening and as he was tired and there was no one about, he had gone straight up to bed. Paul's bedroom door was closed and there was no light showing beneath, so Richard, knowing that Paul had gone to see Alicia after supper, had assumed that his brother was still out. It was not until the following day, when he heard that Paul must have taken the overdose at about ten-fifteen pm, that he realised that if he had indeed looked in on Paul that night, he might well have been able to save his life. He would always regret not having done so.

Verdict: suicide while the balance of the mind was disturbed.

'Nothing too unusual there,' said Thanet, when he had finished reading. 'Sadly, it's a situation which arises all too often.

You get an adolescent under stress because of impending exams, he has an unhappy love affair and it's all just too much for him to cope with.'

'Amazing, isn't it, how after a suicide everyone feels guilty, thinks he could have prevented it if only he'd behaved differently.'

'Understandable, though.'

'You really think all this stuff might be relevant, sir?'

'Who knows? I certainly think it might be useful to talk to these people. We still don't know nearly enough about Alicia.' And Thanet expained what he had been thinking, on the way to work, in the car.

'With respect, sir, I can't see that it'll be much use talking to people who haven't seen her for twenty years.'

'But how do we know they haven't seen her for twenty years, Mike? Even if she lost touch with them during the time her husband was alive, after his death she might well have begun to wish she hadn't. And from there it's only a step to deciding to contact them again.'

'It's possible, I suppose.' But Lineham didn't sound in the least convinced.

'The point is,' said Thanet, becoming exasperated, 'we've got to explore every possibility. Now Sparks is digging away in London, so we'll do some digging here. Where shall we start? With the Leytons? It's about time we had a talk with them.'

'How about going to see that schoolmaster. What was his name . . .?'

'Hollister, you mean? Why?'

'It could be useful to have an impartial opinion of them all, sir.'

'I'm not sure how forthcoming he would be.' Thanet was intrigued with his own reluctance to take up Lineham's suggestion. Was it possible that he was still intimidated by Hollister, after all these years? The mere possibility was enough to clinch the matter. 'Still, you're right. It could be useful. See if you can find his address in the phone book, will you? I know he retired some years ago, but.as he's a bachelor he might well have stayed put.'

While he waited Thanet glanced through the forensic

report. Lineham was right. There wasn't anything of any use to them there. He sighed. They certainly weren't getting much material help. He hated casting around in the dark, like this.

'Here we are, sir. J.C. Hollister. That's him, isn't it?'

'Yes. Where does he live?'

'41 Benenden Road.'

'Give him a ring. No, on second thoughts, don't bother. It's not far, so we won't be wasting much time. If he's out, we can go on to see someone else . . . Is the PM scheduled yet?'

'This afternoon, sir.'

'Good. Then let's go.'

The houses in Benenden Road were of nineteen-thirties vintage: neat, detached and solidly built, with bay windows upstairs and down. Most of them showed signs of the recent boom in home improvement in the way of double glazing or replacement windows, freshly-painted woodwork and even, here and there, the odd burglar alarm. Over the years the Englishman's home has become more his castle than ever, thought Thanet. He wouldn't mind betting that most of these modest houses also boasted central heating, insulated lofts and kitchens which would have made the original owners swoon with delight.

Number 41 stood out like a sore thumb. The tiny front garden was knee-high in nettles and long grass, there were dingy net curtains at the grimy windows and the paintwork hadn't seen a brush in years. An ancient Morris Oxford stood in the drive.

'Can't think how it passed its MOT,' said Lineham, peering at the licence on the windscreen and wrinkling his nose at the rusting metalwork.

Thanet was already on the front doorstep. 'Mike, we're not in traffic division. Come *on*.' He banged the rusty knocker on the peeling wood.

'And I bet the neighbours love that.' Lineham nodded at the overgrown garden.

'He obviously doesn't give a damn.' Thanet couldn't help having a sneaking admiration for someone who so completely disregarded the conventions. He often felt that he himself was boringly conformist. He was beginning to look forward to this interview. He enjoyed eccentrics.

'Who is it?' A muffled voice from within.

'Police, sir. CID.'

There was a moment's silence and then the sound of bolts

being drawn. The door opened a few inches.

'Mr Hollister?'

'What do you want?'

Thanet introduced himself and offered his identification.

'Thanet . . . Weren't you at the Grammar?'

'Yes, sir.' With difficulty Thanet prevented himself from standing to attention under the old man's scrutiny.

'In the police now, eh?' The door opened a little wider.

'Yes, sir. And we were wondering if you could help us.'

'Me? How?'

'We wanted to talk to you about Paul Leyton . . . If we could come into the house, perhaps? It might be a little less public . . .'

'Paul Leyton . . .'

There was a pause, a long one. Then, just as Thanet was beginning to think that he would have to conduct the interview on the doorstep, the door opened wider and he saw Hollister properly for the first time. Confronted with the reality, his mental image of the man abruptly disintegrated. He remembered the classics master as a tall, commanding figure, a man who had been respected if not liked, notorious for the impossibly long homework he set and feared for his rages if his standards were not met. He expected and got the most excellent results and in his time had nurtured several fine classical scholars.

It was difficult to believe that this neglected scarecrow was the same man. He seemed to have shrunk during the intervening years and he was gaunt, stooping, unshaven. He was wearing stained, wrinkled trousers, a creased open-necked shirt and a shabby fawn knitted cardigan. His eyes, however, were as keen as ever, the cold, penetrating grey that Thanet remembered so well.

'I suppose you'd better,' he said grudgingly, and stood back to allow them to enter. As he turned to close the front door behind them Thanet and Lineham could not prevent themselves from exchanging a look of pure amazement. At first glance it seemed that the house was constructed of books rather than of bricks and mortar, wood and plasterboard. Every available wall surface was stacked with books, right up to the ceiling. They even marched up the stairs, piled shoulder high on every riser, up and up into the dimness of the landing above.

'We'd better go into the kitchen.'

They passed two open doors on the way and in both rooms books prevailed, to the degree that there seemed to be little floor space left, just a narrow corridor between encroaching walls of volumes, leading to a single armchair with a standard lamp beside it. How on earth, Thanet wondered, did Hollister ever manage to get at a book in one of the stacks at the back? For that matter, how could he hope to have even a vague idea of where he had put the one he wanted, let alone find it?

The air was fusty, musty, the smell of a second-hand bookshop magnified a thousand times over by dust and neglect. Hollister had evidently become a recluse of the first order, living in a world of his own bounded by the printed page. And the original owner of this house would certainly have recognised this kitchen, Thanet thought. There was the old china sink, the built-in dresser with cupboards below, the white enamel table, chipped and stained with rust, the walk-in larder beside the back door. It was possible, of course, that Hollister himself had bought the house newly-built and, supremely indifferent to his surroundings, had simply never bothered to make any changes.

This appeared to be the one room relatively free of books. A few were piled on the dresser, with little pieces of paper sticking out of them, but that was all. On the table was a sheaf of papers and an open, typed catalogue. A pencil lay nearby. Hollister had evidently been engaged in the pleasurable task of selecting new acquisitions. Where on earth would he put them? Were the bedrooms, too, book depositories? Despite the warmth of the day the back door was firmly shut and the window closed, and there was a smell of drains and stale food.

Any idea that Hollister was in his dotage was quickly dispelled. He sat down on the only chair, gave Thanet a piercing glance and said, 'Now, perhaps you would enlighten me as to your interest in this matter. It is twenty years since Paul Leyton's death and I fail to see how anything I could tell you could be of any possible interest to you.'

84

Thanet wouldn't have expected to find anything as incongruous as a television set here, but a quick glance around had shown him that there did not appear to be a radio, either. Nor, so far as he could see, were there any newspapers.

'Do you remember a girl called Alicia Doyle, Mr Hollister?'

'Of course I do,' snapped Hollister. 'I am far from senile yet, Thanet. She was that little trollop Leyton was running about with. If it hadn't been for her, he would never have killed himself.'

His venom startled Thanet and he wondered, could he by chance have stumbled across Alicia's murderer? That Hollister should speak with such passion after all these years astonished him.

'You may not have heard, sir, but Alicia Parnell — Alicia Doyle, as you knew her — was found dead in the Black Swan on Sunday morning. She had been strangled.'

Hollister didn't even blink. 'Doesn't surprise me. A fitting end, I should think.'

'It would evidently be putting it mildly, to say that you didn't like her.'

'It would. Girls like that should be locked up. The degree of havoc they wreak amongst unsuspecting adolescent males is incalculable.'

'You speak in the plural, sir.'

'I do. Boys may think that their masters are blind, but I can assure you that they're not. Earlier in the year Miss Doyle,' — and he almost spat the name — 'had had her claws into Nicholas Rain. His work, too, was deplorable for a while after she tossed him aside, but it didn't matter so much for him. It had been evident to everyone for a very long time that he was destined for a brilliant musical career. As it transpired, he recovered sufficiently to gain a respectable grade at A level. But Leyton was a different matter. When his work began to deteriorate I didn't realise why, at first. And when I did find out, there seemed to be nothing I could do. He was deaf to reason. It was a tragedy.' Hollister banged the enamel table with a clenched fist, making the two policemen jump. 'I really fail to understand why someone as intelligent as he should . . . That boy had the finest brain I ever taught. And it was addled

— that's the only word for it, addled — by that little chit of a girl.'
Hollister shook his head. 'I couldn't believe he'd been so foolish
as to succumb to her "charms". I'd thought he had enough sense
to realise that at that stage in his life there was no room, no room
at all for dalliance. I'd seen the other one mooning around after
him and it obviously hadn't affected him in the least, so . . .'

'The other one?'

'The one with red hair. Forever following him around like a
love-sick cow.'

Thanet caught Lineham, who was standing behind Hollister,
smothering a grin. It was rapidly becoming obvious why
Hollister had never married. His view of the fair sex was, to put it
mildly, somewhat jaundiced.

'That was Leyton's tragedy,' Hollister went on. 'He was too
well-liked, too popular. If he'd been less sought-after, he'd be
alive today and the Regius professor of Greek, no doubt.'

'You felt that his friends were a distraction?'

'Distraction? Hah, you have a talent for understatement,
Thanet. They distracted him, they distracted each other and,
believe me, they distracted me. If they'd given only a fraction of
the attention to their work that they gave to their social activities,
it would have been a very different story.'

'I don't know about Richard Leyton, Paul's brother, but the
other two men did well enough though, sir, didn't they? Rain has
a fine career and Bassett . . .'

'Bassett was only a hanger-on. It was that sports car of his that
was the attraction.' Hollister snorted. 'Absolutely ridiculous,
giving a sports car to a boy of that age. Asking for trouble.
Parents should have more sense. Over-indulgence and too much
laxity, they're the ills of the modern age.'

It was obvious that Hollister's prejudices were too strong for
him to be of any help to them, and Thanet left as soon as he
decently could.

'So much for an impartial opinion,' said Lineham, when they
were outside. 'Sorry, sir.'

'Don't worry about it.' Thanet grinned. 'To be honest, Mike,
I only decided to interview him because the prospect made me
nervous. After all these years! I just couldn't resist going to see
what he was like.'

'He must have been a real tartar, at school. I'm thankful he never taught me, that's for sure. Classics was never my strong point.'

'Nor mine, alas,' said Thanet. 'And he obviously hasn't forgiven me for it.'

'Pretty weird set-up he's got there. Do you think he spends all day, every day, reading?'

'Looks like it.'

'What a life! I'd go round the bend.'

'Presumably it's by choice, so I shouldn't feel too sorry for him.'

'Where now, then?'

'Oliver Bassett first, I think, as we're so close to his office.'

'He may not be free to see us.'

'Then we'll make an appointment.'

But Bassett would see them in fifteen minutes, they were told, if they cared to wait.

They were shown into a neat, impersonal waiting room.

'Nice little practice he's got here,' said Lineham, shuffling through the magazines on a low table. '*Country Life, Ideal Home, Practical Photographer, The Field, What Micro* . . . all pretty upmarket, and current issues, at that. Perhaps I should have gone into the law.'

'You *are* in the law, Mike.'

'Yes, but . . .'

'Mr Bassett will see you now.'

Bassett's office was on the second floor, overlooking the High Street. Here, too, were the carefully chosen antiques, the air of solid prosperity which had pervaded his home.

They all sat down and Bassett steepled his fingers in what was clearly an habitual gesture. 'What can I do for you?'

'We've come to ask for your help.'

Bassett waved a hand. 'I told you last time, Thanet, any-thing . . . You have only to ask.'

'I'll be frank with you, sir. We are still not sure why Mrs Parnell came to Sturrenden. It's possible that you are right, that she did indeed come simply to attend the concert. But I think you will agree with me that it is very odd that after living away from Sturrenden for twenty years or so, she is murdered just a few hours after she sets foot in it again.'

'True, but possibly coincidental.'

'Also, possibly not. And you must see that while that possibility exists, that she was killed *because* she came back, for whatever reason, it is clearly our duty to take a close look at her former friends and acquaintances.'

'Including me.'

'Including you, naturally. But in fact, we haven't come here this morning to question you further about your own movements . . .'

'About what, then?'

'You were one of Mrs Parnell's closest friends, and . . .'

'Oh, hardly that, I'd say, Inspector.'

Back to formality now, Thanet noted. 'At any rate, one of the group of young people she went around with during the last summer she was here.'

'But we don't know whether that necessarily was when she was last here. During the past twenty years she could well have made other friends who live in this area.'

'Perhaps. And if so, no doubt we'll find out in due course. But frankly, I doubt it. She was very much tied to her home. Her husband was very dependent on her. He was badly crippled in an accident, on the way back from their honeymoon, and confined to a wheelchair for the rest of their married life. He died about six months ago.'

Bassett's prim little mouth had pursed in concern, 'Poor Alicia. I'm sorry to hear that. She didn't have much of a life, did she?'

'Nor death,' said Thanet grimly. 'So anything you could tell me . . .?'

'About what, then, precisely?'

'I would like to know about the relationships within that group of young people, about their attitudes to each other and to Mrs Parnell. Or anything else you think it might be helpful for me to know, of course.'

Bassett didn't like it. He hooked his thumbs into the armholes of his waistcoat and gave Thanet a long, speculative look. 'Strange,' he said, 'but do you know, even after all this time I experience an uncomfortable frisson of disloyalty when you make a suggestion like that.'

'You did promise us your full cooperation.'

'Yes. Rash of me, wasn't it? These people were my friends, Inspector.'

'And Mrs Parnell was one of them.'

'Death alters the boundaries of what is considered acceptable behaviour, you mean?'

'Wouldn't you agree with that proposition?'

'Perhaps. I suppose so. I have to hand it to you, Thanet. You're no mean tactician. . . . Well, I suppose I shall have to put aside my scruples and do as you ask. . . . Where would you like me to start?'

'Wherever you wish.'

NINE

Bassett drummed his fingers thoughtfully on his desk.

'Since you came to my house on Sunday, Thanet, I've been thinking — well, I suppose it's inevitable that when this kind of tragedy occurs, memories of the past are resurrected. And do you know what seems to me the most ironic thing of all?'

Thanet raised his eyebrows interrogatively.

'That of the six members of our group, the two who were most full of life are now dead.'

'And that both died unnaturally.'

Bassett bowed his head.

In acknowledgement or mourning? Thanet wondered. 'You're talking about Paul Leyton, of course.'

'Yes. He and Alicia . . . the rest of us just revolved around them. They were always the leaders, the ones who suggested what we should do, influenced our thinking, our attitudes . . . Not consciously, mind. It just came naturally to them. And they made it such . . . fun.' Bassett sighed. 'That doesn't seem to be a word one hears much these days, amongst the young. Not that I know many young people, but my impression is that they are looking for stronger meat — thrills, excitement. But in those days . . . well, you'll know yourself, it was different.'

'When did you begin to cohere, as a group?'

'At the beginning of my second year in the sixth. We knew each other before then, of course, in ones and twos, and then, in the November of that year, let me see, it would have been . . .'

'1963, I believe.'

'That's right. 1963. A week or two before Paul's birthday he approached me and said he'd like to get up a theatre outing, but it would be too expensive if they all went up by train. Was there any chance that I would be prepared to drive them up to London, as one of the party? I'd been given this car, you see, when I passed my test in the summer of that year. Of course, I agreed. I don't mind admitting that I was flattered to be included. So, on Paul's birthday, off we all went. It was a marvellous evening and on the way home someone suggested another outing the following Saturday — ice-skating, I believe. And it went on from there.'

'It was a very unbalanced group, as far as the sexes were concerned. Four boys and two girls.'

'True. But it didn't seem to matter, to begin with, anyway.'

'How did it come about?'

Bassett shrugged. 'I think it was the natural outcome of our friendships at the time of that first trip. Richard was Paul's brother, and as it was a birthday celebration I suppose he felt he had to ask him along . . . and Richard was keen on Vivienne, even then, so that's why she was asked. Later on he married her. But I suppose you knew that.'

'I had heard, yes.'

'They've got two children now, in their teens. Anyway, that's why Richard and Vivienne came. Nicky — Nicholas Rain — came because he was Paul's closest friend. And Alicia was Nicky's girlfriend. Then there was me.'

Asked because you were able to provide a mode of transport, thought Thanet. 'So both Alicia and Vivienne started out as girlfriends of boys in the group?'

'Yes . . . well, not exactly, perhaps. Vivienne wasn't as keen on Richard as he was on her, at the time. That came later.'

'Much later, I gather.'

Bassett frowned. 'What do you mean?'

'I understood that Vivienne was attracted to Paul.'

'Ah, yes. You're right, she was. In fact, that was half the trouble. Paul was too attractive — to women, I mean.' Bassett shifted a little in his chair and cleared his throat.

Thanet did not betray his sudden interest. Had that last rider been added a shade too hastily? Because if so . . . he glanced at Lineham and their eyes met. So Mike had spotted it too.

'What do you mean, "half the trouble"?'

'Well, to begin with, there was no problem. We knew where we were. Richard was keen on Vivienne, we all knew that, and we also knew that she wasn't as keen on him. Alicia and Nicky were pretty close, and if they wanted to be alone together, they used to go off by themselves. Then it became obvious that Vivienne had fallen for Paul. And Richard wasn't very happy about that, as you can imagine.'

'Paul reciprocated?'

'Oh no. But that didn't seem to put Vivienne off. Quite the reverse, in fact. She didn't seem to have eyes for anyone else. And then, to complicate matters, we noticed that Alicia was falling for Paul too.'

'When was this?'

'Let me see . . . some time in the Easter holidays, I should say. Nicky was still just as keen on her as he had been all along, but it was obvious to us that Alicia had lost interest. It was all very awkward. Nicky was Paul's best friend, after all, and to begin with, Paul didn't respond. Finally, around the end of April, Alicia broke off with Nicky and I suppose Paul felt that there was then no reason why he shouldn't go out with Alicia if he wanted to. She was a very attractive girl and he really went overboard for her. He'd had lots of dates, but he'd never had a steady girlfriend before and the whole thing was a disaster. The timing was all wrong for him, with his A levels coming up, and his work went to pieces. He couldn't seem to think of anything but Alicia. He was . . . obsessed by her.'

Bassett had betrayed himself. The tone of the last few words had been unmistakeable. Like Hollister, Bassett had bitterly resented Alicia's hold over Paul Leyton, if for a different reason.

Now, he caught Thanet's eye, gave a shame-faced little grin and shrugged, lifting his hands in a disarming gesture of surrender. 'We were all furious with Alicia, for what she did to him. Paul was really brilliant, you know. His death was such a waste . . . and so unnecessary. If only Alicia had waited just a few more weeks, until his exams were over, before breaking off with him, he would have been able to cope better. But to tell him then, with his first A level only a few days away . . . it was unforgiveable.'

'You saw him the evening he died, didn't you?'

'You've been doing your homework I see, Inspector. Yes, I did.'

92

Thanet noticed Bassett's hands begin to curl up on the surface of the desk before the solicitor casually folded them together and put them in his lap out of Thanet's sight.

'You gave him a lift home.'

'Inspector, I've gone along with you so far, but I see absolutely no point whatsover in relating to you an experience which is still painful to me. Everything I had to say on the subject I said at the inquest and is available to you in black and white. So if you don't mind . . .'

'Of course, sir. I didn't mean to distress you.'

'I'm sure you'd feel the same, if one of your closest friends had killed himself and you were the last person to see him alive.'

'I'm sure I should,' said Thanet with sincerity.

Despite his plea to drop the subject, Bassett now couldn't leave it alone.

'You're bound to be left wondering what you said to help push him into it, or what you didn't say that could have prevented it . . .'

'I believe many people felt the same, in the case of Paul Leyton.'

'Yes, that's true. I wasn't the only one.'

'In fact, he seems to have aroused very strong feelings in everyone who knew him.'

Bassett was staring at Thanet but not seeing him.

'So what happened afterwards, as far as the group was concerned?'

'Sorry? Oh, we were all badly shaken, of course. And we just drifted apart. Nicky, Alicia and I had our A levels, so we didn't have much time for social activities in any case. Richard and Vivienne were a year below us, but I had the impression they didn't see much of each other either. And then, soon after the end of term, Alicia and her family moved away.'

'This was a sudden decision, to leave the area?'

Bassett shrugged. 'I've no idea. All I know is that shortly after the inquest the Doyles' house went up for sale. Perhaps her father moved because of his work, perhaps they thought it would be best for Alicia if she could put the tragedy behind her . . .'

'She'd intended going to university, I believe.'

'Yes. She had a place at Bristol. She was pretty bright. But she didn't do nearly as well in her A levels as she'd hoped — failed one of them, I believe — so I suppose they wouldn't take her. She was badly shaken by Paul's death.'

Thanet felt that he'd learned as much as he could at this particular juncture, and he thanked Bassett and left.

'All very interesting, I'm sure,' said Lineham as they went down the stairs. 'But where does it get us, that's what I'd like to know.'

'Patience, Mike. I thought one or two interesting things emerged, didn't you?'

'You mean, the way Bassett felt about Paul Leyton, for example.'

'I thought you'd spotted that. Yes. It seems that Bassett was the outsider in more ways than one.'

'You think the others knew?'

'Quite likely, I imagine. No doubt they were prepared to tolerate him because he was useful to them. Also, I find the whole dynamics of the group interesting. Leyton seems to have been the focal point of it all. The two girls were attracted to him, and if we're right, so was Bassett, and the other two boys were jealous of him. I imagine he must have been under considerable emotional pressure — in fact, it wouldn't surprise me if it was a contributory factor in what happened later.'

'His suicide, you mean?'

'Yes. And it's interesting that when Paul killed himself, the group split up. You might have expected them to stick together for moral support, but they didn't. Perhaps they just couldn't face each other. Perhaps they found it possible to cope with their individual feelings of guilt, but their collective guilt was too much for them. In any case they seem to have cast Alicia in the role of scapegoat, and what I'm wondering is . . .'

'What?' Lineham had unlocked the car and was about to open the door. Now he stopped, facing Thanet across the roof.

'Let's get in.'

Thanet waited until they were settled. 'Well, suppose

someone in the group felt very strongly — passionately, even, about Paul. And suppose that someone blamed Alicia for his death . . .'

'You're suggesting he might have killed her for revenge?'

'Why not? It's as good a motive as any.'

'But with respect, sir . . .'

'Mike, will you stop saying that, every time you're about to disagree with me? It drives me mad. If you've a point to make, make it.'

'I was only going to say it's bit unlikely, isn't it, after twenty years when he'd done nothing about it?'

'I'm not so sure. Consider the matter, Mike. Soon after the tragedy Alicia moves away, out of this person's reach. He hopes he'll get over it in time and he does, to the extent that he goes on living a normal life. But underneath the desire for revenge is still there, biding its time. And then, finally, one day that time comes. Quite by chance he sees Alicia again. He knows that she is only here on a brief visit, and that if he is going to act, he must act swiftly . . .'

'By "he", I presume you also mean "she".'

'You're thinking of Vivienne Leyton?'

'Well if she was in love with Paul Leyton, as Bassett claims, she'd certainly qualify, wouldn't you agree?'

'Mike, you've the soul of a romantic after all! You're suggesting that this apparently happily married woman has for twenty years been yearning for her long-lost love!'

Lineham was not amused. His jaw tightened and he glanced reproachfully at Thanet before saying, 'You know perfectly well what I mean, sir.'

'Oh come on, Mike. Don't take everything so seriously. Of course I know what you mean. And I agree with you. Vivienne Leyton should definitely be considered a suspect.'

Lineham gave him a penetrating glance, as if he suspected that Thanet were still teasing him, and then said, 'Except that strangling is not usually a woman's crime, sir.'

'Beware of generalisations, Mike. The case you're dealing with may always prove to be the exception.'

'Then there's Bassett.'

'Yes.' Thanet absent-mindedly started patting his pockets.

Lineham wound down the window.

'Yes,' repeated Thanet, his fingers closing over the stem of his pipe, 'Now Bassett is quite a promising prospect, I should think.'

Lineham watched with resignation as Thanet began to feed tobacco into the bowl.

Thanet waited until it was drawing well before he said, 'If we're right, and he has got homosexual leanings, and he was deeply attached to Paul, has never found anyone to replace him . . . Yes, I could well imagine a desire for revenge burning away in him like a `slow fuse, all these years. . . . He's too conventional, too embedded in respectability, actively to have tried to seek her out, but when he bumps into her, by chance . . .'

'He knew where she was staying, sir.'

'And that she was going to the concert, that night.'

'And we've only got his word for it that she refused his invitation to have supper with him, afterwards.'

'We must put someone on to checking that useless alibi of his, Mike, that walk he claims to have taken by the river in the moonlight.'

'There is one snag though, sir. Surely, even if Mrs Parnell did accept an invitation to meet him after the concert, and they went back to her hotel to pick up a coat or something, she wouldn't have asked him up to her room? He'd have waited downstairs, in the foyer.'

'True.'

'But,' said Lineham, on a sudden note of excitement, 'how about this? That red folder. Suppose it was really Bassett she had come to Sturrenden to see, that if she hadn't run into him by chance, she'd have engineered a meeting somehow. Suppose she *had* to ask him up to her room because she wanted to show him what was in the folder.'

'What are you suggesting was in it?'

'Compromising photographs of him and Paul Leyton? It could fit, sir. Maybe this could explain why she broke off with Leyton so suddenly — because she'd discovered he and Bassett were carrying on together . . .'

Thanet was shaking his head. 'It's no good, Mike. I can't

really see the Alicia we've been hearing about setting out cold-bloodedly to blackmail someone over something that happened all that time ago.'

'I suppose you're right.' Lineham shrugged. 'Ah well, it was a nice theory . . .'

'Still thinking along the lines of a revenge motive, though, Mike, there's Richard Leyton.'

'Paul's brother? I should think he'd have been more likely to be grateful to Mrs Parnell.'

'For causing his brother's suicide!'

'No, for leaving the way clear for him to get the girl he wanted. From what Bassett was saying, Richard didn't have much of a look in with Vivienne, while Paul was still alive.'

'True. Or there's Hollister. He obviously hated Alicia for destroying his great white hope.'

'Unlikely, sir, surely, that he should have bumped into her by chance. I had the impression that he didn't emerge from his book-burrow from one year's end to the next. And I really can't visualise those two meeting by arrangement. The mind boggles.'

'I admit we're scraping the barrel a bit.'

'So, where next?'

'I think it's about time we met the Leytons, don't you?' Thanet glanced at his watch. 'It's ten to twelve, and Leyton's a farmer. With any luck we might catch him at home for lunch.'

Kent is a county of infinite variety. Between the rolling majesty of the Downs in the north and the flat expanse of Romney Marsh in the south lies some of the richest agricultural land in England. In the flattish area in the middle, known as the Weald, grow the hops for which the county is famous and tourists frequently make a point of visiting the celebrated Whitbread Oast houses near Paddock Wood, where there is an interesting museum of Country Crafts and bygones.

But many feel that the most beautiful area of all is the broad swathe of land encircling the Weald, with its little wooded hills and sheltered valleys, its spreading acres of golden corn and the annual miracle of blossom-time in the spring. In this part of Kent, in summer, little notices sprout everywhere, advertising anything and everything which grows. Everyone, it seems, has green fingers and wishes to profit by his talent. Beginning with tomato plants and brassica seedlings, one may trace the progress of the seasons by the produce set out on little tables by garden gates on the roadside: boxes of bedding plants, punnets of luscious strawberries glistening ruby-red in the sunshine, plump cabbages and fresh greenhouse tomatoes with that distinctive, once-tasted-never-forgotten smell and flavour, bunches of stately gladioli and jaunty dahlias and bags of that crisp, juicy king of apples, the Cox's Orange Pippin.

This is the setting for Bickenden, which lies midway between Sturrenden and Ashford, a tiny village of scattered black and white timbered houses and pretty little red-brick Georgian cottages grouped around a traditional village green with duckpond, church and pub.

Pulling up at the latter to enquire the way of an old man sitting on a bench in the sun with pipe and pint, Thanet gathered that Apple Tree Farm still belonged to Richard's father.

The Leytons senior lived in the main farmhouse, Richard and his family in a 'new' bungalow built for them at the time of their marriage. They found it without difficulty, an impressive, one-storey building set in a large garden surrounded by orchards.

'Very nice,' said Lineham, as they turned into the gravelled driveway. 'They can't be short of a penny.'

'We're not here to assess their income, Mike.'

'Still . . .'

Thanet recognised the woman who opened the door at once by her hair, which haloed her small, pointed face in an elaborately frizzed burning bush. If it hadn't been for this, her most striking feature, he would have passed her in the street without a second glance. There was nothing distinctive about her pale, rather close-set eyes and sharp little nose.

'Mrs Leyton? I'm sorry to trouble you.' He introduced himself and Lineham. 'We're investigating the murder of Mrs Alicia Parnell.'

'Oh.' The frown which had already made permanent lines on her forehead deepened. 'But we've already made a statement. Someone called the other day.'

'Yes, I know. And I do apologise for disturbing you again. But there are one or two points I'd like to go over with you and your husband, if you don't mind.'

She still hesitated. 'It's not very convenient. We're having lunch, and my husband doesn't take a very long break. He's up to his ears with the raspberries, at the moment.'

'Who is it, Viv?'

Vivienne Leyton half-turned, opening the door a little wider, and a man came out of a room at the far end of the hall. Briefly, Thanet experienced a moment of confusion. What was Nicholas Rain doing here, sounding so proprietorial? Then the man came closer and he saw that he had been mistaken. Leyton was slightly taller and slimmer, his hair and beard lighter in colour. Thanet would scarcely have recognised him — but then, nothing alters a man's appearance so much as a luxuriant growth of hair on the face, he told himself.

Once again Thanet said his piece.

Leyton shrugged. 'If we must, I suppose. But I really can't think that we'll have anything to add.'

He led them into a room to the right of the hall, a spacious L-shaped sitting room which ran the depth of the house. The patio doors were wide open and beyond them a green and white striped awning shaded a terrace furnished with swing seat and loungers cushioned in the same fabric. It all looked very civilised and inviting.

Not so the atmosphere in the room. Almost at once Thanet became aware of Mrs Leyton's antagonism towards her husband. She had immediately flopped down into one of the deep chairs and folded her arms across her chest, one swinging foot betraying her irritation. Perhaps she was angry because Leyton had not backed her up and had invited them in, or because the food she had cooked was spoiling. Though she didn't look the domestic type, Thanet thought. Her crisp, well-cut white trousers and yellow and white top wouldn't take kindly to housework.

'If you'd like to finish your lunch, we'd be quite happy to wait,' he said, testing his impression.

'No, no. We'd just about finished, hadn't we, darling?' said Leyton.

In contrast to his wife, he was wearing stained jeans and an open-necked shirt with sweat-marks under the arms.

She didn't bother to reply or even to look at him.

'If we could just get on with it, Inspector.' She spoke in a slow, maddening drawl.

Out of the corner of his eye Thanet saw Lineham tense. The sergeant was less phlegmatic than Thanet, less able to control his reactions. It would be good experience for him to conduct what was obviously going to be a tricky interview. Thanet could always bale him out, if necessary.

'My sergeant has some questions he would like to put to you.' Thanet grinned inwardly at Lineham's quickly suppressed surprise.

'Yes, well . . .' Lineham leafed through his notebook, clearly giving himself a moment or two to collect his thoughts.

Vivienne Leyton gave an exaggerated sigh and rolled her eyes.

'Perhaps we could begin by running quickly through your account of your meeting with Mrs Parnell.'

'Oh, really! But we've been through all that once. What's the point in going over it again?'

'We often find that the second time round, people remember things they didn't the first time, Mrs Leyton.'

'But we were only with the woman a matter of minutes!'

'Nevertheless . . .'

'Come on, Viv,' said Leyton. 'Why waste time prevaricating? The police have their job to do and it won't take long . . . It's all very simple, Sergeant. My wife and I arrived at the Swan at about six-thirty on Saturday evening, for a Rotary Club Ladies' Night. Guests were not due to arrive until seven, but we were early because I had helped to organise the affair, and I had one or two things to see to. Just before seven o'clock we were standing in the foyer when Alicia — Mrs Parnell — came out of the lift, put her key on the reception desk and started to walk towards the door. We'd known her well at one time, before she moved away from Sturrenden, and I recognised her at once — it was astonishing how little she had changed. I pointed her out to my wife and we moved to meet her as she came towards us. We all said hullo, how surprising to see you after all these years, how are you, what are you doing here and so on . . .'

'What did she say, when you asked her that?'

'Said she had some business to attend to.'

'Did she say what it was?'

'No, and I didn't enquire. Then we asked how long she was staying, and she said, just for the night. She told us she was going to the concert. Nicholas Rain was playing in Sturrenden that night and he was a mutual friend. We'd probably have been going ourselves, if it hadn't been for the Ladies' Night, and I said so. Then we said how nice it had been to run into each other, and that was it.'

'Didn't she say something about Mr Bassett?'

'Oh sorry, yes. She said how amazing it was that she'd only been in Sturrenden a few hours and she'd already seen three people she knew. Then she told us she'd run into Bassett in the High Street, earlier on, on her way from the station. And that he was going to the concert too. And that really was it.'

'How did she seem?'

'What do you mean?'

'What sort of a mood was she in? Depressed? Excited? Nervous?'

Leyton frowned and began to stroke his beard. 'I don't know. I hadn't thought about it. She seemed perfectly normal to me. Except that, well, perhaps I'd say she was more subdued than she used to be. But that didn't strike me as surprising. She was much older, after all. What do you think, Viv?'

Mrs Leyton shrugged, the picture of indifference. 'I didn't take much notice, I must confess. She looked older, of course, and her hair was different, she always used to wear it long.'

'Did you happen to notice what she was wearing, Mrs Leyton?'

Vivienne Leyton raised one well-plucked eyebrow. 'Naturally. Black dress, cream jacket, high-heeled black patent sandals.'

'You're very observant. Was she . . .'

'Women always notice clothes, Sergeant. If they take an interest in them themselves, of course.' And she glanced down complacently at her own, brushed an imaginary speck from one white-trousered leg.

'Did you happen to notice if she was carrying anything?'

'A black patent clutch handbag.'

'Nothing else?'

'No.'

'You're certain?'

'Sergeant, if I say she wasn't carrying anything else, she wasn't.'

This was confirmation of what the receptionist had said. So, no red folder, thought Thanet.

'If she had been, I'd certainly have noticed. Why? Should she have been?' For the first time there was a spark of curiosity in Vivienne Leyton's eyes.

Lineham was non-committal. 'We just wanted to check, that's all. You're sure there's nothing you'd like to add to what your husband has said . . .? In that case, perhaps we could move on, to later.'

'What do you mean, later?'

Had there been a hint of wariness in her voice, just then?

Alerted, Thanet studied her closely. She was, he observed, giving Lineham her full attention for the first time, behind a mask of pretended indifference. She ran a hand casually through her mop of hair, stretched out her legs and studied her scarlet toenails — but glanced covertly at her husband, apparently to gauge his reaction to Lineham's question.

'We understand that the dinner ended at ten-fifteen, and that most of the guests then left the Fletcher Hall to . . . er . . . powder their noses and so on, while the room was cleared for dancing.'

He'd have to speak to Lineham about that ridiculous euphemism, thought Thanet.

'So?'

'Is this what you did?'

'Certainly. But I really don't see . . .'

'And you, sir?'

'Yes, certainly.'

'So you split up.'

Vivienne Leyton gave a sarcastic smile. 'Brilliant deduction, Sergeant. Of course, you've noticed that the Swan does not have unisex lavatories.'

'Viv, please. There's no need . . .'

But his wife ignored him. Swinging herself up out of her chair she glared at Thanet. 'Really, Inspector, I simply cannot see the point of sitting here wasting time answering pointless questions. Besides, my husband has to get back to work and I have an appointment in Ashford at one-fifteen, so if you don't mind . . .'

What was she afraid of? Thanet wondered. 'Do sit down again, Mrs Leyton,' he said patiently. 'We realise how very irritating this must be for you, but you must understand that this is a serious business. Mrs Parnell, a former friend of yours, has been *murdered*. Now I'm quite sure that if you had been murdered, your husband would expect us to explore every possible avenue . . .'

'Aha. I see. So that's it, is it? It's her husband who's pushing you . . .'

'No one is pushing me,' said Thanet. His voice had become ominously quiet and Lineham gave him an apprehensive glance. Thanet invariably treated witnesses with courtesy and his patience was legion, but press him too far and he became formidable.

'So you *say*.'

'*Viv!*'

But she was not to be deterred. 'She was wearing a wedding ring, I noticed. And a flashy engagement ring . . .'

'Mrs Leyton! Mrs Parnell's husband is dead. He was a cripple. They were in a serious accident on the way back from their honeymoon and Mrs Parnell spent the rest of her married life nursing him. Apart from an elderly father who is away on holiday and still doesn't know of his daughter's death, there is no one, no one at all, to take an interest in whether we solve this case or not. Sergeant Lineham and I are, believe it or not, merely trying to do our job, and it is our experience that most members of the public are prepared to be cooperative in making that job as easy as possible for us. So we'd be grateful if *you* would stop wasting *our* time and answer our few remaining questions as succinctly as possible.'

There was a dead silence, then Vivienne Leyton tossed her head. 'My word, what have we here? A dedicated policeman, no less . . .'

'Viv, for heaven's sake!'

'Oh, very well. I can see that you're not going to go away until you're satisfied, so let's get on with it, shall we?' And she plumped down in her chair again, her face settling into familiar lines of sulkiness and frustration.

Thanet allowed himself a moment or two to regain his composure.

'You were with a party of friends, at the dinner?'

'Acquaintances, Inspector, not friends. But yes, we were.'

'Their names and addresses, please.'

'Oh, really . . .'

'I'll write them down for you,' said Leyton, rising. He took a sheet of paper from a writing desk in the corner and began to scribble.

'And after the dinner was over, the ladies and gentlemen parted company?'

'To powder our noses, as your sergeant so delicately put it.

Yes. At least, the ladies did, I'm not sure about the men. Make-up isn't much in their line.'

Leyton shot a furious glance at his wife. 'We went to the men's room, yes, Inspector.'

'And did you both stay with the other members of your party throughout the interval?'

'I didn't,' said Leyton. 'I had to go and check on the arrangements for the raffle.'

'And that would have been at what time?'

'Around ten-twenty-five, I should think. Dancing began at ten-forty-five.'

So Leyton had been free to wander around the hotel at will, at the very time when Alicia must have arrived back from the concert. Had they run into each other a second time?

'Did you see Mrs Parnell at any point, during the interval?'

'No.'

'Did you, Mrs Leyton?'

'Absolutely not. And if you want to know what I was doing during that vital half an hour, I really can't remember.'

Her mocking, dismissive tone infuriated Thanet, but he didn't show it. He'd already once given her the satisfaction of knowing just how much her deliberate needling was annoying him, and he had no intention of allowing it to happen again.

'Try.'

She gave him a defiant look. 'I have. And I told you, I really can't remember.' She lifted one languid hand and made a vague gesture which was clearly intended to convey the haziness of her recollection. 'We'd had rather a lot to drink, at dinner. I expect I drifted around chatting to people I knew. That's what one usually does on such occasions.'

'Here you are, Inspector.' Leyton handed Thanet the sheet of paper.

There were six names on it, three married couples, by the look of it.

'Thank you . . . Well, I think that's all, for the moment.'

Vivienne Leyton sat up. 'What do you mean, "for the moment"? We've told you all we know, every last, trivial detail . . .'

Thanet was folding the paper and putting it in his wallet.

'It hasn't struck you as strange, that after being away from Sturrenden for twenty years, Alicia Parnell returns and almost at once is murdered?'

'Strange? What do you mean, strange?'

'Too much of a coincidence, perhaps?'

'What are you implying?'

She was afraid. He knew it. Behind that implacably hostile façade, she was afraid. But, of what, exactly? Was she his quarry? 'I should think, Mrs Leyton, that the implication is obvious. Someone in Sturrenden had some kind of grudge against her.'

Vivienne Leyton gave a harsh laugh. 'A grudge that's lasted twenty years? What a ridiculous idea!'

'In any case,' said her husband, 'what conceivable grudge could anyone have had against Alicia?'

'That's what I'm hoping someone will tell me. Has either of you any suggestions?'

Leyton shook his head and his wife muttered, 'Preposterous idea . . .'

'Is it, Mrs Leyton?' Thanet looked at her husband. 'I understand a lot of people blamed her for your brother's suicide.'

Leyton didn't flinch, but the edges of his eyelids twitched, almost imperceptibly. 'My brother has been dead for *twenty years*, Inspector. That's all long past, long forgotten.'

'Is it? People have long memories, you'd be surprised.'

'Who've you been talking to?' said Vivienne Leyton sharply. 'Nicky? No, he wouldn't stoop so low. Oliver, then. It must be Oliver, Oliver Bassett. Am I right?'

Thanet said nothing.

'You see, Richard,' she said, with a triumphant glance at her husband. 'He can't deny it — either that, or he hasn't got the guts to admit it, it comes to the same thing. Well, Inspector, I must say I certainly don't envy you your job, going around digging up dirt that's twenty years old.'

'Every job has its unpleasant aspects, Mrs Leyton.'

'And some more unpleasant than others, eh? Well, dig all you like, you won't find anything that rebounds on us, will he, Richard?'

'Is it really necessary, to . . . to go into all that again,

Inspector?' The skin around Leyton's eyes had gone very pale, in contrast to his deep tan.

'To be honest with you, Mr Leyton, I don't know. But you can be sure that I mean to find out. Thank you for your help. We can see ourselves out.'

Outside, Lineham said, 'My God, what a woman! Imagine . . .'

Thanet laid a hand on his arm. 'Shh . . . Listen, they're not watching, so walk across to the car, making as much noise as you can on the gravel, get in and drive off, tooting your horn at the gate, to make sure they think you've gone. Go a hundred yards or so down the lane, then find a convenient place to park. I'll be with you as soon as I can.'

'What are you going to do?'

Thanet shook his head impatiently. 'Tell you later. Just do as I say, will you?'

ELEVEN

While Lineham crunched across the drive Thanet moved quietly along the paved path which ran along the front of the house, conscious of the pungent scent of rosemary as his legs brushed the low bushes on his right. At the corner he waited while the sergeant got into the car, then used the crackle of tyres on gravel to cover the sound of his movement along the side of the house as far as the open patio doors.

As he had guessed, Richard and Vivienne Leyton were in the middle of a full-scale row. He didn't like what he was doing, disapproved of eavesdropping, and would consciously have gone out of his way to make his presence felt if he had found himself in this sort of situation in his private life. But this was murder, the most heinous crime in the book, and he was certain that Vivienne Leyton had been covering something up. This way, he might find out what it was. He prayed that no one would spot him, and quickly thought up a specious question to ask, if he were discovered.

'. . . don't care what you say, if you hadn't insisted on going to talk to the bloody woman in the first place, none of this would be happening.'

'Oh come on, Viv, be reasonable. I just thought it would be nice to say hullo to her. I didn't think . . .'

'Oh God, you're so naive . . . No, you never do think, do you, that's half your trouble. Jump in first and regret it afterwards, that's you all over. I told you at the time I'd rather not have anything to do with her, but oh no, you have to have your own way . . .'

'You didn't protest that much, as I remember.'

'Well of course I bloody didn't! What d'you expect me to do, make a scene in the middle of the foyer? But I told you I didn't want to talk to her, and that should have been enough.'

'Oh it should, should it? And don't I get any say in the

matter? What about what I want? I admit that as it's turned out, it would have been better if we hadn't spoken to her, but how was I to know that she would get herself murdered later on the same night?'

'Oh, so you do admit that you might just have been wrong?'

'For wanting to say hullo to an old friend? No, why should I?'

'Despite the fact that she just happened to be the "friend" who drove your own brother to his death?'

'Ah, now we're getting to the heart of it, aren't we? That's the point, isn't it? You've never forgiven her for what she did to your precious Paul.'

'My precious Paul! Well, I like that! He was your brother, too, remember. I shouldn't have thought you'd exactly be eager to get down on your knees and thank her . . . Or perhaps that's it. Perhaps you *were* grateful to her, have been grateful to her all these years. Yes, I'd never thought of it quite like that before, but I see, now . . . You'd never be where you are today, would you, if Paul had still been alive? After all, he was the eldest son . . . You wouldn't now be expecting to inherit your father's farm, would you, if Paul were still with us, he'd either have got the lot or you'd have been forced to sell up to give him his share . . .'

'For God's sake, Viv, Paul wasn't interested in farming, and you know it. All he cared about was his work . . .'

'Your parents wouldn't have been able to afford to build this house for us, either, would they, if they'd had to see Paul through Oxford. . . . And one thing's for sure, you wouldn't have got me, either.'

Leyton murmured something inaudible.

'What did you say? Go on, say it aloud, like a man.'

'I said, perhaps you weren't much of a bargain, after all.'

'Oh, so the worm's turning at last, is he? Well, let me tell you this, you're not half the man your brother was, you never have been and you never will be. You don't measure up to him in any way, in brains, in looks . . .'

'And in bed?'

Leyton's voice was very quiet and Thanet had to strain to hear him. Was this a scene which had been enacted many times before between these two, over the years? What a soul-destroying way to live, he thought.

'Unfortunately I nèver had that pleasure, as well you know. Alicia,' and she spat the name out, 'got there first.'

'Are you sure of that?'

'What do you mean?'

'Do you *know*, are you absolutely certain, that Alicia went to bed with Paul?'

'Not *know*.' For the first time Vivienne Leyton sounded unsure of herself. 'I just assumed . . .'

'Ah, I thought so.'

'What's that supposed to mean?'

Silence.

'What do you mean, "I thought so"?'

Still no response from her husband.

'Richard, you can't just stop there. You can't drop mysterious hints and then just back off, refuse to speak. What did you mean? What were you implying?'

'It doesn't matter.' Leyton's voice was scarcely more than a murmur.

Vivienne Leyton gave a little moan of exasperation. ' "It doesn't matter", he says. You make me mad!' she went on in a low, furious voice. 'You make me so mad I feel as though I'm going to explode with sheer frustration. You're always doing this, winding me up and then pulling out . . . I suppose you just haven't got the guts to see it through. You're pathetic, do you know that, pathetic . . .'

Her voice had been rising and now Leyton had to shout to make himself heard. 'All right! I'll tell you!'

There was a sudden silence in which Leyton's last words seemed to echo, and it was only now that Thanet became aware of their complex tone. There was desperation in them, mingled with despair and yes, too, a hint of satisfaction. Whatever else had been said during this conversation, this, at least, was going to be news to Vivienne Leyton. And she wasn't going to like it one little bit.

'You blame Alicia for Paul's death, don't you, Viv? You always have.'

'Yes. Well, everybody did. The inquest . . .'

Leyton laughed, an unpleasant sound. 'The inquest. Ah, yes. But you see, my dear Vivienne, the fact of the matter is that the whole truth did not come out at the inquest.'

'What do you mean?' She was beginning to sound alarmed. 'And how do you know?'

'I know because I was the one who withheld the information.'

She was silenced at last.

'Shall I tell you what that information was, my darling? Very well, I will. Yes, I can see you want to hear. You do, don't you? *Don't you?*'

'Yes! Yes, of course I do.'

'Of course she does!' mocked Leyton.

He was certainly enjoying the prospect of this revenge, whatever it was, thought Thanet. And by now he had an inkling of what was coming.

'Very well, I'll tell you . . . my dear brother Paul didn't kill himself because Alicia had broken off with him. He killed himself because that very night he had discovered that it was *men* he was attracted to.'

Dead silence.

Then Vivienne Leyton made a little choking sound. 'I don't believe you.' The words were almost a whisper. 'You . . . you're making it up.'

'I am not.'

'Yes you *are*!' She had found her voice again and almost shrieked her distress and disbelief. 'You're lying. You're just trying to . . . to besmirch Paul's memory, that's all. You've always resented the fact that he was cleverer than you, more popular than you . . . and that I loved him, I've always loved him.'

'Maybe that's true. Maybe I have always resented those things, as you say. But, my dear wife, I am not lying about this. I actually saw them in bed together, him and Oliver Bassett.'

'No!'

'Yes. Come on, take your hands away from your ears. All these years I've had to listen to you telling me how inferior I am to Paul, now you listen to me for a change . . .'

111

'No . . . it's not true . . . I don't believe you. . . . Let go of my hands, let *go* . . . you're hurting me!'

Thanet braced himself. He didn't want to intervene, had no real right, even, to interfere in a row between man and wife in their own home. But he couldn't just stand by while violence was done only a few feet away . . .

'Sit down,' shouted Leyton. 'Go on, sit *down*. . . . Right, now whether you like it or not, you're just going to sit there and listen until I've finished what I've got to say. And it's in your own interests to hear it. After all, if you don't, you'll never know whether I was telling the truth or not, will you? You can judge for yourself. That's better . . .'

Thanet relaxed a little. It sounded as though the threatened flash-point had been averted, for the moment at least.

'Well now, if you remember, after leaving Alicia that night, Paul ran into Oliver, and Oliver gave him a lift home. Now, according to what Oliver said at the inquest, when they arrived at our house, Paul asked him in for a cup of coffee. Do you remember all this?'

Vivienne Leyton must have nodded.

'Then you probably also remember that I said I'd got home about ten-fifteen that night, that my parents were out and I went straight up to bed. The light was out in Paul's room, I said, the door was closed and I thought he must still be out with Alicia. So I never looked in. Agreed?'

Again, he must have waited for her nod.

'Well, now I'll tell you what really happened. . . . It was nearer a quarter to ten than a quarter past when I got home. I'd seen Oliver's car outside, of course, so I knew he was there, but when I got in there was no sign of either him or Paul. But I could hear music, upstairs, and I thought they must be playing records in Paul's bedroom. So I went up. Paul's door was shut, but the light was on, so I looked in. And I saw them . . . No, just listen. You *will* listen. I *saw* them, I tell you, with my own eyes. On the bed. And there was no mistaking what they were doing . . .'

'No!' shrieked Vivienne Leyton. 'I don't believe you. You're making it all up. You're jealous of Paul, you've always been jealous . . .'

112

'Maybe I have,' shouted Leyton, 'but this is the *truth* I'm telling you. Every word is the truth, I swear it. And Paul saw me. I . . . I didn't wait, I just backed out, quickly, and shut the door behind me. I couldn't believe it. I was shocked, disgusted, upset . . .'

'Upset!'

'Yes, upset! Of course I was bloody upset! I was only seventeen and he was my *brother* . . . I went into my room and locked the door. A little while later I heard Oliver leave. My parents still weren't home, and a few minutes later Paul came and knocked at my door. I didn't answer. He had to talk to me, he said. What I'd seen . . . it had never happened before and it wouldn't happen again . . . I just couldn't bring myself to let him in, face him. I couldn't get that picture of him and Oliver on the bed out of my mind . . . I buried my head in the pillow and in the end he gave up, went away.'

'So it was your fault! Your fault, that he killed himself! I expect he thought you'd go sneaking to your parents in the morning . . .'

'Rubbish. I'd never have done that, and he knew it.'

'He thought he wouldn't be able to face you, then . . .'

'You didn't really know Paul very well, did you, Viv? If you had, you'd know that that wouldn't be what was worrying him. It was himself he couldn't face.'

'Anyway, I don't believe a word of all this. It's nonsense, it's rubbish, you're making it all up, out of spite . . .'

'You can believe it or not, as you like. But it's the truth. And what's more, inside, I bet you know it. You know me. Faults I may have, like anyone else, but spiteful I am not. And what possible other reason could I have, for making up a story like this?'

'Perhaps you thought that if you managed to destroy Paul in my eyes, I might forget about him, and turn to you . . .'

'Oh, Viv,' and there was a profound sadness in Leyton's voice, 'do you think I could ever really hope for that? You've made it pretty obvious, over the years, what you think of me . . .'

'All right, then, just tell me this. If all this is true — and I'm only saying "if", mind — why haven't you come out with it before? Why wait till now?'

'What was the point of telling you? I certainly had no intention of letting it out at the inquest. The row with Alicia was
evidence enough for them . . . I had to think of my parents,
too. Imagine how upset they would have been, if it had been
made public. And then, later . . . well, as I say, there didn't
seem to be any point. I felt a loyalty to Paul . . . Oh, there's no
need to look at me like that, I did, I tell you. And he wasn't
here, to defend himself . . . I don't suppose I would ever have
told you, if it hadn't been for this Alicia business, resurrecting
it all. Viv, don't look at me like that. . . . Don't cry. Don't.
I'm sorry. I suppose I shouldn't have told you, even now. It's
just that I was sick and tired of you holding him up as some
sort of model of perfection . . . Viv, please . . .'

'Leave me alone.' She was crying openly now, noisy, tearing sobs. 'Get away from me, don't touch me . . .'

There was a flurry of movement, a door slammed, and then
silence.

Thanet moved quietly away from the patio doors, ran
across the lawn to the front gate and hurried down the lane to
the car, where Lineham was waiting.

Lineham opened the door for him, from inside. 'What was
all that about?'

'I could tell a row was brewing, and I knew Mrs Leyton was
holding something back. I thought I might find out what it
was.'

'And did you?'

'No. She was deflected.' And Thanet told Lineham what he
had heard.

Lineham pursed his lips. 'So we were right about Bassett.'

'So it seems.'

'If Leyton was telling the truth. D'you think he was?'

'Yes. It all hangs together, makes sense. And if you could
have heard him . . . Oh yes, he was telling the truth, all right.
Twenty years ago homosexuality was a very different matter
from nowadays. Shrouded in shame and secrecy.'

'I don't know that things have changed all that much, actually. I often think that despite all the noise the "gay" groups
make, ordinary people still feel pretty much the same about it.'

'In a small town like this, anyway, yes, I tend to agree. It certainly wouldn't have done Bassett any good, if the truth had come out.'

'Anyhow, it seems that Mrs Parnell didn't come down just to go to the concert. What do you think she meant, by "business to attend to", sir?'

'Your guess is as good as mine. It's a deliberately vague expression, isn't it? One thing's certain, though. There was a good deal of pretty strong emotion floating about in that group of youngsters, and a lot of it is still about today. We should never underestimate the power of the past, Mike. If you'd heard those two going at each other, you'd never have believed they were talking about something that happened all those years ago.'

'But they're different from the others, sir, in that they're married. They'll have had twenty years of other arguments — pretty unhappy years, by the sound of it — to fuel a row like the one you just heard.'

'True. Nevertheless I wouldn't mind betting that this particular issue — Vivienne Leyton's idolisation of Paul — is the one that has underlain all those other disagreements over the years.'

'Well, if she still feels as strongly as that, we certainly shouldn't rule her out as a suspect, strangling or no strangling.'

'I agree.'

'Though if what Richard Leyton says about the night of Paul's suicide is true. I'm not sure it doesn't rule Bassett out.'

'I don't follow you, Mike.'

'Well surely, in the circumstances he'd be blaming himself, more than Alicia Parnell . . .'

'I don't see why. Richard Leyton didn't say that Bassett had seen him, when he put his head into Paul's bedroom, that night. Bassett may well have known nothing about it. He may still simply think that his attempt at "consolation" failed.'

Lineham's bleeper sounded. 'Wonder what that's about.'

They drove back to the village and Thanet waited in the car while Lineham phoned. The sergeant made two calls, and was frowning when he emerged from the phone box. He had left the receiver off the hook, Thanet noticed.

'What is it, Mike?'

'It's Louise. Apparently she saw a house she really fell in love

115

with, this morning. It's just what we're looking for, she said, and I must say it sounds almost too good to be true — right type, right size, good position, fair price . . .'

'The one in Frittenden Road you were telling me about on Sunday?'

'No. That was hopeless. We only got the details of this one this morning.'

'So what's the problem?'

'Someone else was shown over it before Louise and they're coming back this afternoon — it's not an agent's ploy, she actually saw the woman and heard her say she'd like her husband to see it. She's afraid they might get in first, with an offer.'

'So she wants you to take a look at it?'

Lineham nodded sheepishly. 'I'm sorry, sir, I told her I didn't think I could get off, but she insisted I ask you . . .'

'Where is it?'

'In Market Cut.'

'That little cul-de-sac off Market Street?'

'That's right.'

'Very nice, too. Well, there's no difficulty there. We haven't had anything to eat yet, so if you want to go hungry and spend your lunch hour looking at houses . . . Tell her you'll be there in ten minutes.'

'Thank you, sir.' Lineham ran back to the phone box and returned beaming.

'If you like the place as much as she does, you can get it all sorted out on the spot. I'll drive, then I can drop you off and you can walk back to the office afterwards.'

The Market Square in Sturrenden lies at the lower end of the town, just before the river bridge, a broad, cobbled area which is really an extension of the High Street. Market Street leads off it at right angles, following the curve of the river and eventually leading out into open country. The houses here are very old, many of them falling into disrepair, and it has been rumoured that one day in the not too distant future they will all be pulled down to make way for a new leisure complex. Thanet hoped that that day would never come. He loved the picturesque juxtaposition of lathe and plaster, ancient beams, mellow stone and rosy brick, the irregular peaks and slopes of the roofs of old red Kentish peg tiles, the encapsulated history of Sturrenden which these houses still preserve for the seeing eye to read.

Market Cut was once, as its name implies, a link between two streets, but when the inevitable one-way system was introduced into Sturrenden some years ago, one end was blocked off with bollards to prevent traffic siphoning off into the chaos that is Market Street on market days, and it is now a pleasant little cul-de-sac of a dozen Victorian semi-detached houses facing each other demurely across wide pavements planted with cherry trees which are a froth of pink blossom in the spring. The situation is ideal, within walking distance of the High Street and the river, yet tranquil, undisturbed by the noise of passing traffic.

Thanet said so.

'Handy for work, too,' said Lineham with a grin.

The For Sale notice was half-way along on the left-hand side and Louise was waiting outside with the estate agent, her sturdy figure in its bright cotton sundress a splash of vivid colour in the shade cast by one of the cherry trees. She ran to the car as they pulled up, and spoke through the open window. 'Oh, Mike, I'm so glad you could come. You'll love it, I know you will. It's exactly what we've been looking for.'

Her cheeks were flushed with excitement, her eyes shining.

Thanet was surprised that she should betray her enthusiasm to the man waiting at the gate. Louise was normally cautious, sensible, restrained. But then, if there really were other prospective purchasers in the offing, she and Mike would probably have to offer the full price anyway. And it was good to see her so animated. She was smiling at Thanet, now.

'It's kind of you to spare him.'

Thanet smiled back. 'It's his lunch hour. I told him, if he wants to starve, that's his affair. See you back at the office, then, Mike.'

'Right, sir.'

Bentley pounced on Thanet the moment he stepped through the door.

'There's a girl waiting to see you, sir. Been here for an hour or so. A Miss Carol Marsh.'

117

Carol . . . The girl from Jobline? The one Jessica Ross didn't approve of? 'What's it about, do you know?'

'She wouldn't say. She works in Mrs Parnell's employment agency.'

She must have come down from London especially to see him. Excitement flared. She wouldn't have bothered, if it hadn't been important.

'Where is she?'

'In interview room three, sir.'

'Tell her I'll be with her in a quarter of an hour. I just want to see what's on my desk. Offer her something to eat, and a cup of tea. Oh, and see if you can get Doc Mallard on the phone for me, will you? The PM should be finished by now.' Not that he expected anything very startling there, but you never knew.

He took the stairs two at a time. The phone was ringing in his office. He snatched it up.

'Luke? Mallard here.'

'That was quick.'

'Don't know what you mean. It took the usual length of time.'

'Not the PM. Finding you.'

'Finding me? What are you talking about?'

'I asked . . . Oh, never mind. Anything interesting?'

'You could say that.'

'Oh?'

'Cause of death was asphyxia, of course, as we thought. Manual strangulation. The hyoid was broken.'

'And?'

'This is the interesting bit.'

Thanet listened intently and when he had put the phone down, sat for a few moments staring into space.

He wondered what Lineham would make of this.

TWELVE

Perched on one of the metal chairs in the grey anonymity of the interview room, heels hooked over the lower rung and shoulders hunched, Carol Marsh looked like a dejected budgerigar. The spikes of her orange-dyed hair were limp at the tips as if fierce emotion had melted the wax with which she had stiffened them, and copious tears had streaked her cheeks with mascara. Her skimpy mini-dress, boldly striped in green and yellow, emphasised her skinny body, sharp elbows and stick-like legs. She looked up as Thanet entered and slowly her red-veined eyes focused on his face.

He smiled at her. 'Miss Marsh?'

She gave an almost imperceptible nod.

'I believe you wanted to see me. Detective-Inspector Thanet.'

'You're in charge of the . . . you're investigating the . . .' But she couldn't bring herself to say it. More tears welled up, spilled over and began to roll down her cheeks. She dabbed at them with a sodden, balled-up handkerchief, shook her head hopelessly and said, 'I'm sorry, I just can't seem to stop.'

'That's all right. Don't worry about it. I quite understand.'

Thanet turned to the Woman Police Constable standing patiently near the door and said in an undertone, 'Fetch a box of tissues, will you?'

He waited in silence until she returned. Carol Marsh took the box with an attempt at a smile. 'Ta.' She pushed her wet handkerchief into her white plastic shoulder bag.

When she had mopped at her eyes and blown her nose Thanet said, 'I'm in charge of the enquiries into the death of Mrs Parnell, if that's what you wanted to know.'

'Yes,' she said gratefully. She was looking a little more composed now. 'Sorry to be so stupid.'

'I told you. Don't worry.'

'I've been off sick, so I didn't hear about it till this morning.' She shook her head. 'I just couldn't believe it.' The tears threatened again and she straightened her shoulders, drew a deep breath.

'You were obviously very fond of Mrs Parnell.'

'She was . . .' Carol took another deep breath, tried again. 'Yes, I was. She was very good to me.'

'In what way?'

The thin shoulders lifted, fell. 'All sorts of ways. This was the first job I ever really wanted to make a go of, you see, and I was scared stiff of making a mess of it.'

'How long have you worked at the agency?'

'Just over a year, now.' She was beginning to relax and she gave an incredulous little laugh. 'Can you believe it? A year! Who'd ever have thought I'd have stuck at any job that long! Not me, that's for sure. Do you know, before I went there, I'd had twenty different jobs in six months?'

'You're saying that it was because of Mrs Parnell that you stayed?'

She scowled. 'Well it certainly wasn't because of Miss High-and-Mighty Ross, that's for sure. But Mrs Parnell . . . Right from the very first day she was really good to me. Started off by saying not to worry if I made mistakes at first, it was pefectly natural in a new job, everyone did, and she was sure I'd soon get the hang of things . . . Catch Miss Ross saying something like that! I won't be staying on there now, that's for sure. I don't think I could stand it.'

'Why not?'

'She's always breathing down our necks, checking up on what we're doing. And it makes me nervous, so I keep making mistakes. And if I do . . . oh boy, the fuss she makes . . . I should think they could hear her at the other end of the Fulham Road. But Mrs Parnell . . . Oh God, here we go again,' she said, as the tears suddenly spilled over once more. She shook her head hopelessly. 'I just can't seem to stop,' she said again.

It occurred to Thanet that this strange little waif-like creature was the first person he had met who could truly be said to mourn Alicia's death. He waited until she had calmed down, then said, 'Do you feel able, now, to tell me why you've come?'

She nodded. 'When I heard about Mrs Parnell . . . and saw *her* lording it over everything . . . I felt I just had to tell someone.' She blew her nose and sat up straighter in her chair. 'About the rows, I mean.' There was defiance in her voice, as if Jessica Ross were present and still exercising authority over her.

'Between Mrs Parnell and Miss Ross?'

'Yes. Old cow,' she muttered. 'She's got no . . . no . . .' She sought for the word and found it, triumphantly. 'No *humanity*, that's what. She knew how Mrs Parnell had felt about Mr Parnell. He was terrific. You knew he was in a wheelchair, had been for years?'

She waited for Thanet's nod before continuing. 'Not that you'd ever hear him complain, mind. Mrs Parnell did everything for him, you know. It was really lovely to see them together, you could tell just by looking at them how fond of each other they were.'

Her eyes were dreamy now and Thanet could see how deeply she had been touched by the Parnells' devotion. He found himself wondering what kind of background this girl had come from. A tough one, probably, possibly a broken home or at any rate one where love and tenderness were totally lacking. Which was perhaps why she needed to shout her identity with that hideous hair-style, those shrieking colours . . . He refocused his attention on what she was saying.

'. . . so upset, when he died.'

'This was about six months ago, wasn't it?'

'In February, yes. I'd seen the difference in him myself, since I first started at Jobline. He was ill more and more often and then, towards the end of January, he got this chest infection he just couldn't shake off. In the end it turned to pneumonia and he had to go into hospital. He died two days later. Mrs Parnell was that upset . . . She more or less lived at the hospital, while he was in, and then afterwards she just shut herself away in her flat, didn't want to see anyone. I put a note through the door, saying if she wanted me to do anything, anything at all, she only had to ask — shopping, cleaning, anything, but she just wrote me a few lines back saying she preferred to be by herself for the moment, she had to get used to living alone and she might as well start now. And that Miss Ross . . . well, you could see she enjoyed being in charge, bossing us around and throwing her weight about. . . . Of course, when Mrs Parnell came back to work Miss Ross didn't dare carry on like that, and it used to make me mad, it really did, to see how different she was with her, all smarmy and helpful, when behind her back . . . I really can't think why Mrs Parnell made her a partner. I should think it was the worst thing she ever did.'

'Maybe she was grateful to Miss Ross for taking the weight of the business off her shoulders, while she was unable to cope.'

Carol shrugged. 'I dunno. It's beyond me. Anyway, Faith and me weren't suprised when, once Miss Ross had got what she wanted, got that partnership, she started acting different towards us in front of Mrs Parnell — oh, only in little ways at first. But Mrs Parnell noticed. Sometimes I'd see her look at Miss Ross in a funny way, as if she didn't quite recognise her. And then, of course, Mrs Parnell started slipping up herself — only in small things, mind, and anyway it wasn't surprising, was it, after what she'd been through?'

'It takes a long time to get over the death of someone you love, especially if you've been as close as Mr and Mrs Parnell obviously were.'

'Just what I said to Faith! But do you think Miss Ross understood that? You bet she didn't! I don't suppose that woman has ever loved anyone but herself in her whole life. I mean, you couldn't really expect Mrs Parnell to be able to concentrate on her work as if nothing had happened, could you? But Miss Ross did. And of course, it made her mad when Mrs Parnell made mistakes and even more mad because she didn't dare show it. She used to take it out on us instead. But things weren't too bad until Mrs Parnell began leaving the office without telling Miss Ross. And then . . . Well, you can imagine, can't you? Talk about thunderstorms! Miss Ross used to carry on like crazy, banging about the office and muttering to herself about irresponsibility and so on. Faith and me hardly dared breathe, let alone open our mouths. As I said to Faith, who could blame Mrs Parnell for wanting to get out of the place from time to time? And if she didn't choose to give explanations, why should she? She was the boss, after all.'

'Do you happen to know where Mrs Parnell went, on those occasions?'

Carol shook her head. 'No idea. It wasn't my business and as far as I was concerned she could go off as much as she liked. If it meant extra work for the rest of us, that was just too bad. And Faith felt the same . . . Anyway, as I say, the atmosphere got worse and worse. And then, for no reason that we could see, Miss Ross suddenly started being all sweetness and light again.'

'When was this?'

'About a month ago. Faith and me couldn't believe it. Before then, if Mrs Parnell had gone out without telling her, Miss Ross would have been giving her black looks for the rest of the day, and you could have cut the atmosphere with a knife. And then, as I say, suddenly, no complaints, nothing was too much trouble . . . We wondered what she was up to, I can tell you.'

'You thought she had an ulterior motive?'

'That woman wouldn't be nice to her own grandmother unless she was hoping to get something out of her. And then, last week, I found out what was behind it all.'

Carol sat forward on her chair, lowered her voice, as if Jessica Ross were listening outside the door. 'It was on Wednesday, late in the afternoon. Faith and me had both finished work for the day, and left. I'd only gone a few yards down the road when I realised I'd left behind the book I'd bought in my lunch hour. I'd put it in the drawer of my desk. Well I'd been looking forward to starting it that evening — it was the new Danielle Steel, she's my favourite author — so I went back for it. The office wasn't locked up yet, so I just walked in, and I heard them arguing straight away — well, I heard Miss Ross, that is. The door of the inner office was ajar and the outer office is carpeted, so they didn't hear me.'

She paused dramatically and then said, 'They were arguing about the will.'

'Mrs Parnell's will?'

Carol nodded solemnly. Her eyes, Thanet noticed, were beautiful, a clear green flecked with gold.

'Don't you *see*?' she said impatiently.

Thanet saw several things. He saw the implication of what she was saying, but he also saw that Carol was deeply distressed by Alicia's death and anxious to see her murderer brought to justice. He saw too that she was very anti-Ross and that her feelings might have caused her to jump to a conclusion which had little foundation in fact.

'I think I'd like to hear more, first, before I can say that I "see" anything.'

She shrugged. 'Fair enough.'

She leaned back in her chair, hooking one bony knee over the other and smoothing the cheap cotton material over her thighs. Now that she had overcome her initial distress her natural ebullience was reasserting itself, and despite the gaudy colours Thanet thought that if he had met her now he would have likened her to a pert little Cockney sparrow rather than a budgerigar. There was something very engaging about her, something which aroused both his sympathy and his admiration and at the same time made him feel curiously protective towards her. He could understand why she had quickened Alicia's maternal instinct.

'Well, as I said, they were talking about Mrs Parnell's will. Miss Ross was saying that she thought they ought to . . . how did she put it? Now let me get this right . . . She thought they ought to regularise the position, that's it. By which she meant, make a will in each other's favour.'

'She actually said so?'

'Yes.'

'You're certain of this?'

'Course I am. Oh, I see. I know what you're thinking. You think I'm making it all up, because I can't stand Miss Ross.'

'I didn't say that . . .'

'You didn't have to, did you? Well you're wrong, see. I'll tell you exactly what they said, and you can make up your own mind. Like I said, Miss Ross was talking. And what she said, *her very words*, was, "I think the only satisfactory thing to do would be for both of us to leave our share to the other. Then we'd both be secure." '

Carol had caught the imperious, overbearing tones of Jessica Ross's voice exactly, and Thanet had to suppress a smile.

'And what did Mrs Parnell have to say to that?'

'She said — and I'd never heard her sound so cross before — "I would remind you, Jessica, that Kenneth and I spent many years building this business up. You and I are not equal partners and I'm really beginning to wonder if I've made a serious mistake, in offering you any kind of partnership at all." Then Miss Ross tried to say something and Mrs Parnell said, "No, Jessica, *you* listen to *me*. I shall make my will when I'm ready to do so, and not before. But I can assure you of this. When I do, you will not be a beneficiary. I have my own family to think of." And Miss Ross burst out, "But your father's *old*. He's in his seventies. What if he . . ." And Mrs Parnell said, "I'm not referring to my father. And now, if you don't mind, I've had just about enough of this . . ." Well, I didn't wait to hear any more. I just grabbed my book and left.'

'Yes. Yes, I see.'

'Well, what d'you think? You see what I mean?'

'I do, of course. And I'm grateful to you for taking the trouble to come all the way down here and tell me about it.'

'Yeah, well, it was the least I could do, wasn't it? For her, I mean.' Carol stood up and put the box of tissues on the table.

'There's just one other thing . . .'

'What?' Carol tilted her head and looked at him expectantly.

'Mrs Parnell. Did she have any friends that you know of, outside the agency?'

The orange spikes swung from side to side as she shook her head vigorously. 'Didn't have time to make any, did she? Looking after Mr Parnell was a full-time job.' Without warning the tears brimmed over again. 'She didn't *deserve* to die like that.'

THIRTEEN

Lineham was just coming in as Thanet left the interview room.

'Well, how was the house?'

'Terrific! Exactly what we've been looking for. I can't believe we've actually found it. I was beginning to believe it didn't exist.'

'You've made an offer?'

'Yes, a written one. We're taking no chances. Subject to survey and contract, of course.'

'Good. Excellent.'

Lineham enthused over the house as they walked upstairs. 'Anything interesting been happening here?'

Thanet grinned. 'You could say that. I had a visitor. From London.' And he told Lineham Carol Marsh's story.

'You think she was telling the truth, sir?'

'Yes, I do.' Thanet gave a reminiscent smile. 'She was an excellent mimic.'

The office smelt stale, stuffy with stored-up heat. 'Open the window, will you, Mike?'

Lineham struggled with the sash window, eventually managing to lower the upper section two or three inches. 'That's the best I can do, I'm afraid, sir.'

'One of these days they'll come in here and find we've collapsed for lack of oxygen . . . Open the door for a while, instead.'

'What d'you think Mrs Parnell meant by "I have my own family to think of"? And, "I'm not referring to my father"? Who else was there for her to leave it to?'

'Ah, now this is where things get interesting, Mike. I had a word with Doc Mallard just before I saw Carol Marsh.'

'About the PM?'

'Yes.'

'And?'

Thanet said nothing, simply raised his eyebrows and waited for Lineham to make the connection.

'Mrs Parnell had had a child!' said Lineham.

'Full marks, Mike. She had.'

'So that's who she was referring to.'

'Seems highly likely, don't you think?'

'It couldn't have been her husband's or we'd have come across some reference to it before now, so she must have had it before they were married, and had it adopted. So it must be — what? — at least thirteen by now, possibly much older.'

'Quite. So we now have to find the answers to three questions — when did she have the baby, who was the father and what is the child's new identity?' Thanet sat down at his desk, took out his pipe and started to fill it. 'I was thinking, Mike, everyone has always assumed that Alicia and her family moved away from Sturrenden because of Paul Leyton's suicide. But suppose that's not true.' He lit up, waited until he was satisfied that the pipe was drawing well. 'Suppose they really moved because she had discovered she was pregnant. Now, according to Bassett, Alicia was still going around with Nicholas Rain until the end of April of that year. And on June 4th she broke off with Paul Leyton. I was thinking . . . suppose that the real reason for her breaking off with him then was because she had just discovered she was pregnant?'

'Could be. That would explain why her timing was so bad. I mean, everyone said they couldn't understand why she didn't wait until after his exams were over. Maybe she felt she just couldn't continue to go out with him if she was already pregnant by someone else.'

'And she would have been worried stiff, of course.'

'Quite. There couldn't have been any question of a legal abortion, the new act didn't come in until 1967.'

'Not only that. You're forgetting something, Mike. She was a Catholic.'

'Of course . . . abortion would have been out of the question anyway. And you're suggesting Rain was the father?'

'It's certainly a possibility, wouldn't you agree?'

'But only one. After all, we're simply speculating about the

Doyles' reason for leaving Sturrenden. It could genuinely have been because they couldn't face all the talk after Paul Leyton's death, or because Mr Doyle had got another job. In which case she might have become pregnant long after she left Sturrenden — it was another seven years before she got married.'

'True. Or she might not have known she was pregnant when they moved, and Paul Leyton was the father, despite what his brother says about him being a homosexual. Though . . .' Thanet abruptly stopped talking and his eyes glazed.

Lineham had seen that look before. 'Sir?' he said, on a note of excitement.

'It's just occurred to me, Mike. If — and I know it's only "If" — the pregnancy was confirmed at the beginning of June 1964, and if we assume that Alicia was then around eight weeks pregnant, then the baby would have been born the following January, January 1965, and would now, by my calculations, be twenty years old.'

'So?'

'Think, Mike, think.'

'I *am* think . . .' Lineham broke off as he suddenly realised what Thanet was getting at. There was a moment's stunned silence and then, 'Penny Rain . . .' he breathed.

.Thanet nodded slowly. 'Penny Rain.'

The two men stared at each other, considering the implications.

'She's the right age,' said Lineham at last. 'I distinctly remember Doc Mallard saying she's twenty.'

'So do I. I wonder if he knows exactly when she was adopted.' Thanet was already reaching for the telephone. 'Get Doc Mallard for me, will you?' He replaced the receiver. 'The baby wouldn't have been put out for adoption until it was at least six weeks old, so if it was born in January the chances are that it would first have gone to the adoptive parents some time in late February or early March.'

'Do you think it would have been arranged privately, or done through conventional channels, via an adoption agency?'

– Thanet shook his head. 'Not through an agency. They rate anonymity very highly and I should think they'd consider this

128

kind of arrangement to be fraught with future complications. No, if the Rains did adopt Alicia's baby, I would think it much more likely that the whole thing was quietly set up by the two families.'

'But surely people like the Rains wouldn't have entered into an illegal arrangement like that?'

'You know as well as I do that when people are desperate they don't act rationally. And there would have been a lot of desperation involved here.'

The phone rang.

'Mallard here. You wanted a word?'

'Yes. You know you told me Alicia Parnell had had a child at some point? Well we've just come up with a rather interesting idea.' Briefly, Thanet explained.

When he had finished there was dead silence at the other end of the line. 'Are you still there, Doc?'

'Yes, of course I'm here,' snapped Mallard. 'I'm just trying to make up my mind if there could possibly be any truth in what you're saying.'

Thanet took the hint and waited.

Eventually, 'My immediate reaction is to say "Stuff and nonsense".'

'But?'

'I told you. I'm thinking about it. You do want a *considered* opinion, I suppose?'

Mallard had known the Rain family well and Thanet was interested to know what he thought. 'Of course.'

There was another, longer silence.

'Well,' said Mallard reluctantly, at last, 'I suppose it's *possible,* all things considered. But it would have had to be a private arrangement, you realise that. No adoption agency would have touched it.'

'Yes, I know.'

'Anyway, I don't flatter myself that you just wanted my opinion . . . . What else did you want to ask me?'

'Well, in view of the fact that Alicia was not obviously pregnant when the Doyles moved away in the summer, we worked out that if Nicholas Rain was the father, the baby would probably have been conceived towards the end of her association with him, say between the middle and end of April 1964. In which case it would probably have been born some time in January 1965 and would have been ready for adoption around the end of February or early March. We were wondering if you can remember exactly when Penny arrived in the Rain household.'

'I can do better than that. I can tell you when Penny's birthday is — not the precise date, but within a few days. And I must admit it supports your theory. I only know because I ran into her and her mother on the train back from London one day. I'd been up to a meeting and they'd been shopping for a coat for Penny's birthday, in the January sales. She was joking about it, saying that she hated having a birthday only three weeks after Christmas, that the only advantage she'd ever discovered was that she could often find a really nice advance birthday present in the sales, something her mother would not normally be able to afford.'

'So, mid-January, then.' The excitement which Thanet had deliberately been holding in check now pricked at his scalp, raised gooseflesh on his arms. *Careful,* he told himself. *Don't get carried away.*

'And you did say she was twenty, didn't you?'

'I did . . . . I suppose if you're right about all this, it would explain a lot.'

'Such as?'

'Well, I was saying to you the other day how well Penny fits into the family. There's a really close bond . . . she even looks like her adoptive mother — same build, same colouring . . . . But if Mrs Rain is really her grandmother . . . I always thought the resemblance was just a happy accident.'

'Which it might well still be, of course. At the moment this is all pure speculation.'

'Still . . . Let me know how you get on, would you?'

'Of course.'

Thanet thanked him and rang off. Then he told Lineham what Mallard had said.

'So Penny Rain really could be Nicholas Rain's daughter, not his sister.'

'*Could* be, Mike, remember that.'

'But if she was . . . . You could just see how it might have come about, couldn't you, sir? If you think about it, it would be the natural outcome of the whole situation. Alicia would be free to start a new life unencumbered by an illegitimate child, and both she and the Doyles would know that the baby would be brought up in a secure, happy home by people who were actually blood relations and would have her welfare at heart.'

'Also, of course, the Rains were Catholics, like the Doyles. I imagine that would have been an important point in their favour.'

'And from the Rains' point of view, it must have seemed the perfect answer. Mrs Rain couldn't have any more children, but this way she'd get a granddaughter instead of the daughter she'd always longed for, and no one any the wiser.'

'True.'

'*And,*' said Lineham, becoming really excited now, 'if Mrs Parnell was Penny Rain's mother, it would explain something that's puzzled us all along — why she came to Sturrenden on Saturday.'

'Because of the accident, you mean? But you're forgetting, Mike. The manager of the Swan told us she made the booking for Saturday night a fortnight before.'

Lineham's enthusiasm received only a temporary check. 'But the accident could be the reason why Mrs Parnell seemed upset on Saturday morning, sir, and why she wanted to get off early.'

'Possibly.' Thanet's pipe had gone out in all the excitement and he took time now to relight it. 'I wonder why she booked ahead for that one particular night.'

'Sir! It could have been because she knew Rain would be in Sturrenden on Saturday. I know the concert was mentioned in the papers when his engagement was announced, because I saw it myself. Perhaps, since Mrs Parnell's husband died, she'd been thinking more and more about getting in touch with Penny. She mightn't have felt she could, before. If she didn't tell him about the baby before they were married she probably wouldn't have felt she could, afterwards, because he couldn't give her any children himself and she wouldn't have wanted to hurt him. But after his death, when

131

she was alone, with a lot of time to think, I suppose it would have been natural for her to start thinking about the baby and wondering what she was like, how she'd grown up. And from there it's only a step to deciding to try to find out. Then she'd have had to work out the best way to go about it, and she must have thought she'd begin by getting in touch with Rain. The problem is that he must be very difficult to pin down. His career takes him all over the world. Then, with all the publicity over his engagement, she learns that he will be giving this concert in Sturrenden last Saturday. So she books a room at the Swan, buys a ticket for the concert and then, when she gets here, decides it's too important to leave the meeting to chance. So she rings him up — that could be the local call she made, soon after she arrived.'

Lineham paused, grinned. 'How'm I doing, sir?'

'Magnificently, Mike. Carry on.'

'Well, Rain is very tied up because he's spending so much time at the hospital and the only time he can suggest is after the concert. They meet in the foyer and she tells him she must talk to him urgently, in private, about Penny. She doesn't say so, of course, but the news of Penny's accident has made her even more determined to re-establish contact with her daughter. Anyway, he agrees, reluctantly no doubt, and he fobs off his fiancée and her parents by telling them he wants to go straight back to the hospital, then he and Mrs Parnell go back to the Swan. Or they could have gone separately, arranged to meet there.

'Once they're in her room she tells him she's decided she wants to make herself known to Penny. The idea really horrifies him. He knows that if Penny finds out that her adoptive mother is really her grandmother and her adoptive brother is really her father, and realises that they've been deceiving her about this all her life, she might never trust them again. It could ruin what until now has been an exceptionally close and happy family. Somehow he's got to persuade Alicia to change her mind. He begins to argue with her, but she won't listen. The trouble is, Rain is already in a pretty fragile state. He's worried sick about Penny and his mother, especially his mother, and he's just been through the tension of a concert

132

performance. The argument becomes a quarrel, the quarrel escalates, Rain loses his temper and . . .' Lineham waved a hand. 'That's it.'

Thanet had never heard Lineham so eloquent. He had worked out much the same scenario himself, but had no intention of saying so. Instead he clapped. 'Bravo, Mike. Convincing. Very convincing, in fact. And the red folder?'

'Rain had to take it away with him because it contained proof of Penny's true identity — birth certificate, letters, perhaps . . . He just couldn't risk leaving it there for us to find.'

'And proof, of course, is precisely what we now need, for this theory to stand up.'

'Of Penny's true identity, you mean.'

'Not exactly. Proof, rather, that she is in fact Alicia's daughter.'

'I see what you mean. If they're one and the same, fine. If not, our case falls apart, right?'

'Right. The question is, how to go about finding out? We daren't risk asking Rain, of course. If he is guilty, that would simply alert him to the fact that we were on to him. And the only other people who would know are Mrs Rain, who's in a coma, and Alicia's father, who's still away on holiday.'

'Old Mr Doyle is the only possibility, really, isn't he?' Lineham frowned. 'Looks as though we'll have to wait until Saturday.'

'Yes. Just a minute, though. Alicia's solicitor might know. We've got an appointment with him tomorrow. Looks as though that might be quite an interesting interview, in view of what Carol Marsh told me.'

'That certainly puts Miss Ross in the running too, don't you think?' Lineham clapped a hand to his forehead. 'Hell.'

'What's the matter?'

'I've just realised. You asked me to put someone on to checking overnight accomodation in Sturrenden, in case she followed Mrs Parnell down and stayed here on Saturday night, and I forgot. Sorry, sir. I'll get Bentley on to it first thing in the morning. Did you remember to ask Sparks to check if she's got a car, or can drive?'

'Yes. I wonder how he's getting on.'

Lineham grinned. 'Having the time of his life, I should think . . . . To get back to Miss Ross, though. Reluctant as I am to admit it, on second thoughts I can't see that what Carol Marsh told you strengthens the case against her that much.'

'Why not?'

'Well even if Miss Ross and Mrs Parnell did quarrel about the terms of the will, I can't really see that Miss Ross had much to gain by preventing Mrs Parnell from making a new one. Presumably the terms of the original will now stand, and as her husband is dead, her share in the business will go to her father.'

'Precisely. And he's an old man. Jessica Ross might well think it would be easier to get a better deal from him than from a legatee who is an unknown quantity.' Thanet glanced at his watch. A quarter past five already, and he had promised Joan that he'd try to be home early so that they could have that talk with Ben . . . 'Anyway, there's not much point in discussing it further at the moment. We might know more tomorrow, after seeing the solicitor. I'm going to write up my reports now, then go home.'

'Anything else you want me to do, sir?'

'Yes. Come on, Mike, don't look so crestfallen.' Thanet grinned. 'It'll make up for you actually having the nerve to take your lunch hour off. The thing is, I'm not too happy about Vivienne Leyton. She obviously hated Alicia and was bitterly jealous of her. And I'm still convinced she's holding back on something. I want you to talk to the party of friends the Leytons were with on Saturday night, see if they can tell us anything helpful. Oh, and make sure you get a description of the dress Mrs Leyton was wearing.'

'Right, sir.'

Two hours later Thanet sat back with a sigh, flexed his aching spine. The reports had taken longer than he had hoped, but he would still be home early enough to carry out his promise. He wasn't looking forward to the coming confrontation one little bit, but it was obviously vital to find out the truth of what had been going on. Thanet prayed that Ben had never actually been drawn in to experimenting with glue-sniffing. But what if he had? What if he had more than experimented, was on the way to becoming an addict?

Don't be stupid, Thanet told himself as he drove home through the familiar streets. *If he had, Joan or I would surely have noticed the symptoms.* But how evident were they in the early stages of the addiction?

He began to rehearse what he was going to say to his son.

FOURTEEN

Joan came to meet him in the hall and he kissed her, put his arms around her. Their shared anxiety gave this ritual embrace a deeper significance tonight and they stood motionless for a few moments, each drawing strength from the other's closeness.

Then Thanet pulled back a little, looked into her troubled grey eyes.

'How is he?'

She gave a little shrug. 'All right, I suppose. Quiet.'

'Has he mentioned Andy at all?'

'No.'

'And what about Sprig? How's she?'

'Seems fine.'

'Where are they?'

'Ben's just got into bed, Sprig's in the bath.'

'Good.' Perfect, in fact. Much as he loved his daughter, Thanet would prefer not have this talk with Ben interrupted. 'Shall we go up, then?'

To his surprise, Joan hesitated. 'Luke, I was wondering . . . do you think it would be better if you saw him by yourself?'

For a moment he was annoyed that she should be deserting him, leaving him to deal with this delicate situation alone, then commonsense reasserted itself. If Joan made a suggestion like this, she had good reason for it.

She must have glimpsed his fleeting anger and before he could speak she flared up in response. 'I'm not just chickening out, you know.'

He put out his hands and held her lightly by the shoulders. 'I do know. I was just being stupid.' He kissed her on the tip of the nose. 'Come on, darling, calm down. We're both on edge.'

He felt the tension leave her body and she gave a rueful smile. 'You're right. I'm sorry. . . . It's just that Ben and I don't seem to be getting on too well together at the moment and I thought he might be more prepared to open up if you saw him alone. Also, I thought he might find it a bit overwhelming, if we both tackled him about it.'

'You're right. He probably would. I don't in the least mind seeing him by myself.'

Thanet wished that this were true. As he climbed the stairs he wondered which was worse: to have this terrible sinking feeling in the pit of his stomach at the thought of the next half an hour, or to be stuck in the kitchen downstairs, knowing that whatever happened you were not going to have any control over it. Ben's door was ajar and Thanet popped his head around it. 'Boo!'

Ben did not shriek with laughter, jump out of bed to run and throw his arms around his father, or even smile. He just looked up and said listlessly, 'Hullo, Dad. I didn't hear you get home.'

'What are you doing?' Thanet approached the bed and sat down. It was painfully obvious that Ben was not doing anything. A discarded electronic game lay on the bedspread.

Thanet picked it up. 'Playing with this?'

Ben shook his head. 'Didn't feel like it.'

He looked so small and lost, it was all Thanet could do not to gather him up and hold him fiercely, protectively, reassure him that everything was all right, Daddy was here. But that would achieve nothing. Not yet, at any rate. Did all parents feel like this, he wondered? Obviously not. Child-battering was on the increase and every day stories of child abuse and neglect found their way into the newspapers. And yet, he believed, the majority of parents did care for their children. How could it be otherwise? They were, after all, extensions of their parents' bodies, their physical characteristics and their genes only one link in the endless chain of creation and procreation which joins a man indissolubly to his ancestors and to all those future generations as yet unborn. How painful it must be, he thought, to lose a child. Small wonder, then, that the most harrowing battles in the divorce courts were fought over custody of the children, or that someone like Alicia, who had lost her child at birth, might in later life seek to re-establish that most fundamental of relationships. *Your pain is my pain, Ben,* Thanet said silently, *your sorrow my sorrow. If I could only bear it for you. . . . But I can't. My job is to teach you to bear it yourself.* But, how to go about it, that was the problem.

'Ben,' he said, tentatively.

'Yes, Dad?'

'We have to talk.' *Gentle but firm, that was it. But above all don't make him clam up before we get to the important bit.*

Ben said nothing, but his eyes clouded and he looked away.

'About Andy.'

Ben frowned and bit his lip.

Thanet took his son's hand and held it, gently. 'I'm sorry, I know it hurts you even to think of him — how upset you must be feeling . . . But it is important to talk about it, just the same. You see, Andy died because, well, because he didn't realise just how dangerous glue-sniffing is . . .'

He'd lost him. He could tell by Ben's eyes that the boy had blanked him out. He didn't want to hear, was too frightened to listen, perhaps. He would have to back off, change tack.

He stood up, walked across to the window, hoping that the movement would attract Ben's attention, tug him back again.

Outside, flowers and shrubs, trees and grass basked peacefully in the evening sunshine. The white Iceberg roses beneath the weeping pear which Joan had planted at the far end of the garden were luminous in their patch of shade, their great clusters of blooms nodding gently in a little breeze that had sprung up.

'Ben, what would you say if I gave you a gun to play with? A real gun, with bullets in it?'

He had Ben's attention now, all right. 'What if I gave you this gun and said, "There you are Ben, it's yours, now run away and play with it"?'

Ben didn't know how to reply. 'But you wouldn't,' he said at last.

'Why not?'

'Because it might go off by accident.'

'And you'd hurt yourself.'

The boy nodded, still puzzled. 'Anyway, it would be illegal, wouldn't it?'

'You're quite right. It would. Perhaps it was a bad example.'
Thanet returned to his perch on the edge of the bed. 'Take a bottle of paracetamol, then.'

'What do you mean?'

'Well, as you know, Mum and I have always told you that you are never to take any kind of medicine or tablets that have not been given to you by us.'

'Everyone knows that.' Ben was scornful. 'It's written all over the labels.'

'Exactly. But what if, before you could read, Mum and I hadn't bothered to warn you how dangerous these things are, and then we'd left a bottle of paracetamol somewhere where you and Sprig could easily get at it . . .'

'You wouldn't have!'

'No, but if we had . . .'

'You never would.'

'Right. Because we do try, very hard, to make sure that you are aware of such dangers. We'd be very bad parents if we didn't. But I'm very much afraid, Ben, that we *have* been bad parents.'

'No, you haven't!' Ben was sitting bolt upright now, looking fierce.

'In one respect we have. We have not taken care to make sure that you and Sprig were fully aware of the dangers of gluesniffing.'

Ben's eyes dropped and he shrank down a little on to his pillows. 'The trouble is, you see, Ben, that glue seems such ordinary stuff. You find it in every household and for years and years we've taken it for granted. It's difficult to take seriously the idea that it might be dangerous. Parents wouldn't dream of giving their children loaded guns to play with or leaving bottles of dangerous drugs around for them to take by accident, but they leave glue openly in the kitchen drawers or cupboards and don't think twice about it. And I think that's why many children simply don't realise how dangerous it is. The problem is, also, that it's addictive. Do you know what that means?'

Ben shook his head.

'It means that once you start doing it, it becomes harder and harder to stop.'

The fear that flared in Ben's eyes made Thanet's throat go dry and his stomach clench. 'I don't mean to say that if you've just done it once or twice, and then you realise how dangerous it is and decided to stop, that you won't be able to stop, just that the more often you do it, the harder it becomes to stop and in the end you can't and that's when you get the kind of terrible accident that happened to Andy.'

Why wasn't Ben saying anything?

'So you see, Ben, that's why I'm saying that in this respect, Mum and I have been bad parents. We should have warned you, properly. And because we didn't, I don't feel we could blame you if you'd had a sniff yourself, once or twice . . . Have you?'

Thanet had put the crucial question in as casual a manner as possible and now he held his breath. His heart was pounding in his ears like the beat of a distant drum. *Please God, let him say no.*

The silence stretched on and on. Ben was staring down at the bedspread, either thinking over what Thanet had said or plucking up the courage to reply. Eventually he shifted uncomfortably and, without looking up, muttered, 'Well, once or twice.'

Thanet forced himself to sound calm, matter-of-fact. 'More than that, perhaps?'

'Three times, actually.'

'So why didn't you go on?'

'I didn't like it!' Ben burst out. 'I didn't like what it made the others do. They looked stupid, all falling about, as if they were drunk. And one of them spewed up all over the place. *Yuk!'*

Relief exploded in Thanet's brain, the shockwaves spreading out and down in tingling waves through torso, arms and legs. For a moment he felt light-headed. Then he took a deep breath. 'Congratulations,' he said, and ran his hand caressingly over Ben's hair.

'What for?'

'It's the hardest thing in the world to say 'No', when a group of friends is urging you on. I want you to know that I'm really proud of you, Ben.' *And relieved. Oh, so relieved.*

Ben had flushed with pleasure and now he muttered, 'They were a load of wallies anyway. Except for . . .'

'I know. Except for Andy.'

'So why did he do it, Dad? Go on sniffing glue? *Why?*'

'The thing is, Ben, when people are unhappy it makes them do silly things, things they wouldn't normally do. And I think this is what happened to Andy.'

Ben was listening intently, his eyes huge and solemn.

'Remember when you asked me, a few months back, why Andy's parents were getting divorced, and we had a long talk about it? Well, I think that was why Andy was unhappy. And I think that was why he started getting into trouble at school and so on . . . The glue-sniffing was only one aspect of it.'

Ben began to cry. 'I told him!' he sobbed. 'I told him it was stupid. I tried to make him stop. But he told me to leave him alone, he couldn't care less what I thought . . .'

Thanet put an arm around Ben's shoulders and pulled him close. 'I'm sure that wasn't true, Ben. As I said, Andy was very unhappy and that would have made him say things he didn't really mean . . .'

The conversation went on and on, round and round, with Thanet reassuring and Ben at last able to talk his hurt, anger, distress and bewilderment out of his system. By the end of it Thanet was exhausted and Ben's eyelids drooping where he sat. Enough was enough, Thanet decided. Ben would be all right now.

'Come on,' he said firmly. 'Time you settled down, and went to sleep. Would you like a story?'

'Yes, please.'

'Daddy!' Bridget flew into the room and flung her arms around his neck. Her skin was still damp from the bath and she smelt like sunshine and flowers.

'I was beginning to think you must have been washed down the plug-hole,' said Thanet teasingly.

'I was reading . . .' She stood up, tugging at his hand. 'Come and see my photos of Princess Diana. Mummy got them done Express. They're terrific!'

'In a minute,' said Thanet, smiling up at her. 'I'm just going to read Ben a story.'

'I'll listen too.' She flopped on to the bed on her stomach, propping her chin on cupped hands.

'Right. What shall we have? You choose, Ben.'

The story over and the photographs duly admired, Thanet returned downstairs.

Joan was tossing salad in a big green pottery bowl. She stopped, turned, her face apprehensive. 'How did it go?'

'Not too badly.'

'Really?'

'Really,' said Thanet, smiling at her and holding out his arms. She came into them and laid her head against his shoulder. 'What a relief! And did you find out . . . ?' She pulled away. 'No, come on. Let's carry these things through and you can tell me all about it over supper. Hope you don't mind having salad again.'

'It's what I prefer in this hot weather, you know that.'

'I've got some really good roast beef . . .'

While they ate he related to her his conversation with Ben, in detail.

'So you really think he's in no danger?'

'I'm pretty certain he was telling the truth. In fact, I *am* certain.'

'What a relief!' she said again. 'I was so afraid . . .'

'I know. So was I.'

They continued their meal in a companionable silence for a while and then began to talk about the day's work. The mother of Tracey, the pregnant fourteen-year-old, was still refusing to have anything to do with her and the girl was still determined to have the baby and bring it up herself. After endless phone calls Joan had at last managed to find a mother and baby home willing to take her.

'Interestingly enough,' said Thanet, 'it's beginning to look as though the Parnell case might revolve around a similar sort of situation.' And he explained the elaborate theory which he and Lineham had worked out about Alicia and Penny Rain.

'I suppose the adoption could have happened that way,' said Joan. 'That kind of arrangement is not unprecedented. I'd no idea Penny Rain was adopted, though.'

'There's no doubt about that, according to Doc Mallard. I

didn't know you knew her. What's she like?'

'A very nice girl. I don't know her well, mind. It's just that she helps out occasionally at the Youth Counselling Centre.'

'As a counsellor?'

'Oh no. She serves refreshments, plays table-tennis with the kids, that sort of thing. She looks so like her mother I'd never have . . . Oh, of course, how stupid of me. If what you say is true, Mrs Rain is really her grandmother.'

'Yes. If.'

'You really don't sound too certain about it.'

'I can't be, yet. We might know more after we've seen Alicia's solicitor tomorrow. The whole case seems so complicated.' And he told her about Carol Marsh's visit, about Vivienne and Richard Leyton and about Oliver Bassett and Paul Leyton.

'I see what you mean. Of course, even if Penny Rain is Alicia's daughter and Alicia did come down to Sturrenden with the intention of telling Nicholas Rain that she was thinking of making herself known to Penny, that still doesn't necessarily mean that Mr Rain killed Alicia, does it? It doesn't sound as though anyone saw them together after that brief conversation at the concert hall, and for all you know they might just have been arranging to meet the following morning. That would have been much more likely, surely. After all, you don't just go up to a boyfriend you haven't seen for twenty years and invite him back for an urgent meeting in your hotel bedroom, especially if he has a fiancée and prospective parents-in-law in tow.'

'We're not just talking about any boyfriend, Joan. If we're right, this was the father of her child. Surely that would give her a strong claim on him.'

'True. But I still can't see why the matter should have been sufficiently urgent for her to press him to go back with her then and there. Where's the hurry? Alicia hadn't seen Penny in twenty years, why should she worry about a few more hours?'

Thanet sighed. 'I suppose you're right. Anyway, as I said, it's all pure speculation at the moment. All we really know is that Alicia had a child. We don't know when, or where, or by

143

whom, or even if the child is alive or dead. Besides . . .'

'What?'

Thanet shook his head. 'Nothing.' Which wasn't strictly true. There was something, some tiny piece of information that was nagging at him, eluding him, stubbornly remaining just beyond the reach of his conscious memory. Was it something someone had said, or something that he had noticed? He shook his head again.

Joan was watching him. 'Trying to remember something?'

'It won't come.'

'Think of something else, then.'

'It's infuriating . . . Right. Is there anything interesting on television? Or shall we have some music?'

'Music, I think. But I'd like to clear away, first.'

They did the washing up together and went back into the sitting room. Thanet put Vivaldi's Four Seasons on and then went and lay on the settee, his head in Joan's lap, easing himself into a more comfortable position as the taut muscles of his back relaxed. He closed his eyes and the intricate, ordered music flowed around him, soothing and restoring him.

But that elusive memory continued to remain tantalisingly out of reach, destroying his peace of mind.

FIFTEEN

DC Spark's report on his activities in London the previous day was waiting on Thanet's desk when he arrived in the office next morning. It was, predictably, everything a report should be: thorough, succinct and immaculately typed, without a single error of grammar, spelling or punctuation.

Thanet accorded it the respect which it deserved. He read it through quickly, first, then again, slowly. After that he checked once more on certain points which had caught his interest. Then he sat back and thought about Jessica Ross.

Sparks had managed to talk to most of the other tenants of her block of flats, returning in the evening to question those who had been out at work earlier in the day. The consensus of opinion was unanimous: Jessica Ross had been away on Saturday night.

As well as the old woman to whom Thanet had spoken on Sunday, one other neighbour had seen Miss Ross depart for work at eight-fifteen on Saturday morning. After that the flat had been silent until late on Sunday afternoon — no plumbing noises, no radio or television and, despite the heat of the day, no window open. One neighbour had noticed Miss Ross's daily pint of milk still standing outside at midday on Sunday and as it was such a warm day had taken it in to put it into her own refrigerator. Jessica Ross had knocked on her door at five o'clock to enquire if this was what had happened, and had explained that she had been in bed all day with a migraine. The neighbour had been surprised to hear this. She had never heard Miss Ross complain of a migraine before and in any case had been convinced that Miss Ross had been away for the weekend, even though this would have been unusual — unprecedented, in fact. Miss Ross hardly ever went out, or had friends in, and this was why the neighbour had been convinced of her absence. She was used to noises from next door and could more or less chart Miss Ross's routine from them. This was why they had been so conspicuous by their absence. The woman herself had been in all weekend except for an hour and a half on Sunday, when she had gone to lunch with a friend — which was presumably why Thanet himself had missed her.

From other neighbours Sparks had learnt that Jessica Ross 'kept herself to herself' and was generally regarded as having no interests in life apart from her work. No one had ever seen her have a visitor and it was generally believed that she had no family.

But this was apparently not so. Sparks had managed to manoeuvre a long conversation during the lunch hour with Faith Bevan, the other girl who worked in Jobline — Carol Marsh, of course, had been in Sturrenden talking to Thanet. According to Faith, Jessica Ross had come from a large family of seven children. Faith assumed that it was a working-class background because Jessica's father had insisted that she leave school at sixteen to start work, and she had had to go to night classes to earn her secretarial qualifications. It had been a long, slow process, but she had been determined to see it through, and to achieve the kind of standards which would be attractive to prospective employers. Faith accorded her a grudging admiration for this perseverance, but was tired of having it 'rammed down my throat' and, like Carol, was resentful of Jessica Ross's highly critical attitude not only towards the two girls but also, behind her back, towards Mrs Parnell. Miss Ross, she said, was two-faced and also very jealous of Mrs Parnell's looks and pleasant personality. Faith had no idea where the rest of the Ross family lived, so Sparks had been unable to find out more about them.

There was one other interesting piece of information: Jessica Ross had never learned to drive.

Lineham came in looking like a thundercloud.

'Just been finishing this report on Mr and Mrs Leyton's party of friends on Saturday night, sir.' He handed it to Thanet.

'Thanks. What's the matter, Mike? You look as though you've just had an unpleasant conversation with your bank manager.'

'Not with my bank manager, with my estate agent. We've been gazumped.'

'Oh, no.'

'Oh yes. By five hundred.'

'It really is time something was done about this. It's iniquitous. In my opinion, if you've made a written offer for the full asking price, that should be it.'

'Yes, well there we are. Iniquitous or not, it hadn't been accepted in writing by the vendor and these other people got in fast. She seemed so nice, too, the woman who was selling. She's a widow, so I suppose you can't blame her for wanting to make as much as she can get, but we're going to be out on the street at this rate, if we're not careful.'

'So what are you going to do?'

'I don't know. I only just heard, a few minutes ago. I haven't even told Louise yet.'

'Can you afford to raise your offer?'

'I'm not sure. We'd have to bid at least five hundred more than these other people, which means a thousand more than we'd bargained for.'

'You'd better give Louise a ring, see what she thinks. Perhaps while we're in London she could get on to the building society, see exactly what it would mean in terms of mortgage repayments.'

'Would you mind, sir . . .?'

'I told you, go ahead. I'll glance at this, while I'm waiting.'

Lineham's report made interesting reading. According to the other members of their party, Vivienne Leyton had sniped at Richard throughout dinner in a way which had created a very uncomfortable atmosphere and spoiled everyone else's enjoyment. The impression was that the couple had had a row earlier in the evening and Vivienne wasn't going to let Richard forget it.

After the dinner was over the men and women had split up to go to their respective cloakrooms and then, between around twenty-five past ten and twenty to eleven, both Richard and Vivienne had disappeared. When the party had reassembled for the dancing at ten-forty-five, the Leytons had returned together, and everyone had assumed that they had gone off

147

somewhere during the interval to sort out their disagreement, because for the remainder of the evening the sniping had stopped. Vivienne had been much more subdued and Richard, although somewhat wary of her, more convivial.

'Louise seems to think it's worth going into,' said Lineham, putting the phone down.

'She's going to see what she can do?'

'Yes. I hope she doesn't get too carried away. She really has set her heart on that house.'

'I think we can safely leave it in her hands. Louise is a very capable woman.' Thanet tapped Lineham's report with one finger. 'This is interesting.'

'Yes, isn't it? I wonder what those two were really up to.'

'Paying a little visit to Alicia, perhaps? I wonder if we were wrong, Mike, and it was Richard Leyton who was the father of Alicia's child.'

'But no one has ever suggested that he had even the slightest interest in her.'

'No, but if he had, there are all sorts of interesting implications, aren't there? Let's just suppose for a moment that he took up with Alicia, however briefly, in between the time she broke off with Rain and started going out with Paul . . . . Perhaps he was fed up with mooning around after Vivienne, even thought she might sit up and take notice of him if he went out with another girl, especially one as attractive as Alicia . . . Anyway, at the time I don't suppose it would have mattered much to Vivienne. She had eyes for no one but Paul. But then Alicia starts taking an interest in Paul and, worse, Paul reciprocates — goes overboard for her in fact, and our faithful Vivienne is left high and dry. She is furiously jealous of Alicia. Then comes Paul's suicide and in Vivienne's eyes Alicia and Alicia alone is responsible for Paul's death . . . Richard meanwhile has reverted to the role of adoring lover and later, much later, perhaps, Vivienne at last gives in and marries him. But it infuriates her to think that even Richard, whom she had regarded as her own exclusive property, had at one time succumbed to Alicia's charms. Over the years she never forgets Alicia, and those feelings of jealousy and hatred fester away at the back of her mind, poisoning her marriage. And then, one day . . .'

'One day,' said Lineham eagerly, 'Alicia contacts Richard and says she has to see him. They arrange to meet some time over the weekend, but she doesn't realise that he's going to be at the Swan on Saturday evening for the Rotary Club Ladies' Night, and they bump into each other in the foyer . . . No, this won't work, sir. In that case, Leyton would surely not have insisted on going to talk to her. He would have pretended not to notice her . . .'

'Not necessarily. You're not allowing for human nature, Mike. It's obvious that Leyton's wife treats him like dirt most of the time. He might have insisted on dragging her across to see Alicia through sheer perversity or from a desire to punish Vivienne, or stir her up . . .'

'He certainly succeeds in doing that, anyway. She's a real bitch all through dinner . . .'

'So much so that he thinks, what the hell . . . And decides to slip up to Alicia's room during the interval, if he can manage to get away. He knows the concert will be over by then . . .'

'They could originally have arranged to meet then, for that matter.'

'Unlikely, I should think, Mike, but possible . . . Anyway, up he goes. And Vivienne, who's been keeping an eye on him, sneaks up after him.'

'Or it could possibly have been the other way around. Perhaps it was Vivienne who decided to go and pay a little visit to Alicia during the interval, and her husband who followed her . . .'

'True. But in any case there they are, one or the other or both. And then . . . well, then the situation is open to all sorts of permutations . . . Not much point in going into them all now, not until we have some kind of verification. . . . We'll have to question the hotel staff and guests again. That dress she was wearing . . .'

' "The colour of a copper beech leaf, with lurex in it," ' quoted Lineham. 'That's that glittery stuff, isn't it?'

'Yes. That's what I mean. It was pretty striking, by the sound of it.'

'Long and slinky. And with that hair of hers . . . She wouldn't have been exactly unobtrusive.'

'We'll get Sparks on to it. He made a good job of that report on Jessica Ross. Have you seen it?'

'Just glanced at it before I went downstairs, yes.'

'Get him in.'

Spark's thin eager face flushed with pleasure when Thanet complimented him on his day's work and the excellent report.

'I've got another job for you today, while Lineham and I are in London. We're going to see Mrs Parnell's solicitor.' Thanet explained what he wanted Sparks to do. 'Take your time. It could be very important. Fortunately Mrs Leyton has a pretty distinctive appearance, but Leyton is more difficult. The place was crawling with men in dinner jackets.'

'His beard might help, sir. Anything else?'

'Just one point. Two couples checked out of the Swan early on Sunday morning, before Mrs Parnell's body was found, and one of them had a room two doors away from Mrs Parnell. We still haven't managed to contact them — we think they must be touring — and obviously their evidence could be important. Have another go at getting hold of them, will you? Here's their address.'

'Right, sir.'

'That's all then.'

But Sparks was hesitating.

'What is it, Sparks?'

'When you sent for me, sir . . . I was just on my way up. To show you this.'

'This' was an excellent photograph of Jessica Ross.

'Where did you get it?'

'I printed it myself, sir. Last night, when I got back.' Sparks shifted his feet a little, uncomfortably, as if he were afraid that he had exceeded his brief. 'I took my camera with me yesterday.'

Thanet had difficulty in hiding his amusement. 'Hmm . . . Yes, well as it happens, it'll come in very handy. I was going to send someone around the hotels and boarding houses this morning, to check if she stayed in Sturrenden on Saturday night.'

'That's what I thought, sir . . .'

'I'll put Bentley on to it. Send him in, will you, on your way out.'

'Yes, sir.'

When he had gone Thanet and Lineham grinned at each other.

'Keen as mustard, isn't he, sir?'

'Enterprising, too. And versatile. He even printed it himself! If we're not careful we're going to be outclassed.'

'Worry you, sir, does it?'

'No need to be impudent, Mike. No, I'm afraid I never was very ambitious. I like things just the way they are.' Thanet glanced at his watch. 'If we're going to catch the ten-ten we'd better get a move on. As soon as we've seen Bentley, we'll be off.'

SIXTEEN

The offices of Thrall, Hardy and Blythe were a complete contrast to the Georgian elegance of Wylie, Bassett and Protheroe. They were housed in a brand new high-rise office block near Paddington station, some floors of which were still untenanted.

Thanet and Lineham were whisked up to the sixth floor in a lift and found themselves in a spacious, air-conditioned foyer artfully divided into separate areas by exuberant potted plants and plate-glass screens. The receptionist matched the decor. She was sleek and well-groomed, her manner a well-tutored blend of politeness, warmth and efficiency.

'Someone's been watching too much "Dallas",' whispered Lineham.

Thrall came out to meet them hand extended. Unerringly, he picked Thanet as the senior.

'Inspector Thanet?'

He was in his thirties, plump and smiling, dressed in a sleek pale grey dacron suit, pale pink shirt and deeper pink tie. 'And this is. . .?'

'Detective-Sergeant Lineham.'

Thrall shook Lineham's hand too, then led the way into his office. 'I apologise for being unable to see you before now. I've been very tied up, this week. Do sit down.'

He ignored the enormous desk with its padded executive-style swivel armchair and led them to the other end of the room, where there was a small seating area furnished with a comfortable leather bench-settee and matching armchairs.

'It was a terrible shock, to hear about Mrs Parnell. Ah, thank you, Marcia.'

The receptionist had entered with a tray. Not just cups of coffee, Thanet noted, but a glass jug and attractive pottery cups and saucers. Thrall and partners obviously believed in attention to detail. A delicious aroma of freshly ground coffee filled the air as Marcia poured and handed cups around.

'A tragic business,' said Thrall when the girl had gone. He helped himself liberally to brown sugar.

'You knew Mrs Parnell well?'

'Not well, exactly. One doesn't really see clients often enough to know them well. But we have dealt with Mr and Mrs Parnell's business for some years — perhaps I should explain that before our lease expired our premises were also in the Fulham Road. One does rather feel that Mrs Parnell had a raw deal in life. First Mr Parnell's accident — you know about that, of course? — then his death, then her mother's death, and now this . . . She was a charming woman, you know.' Thrall shook his head mournfully and sipped his coffee. 'But of course,' sip, 'you haven't come here to hear all this,' sip, 'you've come, I presume, to find out about her will?'

'If there was one.'

Thrall finished his coffee. 'More coffee, Inspector? Sergeant? No?' He poured some for himself and sat back, nursing his cup. 'Yes, there is one.'

'But not the one she'd intended leaving, I believe?'

Thrall gave Thanet a sharp, assessing glance. 'That's true, yes. She was on the point of making a new one.'

'In favour of the child which she had given away for adoption, at birth.'

Again that shrewd look. 'I see you've been busy, Inspector.' Abruptly Thrall leaned forward and set his cup down on the table. 'I'll be frank with you, Inspector. I was dead against it. I don't believe in stirring these things up. It causes nothing but trouble. When a child has been settled for years in one family . . . If she is unaware that she is adopted, such a legacy could be a considerable shock.'

Thanet noted the 'she' with satisfaction.

'So you tried to persuade Mrs Parnell not to change her will in favour of her daughter.'

'I did. But she wouldn't listen.' He lifted his hands helplessly. 'What could I do? One can only advise . . . If a client then chooses to ignore that advice, one has no option but to follow his instructions. It was understandable, I suppose, that

153

she should wish to dispose of her property in this way. She had no one else to leave it to. There's her father, of course, but in the normal way of things, one would have expected Mr Doyle to die first.'

'When did she first mention this matter to you?'

'Soon after her mother died — about three months ago, I suppose. Mrs Parnell came to see me. She wanted me to advise her. She told me that she had had this child when she herself was still in her teens, way back in January 1965. She had never told her husband about it. . . . She was very devoted to Mr Parnell, and I think she felt that he would have been deeply hurt to know that she had had a baby by another man, especially in view of the fact that he himself had never been able to give her one. So until now she had never thought of trying to trace the child, and indeed . . .'

Thanet and Lineham exchanged glances.

'Just a moment. Sorry to interrupt, but did you say, "trace the child"?' Thanet could see their carefully constructed theory tumbling about their ears.

'Yes. Why?'

'You're saying that Mrs Parnell had the baby adopted through conventional channels and had no idea of its new identity?'

'Naturally. Do I gather you thought otherwise?'

Thanet waved a hand. 'Just an idea we had, Mr Thrall. It doesn't matter. Do go on.'

But it did matter. It had been a beautiful theory — neat, convincing, satisfying. And now . . . Thanet's hand strayed in the direction of his pocket. Dare he pollute Thrall's opulent premises with clouds of unhygienic smoke? Probably not. Yet of its own volition his hand emerged from the pocket clutching his pipe.

Thrall noticed at once. 'Do smoke, if you wish, Inspector. I'm a pipe man myself. That's why the ashtrays in here are so solid.' And he leaned forward and pushed in Thanet's direction a chunk of quartz with something resembling a volcanic crater in the middle.

Thanet picked it up. 'Very nice,' he said.

'It's a piece of the Atlas Mountains. Picked it up in Morocco.'

Thanet set it back on the low table and began to fill his pipe. 'Sorry, we're digressing. You were telling us about Mrs Parnell's visit . . .'

'Yes. Well, I think that at that point she was feeling desperately alone. She'd lost her husband and her mother within the space of three months, and either loss is enough for anyone to cope with. . . . There was her father, of course, but he lives in the Midlands, as you probably know, and there was no one else to turn to. Because of Mr Parnell's disability she and her husband hadn't had much of a social life — they could have, of course, if they'd wanted to, but they didn't seem to need other people, they had a very special relationship, a kind of mutual interdependence which was very touching. But it did mean that when Mr Parnell died, she found herself with this enormous void. She had her work in Jobline, but I think it reminded her too much of her husband — they'd built it up together . . . Anyway, when she was sorting through her mother's papers she came across an old letter from the agency which had arranged the adoption. And this triggered off what in the end became something of an obsession with her. I think she found the thought of a grown-up daughter irresistible.'

'You said she wanted you to advise her . . .'

'Yes. She wanted me to tell her how to find her child, and I don't mind admitting that I was glad that in this particular matter I couldn't help her. Adoption procedure is designed specifically to protect the child against this situation — quite rightly so, in my view. Apparently she had written to the adoption agency and they'd told her that the only way in which the natural mother can get in touch with her child is by the agency writing to tell the adoptive parents that she wishes to do so. Then, if the child is over eighteen, it's up to him or her to decide whether or not to follow up the contact. Unfortunately, in Mrs Parnell's case, this procedure couldn't be followed, because in 1972 the agency which arranged the adoption had a serious fire, and all their records up to that date were destroyed.'

'Wouldn't it have been possible to trace the child through Public Records?'

Thrall shook his head. 'Mrs Parnell had tried. The

Adoption Register is inaccessible to the natural mother. The only thing she can do is go to St Catherine's House and inspect the Index to that Register, which gives the new, adoptive name of each child, its date of birth and the date of the adoption. Mrs Parnell had done this, but the only piece of information which was of any use to her was the date of birth. I believe she made many visits to St Catherine's House to go through the Index, noting down the names of all the female children born on the correct date, but of course all she ended up with was a very long list and absolutely no means of telling which child was hers.'

So here, no doubt, was the explanation of Alicia's mysterious and erratic absences, of her absent-mindedness and lack of interest in the affairs of the agency. The search for her child had enabled her to cope with her double bereavement by providing her with a goal to work towards, a hope to sustain her. Thanet could understand the degree to which that search must have obsessed her, her growing despair as she slowly came to appreciate the impossibility of the task.

'That was why I was so astounded when she rang up a little while back to say that she'd at last actually managed to trace her daughter,' said Thrall.

Thanet's attention snapped back. 'What? But how?'

Thrall shrugged. 'I've no idea. She rang me up, early one morning. She sounded very agitated.'

'She'd actually made contact with the girl?'

'Oh no. She said she'd discovered her daughter's new identity by pure chance, that she'd tell me the whole story when she came in to see me. She said she was trying to make up her mind about the best way to contact her — she didn't want to rush in, she said, and regret it later. But meanwhile she was ringing because despite what I'd said when we first discussed the matter, she had definitely decided to make a will in the girl's favour, and she'd like me to draw up a rough draft so that we'd have a basis on which to work when she came to see me. She'd ring for an appointment in a week or two, she said, when she'd had time to think the matter over. Of course, she never came.'

'Did she ever tell you who the child's father was?'

'No.'

'Or the girl's new name?'

'I'm afraid not.'

A pity. Even though it looked as though the matter was irrelevant, a side-issue, for his own satisfaction Thanet would have liked to reassure himself that it had nothing to do with the case.

'So the original will still stands?'

'Drawn up at the time of her marriage, yes. As her husband predeceased her, everything will now go to her father.'

'I see.'

There was a knock at the door and the delectable Marcia put her head in. 'Sorry to disturb you, Mr Thrall, but there's a call for Inspector Thanet. Urgent, apparently.'

It was Bentley. 'Glad I managed to catch you, sir. Have you been to see Miss Ross yet?'

'Not yet, no.'

'Good. I thought you might like to know, before you saw her, that she was in Sturrenden on Saturday. She spent the night at the Three Horseshoes, opposite the Black Swan. Checked in at about four-forty-five on Saturday afternoon, under the name of Jennifer Rawlings. She asked for a room at the front, and left shortly before twelve on Sunday morning.'

'This is definite?'

'The landlord was positive, sir. Said the photograph was an excellent likeness.'

'Thank you, Bentley. Well done. Tell me,' he said to Thrall as he replaced the receiver, 'did Mrs Parnell have a partnership agreement drawn up between herself and Miss Jessica Ross?'

'Yes, she did. I arranged it myself, as a matter of fact.'

'Mrs Parnell retained the major share in the business?'

'Yes. It was a sixty/forty arrangement. I strongly advised it. To be frank, I wasn't too happy about the partnership. I wasn't particularly impressed by Miss Ross and I felt that Mrs Parnell should delay making such an important decision, until she had fully recovered from the trauma of a double bereavement, but I couldn't get her to change her mind. She said Miss Ross had had to carry much of the weight of the business alone during the last months of Mr Parnell's life, and afterwards

157

too, for that matter, while Mrs Parnell was recovering, and she felt she owed it to her.'

'Was there any arrangement as to what should happen in the event of the death of one of the partners?'

'The other was to be given the first option to purchase the other's share, after an independent assessment as to market value, should the legatee wish to sell.'

'And if the legatee did not wish to sell?'

'Then the business would presumably continue under the new partnership.'

'I see. Thank you.'

Outside, Thanet decided to be extravagant and take a taxi.

'Bang goes our lovely theory,' said Lineham gloomily.

'That Penny is Rain's daughter, you mean. Yes, looks like it, doesn't it. I simply cannot believe that any reputable adoption agency would collude with the parents of the natural mother to place the child in the family of the natural father without her knowledge. Nor can I believe that Alicia's child should have been placed with the Rain family by sheer coincidence. It's just too much to swallow. No, I'm afraid that as you say, bang goes our lovely theory.'

'And it doesn't look too promising as far as Jessica Ross is concerned, either, if there has to be an independent market assessment of the value of Mrs Parnell's share of the business before Miss Ross can purchase.'

'I shouldn't be too sure about that, Mike. There are all sorts of ways of milking a business. Jessica Ross could still be in a pretty strong position now. I don't imagine Alicia's father would be anything but a sleeping partner, and a sleeping partner who's in his seventies and lives a convenient couple of hundred miles away would be a pretty attractive proposition to someone like her. Besides, I had a very interesting phone call just now. From Bentley.'

'You mean . . . Miss Ross really was in Sturrenden on Saturday?'

'No doubt about it, according to Bentley. Checked into the Three Horseshoes at around four-forty-five on Saturday afternoon, under the name of Jennifer Rawlings. Sharp's photograph came in handy. The landlord recognised her immediately. She asked for a room at the front, too'.

'Overlooking the entrance to the Swan! Terrific!' Lineham's eyes were already alight with enthusiasm.

Thanet smiled indulgently. Lineham's ability to pick himself up after disappointment and throw himself wholeheartedly into the next project was one of the sergeant's most endearing qualities.

'Four-forty-five, you say? Then she must have followed Mrs Parnell down, as we thought. I bet that's why she made a fuss when Mrs Parnell said she'd like to leave work early — she wouldn't have been able to follow her, if she had. I bet she'd been dying to know where Mrs Parnell used to go off to, those times when she left the office without telling anyone where she was going, and this time she thought she'd do a bit of detective work for herself. She'd have brought her night things with her when she left home that morning — remember the squashy bag that neighbour mentioned . . .'

'Following her out of curiosity is still a long way from killing her, Mike.'

'But it's the first step, isn't it? And you know what you're always saying . . .'

' "It's the first step that counts", you mean. Well, maybe, but . . .'

'Even if she hadn't intended killing her when she set off, even if she was just following her out of curiosity, perhaps when she saw the set-up she realised how perfect it was . . . All those people milling around in the hotel . . . it would have been so easy to slip in and out undetected, mingle with the crowd, especially around the time when Mrs Parnell got back, after the concert.'

'Maybe. But just remember, the same applies to anyone else. No, the fact remains, Mike, that what we need is some good, hard evidence.'

The taxi was pulling up and Lineham leaned forward with alacrity to open the door. 'I know that, sir. All the same, I'm looking forward to seeing her try to wriggle out of this one.'

When Thanet and Lineham walked in, both Carol and Faith were busy at their desks. Carol immediately jumped up.

'Morning, Inspector.'

He was glad to see that she was looking much better today, though her shrieking scarlet and emerald green mini-dress made him blink. The orange spikes were poker-stiff and the mint-green eyes elaborately made-up.

'I'm working out my notice,' she said, lowering her voice and glancing at the inner door, which was shut. 'We both are.'

'You've definitely decided to leave, then?'

'You bet.'

'Is Miss Ross in?'

'You come to arrest her?' she said eagerly. 'See, Faith, I told you, didn't I?'

'Just to talk to her,' said Thanet, smiling.

'Oh . . .' She shrugged. 'Well, it's early days yet, isn't it? Yes, she's in. Got a client with her.'

'Will she be long, do you know?'

'Half an hour or so, I should think.'

Thanet glanced at his watch. Half past twelve.

'Would you tell her we'll be back at one-fifteen?'

In the street Thanet said, 'Thought we might as well get something to eat while we're waiting. I noticed a sandwich bar just down the road.'

The pavements were crowded with people hurrying about to make the best use of their lunch break.

'I'd hate to live in London,' said Lineham as they dodged their way along the pavement.

'Me too. Here it is.'

They had to queue of course, first to order, then to find somewhere to sit down, and it was a scramble to be back at Jobline on time. Faith was alone in the office. Presumably the girls' lunch hours were staggered so that the office could remain open throughout the day.

'Is Miss Ross free now?'

Faith nodded and crossed the room to knock on the inner door.

Jessica Ross was not pleased to see them. 'I hope this isn't going to take long, Inspector. I'm very busy.'

Today she was wearing a summer dress with long sleeves and tie-neck in a silky fawn material patterned with brown scribbles. It was an unfortunate choice of colour, emphasising the sallowness of her skin.

'That rather depends on you, Miss Ross.'

'What do you mean?' She plumped herself down in the chair behind the desk and waved an irritable hand. 'Do sit down.'

'It seems you've been rather less than frank with us.'

'I don't know what you're talking about.'

'Don't you, Miss Ross? Why didn't you tell us you'd spent Saturday night in Sturrenden — and under an assumed name? And don't bother to deny it. It really isn't worth the trouble.' Thanet nodded at Lineham who flicked open his notebook and read off an imaginary script.

'Jessica Ross. Positively identified by the landlord of the Three Horseshoes in Sturrenden as having registered under the name of Jennifer Rawlings at four-forty-five on Saturday the fourteenth of July. Checked out at eleven-fifty-five on Sunday the fifteenth.' Lineham closed the notebook with a snap.

'What absolute rubbish! I told you, I was at home in bed with a migraine. . . . There's some mistake . . . how could anyone possibly have identified me as this Rawlings woman? I've never even heard of her.'

'There's been no mistake, Miss Ross, I assure you.'

'But there must have been! How could you possibly . . .?'

'Never mind how,' snapped Thanet. 'And let's stop wasting time, shall we? Or perhaps you'd prefer to come down to Sturrenden with us and take part in an identification parade. I'm sure the proprietor of the Horseshoes would be only too happy to oblige.'

Jessica Ross stared at him. Her pale blue eyes were blank,

but Thanet sensed that underneath she was desperately twisting and turning, this way and that, seeking a way out. He waited patiently. He had her and he knew it.

Suddenly her eyes filled with tears and she snatched at her handbag, took out a handkerchief. She dabbed at the corners of her eyes — carefully, Thanet noticed, so as not to smudge her make-up — and blew her nose. 'Oh,' she said, in a tremulous voice, 'whatever will you think of me, Inspector?'

So it was to be a bid for sympathy. Well, she wasn't going to get it. Thanet glanced at Lineham, who rolled his eyes and cast them up at the ceiling. Thanet said nothing, just waited.

'It was only that I was so worried . . . I mean, Alicia had been behaving so strangely. . . . And, as I told you, she had been neglecting her work, going off without warning and giving no explanation when she came back . . . I was getting very concerned about her.' Miss Ross gave a final dab and then sat up with a self-righteous little twitch of the shoulders. 'And she had no one else to take an interest, no one at all.'

'So you thought it was your duty to find out what she was up to?'

'Yes. No. I mean . . . I thought I might be able to help her, if I knew.'

'How?'

Jessica Ross blinked at the staccato question. 'Well . . . I thought it might help me to take the right attitude, in deal . . . in talking to her.'

'Oh, come on, Miss Ross. We're not complete fools, you know. Why not admit it? You were intrigued by those erratic absences of hers, fed up with them, too. You wanted to find out what she was up to. So, when you discovered she was going away for the weekend, you decided to follow her out of sheer curiosity.'

Jessica Ross's puddingy face hardened, took on greater definition. Her nose suddenly seemed sharper, her heavy jaw more prominent than ever. 'Well, what if I did? There's no law against that, is there?'

'No one has ever suggested that there is,' said Thanet amicably.

'Well then . . .'

'Precisely. "Well then . . .". Why bother to cover it up?'

'Because when I heard . . . when I discovered that Alicia had been . . . murdered, I panicked. I thought that if you knew I'd followed her down there, you'd think I'd . . . I'd . . .'

'Killed her.'

'Yes.'

'And did you?'

Her head snapped up. 'Certainly not!'

Thanet folded his arms. 'Convince me.'

Her mouth gaped a little, then snapped shut. 'You'll just have to take my word for it, I'm afraid.'

'Why should I? You've already lied to us once.' Thanet leaned forward in his chair. 'Look, Miss Ross, I'm tired of all this skirmishing. It is time-consuming and time-wasting, and frankly, I can't be bothered with it. I want a clear, precise and *truthful* account of your movements on Saturday and Sunday, and if you're not prepared to give them to me, here and now, then I really shall have to ask you to accompany us back to Sturrenden, when I shall be able to question you at my leisure.'

Silence.

'Very well,' said Thanet, standing up. 'If you'd just get your coat . . .'

'No!' Her voice was harsh with anger, frustration, fear and defeat. 'No,' she repeated, less violently. 'Very well, I'll tell you.'

Slowly, Thanet sat down again.

'This is outrageous!' she began furiously, then caught Thanet's eye. She clasped her hands as if to contain her anger and took a deep breath, straightened her shoulders. 'As you said, I knew that Alicia was going away for the weekend, and I wanted to know why. I felt I had a right . . .' She faltered as Thanet shifted impatiently in his chair. 'When I left home on Saturday morning I brought my night things with me. When I got here Alicia seemed upset, as I told you, and said she wanted to get off early. Naturally I was against it — it would have upset my plans. So I said it really wouldn't be fair on Faith and myself if Alicia left early — which was true, as a matter of fact,' she added defensively. 'We were short-handed as it was, with Carol away sick. Also, there were a number of appointments already arranged and Saturday morning is always the busiest time of the week. So many people come in because it's their only day off . . . So I made an issue of it, and she agreed to stay.

'It's my job to lock up, so at lunchtime I made sure that Faith left promptly, and then I waited until Alicia came out of her front door. She took a taxi, and I followed in another. She went to Victoria and I managed to overhear her destination, when she bought a ticket to Sturrenden. There were a lot of people about and she seemed very preoccupied, so it wasn't difficult. Then I caught the same train, the two-thirty. When we got to Sturrenden I expected her to take another taxi, but she didn't. I didn't realise then how small the town was, I'd never been there before. I'd been wondering how difficult it would be to follow her without her spotting me, but I needn't have worried. There were crowds of people about and later I heard that the Princess of Wales had visited the place earlier in the day. So, there was no problem. She went straight to the Black Swan. She stopped once, on the way, to talk to someone for a few minutes — a tall man, well-dressed — but that was all. I'd already made up my mind that if she went to a hotel I wouldn't be able to risk registering in the same place, and I spotted this pub across the street, the Three Horseshoes — well, you know that already. I asked for a room at the front, and got one.' Miss Ross's large nose wrinkled in distaste and her mouth turned down at the corners. 'Scruffy place it was, too. But it did have a good view of the entrance to the Black Swan, and that was what I wanted. I settled down by the window and waited. Over two hours. Then Alicia came out. She was obviously going out for the evening. I hurried downstairs, afraid I might lose her, but once again she walked.'

'She went to a concert. Did you go, too?'

'I bought a ticket. Waste of money, the stuff they were playing wasn't my cup of tea, but I wanted to see if she was going to meet anybody. But when she sat down she was alone. The seats on either side of her were already occupied, but she didn't speak to anyone, just settled down to read her programme, so I assumed she could safely be left there until the

164

concert ended, and I went out again. I was starving. I'd had nothing to eat or drink, not even a cup of tea, since mid-morning. On the way out I enquired what time the concert ended and well before ten o'clock I was waiting outside.'

Thanet did not glance at Lineham or betray his excitement. Jessica Ross might well be innocent of nothing more than an intrusive curiosity, and if that were so, and she had seen Alicia leave with someone . . .

'I stood there for three-quarters of an hour, until everyone had left and they were locking the place up. I'd missed her.'

Jessica Ross was too engrossed in reliving her own disappointment to notice Thanet's.

'There'd been a rush of people leaving around a quarter to twenty past ten, and it'd been impossible to check them all. I hadn't dared get too close, in case I ran into Alicia. I was furious that I'd missed her, like that. . . . I walked back to the centre of the town and hung around for a while outside the Black Swan, trying to decide whether or not to go in and enquire if Alicia was back yet, but I was afraid I might run into her. . . . In the end I went back to my room. Next morning I got up very early and was at my window by seven-thirty. As it was Sunday morning everything was very quiet in the street outside until around nine-thirty, when a police car arrived and drove into the car park of the Black Swan. I didn't connect it with Alicia, of course. Then more cars arrived, and an ambulance . . . Naturally, I was very curious by now, but I didn't dare leave the window in case Alicia came out and I missed her again.

'At a quarter past eleven, when there was still no sign of her I went downstairs. There was a woman cleaning the bar, and I asked her if she knew what was going on across the street and she told me one of the guests had been murdered. A woman from London, that was all she knew. I still didn't think it could be Alicia — well you don't, do you? You never think it could be someone you know. . . . I didn't dare go into the Swan and ask for her. If she was in I wouldn't be able to say why I'd suddenly changed my mind about wanting to see her and if by any chance it had been her who'd been murdered, I'd simply be drawing attention to myself. So in the end I waited until there were several people in the foyer, then I went in and started to chat to some of them, pretending that I was a guest there too. I said what a shocking business it was then I asked if they knew who the dead woman was. They said her name was Parnell. . . . So I went back to the Horseshoes and checked out, caught the first train back to London. And that's it.'

'I see. So between ten-fifteen and ten-forty-five you were standing outside the concert hall, waiting for Mrs Parnell?'

'That's right. Why? Was that when . . .?'

'Is there anyone who could confirm this? Did you speak to anyone, do or say anything which might make anyone remember you?'

'No, of course not. The whole point was that I was trying to make myself as inconspicuous as possible.'

'What were you wearing?'

'A navy blue summer coat and a navy and turquoise scarf over my hair.' She touched the carefully arranged blonde waves with a complacent hand. 'I thought it might be too noticeable.'

'Pity. Well, Miss Ross, you must see that this doesn't really give you much of an alibi. We'll do what we can to check it out, but it's going to be extremely difficult. I must ask you not to leave town, at present, and to make sure that you will be available for further questioning, should we need to see you again.'

'But . . .' For once she was at a loss for words, and her sallow skin was the colour of dough.

'If you are innocent, you have nothing to be afraid of.'

'Of course I'm innocent!' She thumped the desk with a balled fist.

'In that case, as I said, you have nothing to worry about.' Thanet rose and Lineham followed suit. At the door Thanet turned. 'We'll be in touch.'

They left her sitting motionless at her desk.

'She could have done it,' said Lineham. 'As I said, if she did follow Mrs Parnell into the hotel, no one would have noticed her in all that crush. And although Mrs Parnell would have been surprised to see her, she'd almost certainly have invited her into her room.'

'True. But there's still no scrap of proof and if we don't get any, she'll be a hard nut to crack. And what about that red folder?'

Time was getting on. They took another taxi back to Victoria and were in the train before Lineham said, 'That folder, sir . . .'

'What about it?'

'If Jessica Ross is guilty, and took that folder away, the implication is that there was something in it which she wouldn't have wanted us to see, right?'

'So?'

'I was trying to think what it could be. . . . Suppose she'd been trying her hand at a spot of embezzlement, while Mrs Parnell was out of touch with things . . .? Say Mrs Parnell found out, told Miss Ross she'd done so, and also told her she was going away for the weekend to think things over before deciding what action to take . . .'

'And the folder contained incriminating papers . . .'

'Yes. What d'you think, sir?'

'Within the bounds of possibility, I suppose, given the personalities concerned.'

'You think it might be worth looking at the agency's books, then?'

'It might. Let's mull it over for a while, first. In any case I think we'll get the men to show that photograph of Jessica Ross to the guests at the Ladies' Night, just in case one of them happened to notice her. She wasn't in evening dress, remember.'

'It'll be a long job.'

'That can't be helped.' Thanet shifted uncomfortably in his seat. 'I don't know, Mike, I feel we're not really getting anywhere in this case. It's not that we're not making any progress, just that as soon as we think we're getting a clear lead on one person, something crops up and we have to focus on someone else.'

They were both to remember these words when they got back to Sturrenden. Sparks was hovering, obviously bursting to impart some important information. Apparently the couple who had spent Saturday night in a room two doors away from Alicia's were now at home, their holiday over, and Sparks had

167

had a long telephone conversation with the wife, a Mrs Dora
Brent. When asked to describe anyone she had seen in or near
the third-floor corridor that evening, she had at once come up
with an immediately recognisable description of Vivienne
Leyton.

'You're sure?'

'Yes, sir. That hair and that dress . . . the combination is
unmistakable.'

'What time was this?'

'Around ten-forty-five, sir.' Sparks was triumphant.

'How can she be so precise?'

'Well apparently she was fed up with the noise and all the
people from the dinner-dance milling about downstairs, and
she suggested to her husband that they have an early night. He
said it was only twenty-five to eleven and he had no intention
of going to bed at that ungodly hour, so she went up alone.
When she got out of the lift Mrs Leyton was just hurrying
past, and disappeared down the stairs at the right-hand end of
the corridor.'

'I see. Good. Where do these people live, Sparks?'

'Cirencester, sir.'

'Better contact the local police, get them to send someone
round to take a statement.'

'I already have, sir.'

I might have known, thought Thanet with amusement.

'Right, Mike,' he said, when Sparks had gone. 'I think
we're due for another visit to Vivienne Leyton, don't you?'

The telephone rang.

'There's a Mr Knight in reception, sir. Very anxious to see
you.'

The father of Rain's fiancée. Thanet hesitated. He put his
hand over the receiver. 'Mr Knight wants to see me,' he said to
Lineham. He raised his eyebrows, shrugged. 'All right, send
him up.'

'I wonder what he wants, sir.'

'Can't imagine, but we're about to find out.'

There was a knock at the door.

'Come in.'

EIGHTEEN

A uniformed constable ushered Mr Knight into the room. Melanie's father was wearing a well-cut track suit and expensive running shoes and his fair hair was damp with perspiration.

'Excuse my informal attire, Inspector. I needed an excuse to get away, to see you . . .'

'Please. Sit down.'

'I hope you don't mind my bursting in upon you like this, without an appointment.'

'Not at all. How can I help you?'

'I feel a bit foolish, really, coming here . . . It's just that . . . Well, to be frank, Inspector, I've come to see if you've made any progress in your enquiries.'

'Into the murder of Mrs Parnell?'

'Yes.' Knight wiped the sweat from his forehead with his sleeve. 'I know I have no right to ask, really, but . . .' His eyes pleaded for understanding. 'It's just that it's so unsettling for us all. And Nicholas, of course, is already under considerable strain, with his mother still in a coma.'

'I know. It must be a very difficult time for him. And I'm sorry to have had to add to his burdens by having to question him. Though I must say that he didn't seem to be particularly bothered by it.'

Knight had scarcely heard a word Thanet said. 'Melanie's our only child, you see, and we love her dearly. We can't bear to see her miserable, like this.'

'But I don't quite see . . .'

'They were so very happy together. And of course, my wife and I were delighted about the engagement. It seemed such a very suitable match. I know he's much older than her, but that's no bad thing in a husband, it makes for stability, and of course, they have a mutual passion for music . . . Have you ever heard them play together?'

'I'm afraid not.'

'They're both wonderful musicians, and although Melanie is still only at the beginning of her career . . . I'm sorry, you don't want to hear all this.' Knight mopped at his forehead again. 'It's just that . . . I'm trying to make you see how important this is to us.'

'Of course. But I still don't quite understand . . .'

'He's changed, you see. Nicholas, I mean. Since all this began. Well, since the accident, really. Before, he . . . well, he couldn't see enough of Melanie, but now he seems to spend most of his time at the hospital — well, that's understandable, I suppose — but even when he is with her, with us, he seems preoccupied, distant . . .'

'But as you yourself just said, that is understandable, in the circumstances, surely. I'm told that Mr Rain is devoted to his mother.'

'I know, I know. It's just that . . . well, I can't help wondering if this other thing is playing on his mind, too.'

'That he feels he's seriously under suspicion of murder, you mean?'

'Yes,' said Knight, with relief. 'And what I have really come to ask is, is he?'

'Ah, well now, it's a little difficult to answer that question, Mr Knight. You must appreciate that we have to follow up every possible lead. And we can't get away from the fact that Mrs Parnell was last seen alive talking to Mr Rain at five past ten on Saturday night.'

'And those are your only grounds for suspecting him?'

Thanet shook his head. 'I'm sorry, you must see that I can't possibly answer that question.'

'But . . . Look, Inspector, I'm only too well aware that I shouldn't be pressing you like this. But . . . have you by any chance got a daughter?'

'As a matter of fact, I have. And I can guess what you're going to say . . .'

'Nevertheless,' said Knight eagerly, leaning forward in his chair to emphasise the importance of this point, 'you must be able to imagine . . . Put yourself in my position. If your daughter was engaged to a man under suspicion of murder . . .

It's tearing her apart, Inspector, and naturally her mother and I are desperately worried in case there is anything in it. Not that we really believe there could be, of course, but all the same . . .'

'I do understand, Mr Knight, believe me. But I'm afraid that at the moment I simply cannot give you the reassurance you need.'

'You mean that Nicholas . . .'

'I mean that at the moment Mr Rain is only one of a number of people whose connection with Mrs Parnell is under scrutiny. And I really cannot tell you any more than that.'

The note of finality in Thanet's voice must finally have persuaded Knight that it was pointless to persist. He was silent for a moment and then slumped back in his chair, gave a resigned shrug. 'Very well, if you can't, you can't.' He stood up. 'Thank you for seeing me, anyway.'

Thanet watched him go and then said, 'That's the trouble with murder, Mike — or any serious crime, for that matter — the number of innocent people who are affected. We come and go in their lives, and that's it, as far as we're concerned. It's only too easy to forget the havoc we might leave behind.'

'But it has to be done, sir.'

'True. But we should always be aware of the fact that long after the case is over, these people have to go on living with the effects of the distress they may have suffered unnecessarily. I tell you, it's one of the aspects of this job which really gets me down, sometimes.'

'But if they're innocent . . .'

'That doesn't eliminate the pain of uncertainty, the days, weeks or even months of anxiety.'

'I think he had a nerve, as a matter of fact, coming here like that and trying to squeeze information out of us.'

Lineham's indignation was, Thanet knew, partly over the effect that Knight's visit had had upon Thanet himself, and for the millionth time he asked himself if he was in the wrong job. He loved the excitement of the chase, the knowledge that he was working to enforce a moral as well as a legal justice, but at the same time he was constantly aware that he himself was perhaps too sensitive to be able comfortably to tread the tightrope between objectivity and emotional involvement with the people he met during the course of his investigations. There was, he felt, a softness at the core of his nature inappropriate to the work he had to do, and try as he would to suppress it, like a many-headed hydra it kept popping up when he least expected it. Ten minutes ago he had been full of eagerness to pursue their latest lead and now . . . With an effort he forced himself back into briskness.

'Oh, I don't know, Mike. It's understandable that he should be concerned, in the circumstances. As he said, wouldn't you be?'

Lineham shrugged. 'I suppose so . . . Anyway, do you want me to give Mrs Leyton a ring before we go?'

'No. She's sure to be there at this time of day. We'll surprise her.'

It was now half past five in the afternoon and Thanet was banking on the fact that by this hour most women were at home and thinking of preparing the evening meal. Vivienne Leyton didn't have a job, so far as he knew, and Richard Leyton would presumably soon be arriving home hungry from his day's work on the farm.

But he had miscalculated, it seemed. When they arrived at the bungalow all the doors and windows were shut, and the double garage stood open and empty.

'Do we wait, sir?'

'Let me think . . . Let's enquire at the main farmhouse. Perhaps her mother-in-law will know where she's gone.'

It was a typical Kentish farmhouse, brick and tile-hung with a well-kept garden and yellow roses smothering the open-fronted porch. Mrs Leyton senior was languidly elegant in a flowered Tana lawn suit.

'She's gone to town for the day. Shopping, with a friend. Mad, going to London in this heat, but there you are . . .'

'Have you any idea what time she'll be back?'

'She hoped to catch the five-ten, I believe.'

So it would be at least another hour and a quarter before she returned.

'I see. Thank you, Mrs Leyton. We'll come back later this

evening, around seven-thirty. Perhaps you could give her the message.'

'If I see her. I could give her a ring, I suppose.'

'Some people!' said Lineham as they returned to the car. 'Give her a ring, indeed, when the house is only a hundred yards away!'

'Pity. I was hoping to catch Vivienne without her husband. He's sure to be home before then.'

'So what now, sir?'

'Might as well do something useful. We'll go and have a word with Rain, I think. We should be in good time to catch him before he leaves for evening visiting time at the hospital.'

They drove in silence for a little while and then Thanet said, 'Pull in for a minute, will you Mike?'

Lineham did as he was asked and switched off the engine. They were in a lay-by in a narrow country lane which ran along the top of a ridge. They both wound their windows right down and the fragrant country air flowed into the car, laden with the mingled scents of lush green vegetation and the faint, sweet smell of strawberries from the field below on their left. At the bottom of the slope a lorry was being loaded with the last pickings of the day, ready for its trip to New Covent Garden.

Thanet stirred. 'I've been trying to work out how this baby business fits in — or if it fits in at all.'

'We can't just ignore it.'

'I know. And I agree, Rain does seem the most likely candidate for the father, in view of the timing. But it has occurred to me that if he is innocent he really may have known nothing about the baby, still be unaware of its existence.'

'If. But if he did kill Mrs Parnell, the baby could still be the precipitating factor, whether he knew about it originally or not.' Lineham warmed to his theme. 'Say Mrs Parnell had kept in touch with him through the years, and after her husband died had hopes that she and Rain would get together again. Then she reads about his engagement, and she's furious that even though she's now free herself, he's still not going to marry her. So she comes down to Sturrenden and threatens to tell Miss Knight about the child, if he doesn't break off with her.'

'I just don't like it, Mike. It doesn't sound like the Alicia we've been hearing about. Nothing anyone has said to us has even hinted that she'd be the type to resort to blackmail in a matter like this — nor that she ever had eyes for anyone but her husband.'

'True.' Lineham chewed his lip for a few moments, gazing out of the window at the fruit lorry, which was just moving off. 'Are you saying, then, that you really think Rain is in the clear?'

'I just don't know. And I agree, we have to go on investigating this particular avenue. But we mustn't forget that it's quite possible that one of the others was the father of Alicia's child.'

'But which?'

'Who can say, at this stage?' Thanet sighed. 'It was all so long ago. A lot can happen in twenty years. People change, they forget . . . Alicia was different then — young, flirtatious, even a bit flighty, perhaps. If so, the experience of having the baby would have sobered her up considerably. And I think you'll agree that, despite the fact that she had more than her fair share of tragedy, by all accounts she became a pretty fine sort of person. I don't know . . . I suppose we'll have to see Rain, tackle him about the baby, to see how he reacts, but I honestly wonder if we're doing the right thing.'

'But why, sir? I don't see what you mean.'

'Well, remember what I was saying just before we left the office? About disrupting the lives of innocent people? If Rain is innocent, if he didn't even know about the child, and his contact with Alicia on Saturday night was limited to those few minutes in the foyer after the concert, have we any right to give him further pain by telling him that he could be the father of a child he didn't know about and will never see? He has enough troubles of his own at the moment, without our adding to them unnecessarily.'

'With respect . . .'

'Mike!'

'Sorry, sir . . . I was only going to say that although I can see the point you're making, I don't think we can *afford* to have scruples like that. This is a murder investigation, after all.'

Thanet burst out laughing and slapped Lineham on the

shoulder. 'Spoken like a true policeman, Mike. And you're absolutely right, of course.' He sat back, folding his arms. 'Well, what are you waiting for? Drive on.'

'We're going to tackle Rain about the baby?'

'We're going to tackle Rain about the baby.'

NINETEEN

Nicholas Rain was mowing the lawn, describing slow, controlled arcs with a Flymo. He looked up as the police car pulled into the drive, cut the engine of the motor mower and walked slowly across the grass towards them. He was wearing tee shirt, jeans and walking boots. Thanet noted the latter with approval. Rain was obviously a practical man as well as an artist. Flymos should be treated with respect.

'Sorry to trouble you again, Mr Rain.'

Rain gave a resigned shrug. 'D'you mind if we stay in the garden? Then I won't have to unlace these.' He gestured at his boots.

'Not at all.'

Rain led the way around the side of the house to a paved terrace where comfortable cedarwood chairs with plump blue and white cushions were set around a slatted table of the same wood. On it stood a tray with a small flowered teapot, a single cup and saucer and, a bachelor's touch, a milk bottle. It was a pleasant place to relax on a warm summer evening. Low shrubs and variegated ornamental grasses spilled over on to the mellow slabs of york stone, softening the hard lines of the edges, and little clumps of low-growing thyme and rock plants grew here and there in spaces left between the paving stones. Beyond the terrace was the lawn, flanked by herbaceous borders, their curving edges leading the eye to a small cedarwood summerhouse with a conical roof, artfully set off centre at the far end of the garden. Behind, mature beech and chestnut trees provided a majestic backdrop.

'You have a beautiful garden,' said Thanet.

'It's my mother's pride and joy.' Rain's eyes clouded. 'She spends most of her time out here, especially in the summer. I feel I must try and keep it up until I can get someone to look after it for her.'

'How is she?'

'No change, I'm afraid.'

'And your sister?'

'Making good progress, now. Look, Inspector, much as I appreciate your asking, we both know that you haven't come to enquire about my mother's health. What do you want this time?'

Might as well be equally direct, thought Thanet. 'Did you know that Alicia Doyle was pregnant when she left Sturrenden in 1964 and had a baby the following January?'

Rain sat up with a jerk and his elbow caught the corner of the tray, knocking it off the table. The crockery shattered, scattering pieces of flower-sprigged porcelain all around them. Despite his previous determination to watch Rain's reaction to his question closely, Thanet's attention involuntarily switched to the falling tray and by the time he realised what had happened it was too late and Rain was murmuring apologies and picking up the pieces, helped by Lineham.

Cursing the accident — if that was what it was — Thanet waited until most of the fragments were retrieved and then said, 'If we could continue . . .'

Rain deposited a handful of broken china on the tray and sat down. 'Yes, of course . . . Sorry about that, clumsy of me . . . No, I'd no idea. No one knew, I'm sure of that, or I'd have heard . . . So that was why she moved away. We'd been told it was because her father had a new job, but we all assumed it was really because of Paul Leyton's suicide . . . You'd remember that, of course.'

'Yes, I do. But in view of this new information, the next question we naturally have to ask ourselves is, who was the father of that child?'

Rain stared at him. 'My God, you're not suggesting . . .?'

'Work it out for yourself. The baby was born in January 1965. Which means that it would have been conceived in April 1964. Who was Alicia Doyle's boyfriend at that time?'

Rain was still looking stunned. He was either a very good actor or genuinely taken aback, Thanet couldn't decide which. Thanet glanced at Lineham, who was sitting slightly behind Rain's line of vision, but the sergeant shrugged, obviously as uncertain as Thanet.

'I don't believe it.' It was scarcely more than a whisper.

'But it's true, nevertheless. I assure you we don't play games with this kind of information, Mr Rain.'

'I'd no idea . . . I really had no idea . . .' Rain passed a hand across his forehead and shook his head in disbelief. 'I'm sorry, Inspector, but this has . . . this is . . . It's a bit of a shock, to learn you might be a father, twenty years on.' He looked up, suddenly intense. 'What happened to the child?'

'We were hoping you might be able to tell us that.'

'Me!' Rain gave a derisive laugh and spread his arms wide. 'I assure you, Inspector, if it hasn't become obvious to you already, that I had no knowledge of the existence of any child, let alone its whereabouts. . . . Didn't Alicia bring it up, then?'

'No. The baby was adopted.'

'Was it a boy, or a girl?'

'A girl.'

'And you've really no idea where it . . . where she is?'

'Not as yet. But one never quite knows what will turn up. It seems that Mrs Parnell had been trying to trace the child for some months, and that a couple of weeks before she died she found out the girl's new identity quite by chance.'

'How do you know this?'

'Mrs Parnell's solicitor told us. Apparently she intended making a new will, in the girl's favour.'

'So she told him her name?'

'No. I gather she didn't want to rush things. She wanted to make contact with her daughter first, see how things went.'

'And you haven't found any clues to her new identity, among Alicia's papers?'

'Not so far.'

Rain frowned and then gazed abstractedly down at his clasped hands. He began absentmindedly to rub the tip of one thumb across the ball of the other. The silence stretched out until eventually he stirred, shook his head and raised it to look at Thanet again.

'I'm sorry, Inspector, but I find myself quite at a loss. As I said, it's rather a shock to learn that one might have been a father for twenty years without being aware of the fact. And at this stage . . . To be honest, I don't know whether to be glad or sorry that you don't know the girl's name, or where she is.'

'I can understand that.'

'Perhaps . . . if you do find out, in the course of your investigation . . . You'd let me know?'

'I can't promise that, I'm afraid. It would depend very much on the circumstances.'

'Yes, I can see that. But you'll bear it in mind?'

'Of course.'

There was nothing further to be said on the subject at the moment, and they left.

'What do you think, sir? Do you think he genuinely didn't know about the baby?'

'I'm not sure.'

They drove back to Vivienne Leyton's house in silence.

It looked as though she was home, this time. Some of the house windows were open and a metallic green Metro stood in the drive.

Before they had a chance to knock, the front door opened with a jerk and Vivienne Leyton stood glaring at them. She was wearing a beige linen safari-style suit, with a beige and white striped cotton blouse and high-heeled, strappy sandals. Her blazing mop of hair seemed to crackle with indignation.

'Really, Inspector, this is outrageous! It's too much! I've been up in town all day, I've only just got back, I have to prepare my husband's dinner and what do I find? An arbitrary message informing me that you will be calling to see me at seven-thirty. No "Is it convenient?" or anything like that, I'm just expected to be at your disposal regardless . . .'

'Yes, but . . .'

'It can't possibly be anything so urgent that it can't wait till morning, so if you don't mind . . .' And she started to close the door.

Thanet put out his hand to prevent it being slammed in his face. 'I'm sorry, Mrs Leyton, but I do mind.'

'Really! What right have you got, to come forcing your way in like this?'

'I am not forcing my way in. Indeed, if you would prefer not to have us in the house, that is your privilege. In which case, perhaps you'd be so kind as to accompany us to the

179

police station, and we can talk there.'

This case was bedevilled by aggressive, recalcitrant women, Thanet thought. It was degrading to have had to wield the same big stick twice in one day, but in the circumstances it seemed the only thing to do. And the threat seemed as effective with Vivienne Leyton as it had been earlier with Jessica Ross.

She stared at him, taken aback. 'You can't be serious . . .?' She glanced from Thanet to Lineham. 'You can't possibly mean . . .' Suddenly, she was alarmed. 'You're not *arresting* me?'

'No. We merely want to talk to you. And I repeat, I do apologise for the inconvenience.'

She stepped aside. 'You'd better come in,' she said, on a note of defeat.

She led the way once more into the sitting room and perched on the arm of one of the chairs. 'If we could just get on with it, then.'

'You will recall,' said Thanet, sitting down on the long, deeply-upholstered couch, 'that the last time we were here we asked you about your movements during the interval between the dinner and the dancing on Saturday night — between a quarter past ten and a quarter to eleven, that is.'

'So?'

'You told us, if you remember, that your recollection of what you did after leaving the powder room was rather hazy, but that you thought you had probably "drifted around" chatting to people you knew.'

'If you say so.'

'Now that you've had time to think about it, can you recollect the names of any of these people?'

'I don't know what you mean by "Now that you've had time to think about it". I lead a very busy life, Inspector, and I have better things to do than spend my time fruitlessly mulling over a particularly boring half an hour during a singularly uninteresting evening.'

Thanet sighed. 'Very well, Mrs Leyton. I see you're determined to be uncooperative. I have given you ample opportunity to offer me the information voluntarily and I will, in fact, ask you just once more. Are you sure that there is nothing you want to tell me, nothing at all to add to your statement about how you spent your time during that interval?'

There was no doubt about it, his formal tone had frightened her, though she was doing her best to hide it. She put up her hand as if casually to stroke her throat, but not quickly enough to hide the involuntary swallowing movement which betrayed her fear.

'I don't know what you mean.'

'Don't you? I would remind you that it is a serious offence, deliberately to withhold information from the police, especially in a case as serious as murder.'

A tense shake of the head.

How could he make her tell him, without revealing just how little he knew? 'In that case, perhaps you might change your mind when you hear that we have a witness, an independent witness at that, someone who could have no possible reason to lie . . .'

She opened her mouth. 'A wit . . .' Her voice emerged as a croak and she had to stop, clear her throat. 'A witness to what?' Her eyes were agonised.

Was it possible that she thought he meant, a witness to the murder? Had her unrelenting hostility been not merely the natural outcome of her aggressive nature but a smokescreen to hide her guilt? For the first time Thanet began seriously to entertain the possibility that Vivienne Leyton was their quarry. His eyes went to the hand which was still clutching her throat. Her nails were painted, yes, but short, very short, in fact. . . . Surely she wouldn't have had sufficient strength to overpower another woman of her own size? And yet, it was astounding just how much physical strength may be summoned up if the passions directing it are sufficiently powerful. . . . He became aware that she was still awaiting his reply.

'A witness to what?' she repeated.

'Oh come, Mrs Leyton, there's no need for me to spell it out for you.'

But still she said nothing.

It was no good. He would have to acknowledge defeat on

181

this point, in order to move forward. 'You were seen, Mrs Leyton. In the corridor outside Mrs Parnell's room.'

'Ah. I see.'

Was that *relief* he had glimpsed in her eyes?

'Well, Mrs Leyton?'

'Well, what?'

Keep cool, Thanet told himself. Don't let her rile you. 'I'm waiting for an explanation. And please, don't say, "Explanation of what?" To spell it out for you, I want to know exactly when you went upstairs, and precisely what you did when you got there. And,' he went on quickly as she glared at him defiantly and opened her mouth to interrupt, 'I must make it clear that I am not prepared to be fobbed off. I want answers to these questions, Mrs Leyton, and however long it takes, Sergeant Lineham and I are not going to leave until we get them.'

She glowered at him and folded her arms with a brusque, impatient movement, as if trying to contain her anger and frustration. For a full minute they held each other's eyes, locked in wordless combat. Thanet found himself willing her to capitulate. *Give in, go on, give in . . .*

Finally, recognising perhaps the degree of his determination, understanding that she could not hold out indefinitely, she gave a nonchalant little shrug and said, 'OK, you win, Inspector. Though I think that when you hear what I've got to say, you'll agree that it wasn't worth all the fuss. In fact, I can't think why I didn't tell you in the first place . . . I suppose because I thought it would save a lot of hassle . . .' She laughed. 'Big joke, in the circumstances. Anyway, it's very simple, really. I went up to Alicia's room, knocked at the door, got no reply, and came down again. And that's it. Satisfied?'

'Not quite. I'd like to take it a little more slowly. What time did you go up?'

She shrugged. 'Some time between half past ten and a quarter to eleven.'

'How did you know which room she was in?'

'Elementary, my dear Watson. I took a peek in the hotel register. It was lying open on the counter at the reception desk, and there were so many people about that no one noticed.'

'You went up in the lift?'

'Yes.'

'Then what?'

'I told you, I knocked at her door, got no reply, came down again.'

'In the lift?'

She fell straight into the trap he had set for her.

'Yes.'

'Why did you want to see her?'

'For a chat. Well, to be honest, I felt I'd been a bit off-hand with her, earlier on in the evening, and I wanted to make amends.'

'To apologise for your earlier behaviour, then?'

'That's right. Just to show there were no hard feelings.'

'Over what?'

'We parted on, shall we say, a sour note, many years ago. During dinner I kept on thinking how childish it was, to have behaved as I had, in the foyer . . .'

Thanet didn't believe a word of it. In his view, Vivienne Leyton just wasn't the sort of woman to go out of her way to apologise to a woman she hadn't seen for twenty years and would probably never see again.

'I'm sorry, I don't believe you. And I've had more than enough of this prevarication. As I told you, we have a witness who could have no possible reason to lie. And I know, I repeat, I *know*, that you are lying now.'

Vivienne Leyton's eyes flickered briefly in the direction of the door. Then, to Thanet's surprise, she burst into tears.

His astonishment did not last long. The next moment the sitting room door opened and Richard Leyton came into the room. She must have heard him arrive.

'What the hell . . .?' He hurried to his wife's side and put his arm around her shoulders, gathering her to him. Then he glared at Thanet. 'What the devil's going on here? How dare you invade my home and bully my wife like this? I shall report you to your superiors, have no doubt about that.'

'Do, by all means, Mr Leyton, but I think you will find that you have no legitimate grounds for complaint.'

'No legitimate . . .'

'Withholding evidence is a serious matter, especially in a murder case. And I'm sorry to say that this is precisely what your wife has been doing.'

'That still gives you no right to browbeat her!'

'I was not browbeating her, as you put it. I was simply informing her that I knew she was lying to me.' Thanet held up his hand. 'And before you make any further complaint, allow me to inform you that the reason why I didn't believe her story is because we have an independent — *independent* — witness, Mr Leyton, whose story disagrees with hers.'

Leyton stared at Thanet and then glanced down at his wife. Her tears had stopped now — perhaps, Thanet thought, because she wanted to be able to hear her husband's reactions to all this.

'Is this true, Viv?'

'Lend me your handkerchief, Richard, will you?'

'Of course.' He took it out and handed it to her, waited while she wiped her eyes and blew her nose. 'Viv?' he repeated.

'That's what he *claims*. I don't know what he's talking about. I just told him the truth, that I went up to Alicia's room during the interval on Saturday night, knocked, got no reply and came down again.' She was gazing up at her husband as she spoke and it was clear to Thanet that there was some kind of message, or appeal, in her eyes, but whatever it was Leyton hadn't received it. He was merely looking puzzled.

'You went up to see Alicia? But why?'

Vivienne Leyton tossed her head impatiently. 'Why not? Oh well, if you must know, because I felt I'd been a bit off-hand with her when we'd met, earlier in the evening. That's true, isn't it?'

'Well yes, but . . .'

She cut him off. 'There you are, then. I thought she might be back from the concert by then and I'd just pop up and apologise.'

'And then you went back down. In the lift,' said Thanet.

'Yes.'

'Sergeant Lineham, just read that statement out, will you?'

Lineham shuffled his papers obediently and for the second

time that day pretended to read from an imaginary script. 'Statement of Mrs Dora Brent, occupant of room number 105, the Black Swan on Saturday July 14th . . . Do you want it all, sir?'

'Just the relevant bit.'

'Ah, here we are. "My husband said it was only twenty-five to eleven and he didn't want to go to bed yet, so I went up alone. I had to wait a couple of minutes for the lift and when I stepped out on the third floor a woman passed me. I didn't see her face, but I noticed her because even from the back she was very striking. She was wearing a beautiful long, narrow, copper-coloured evening dress threaded with gold lurex and she had a mass of red hair, frizzed out in a great bush. She disappeared down the staircase at the end of the corridor" . . .'

Lineham paused significantly and both policemen looked at Vivienne Leyton.

Her face still wore an expression of expectancy which gradually turned to puzzlement as she realised that Lineham had finished.

'I'm sorry,' she said, 'I must be dim, but . . .'

'The staircase!' said Leyton. 'That's what you mean, isn't it, Inspector? The statement says you went down the staircase, Viv, and you told us you'd gone down in the lift.'

'Oh. I *see*.' Suddenly she was transformed, her face vivid with relief. 'Is that *all* . . . But I made a mistake, it's as simple as that. I'd just forgotten I used the stairs, on the way back down.'

'Why was that, Mrs Leyton?'

'What do you mean?'

'Why did you use the stairs, instead of the lift?'

She shrugged. 'I just felt like it.' She gave him a pert smile. 'Exercise is good for you.'

Thanet refused to allow himself to be provoked. He was still convinced that there was more to it than that. And yet, he was inclined to believe her, when she said that she had knocked at Alicia's door and got no reply. There had been the ring of truth in her voice. So what had he missed? Missed . . . Not what she had done, perhaps, but what she had *seen* . . .

According to Mallard, the murder had taken place between

ten and eleven on Saturday night. Alicia couldn't have got back to the Swan after the concert before ten-fifteen at the earliest. Vivienne Leyton claimed to have gone up in the lift at around ten-thirty, give or take a few minutes. Mrs Brent had seen her in the third floor corridor at around twenty to eleven. Assuming that Vivienne herself had not committed the murder, what would the murderer himself have been doing at that time? There were various possibilities, the least interesting being that he had not yet arrived. But equally, he might have been in Alicia's room, talking to her; the murder might actually have been taking place; it might already have happened, and he could have been preparing to leave; or — and as far as Vivienne was concerned, these were the two most intriguing possibilities of all — he might just have been arriving at her room, or leaving it, when Vivienne appeared on the scene. *In which case she could have seen him.*

Thanet realised that everyone was looking expectantly at him. He cleared his throat, which was suddenly dry with excitement. He felt as though he himself had been given a glimpse of the murderer, an oblique, tantalising glimpse, no more than a blur of movement at the very edge of his vision . . .

'Very well, Mrs Leyton. Say I accept that you might have walked back down because you just happened to feel like it, and that until a moment ago you'd forgotten you'd done so . . .'

'Just a moment, Inspector,' Leyton cut in. 'Aren't you forgetting something?'

'What, Mr Leyton?'

'I think an apology is in order, don't you? You reduce my wife to tears and then, when you find she hasn't been lying to you after all, that it was a simple mistake in memory on her part, you just barge on . . .'

'By all means.' Apologies cost nothing and were frequently a good investment. 'Mrs Leyton, if I have upset you unnecessarily, I apologise.'

Vivienne Leyton glanced up at her husband and gave an uneasy little laugh. Richard Leyton looked mollified. He stood up. 'Now that that's settled . . .'

'I'm sorry, Mr Leyton, I'm afraid I haven't quite finished.'

Leyton frowned, took his wife's hand, but said nothing.

'You've told us what you *did*, Mrs Leyton. Now I'd like you to tell us what you *saw*. From the moment you stepped out of the lift on the third floor, to the moment you arrived back downstairs.'

On target. Thanet could tell, by the flash of terror in her eyes before she looked down at her lap, the sudden curling of her toes in those pretty, open sandals. Could he be right? Had she really seen the murderer? But if she had, why hadn't she said so? Unless . . .

Thanet looked at Leyton, who was gazing protectively down at his wife. Could it be her husband, whom she was trying to protect? If so, this would explain the unspoken message which Vivienne had tried to convey to Leyton just now. *I was there, and I know it was you*, she could have been saying. Yet Leyton hadn't understood, Thanet was willing to swear to that. Unless that misunderstanding had been deliberate, a display put on for Thanet's sake.

They were all looking at Vivienne Leyton in expectant silence. Eventually her husband nudged her. 'Come on, Viv. We're waiting.'

Again she glanced up at him with that appeal for complicity and once again there was no response.

'I'm trying to remember,' she said irritably, sliding her hand out of his grasp. She began to pluck at one corner of the handkerchief balled up in her left hand, quick, jerky little movements which betrayed her inner tension. Finally she shook her head. 'There was nothing. I didn't see anything. It was extraordinary, the contrast . . . Downstairs you could hardly move for people, but upstairs it was quiet, quiet and empty . . .' An involuntary shudder coursed through her body and she bit her lip, hard.

'So why does the memory upset you?' said Thanet. He was beginning to think that it really would be sensible to take her in for questioning. If he was right, and she really had seen her husband up there, she was never going to say so with him sitting beside her, monitoring her every word and displaying so much solicitude.

187

'Viv?' said Leyton. And he passed one hand gently over her head in a soothing gesture. 'Did you see something?'

Had he detected a note of warning in Leyton's voice? Thanet wondered. Or had it merely been concern?

Vivienne Leyton took a deep breath. The tension in the room was almost palpable.

She raised her head and looked straight at Thanet. 'No,' she said. Suddenly she began to tremble. 'It's just that . . . It was so horrible, to think that I was up there and Alicia . . . Alicia was . . . just on the other side of that door . . .'

She began to weep again, noisy, racking sobs which convulsed her whole body. Richard Leyton put his arm around her again. 'Viv . . .' He glanced at Thanet and said fiercely, 'There's your answer, Inspector. Now will you please leave my wife alone and get out?'

They had no choice but to comply.

TWENTY

'I still think we ought to bring her in for questioning,' said Lineham.

It was the following morning and Thanet and Lineham were arguing about Vivienne Leyton. Like Thanet, Lineham had worked out that she must have been protecting her husband — unless, of course, she was guilty herself.

'What's the point?' said Thanet wearily. 'She's obviously made up her mind that she's not going to tell us, either way.'

'But if we saw her alone . . . Obviously she wasn't going to say anything last night, with him there, but without him we might manage to persuade her.'

'I doubt it. She's a very stubborn woman, and a very determined one. Oh, I agree we'll have to see her again, but I still feel it would be best if we had some sort of evidence to confront her with, when we do.'

'If she is protecting him, I can't think why she's so set on it. They're not exactly on the best of terms, anyone can see that. And that conversation you overheard . . .'

'Maybe it's just self-interest, pure and simple. She doesn't want to lose her comfortable life-style . . . Or maybe she wants to have an extra stick to beat him with, in the future . . . Who can tell? Maybe they both enjoy the way they live. Maybe conflict is the spice of life for them — or for her, anyway.'

'I don't see what evidence you hope to get against either of them anyway. I don't see what else we can do. It's so frustrating.' Lineham thumped the edge of his desk with a closed fist.

'Looks as though you two need a referee.' Mallard had poked his head into the room in time to hear Lineham's last words.

'Come in, Doc.' Thanet grinned. 'I was just saying that for some people conflict is the spice of life.'

'As you are demonstrating, presumably. I just called in to ask if you'd had any confirmation of that adoption theory of yours.'

'That Nicholas Rain was really Penny's father, you mean? Sorry, I forgot to let you know. No, that all fell through.'

'Suspected as much,' said Mallard with satisfaction. 'In fact, the more I thought about it, the more cock-eyed it seemed. The Rains were sensible people, they'd never have gone in for some hole-in-the-corner arrangement like that. It's too risky for everyone concerned, too much could go wrong. Far better to do it properly, with guaranteed anonymity on both sides.'

'Quite.'

'So you're stuck, are you?'

'No need to look so pleased about it. But no, we're not, as a matter of fact. Just one or two temporary difficulties, that's all.'

'Pleased about it? Don't be insulting Luke. I wasn't gloating over your lack of progress, I was merely endeavouring to spread a little sweetness and light.' And Mallard gave Thanet such a hearty clap on the back that glowing flakes of tobacco from his newly-lit pipe cascaded over his lap and he leapt up, beating them out. Joan was forever reproaching him for the minute holes which appeared with monotonous regularity in his clothes.

'Sweetness and light isn't all you'll be spreading if you go on like that, Doc,' he grumbled.

Mallard was grinning. 'Serves you right. Filthy habit. Been trying to break you of it for years.' He glanced at Lineham, who was watching with amusement. 'You ought to take a leaf out of Lineham's book. Bet he could beat you hands down on fitness, any day.'

'When you've quite finished the lecture . . .'

'All right.' Mallard held up his hands. 'No need to say any more. I know when I'm not wanted.'

But he was still smiling as he left.

'He seems unusually cheerful this morning,' said Lineham.

'Hmm. Anyway, what were we saying?'

'We were talking about the Leytons.'

'Ah, yes. And you were doing a bit of table-thumping, as I recall.'

'Well it is infuriating.' Lineham was looking frustrated all over again. 'Every time we get a clear-cut lead on any of them, something crops up to stop us going ahead, or it fizzles out, or one of the others suddenly seems a better bet.' He sat up, assumed the pose of a race commentator clutching a microphone and began to talk in a rapid monotone. 'They're off! And it's Richard and Vivienne Leyton pulling away, with Bassett close behind, followed by Ross and Rain. Now, suddenly it's Rain, Rain is pulling away, but no, Ross is overtaking him, Ross is taking a clear lead. But no, Rain is coming up behind and here's an outsider coming up, it's Hollister, Hollister, no, he can't make it, he's dropping behind and yes, he's fallen, he's out of the race, it's Bassett instead, yes, it's Bassett, no, the Leytons are making headway, followed by Ross and Rain, it's going to be a very close thing . . .' Lineham made a disgusted sound in his throat and sat back, folding his arms. 'Makes you sick,' he said.

'Feeling better, Mike?' Thanet had been watching his sergeant indulgently. It had been a harmless enough way for Lineham to vent his feelings. 'All right, so at the moment it's anybody's guess. Now, let's stop fooling around and get down to it. We're both agreed, I think, that this was no casual crime committed by an outsider.'

'Because Mrs Parnell's money and jewellery were not touched, and that red file mysteriously disappeared.'

'Yes. So our chief suspects would appear to be Jessica Ross, the two Leytons and Nicholas Rain.'

'With Bassett as an outsider, sir.'

'True. All right, we won't forget Bassett. Though there's very little, so far, to implicate him.'

'He's got a possible motive, sir, if he really was as attached to Paul Leyton as we think.'

'Revenge. Yes. And no alibi, either. Perhaps we have been rather remiss, there. We'll get hold of a photograph and see if anyone who was at the Swan on Saturday recognises him.'

'If only there hadn't been that Ladies' Night, and all those people crowding the place out just at the wrong time . . .'

'No point in saying, "if only", Mike.'

191

'And you're still not discounting Mr Rain, sir?'

'I don't think we can.' Thanet leaned back in his chair, clasping his hands behind his head. 'As we've said before, the fact is that unless Alicia was killed by Jessica Ross, for gain, there just doesn't seem to be anyone in her present life who's even a remote possibility. In which case it seems most likely that she was murdered by someone local, for a reason connected with her past. So we have to continue to look at Rain. For all we know there's some other reason, a reason we haven't begun to guess at yet, why he might have wanted to get rid of her.'

'I still think we can't discount the possibility that he and Mrs Parnell might have kept a relationship going all these years. After all, she was an attractive woman, sir, and as her husband was incapable of making love to her . . .'

'We don't know that he was incapable.'

'But he was paralysed from the waist down! And Mr Thrall said that she had told him that her husband couldn't give her any children.'

'Not quite. He'd never *been able* to give her a child, was the way Thrall put it. And that's not necessarily the same thing at all. Anyway, that's not the point. The point is that Parnell might have been paralysed, might have been sterile, too, but he could still have been capable of making love. It depends, I understand, on the nature of the injury. If it's a spinal injury only, it might still be possible, with stimulation. You remember that furore over that Catholic couple who were initially refused permission to marry by their priest, because, he said, they would be incapable of consummating the marriage?'

'Yes. They did get permission in the end   gh, didn't they?'

'Exactly. There must have been good reason, for the Church to change its mind like that. I remember that at the time I heard an item on the radio, by a doctor who specialised in the sexual disorders of paraplegics, and he seemed to think they might well be able to manage it. So I think that as far as the Parnells are concerned we simply can't take it for granted that he was incapable of making love to her, and that she would have been driven to take a lover through sexual need.'

And the other thing is that from all we've heard about her, it wouldn't have been consistent with Alicia's character or with her relationship with her husband, for her to have been carrying on an affair for years behind his back.'

'Maybe. But surely we still have to take it into account as a *possibility*. In which case the reason why she would have seemed especially on edge for the couple of weeks previous to her death would not have been because she was wondering how best to approach her daughter, but because she'd seen Rain's engagement announced in the papers and was nerving herself to tell him that if he didn't break it off she'd tell Miss Knight about the affair and also about the baby. In which case, the red folder could have contained documentary evidence — photographs, love letters perhaps, even the baby's birth certificate — which she could have threatened to show Miss Knight.'

Thanet was shaking his head. 'It's no good, Mike, I still can't see Alicia as a blackmailer either. But I do agree that what you're saying all hangs together, and that we can't afford to ignore the possibility that it did happen like that. All right. We'll make further enquiries in London, see if there's anything even remotely resembling a whisper that Alicia and Rain have ever been seen together.'

Thanet made a note, then laid his pen down again. 'So much for Rain. Now, Jessica Ross. How are the men getting on with showing her photograph to guests at the Ladies' Night?'

'Slowly, I'm afraid. And with no luck so far. There were about two hundred people there.'

'They've got the description of what she was wearing?'

'Yes.'

'So we'll just have to be patient, see what comes up. Pity we didn't think of getting them to show Bassett's photograph at the same time. We slipped up there, Mike. Anyway, that leaves us with the Leytons.'

'I still think . . .'

'Mike, I know what you think. You've made it abundantly clear. And I've also stated my reason for disagreeing with you. Mrs Leyton is a tough nut to crack and before we tackle her I want some good, clear, irrefutable evidence so that I can lay it

in front of her and say, "There, explain that away." Besides
. . .' He frowned.

'What, sir?'

'Something's been nagging at me for days. If only I could
think what it was . . .'

'Try thinking of something else.'

'What do you think I've been doing!' Thanet shook his
head, as if to clear it, massaged his temples.

The telephone rang. Thanet answered it and raised an eyebrow at Lineham.

'Send them up.'

He replaced the receiver. 'Well, it looks as though you've
got what you wanted, Mike. The mountain has come to
Mohammed.'

'Mrs Leyton?'

'The same. Accompanied by spouse.'

'Really? I wonder what they want.'

'Intriguing, isn't it? A united front isn't exactly their strong
point.'

'Perhaps she's come to confess, and wants him to hold her
hand.'

'The trouble with you, Mike, is that you have an over-
optimistic nature.'

Thanet's guess was that possibly, overnight, Leyton had
managed to get out of his wife the reason for her prevarication
of the previous day and had persuaded her to tell the truth at
last. Thanet's pulse quickened. Vivienne Leyton had actually
been there, on the spot, round about the time the murder had
been committed . . .

The Leytons looked nervous, apprehensive, and Vivienne
Leyton avoided Thanet's eye as they sat down. It was the first
time Thanet had seen Leyton out of his working clothes and
they looked a handsome, prosperous pair, he in a light grey
summer suit, striped shirt and sober tie, she in an eye-opening,
sizzling pink cotton dress which Thanet would have expected
to clash with her hair, but for some reason didn't.

'It's good of you to see us without an appointment, Inspector,' said Leyton.

'Not at all. What can I do for you?'

'First of all, I feel I owe you an apology. I'm afraid I was abominably rude to you last night.'

Now that they had come to him voluntarily Thanet could afford to be generous. 'Forget it. It's an occupational hazard, I'm afraid. I've experienced far worse, I assure you.'

'All the same . . .'

'Please. I mean it.'

'Very well. Thank you.' Leyton shifted in his seat, glanced anxiously at his wife. 'We've come to see you because . . .' He cleared his throat, began again. 'It's just that after you'd gone, last night, well, we . . . I couldn't help feeling that you were right, that my wife was rather more upset than . . . than the occasion seemed to warrant. So in the end I persuaded her to tell me what was the matter.'

So he had been right. Thanet experienced a spurt of satisfaction, and the nape of his neck prickled with excitement.

Leyton sat up a little straighter and squared his shoulders, as if bracing himself against an anticipated onslaught. 'The truth of the matter is, that she was behaving as she did out of mistaken loyalty to me.'

'I see . . . at least, I think I do. Could you clarify a little?'

'Certainly. I . . .'

'Or perhaps we could hear this from Mrs Leyton herself?'

The Leytons consulted with a glance, then she nodded. 'All right. It was stupid of me, really. I should have realised that Richard . . . that I was mistaken. I . . . I thought, you see, that as I stepped out of the lift on the third floor that night, I saw Richard moving away from me towards the stairs at the far end of the corridor.'

Once again Thanet experienced that tantalising sensation of catching a fleeting glimpse of the murderer.

'What time was this?'

'I worked it out. It must have been about twenty-five to eleven.'

'And at the time you concluded . . .?'

'That he must have come up to see Alicia.'

'Why did you think he might have done that?'

She caught her lower lip beneath her teeth. 'Because . . . well, I don't like airing these things in public, Inspector, but I suppose . . . The truth is, as I told you, that I hadn't particularly wanted to speak to Alicia earlier in the evening, but Richard had manoeuvred me into it and I'd been . . . well, rather cross with him, all evening. I thought . . . I thought he might have gone up to see Alicia during the gap between dinner and the dancing just to . . . well, just to spite me.' She gave her husband an apologetic smile. 'I really should have known better. Richard isn't like that.'

'So what did you do?'

'Do?'

'When you thought you saw him?'

'I opened my mouth to call him, and then I thought, no, I'd wait and see if he said anything, later.'

'And then?'

She shrugged. 'The rest of what I told you was true. I went and knocked at Alicia's door, but there was no reply. I listened for a moment, but there was no sound from inside. I tried the handle, but the door was locked and I assumed she hadn't yet got back from the concert. I was still a bit shaken from seeing Richard, as I thought, and to give myself time to think I decided to walk back down, instead of taking the lift. I used the stairs at the opposite end of the corridor from the ones I thought I'd seen Richard go down, just in case he'd got held up, and I bumped into him. But I needn't have worried. When I got downstairs he was talking to someone, in the foyer.'

'And you decided not to mention this little episode to him.'

'I told you, I was waiting to see if he would say anything to me.'

Unlikely, Thanet thought. It was much more probable that she had wanted to have a weapon which she could use against her husband at a time when she needed one. And yet, there was a curious bond between this pair.

Everyone looked at Leyton and he burst out, 'Don't you see, Inspector? It's all been a terrible misunderstanding. . . . I didn't go up to see Alicia during the interval, I can assure you of that. The thought never entered my head. Why should it? I hadn't seen the woman for twenty years and I couldn't have cared less if I didn't see her for another twenty. . . . My wife was mistaken, that's all. And what's more, I can prove it.' He fished in his pocket and produced a piece of paper. 'That's why we're here. To get this ridiculous misunderstanding cleared up for once and for all. I've been up half the night, thinking back over the interval on Saturday evening, doing one of those total recall tricks — you know, you shut your eyes and take yourself back through something step by step. Here's a consecutive list of all the people I spoke to from the moment we came out of the dinner until the moment we returned to the Fletcher Hall for the dancing. I've given names, times, topics of conversation. And I think — no, I *know* you'll find that they tally with other people's accounts, and that I simply wouldn't have had time to go making social calls up on the third floor.'

Thanet took the paper. 'Thank you. As a matter of interest, Mrs Leyton . . . next day, when you heard about Mrs Parnell's death, why didn't you mention this to your husband then? If you believed that he had gone up to see Mrs Parnell at the very time when she had been killed, then this was now a very serious matter.'

'I panicked. It really was very stupid of me, I see that now. I honestly didn't think for one moment that Richard . . . that my husband could have had anything to do with Alicia's death, but . . . I don't know, I just wanted to pretend that it had never happened, that I hadn't been involved in any way, that the whole thing was nothing to do with me . . .'

All her ill-temper and arrogance were gone and two pairs of eyes, one blue and one brown, pleaded with Thanet to believe their story.

And he did. This time he was sure that she had at last given him the truth, and so had her husband. He glanced down at the piece of paper. It was all there, in immense detail. He looked up at them again and suddenly there was a pressure in his head. It was a physical sensation, as intrusive as a headache, only different. The skin of his arms tingled with excitement, as if he had received a minor electric shock. Past experience had taught him that this particular sensation of pressure usually heralded some breakthrough in understanding. He mustn't focus on it, though, or it would go away. He became aware that Lineham was watching him and that the

Leytons were still awaiting a response. With an effort he forced his attention back to the conversation.

'This man you saw, Mrs Leyton.' *Blue eyes, brown eyes*, 'How far away from you was he, down the corridor?'

She frowned. 'I'm not very good at distances. He was a few paces away from the top of the stairs.'

'Tell me what you can about him.' The pressure was still there, mounting as steadily and as inevitably as an approaching orgasm.

'There's not a lot to tell.' She gave a nervous little laugh.

Thanet closed his eyes as enlightenment burst upon him and a succession of images raced through his mind, like speeded-up film. Of *course*, this was what had been eluding him for days, that one crucial fact, staring him in the face, its significance recognised by his unconscious mind but submerged until now. He knew, with a complete and absolute certainty that the case was solved and he felt humble, grateful and above all exultant. He would have liked to leap out of his chair and bound about the room, shouting his triumph. Instead he opened his eyes to a disconcerted silence.

Vivienne Leyton had obviously been telling him something; her last words still hung upon the air, unacknowledged. He could tell by her face that she had thought them significant, that she had expected a positive response from him.

'I'm sorry, I was thinking. I wonder if you'd mind repeating that.'

But it wasn't really necessary. He already knew what she was going to say.

TWENTY-ONE

Thanet and Lineham led the way through the narrow country lanes and two more police cars followed on behind, sensibly spaced out. There was no desperate hurry. A telephone call had ensured that their quarry would be there waiting for them, in blissful ignorance of the real nature of their errand. The search warrant which would, Thanet devoutly hoped, set the seal on their success, was safely tucked away in his breast pocket. He was convinced that the evidence he hoped to find still existed. Lineham had been dubious.

'He'll have destroyed it, sir, surely. It would have been madness to keep it, in the circumstances.'

'People don't always do the sensible thing, Mike. I don't think he would have been able to bring himself to destroy these particular papers.'

He only hoped that he was right, that he was not about to make a monumental fool of himself. He had certainly had enough of a struggle, convincing the Super.

'You know as well as I do, Thanet, that you can't possibly be granted a search warrant in these circumstances. If you'd arrested the man, yes, or if you were applying under the Theft Act . . .'

He was right, and Thanet knew it. Desperation brought him inspiration.

'But sir, what we shall be looking for *is* stolen property. Not in the conventional sense, perhaps, but . . .'

Superintendent Parker had looked thoughtful. 'Hmm. I see what you mean.' Then he had lapsed into silence, tapping a pencil on his blotter and gazing away out of the window, as if his view of All Saints' spire would provide him with spiritual guidance.

'This is a very delicate situation, Thanet. Very delicate. The man's a highly respected citizen. If you're wrong, there could be hell to pay.'

'We have an eye-witness, sir . . .'

The Superintendent had given a contemptuous snort. 'Eye-witness! You know precisely the degree to which we can afford to rely upon eye-witnesses — not at all! And this one . . . a momentary glimpse, seen in a hotel corridor at night, with the man's back to her. . . . Defence counsel would make mince-meat of it. She didn't even identify him to begin with, though she knows the man.' Another snort. 'Thought it was her own husband, if you please!'

'I told you, sir, they're very alike. They . . .'

The Superintendent waved an impatient hand. 'Yes, yes, I know. We've been through all that once, already.'

'I'm absolutely convinced I'm right, sir.'

'You have made that very plain, Thanet, but the fact remains that you're not the only one who'd be sticking his neck out, if I let you go ahead with this. All this airy-fairy stuff is not enough. What we need is some positive evidence of the man's guilt, then we'd be home and dry.'

Thanet felt as though he would explode with frustration. Talk about vicious circles! 'But sir, the whole point of this search is to find that very evidence!'

Parker glared at him. 'All right, Thanet, I'm not a complete idiot, you know. I can see your dilemma. But you must recog-nise that I have mine, too.'

Thanet realised that anything else he said might jeopardise his chances of success. Besides, the Super was right. It would be a risk, and if anything went wrong Parker would ultimately be held responsible. And he had more to lose than Thanet.

The Superintendent took his time, tapping his pencil on the blotter again and scowling at All Saints' spire as if it were failing in its duty by not providing him with an immediate and acceptable solution. Finally he said, 'Very well then, Thanet. I'll back you. But you'd better start praying now that you're right about all this.'

The devil of it was, thought Thanet as the little procession neared its destination, he was almost praying that he was wrong. As far as his professional pride was concerned then yes, he needed that evidence, but privately . . . He couldn't ever remember approaching an arrest so reluctantly.

They had arrived. The three cars swept up the drive and parked side by side. It was a morning of bright sunshine and clear blue skies, and the garden of Three Chimneys had never looked more beautiful, nor more inviting. The cool green velvet of the lawn, the glowing swathes of colour in the herbaceous borders, the harmonious juxtaposition of foliage, shape and line which is the hall-mark of the gifted gardener, provided a visual feast enhanced by the scent of roses and by the cascade of music which flowed through an open window. Thanet stood for a few moments absorbing the almost unbearable sweetness and poignancy of the pure, liquid notes. Was this Rain's swan song? Had he guessed the reason for their visit?

By prearrangement the other men remained in their cars while Thanet and Lineham approached the front door. The music cut off abruptly in mid-phrase when they knocked and Rain was still carrying bow and instrument when he opened the door.

'Sorry, I didn't hear you . . . Come in, Inspector.' His gaze took in the other cars, the waiting men, then returned to Thanet. There was no surprise in his face, no outrage, merely resignation, a weary acceptance.

'We have a warrant to search these premises, Mr Rain.' Thanet took the paper from his pocket and presented it for Rain's inspection.

Rain barely glanced at it before shaking his head. 'That won't be necessary. I know what you've come for. You can tell your men to stay where they are.'

And without waiting for Thanet's reaction Rain turned and walked back along the passage.

Lineham raised his eyebrows and Thanet nodded. The sergeant hurried across the gravel to the cars and Thanet followed Rain into the sitting room. The violinist laid his instrument gently down in its case, then loosened the bow. He seemed completely absorbed in the little ritual, a ritual which he must have performed thousands, perhaps hundreds of thousands of times before. What was Rain thinking? Thanet wondered, as he watched him slide the bow carefully into position in the lid.

lovingly folding around the mellow, gleaming wood of the violin the silk scarf evidently kept in the case specifically for this purpose. Had this little sequence of actions, no doubt as automatic to Rain as brushing his teeth, suddenly acquired a special significance, become a private farewell to his art? Once again Thanet was overwhelmed by a sense of the significance of what he was about to do. What right had he, an ordinary, humdrum mortal with no special contribution to make to society, even to contemplate depriving the world of a gift like Rain's?

Lineham came quietly into the room, shutting the door behind him. Rain closed the lid and snapped the lock, his hand lingering for a brief caress on the worn black surface of the case. Then he sat down heavily in the nearest chair, as if his legs were suddenly incapable of bearing his weight a moment longer.

'When you rang, a little while ago, to say you were coming . . . I almost told you then.'

Quietly, unobtrusively, Thanet and Lineham sat down.

'Told me what?' Thanet couldn't believe that it was going to be this easy. And yet . . .

'That I had killed Alicia.' Rain dropped his head in his hands.

So there it was. This was no false confession, made for sensational or irrational reasons. It should have been a moment of triumph and it was true that Thanet did experience one brief spark of relief that he had been proved right. But it was immediately extinguished by pity, for here was a man driven by force of circumstance into tragedy. It was true that he himself had initially been responsible for setting into motion those forces which would ultimately bring about his downfall, and also that in trying to avoid the consequences of his behaviour he had committed the ultimate crime against humanity. But despite all this, Thanet could not help feeling sorry for him and envious of Lineham who, notebook calmly at the ready, was prey to no such inconvenient emotion. At his signal the sergeant rose and spoke the formal words of the caution. Thanet doubted that Rain even heard it properly. His face was expressionless, his eyes dull.

'If we could have the folder now, Mr Rain . . .'

Rain looked blankly at him, as if he had no idea what Thanet was talking about, and Thanet experienced a brief, irrational stab of panic. What if they had been talking at cross-purposes all along? Yet Rain's confession had been specific enough . . .

No, Rain was rising, sliding aside a painting to reveal a wall-safe. In a matter of seconds he was turning, the red folder in his hands. Without a word he gave it to Thanet, then returned to his chair.

Thanet slid out the flap, extracted the slim sheaf of papers. And yes, here was the confirmation he had been seeking, the visible, tangible proof that his theory was correct. First, a list of names, sheets of them, all of female children born on the same date in January 1965, January 10th. One of those names was ringed.

Next came a birth certificate, the child's original birth certificate, naming Alicia Mary Doyle as the mother, the child as Alice; father unknown. Thanet remembered that the father's name was entered only if he had acknowledged paternity to the adoption agency. Rain, then, had probably been telling the truth when he had professed that he had originally been ignorant of the child's very existence.

Finally there was a small brown envelope. It contained the two crucial pieces of evidence. One was a newspaper cutting. What must Alicia have felt when she had picked up the paper one morning, and had been confronted with this? Thanet stared at it, Jessica Ross's words echoing through his mind . . . *She was pale, shaking, as if she'd seen a ghost*. Not a ghost, alas, but flesh and blood, her own.

The other vital piece of evidence was a faded photograph. On the back was written *Alice, February 12th 1965*. Taken, no doubt, just before Alicia had parted with the child. Thanet turned it over. The baby smiled up at him. Babies, Thanet thought, usually looked very much alike and he would have been hard put to it, to distinguish between them.

Except in this case.

For Alicia's child had had one unique, identifying feature, as individual as a fingerprint: a clearly-defined, perfectly heart-shaped birthmark on her right cheek.

TWENTY-TWO

Thanet passed the newspaper cutting and the photograph to Lineham, who compressed his lips and nodded solemnly. Rain had reverted to his former posture, knees apart, head in hands. Now, he stirred.

'I'd better explain . . .'

'If you wish. But as you have been told, you have the right to remain silent.'

Rain shook his head, ran a hand through his hair. 'No, I'd rather . . . It's been impossible, carrying this alone.'

Especially with the added anxiety over Mrs Rain, thought Thanet.

'And I can assure you, Inspector, that I would give anything, anything at all, to be able to put the clock back.' He attempted a wry smile. 'I suppose all . . . murderers,' and he brought the word out as though it were choking him, 'say they never meant to do it.'

'Far from it, I assure you.'

'Nevertheless . . . I still can't believe that I . . . that Alicia . . . I know I lied to you, Inspector, and I don't see why you should believe me now, but I was only trying to protect Melanie. No, that sounds far too deliberate, and the truth is, it all happened so fast that . . . What I mean is, I can only assume that it was the thought of what it would do to Melanie that made me lose control . . . If she ever found out that I was her . . .' and he swallowed, as if to control rising nausea, 'her father, I mean.'

'I know.'

Rain focused suddenly and fiercely upon Thanet, directing the whole weight of his formidable personality and intelligence upon him. For Thanet, the effect was as dramatic as if he had been walking along a dark alley at night and someone had suddenly shone a searchlight in his face.

'Yes,' said Rain wonderingly. 'I believe you do. I really believe you do . . . What I told you yesterday was true, you know. I had no idea that I had made Alicia pregnant, that she had had a baby before she was married. That alone was shock enough, but when she told me . . .' He ran his hand through his hair and took a deep breath. 'She rang me up, you see, on Saturday afternoon. About half past four. Said she wanted to come and see me, that it was really urgent. I was astounded, naturally. After all, I hadn't seen or heard from her for twenty years. . . . I told her it wasn't very convenient at the moment, that my fiancée and her parents were here, but if it was all that urgent she could come if she wished. But she said no, she didn't want to butt in or cause any awkwardness — I realised later, of course, that the last thing she wanted to do was meet Melanie for the first time under those circumstances. . . . Anyway, I was so tied up one way and the other that the only possible time we could manage to meet was after the concert, in the foyer.

'Even then, we had only a few minutes. Melanie and her parents were waiting — we'd arranged to go out for supper, afterwards. But Alicia wanted me to go back to the hotel with her. . . . She was so pressing . . . said she had something to show me, that it was absolutely essential I see it, a matter of life and death, almost. By now I was beginning to wonder if she was quite stable. She seemed so tense, so desperate . . . I didn't feel I could just shake her off, abandon her. She was so obviously in some kind of trouble . . . I suggested we meet the following morning, but she wouldn't be put off. She told me that the reason why it was so urgent was because it concerned Melanie, that it was a matter of Melanie's welfare . . . I still couldn't imagine any connection, but by now I was thinking that the simplest thing would be to humour her. I was afraid that if I didn't she would create a scene, there and then, in the middle of the foyer . . . and anyway by now I was becoming intrigued.

'So, I told Melanie and her parents that I'd decided to go back to the hospital after all, and I put them in a taxi. I hated deceiving them, they were very understanding . . . Then I went back to the Swan with Alicia.'

205

'Sorry to interrupt you, sir,' said Thanet, 'but there is just one question I'd like to ask, at this point. . . . When you left the concert hall, did you go out by the main entrance?'

'No, via a rear entrance which opens on to the small car park at the back of the hall.'

Which was why Jessica Ross had missed Alicia, despite her vigilance.

'Thank you. Do go on.'

'The Swan was crawling with people, there was some kind of function on — I suppose if there hadn't been, someone would have noticed us, but as it was we went up in the lift and when we got to her room she went straight to her overnight case and took that out.'

His eyes lingered for a moment on the red folder.

'Then she told me . . .' He dropped his head in his hands again and began to tug at his hair with tense, plucking movements. His voice became jerky, the words forced out in irregular spurts. 'She told me first . . . about the baby . . . and then she . . . she opened the folder and showed me . . . showed me the photograph. That, she said, was *our child*.' Rain sat up, met Thanet's eye. 'Well, you've met Melanie, you've seen that birthmark of hers for yourself. . . . To think I always liked it, thought it rather distinctive . . .' Rain shook his head in disbelief and gave a bitter little laugh. 'Anyway, when Alicia showed me that photograph, I couldn't believe what I was seeing . . . I'd known Melanie was adopted of course, she'd told me soon after we met, but this . . . I didn't want to believe it, couldn't *bear* to believe it. Melanie and I, we'd been . . . sleeping together. We were *engaged*, for God's sake . . .'

The atmosphere in the room was thick with emotion. Rain was crying now, raw, gasping sobs which tore at his throat and made him incapable of further speech. Thanet couldn't bear to sit still any longer. He rose, went to lay a sympathetic hand on Rain's shoulder, then crossed to look out of the window. Outside the garden glowed in the midday sun, its beauty and serenity a poignant contrast to the pain which filled the room. The men who had accompanied them were standing about by the cars, still awaiting orders. Thanet had forgotten about them. Quietly, he went to murmur in Lineham's ear. They could return to Sturrenden, they wouldn't be needed now. Then he sat down again.

Rain was calming down and by the time Lineham returned a minute or two later, he had regained control of himself. Eventually he said, 'I truly don't know how it happened, Inspector. One minute she was standing there, talking to me, and the next my hands were around her throat and she was . . . dead. I laid her on the bed and tried to revive her, but I could see that it was pointless. The folder had fallen to the floor and I picked it up. Then I left. I'd only been in there a matter of minutes. Minutes!' Rain shook his head incredulously. 'At times, since, I couldn't help wondering if I'd imagined the whole thing, if it was all some terrible nightmare. But I'd only have to look at that, to know it wasn't.' And he nodded at the folder.

No jury could fail to be moved by such a story, Thanet thought. Rain would get away with manslaughter. The anxiety over his mother's condition would work in his favour, too. . . . He would get a relatively short sentence, possibly even a suspended one.

And then what? What would happen to Melanie, the innocent victim of this whole sorry tale, when all this came out in court? How would she be able to cope with the knowledge that she had, all unwittingly, committed incest, how could she reconcile herself to the loss of mother, father, husband and emerge emotionally unscarred?

'Naturally,' said Rain, 'I shall plead guilty.'

It was as if he had tuned in to Thanet's thoughts.

'That way,' Rain went on, 'none of this need ever be made public.'

'You realise that in those circumstances you would get a life sentence?'

'Of course.' Rain lifted his head proudly. 'And that, I would say, seems only fair. A life for a life. Mine for Alicia's. I think, in a way, I shouldn't be able to live with myself if I didn't have to pay. If indeed I shall ever be able to anyway. But that's not the main reason why I've decided to plead guilty. As I said, if I do it this way, none of this need ever come out. Melanie need never know of our true relationship. This way, her innocence will be preserved. And my going to prison will also, I hope, have the advantage of helping her to forget me. Knowing her, she'll probably try to remain loyal. But I shall make it impossible for her to do so. I shall refuse to see her. She's young and in time she'll meet someone else, someone more . . . worthy of her. It's the best way, the only way, to salvage what we can out of this whole sorry mess. This was why, even before you rang up, earlier on, I'd already decided to make a confession.'

Nothing was going to make Rain change his mind, Thanet could see that. And he was probably right. This way would cause the least damage. The average length of a life sentence was nine years. With remission for good behaviour, Rain could be out in far less time than that.

There was nothing more to be said. He nodded. 'Sergeant Lineham will accompany you upstairs, while you put a few things together.'

While they were gone, he shut the downstairs windows and locked the back door, then went on ahead to wait beside the car. When they appeared he reached sideways and down to open the door — and found that he couldn't move.

His back had gone again.

TWENTY-THREE

Thanet lay flat on his back in bed, seething over the injustice of it all. What had he done to deserve this? It wasn't as though he had been rash, or careless . . . He squirmed at the memory of having to be manoeuvred into the car by his prisoner and his sergeant, of arriving back at the station as twisted as a corkscrew. The attitude of his physiotherapist had been the last straw.

'Been heaving your lawnmower about again, Mr Thanet?'

'No! I didn't do *anything* I shouldn't. Just bent to open the car door, that's all.'

'Well I did warn you. Once a disk has been misplaced, it can easily pop out again.'

Pop out! She made it sound so trivial, so insignificant! Not trusting himself to speak Thanet had managed to heave himself on to the couch and had once more yielded to the discomfort and indignity of being manipulated as if pain were an abstract and his body no more animate than a lump of dough.

And now here he was, his comfortable bed transformed into an instrument of torture by the planks which Joan had inserted beneath the mattress and with the prospect of forty-eight hours of boredom. He worked it out. Two thousand eight hundred and eighty minutes. Or a hundred and seventy-two thousand eight hundred seconds . . .

He reached out and switched on the tape he had made earlier, listened critically while it ran. He wondered how Lineham had handled the interview with Melanie's parents, how Melanie herself had taken the news of the arrest and whether she had already had to face the shock of Rain's refusal to see her. He wondered how Rain was taking his first night in the cells and whether there was any improvement in Mrs Rain's condition . . .

He glanced at the clock. Six-thirty. Which meant, in fact,

that his forty-eight hours was now down to forty-six; two thousand seven hundred and sixty minutes or a hundred and sixty-five . . . Was that the front door bell? He strained to hear above the muffled noise of the television from the living room below, the distant whine of the washing machine from the kitchen. Lineham had promised to call around and in Thanet's view the visit was long overdue.

There were voices in the hall. Yes, it was Lineham. Thanet listened enviously as his sergeant took the stairs two at a time.

'How are you feeling, sir?'

'Frustrated. Pull up a chair.'

Lineham complied. 'Your wife tells me you've got to stay flat on your back for forty-eight hours.'

'Another hundred and sixty-five thousand, five hundred and twenty seconds, to be precise. Comes to something, when I've nothing better to do than mental arithmetic. Which reminds me . . .' Thanet handed Lineham the tape. 'My final report on the Parnell case. Get it typed up for me, will you? How's Rain?'

Lineham put the tape in his pocket and pulled a face. 'Resigned. Quiet. Even more so since we had the news from the hospital. His mother died at five o'clock this afternoon.'

So, yet another blow for Rain, Thanet thought. The violinist must be feeling that his world had collapsed around him, his fiancée, his career and now his mother, all lost within the space of a few short hours. Perhaps worst of all, his self-respect had gone. A man at peace with himself has inner reservoirs of strength upon which he can draw in time of need, but because of those few fatal moments when Rain had lost his self-control, he had forfeited even this.

'And Miss Knight is terribly upset, of course, that he won't see her.'

'She's been into the office?'

'Asking for you, sir, yes. She wants you to use your influence on Rain, to persuade him to allow her to visit him. I told her I'd speak to you about it, but that I really didn't think there was any prospect of him changing his mind. I hope I did the right thing.'

'I don't see what else you could have done, in the circumstances. Poor kid, she must be not only completely shattered but totally bewildered by it all. It's fortunate her adoptive parents are here to see her through. The awful thing is, she'll have to live with that incomprehension for the rest of her life. If she ever learnt the truth it would make a nonsense of the sacrifice Rain is making, and the tragedy is that she can never know that that sacrifice exists, let alone that it's entirely on her behalf.'

'Let's hope she never does find out. It's pure luck that so far no one has ever mentioned Mrs Parnell's maiden name. If they did, she'd be bound to recognise it. The Knights tell me she's been shown the original birth certificate.'

'So it's true. She really was Alicia's daughter.'

'Yes.'

The news was a relief. There'd always been the niggling doubt that it had all been some terrible, ironic twist of fate, the fear that everyone might have put two and two together and come up with five, and that Melanie had not been Alicia's daughter after all.

'How are they taking it?'

Lineham grimaced. 'They're very shocked, of course. And it's difficult for them to know quite what to say to Melanie. In the circumstances they fully understand why Rain is refusing to see her, but of course they can't explain this to her.'

'They agree that it's best to keep it from her?'

'Oh yes, wholeheartedly. Though of course there's no guarantee that some nosy reporter won't dig up Mrs Parnell's maiden name and print it.'

'If that happened I'm sure the Knights would do their best to make sure she didn't see it. Though I don't know . . .'

'What?'

'It's just occurred to me . . . We're all falling over ourselves to make sure Melanie doesn't find out the truth . . .'

'Well it's what he wants, isn't it? If she did find out, it would make a nonsense of the sacrifice he's making.'

'Maybe. And we've automatically gone along with him, assumed he's right. But I don't know whether we've ever actually asked ourselves if it's necessarily the best thing for her.'

'But wouldn't any parent do the same thing, in circumstances like this? Wouldn't you?'

'I suppose so.' Lineham was right. Of course he would. He remembered that fierce, intense protectiveness which he had experienced in Ben's bedroom the other evening and ceased to marvel at Rain's determination to shield Melanie from the truth regardless of the cost to himself. He could imagine too the horror with which Alicia must have looked at the engagement photograph of Rain and of Melanie, right cheek with that tell-tale birthmark presented to the cameras. She must have spent a tormented couple of weeks worrying about how best to tackle Rain, when he returned from his concert tour in Canada, wondering if she was already too late to prevent incest. It wasn't surprising that she had been so distracted at work, or that she had wanted to leave early on that last morning. She must have found the prospect of even a few more hours in the office intolerable, must have longed to prevent Melanie from learning the truth at all costs, as Rain did now. And yet . . .

'I don't know, Mike. I'm not sure. Just think for a minute. If Melanie did find out she would be very distressed, yes, but she is twenty years old, after all. Her adoptive parents obviously believed her to be sufficiently mature to make a decision to marry. And yet here we all are, treating her as a child, to be protected from the truth at all costs . . . The more I think about it, the more I wonder why we're all colluding like this . . . It could be even worse for her, never to know what went wrong, and why. If she did know, she might one day be able to put the tragedy behind her, but this way I'm not sure that she ever could.'

'So what are you suggesting? That we tell her ourselves?'

'I don't think we could do that at present. But I do think that perhaps, when I'm up and about again, I might talk to Rain about this, see if I can get him to look at it differently. And talk to the Knights, too.'

'I suppose one big advantage of telling her the truth would be that Mr Rain could change his plea to not guilty. And in the circumstances I should think he might well get pretty lenient treatment.'

'Quite. Anyway, there's no immediate rush. We can think about it. Thank you for coming in, Mike.'

Lineham stood up. 'Well, I'd better be off. I told Louise I'd try to be on time for supper, for once.'

212

'Did you ever manage to get the matter of the house settled, by the way?'

'Oh yes, didn't I tell you? The building society agreed to the increased mortgage, subject to survey. And we have the old lady's assurance that there'll be no more gazumping. I think she felt quite guilty about it, really.'

'Excellent. Louise is delighted, I expect.'

'I should say, We're both praying, now, that nothing goes wrong for the people who are buying ours. I shan't feel we're home and dry until both sets of contracts have been exchanged.'

Lineham had been gone only a few minutes when Joan came in and plumped down on the chair he had vacated.

'Bridget and Ben are making us a surprise supper.'

Thanet grinned. 'I'm supposed to be pleased?' But he was, grim though the gastronomic prospect might be.

She returned his smile, then leaned forward, touched his arm and said, 'This case has depressed you, hasn't it?'

He'd given her a brief account of the arrest and of the reason for it, earlier.

'Yes, it has. Despite the fact that he's a murderer, I liked Rain. And I can't help respecting what he's doing. Though as I was saying to Mike just now, I'm not sure if it's the right thing.' And Thanet explained his reservations to her.

Joan was silent for a while. At last she said, 'I'm just trying to imagine how I would have felt, if I'd found myself in Melanie's situation, at her age. It would be a terrible shock, of course, but I think I'd have liked to know the truth. And yes, I think you're right. I think there'd be a better chance of her coming to terms with what's happened if she did know. Otherwise, as you say, she'll just go on and on in a fog of incomprehension and distress. Also, it would ensure that she gives up any idea of waiting for Mr Rain and marrying him when he comes out of prison.'

'Quite. Though I don't know if I'll be able to persuade Rain to see it like that.'

'I'm not so sure. You might well find that now that the worst has happened, and he's actually been arrested, he might be able to look at it differently. I imagine that up until now he

213

hasn't been able to think beyond confessing.'

'And beyond preventing Melanie from learning the truth, at all costs.'

'Yes, but if he can be made to see that this might not necessarily be the best thing for her . . . He does seem to care very deeply for her, or he wouldn't be prepared to go to these lengths to spare her.'

'Oh yes, he does, I'm sure of that.'

'Well, then . . .'

'You may be right. I'll have to see what I can do. Perhaps it's as well that I'm out of commission for a day or two. It'll give him a chance to get his breath back . . . Did Mike tell you, by the way? Mrs Rain died this afternoon.'

'Oh dear. Poor man. Not that, on top of everything. And poor Penny.'

Poor Alicia, too. It was difficult to reconcile his memories of the vivid girl he had once known with the sad, gentle Alicia of her later years, and tragic to think that her seventeenth summer, that time which had seemed so full of golden promise, had proved instead to be the fulcrum around which she had swung into the downward spiral which had culminated finally in her death.

'What's the matter, Luke?'

'I was thinking about Alicia. And how sad it was to think that an adolescent love affair could have led to all this . . . Which reminds me. Her father doesn't even know she's dead, yet. He's not due back from holiday until Saturday.'

'Will you tell him why she was killed?'

'I don't know. Perhaps. The trouble is, if I do tell him he'd be bound to feel partly responsible . . . knowing that the adoption which he no doubt encouraged eventually caused Alicia's death.'

'But he couldn't possibly think it was his fault! How could he, by any stretch of the imagination, have foreseen that Melanie would ever even meet her real father, let alone fall in love with him.'

'He couldn't, of course. But you know, as well as I do, that in circumstances like this people aren't rational. He'll tell himself that if he'd insisted Alicia keep the baby she'd still be alive today.'

'In fact, you know, it does seem the most extraordinary coincidence that Melanie and her father did meet.'

'Not if you think that they're both professional musicians. That's a relatively small world, I imagine, especially as far as soloists are concerned. She must have inherited her talent from him. They even play the same instrument.'

'Yes, that's true . . . Incidentally, talking about the adoption, you haven't yet told me how you came to cotton on to the fact that Melanie was Alicia's daughter.'

'Ah, that was a bit of luck, really.' *No, nothing as casual as luck.* 'You remember that programme on genetics we saw a couple of months ago?'

'Vaguely.'

'Well, after I met Melanie and the Knights, almost at the beginning of the case, I knew that something was worrying me. But I couldn't put my finger on it. It went on nagging at me for days — you remember? I mentioned it to you at one point. And then, suddenly, I realised what it was.'

'Go on. I'm fascinated.'

'Apparently it's not genetically possible for two blue-eyed parents to produce a child with brown eyes. Something to do with recessive genes.'

'Oh, I *see.* I gather that both the Knights have blue eyes, and Melanie's are brown?'

'Precisely. Anyway, I was interviewing the Leytons when it dawned on me. Leyton has brown eyes, his wife has blue. They were both sitting there, staring at me across my desk and I simply couldn't work out why it was bothering me so much. Then I realised, and suddenly the whole thing made sense. If Melanie was adopted, and it was she, not Penny, who was the daughter of Alicia and Nicholas Rain . . . I saw how it could all have come about. Alicia would have seen the announcement of the engagement in the papers, would have recognised Melanie by that very unusual birthmark on her cheek . . . She'd never told Rain about the child, and naturally she would have been desperate to see him at the first possible opportunity. As it was, she had to wait a fortnight, because he was away on tour in Canada. She must have been out of her mind with worry. She'd have known he was giving this concert in

Sturrenden — it was mentioned in all the engagement announcements, because he and Melanie were playing in it together — so she booked a room at the Swan and persuaded him to go back with her after the concert, so that she could show him the proof of what she was saying . . . As I say, I saw it all, and then something else that had puzzled us suddenly made sense. You see, Vivienne Leyton had been lying about her movements on Saturday evening because when she went up to Alicia's room she thought she saw her husband coming away from it. In fact, of course, it wasn't her husband, it was Nicholas Rain. They're much of a height and they both have brown hair and beards. And I remembered that the first time I saw Leyton, in the semi-darkness of the hall at his home, just for a split second I thought he was Rain.'

'But she surely wouldn't have mistaken her own husband for someone else?'

'You'd be surprised at the tricks the mind can play, where recognition is concerned. We've done tests on eye-witness credibility and the results were pretty staggering. We see, above all, what we *expect* to see. And our judgement can also be affected by a state of heightened emotion. So Vivienne was ripe for a mis-perception. What was more, both Leyton and Rain were formally dressed, her husband because of the dinner dance, Rain because of the concert. The fact that one was wearing a dinner jacket, the other tails, was immaterial. The impression was one of black and white, formal evening attire, and if you add this to the rest of what I've been saying . . . Oh no, I think her mistake was all too understandable.'

'Put like that . . . Yes, I see what you mean. So what made her realise that it had been a mistake?'

'Well, when Mike and I went out to see her last night it was perfectly obvious to everybody, including her husband, that she was holding something back and after we left he managed to get her to tell him what it was. So then, of course, they got it all sorted out. When, finally, he'd managed to convince her that he really hadn't been anywhere near the third floor that night, they decided the only thing to do was to come to me and make a clean breast of it. And once they'd cleared up the misunderstanding, the way was open for her to search her memory again and come up with a different answer.'

'She actually identified Nicholas Rain?'

'Not at first. But eventually she worked it out for herself. By this time, of course, it had dawned on me what had happened and I had to be very careful not to influence her . . . Even so, I'm not too sure how her evidence would have stood up in court. Still, her identification, tentative though it was, did support my theory and helped to persuade the Super to back me in my application for a warrant to search Rain's house.'

'Sorry, I must be a bit dim. What were you hoping to find?'

'The red folder which was missing from Alicia's hotel room. I was pretty certain it must contain proof of Melanie's real identity, and that was why he'd had to take it away with him.'

'I see. But I still don't understand why you were so sure you'd find it? Surely the first thing he would have done, afterwards, would have been to destroy it? He must have known it would be pretty damning evidence against him.'

'I know. But I was banking on the fact that he hadn't, for various reasons. To begin with, I thought he might well have been unable to bring himself to destroy Melanie's original birth certificate and the photograph of her as a baby, for sentimental reasons. The photograph, especially, was irreplaceable, I imagine. And you must remember that he was in a state of shock. He told me himself that he couldn't really believe it had happened, that he felt it must be some terrible nightmare from which he would eventually wake up. I felt he would almost have *needed* to keep that folder, partly to remind himself that it had not in fact just been a bad dream, but also to convince himself that there had been a valid reason for his having gone over the edge as he did.'

'I suppose, too, that from a purely practical point of view, he might have kept it because if ever he were arrested, it would uphold his story.'

'There's that, too, yes . . . But I'm not sure that he was ever particularly interested in saving his own skin. As I say, I think that right from the beginning he was genuinely shocked, genuinely horrified at what he had done and I think he lied to us because his first instinct was to protect Melanie. As he saw it, the only way to do that was by trying to convince us that he

217

was in the clear. And really, at the point when we applied for that search warrant, we had nothing beyond Vivienne Leyton's rather shaky identification to justify taking such a drastic step.'

'You were rather sticking your neck out, weren't you.'

'I know. If the folder hadn't turned up, I really would have looked a bit of an idiot.'

'You trusted your instinct.' Joan took his hand. 'And you were right, as usual.'

'Luck, that's all.'

'Not luck. Judgement. And there's no point in waving your hands about and trying to deny it. It's what makes you a good policeman.'

He smiled at her. 'The trouble with you is that you're biased.'

She bent to kiss him. 'And why shouldn't I be? You're my husband, aren't you?'

There were noises on the stairs and a moment later the door was flung open.

'First course,' announced Ben.

'Good. I'm starving.' Thanet eased himself into a sitting position and Joan plumped the pillows up behind him. Bridget put the special bed-tray in front of him, the one with legs, and he was touched at the trouble she had taken. She had found a pretty tray-cloth embroidered with forget-me-nots, had given him their best china and cutlery, and had poured him an ice-cold lager in a tall glass beaded with moisture. The first course was half a grapefruit with a cherry in a middle.

'This looks terrific, Sprig.'

She beamed at him as Ben returned with three more servings of grapefruit and they began to eat, Bridget and Ben sitting cross-legged on the floor. Throughout the entire meal (cold ham and salad followed by raspberry ice-cream with fresh raspberries from the garden) Thanet was aware that he was the focus of their attention, that their efforts were being directed solely towards comforting him for his misfortune. By the time they had finished eating he was thoroughly ashamed of himself. This was only a temporary injury, after all. In a couple of days he'd be up and about again. Why didn't he make the best of the enforced break, instead of mumping and moaning about it? He could read, listen to music, talk to the children, have leisurely conversations with Joan — do, in short, all the things he never normally had time to do. He reached for Joan's hand.

'Sorry I've been such a bear.'

She smiled back, leaned forward to ruffle his hair. 'Good. You're beginning to look human again.'

'Food always does that for me. Congratulations, you two. That was a really delicious meal.'

Bridget and Ben looked gratified and Ben, ever the opportunist, said, 'How about a game of scrabble, Dad?'

'We've got to wash up first.' Bridget began clattering the dishes together.

Thanet saw Joan wince. It looked as though their best dinner service wasn't going to last the night.

'I'll do that,' she said hastily. 'Fair's fair. You prepared it all. Now it's my turn. Though I don't know if your father can manage scrabble. He's supposed to be flat on his back.'

'I could keep the score,' said Thanet, reluctantly sliding down in the bed.

Bridget fetched paper and pencil and they set up the scrabble board on Thanet's stomach.

'Hey!' he protested. 'I won't be able to move.'

Ben grinned. 'You're not supposed to anyway. I heard Mum say.'

They perched on either side of him and the game began. They were half way through when Ben's face lit up with excitement. Then, frowning with concentration he laid out his counters on the board, pausing twice for readjustments. 'Thirteen letters!' he said at last, triumphantly.

'Let me see.' Bridget swivelled the board around. 'That's not how you spell it,' she said. And then, reproachfully, 'Oh Ben.' She glanced at Thanet, then back at her brother and there was an amused complicity in the look they exchanged.

'What's the joke?' said Thanet. 'What's the word?' And he craned to see, wincing as pain immediately stabbed at the base of his spine. 'It's no good. I can't lift my head far enough. What is it?'

They grinned at each other and Bridget said, 'It doesn't count, anyway. He's spelt it wrong.'

'I haven't!'

'Yes you have. There should be a "y" there, not an "i".'

'There shouldn't! You're making it up.'

'No I'm not!'

'When you two have quite finished squabbling, perhaps you'd tell me what it is. Then I can decide whether Ben's spelt it wrongly or not.'

'Yes, go on,' said Bridget. 'Ask Dad.'

Silence.

'Well?' said Thanet, beginning to wonder what on earth Ben could have put.

Ben gave him an assessing look, and then, in a tone which begged him to share the joke, said, 'Physiotherapy.'

With a straight face Thanet spelled it for him and then, unable to contain his amusement, began to laugh.

Scrabble counters flew everywhere as the children joined in

DEAD ON ARRIVAL

To Pat and Ailsa

ONE

The house was unnaturally silent. Thanet stood in the hall, head cocked, listening: no sound from the television in the living room, no movement or clatter of pans from the kitchen, no muffled, rhythmic thump of distant pop music from Ben's room . . . He glanced at his watch. Ten to six. Where were they all?

He moved to the foot of the stairs. 'Anyone in?' he called.

No reply.

He shrugged, went into the kitchen and put the kettle on, feeling disgruntled. Not so many years ago he would have arrived home to a rapturous welcome. Bridget and Ben would have rushed to greet him, faces aglow, reaching up to kiss him, competing for his attention. Unconsciously, he sighed. He certainly wouldn't expect such behaviour of an eleven- and a thirteen-year-old, but he had to admit that he sometimes regretted that they were growing up so quickly. In just a few years they would be independent, leaving home . . .

The front door slammed.

'I'm home!' Bridget's voice.

Thanet rose with alacrity, went into the hall. 'So I gather,' he said, smiling.

'Dad! Hi! What are you doing home?' The wind had whipped colour into her cheeks, tousled the fine blonde hair which recently (to Thanet's regret) had been cut fashionably short.

'Finished early for once.'

'Wonders will never cease.' Bridget shed her coat, hung it in the cupboard under the stairs and followed Thanet into the kitchen. 'It's nice to get into the warm.'

It was a Tuesday in late November, and since early morning an icy wind had been blowing from the east, bringing

7

a warning of early snow and the prospect of a long, hard winter.

Thanet handed her a steaming mug of tea. 'I was beginning to wonder where you'd all got to.'

'Thanks.' Bridget cupped her hands around the mug and sipped appreciatively. 'Mum'll be a bit late tonight. She forgot to tell you.'

Joan, Thanet's wife, was a probation officer, and her working hours were sometimes inconveniently unpredictable.

'So I went round to Susan's. And Ben's at Paul's, watching a video.'

'What video?' said Thanet sharply. He was only too well aware of the ready availability of the pornographic and sadistic video films which, despite every attempt to stem the flood, continued to pour into the high street rental shops in a seemingly never-ending stream.

Bridget grinned. 'Cool it, Dad. It's nothing unsuitable. Just some documentary on photographic techniques which Ben missed because he was at Scouts.' She put her mug on the draining board. 'I must get on. I want to try another way of decorating that lemon flummery.'

Thanet hid his dismay. Much as he enjoyed that particular pudding, a fluffy concoction half-way between a mousse and a cream, this would be the fourth night in a row they'd had to eat it.

'Still not satisfied? I thought last night's looked terrific.'

Bridget frowned at the dish she had taken from the fridge. 'I've got to get it just right.'

About a year ago Bridget had developed an interest in cooking. Her mother was an excellent cook, but ever since Joan had started working full-time she had had neither the time nor the inclination to expend much energy in the kitchen. Thanet had watched with approval as Bridget rapidly developed an astonishing degree of expertise. On Friday she was to take part in the regional heats for the Junior Chef of the Year, her first competition.

'Nervous?' he asked, watching with admiration as she whipped cream, carefully selected the appropriate nozzle for the piping bag and began to decorate the pudding with minute, glistening whorls.

'A bit, I suppose.'

'You're going to win, I know it.'

'You're biased, Dad. But thanks for the vote of confidence, all the same.'

The front door slammed again and Ben appeared in the kitchen doorway. 'Oh no, not yukky lemon flummery again.' And he stuck out his tongue and pretended to retch.

'That's enough, Ben. If it'll help Sprig to win we'll eat it until it comes out of our ears.'

'It's already coming out of mine!'

'Good programme?'

'Great. Dad, when *are* we going to get a video? *Everyone's* got one.'

'Not everyone. *We* haven't. And as I've said before, there's no point in going on about it, we've no intention of getting one.'

'But why? It's so useful. Just think, when you got home late from work you could watch all the things you've missed earlier on in the evening.'

'When I get home late from work all I want to do is go to bed. Apart from which, so far as I can see, there's never anything on worth watching, these days.'

'That's not true,' they chorused. 'There's . . .'

Thanet held up a hand. 'No. I don't want to hear, thank you. As far as I'm concerned, kids nowadays have far too much potted entertainment, and I'm not going to provide you with the potential for yet more.'

'But if we don't see it here, we only go and see it at someone else's house,' objected Ben.

And this, Thanet had to admit, was the one potent argument for having a video recorder of their own. Here, at least, he and Joan would have some control over the sort of material the children watched. But he wasn't going to

9

strengthen Ben's case by saying so. 'In that case, what are you complaining about?'

The front door slammed once more, and Thanet went to greet Joan, his heart lifting, as always, at the sight of her. Tonight, fuelled by the memory of the emptiness which had marred his return home, his kiss was even more enthusiastic than usual.

Joan pulled away a little, laughing. 'Hey, what did I do to deserve that?'

He kissed her again. 'Do I have to have an excuse?'

Her arms tightened around his neck for a moment, then she wriggled out of his grasp, began to unbutton her coat. 'I must get on with supper. I'm all behind.'

'I was wondering if you'd like to go out for a change. Nowhere elaborate. Pizzaland, for instance?'

'Luke! That would be lovely. With the children?'

'Why not?'

'What are we celebrating?'

He came closer, put his mouth against her ear. 'Sprig is decorating yet another lemon flummery. I don't think I can face it.'

Joan laughed. 'That makes two of us.'

They all enjoyed the unusual treat of a family outing mid-week, and it was not until a quarter to eleven, when Thanet and Joan were thinking of going to bed, that the telephone rang.

Joan pulled a face. 'Guess who that's for.'

Thanet went reluctantly to answer it.

'Thanet here.'

'It's Bentley, sir. We had an anonymous phone call, at ten twenty-five, reporting a murder at number three, Hamilton Road. We sent someone round, and it's just been confirmed. Young man in his twenties. Head bashed in.'

And Lineham's not here . . . 'Better get everything laid on. You know what to do. Has Doc Mallard been informed?' *I'll have to get Lineham back, as soon as I can. Hines isn't going to like this one little bit.*

10

'Yes. He's out on a call apparently, but a message was left on his answerphone.'

'Let's hope he won't be too long. I'll be over there as soon as I can.'

Thanet rang off. He'd better get on to Hines right away. No, he'd wait until he'd seen what the position was for himself.

Joan was in the kitchen, pouring boiling water into a thermos flask.

'Coffee,' she said. 'It sounds as though it might be a long night.'

' 'Fraid so. Thanks, love.'

Outside, the wind tore at Thanet's raincoat. It was beginning to rain and by the time he turned out of his driveway on to the road heavy drops were hurling themselves against the windscreen in gusting sheets.

'That's all I need,' he muttered as he switched on the windscreen wipers. It was at times like these that he paid lip-service to the idea that it would be nice to have a comfortable, nine-to-five office job with weekends off and plenty of guaranteed leisure. But underneath he knew that such work would have bored him stiff. He loved his job, enjoyed its unpredictability, the constant challenge, the thrill of the hunt, the unique satisfaction of victory. There were disadvantages, of course, and he was grimly aware that one of them was imminent, something far more difficult for him to cope with than the inconvenience of being called out at an hour when most people were thinking of getting comfortably tucked up in bed.

For the truth was that, despite all his years on the force, Thanet had never been able to harden himself against his first sight of a corpse. He had tried every trick in the book, from disassociation to levity, but nothing had worked, ever. In the early years he had told himself that familiarity would breed if not contempt, then at least indifference, but it had never happened and by now he began each case with resigned dread and an acceptance that those few moments of acute discomfort were the necessary prelude to the work in which he found such satisfaction.

Hamilton Road was a wide, tree-lined street leading down to the river. The houses were huge Victorian redbrick monsters, built by prosperous tradesmen in the days when servants were plentiful and labour cheap. They had long ago been converted into flats and their original owners would have been appalled to see the dirty windows, peeling paint, sagging gutters, and overgrown gardens. Tonight the façades were punctuated by uncurtained oblongs of yellow light against which were silhouetted the heads and shoulders of neighbours curious to know what was going on. At least the weather should prevent the usual crowd of ghouls, Thanet thought with satisfaction.

It was easy to pick out number three by the police cars parked outside. Thanet cursed as the wind tore the door-handle from his grasp, straining the hinges. He ran through the pelting rain along the short, curving drive to the front door, where a uniformed PC in a waterproof cape was stamping his feet in a fruitless attempt to keep warm.

'Evening, Johnson. Filthy night.'

'Certainly is, sir.'

'Where's the body?'

'First floor back, sir.'

Thanet pushed open the stained-glass inner door and stepped into a spacious hallway which ran the depth of the house to a rear door at the far end. It was cluttered with prams and bicycles and only the curving hand-carved banister and the ornately patterned ceramic tiles on the floor spoke of the gracious way of life for which it had been designed. An unshaded, low-wattage overhead bulb cast a sickly yellow light on flaking plaster and grubby, distempered walls.

Head bashed in. Conscious of the tightening muscles in his abdomen, Thanet ran up the wide, uncarpeted stairs, trying not to think of all the other head injuries he had seen, some of them stomach-churning by any standards. *Another few minutes and the worst will be over*. A door immediately in front of him was ajar and from within came the unmistakable sounds of police activity. Thanet took a deep breath and walked in.

Carson was standing just inside the door, keeping out of the way of the photographers. The room was stiflingly hot.

'Evening, sir.'

Thanet nodded a greeting. 'Where is he?'

'Over there, sir. On the floor in front of the settee.'

Avoiding what looked like a smear of blood on the carpet, Thanet walked around the side of the settee, which stood with its back to the door half-way across the room. Then he took another deep, unobtrusive breath and looked.

The dead man lay face down on the floor in front of the settee, his knees curled up, one arm outflung. He was wearing jeans, a dark blue sweater and shabby plimsolls.

After the familiar rush of compassion, the pang of anger and regret at this wanton waste of human life, Thanet's first emotion was one of relief. Often, with head injuries, there is a great deal of blood, but in this case there was only a small, glistening streak in the man's hair.

'A single blow?' he murmured to Carson.

'Looks like it, sir.'

'And with something pretty blunt, by the look of it. Flat, even.'

Which made this case a little unusual. Thanet knew that in the majority of cases of death by head injury more than one blow is struck — which results in a lot of very quick bleeding and much splashing of blood. If, however, the victim is hit by something flat, the impact is distributed over a large area. There may be local damage to the brain under the point of impact, the skull may be fractured and there may be a large area of bruising, but the skin may not even necessarily split and there may thus be no external scalp bleeding.

Thanet was beginning to sweat. The gas fire was on full blast.

Carson followed Thanet's glance. 'Thought I'd better leave the fire on until the doc's been.'

13

Room temperature is an important factor in estimating time of death.

'Quite right . . .' Thanet shrugged out of his coat and slung it over his shoulder.

One of the Scenes-of-Crime officers approached. 'All right if I take samples now, sir? I wanted to leave him *in situ* until you'd seen him.'

'Finished the photographs?'

'Of the body, yes, sir.'

'Fine. Carry on, then.'

Thanet began to wander around the room. The shabby settee, sagging armchair, cheap table scarred with innumerable cigarette burns and white rings on its once-glossy veneered surface, all spoke of a room which had been rented furnished to countless careless tenants. And yet, Thanet noticed, attempts had been made to brighten the place up. There were new, brightly coloured cotton curtains at the tall window, matching cushions on the settee and armchair. A wife, then? Or live-in girlfriend? If so, where was she? There were two birthday cards on the mantelpiece and he crossed to look at them. One, with a sentimental verse, was signed Sharon, the other, a bawdy, humorous one, was from someone called Geoff.

Carson had been following Thanet about, walking a pace or two behind like a faithful retriever.

Thanet glanced back at him. 'Do we know anything about him?'

'Not much. I had a quick word with a Mrs Bence, who lives in one of the downstairs flats, the one below this. She's a sort of caretaker, and has spare keys to all the flats in case of emergency, so it was her who let us in. She's a funny old bird. She says his name is Steven Long.'

'Married?'

'Yes.'

Sharon, perhaps?

'But they split up recently. Not surprising, according to Mrs Bence. She was quite friendly with the wife, but didn't have much time for him.'

14

'Why not? No, it doesn't matter, I'll have a word with her myself, later. How old is she?'

'Mrs Bence? Early sixties, I'd say.'

'Good. Time on her hands to be nosy, then.' Thanet was missing Lineham. It wasn't that Carson had been crass, or inefficient, quite the contrary. He was careful, solid, reliable, where the sergeant was eager, impulsive, volatile. But Thanet was so used to working with Lineham that it was almost as if a part of himself were missing. Was this what it would be like if Lineham got his promotion to Inspector? Thanet wondered. Would it be impossible to adjust to working efficiently with someone else, after all these years?

'Tell me what you think happened here, Tom.'

'Well, I was thinking about it while I was waiting for you to arrive, sir, and I reckon he was sitting on the settee when it happened. I think he was bashed from above and behind.'

'What with, do you think?'

Carson shrugged. 'Doesn't seem to be anything likely lying about. Chummy must've taken it with him. I was wondering . . .'

'Yes?'

'Well, that smear on the carpet, half-way between the door and the settee . . . Looks like blood.'

'Yes, I'd noticed. What about it?'

'Well, I reckon he must have dropped the murder weapon, after hitting the victim, sir, then decided it was safer to take it away with him.'

'Could be.' Thanet already had a theory about what that weapon had been but he did not comment, simply gestured at the object which dominated the room, a huge colour television set, complete with video recorder on a shelf below. 'He can't have been too hard up.'

Carson grinned. 'It was probably on the HP.'

'Even so . . .'

There was a flurry of movement on the stairs. Reinforcements had arrived. Thanet gave Carson the thankless task of tracing and notifying the next of kin and then went out on to the landing and set about deploying his men. He had just finished when the stained-glass front door opened again and Mallard came in, taking off his hat and shaking it, spattering the floor with raindrops which made dark circles in the dust.

Usually the lateness of the hour or the inclemency of the weather would have elicited some sarcastic comment from the little doctor, but tonight he merely glanced up at Thanet and said, 'Up there?'

Thanet nodded. 'Evening, Doc. Sorry to drag you out on such a filthy night.' He ushered Mallard into Long's room.

The SOCOs had finished with the body for the moment and after Mallard had examined the head wound, he and Thanet gently turned Long over.

It was the first time Thanet had seen the dead man's face, and he studied it while Mallard made his examination.

Steven Long had been in his mid-twenties, with a narrow face, beaky nose and dark blue eyes beneath straight brown hair brushed back from a bony forehead. In his lifeless sprawl he looked, Thanet thought fancifully, as pathetic as a dead sparrow abandoned at the roadside. But this had been no accident, and Steven Long no sparrow. Thanet's fists clenched involuntarily. At moments like this he invariably experienced a painful mixture of anger and compassion.

'Can't give a final verdict until after the PM, of course,' said Mallard, 'but there doesn't seem to be much doubt about cause of death.'

'The blow to the back of the head?'

Mallard nodded.

'Any guesses about the murder instrument?'

Mallard heaved himself to his feet. 'Something flattish, by the look of it, heavy, with a rim around the base which broke the skin and caused that slight bleeding.'

'An ashtray, perhaps?'

Mallard shrugged. 'Possible, if it was weighty enough. One of those heavy glass or pottery ones. Why, have you found it?'

'No, but come and look at this.'

Thanet led Mallard to the battered oak sideboard which

16

stood against the wall to the right of the door. In the thin layer of dust which covered it was a clean, circular patch about five inches in diameter.

'I can't see anything in the room to match it. Could have been a heavy vase, I suppose,' Thanet added.

'It's about the right size, certainly.'

'I'd like several shots of this,' Thanet said to the photographer. 'Make sure you give a clear impression of its size.'

'Right, sir.'

'You can turn that fire off, too,' said Mallard, mopping at his forehead and running his handkerchief over his bald head. 'Place is like a tropical greenhouse.'

'We left it on because . . .'

'Yes, yes.' Mallard waved a dismissive hand. 'But I've finished, now. Turn the damned thing off, for God's sake.'

Thanet did so, then returned to Mallard, who had finished packing his things away and now closed his bag with a snap.

'Where's Lineham?' he said. 'Unusual not to see him here. Still on maternity leave, so to speak, is he?'

Lineham's wife Louise had just given birth to their second child, a daughter this time, and the sergeant had taken ten days of his annual leave to help out.

'No, he's been back at work for a week now.' Thanet scowled. 'He's on loan to Chief Inspector Hines for the investigation into that murder over at Coddington Woods on Sunday night.'

'Ah yes. Nasty business, that. You realise she was still alive when they found her, on Monday morning?'

Thanet grimaced. 'So I heard. Died in the ambulance on the way to hospital. I understand they think she was thrown out of a car and cracked her head on a big stone at the side of the road.'

'Having been half-strangled first,' said Mallard.

'I didn't know that. Anyway, Mr Hines is rather short-handed at the moment, and as things were very quiet here, I agreed to let him borrow Lineham. I'm kicking myself now, of course.'

17

'You'll get him back, though, surely.'

'I certainly shall,' said Thanet. *With difficulty.*

Mallard was putting on his coat.

'There's just one more question, Doc.'

Mallard frowned at Thanet over his half-moon spectacles. 'Don't tell me. The usual. Time of death.'

'Well . . .'

'Impossible to be accurate, in the circumstances. The temperature in here would have affected the cooling of the body considerably, and as it's lying right in front of the fire . . . Well, you can see the problem for yourself.'

'Could you hazard a guess?'

'Not really. I'm sorry, Luke, I'm usually prepared to stick my neck out, as you know . . .'

Normally, Thanet would have left it there, but Mallard's unusually amiable mood encouraged him not to give up just yet. 'Some time this evening, anyway?'

Mallard gave a mischievous smile. 'Some time today, I'd say. And I refuse to commit myself any further.'

Thanet had to leave it at that. He had expected something of the sort and it certainly wouldn't help. But it wasn't the doctor's fault and he simply nodded his thanks and escorted him to the front door, wondering why Mallard had been so relatively civil this evening. The police surgeon's ill-humour was a legend in the force. Thanet did his best to ignore it, having known Mallard in the days before his wife had died a slow, lingering death from cancer, many years ago. The little doctor had never managed to come to terms with his grief and his irascibility was his way of venting upon the world the anger and despair he still felt at her loss. Lineham would certainly have noticed this change in Mallard's behaviour, and together they would have speculated as to its significance. Once again Thanet wished that the sergeant were present, and decided that he would make that phone call his first priority.

They had just reached the front door when it burst open: Brent, one of the new young DCs.

18

Mallard staggered a little and Thanet put a hand under his elbow to steady him. 'For God's sake, man, be careful.'

'Sorry, sir. Sorry, Doc. Sir . . .' Brent's eyes were sparking with excitement.

'Take a deep breath and count to five. Then tell me.'

Brent did as he was told, but even so the words tumbled out in his haste. 'Sir, there's a car parked just along the road. It's been there all evening, I gather. We were just checking it, as a matter of routine, and we found a man inside, half sozz . . . pretty drunk, sir. He's mumbling threats against Long. And he's crying.'

Until now the other inhabitants of the house had reluctantly obeyed orders and stayed in their rooms, but DC Brent's precipitous entry had created a new surge of curiosity. Thanet was aware of doors opening, of murmured conversations, and of people peering down into the hall.

He and Mallard exchanged glances.

'You want me to hang on for a few minutes?' said the little doctor in a low voice.

'Thanks, yes. Just till we see what sort of state this man's in. Where is he, Brent? Still in the car?'

'At the moment, yes, sir. We didn't know if you'd want him brought in here or taken back to the station.'

'From what you say it doesn't sound as though I'll get much sense out of him, but I'd better have a quick word with him, then you can take him back to the station.' But where to talk in privacy, that was the problem? He couldn't conduct an interview here, in the hall, it was much too public, and Long's room was out of the question.

Thanet glanced around. The door to the right of the stairs remained shut, but a middle-aged couple was peering curiously from the one on the left and at the back of the hall, arms akimbo, wrapped in a brilliant scarlet kimono with a gold dragon emblazoned from shoulder to hem, stood a squat little figure squinting at them through the smoke from the cigarette hanging from her lower lip; Mrs Bence, presumably.

There appeared to be no choice.

Thanet turned back to Brent. 'Bring him in. But first I want all these people back inside their rooms again. And make sure they stay there, this time.'

Thanet and Mallard waited while these orders were carried out and within minutes the newcomer was half-led, half-carried into the house and propped against the wall, supported by a man on either side.

He was in his late forties, Thanet guessed, short, burly, and dressed in a good-quality dark grey worsted suit, blue and white striped shirt and blue silk tie. There were well-defined creases in his raincoat, as if he had been sitting in the same position for some hours. He looked like a successful business-man, but somewhere along the way something had gone badly wrong: the skin of his face was the colour of dough, his eyes red-veined and puffy with recent tears. A sour reek of whisky hung in the air. He seemed unaware of his surroundings.

'Could you give me your name, sir?'

Somewhere at the back of the man's eyes awareness flickered briefly, and was extinguished.

'Sir?'

Still no response.

Thanet stepped forward and gently removed the man's wallet from his inside pocket. There was no reaction.

Thanet flicked through it and extracted a driving licence: Harry Ronald Carpenter; address: Smallwood, Benenden Drive, Sturrenden. Benenden Drive was an exclusive residential area of large, relatively new detached houses on the far side of town.

Thanet frowned. Carpenter . . . The name rang a bell, but Thanet couldn't think why.

'You were talking about Mr Long, sir . . .'

The man's body jerked, as if an electric current had been passed through it. His head lifted, his eyes narrowed, his mouth twisted. 'Bastard,' he said thickly. 'Kill him . . .'

'Why?' said Thanet. 'Why should you want to kill him, Mr Carpenter?'

'Kill him,' repeated Carpenter. 'Kill him. Only thing to do.' Suddenly he began to struggle, working his shoulders up and down to release himself from the restricting grip on his arms. 'Where is he?'

'He's dead, Mr Carpenter. Upstairs.'

Carpenter stopped struggling as abruptly as he had begun

21

and peered at Thanet as if he were trying to see clearly in dense fog.

'Dead?'

'Yes. Upstairs.'

Carpenter's eyes rolled up in his head and he collapsed, his sudden dead weight causing the men to stagger. They lowered him gently to the floor and Mallard squatted to examine him.

'Passed out,' he said, after a moment.

'Heart attack?'

Mallard shook his head. 'I don't think it's anything serious. Just a shock, on top of too much to drink. But to be on the safe side I think we'd better put him into hospital for the night.'

'Ambulance outside?' said Thanet to one of the men.

'Yes, sir. Waiting to remove the body. It arrived some time ago.'

'Good. It can take Mr Carpenter first, then come back. Stay with him and let me know the moment he's fit for questioning.'

When Carpenter had been removed and Mallard had left, Thanet glanced at his watch: twelve thirty. Was it too late to make that phone call about Lineham? Hines had probably gone home by now. But even if he hadn't it might be better not to arouse his antagonism unnecessarily by breaking the news of Lineham's imminent withdrawal at this hour of the night. The little patience Hines possessed would be at its lowest ebb. Reluctantly, Thanet decided to wait until morning.

So, what now?

As soon as the SOCOs were finished upstairs, Thanet wanted to take a really good look at Stephen Long's room, but meanwhile it might prove fruitful to have a chat with Mrs Bence. According to Carson she had known the Longs quite well. And Thanet had been intrigued by that brief glimpse of her just now.

He walked along the short passage beside the staircase and raised his hand to knock on her door, but before his knuckles had made contact with wood it had opened. She must have been standing on the other side, listening. 'Mrs Bence?'

'Who wants to know?'

22

Her grey hair was short, unevenly hacked off just below the ears, and a cigarette still drooped from her lower lip. She was looking him up and down as if he were the prize turkey she wasn't sure whether to buy for Christmas. But there was no aggression in her gaze, only appraisal, and she must have approved of what she saw because she removed the cigarette and grinned to take the sting out of her words, revealing teeth the colour of old piano keys.

Thanet introduced himself. 'I understand you knew the Longs. I'd like to talk to you, if I may.' Ordinary members of the public, he found, invariably responded well to courtesy.

Mrs Bence was no exception. She stepped back.

'Come in, ducks. Welcome to my humble abode. And you can call me Dara.'

'Dara,' repeated Thanet. But he hadn't taken in the outlandish nature of Mrs Bence's Christian name; he was too preoccupied with trying to absorb the extraordinary atmosphere of her sitting room.

Every available inch of wall-space was taken up with posters, hand-bills and photographs large and small. The former all advertised the imminent arrival of BENJY'S, THE GREATEST LITTLE CIRCUS IN THE WORLD. Prominently billed was DARA, THE MOST SENSATIONAL HIGH-WIRE ACT THE WORLD HAS EVER SEEN. The photographs showed Dara, glamorously attired in spangles and tights, at some of the most sensational moments of her act: flying through space with the grace of a swallow, tightly curled up in the now-familiar ball of the triple somersault, suspended by the teeth from a gossamer wire high, high above the upturned faces of the awed spectators.

'Never believe it was the same woman, would you?'

Thanet turned. She was standing in the middle of the room watching him, enjoying his astonishment and absorption. What could he say? The truth was that no, he could scarcely believe it.

She waved her hand. 'Oh, don't bother to deny it. I don't want to put you in a spot. 'Specially as I like the look of you.'

23

She lowered herself into a huge, sagging leather armchair and lit another cigarette from the stub of the old one. 'Take a pew.'

The 'pew' was an ancient monster of tan moquette, bald and shiny with years of wear. Seen in a better light the scarlet kimono, too, was stained and faded, a mere reflection of its original splendour.

'Want a fag?'

Thanet shook his head, his hand unconsciously straying to his pocket.

'Smoke a pipe?'

He nodded. So she was observant. Good.

'Carry on, then. Light up, if you want to. My old man used to smoke a pipe. I miss it. Used to complain like hell at the time, but now . . . What d'you think of it all, then?' And she waved her hand at the display on the walls.

'Amazing,' said Thanet with sincerity, feeding tobacco into his pipe. 'Really amazing.'

'Them was the days,' said Mrs Bence with a sigh. 'I still miss it, you know. There's nothing like it in the world – the people, the animals, the atmosphere, the excitement, and above all, the smell . . .' She closed her eyes in ecstatic reminiscence. 'Sweat, sawdust . . . If Benjy's hadn't folded, I'd probably be there still, helping out in some way . . . But you don't want to hear all this.'

'On the contrary.' Thanet paused to apply the first match. 'It's fascinating,' he said, waving his hand to dispel the clouds of smoke.

She peered at him through the haze. 'You mean it, don't yer?'

Thanet nodded, smiled. 'All the same, there's a lot to do. So if you don't mind . . .'

'Carry on.'

'I'd like you to tell me about the Longs.'

'What sort of things d'you want to hear?'

'Anything. Whatever comes into your head. Then, if there's anything else I specifically want to know, I'll ask you.'

Mrs Bence frowned, lit yet another cigarette. 'They've been

here about, let me see, oh it must be eighteen months, now. And I gather from Sharon – that's his wife – they'd been married about six months before that. If you ask me it's a miracle she stuck it as long as she did.'

'They're separated, I gather.'

'Yes. She's been gone about three weeks now. Found herself another boyfriend.'

'How did Mr Long take that?'

'Didn't like it one little bit, did he?' The thought obviously gave her satisfaction. 'Didn't realise what he'd got until he'd lost it.'

'You liked Mrs Long, obviously.'

'Yes. Nice little thing. Kind, sweet-natured – she must've been, or she'd never have put up with him.'

'But you obviously weren't too keen on him.'

'He was a real . . .' She paused, trying to find a word which would sum Long up to her satisfaction. 'A real *bleeder*,' she concluded triumphantly.

'In what way?'

'In every way. You should have seen how he treated that poor girl. Ordered her about as if she was a skivvy. "Do this, fetch that . . ." And bad-tempered! I've had her down here more times than I care to tell, in tears . . .'

'He was violent?'

'Oh no, I'll grant him that,' said Mrs Bence grudgingly. 'Far as I know he never laid a finger on her. But there's more ways than one of being cruel, as I'm sure you know full well. I don't know how she stood it. It wasn't even as if he brought home the bacon, either – not regular, anyhow. Poor kid didn't know where she was half the time, far as money was concerned.'

'He was out of work?'

'Not at the moment, no. But he was in and out of jobs like a yo-yo. He was a mechanic – a good one, Sharon says, but unreliable, and people would get fed up with him being late for work or just not turning up, if he fancied a day off . . .Well, about three weeks ago he lost his job yet again, because he'd been late five days running. He'd been warned, but he just didn't pay attention . . . He got himself another one, since, but by then it was too late, she'd gone, and she didn't come back. She'd had enough, I reckon.'

'What about the boyfriend?'

Mrs Bence shook her head. 'Don't know nothing about him.' She heaved herself out of her armchair, crossed to the sideboard and held up a bottle enquiringly.

'No, thanks.' Thanet grinned. 'Got to keep my head clear.'

She poured herself a generous half-tumbler of gin, then returned to her chair.

Thanet re-lit his pipe, which wasn't drawing very well. 'Did they have many visitors?'

'No. Not surprising, considering the way he went on. Sharon told me he come from quite a big family, but I never set eyes on any of them.'

'On bad terms with them, was he?'

'Must've been.'

'How many brothers and sisters did he have?'

'Not sure. One brother's a schoolteacher, I think. Don't know about the rest.'

'What about his wife . . . er, Sharon?'

'Father's dead and she's got one sister. Does she . . . Anyone broke the news to her, yet?'

'I should think she's probably heard by now, yes.'

'Poor kid. She'll be real upset, I expect.'

'Even though they were separated?'

'I told you. She's a real sweet girl. She'll be upset, all right.'

And even more so in the morning, after the unpleasant task of formal identification of the body, thought Thanet.

'Did you by any chance see Mr Long this evening, Mrs . . . Dara?'

'He was going out as I came in. About a quarter to seven.'

That was a help. So he'd been alive until quite late. 'You heard him come in again, later?'

She shook her head.

'But his room is directly above yours, isn't it?'

26

'Yes. I might've been cooking my bit of supper in the kitchen when he came in, I suppose. Anyway, I can't hear everything that goes on upstairs. If they're walking around a lot, or playing that awful pop stuff then yes, I can hear the thump, thump, thump, but otherwise this house is built pretty solid, not like the modern rubbish they put up these days. And I had the telly on most of the evening. Next time I saw him was flat out on the floor, when I let the policeman into his room. I has a spare key to all the rooms, in case of emergency. One thing I wanted to ask you . . .'

'Yes?'

'How did the police know there was anything wrong? I mean, there'd been no row, nothing to let on . . .'

No reason why he shouldn't tell her. 'Someone rang in, to let us know.'

'And I bet he didn't give his name and address, neither.'

'You missed your vocation, Dara,' said Thanet, smiling. 'You should have been a detective.'

She gave a snort of laughter and the long worm of ash on her cigarette dropped into her lap. She brushed it away, leaving a smear of grey on the scarlet silk. 'That'd be the day!'

'So you have no idea what time Mr Long returned home?'

'Not the faintest.'

'Did you happen to see any strangers in the house this evening?'

'Once I shut the front door behind me, that was it, I didn't poke me nose out again until I heard that policeman hammering away at Sharon's door.'

Pity. 'Did either of them ever mention a man called Carpenter?'

Mrs Bence looked at Thanet sharply and fumbled in the pocket of her kimono for her packet of cigarettes. 'Oh,' she said. 'So that's the way the wind blows, is it?'

'What do you mean?'

She waited until she had lit her cigarette. 'Soon after they came here, the Longs, he was involved in a car accident . . .'

The words 'car accident' were enough, in this context, for

Thanet immediately to realise why Carpenter's name had seemed familiar. About a year ago, in the neighbouring town of Ashford, Carpenter's wife and daughter had been involved in a car crash. Mrs Carpenter had been killed instantly, but the little girl had been taken from the wreckage unconscious and had remained in a coma ever since, kept alive by life support machines. Although the driver of the other car had been prosecuted for dangerous driving, his defence counsel had come up with a witness whose testimony had laid part of the blame for the accident on Mrs Carpenter, and there had been a nasty scene in court when the young man had got off with a fine and a driving licence suspension of nine months. Carpenter, Thanet had been told, had had to be forcibly restrained from attacking the accused there and then. So that other driver had been Steven Long . . .

But why should Carpenter wait a year to take his revenge? It just didn't make sense. And if he were the murderer, why should he be sitting outside, some time later, still uttering threats against his victim? Had he been too drunk to know that he had already killed him? Thanet made a mental note: get hold of the clothes Carpenter was wearing, and run tests on them.

Thanet waited until Mrs Bence had finished talking, asked a few polite questions, then stood up. 'Well, thank you, Dara, you've been a great help. I'll leave you now, to get your beauty sleep.'

She grinned, stubbed out her cigarette and levered herself up out of her chair. 'At my age what you need is the beauty, not the sleep.'

'Look,' said Thanet. 'Would you mind if I came back some time, and you told me all about the circus?'

She frowned in disbelief. 'You're having me on.'

'I most certainly am not. I'd really like to.'

She was suddenly radiant and Thanet caught a fleeting glimpse of the vivid creature she had once been. 'I'll have to shake the moths out of the red carpet,' she said.

THREE

'Hurry *up*, Ben!'

It was Joan's turn to take the children to school, and as usual Ben was late. She and Bridget were standing in the hall, muffled up in coats and scarves against the biting cold which awaited them outside. Thanet, still sluggish after only a few hours' sleep, was sitting at the kitchen table with a cup of black coffee.

Hurrying footsteps on the stairs told him that Ben was ready at last, and he got up and went into the hall to say goodbye. Hasty kisses from Joan and Bridget, a wave from Ben and they were gone. Thanet returned to the kitchen and sat down again, feeling for his pipe. He needn't leave for another five minutes yet. He made a conscious effort to think about the day's work, to force his brain to start ticking over at the necessary speed. At the beginning of a case there was always so much to do, it was essential to decide on priorities. And the first, of course, would be to get Lineham back.

The radio was on and although Thanet hadn't been listening properly a familiar name suddenly attracted his attention.

' . . . Carpenter, in a coma for over a year, ever since the tragic road accident in which her mother was killed, has died. After many months of discussion the decision was finally taken yesterday to switch off Christine's life support machine. Her father, Mr Harry Carpenter, was not available for comment.'

So here was the explanation of Carpenter's behaviour last night. Thanet could imagine the man's grief after the long months of hoping, his need to vent his anger against life for the cruel blow it had dealt him. What more natural than that that anger should have found its focus in the man who had been driving the other car? It seemed possible that Thanet would need to look no further for his murderer.

29

All the same, he couldn't afford to take Carpenter's guilt for granted. An interview with him was obviously a matter of urgency, but if Mrs Bence was to be believed, Steven Long had been the kind of man to make enemies rather than friends. Who could tell, at this stage, what other, equally powerful motives might turn up?

It was time to go. Thanet adjusted the time-clock on the central heating so that the house would warm up before the children got home from school, then left.

The streets of Sturrenden, the small country town in Kent where Thanet lived and worked, were unusually deserted for this hour of the morning, and the few pedestrians were hurrying along with heads down, eyes watering in the persistent wind. Along the banks of the river the last remaining leaves had been stripped from the flowering cherry trees, and between banks slick with mud the water ran swift and treacherously, the colour of molten pewter.

In the office a stack of reports awaited him, but he reached for the telephone, pushing them to one side.

Harry Carpenter, he learned, was not yet fit for questioning. He was conscious but still in shock, unresponsive and silent. Thanet arranged for a rota of men to await the moment when he could be interviewed, then rang Chief Inspector Hines.

'Hines here.'

Hines's brusque bark was painful to the ear and Thanet winced, held the receiver further away.

'Good morning, sir. Thanet.'

'Ah, morning, Luke. Had a spot of trouble over there, I gather.'

'You've heard about it, then. That's why I'm ringing.'

'Don't tell me you're stuck already.' Hines's hearty guffaw sent shock vibrations through Thanet's ear-drum.

Don't let him rile you. 'Not exactly, sir. It's just that I need DS Lineham back.'

'Ah. Well now, we have a slight problem there, I'm afraid.'

'Oh?'

'Lineham's already been briefed this morning, and won't be back until lunch time.'

Thanet silently ground his teeth. If Hines had heard about Long's murder, he must have known that Thanet would be requesting the sergeant's return. He was being deliberately obstructive. 'That's a pity.' *Pity!* 'I really am very short-handed here. I don't suppose there's any chance of recalling him?' *Damn. Shouldn't have put it like that. Asking for the answer 'No'.*

'No,' said Hines, trying but failing to keep the satisfaction out of his voice. 'He's been given a job to do, he'll have to finish it.'

'So he'll be reporting in around midday?' Knowing Hines of old, Thanet was determined not to let the conversation end without some definite arrangement being made.

'Somewhere around then, I should think.' Hines wasn't enjoying being forced into a corner.

'So I can expect him back here by, say, two o'clock, at the latest?'

'Unless anything unexpected crops up.'

Thanet was satisfied. Both men knew that Hines was now committed to returning Lineham and was just going through the motions of demonstrating that he still had the whip hand. 'Thank you, sir.'

Mission accomplished, Thanet could afford to be generous. Besides, he was genuinely interested. 'How's the case going?'

'Well enough, Luke, well enough. We have an identification now, so it's just a matter of time, I expect. You know how it is.'

'Quite. Good.'

A few more pleasantries and Thanet rang off, relieved that the call had gone off relatively smoothly. It would be a nuisance having to manage without Lineham again this morning, but the inconvenience was a small price to pay for avoiding a head-on confrontation with Hines, whose over-bearing, perverse nature had made him universally unpopular.

Thanet arranged for Carpenter's clothes to be brought in

for examination, then settled down to read the reports. Carson had managed to trace both Long's mother (too drunk to take the news in properly) and his wife (very distressed, almost hysterical). He had arranged for someone to pick Sharon up this morning and bring her in to identify the body. There was a separate note from Carson informing Thanet that the post-mortem was scheduled to take place today.

A number of people who lived in Hamilton Road reported seeing Carpenter's car parked there last night. The earliest time mentioned was around six thirty, shortly before Mrs Bence had seen Long go out.

Thanet tried to work it out.

If Carpenter had gone to Hamilton Road determined to revenge himself, he obviously hadn't killed Long when he first arrived because at a quarter to seven Long had been alive, kicking and apparently unscathed.

But Carpenter hadn't struck Thanet as being a naturally violent type. Perhaps he hadn't gone up to the flat immediately, but had sat in the car, drinking, to bolster up his courage. The police had found a large empty whisky bottle in his car. If so, then surely he would have seen Long go out.

But no, not necessarily. For one thing it was dark, and for another, Long might have left by car and Carpenter might not have been able to see who was driving.

Thanet made a note to find out about Long's car, and where he usually parked it.

In that case, Carpenter might eventually have gone up to the flat and found it empty, returned to the car and proceeded to drink himself senseless. On the other hand, Long might have been back by then, and this could have been when Carpenter finally attacked and killed him . . .

Thanet shook his head in self-admonition. It was pointless to waste time speculating like this. He really ought to know better. He didn't have nearly enough facts at his disposal, as yet.

Thanet read on.

Long's neighbours reported having heard more than one

person knocking on his door last night, but wouldn't commit themselves to exact times, and with one exception hadn't actually seen any of the visitors. Nor did they know whether any of them had been admitted.

But someone had seen a man turning away from Long's door 'getting on towards half past eight', as he himself was coming up the stairs. And there was a good description: early twenties, heavy build, around five feet ten, with longish, dark curly hair and a moustache. Wearing jeans, dark blue anorak, heavy brown leather trainer-style shoes.

Excellent. Full marks for observation, thought Thanet, noting that the description could not by any stretch of the imagination apply to Carpenter. One of Long's brothers, perhaps?

The obvious way to find out about Long's family would be to talk to his mother. Even if she had a job it would be most unlikely that she would be going in to work today. Thanet found Carson's report and scribbled down the address: Mrs Lena May, 21 Orchard Road, Sturrenden. A different surname, Thanet noted. She must have married again.

Suddenly he was eager to be off, out of the confines of his office, away from the administration and paperwork which was for him the least interesting part of his job.

In a matter of minutes he was on his way.

FOUR

Over the years Sturrenden had gradually expanded. Typical of many small Kentish towns, its architecture mirrored the centuries of change through which it had passed. In the centre, black and white half-timbered buildings rubbed shoulders with elegant sash-windowed Georgian houses of mellow red brick which gradually gave way to larger, Victorian tradesmen's houses and rows of terraced cottages.

Around this older core the twentieth century had tacked on a hotch-potch of housing estates, both private and council-owned. The Orchard Estate was one of the latter and like most council estates demonstrated the varying attitudes of council tenants towards the accommodation provided for them, from pride to indifference. By the look of it, Mrs May was well down in the spectrum: the windows of number 21 were grimy, its garden overgrown.

The woman who answered the door matched the exterior. Her pink satin dressing gown was grubby and stained, her slippers down at heel. She was, he guessed, in her fifties, with improbably bright blonde hair, deeply scored frown lines and a sour, discontented expression. Thanet could detect no signs of grief. She was heavily made up with startlingly blue eye-shadow and pillar-box red lipstick which emphasised the sallowness of her skin. As soon as she saw Thanet she gave him a coy smile, folded the pink satin more closely about her, emphasising her bra-less breasts, and gave what she obviously imagined was a seductive little wriggle. 'Yes?'

Thankful that he had had the foresight to bring Carson, who until now had been out of her line of vision, Thanet introduced himself, shuffling sideways so that his companion was visible.

When she saw the detective constable her smile didn't so

much fade as switch off, like a light going out. 'Oh, it's you again. So I didn't imagine it, last night.'

'May we come in?' said Thanet.

She shrugged. 'If you must.'

Thanet and Carson exchanged glances behind her back as they followed the pink dressing gown along a narrow passage beside the stairs. She opened the door ahead of them and stopped so suddenly that Thanet cannoned into her.

'Sorry.' Over her shoulder he glimpsed a squalor which made him shudder: a floor so dirty that it was impossible to tell what kind of floor-covering had been used, unwashed dishes piled on every available surface, and a rank, sour smell that was a combination of blocked drains, unwashed dish-cloths and rancid fat.

'Haven't had time to clear up this morning yet,' she muttered. 'We'd better go in the other room.' She shut the kitchen door and opened the one at right angles to it.

Chill air gushed out to meet them, laced with stale alcohol. The curtains were still drawn and she hurried across the room to open them. Some time in the distant past an attempt had been made to brighten the place up, but the swirling orange and black abstract design in the wallpaper had faded, the pink and green cabbage roses in the carpet were stained and worn, the orange stretch slipcovers on the settee and armchairs were greasy along the arms and marked with dark, circular patches on the backs where countless unwashed heads had rested.

Mrs May stooped to light the gas fire. 'Bloody freezing this morning, in't it?' She stood rubbing her arms and watching the fire, as if willing it to warm the room up quickly. 'I hope this won't take too long, I was just getting ready to go to work.'

The morning after her son had been murdered?

Perhaps she had picked up Thanet's unspoken disapproval because she shot him a defensive glance and sat down. 'Got to earn a living, haven't I? No one else is going to pay the rent, that's for sure.'

Thanet perched on the edge of the settee and Carson sat down alongside him. 'Your husband . . .?'

She laughed, a harsh, ugly sound. 'What husband?'

Thanet said nothing and she fished a packet of cigarettes out of her pocket and lit one, inhaling deeply and blowing the smoke out in a long stream. 'Scarpered, didn't he? Like the last one.'

'You've been married twice?'

She nodded. 'Bastards, both of them. Just my luck. First time I was just sixteen. Fred was eighteen. We never had a chance. Only been married five minutes and along come twins. Twins, I ask you! And me hardly knowing which end of a baby was which. 'E wasn't very pleased, I can tell you. Really gave me gyp. As if it was my fault!'

'How did you cope?'

'I didn't. My sister took one of them. She'd been married several years and they'd given up hope. Hope! Some word, that. If you ask me, it's all one big con.'

'What is?'

'The idea of babies being sweet and cuddly and all that. If they're not screaming they're puking or shitting, and as for having a good time, any hope of that is gone, bang, out of the window . . . And of course, it was just my luck that I picked Steve . . .'

'Just a moment. Let me get this straight. You're saying that Steven Long, the man who was . . . died yesterday, was one of the twins?'

She nodded.

'Identical twins?'

'Yes. And he was trouble from the word go, believe me. Never stopped screaming, day or night. If it hadn't been for him Fred might never have left me. He just couldn't stand it no longer.'

'What is the name of the other twin?'

'Geoff. Geoffrey.'

Thanet remembered the bawdy birthday card on Long's mantelpiece. 'And he's still living with your sister?'

'No. She died a couple of months ago.' For the first time a shadow passed briefly across Mrs May's face.

'I'm sorry.'

'Who for? Her or me?' Mrs May gave that harsh, cynical laugh again. 'You certainly needn't be sorry for her. She may have had it short, but she did have it good.'

'She married well, you mean?'

'Better'n I did, that's for sure, even first time round. Then, the second time, she hit the jackpot. Married her boss.'

It took a little while to get Mrs May's tangled family relationships sorted out.

Shortly after the departure of her first husband, Fred Long, Mrs May had found herself another man, Stanley May, whom she eventually married. They had had two more boys, Christopher and Frank, both now married and living in Sturrenden. Carson took down their addresses.

'How did Steven get on with his half-brothers?' asked Thanet.

'He didn't. Full stop.'

'They argued?'

'All the time. You got any children?'

'I'm not sure what that has got to do with it.'

'You would if you had more than one boy. Squabble squabble all day long. Drives you round the bend.' Mrs May was getting restless, crossing her legs first one way, then the other, twiddling hair around her fingers, picking at a loose thread on the arm of her chair.

'Didn't they get on better as they grew up?'

'Not so's you'd notice. It was Steve's fault, really.'

'What do you mean?'

'Well, Frank and Chris didn't go looking for trouble, if you see what I mean. Steve did, always . . . Fancy a little nip, Inspector?'

'It's a bit early for me, I'm afraid. But you go ahead, if you want to.'

She jumped up with alacrity and crossed to the sideboard. 'It's so bloody cold in here . . .'

By now the room was stifling. Thanet and Carson exchanged glances as she poured herself one glass of neat gin, tossed it off and poured another.

She returned to her chair with the second drink. 'That's better . . . What were you saying?'

'You were saying that Steve always went looking for trouble.'

She drank, nodded. 'S'right. Always did, even as a little'un. Used to needle you. Go on and on until you . . .' She stopped.

'Exploded?'

'Sometimes.' Her eyes were evasive.

'So you think that's what might have happened, last night? He provoked someone beyond endurance?'

She shrugged. 'I haven't set eyes on him for months. How should I know?'

Or care. The unspoken words hung in the air, almost audible.

'What about his twin? Geoffrey? How did Steve get on with him?'

'A bit better than with the others, I suppose. Not much.'

'I thought there was supposed to be a closeness between identical twins.'

'You could have fooled me. Perhaps it was because they never saw each other till they were . . . oh, let me see . . . must've been when they were nine or ten.'

'Why was that?'

When Mavis, Mrs May's sister, had adopted Geoffrey, the other twin, she had been married to an insurance salesman called Hunt. Soon afterwards his work had taken him to another part of the country, where they had remained until his death, ten years later. Mrs Hunt and the boy had then returned to Sturrenden, where she had found a secretarial job in a small but prosperous firm which manufactured engineering components. Her boss, the owner, was a widower and a year later they married.

'In clover, she was. He bought her a big house in Brompton

38

Lane, then conveniently popped off, a couple of years later. Heart attack.'

Thanet knew Brompton Lane well. He'd had a case there, once. The houses were Victorian, solidly built and spacious.

'He was jealous as hell, of course,' she added.

It took Thanet a moment to realise who she was referring to. 'Steve, you mean? Jealous of Geoffrey?'

'Can you blame him?' She waved her hand at their sleazy surroundings. 'He wasn't the only one.'

'How did Geoffrey react to that?'

'How should I know? They were hardly ever together and when they were I had better things to do than sit around staring at them.'

'Were they much alike? In character, I mean?'

She frowned, as if she had never considered the question before. 'No. Well . . . I dunno. A bit, in some ways, I suppose.'

'What ways?'

'They both liked messing around with cars . . . Look, Inspector, I don't want to be rude, but is there any point in all this? I mean, I can see you've got to ask questions, but like I said, I got to get to work. I'm on at eleven thirty and it's ten past now.'

She worked as a barmaid, apparently, in a pub on the housing estate.

'Just one more question, then, Mrs May. Do you know anyone fitting this description?' And Thanet described the young man seen coming away from Long's flat the previous evening.

As soon as he began Mrs May's face went blank. She waited until he had finished then said, 'Dozens of 'em. Could fit half the customers I see every day.'

'No one you know personally?'

'I know most of them personally. Why d'you want to know, anyway?'

'Just wondered,' said Thanet, vaguely.

'Hard as nails, that one,' said Carson as they walked back to the car.

'I know.' Thanet turned up the collar of his coat. The sky was an unbroken, leaden grey and it was beginning to rain again.

'And she recognised that description all right, didn't she? She just wasn't letting on.'

'I'm sure of it. I'm not too worried, though. We'll find out which of them he is, soon enough.'

Once again Thanet was missing Lineham and the ritual discussion after interviewing a witness. He felt like a boxer trying to fight with one arm tied behind his back. *Hines had better keep his word, or there'll be fireworks.*

'Where now, sir?'

'When you talked to Mrs Long last night, did she tell you when she last saw her husband?'

Carson grimaced. 'I didn't have a chance to ask her anything at all, sir. As soon as I broke the news to her she just fell apart. Of all the jobs we have to do, that's the one I hate the most.'

'Me too. Well, I suppose we'd better try and have a word with her. Though I don't suppose she'll be in much of a state to talk, after doing the identification. What time was she being picked up?'

'Nine thirty.'

So she should be back by now. It wouldn't be the ideal time to interview her but Thanet did at least want to introduce himself and establish some kind of initial contact with her.

The block of flats in which Sharon Long's boyfriend lived had been put up in record time a few years ago by a speculative builder, and had been the subject of a never-ending stream of complaints ever since. Chunks of ceiling fell down, the plumbing didn't work, and fixtures and fittings worked their way out of crumbling plaster. By now a number of the flats were empty and only the desperate moved in. Anything was better than being crammed in with in-laws, Thanet supposed, but looking around he sent up a silent

40

prayer of thankfulness for his own comfortable, well-ordered home.

There was no answer to their knock and they were about to turn away when the door across the landing opened and a young woman came out, struggling with two toddlers and a push-chair.

'You looking for Sharon?'

'Yes.' Thanet held up his warrant card. 'Detective Inspector Thanet, Sturrenden CID.'

'That'll be about 'er 'usband, I suppose. Terrible wasn't it. Stop it, Darren.'

Darren was jiggling the handle of the push-chair.

'Sharon was that upset . . . Though I dunno, you'd think that, you know, her living with Ivor and all that . . . Will you stop that, Darren!' The baby's face was beginning to crease ominously. 'She's out. Gone to 'er mum's for the day.'

'Where does her mother live, do you know?'

'Nightingale Road. Don't know which number. Darren, if you don't stop that I'll give you to the policeman and he'll take you away.'

Thanet winced inwardly. He hated being used as a bogeyman by ineffective parents. All the same, he sympathised with the girl. Three children under the age of five were enough for anyone to cope with and it couldn't be much fun struggling to do it here, with your home disintegrating around you and three flights of stairs to struggle up and down every time you went out because the lift was permanently out of order.

'Do you happen to know her mother's surname?'

'Sorry, no.'

'Not to worry. I'm sure we'll find her. Do you know Mrs Long well?'

'Not really. She's out at work all day. And they've only been here a coupla weeks. Darren, I told you . . .'

The baby had had enough. It began to cry and the girl gave her recalcitrant son a half-hearted slap on the bottom. His wails combined with the baby's to echo deafeningly off the bare walls of the landing and stair-well.

'Shall we give you a hand down with the push-chair?' Thanet had to shout, to make himself heard.

'Oh, ta.'

At the bottom of the stairs she smiled gratefully at them before setting off into the wind and rain, head down, one toddler clutching at the push-chair handle on either side.

If there had ever been any of the fabled birds in Nightingale Road they had long since disappeared. Carson went off to knock on doors and track down Sharon's mother and Thanet stood looking about him. It was a short street of neat little early Victorian cottages, obviously owned by a conscientious landlord: the roofs were in uniformly good repair, identical replacement windows punctuated the well-pointed façades, and all the front doors were the same serviceable shade of milk chocolate.

Strange, thought Thanet, his imagination kindled by the poetry of the name, to think that this very spot where I am standing was once deep in the heart of the great forest.

This, he knew, had stretched a hundred and twenty miles from east to west, thirty miles wide, from behind Folkstone right across Kent into the neighbouring county of Sussex, a wild, virtually uninhabited region of giant oaks, deer and wild boar.

'. . . sir.'

He became aware that Carson was speaking to him. 'Sorry, Tom. What did you say?'

'Her name's Mrs Pinfold, sir. Lives at number 14.'

The woman who opened the door reminded Thanet of a boxer dog: square jowls, pugnacious expression, solid build.

He introduced himself, but she was clearly reluctant to let them in.

She folded her arms belligerently. 'My daughter's not well. She's very upset. She's only just got back from the mortuary.'

'We are aware of that, Mrs Pinfold,' said Thanet gently. 'And we do understand your concern for her.' With a non-criminal aggressive witness he invariably retreated into

42

mildness. He found it by far the most disconcerting way to react.

As now.

Mrs Pinfold shifted uneasily and said, 'Yes, well . . .'

'I assure you that I have no intention of interrogating her. But as I am in charge of the investigation into her husband's death, I thought it only proper to introduce myself . . . I just wanted a word with her about the identification this morning . . . And to ask her, at this stage, just one question.'

'What question?'

'Whether or not she saw him, yesterday. We are trying to build up a picture of his movements, you see, so far without much success. It really would be very helpful if we could . . .'

'All right, then,' said Mrs Pinfold ungraciously. 'But only for a few minutes, mind.'

She led them into a room of formidable cleanliness and neatness. Furniture gleamed, the window sparkled, even the aspidistra leaves looked polished, and everything was geometrically arranged: chairs at right angles to the fireplace, television exactly parallel to the wall.

'I'll fetch her,' she said grudgingly.

The girl who came into the room a few moments later was a complete contrast to her mother; small and slim, she looked as though a strong wind would blow her right away. Her face was chalk-white, with dark hollows of grief and sleeplessness around the eyes. Her hair, though, was beautiful, an airy cloud of filigree-gold curls.

Mrs Pinfold was close behind, steering her protectively with one hand.

They all sat down and Thanet chatted quietly for a few moments, to put Sharon at her ease. He would have liked to talk to her at length, but that would have to wait for another day. She was, he noticed, very fond of jewellery. She was wearing gold hoop earrings, three gold necklaces of varying lengths and thicknesses, and rings on most of her fingers.

'I expect your mother told you why I wanted to see you?'

She nodded. She had rolled her handkerchief up into a ball

43

and was turning it over and over, tugging incessantly at one corner.

'I'm sorry to have to ask you to go back once more over what must have been a very distressing experience for you, but I'm afraid circumstances make it necessary . . . The identification this morning . . . You're absolutely certain it was your husband?'

She nodded again, a single, jerky movement. She was having to exert all her self-control to contain her emotion.

'I have to ask you, you see, because we understand that he has a twin brother.'

She immediately understood the implication. Her head snapped up. 'You mean . . .?' Hope flared briefly in her eyes, followed by a gleam of calculation, then resignation. She shook her head, sadly. 'No. It was Steve, I'm certain of it.'

'I'm sorry . . . You do understand why I had to ask?' Thanet waited for her nod before going on. 'I won't trouble you much longer, but there is just one more point I'd like to raise with you. We're trying to get some idea of your husband's movements yesterday, and we haven't had much luck so far. We were wondering if you could help us. Did you by any chance see him, at any time yesterday?'

'Yes.' She glanced apologetically at her mother. 'Just for a few minutes.'

Mrs Pinfold's lips tightened.

'When was this?' asked Thanet.

'He came straight from work.'

'And he finished work at what time?'

She shrugged. 'I'm not sure, with this new job. But it must have been half five, I think. He was there about twenty to six.'

'And he stayed how long?'

'Five minutes, ten at the most. I . . . He . . .'

'Always pestering her, he was,' burst out Mrs Pinfold. 'Just wouldn't leave her alone. You'd think he wouldn't have the nerve, after the way he treated her . . .'

'Mum,' said Sharon wearily. 'Leave it out, will you?'

'What did he want?' said Thanet.

44

'What he usually wanted, of course,' said Mrs Pinfold, undeterred by Sharon's request. 'He was always on at her to go back to him.'

'It don't do no good, going on like that, Mum. Don't you understand? He'll never be coming round again.' Sharon jumped to her feet, tears starting to her eyes, fists clenched as if to fight the onrush of pain. 'He's dead. *Dead*, do you hear me?' Her voice had risen but now she broke off, sinking down on to her chair like a puppet whose strings have just been released. She buried her face in her hands and began rocking to and fro, shaking her head.

Mrs Pinfold stood up and shot Thanet a furious glance. 'Now look what you've done. Just when she was starting to pull herself together, too.'

He opened his mouth to protest, then decided it wasn't worth it.

'I think we'd better go.'

He and Carson rose. As they walked to the door Thanet laid a sympathetic hand on Sharon's shoulder.

At least one person, then, truly mourned Steven Long's passing.

FIVE

It was twenty past two by the time Lineham walked into the office.

'Mike! I was just about to ring Mr Hines, to find out where you'd got to.'

Lineham grinned. 'I'm afraid you're not too popular in that quarter, sir.' He sat down and put his hands proprietorially on his desk. 'It's good to be back.'

'Any news yet?'

They both knew what he was referring to. After much heart-searching Lineham had finally decided to take the plunge and try for promotion to Inspector. He had taken the written examinations, had waited the usual interminable three or four months for the results to come through, and had passed. Unfortunately, promotion was not thereafter automatic, especially in Kent, where there is always a great press of applicants. Of the one hundred and fifty men who had passed the examinations, only a third would be called to the Selection Board, and Lineham was waiting to hear if he would be one of them. A further sifting would then take place and approximately twenty-five candidates would attempt the final hurdle, the Promotion Board. Only five or six of these would finally make the grade.

Thanet had very ambivalent feelings about the whole business. He didn't want to stand in Lineham's way, had even positively encouraged him to go ahead, once the sergeant had made up his mind to do so. But he suspected that it was Louise who had pushed Lineham into seeking promotion and that left to his own devices the sergeant would have been content to leave things as they were. Thanet himself very much doubted that Lineham would make it, and sincerely hoped that the sergeant's self-esteem, always somewhat precarious, would not be too badly damaged by the failure, if it came.

Lineham shook his head mournfully. 'Not yet. It's really beginning to get me down.'

And the sleepless nights inevitable with a new-born baby couldn't be helping either, thought Thanet. Lineham was very pale, with dark smudges beneath his eyes.

'Come on, cheer up. It'll be any day, now.'

'Louise says if the suspense goes on much longer she'll run round the town screaming.'

Thanet laughed. 'That would make the headlines all right. Perhaps it would make the powers-that-be hurry things up a bit. Tell her I think she ought to try it.'

Lineham grinned back. 'I'll do that.'

'How are things going over in Coddington?'

'Quite well. You heard we'd identified the body?'

'Yes. Mr Hines told me. Who was she?'

'A woman by the name of Marjorie Jackson. Known as Marge. She lived in Barton. Around forty-five, divorced, with a local reputation as a prostitute.'

'And Mr Hines thinks one of her clients might have killed her?'

'Seems possible. We had a stroke of luck. She was seen leaving the Fox and Hounds in Coddington with some bloke. Unfortunately the pub was crowded – there was a local darts match on – and we didn't get much of a description – average height, slight build, youngish. The one useful item of information was a description of the man's jacket. It was very unusual, apparently – grey leather, with the head of a dragon embossed on the back, in red.'

'Sounds pretty distinctive. There shouldn't be too many problems in tracing it.'

'No. Especially since TVS ran a photograph of it on *Coast to Coast* last night. We've been swamped this morning with calls from people who were in the Fox and Hounds on Sunday night and we've all been working flat out, interviewing them.'

'Pity you couldn't have seen it through.'

Lineham grinned. 'Don't worry, I'd much rather be here, working with you. What's the story?'

47

Thanet told him, in detail.

'So what d'you think, sir?' said the sergeant when Thanet had finished. 'Do you reckon it might have been Carpenter? Sounds more than likely, to me.'

'I know, and I agree, it does sound probable. But as I said, the trouble is that Carpenter is incommunicado at the moment. I've got someone with him, and I'll be informed the minute he's fit for questioning, but meanwhile I don't feel we can just sit around doing nothing, in case he's innocent.'

'Yes, I can see that. So presumably the next thing is to trace the bloke seen coming away from Long's flat . . . You think he might be one of the brothers?'

'Could be. Or it might be Mrs Long's boyfriend, Ivor Howells. If Long kept on pestering his wife to go back to him, Howells might well have decided he'd had enough, gone around to tell him so, and lost his temper.'

'Yes. Though from what you say about the position of the body, it sounds as though whoever did it struck in cold blood, deliberately, from behind.'

'True. All the same, it did occur to me that for an estranged wife, Mrs Long's behaviour seems a little extreme. You can understand her being pretty upset, of course, but she's behaving as though she was still passionately in love with her husband. If that was so, and he kept on pestering her to go back to him, it's difficult to see why she didn't.'

'Oh I don't know, sir. She might have been in love with him, but had finally decided that it simply wouldn't work and there was no point in trying again.'

'Yes, possibly. But I was wondering if there's a little more to it than that. Now if she were feeling at all guilty, that could account for her somewhat hysterical attitude.'

'Are you suggesting she might have killed him?'

'I shouldn't think so, for a moment. But if her boyfriend had got fed up with Long pestering her, she might either know or be afraid that it was Howells who killed him, and feel herself responsible. I certainly think we ought to take a good look at Howells, question the neighbours. If there'd been any

48

quarrels they might well have heard something, the walls of those flats are paper-thin.'

'I'll get someone on to it right away.'

'Meanwhile, what I want to do is try and interview all of them today – the three brothers, including the twin, then Howells and, if he's up to it, Carpenter . . . You know what strikes me as odd, Mike?'

'What, sir?'

'Well, according to Mrs Bence the Longs never had any visitors, but all of a sudden, on the very night Long was murdered, the place was crawling with them.'

'True. I wonder what was going on.'

Thanet had every intention of finding out.

SIX

Thanet and Lineham were just about to leave when Mallard arrived.

'Ah, *good* afternoon, Luke, *good* afternoon, Mike. Back from the wilds of Coddington, I see.' He was beaming at them over his half-moons and rubbing his hands together as if in anticipation of some long-awaited treat.

He registered their raincoats. 'Going out?'

'If it's about the PM, nothing that can't wait,' said Thanet, hastily shedding his coat and wondering what on earth could be coming, to have put the little doctor in such a good mood. Usually any hint of cheerfulness on Mallard's part heralded the announcement of some especially significant medical evidence.

'Just a preliminary report,' said Mallard. He crossed to the window and stood bouncing gently on the balls of his feet and gazing out benignly, as if he were contemplating the Elysian Fields rather than the deserted streets of Sturrenden swept by sheets of driving rain on a bleak November afternoon.

Behind his back Thanet and Lineham raised eyebrows at each other.

'Won't you sit down, Doc?' said Thanet.

'Don't want to delay you.' But Mallard took a seat, all the same. 'Nothing very interesting to say, anyway.'

'Oh?' Thanet was puzzled. In that case, why all the bonhomie?

'Cause of death was that blow on the head, as we thought. Apart from that, nothing. He was in good health and in the normal way of things should have lasted another fifty years or so, poor devil. You'll get the written report, in due course, but I'm afraid you won't find it much help.'

'I see. Ah well, pity, that.'

There seemed little more to say, but Mallard was inclined to linger.

'How's it going?' he said.

Thanet shrugged. 'So so. There are one or two leads to follow up, but nothing very concrete as yet.'

'What about the man who was picked up outside the house last night, Carpenter?'

'Still in a state of shock, apparently. Conscious but doesn't respond when talked to.'

'You realise what's the matter with him?'

'Yes. Heard it on the local news this morning.'

'So did I. Sad case, that. It's possible that you might not have to look much further for your murderer. The strain has obviously been too much for him. It might well be a day or two before he's fit to talk, though. The body has its own mechanisms for ensuring a proper period of recuperation, in circumstances like that.'

'Yes.'

Lineham shifted restlessly and Thanet knew that, like him, the sergeant was anxious to be off, now that Mallard had passed on the information about the PM. But Mallard, leaning back comfortably in his chair, fingers hooked into the armholes of his waistcoat, showed no sign of moving. What to do? Thanet didn't want to be discourteous and bring the conversation to an abrupt end, especially with Mallard in this unusually amiable mood.

The silence stretched out and began to be uncomfortable. Thanet cast desperately around for a suitable topic of conversation.

'Long was an identical twin, we discovered.'

'Really?' Mallard's face was alert with interest. 'No chance you've got the wrong body, I suppose?'

'The possibility had occurred to me. But his wife seemed positive enough that the dead man was her husband, and she ought to know, if anyone does. We know very little about the twins yet, except that they were separated at birth.'

'But the other man lives locally?'

'Yes. In Brompton Lane.'

'Brompton Lane, eh? Well, well. A step up in the social ladder from Hamilton Road.'

'Quite.' Briefly, Thanet explained the circumstances which had led to the twins' separation, and their subsequent difference in life-style.

'Interesting, that. There's a fascinating book, you know, by a man called Shields, James Shields. It's a study of monozygotic twins, brought up together and brought up apart.'

'It does sound interesting. Er . . . What did you call them?'

'Monozygotic. Identical.'

'I've never quite understood the difference, myself,' said Lineham. 'Medically, that is. I mean, why is it that some twins are identical and some aren't?'

'Twins are conceived either as a single egg which splits into two within a few days of conception, which results in monozygotic or identical twins, or as two eggs which have been fertilised on the same occasion by two separate male sperms, which results in dizygotic or fraternal twins.' Mallard was enjoying his lecture. 'Fraternal twins are therefore no more alike than any other siblings – brothers and sisters – with the same parents.'

'So what were the book's findings?' asked Thanet. 'In terms of the identical twins who had been brought up apart?'

'You can read it for yourself, if you're really interested. I've got it at home, somewhere. I'll look it out for you.'

'Thanks, I would be, very. But briefly . . .?'

'It was astounding how little difference there was between them in terms of mental and behavioural similarities, mannerisms and gestures, interests, drinking and smoking habits, even in type of occupation.'

'Really!'

'On the other hand, there were some intriguing findings. For example, it was found that the twin who stayed with the mother and was often brought up with brothers and sisters was frequently more neurotic than the one who was adopted and had been brought up as an only child, by older parents and probably in somewhat better social circumstances. And it was interesting that when they met, later on in life, they sometimes didn't get on at all.'

'As in this case, to a certain degree, apparently. According to the mother, anyway.'

'Fascinating.' Mallard took out his pocket watch, flicked it open. 'Good grief, is that the time? I must go.' He jumped up out of his chair, said goodbye and was gone, in a matter of seconds.

Thanet and Lineham looked at each other, bemused.

'What on earth's got into him?' said Lineham.

'Search me. He was like this last night, too – well, perhaps it wasn't quite so obvious. But noticeable, all the same. D'you know, Mike, if it were any other man, I'd say . . .' Thanet paused. He had been going to say 'he's in love', but somehow, with reference to Mallard, the words sounded slightly indecent, insulting, almost. Mallard had loved his wife with a loyalty and devotion that caused him to treat all other women with polite indifference. Was it possible that he had at last found someone to replace her? Thanet sincerely hoped so. But he wasn't going to voice his suspicions to Lineham, not yet, anyway.

'What?' But Lineham wasn't really interested. He was already buttoning up his coat, eager to be gone.

'Nothing.' Thanet, too, hurried into his coat. There was a great deal to get through, today.

Just as they reached the door the telephone rang. A further delay? But it could be important and they couldn't afford to ignore it. Reluctantly, Lineham turned back.

'DS Lineham.'

He listened intently for a few moments.

'Yes. Yes, I'm afraid it's true, sir, and I'm sorry you had to hear the news like that. Yes, very distressing for you . . . Just one moment, sir.' He covered the receiver and said quickly, 'It's the twin brother, sir, Geoffrey Hunt. Very upset. Just heard the news on Radio Kent. Do you want to speak to him?'

Thanet shook his head. 'Tell him we were hoping to have a

53

word with him some time today. Fix up an appointment, if you can.'

Lineham spoke again, listened, covered the mouthpiece once more. 'Says he's free now, if we'd like to go along.'

'Tell him we're on our way.'

SEVEN

The last time Thanet had seen this face the eyes had been sightless, the features slack in death. Intellectually, of course, he had been prepared for the resemblance, but emotionally the impact was both unexpected and disconcerting; it was eerie, positively uncanny, to see the dead man standing before them in apparent good health.

'Inspector Thanet?'

'That's right.' Thanet introduced Lineham, studying Hunt for ways to distinguish him from his brother. Here was the same thin face, beaky nose and very dark, almost navy-blue eyes. Geoffrey was a little thinner than Steven had been – or perhaps it was simply that he had been ill, and lost a little weight recently, for his jeans hung loosely on him. Thanet remembered the FOR SALE board by the gate and recalled that Geoffrey's adoptive mother had died only a couple of months ago. Perhaps grief – or perhaps simply a bachelor existence – had thinned him down.

'Ah yes. It was you I spoke to on the phone,' Hunt said to Lineham. 'Come in, won't you?'

Most of the houses in Brompton Road were Victorian, but this one was of nineteen thirties vintage. Its rooms were spacious, its proportions generous, its one fault the stupefying dullness which seems to have hung like a pall over the domestic architecture of the period. Everywhere was evidence of material prosperity – thick fitted carpets, original paintings, antique furniture. Outside, in the double garage, was a new Scimitar SS1.

Lineham, always a car enthusiast, had come to an abrupt halt.

'Look at that, sir!'

'Very nice.'

'Nice! 0–60 in 9.6 seconds, maximum speed 110 mph . . .'

'I can never see the point in being able to go that fast if it's illegal.'

'It's just the knowledge that you've got the power, sir.'

'Mike, come *on*. We've got a job to do.'

'Costs around £7000, you know. And look, there's a hydraulic lift and a proper inspection pit . . .'

'A very fortunate young man,' said Thanet drily. *Obviously over-indulged by an adoring mum.* He put his forefinger firmly on the front door bell and concealed a grin at Lineham's undignified scamper to catch up with him. 'But we knew that, already.'

Hunt led them into a pleasant drawing room which ran the depth of the house, with windows on three sides. At the back, tall glass patio doors – obviously a recent innovation – opened on to a paved terrace and an extensive lawn which petered out in a little coppice of silver birch, their few remaining butter-yellow leaves valiantly clinging to the delicate, wiry branches.

The room was in a considerable state of disorder. A pile of bed-linen topped by two multi-coloured Welsh blankets still in their polythene bags stood beside two packing cases, one full of books, the other half-filled with objects wrapped in newspaper. The book-shelves were almost empty and bundles of discarded books tied up with string were stacked near the door. A number of the smaller pieces of furniture had labels tied on to them.

'Sorry about the mess. I'm in the process of packing up, as you can see.'

'Please, don't worry about it.'

'Sit down, Inspector, Sergeant.'

Hunt crossed to the low coffee table which stood in front of the settee, and piled on to a round silver tray the pair of coffee cups and two brandy glasses evidently left over from last night.

So Hunt had had company the previous evening, thought Thanet. Female? Probably. Two male companions would be more likely to have occupied separate armchairs and to have skipped the coffee.

Thanet took an armchair and Lineham chose a corner of the settee.

Hunt, after a moment's hesitation, deposited the tray clumsily on a small table near the door, knocking off a small china figure in the process. He grabbed for it, but missed it. It bounced harmlessly on the carpeted floor and he picked it up, restored it to its original position, then sat down in one of the other armchairs.

He shook his head. 'I still can't believe it. It said on the radio he was found in his room . . . How did it happen?'

'He died from a blow to the head. I'm sorry. You must feel it especially, as a twin.'

Hunt folded his arms across his chest and hunched forward, as if to try to contain his grief and pain. 'It's difficult to describe . . . It's as if part of myself had died.'

'Though you weren't especially close, I gather.'

Hunt's head came up sharply. 'Who told you that?'

'Your mother.'

Briefly, Hunt looked disbelieving. 'My . . . Oh, you mean my natural mother, of course. I'm afraid I never think of her as my mother. My own mother died, nine weeks ago.' He glanced around. 'That's one of the reasons why I decided to move. This place is much too big for one person. Well, it was too big for two, really, but she was very fond of it and wanted to stay on, after my step-father died.'

'Quite a big job, clearing out a house of this size.'

'Oh, I'm not doing it all. I'm just packing up the things I want to take with me. I've bought a flat and most of the stuff here is much too big.'

'Where are you going?'

'Tamworth, in Staffordshire. I had a job offer that was too good to turn down.'

'A large company?'

'It's with Scimitar, actually. I've always had a love affair with Scimitars – you may have noticed that I've got one.'

'Yes, I did. Beautiful cars, aren't they? So you're moving quite soon?'

'Tuesday of next week. At least, I was going to. But now . . . I shall have to stay on, for the funeral, of course. How soon do you think that's likely to be, in the . . . in the circumstances?'

'Not for some time, I should think. You'll be able to complete your move and then come back for it.'

'Good. I was going to come back anyway. All the stuff I don't want is going to auction, and there are various other things to attend to . . . Oh God, what am I doing, talking about moving and auctions, when Steve . . .' Hunt raked his hair with hooked fingers. 'I just can't believe it, that's why. It doesn't seem real. Who would want to do a thing like that?'

'That's one of the questions we wanted to ask you.'

'Me?' Hunt stared at them. 'How should I know?'

'You were his brother.'

'Yes, but . . . We lived very different lives, Inspector. Our paths did cross occasionally, yes, but we weren't close, I really have no idea who Steve's friends were – if "friends" is the right word, in the circumstances.'

'You know his family, though? His . . . your half-brothers?'

'I certainly never think of them as my half-brothers, I assure you! But yes, I know them, of course.'

'Well?'

'Not especially, no.'

'But enough to tell me a little about them?'

'Depends what you want to know.'

Thanet waved his hand in an all-encompassing gesture. 'Anything. Anything at all. I haven't met them yet.'

Hunt frowned and shifted restlessly in his chair. 'Well . . . er . . . There are two of them, as you probably know, Chris and Frank. Chris is the older.'

'How old?'

'Twenty-three. Frank's twenty-two.'

'And Steven was . . .?'

'Twenty-seven.'

'Sorry, go on.'

'Chris is, well, of the three of them, I suppose you could say Chris is the odd man out.'

'In what way?'

'He's the only one who's managed to make something of his life.'

Thanet's attention sharpened. Had there been a hint of bitterness there? If so, why? Hunt himself had no reason to be envious. He was obviously in a very comfortable position.

'I can see you're wondering why I sounded rather bitter, Inspector,' said Hunt, with disconcerting accuracy. 'It was because I couldn't help resenting the fact that Steve never had the same chance.'

'Why was that?'

'Chris was the favourite. So he was allowed to stay on at school when the other two were made to go out to work the minute it was legal for them to leave. Chris therefore went to university, got a good degree and is now teaching at the Grammar School, whereas Steve ended up as a mechanic and Frank as a delivery man.'

'At least they all have jobs. That's not bad going, these days.'

'That's not the point!' Hunt was getting angry. The navy-blue eyes were almost black and his hands were clenched into fists. 'The point, Inspector, is that Steve was capable of so much more. And he never had a hope in hell of achieving it.'

'You really cared about him, didn't you?'

'Yes, I did. And if you're wondering why I get so hot under the collar about it, believe me, I could tell you some stories about the way Steve was treated that would make your hair stand on end.'

'What stories?'

Hunt shook his head. 'I shouldn't have said that. Steve told me in confidence. Besides, of what possible interest could they be to you?'

'You'd have to let me be the judge of that.'

Hunt shook his head again, vehemently this time, and it was obvious that he wasn't going to change his mind.

'You were telling me about Chris and Frank.'

'There's not much more to say about Chris. As I say, he

teaches at the Grammar School, he's married, to another teacher.'

'What about Frank?'

'Frank's a very different kettle of fish. Not very bright, and he was on the dole for years, after leaving school. Then, just over a year ago, he got a job at last, at Passmore's, delivering furniture, and on the strength of it he got married. His wife's expecting their first baby soon.'

Passmore's was Sturrenden's only department store.

'Does either of them fit this description?' And, once again, Thanet described the man seen coming away from Steven Long's door the previous evening.

'Why?' said Hunt, warily.

So the man had been one of the two half-brothers. 'Because this man was seen outside Steve's flat last night.'

'That doesn't necessarily mean he killed him.'

'I'm aware of that, Mr Hunt. Nevertheless, you must see that we have to trace him.'

'You'll find out sooner or later, I suppose, whether I tell you or not . . . It sounds like Frank.'

'I see . . . How did Steven get on with Chris and Frank?'

'Well enough, I think. He used to see them from time to time, but I wouldn't say they were exactly close.'

'What about his wife?'

'Sharon?' Hunt shrugged. 'You know they were separated?'

'Yes. How did Steve feel about that?'

'About the separation?' Hunt shrugged again. 'He was put out at first, but I think he'd got used to the idea.'

'He wasn't trying to persuade her to come back to him?'

'Not to my knowledge.'

'That's not the impression we had from Sharon herself, or from her mother.'

'Her mother!' Hunt gave a cynical laugh. 'Well, that doesn't surprise me. Sharon's mother thinks that Sharon is God's gift to man, and if you ask me she was more responsible for the split between them than anything else. She never could stand Steve, and was against the marriage from the start.'

60

Lineham, who had himself suffered much from an over-possessive mother, shifted uncomfortably.

'So you don't think he was too upset about his marriage breaking down?'

'I told you, no.'

'He used to go and see Sharon, though. Yesterday, for example, he went straight round after work.'

'I don't think he was too happy about the bloke she's living with.'

'Ivor Howells, you mean. In what way?'

'Well, Sharon's very sweet, but she's not exactly a strong personality – not surprising, when you look at her mother – and I think Steve was a bit concerned that Howells would be too much for her.'

'Too dominating, you mean?'

'Yes.'

'So you think that the reason why Steve used to go and see her was because he was hoping to persuade her to leave Howells, rather than that he was trying to get Sharon back for himself?'

'Possibly. I don't really know. I told you, we never actually discussed it. This is just what I picked up, reading between the lines, so to speak.'

'Tell me what he was like.'

'Steve?' Hunt frowned. 'It's always difficult to describe someone you know well. He was a brilliant mechanic, had a real feel for machines. I mean, I've got a degree in mechanical engineering, but I've never had his flair. You could have a really tricky problem, one that's really been bugging you, and Steve would come along, have a listen and say, "Ah yes, that'll be the . . ." whatever it was. And he'd be right, every time. That's why he never had problems in finding a job.'

'He seems to have changed jobs rather often.'

'He got bored, easily. The truth is, he was never stretched, never had a chance to reach his full potential.'

'Not like you?'

'I was lucky.' For the first time Hunt smiled. 'You know

61

what Steve used to call me? "The one who got away".'

'Did he resent the difference in your circumstances?'

'A bit, I suppose. Understandable, of course.' Hunt glanced compacently around. 'Not that he ever *said* anything . . .'

'And it caused trouble between you?'

'Depends what you mean by trouble . . .' Hunt leant back in his chair and smiled. 'If you mean, did we get on so badly that I went round last night and bashed his head in, then the answer's no.'

'What did you do last night, Mr Hunt?'

'Oh, so it's alibi time, is it?' Hunt stood up and strolled across to the french windows. 'What time did you say Steve was killed, Inspector?'

'I didn't.'

'Ah.' Hunt swung around to face them. 'And I don't suppose you're going to tell me, are you?'

Thanet said nothing, remained impassive.

Hunt shrugged. 'Well, I've nothing to hide, so why should I worry?' He returned to his chair, sat down and folded his arms.

With a hint of defiance? Thanet wondered. What was coming?

'As a matter of fact I went to see Steve myself, last night.' His eyes were watchful, assessing the effect of his words on the two policemen.

Thanet was deliberately non-committal. 'Really? What time was that?'

'I arrived at about, oh, a quarter to twenty past six. And left at about twenty to seven.'

And Mrs Bence claimed to have seen Steve leave at a quarter to. Was it possible that it was Geoff she had seen? If so, Steve might already have been dead . . .

'Why did you go to see your brother last night, Mr Hunt?'

'I was a bit concerned about him.'

'In what way?'

'Well, I'd last seen him on Sunday evening – it was our birthday, and I called round to wish him many happy returns.

62

I thought he seemed a bit low, rather depressed.' Hunt lifted his shoulders. 'So last night I thought I'd just pop round to see how he was.'

'And how was he?'

'All right, I suppose. I wouldn't say he was exactly full of the joys of spring, but then he hasn't been for some time.'

'Why was that, do you think?'

Again the shrug. 'I never actually asked him, outright. I just used to, you know, try to jolly him along . . . I suppose it was partly because of his marriage going wrong, partly because he could never really settle to a job for long, partly because . . . oh, I don't know, I suppose it was general, really, an overall feeling of disappointment in life, a sense of, well, failure, perhaps . . .'

'But he never actually discussed these things with you?'

'Not in so many words, no.' Hunt hesitated. 'He wasn't the sort of man to discuss his feelings. He'd be much more likely to try and cover them up.'

'So what did you talk about, last night?'

'Nothing much. Cars – we always talked about cars . . . A job he'd been doing at work, how I was getting on with the packing . . . Nothing special, really.'

'And how did he seem?'

'Rather more cheerful than he was on Sunday, I thought.'

'That was why you stayed for only twenty minutes or so?'

'Partly. But also because I had a date.'

'Oh?'

Geoffrey Hunt's date had been with a girl called Caroline Gilbert, who worked as a secretary in Sturrenden. After leaving Steve, Geoffrey had returned home for a quick shave and had then picked Caroline up at home, at half past seven. He had taken her out to dinner and later they had returned to Geoff's home for coffee and a final drink. Just before midnight he had taken her home.

'We shall have to check with Miss Gilbert, of course.'

'Of course,' echoed Hunt. 'Do, by all means.'

Thanet rose. 'Well, I think that's about it, for the moment,

Mr Hunt. If you could come into the station to make a formal statement some time today . . .?'

'Certainly.'

'Good! In that case we'll leave you to get on with your packing. But . . .'

Hunt held up a hand. 'Don't tell me! "Don't leave town without informing us." '

Thanet smiled. 'You've been reading all the right detective stories, Mr Hunt. Don't bother to come to the door. We'll see ourselves out.'

Thanet and Lineham walked back to the car, got in and sat in silence for a few minutes, thinking back over the interview. Eventually Thanet stirred.

'Well, what d'you think, Mike?'

'I certainly think he ought to go down on our list. After all, he was there, last night. And I did wonder . . . D'you think it was him, not Steve, that that witness saw leaving at a quarter to seven?'

'I wondered too. Could well have been. We'll have to see how things shape up. So far we haven't come across anyone who's seen Steve alive after that time. In which case . . .'

'He might have been dead before Geoff left . . . If only that gas fire hadn't been left on full blast, we'd have a much better idea of the time of death. Do you think it might have been left on on purpose, sir?'

'To mislead us? Quite possibly. But it's equally possible that it was pure coincidence. It was very cold last night, if you remember. It would have been perfectly normal for Steve to have turned it on full when he got in, to warm the place up.'

'Though I can't for the life of me see why Geoff should have wanted to kill Steve. After all, he's got everything going for him – plenty of money, a new job he's really looking forward to . . . I'll check with Scimitar, shall I, sir?'

'Put Bentley on to it. We've got too much to get through today. Anyway, I can't think he'd lie about a thing like that, because it's so easily checked. This move of his has obviously been under way for some time. You might get Bentley to give

64

the estate agents a ring too, though, just to be certain.'

'What about Miss Gilbert, sir?'

'We'll send Carson. Hell, I suppose it would be simpler to nip back to the office and get all this organised, before our next call.'

'Who are we seeing next, sir?'

'Frank, I think. He's the only one on whom we have something definite.'

But when they got back to the office Thanet changed his mind. The house-to-house enquiries in the block of flats where Ivor Howells lived had produced an interesting piece of information: on Sunday evening, two days before the murder, Howells and Steven Long had had a blazing row, and Howells had been heard threatening to 'chop' Steve if he ever came near Sharon again.

EIGHT

Ivor Howells was employed by Sturrenden Council and a phone call ascertained that he was at present working on road repairs between Sturrenden and Nettleton, a couple of miles away.

It had stopped raining a little while ago but the landscape looked half-drowned, the branches of trees still drooping with the weight of unshed water, the bare earth of newly ploughed fields glistening like Christmas pudding. Sodden leaves lay in pulpy russet ribbons all along the edges of the road, their autumn glory prematurely extinguished, and the rolling curves of the North Downs were swathed in mist.

'Who'd be a cow, in this weather?' said Thanet as they passed a mournful-looking animal poking its nose through a five-barred gate.

'Light's beginning to go already.' Lineham switched on dipped headlights. 'Let's hope they haven't packed up and gone home. Shouldn't think they'd have been able to do much in these conditions anyway.'

'There's the sign now.' Thanet nodded at the familiar ROAD WORKS AHEAD board propped at the side of the road.

Lineham was right, the men had obviously decided to give up for the day. Some of them were loading equipment into a lorry and one was walking along the side of an open trench half-full of water, checking that the warning lights were in position and functioning.

'Just in time, by the look of it.' Lineham pulled up and they both got out.

'Hul*lo*.' One of the men, a tall, lanky individual with a drooping moustache, noticed their arrival and nudged the man next to him. 'What have we here, then? Trouble?'

Four wary faces watched their approach.

'Is one of you Ivor Howells?' said Thanet.

66

Without taking his eyes off Thanet the lanky man turned his head to call over his shoulder. 'Taff? Visitors.'

The man who was adjusting the warning lights looked up, gave the last light a final nudge with his foot and started back towards them.

Thanet moved to meet him.

'What you been doing then, Taff? Robbing the bank?' shouted one of the men, and they all grinned.

Howells said nothing. He was of medium height and Thanet guessed that under his bulky waterproof clothes he would be slim, but he loped along with a controlled, muscled power that reminded Thanet of a tiger in the jungle. As he drew closer Thanet could see that beneath the anorak hood his hair was dark, his skin sallow and that on his right cheek he bore the bluish scar that is unique to the coal-miner.

'Mr Howells?' Thanet introduced himself. 'I'm in charge of the investigation into the death of Mr Steven Long.'

'So?'

'I'd like to have a talk with you. There's a transport café back there . . . We could give you a lift back to town, afterwards.'

Howells shrugged and began to walk towards the lorry.

The men had finished loading up now and stood watching as he approached.

'No point in you all hanging on waiting for me,' said Howells, and Thanet heard the strong Welsh lilt in his voice for the first time. 'You go on back to the depot and I'll cadge a lift.'

'You're sure? We can wait, if you like,' said the tall man, and the others nodded and shuffled a little closer together, unconsciously demonstrating their solidarity.

'No, not to worry, boys. See you tomorrow, then?'

They nodded, packed themselves into the lorry and departed.

'Have you been working in Kent long?' said Thanet conversationally, as they drove the half a mile or so back to the café.

67

'Since '84.' Howells could not conceal the bitterness in his voice.

Ah yes, the miners' strike. That long, disastrous struggle which had split the mining union right down the middle, turned miner against miner, father against son, and destroyed the unique community spirit of many mining villages, perhaps for ever. It had also left a strong residue of bitterness against the police. Thanet looked at Howells's profile and wondered: had he been amongst the pickets who had faced the riot shields? If so, Thanet had a tough task ahead of him.

At this time of day the café was empty. It was warm and spotlessly clean, the formica-topped tables gleaming, and the three men cupped their hands gratefully around the steaming mugs of tea.

'We heard about the row you had with Mr Long, on Sunday night,' said Thanet, coming straight to the point.

'So that's it.' Howells had taken off his orange safety waistcoat and his anorak and was hunched over his tea. He slurped at the hot liquid before continuing. 'I might have guessed some nosy-parker'd open his big mouth.'

'D'you mind telling us what the row was about?'

'Of course I bloody mind! But I suppose you'll find out anyway, if you don't know already . . . It was about Sharon, of course.'

Thanet waited and Howells shot him a glance in which the embers of resentment against Long still smouldered. 'Wouldn't leave her alone, would he?'

'He was pestering her?'

'Kept on coming round all the time, trying to get her to go back to him. I'd had it up to here, I can tell you.'

'We heard that he wasn't particularly interested in patching things up between them.'

'Huh! Don't know who's been feeding you that rubbish, but they were lying in their teeth. Not particularly interested . . .! D'you call coming round most evenings after work not particularly interested? Or bringing her presents – rings, bangles, boxes of choc'lates, bunches of bloody flowers, bottles of scent, not particularly interested?'

Howells was working himself up into a fury at the memory.

'And Sharon? How did she react to all this?'

'What do you think? She was fed up to the bloody back teeth, I can tell you.'

Remembering Sharon's distress, Thanet wondered if this were true. Perhaps Howells's anger was fuelled by the fear that Sharon's reaction had been precisely the opposite, and that Long's persistence was showing returns.

'So what exactly happened, on Sunday?'

Howells drank off the rest of his tea, set the mug down on the table with a crash that brought a frown from the woman behind the counter and sat back, folding his arms as if to contain his rage at the memory. 'It was around five in the afternoon. Sharon and me was just having a cup of tea when there's this knock on the door. I went to answer it and there he is, large as life, shoving past me. "Hullo Sharon," he says. "Thanks for the card." He's carrying this white cardboard box, see, and he plonks it down on the table and starts to open it. "I thought you'd like a piece of my birthday cake," he says, bold as brass. The nerve of it! I couldn't believe my eyes, that he'd just barge in like that . . . And I thought, I'll show him where to put his bloody birthday cake . . . I tell you, I'd just about had enough. I decided I'd really put the wind up him, this time . . .' Howells shrugged. 'That's about all there was to it.'

Thanet could visualise it: Sharon, in all her fragility, standing by helplessly while the two men, her husband and her lover, snarled at each other like two dogs over a bone . . . It seemed a miracle to him, now that he had met Howells, that it hadn't come to blows. From the neighbours' accounts it was, not surprisingly, Long who had gone off with his tail between his legs – and yet, he had gone back for more, two days later. The question was, had Howells known of this later visit? He should have been back from work by then but no one, as yet, had reported any kind of disturbance and surely, if he had been there when Long arrived, this time it would have ended in violence.

No, on balance Thanet thought it more likely that Howells had heard about yesterday's visit later, probably from some 'friendly' neighbour. It was unlikely, in the circumstances, that Sharon herself would have told him. And there was also the possibility that he hadn't heard about it at all, was still unaware of it . . .

'What time do you usually get home from work, Mr Howells?'

'About a quarter past five. Why?'

'And yesterday?'

'No, yesterday I was . . .' Howells leaned forward, eyes glittering like anthracite. 'Here, what you getting at?'

'Nothing. As yet. Merely requesting information.'

'Don't feed me that guff.'

'It's true. At the moment. But I would remind you that this is a murder enquiry, and that so far you are the only person known to have been on bad terms with Mr Long.'

'The only . . .!' Briefly, Howells was speechless. 'You just have to be joking!'

Thanet was sure the man's astonishment was genuine. 'You obviously know something we don't.'

Howells was still shaking his head in disbelief. 'The only person known to have been on bad terms . . . You haven't seen Frank, then. Or Chris.'

'Not yet, no.'

Howells jerked his head forward, thrusting his face to within a few inches of Thanet's. 'Then may I suggest, Inspector, that before you start making any accusations here, you go and interview *Mr* Long's beloved brothers?'

Thanet didn't flinch. 'I think that perhaps you are jumping to conclusions, Mr Howells. I am not making any accusations against you or against anyone else until I have satisfied myself that they are justified. I have every intention of going to see both Frank and Chris May as soon as possible, but meanwhile I would like to point out that there is only one way for anyone

– anyone, Mr Howells – to clear himself of suspicion, and that is for him to satisfy us that he could not have done the murder. To which end I shall be asking *everyone* involved for details of his – or her – movements between five o'clock and eleven o'clock last night. And the sooner I get that information from you, the sooner we'll all be able to leave.'

Howells stared at Thanet for a moment, evidently trying to decide whether or not to believe him, then leaned back in his chair and shrugged. 'OK. What d'you want to know?'

Thanet glanced at Lineham. *Take over.*

Now that Howells was disposed to be cooperative it didn't take long to get the information they wanted. He had left work at 4.45 as usual, but instead of going home had, as previously arranged, gone to help a friend shift some furniture into a new house. This had taken well over three hours and it was getting on for half past eight when he had arrived home. He and Sharon had had supper and then they had gone out for a drink with some friends, returning home around eleven fifteen. Lineham took down names, addresses, times, routes, and then glanced interrogatively at Thanet. *Anything else you want to ask?*

There was.

'Did you know that Mr Long went to see Mrs Long after work, yesterday?'

'Yes, she told me. Sent him away with a flea in his ear.'

'After the warning you gave him on Sunday, didn't you feel inclined to go and see him, carry out your threat?'

'What threat was that?'

'To "chop" him.'

'I don't know what you're talking about. I never said any such thing.'

'You were heard to, by one of your neighbours.'

'They don't know what they're talking about. "Stop" him, more likely.'

'Well, didn't you? Feel inclined to go and see him again?'

'No need to, was there?'

'What do you mean?'

'The show I put on, on Sunday night – it was as much for

71

Sharon as for him, see. She was too soft with him, always has been. She can't help herself. So I thought, if I could put over the message that I'd really had enough of him coming round, she might be a bit tougher with him, next time.'

'You wanted to frighten her?'

'Not exactly, no. If she'd really wanted to go back to him, it would have been a different matter, but I knew she only put up with him coming because she felt sorry for him. And I thought it had gone on long enough. When she told me she'd refused to talk to him, last night, I knew I'd won. There was no need for me to go and see him.'

So Sharon hadn't been completely frank with Howells. She had told Thanet herself that Long had stayed five or ten minutes. Whether or not Howells had intended to frighten her, it sounded as though he had certainly succeeded in doing so — if he was telling the truth, that is.

He could, of course, be lying. But there was no point in pursuing this line at present. Howells had his story and it was clear he was going to stick to it.

'You say that Mr Long was on bad terms with most people. Why was that? Did he deliberately set out to rub them up the wrong way?'

'Search me. I'm biased, of course, I admit that, but I could never make up my mind if it was deliberate, or if he just didn't know he was doing it. Or even, if he did know he was doing it and didn't want to, but couldn't help himself, if you see what I mean. Anyway, the end result was the same. I mean, look at Sharon. She's a real sweet kid, very easy-going and that . . . It would take a lot to make her get up and leave anyone, but in the end even she couldn't stand it any longer. Believe me, he was bad news.'

'He seems to have got on all right with his twin brother.'

'Ah yes, Geoff. Well. I've never met him, so I wouldn't know. One of them was enough, two would be a nightmare.'

Thanet rose. 'Well, I think that's all for the moment, Mr Howells. We'll give you that lift.'

When they had dropped Howells opposite the block of flats,

Lineham said, 'Difficult to tell whether he was anti us, personally, or anti the police in general, wasn't it?'

'A bit of both, I imagine.'

'In any case, he's a likely candidate, don't you think, sir? I can just see him bashing someone's head in.'

'But from behind? When the man is seated? I'm not so sure. If it were a stand-up fight, then, yes, I'd agree with you. He's obviously capable of violence. On the other hand there could be circumstances . . . Just suppose, for instance, that he went round to Long's place last night determined to have a showdown. And say Long remained cool, refused to be drawn. I could imagine Howells getting more and more worked up . . . Long sitting there on the settee refusing to be intimidated . . . Howells is walking about in his agitation and suddenly his temper snaps, he grabs the nearest heavy object to hand and . . .'

'Wham. End of Long.'

'Possible, don't you think?'

'Having met him, I certainly do. You could just feel the anger simmering away underneath all the time, waiting to boil over.'

'I know. We'd better get that alibi of his checked.'

'A lot of it depends on Sharon's corroboration, sir.'

'Quite. Meanwhile, let's get a move on. I want to catch Frank May at work, rather than interview him at home with that pregnant wife of his around.'

'We may be too late. It's ten past five now.'

'Passmore's doesn't close till five thirty. We're only a few minutes away. We'll give it a try.'

Lineham parked the car near the loading bays at the back of the store. A number of Passmore vans were neatly lined up, apparently abandoned for the night, and the place seemed deserted.

'Looks as though the drivers have all gone home,' said Lineham, with an 'I told you so' inflection.

'Mm,' said Thanet. He got out of the car and strolled across to the end loading bay, where a faint light spilled out across

73

the tarmac from a small door inset into the larger ones.

He pushed it open. The light was coming from a small, glassed-in office in a corner of the bay. Inside, bent over some papers, Thanet could see the top of a bald head. He walked across and tapped on the glass. 'Excuse me . . .'

The head jerked up, the man's face a caricature of surprise and shock, eyes stretched wide, mouth a perfect O. He was in his seventies, small and bent, with arthritic hands.

'Sorry, I didn't mean to startle you.'

The man's gaze switched to Lineham, who had just stepped through the door into the bay.

Thanet held his identity card up against the glass. 'We'd like a word with Frank May. I understand he works here.'

The man leaned across the counter top to peer at the card. His look of apprehension faded. He slid down off his stool and came to open the door. He was tiny, not much more than five feet, twisted and bent with arthritis. A blast of hot, paraffin-laden air gushed out.

'Come in, come in. It's warmer in here. Shut the door, that's right . . . About that business with his brother, is it?'

A strange way to refer to a murder, Thanet thought. 'What business with his brother?' he said, warily.

'About the telly . . .' He was easing himself backwards up on to his stool as he spoke, his eyes bright with interest.

He looked, Thanet thought, rather like a gnome perched on a toadstool.

His eyes darted from Thanet to Lineham and back again. 'No? What d'you want with Frank, then?'

'Look, Mr . . .?'

'Baines. Harry Baines.'

'Well, Mr Baines, it looks as though we might be at cross purposes here. Perhaps you'd better tell us what you meant. Which brother?'

'I didn't know he had more than one. That Steve, I was talking about.'

'What about Steve?'

'Lost him his job, didn't he.'

'Frank doesn't work here any more?' asked Lineham.

'Only till the end of the week.'

'He's here now, then?'

'No, the drivers knock off at five. Most of the deliveries is finished by then.'

Thanet remembered what Geoff had told him about Frank's years on the dole, the wedding arranged on the strength of this job, the imminent birth of the baby, and realised what a crushing blow this must have been. And a motive for murder? 'So how did Steve lose Frank his job?'

'Tried to pull a fast one once too often. I warned Frank, told him that if he wasn't careful he'd be out on his ear. I know he spoke to him about it, but it didn't make any difference, seemingly.' Baines thrust his chin forward. 'Sixty years I've worked at Passmore's, in this very same department. Started straight from school, at fourteen, and I've seen an awful lot of blokes come and go. Frank's all right, a good lad. Not too much up top, but enough to make a sensible driver, and he was a hard worker, too. And there's that little wife of his, just going to have their first baby . . . Fair makes me sick, it does.' The old man was getting so worked up that spittle was forming at the corners of his mouth.

'I'm sorry,' said Thanet, 'but I still don't understand . . .'

'First of all it were small things. Nicked straight off the vans, they were, while they were being loaded up. I couldn't understand it – like, I've had the odd rotten apple before now, but a number of the drivers seemed to be involved, good lads as I've had for years. So we kept our eyes open, and it soon dawned on us – it were always after that Steve came round looking for Frank that things went missing. I had a word with Frank, and it seemed for a while that that were that . . . Until yesterday, that is.'

The old man paused dramatically.

Lineham fed him his cue. 'What happened yesterday?'

'It was about a quarter past three in the afternoon. I was working here in my office, quiet-like, checking over the day's orders, when there's this disturbance in the yard, outside. I hurries out and I finds Frank and this chap I've never seen before, scrapping away like their lives depended on it. Some of the men were standing around watching. I were real mad, I can tell you. Scrapping, in my yard! So I picked up this bucket of water someone'd been using to wash his van and chucked it over the pair of them.' He rubbed his back reflectively. 'Didn't do my back much good, I can tell you, but it worked.' He grinned at the memory. 'They just stood there, dripping, for a few seconds, then they made as if to start again. But I wasn't having any more nonsense. "Right," I said, "into my office and we'll get this sorted out." It was just bad luck that Mr Passmore himself chose that very moment to come down into the yard – he looks in, from time to time, just to keep an eye on things. "What on earth is going on here, Baines?" he says. "I'm not quite sure myself, Mr Passmore," I says. "I was just about to find out." "Then I'll come with you," he says. "But I'd like to make it clear from the outset that I will not tolerate this sort of behaviour on my premises."

'So then, of course, it all come out. Apparently Frank's brother Steve had gone to this chap, the one Frank was fighting, and said, "Look, I know you want a new colour telly, right? Well, my brother Frank works for Passmore's and he can get a big discount, see. Just tell me what make you want, give me the money in cash, and I'll see you get it." Well, of course, you can't blame the bloke for falling for it, can you?'

'Wait a minute,' said Lineham. 'Are you saying that the whole thing was a con trick? That Steven Long was just after the money and had no intention of asking Frank to get the TV set for this chap?'

'That's exactly what I am saying. Over three hundred quid this bloke gave to Steve, a week ago, and he's been expecting Frank to roll up with the telly every day since.'

'And Frank knew nothing about it?'

'Not a whisper.'

'So what happened, after you'd got all this sorted out?'

'Well, Frank finally managed to convince him that he didn't know a thing about it and hadn't seen a penny of his money and he went off breathing fire and brimstone. But the worst of it was, Frank got the push. Mr Passmore said he simply couldn't risk this sort of thing happening again. Well, you can't blame him, I suppose, he's got the reputation of the store to think of . . . No, the one I blame is that danged brother of Frank's, that Steve.'

'So how did Frank react, to losing his job?'

'How d'you think? Real mad, he was.'

They thanked the old man and left.

'I'd have been mad too, in the circumstances,' said Lineham as they walked back to the car.

'Ditto. Anyway, now we know why Frank went to see Long last night. The question is, just how angry was he?'

'And it's quite likely that one of Long's other visitors was this character he'd swindled. It shouldn't be too difficult to find out who he is. I must say our Steven seems to have had a real talent for stirring things up.'

'Yes, he does, doesn't he?'

'I presume we're now going to see Frank.'

Thanet grinned. 'Full marks for deduction.'

NINE

Frank May lived on a small, relatively new council estate. The gardens were trim, the houses well-maintained, and it was obvious from the rash of sun-porches that some of the tenants had taken advantage of the generous schemes available to those who wished to buy.

Thanet was surprised to find that number 6 was one of the larger houses. He wondered how the as-yet-childless Mays had managed to qualify. Perhaps the young couple was living with her parents.

It looked as though he was right. The door was opened by a comfortable little roly-poly of a woman in her late forties whose pleasant smile faded when Thanet introduced himself.

'You'd better come in. I'm Debbie's mum.'

Debbie, Thanet presumed, was Frank's wife.

'That Steve,' she said as she closed the door behind them. 'I was sorry to hear what happened to him, of course, no one would wish that on anyone, but to be honest I'm not surprised, the way he used to carry on, and I can't pretend I'm sorry he's gone. As far as this family's concerned he was trouble when he was alive and it looks as though he's going to be more trouble now he's dead. Makes me mad. Frank's a good lad and deserves better.'

She opened the door on the right. The smell of food drifted out and Thanet glimpsed a number of people – six? seven? – seated around a long table at the far end of the room, eating mechanically and watching a large television set enthroned on the sideboard.

'Frank? Someone to see you.'

Thanet immediately recognised the man who rose. The description had been accurate: early twenties, heavy build, around five feet ten, with longish dark curly hair and a moustache.

The girl next to Frank swivelled her heavy body around to glance over her shoulder. 'Who is it, Mum?'

Her mother answered the question with a shake of the head and Thanet could imagine the frown and the don't-ask-me-to-tell-you expression, the meaningful glance at the other children. There were, Thanet had worked out, four of them, two boys and two girls in their early to middle teens, all of them engrossed in food and television. Debbie didn't look much more than eighteen herself.

But Debbie refused to be put off. She frowned, heaved herself to her feet and followed her husband to the door. 'What is it? What's the matter?'

Her mother was obviously determined to keep the news of the unwelcome visitors from her other children, if possible. 'It's the police,' she hissed. She tugged first Frank, then Debbie out into the hall and shut the door firmly behind them. 'You'd better go in the kitchen,' she said, beginning to shepherd Thanet and Lineham along the narrow passageway beside the staircase like a nervous sheep-dog.

'Just a moment,' said Thanet, stopping so abruptly that Lineham, who was behind, bumped into him. 'There's no need for your daughter to come.'

The woman hesitated, stepping back to consult Debbie with a glance, giving Thanet his first uninterrupted view of the girl.

He looked for the legendary bloom of pregnancy and failed to find it. Debbie's face and ankles were puffy, her skin sallow, her shoulder-length dark hair lustreless. She looked exhausted, anxious, but determined. She and Frank were holding hands, he noticed.

He gave her what he hoped was a reassuring smile. 'I'd like a few words with your husband alone, first, if you don't mind.'

She edged a little closer to Frank.

'We'd prefer to stay together.'

Frank spoke for the first time. 'I've got nothing to hide, Inspector.'

Thanet looked from one to the other. United we stand, he thought. And divided? Well, if Debbie chose not to be protected he couldn't help but admire her for it . . . He could always see Frank alone later, if necessary.

He shrugged. 'As you wish.'

The kitchen was ridiculously tiny for a house of this size, no more than eight feet square, and by the time the two policemen, Frank and Debbie had all squeezed inside there was little more than a couple of feet between them. There was an overpowering smell of hamburgers and fried onions.

Lineham shot Thanet a resigned glance and wedged himself into a corner, between fridge and washing machine, clearing a space for his notebook on the latter with his elbow.

'If there's anything you want, then . . .' said Debbie's mother incongruously, and backed out, shutting the door behind her.

'Well now, Mr May,' said Thanet, 'perhaps we'd better begin by introducing ourselves. I'm Inspector Thanet and this is Sergeant Lineham, both from Sturrenden CID. And as you'll have guessed, we're investigating the death of your brother, Mr Steven Long.'

'Half-brother,' said Debbie.

'Quite right, half-brother,' conceded Thanet, with a smile. 'And naturally we are having to talk to all those who were connected with him.'

'Well you needn't think it had anything to do with Frank,' said Debbie aggressively. 'Frank wouldn't hurt a fly, ask anyone who knows him, they'll tell you.' And she gave her husband a brilliant, adoring smile which imparted a fleeting radiance to her drabness.

'That may be true. Nevertheless, there are certain questions we have to put to him. It's a fixed and essential part of our routine in such matters.'

He saw Debbie squeeze her husband's hand.

'What did you want to know?' she said.

'There's no point in beating about the bush,' said Thanet. 'I have to tell you that you, Mr May, were seen coming away from Mr Long's flat last night, and that this puts you in a very difficult situation.'

He read dismay in their faces as they exchanged glances, and it was clear that they had been hoping no one had seen Frank in Hamilton Road the previous evening.

'We also know that yesterday afternoon you lost your job, because of your half-brother's deception over the television set . . .'

They stared at him numbly. They couldn't fail to realise where all this was leading.

'So you see, there's no point in pretending that you and Mr Long were on the best of terms. And we can't escape the fact that not only did you have good reason to feel very angry with him, but you were also on the spot around the time of the murder . . .'

There was no mistaking the implication. The blow had fallen and for a moment they stood silent, struggling to recover from its impact. It was Debbie who found her tongue first. 'You can't mean . . . Surely you don't mean . . .' Disbelief gave way to outrage. 'It's not fair!' Her sallow skin was flushed with anger. 'Why should this be happening to Frank? We've never done any harm to anyone. All we've ever wanted is to be left alone to get on with our lives, to work, and save up enough for a little home of our own, for the baby . . .' She clasped her hands protectively over her stomach. 'And now . . . All through no fault of Frank's . . . That Steve, I could . . .'

Kill him? The words vibrated in the air, unspoken, as Frank cut her off. 'Stop it, Deb,' he said sharply. 'It don't do no good carrying on like that. You know what the doctor said. Keep quiet, no excitement . . .'

'There's really no need for you to be here, Mrs May,' said Thanet gently.

She shook her head vehemently. 'I'd rather, thanks.'

'Shall I fetch a chair?' said Lineham solicitously. 'I'm sure we could squeeze one in.'

Louise, Lineham's wife, had had two very difficult pregnancies.

She shook her head. 'No, it's all right, really . . .'

'So, Mr May?' said Thanet.

Frank lifted his shoulders. 'What is there to say? It's true. Yes, I have lost my job because of Steve, and yes, I did go to his flat, to try and see him last night . . .'

'*Try* and see him?' said Thanet.

Frank, it seemed, had made two attempts to see Steve the previous evening. On the first occasion he had gone straight from work, arriving in Hamilton Road at about twenty past five. He knew that Steve didn't usually get home from work until twenty to six so he hadn't gone into the house but had waited outside in the car, listening to the radio. By six o'clock there was still no sign of Steve and Frank decided that his half-brother had probably gone to see Sharon, and that there was no point in hanging around any longer. Also, Debbie would be wondering where he, Frank, had got to. He decided to go home, have his tea, and come back later.

By the time he had broken the bad news about the loss of his job to Debbie, had eaten and had been persuaded to watch their favourite quiz programme, his temper had cooled and it no longer seemed quite so urgent to have it out with Steve. It was therefore not until around half past eight that he had found himself once more in Hamilton Road.

'Just a moment,' said Thanet. 'You said "I". Your wife didn't go with you?'

Frank shook his head. 'She wanted to, but I said no. She's supposed to be resting a lot, she hasn't been too good lately. She went to bed, didn't you, Deb?'

Debbie nodded.

'Sorry. Go on, Mr May.'

'I could see there were lights on in Steve's flat . . .'

Frank had been puzzled, therefore, to get no reply to his knock. The door was locked and there had been no sound from within, so he assumed that Steve had been home and gone out again, forgetting to switch the light off. This was odd, because Frank had checked and Steve's car was still parked in the small car park at the back of the house. Frank had concluded that Steve must have gone out with a friend and he

82

had decided to visit a few of Steve's favourite haunts, to see if he could track him down. En route he had run into one 'mate' here and another one there and had ended up drowning his sorrows in drink, to the degree that he had had to be driven home by a friend.

'Right,' said Thanet. 'Let's go back a bit, then. Why did you assume that Steve had gone to see Sharon, when he didn't come straight home from work?'

'He often did,' said Frank.

'He was always pestering her,' said Debbie. 'Couldn't leave her alone. A pity he wasn't a bit nicer to her when she was living with him, I say, then she mightn't have gone off. Couldn't recognise a good thing when he had it, if you ask me, but then, that was Steve all over.'

'Odd, that,' said Thanet. 'Geoff, his twin, didn't seem to think Steve was all that bothered about the separation.'

'Don't know where he got that idea,' said Frank. 'Steve used to go round there pretty often, after work. Ivor usually calls in to see his mum on the way home, see, she's got a bad heart and he does odd jobs for her ... Steve knew he'd be pretty certain to find Sharon alone.'

'Mind, he used to pretend to other people that he didn't care she'd left him,' said Debbie. 'Act cool, like. But I know Sharon pretty well, and she was always telling me he'd been round to see her.'

'And you believed her?'

Debbie shrugged. 'No reason not to. She used to show me the things he gave her – bits of jewellery, mostly, she's very fond of jewellery, is Sharon. He was forever giving her presents. He was trying to buy her back, if you ask me. As a matter of fact, Frank and me wondered ...'

'What?'

'Well, we did wonder if that's what he might have wanted the money for – you know, the money he got from that man, for the telly.'

'In order to buy Sharon an expensive present, you mean?'

'Yeah,' said Frank. 'Couldn't think why else he'd need that

amount of money in a lump sum. I know he was out of work for a bit after Sharon went, but he soon found another job – he's a real genius with cars – and he only had himself to keep, so he couldn't have been too short of the ready.'

'To tell you the truth,' said Debbie, 'it wouldn't surprise me if she had gone back to him in the end. But the point is, Geoff doesn't know Sharon at all well. I don't suppose he's seen her once since her and Steve split up. And he didn't see Steve all that often either, so it would've been easy for Steve to fool Geoff into thinking he didn't care about getting her back.'

'Steve wouldn't have wanted to let on to Geoff that he was feeling down, see,' said Frank. 'He always used to have to act big with Geoff, on account of Geoff being so posh.'

'He was jealous, really,' said Debbie. 'Couldn't stand the thought that if only he'd been the one who'd been adopted it would have been him up there in that posh house with that posh car. Whenever he'd been to see Geoff he'd come back that bad-tempered . . . You should have heard him taking Geoff off! Real good at it, he was. He could be a real laugh, Steve, when he wanted to.'

'You saw quite a lot of him, then?'

'Well, like I said, Sharon and me've been friends for ages. It seemed natural, like, for us to make a foursome. Not that I've ever been what you might call keen on Steve. Got up my nose, most of the time. Always stirring people up. Like it was some sort of game . . .'

'You think it was deliberate?'

Debbie frowned. 'I dunno, really. Seemed like he couldn't help himself.'

'How did he get on with his other half-brother?'

'Chris?' Frank shrugged. 'So-so.'

'Oh, come off it, Frank. Driving Chris and Clare round the bend, he was, if you ask me,' said Debbie. 'Matter of fact, I bumped into Chris in town late Monday afternoon. He was still steaming about something that'd happened the night before. Him and Clare'd had some neighbours in for supper and Steve barged in, blind drunk, and was sick all over the

84

carpet in front of the guests, while they were eating . . .'

Not a manoeuvre calculated to endear him to anybody, thought Thanet. Judging by the wooden expression on Lineham's face, he was thinking much the same thing.

'Well I think that's about it for the moment, Mr May. What I'd like you to do now is this. I'd liké you to sit down and write out a detailed timetable of your movements last night, from the moment you left here after the quiz programme, to the time you got home, together with the names of the pubs you went to and any names you can remember of the people you met. Bring it down to the station, and we'll get you to make a formal statement at the same time.'

'You're not going to arrest him, then?' Debbie's face was suddenly luminous with hope.

'I shan't be arresting anybody until I am satisfied that there is sufficient evidence of guilt. Oh, there is just one other point, Mr May . . .'

'Yes?' Relief had made Frank eager to cooperate.

'The name of the man Steve defrauded over the television set . . . Do you know it?'

Frank scowled. 'Cooper. Martin Cooper. Lives on the Orchard Estate. Plumtree Road, I think.'

'Thank you.'

'Inspector . . .?' Debbie's face, like her husband's, had clouded at the mention of the incident which had had such disastrous consequences for them. 'There's no chance Frank will have to find that three hundred pounds, pay it back, is there?'

'I shouldn't think so, for a moment – that is, assuming your husband really did know nothing about the deal.'

Frank shook his head vigorously.

'In that case, I shouldn't worry about it. The arrangement was between Steve and Cooper. It's not your problem.'

Outside there was a new crispness in the air and a timid moon was lurking behind high, ragged clouds.

'Looks as though it might be clearing up at last,' said Thanet. Suddenly he felt exhausted. His brain, relieved of the immediate necessity to analyse, formulate, assess, seemed to have ground to a halt and his back, always inclined to play up when he was tired, was aching badly. The prospect of the evening's work ahead stretched endlessly before him – interview Chris May, return to the office, sift through all the house-to-house reports that would have come in, write up his own . . . He needed a break, he decided, if he was to face all this with equanimity.

'Yuk,' said Lineham, as they settled themselves into the car. He sniffed at his coat sleeve. 'I stink of hamburgers . . . D'you think Long was already dead by half past eight, when Frank got there?'

'Possible, by the sound of it. But there again, it might have been as he thought, and Long was out.'

'But he was seen going out earlier, at six forty-five . . . I suppose he could have gone out, then come in again.'

'Unless that was really Geoff.'

Lineham was silent for a few moments and then said, 'I don't know what you thought, but it seemed to me that it's Frank's wife who wears the trousers in that partnership . . . And she's very protective towards him, isn't she? I bet she was really furious when Frank came home with the news that he'd lost his job because of Steve. I'm reluctant to suggest it, sir, but it did occur to me . . .'

'Yes, it occurred to me, too . . . That was why I tried to find out what she was up to last night.'

'Going to bed isn't much of an alibi, is it? D'you think she could have slipped out without anyone knowing?'

'Possible, I suppose. We'd better check. It's only a fifteen-minute walk to Hamilton Road, from here. And she's quite a determined person, I imagine. It's difficult not to let the fact that she's so pregnant and obviously not well get in the way.'

'Toxaemia, by the look of it,' said Lineham. 'Did you notice her face and her legs?'

'Exactly. There's some inner taboo which says no, no woman in her condition could possibly be suspected of murder.'

'But you think she's capable of it?'

'Certainly not cold-blooded, calculated murder. But I could imagine her setting off determined to give Steve a piece of her mind, and being goaded into hitting out at him if his reaction was just to laugh it off. Or perhaps she could have decided to follow Frank because she thought that when it came down to it he'd be no match for Steve. If Frank's story is true and Steve really was out when he got there, Debbie would have arrived at Steve's place long after Frank had left, of course, and by then Steve might well have come back from wherever he'd gone.'

'He seems to have done an awful lot of popping in and out last night,' objected Lineham.

'I know . . . Look, Mike, I don't know about you, but I've got to the stage when I can't really think straight any more. I do want to see Chris May this evening, but I think it might be a good idea if we took a break, went home for supper, and interviewed him later.'

'Suits me. Louise was going to make steak and kidney pie . . . I'll drop you at home, shall I, pick you up later?'

'Thanks. You might give Chris May a ring, to make sure he's there when we call. Let's see, it's a quarter to seven now . . . Make an appointment for eight thirty, if you can.'

Lineham put the car into gear and it leapt forward. 'Louise won't be able to believe her eyes,' he said.

TEN

As soon as he walked into the kitchen Thanet knew that something was wrong. Joan smiled a greeting, returned his kiss as usual, but after fourteen years of marriage he wasn't fooled. By now he could read every nuance of her moods. Something had seriously upset her.

'What's the matter?'

She pulled a face. She was mashing potatoes and she added margarine and a generous seasoning of freshly ground black pepper before putting the lid back on the saucepan and turning to face him.

'It's Ben. I got home a bit early and Bridget said he was around at Tom's, so I went over to fetch him. I thought it was time he got started on his homework. Marjorie wasn't there and the boys – about half a dozen of them – were watching a video.' She paused. '*Driller Killer*.'

'No!' Thanet had seen excerpts from this film and had been disgusted by them. In his work he came across much to sicken and appal, but the presentation of such sadistic and vicious material as entertainment was, he felt, one of the most pernicious evils of the modern age.

'Yes. I couldn't believe it. I was furious, as you can imagine. I really read the riot act, insisted they turn it off and give it to me.' She reached up and took the cassette off a shelf, showed it to him.

'Fortunately they'd only watched about five minutes of it. I can't imagine what Marjorie will say.'

'How did they get hold of it?'

'One of the older boys at school hired it to them, makes a profit, apparently, by sub-hiring . . . Oh Luke, what are we going to do? I can't believe that Ben would want to see this stuff.'

'What does he say about it?'

Joan shrugged. 'That he didn't know what it was going to be about . . . That everybody watches them . . .'

'Where is he?'

'In his room.'

'Right. Give that to me.' Thanet turned and marched upstairs, tiredness forgotten, his mind a cauldron of seething emotion: shock that Ben should wish to participate in such undesirable behaviour, fear that his son's mind might already have been irrevocably corrupted, and the despair familiar to all parents trying to bring their children up decently in the face of the winds of evil which sweep across the face of contemporary society. Finally, there was anger, with Ben for letting him down, with the irresponsible senior who had provided the film and, above all, with himself. Where had he gone wrong? Somewhere along the line he had failed his children.

Ben's door was shut. Usually, Thanet knocked before entering, but tonight he flung it open and walked right in.

Ben was sitting at his desk, books spread about, apparently hard at work. He looked around apprehensively.

Thanet held up the cassette. 'So this is what you get up to behind our backs.'

Ben flinched.

'Well, what have you got to say for yourself?'

Silence.

'I'm waiting.'

'I . . .'

'Well?'

Ben compressed his lips, struggled not to cry.

Oh God, what shall I do? Show me the right thing to do, the right thing to say . . . One thing was certain, anger would get him nowhere, could only be destructive. Thanet sank down on to the edge of the bed, and put his head in his hands. He shouldn't have come rushing upstairs like that. He should have taken time, first, to consider the best way to tackle the problem.

Silence.

Eventually Thanet looked up. Ben was sitting staring miserably down at the floor. The sight of his normally patient and tolerant father in a towering rage had evidently subdued him as nothing else could. Thanet couldn't ever remember being so angry with his son before. Perhaps, after all, it had been a good idea to let Ben see just how much the incident had upset him. The thought was encouraging. How best to capitalise on it, that was the problem.

'OK, Ben, the storm's over. Let's try and get this sorted out. Come here.' Thanet patted the bed beside him.

Sullenly, Ben complied.

'Now then, let's begin by hearing your side of the story.'

'What's the point? You've already made up your mind, haven't you?'

'No, I haven't. If I had, why would I be bothering to ask you to tell me?'

Ben shrugged. 'To make it look as though you're trying to be fair? So I'll agree to whatever it is you decide to do.'

Bang on target. Thanet was shaken, and experienced an uncomfortable mixture of pride and alarm. For his eleven-year-old son to show such perception was one thing; to have to take it into account in dealing with him was another. He'd always tried to be honest with the children, to enable them to understand his motivation, the reasons for his behaviour. Now the chickens were coming home to roost with a vengeance.

'To a certain extent that's true. But it's not just that I want it to *look* as though I'm being fair. I want to *be* fair. Do you believe that?'

Ben looked directly at Thanet for the first time, studied his face. At last he nodded.

'Good. So come on, then, tell me how all this came about.'

There wasn't much to tell. One of the senior boys had discovered the profitable side-line of hiring videos overnight and then renting them out to groups of boys in the school for more than one showing, before returning them to the shop next day. Business was thriving. If a number of boys clubbed together, it could cost only twenty-five to fifty pence to see a film. The trouble was, he was allowing the younger boys to hire from him videos which by law they were too young to rent. *Driller Killer* was a case in point.

'So how often have you joined in watching these things?'

'Three, no, four times. But,' Ben added hastily, 'they haven't been like this.'

'What do you mean?'

'They've been the sort of thing you wouldn't mind me seeing. *Star Wars*, stuff like that.'

Relief washed through Thanet's entire body, leaving a weakness in his legs, a slight dizziness which briefly blurred his vision. He was reminded of the time a year or two ago when one of Ben's friends had died of glue-sniffing, and Thanet had learnt that his son's involvement had been only peripheral.

'Good. In that case, things aren't quite as bad as we thought.'

Thanet stood up and walked across to Ben's desk, seeing but not taking in the scatter of text and exercise books. He turned and looked at his son who was now watching him hopefully. 'The question is, what do I do now? I'll be frank with you, I'm not certain of the best way to deal with this. There are several alternatives. I could put you across my knee and give you a good walloping. But that's not my way, as you well know. I never have thought force a constructive way of imposing discipline . . . I could punish you by saying right, no supper and early to bed, but in my mind this is too important an issue to deal with in such a short-term manner . . . Or I could say, right, if this is the way you use the pocket money we give you and the freedom we allow you, we'll take both away, get a baby-sitter in to stay with you after school until one or other of us gets home . . .'

Ben didn't like this prospect one little bit, he could tell.

'But to be honest, I'm not keen on that idea either, and I'll tell you why.' Thanet returned to the bed and sat down again.

'You see, Ben, the only kind of result I'm interested in is a long-term one, the only kind of discipline the sort that comes from within. Within you, that is . . . What worries me most of all about this business is that we trusted you, your mother and I, and you have betrayed that trust . . . Oh, I know you may think I'm making an awful fuss about something pretty trivial – what's one film, after all – but it's the principle, you see . . . Yes? What were you going to say?'

Ben had looked up as if in protest.

'I'm not sure why you are – making such a fuss, I mean. I know, from the bit we did see, that that,' and he nodded at the cassette which lay on the bed between them, 'isn't the sort of thing you and mum'd approve of, but I can't see why it's that bad.'

Thanet glanced at the cassette. 'Can't you? The best way I can put it is to say that we, your mother and I, believe that this sort of thing,' and he tapped the plastic casing with a fingernail, 'is a sort of poison. It is slow and insidious and, what is worse, it is addictive, like heroin or cocaine, the difference being that it affects the mind.' He sighed. 'I know a lot of people don't agree with us, but parents can only bring their children up in what they feel is the right way, and your mother and I don't want you to have a mind like an open sewer, which is what you would have if you kept pouring this sort of stuff into it. And the process is irreversible, you see. Once these disgusting images are inside your head, they're there for good. And, however much you might laugh off the idea, they are bound to influence your behaviour. Personally I really do believe that a great deal of the mindless violence we are seeing nowadays against the weaker members of our society, the old and the handicapped, is a result of children's minds being warped and twisted by watching this kind of thing. Now do you understand why I'm making such a fuss about it?'

Ben sat for a while, thinking. 'I suppose so,' he said at last, reluctantly.

Thanet stood up. 'Well, I think we'll leave it there, for the moment. Supper's nearly ready, and afterwards I'd like you to have a quiet think about what I've said, and we'll talk about it again another time. OK?'

Downstairs Joan was waiting anxiously.

'Well?'

Thanet grimaced. 'I don't think too much harm's been done. It's the first time he's seen anything like this, and I think I've managed to convince him that it's not a desirable activity . . .'

'Thank goodness . . . I suppose this sort of problem is going to get worse and worse, as they get older.'

Thanet put his arms around her. 'We can only lurch from crisis to crisis and hope for the best,' he said, smiling.

She laid her head against his shoulder. 'Oh, Luke, I feel so guilty.'

He drew back a little, to study her face. '*You* do. Why?'

'If I hadn't gone back to work . . . I'd be here, every afternoon, to welcome them home from school. I sometimes wonder what on earth I think I'm doing. Most of my work is with people who've suffered in varying degrees from parental neglect, and here I am, subjecting my own children to the same thing.'

A tiny voice inside Thanet said, *She's right, you know. You've thought this all along.* 'Nonsense,' he said, with as much conviction as he could muster. 'You're getting things out of proportion. You know perfectly well that our children aren't in the least neglected, and anyway they are old enough, now, and should be responsible enough, to be left for an hour or so in the evening without getting into trouble.'

But she knew him too well. 'There's no point in pretending, Luke. Whatever you say, I know you agree with me, underneath. You never did want me to go back to work, did you?'

'Darling, please. Not that old chestnut again.' He glanced at his watch. Five to eight, already. So much for his relaxing supper at home. 'I hate to say it, but in twenty minutes Mike is picking me up, for an eight-thirty appointment . . .'

'Oh . . .' At once she was contrite, the dutiful wife, and in five minutes they were all seated in the dining room, the picture of a united, happy family. Thanet was relieved to see that tonight they were to be spared the doubtful pleasure of enjoying once again the pork chops with mint which was Sprig's choice of a main course for the competition. The first time he had thought it delicious, as he had on the second occasion, too. By the third his enthusiasm was waning and after that . . . well, after that it had become a matter of stoicism.

His enjoyment of tonight's steak and mushroom pie was marred, however, by the fact that Ben was only picking at his food. Joan glanced at Ben and made a face at Thanet, pulling down the corners of her mouth and raising her eyebrows.

Thanet shook his head. Ben was best left well alone at the moment, he felt.

'Are you all ready for Saturday, Sprig?'

'Oh Dad, I do wish you'd stop calling me that.'

'Why? I always have.'

'It's so *babyish*. I'm *thirteen* now, Dad.'

'Quite an old lady,' he said smiling.

'I'm serious. I do wish you'd stop.'

'All right, if you really want me to.' But he felt sad, as if he were finally waving goodbye to Sprig's childhood. 'Anyway, are you? All ready?'

'Just about.'

'She's checked her list and her equipment at least six times already,' said Joan, smiling. 'I must say it'll be a relief to have the kitchen clear again.'

'I expect you'll be glad to get it over with, now,' said Thanet.

'Sort of, I suppose.' Bridget frowned. 'In a way. It's exciting, though. Just think, three days from now it'll all be over.' She looked anxiously at her father. 'You are coming, aren't you, Dad?'

'You know I can't be absolutely certain, love. But I do promise that I'll do my very, very best to be there.'

Bridget knew he meant it and nodded, satisfied.

Thanet tried to look pleased as the by-now-ritual lemon flummery was brought to the table. 'That looks most attractive, Spr . . . Bridget.'

'You think so?' She frowned anxiously at her latest attempt at decorating it, an exquisitely accurate reproduction of the emblem of Kent, the white horse, rampant.

'Oh, by the way,' said Joan, 'I meant to tell you . . . I ran into Louise today, in the town.'

'Oh?' said Thanet, between mouthfuls. 'How is she?'

'Very well, physically. And the baby's gorgeous.'

'But?'

Joan pulled a face. 'They're having problems with her mother-in-law again. The house next door but one to them has been put up for sale, and guess what?'

'Oh, no.'

Thanet was appalled on Lineham's behalf. Mrs Lineham senior had always been demanding, obtrusive, disruptive of her son's life. Just over a year ago the young couple had moved, taking themselves out of her immediate orbit, and Thanet remembered wondering at the time how long it would be before she followed them.

'I thought, as she hadn't shown any signs of moving till now, she was resigned to their being further away.'

'Apparently not. She's just been waiting for something in Market Cut to come up. It's not certain yet, though, apparently. She may not get enough for her present house, to be able to afford the new one.'

'Or someone might beat her to it.'

'Let's hope so, for their sake.'

The door bell rang.

Thanet scraped up his last spoonful of lemon flummery and wiped his mouth. 'That'll be Mike, now.'

ELEVEN

In the car Thanet lit his pipe. There wouldn't be time for a proper smoke but it would help him to relax. Automatically, Lineham wound down his window. The sergeant seemed subdued, Thanet thought. Perhaps Louise had been going on at him about his mother. Thanet admired the way in which Lineham coped with the two women in his life, both of whom were pretty strong characters, but he didn't envy him the delicate juggling act he was perpetually called upon to perform to keep them both happy. Thanet sometimes wondered why Lineham hadn't chosen a wife with a meeker, more complaisant personality. Perhaps the sergeant needed that edge of conflict in his life. If so, he must get more than he bargained for at times like this, when the interests of wife and mother were diametrically opposed.

'You managed to make the appointment, I presume?'

'More or less. May was out when I rang at seven, but his wife was expecting him home at any minute. So he's sure to be there by now.'

'Good steak and kidney pie?'

'Smashing,' said Lineham, with an obvious effort at enthusiasm.

The sergeant obviously wasn't in the mood to talk and they drove in silence to Merridew Road.

The Christopher Mays lived on an enormous private housing estate which had been under construction for several years now, and was still uncompleted. There had been a tremendous outcry from conservationists when planning permission had first been sought, but it had been granted, nevertheless, and there had been mutterings about string-pulling, undue influence and back-scratching ever since. Even at night, however, it was obvious that a considerable effort had been made to make the place visually attractive. The houses and bungalows varied in size and design, and were set back at different distances from the road, and at varying angles to each other. This section must have been one of the first to be completed; the gardens here were already well-established, the young trees more than mere saplings.

Number 26 was one of the cheaper properties, a semi-detached house of modest size. There were lights in the hall and sitting room, and a wrought-iron lantern over the front door illuminated the path of crazy paving.

'Looks as though he might still be out, sir. There's no car in the garage.'

The garage doors were open, in readiness for the return of their owner.

Thanet tapped his pipe out on the heel of his shoe. 'Never mind. I'd like to talk to his wife anyway.'

The girl who answered the door looked absurdly young, more like a child playing at being a housewife, an impression heightened by her Alice-in-Wonderland hair which streamed down her back and framed her small, pointed face.

'Mrs May?'

She nodded.

'My sergeant rang you earlier to make an appointment to see your husband.'

'I'm sorry, I'm afraid he's not home yet.'

'You're expecting him shortly?'

'Yes, he should have got back some time ago.'

'Could we wait for him?'

She hesitated. 'May I see your identification?'

'Certainly.' Thanet approved of her caution. He handed over his card.

She held it up to the light, actually looked at it properly before handing it back. So many people just gave it a cursory glance.

She opened the door wide. 'Come in. He really shouldn't be too long. He's gone to see his mother.'

They stepped into warmth, light and colour. All along the blank, right-hand wall was a mural: the background was a stylised landscape of distant fields and hills, the foreground a road and on it, a procession. And what a procession! thought Thanet. There were people in wheelchairs, people on crutches, people with groping hands and white sticks, people wasted with illness supported on both sides by companions, mothers carrying deformed children and a small group of Down's syndrome children holding hands, their faces joyous with anticipation.

Thanet couldn't help stopping and staring and Lineham, too, was similarly fascinated.

Clare May smiled. 'It's a pilgrimage to Lourdes,' she said. 'I went, last year – oh no, not for myself, but to accompany a group of handicapped children.'

'You painted this yourself?'

She nodded. 'I teach art.'

'It's . . . amazing. I've never seen anything like it.' He would have liked to linger. The longer he looked at the painting, the more there was to see. The detail was incredible – the doll trailing from a child's hand, the filigree cross on a gold chain around a woman's neck, an able-bodied man stooping to tie a shoe-lace . . . and everywhere, on every face, the same steadfast expression of hope.

She turned a knob and part of the painting became a door which led into the sitting room. Reluctantly, Thanet tore himself away and followed her.

The room was sparsely furnished with a cream carpet square, a black and white portable television set and a nineteen-thirties-style settee and armchair, with loose covers in rough-textured milk-chocolate linen. The curtains were beautiful, cream linen with a flowing hand-blocked design of birds and foliage in shades of brown and black. Mrs May's work again? Thanet wondered.

She gestured to them to sit down. 'It's about Steve's death, I suppose.'

'Yes. Naturally, we are having to talk to all the members of his family.'

'You have no idea yet, who did it?'

'No.'

'It's horrible.' She shook her head, her face sombre. 'Who could have done such a thing?'

'That, obviously, is what we're trying to find out. Did you know of anyone who wished him harm?'

'Not to that extent, no. Steve was . . .'

'Yes?'

'Well, he had this . . . unfortunate knack of getting people's backs up.'

'So we understand. You don't think it was deliberate, then?'

'I don't know.' She separated a strand of hair with her right hand and began to twist it around her forefinger. 'I could never make up my mind. Sometimes I thought, yes, he did it on purpose, and then at other times I'd think he just couldn't help himself.'

'Did you like him?'

She hesitated. 'I suppose it would be more accurate to say that I felt sorry for him.'

'Oh? Why was that?'

'Nothing ever seemed to work out for him. Sooner or later, things would go wrong.'

'Like his marriage, for instance?'

'Yes. That's a typical example. He really loved Sharon, I'm sure of that, and yet, somehow, he couldn't help doing things to set her against him. In the end she couldn't stand it, and she walked out.'

'He was hoping to get her back?'

'Oh yes, I'm sure of that. Whether she'd ever have given in and gone back to him is another matter. And yet, she did love him . . . I just don't know. Perhaps it would have depended on whether or not he could convince her that things were going to be different between them.'

'And do you think they could have been? Do you think he was capable of changing, to that degree?'

'I don't know. I just don't know. Then, of course, there was Ivor, Sharon's boyfriend. He was being very possessive about her. Steve came round here on Sunday, in a terrible state. I

99

felt so sorry for him. It was his birthday, and he'd been to see her, and Ivor threw him out.'

'Yes, we heard about that. Made quite a scene here, I understand.'

'Who told you . . .?' She shrugged. 'Why pretend? Yes, it's true.'

'Your husband must have been pretty angry about it.'

She looked down, veiling her eyes, and shrugged again. 'He's used to it by now.'

'You mean, Steve made a habit of embarrassing your husband?'

'I don't know that I'd put it quite like that . . . Anyway, my husband has always felt very sympathetic towards Steve.'

'For any special reason?'

'There's no point in hiding it. You're bound to hear, sooner or later, talking to everybody like this . . . And I must admit I don't feel any special loyalty towards my mother-in-law, even if my husband does . . . The truth is, Steve was ill-treated as a child.'

'By?'

'By his step-father, my husband's father. I don't know much about it, but I do know that the NSPCC were called in, and that the social services were pretty much in evidence.'

'And the other two boys? Frank and your husband?'

'Oh no, they were fine. It was just Steve . . . So you see, my husband has always felt, well, protective towards Steve.'

So this information had been given them in an attempt to put her husband in a good light. But Thanet wasn't convinced. Compassion was all very well, but it could wear thin if the demands made upon it were too high.

'So it was your husband Steve tended to come to, when he was in need of comfort.'

'Yes.'

What was she hiding? Thanet wondered. Most of the time he had felt that she was being completely frank with him, but for the last few minutes . . .

'And Sunday evening was the last time you saw him?'

She jumped out of her chair as though she had been scalded. 'There's my husband now.'

While she was out of the room Thanet and Lineham raised eyebrows at each other. Why that reaction to Thanet's last question? It could scarcely have come as a surprise to her. She must have realised that at some point she would be asked when she had last seen her brother-in-law.

He and Lineham rose as the Mays came in together. Clare May gave a nervous little smile. 'My husband, Inspector. Chris, this is Inspector Thanet, and Sergeant . . .?'

'Lineham.' Lineham was used to people forgetting his name.

They all sat down and Thanet spent a few minutes on preliminaries, while he studied the elder of Steven Long's half-brothers.

Christopher May was as tall as his brother Frank, but thinner, almost to the point of emaciation. He had the stoop of tall men who are not proud of their physique, and he was all angles – beaky nose, high, bony forehead, sharp knees and elbows. If May's disposition matched his physical make-up, Thanet thought, he must be a very uncomfortable person to live with. His wife, Thanet noticed, was watching him covertly. What was she afraid of?

'Your wife was telling us that you always got on pretty well with Steve – I hope you won't object to my using Christian names, but your family relationships are a little complicated . . .'

'Not at all . . . We got on well enough, I suppose.'

'She was saying . . .' Now, this was tricky. According to Steve's twin it was Christopher who had always been his mother's favourite . . . 'That Steve had rather a tough time as a child – for some reason your father took against him.'

Christopher gave his wife a fleeting glance. *What have you been saying to them?* Almost imperceptibly she shrank back a little.

Did her husband bully her? Thanet wondered. Or was it

101

simply that a man who has managed to haul himself up out of a deprived family into the respectability of a post at the local Grammar School does not like to be reminded of the more sordid aspects of his background. Perhaps both . . .

'Step-fathers often find it difficult to take to step-children.'

A neat side-step. Well, if Christopher May didn't wish to discuss the matter, Thanet wasn't going to waste time trying to pry it out of him. There were other sources available.

'Do you think that, for this reason, Steve was especially jealous of his twin?'

'What do you mean?'

'Well, I would have thought it might have been pretty galling to compare their relative positions – Geoff's adoptive parents seem to have been very fond of him, and since his adoptive mother's second marriage, he's also been pretty well off. That car of his, for instance . . .'

'Well it was only natural that Steve should have been a bit envious. Wouldn't you have been, in his position?'

'Quite. How did Geoff react to this?'

Christopher shrugged. 'Tried to play it down, naturally. He always treated Steve as an equal, in every way. Though of course there's no point in trying to pretend that they were.'

'Steve used to pretend to joke about it,' said Clare. 'But you could tell he didn't really think it was funny. I think you're right, he did find it pretty galling, understandably.'

'They seem to have got on all right, though. I understand they used to see each other from time to time.'

She nodded. 'That was mostly Geoff's doing. I think he's always felt guilty about the difference in their situations.'

'It was all talk, though,' said her husband. 'Since his mother died I haven't exactly noticed him being over-generous with the goodies.'

'I don't suppose he's even got any of the money yet,' said Clare defensively. 'Probate takes ages, always does.'

'Well it's a bit late as far as Steve's concerned anyway, isn't it?' said her husband.

His spitefulness had wounded her. Thanet guessed that she

didn't like her image of him tarnished, and that disillusionment lay ahead.

'Anyway,' said Christopher, 'I'm not sure of the relevance of all this.'

'You never know which pieces of information might come in useful,' said Thanet. 'But to get back to the matter in hand . . . I understand Steve came here on Sunday night, and caused quite a scene.'

'Who told you that?' said Christopher, with an accusing glance at his wife.

'Not Mrs May, I assure you,' said Thanet.

'Debbie, then,' said May. 'I suppose I shouldn't have mentioned it to her . . . My God, if you can't discuss family matters without having them bandied about all over the town . . .'

'For all we know,' said Thanet icily, 'this murder could be a family matter. Most murders are – sixty per cent of them, to be precise.'

'Are you implying . . .?'

'I'm implying nothing. Merely attempting to obtain information, much of which, I am well aware, may turn out to be completely irrelevant, but some of which may not . . . I can't imagine you were very pleased about Steve's behaviour on Sunday night.'

'Would you have been?' May's nostrils were pinched and white with suppressed anger.

'Maybe not. But that's not the point. The point is that your brother – sorry, half-brother,' Thanet corrected himself as May opened his mouth to interrupt, 'has been killed, and I am trying to find out why.'

'You're not seriously suggesting that I would have killed him just because of mere social embarrassment!'

'When did you last see Steve, Mr May?'

There was an instant of shocked silence. Thanet had the impression that the young couple were preventing themselves from consulting each other with a glance only by exercising the most rigid self-control.

103

'Well?'

May exhaled slowly, then sat back with a resigned shrug. Now he did look at his wife and their faces said it all. *We'll have to tell them.*

'I suppose you'll find out sooner or later,' said May. 'We saw him last night.'

TWELVE

So they were at last going to learn something about Steven
Long's movements last night. Thanet was careful not to allow
his satisfaction to show in his face. Instead he deliberately
settled back into his chair and appeared to relax.

'What time was this?'

'About seven o'clock, wasn't it?' May glanced at his wife for
confirmation, and she nodded.

'Tell me about it.'

'There's not much to tell.'

This was patently untrue. May clearly found the memory
disturbing. His lips were compressed, his nostrils pinched
white again, his eyes angry.

'All the same . . .'

May shrugged. 'If you must know, he made a scene.
Outside.'

'Outside?'

So this was why May and his wife had shied away from
admitting to seeing Steve last night. It was equally obvious
that May had decided to get in first with his version, rather
than allow Thanet to hear about the incident from neighbours.

'I'd made it quite clear, after that performance on Sunday
night, that we didn't want him here again.'

'So you refused to let him in?'

'Yes.' May was sullen but defiant. 'I was fed up with him
making a laughing-stock of us in front of our friends. Sunday
was the last straw.'

'It's got worse and worse since Sharon left him,' said May's
wife, determined as ever to present her husband in as good a
light as possible. 'Some of the things he's done have been
pretty awful. He even went up to the school . . .'

'The inspector doesn't want to hear about that,' cut in May.

105

'Oh, but I do. I'm interested in hearing anything which will help me to understand Steve better.'

May gave his wife a quick glance. *Now look what you've done.* 'My wife,' he said tightly, with barely controlled irritation, 'is referring to another occasion when Steve had had too much to drink. He rolled up to the school, insulted the secretary and humiliated me in front of a class of thirty fourth-formers.'

'That must have been very unpleasant for you.' Thanet was genuinely sympathetic. Any teacher would have found such a situation humiliating. And May, to whom respectability obviously mattered so much? Thanet was beginning to wonder if, in the case of this man, repeated doses of extreme humiliation could indeed have finally driven him to violence.

May gave a brief, cynical bark of laughter. 'Unpleasant! Talk about understatement! Anyway, as I said, Sunday was the last straw, as far as I was concerned. Steve could look for moral support elsewhere.'

Thanet couldn't make up his mind whether this moral support, of which both May and his wife had spoken, had been real or imaginary. It was difficult to tell. On the face of it, it would be difficult to conceive of a less comforting person to turn to than May. But even the prickliest of people are capable of compassion, especially towards those even more vulnerable than themselves, and perhaps, when Steve had been less extreme in his behaviour, less desperate . . . Yes, that was it. Thanet felt as though he had groped his way towards a significant insight into the dead man. Steve had been desperate . . .

He became aware that the silence had become too protracted, that they were all looking at him expectantly. With difficulty he forced his mind back to what May had been saying.

'Was that what he came for, last night? Moral support?'

May shrugged. 'Probably. Ostensibly, he came to apologise.'

'For his behaviour on Sunday?'

'Yes. Unfortunately, past experience has shown that his

contrition would only last until the next time he needed to make a spectacle of himself in front of me. So I told him that this time I'd really meant what I said. He just wasn't welcome here any more.'

'Needed,' murmured Thanet. 'You said, "the next time he *needed* to make a spectacle of himself . . ." Was that true, do you think?'

May hesitated. His face softened and briefly Thanet glimpsed the young man May's wife had fallen in love with. 'Yes,' he said slowly. 'If Steve was hurt, or upset, he'd usually try to make light of it by turning it into a joke. He'd start fooling around, making people laugh . . .'

'It was his way of dealing with pain.'

'Yes . . . But lately, it always seemed to misfire. It just wasn't funny any more. The way he'd do it was all wrong. He'd have a few drinks to cheer himself up, try and get himself into a light-hearted mood, but it didn't seem to work and he'd end up drinking too much . . .'

'He was drinking steadily?'

'Oh no, don't get me wrong. He only ever used to drink if something had especially upset him. On Sunday, of course, it was that visit to Sharon. Ivor threw him out.'

'And it was his birthday, too,' said Clare May. 'Steve's, I mean. It was so sad. You could see how miserable he was, but it was so difficult. He really was very drunk. We had some friends here to supper, and he . . .'

'No need to go over all that again,' said May sharply. 'The long and the short of it was, he'd gone too far this time, and I wasn't going to change my mind – not for a while, at least. Not that I told him that, mind. As far as he was concerned, that was it. But I thought it might teach him a lesson, pull him up short, show him you can't go around barging into other people's lives, embarrassing them right left and centre, without paying for it in some way. Then, after a while, I'd have relented . . .'

Now it's too late. The words hung on the air as clearly as if they'd been spoken.

'So what did he do, last night, when you refused to let him in?'

'Wouldn't take me seriously at first. Then he began to argue. So I . . . I shut the door in his face . . . I should have known better, really.'

'That was when he made a scene?'

'Yes.' May was hunched in his chair, frowning as he brooded over the memory. 'Banging on the door . . . shouting . . . kicking at it . . .'

'You opened it, eventually?'

'No,' snapped May 'What was the point? He'd roused the whole street by then, things couldn't have got any worse . . . He went on and on, for a good ten minutes, then he left.'

'Had he been drinking?'

'No, I don't think so. If he had, it certainly didn't show.'

'What was he wearing?'

May frowned. 'Jeans and a navy anorak, the one he usually wore.'

'Shoes?'

'I didn't notice. Probably those scruffy old plimsolls of his.'

'And he came by car, presumably.'

'I assume so.'

'It wasn't parked outside?'

'I didn't notice. I was merely concerned with getting rid of him as quickly as possible.'

'So he would have left about, what, ten or a quarter past seven?'

'Around that, yes.'

'So what did you do, after he left?'

'What do you mean?'

There was tension in the air again and Thanet sensed that both May and his wife were being careful not to look at each other. Had they quarrelled after Steve left? Thanet could well imagine that they might have. May would have been tense, angry over the commotion which Steve had caused, and his wife might well have disagreed with her husband over his treatment of Steve. It would have taken only a hint of reproach from her for May to have exploded, perhaps even have flung out of the house in anger . . .

'Did you stay in, for the rest of the evening?'

'No. As a matter of fact, I went to see my mother.'

'What time did you leave?'

'What are you getting at?'

'Mr May, I don't have to remind you that this is a murder investigation. It is a matter of routine that we should find out the movements of everyone connected with your half-brother. Everyone.'

May shrugged. 'Well, I've nothing to hide. I left around eight thirty.'

Well over an hour later. So, if there had been a row after Steve's departure, it had probably been patched up.

'And what time did you get back?'

'About a quarter to ten.'

So May had been out for an hour and a quarter. Plenty of time to have called in at Steve's flat, either on the way to or from his mother's house.

'You visit your mother often?'

According to Geoff, Chris had been his mother's favourite. All the same, from the little Thanet had seen of either Chris or Mrs May, it was difficult to imagine them having much in common.

'From time to time. I wouldn't normally go around two evenings running, but tonight, of course, I thought she might be upset about Steve.'

Thanet wasn't sure whether he believed this, but he was prepared to let it pass. 'Last night . . . Did you call in at Steve's flat, on the way?'

'No! Nor on the way back, either.'

Thanet suspected that May was lying, but he decided to leave it at that, for the moment.

Before returning to the car he and Lineham separated to question the neighbours on either side. In both cases May's story was confirmed, Steve having made enough noise to bring most of the people in the street to front doors or windows. But although there was plenty of parking space, neither re-membered seeing Steve's car outside, and one of them was certain that after abandoning his assault on the Mays' front door, Steve had walked off down the street and around the corner.

'Odd,' commented Thanet, when Lineham told him this. 'If that was Steve, not Geoff, who was seen leaving Steve's flat at a quarter to seven, he must have come by car to have arrived here by seven. Unless he got a lift, of course. And why should he have done that, with a car of his own sitting outside?'

'It could have been temporarily out of action.'

'It was working all right earlier, when he went to see Sharon. At least, we've assumed it was. Perhaps we'd better check with her.'

'Well, at least we're a little bit further on with finding out what he did last night. I wonder where he went next.'

'Back home, perhaps? I shouldn't have thought he'd have left the lights and the television on in the flat while he came to see Chris May. In which case, he must have gone back afterwards, because they were both on when Frank got there at half past eight. Though I suppose we can't assume anything. We'd better check, with the neighbours. And another thing . . . I can't recall seeing a navy anorak in the flat.'

'Perhaps he left it wherever he went to later. If he did go out, later.'

'Possibly.' It was another small discrepancy.

'Where now then, sir?'

It was ten o'clock, and there were still reports to be done. Remembering all the interviews they'd conducted today, Thanet quailed at the thought. The impetus which had carried him through the session with the Mays had suddenly ebbed and he wanted nothing so much as to go home, have a hot drink, go to bed and sink into oblivion. His back was crying out for the luxury of a horizontal position. He sighed. 'Better have another word with May's mother, I suppose, see if she confirms his story. It would be nice if we could go to bed

110

tonight knowing that the alibi of at least one suspect has checked out.'

'Shouldn't think there's much hope of that at this time of night,' said Lineham as he started the engine. 'I should think she'd be pretty well sloshed by now, on past performance.'

Thanet groaned. 'You're right. I'd forgotten. Still, we'd better go through the motions, I suppose.'

There was a light on in the hall of Mrs May's house, but no answer to their knock.

'Perhaps she's working at the pub tonight,' suggested Lineham.

'Possibly. Let's take a look around the back.'

The light was on in the squalid kitchen but they could see through the uncurtained window that the room was empty and once again there was no response to their knock.

'She's probably in the living room.' Lineham nodded at the slash of yellow light which fell across the back yard.

They both moved to peer through the gap in the curtains.

Mrs May, wearing a tight black skirt, frilly red blouse and black tights, was lying in one of the orange armchairs, head thrown back, eyes closed, mouth open. Even from here they could hear her snoring. Her right hand still limply clutched the glass in her lap and beside her on the floor was an almost empty gin bottle.

'Dead to the world by the look of it,' said Lineham.

'It's pointless to try and talk to her now. We'll have to come back in the morning.'

THIRTEEN

During the night the last of the rainclouds had finally moved away and when Thanet drew the curtains next morning he saw that it was a clear, crisp, frosty day. Impulsively he opened the window, leaned out, and took several deep breaths of the icy air. Over to the right the orange globe of the winter sun was just beginning to peep over the horizon and the sky was suffused with an apricot glow which became more and more spectacular by the second.

'What are you doing, Dad?' Bridget had paused by the open door.

'Admiring the sunrise,' he said, with a grin.

She smiled back. 'I hate to say it, but it is ten to eight, and it's your turn to take us to school.'

'Time you started taking yourselves,' he grumbled, closing the window.

'When you have to pass the school gates on the way to work? You know your conscience would never allow it.' She skipped out of the door and down the stairs as Thanet advanced on her in mock anger.

As always the prospect of a sunny day had raised Thanet's spirits, and despite the fact that for the second night running he had had very little sleep, by the time he had done his back exercises, shaved, showered and dressed, he was eager to get back to work.

Sturrenden was looking its best this morning and people were walking briskly, shoulders back, faces turned to the sun. Just inside the school gates a winter-flowering cherry was coming into bloom, its delicate clusters of blossom sugar-almond pink against the clear blue of the sky. Thanet dropped the children off and arrived at the office in good time. Even so, Lineham was before him.

'Morning, Mike. What's new?' Thanet sat down and began to fill his pipe.

'Morning, sir. Not a lot. Bentley's been checking up on Geoffrey Long and Scimitar confirms that he'll be starting work with them a fortnight on Monday. Also, the estate agents say that the house was put on the market six weeks ago – presumably just after he knew he'd got the job in Staffordshire. The PM report's in, but there's nothing there that we didn't know already. I put it on your desk, in case you want to look at it. Oh, and there's good news from the hospital. Harry Carpenter is showing signs of getting back to normal and if the doctor who's been looking after him gives the go-ahead, we'll be able to talk to him today.'

'When will the doctor be seeing him?'

'Later on this morning.'

'Good.' Thanet was skimming through the PM report, but as Lineham had said, there was nothing new in it. He tossed it on to the table and sat back in his chair. 'Well, Mike, I think we'd better try and sum up where we've got to.'

Lineham put down the report he was reading. 'Not very far if you ask me.' He yawned and rubbed his eyes wearily.

'Bad night?' asked Thanet sympathetically. The sergeant was, he thought, looking distinctly the worse for wear. Lineham's eyes were bloodshot, sunk into dark hollows of strain and sleeplessness. He couldn't have been in bed before three, and the baby would have woken to be fed at six . . . Then there was the anxiety over the question of whether his mother would soon be moving in nearby and the strain of waiting to hear about the selection board . . . Thanet deliberately hadn't enquired about that this morning. Lineham would be sure to tell him, the moment the news arrived.

Lineham grimaced. 'The baby woke us at five, and I couldn't get back to sleep again. I started thinking about the case . . . In the end I got up and came in to work early.'

'Did you reach any conclusions?'

'Not really. As I said, I don't really feel we've got very far, yet.'

'Oh, I don't know. We're beginning to get some idea of what Steve was like, and of the various people involved.'

'Yes . . . Sounds to me as though he was a pretty miserable sort of bloke, one way and the other. Seems as though he had everything going for him – he was a first-rate mechanic, which meant he'd always be able to find a job, he had a nice wife who by all accounts was pretty fond of him . . . but he just couldn't seem to make it work. It's almost as though . . .' Lineham trailed off, sat frowning into space.

'As though what?'

'I'm not sure. As though . . . Well, as though he had to *make* it go wrong, somehow.'

'Yes, I'd come to pretty much the same conclusion myself.'

'And he seems to have had a real talent for putting people's backs up . . . Look at what he did to Frank, for example. I mean, he wasn't stupid, he must have known he'd be putting Frank's job at risk, with that business of the television set . . . And Chris, too. I can't say I liked the man, but some of the tricks Steve pulled on him must have made him feel pretty sick. You couldn't blame him, really, for washing his hands of him . . . Then there's Howells. Oh, I know Steve had every reason to be jealous of him, but to walk in on Sharon with that birthday cake as if Howells didn't exist . . . I just can't make up my mind whether he was simply unaware of his effect on people, or if he did it on purpose to needle them, or if he knew what he was doing but simply couldn't help it.'

'I know. But the interesting point is, that whatever the reason for his behaviour, the effect was the same. The question is, was that effect sufficiently drastic for any of them to have killed him?'

Lineham frowned. 'If so, I would have thought it probably happened in the heat of the moment. I can't really see any of those three deliberately setting out from home with the intention of killing him – with the exception, possibly, of Howells. But what I can imagine is that if either Frank or Chris went to have it out with him, his attitude might have goaded them into violence. I can just see him sitting there refusing to take them seriously, trying to laugh it off, and them getting more and more angry . . .'

'I agree.'

'And I don't know what you think, sir, but it sounds to me as though the situation had steadily been getting worse ever since his wife left him. I think the separation hit him pretty hard. His behaviour became more and more extreme . . .'

'Except with Geoff.'

'Yes, that's true. Though by all accounts they didn't get on all that well.'

'Maybe. But Geoff himself seemed quite sympathetic towards him, I thought.'

'Perhaps it's something to do with the fact that they're twins. Anyway, it was easy enough for Geoff to feel sorry for Steve. He was the one who got the best of the bargain, by far.'

'And Steve resented it, by the sound of it.'

'Can you blame him, sir? After all, it must have been pretty galling to compare their circumstances, and to know that it was pure chance that their positions weren't reversed.'

'All the same, there seems to be general agreement that there weren't any major rows between them, and we've heard nothing about Steve playing Geoff up in the same way as the others.'

'True. Anyway, now we know that Steve didn't leave Chris May's house until around seven fifteen, it looks as though Geoff's in the clear.'

Lineham got up and began to leaf through the reports stacked on the corner of Thanet's desk. 'I forgot to tell you. Carson interviewed the girl, and Geoff's alibi checked out. Here we are.'

Thanet glanced through the report. As Geoff had claimed, he had picked up Caroline Gilbert from her home at half past seven. He had taken her out to dinner at the String of Beads, a new restaurant out on the Canterbury Road. They had returned to Geoff's home for coffee and brandy, and had listened to records until just before midnight, when he had driven her home. She was most emphatic that they had been together all evening. There was no question that she was lying to protect him through long-standing loyalty, as they had only met the previous week and had gone out together for the first time on Sunday. Carson was as sure as he could be that the girl was telling the truth.

'You're right,' said Thanet. 'Steve couldn't have got home from the Mays' house, even by car, until twenty-five to half past seven. So if Geoff collected this girl from – where was it? Hillside Road – at half past seven, and stayed with her all evening, there's no way that he could have committed the murder. All the same, I think we'd better interview the girl again. This timing is pretty crucial, if we're to eliminate Geoff as a suspect, motive or no motive.'

Lineham made a note. 'Right, sir. Will we go and see her ourselves?'

'Possibly. It depends on what else we have lined up today. Which brings us back to Carpenter. All this,' and Thanet waved his hand at the stack of reports, 'may prove to have been unnecessary. Of all the possibilities, the likeliest, on the face of it, is that Carpenter, distraught after his daughter's death, went round to Steve's flat and killed him. Then he went out, sat in his car and drank himself into a stupor.'

'Maybe. But it could still be tricky proving it. So far forensic haven't come up with any sign of Carpenter's prints in the flat. And where's the murder weapon? The ashtray or whatever it was the murderer grabbed to hit Steve with? It hasn't turned up in the garden or along the road, and it wasn't in Carpenter's car.'

'True. Make a note, Mike. When we send someone to check with Sharon whether or not Steve took his car when he went to see her after work that night, we must also find out exactly what it was that fitted that clear patch in the dust. It would be useful to know if we're right about it being the murder weapon, and if so, exactly what we're looking for.'

'Right, sir.'

'Meanwhile, we've got a lot of checking to do. I want someone to check timings with the friend Howells claims to have helped move furniture, and I also want Sharon asked about the time he arrived home. I want the names of the friends they had a drink with and details of the evening. I want details of his car, Frank's car, Chris's car, and I want further house-to-house visits to ask more questions about that anonymous phone call, about all the cars seen in Hamilton Road that night, and whether or not anyone noticed lights and noise coming from Steve's flat and when. I want someone to check on the movements of Cooper, the man Steve swindled over the television set . . .' On and on it went, the endless list of queries, a boring but essential part of any murder enquiry. Every good policeman is aware of the fact that many a difficult case has been solved by just such meticulous attention to detail, and it is the constant hope of alighting upon such a crucially important but apparently insignificant piece of information that keeps many a policeman on his toes, especially since the cases of the Yorkshire Ripper and the Railway Rapist.

Thanet came to the end at last and Lineham laid down his pen and massaged his aching hand.

'We need three times as many men as we've got,' he said gloomily.

'Well, there's no prospect of getting them,' said Thanet. 'So we might as well resign ourselves to doing the best we can. I'd like to see the mother myself, and I want you to come with me, but after that we can split up, if necessary. Apart from that, well, let's see how we can best get this covered.'

Both men were pouring over Lineham's list when there was a knock at the door and Mallard poked his head in.

'Busy?' he said, with a beaming smile. He didn't wait for an answer but advanced into the room. Once again, this morning, he was looking distinctly pleased with himself. 'Brought you a present,' he said to Thanet. 'Well, a temporary one, as I'll want it back.' He held up a book. 'The one you said you'd like to read. On twins.' He handed it over.

'Thanks, Doc. It's very kind of you to remember.' Thanet opened it at random. 'Looks fascinating.'

Mallard gave a gratified smile. 'Oh, it is, it is. Er . . . how's it going?'

'So-so. Nothing very startling at the moment. We're just plodding on with all the routine stuff . . .'

Mallard nodded. 'Good, good . . . Well, I'll leave you to it, then. Hope you enjoy the book.'

If I ever get time to read it, thought Thanet gloomily.

'I must say I never thought the day would come,' said Lineham, when Mallard had gone.

'Which day?'

'When Doc Mallard would go around spreading sweetness and light.'

'Mmm.' Thanet grinned. 'He didn't even complain about the fug in here.'

'That's what I mean! Mark my words, sir, something's up.'

'Such as? No, don't bother to answer that. We've better things to do than sit around gossiping. Come on, let's get all this organised.'

Half an hour later they were parking in front of Mrs May's neglected council house.

'Let's hope she's up,' said Lineham.

'You haven't met her yet, have you?'

Lineham shook his head.

'You're in for a treat.'

Mrs May answered the door wearing the sleazy pink satin dressing gown. Once again she was heavily made up, with green eye-shadow this time, and orange lipstick. Thanet was startled to see that today her hair was a bright, glossy brown and much longer, falling in elaborate curls about her shoulders. A wig, then. He wondered what her own hair was like.

'Oh, it's you again.'

She led them into the sitting room. The gas fire was on and the room was stiflingly hot. A plate covered with toast crumbs and a half-empty cup of coffee showed that she had been having her breakfast.

'Want a cup?'

Thanet shook his head. 'This won't take long.'

'Take a pew.' She drained the cup, fished a packet of cigarettes out of her pocket and lit one. 'What is it this time?'

'The night before last ... Could you tell us where you were?'

Her eyes narrowed and she blew out a long, thin stream of smoke before answering. 'The night Steve was killed, you mean? What are you getting at?'

'Nothing. Just checking something, that's all.'

She shrugged. 'What's the odds? I got nothing to hide. I was here, of course. Where else would I have been?'

Thanet smiled. 'Bingo? Darts match? Having a drink with friends?'

Her mouth twisted. 'What friends?'

She glanced at the new bottle of gin on the sideboard and Thanet heard the words as clearly as if they had been spoken. *That's the only friend I've got.*

'So you stay in most evenings?'

'Yeah. Anything wrong in that?'

'Oh no, not at all. And you're sure you were here on Tuesday?'

'I told you.' She stubbed out her cigarette, glanced at the sideboard again and laced her fingers together so tightly that the knuckles gleamed white.

Thanet recognised the signs. She wanted a drink. Badly.

'Did you have any visitors that night?'

She stared at him. 'Visitors?'

He nodded, waited.

She frowned and her eyes glazed as she thought back, trying to penetrate the alcoholic haze in which her evenings were spent. 'No,' she said at last.

'You're sure?'

'I was tired,' she said defensively. 'I fell asleep, in my chair. If anyone came, I didn't hear them.'

'And last night?'

'My son came to see me.' Her expression softened. 'Chris. Thought I might be upset, you know, about Steve.'

So there were still vestiges of maternal feeling beneath that unlikely exterior. Thanet was glad that he had not asked her outright if Chris had been here the night Steve died. It looked as though she would be prepared to lie, to protect him.

Outside, at the gate, Thanet paused. 'Well, Mike, either he didn't come at all, or he came and she didn't hear him, or he came, spent some time with her and she was so drunk she doesn't remember. Take your pick.'

'She remembered him coming last night, all right.'

'I agree, the third possibility is the least likely.'

Lineham shrugged. 'If he did come, and she didn't hear him knocking, he obviously didn't mention it when he saw her last night.'

'That could be significant. It might well mean he's innocent and it simply didn't occur to him that he'd need an alibi. If he were our man and knew he would need one, I'd have thought it would have been easy enough to persuade her into thinking either that he did come and spend some time with her the previous evening but she simply didn't remember, or to lie outright to protect him. Anyway, we might as well try and check, while we're here. You take the next couple of houses on that side, I'll take this.'

As Thanet approached the front door of the house next to Mrs May's he saw the curtains twitch at the downstairs window. Good, a nosy neighbour, he thought. Just what I need.

He had to wait several minutes before the door opened on the chain. A segment of wrinkled cheek and a wisp of grey hair appeared in the crack, and a bright eye peered up at him.

'Yes?'

Thanet introduced himself and produced his warrant card, cursing a society which forces its frail and elderly to bar themselves into even greater isolation than old age already brings, through fear of violence.

A little claw of a hand plucked it from him and he saw the dull yellow glow as the hall light went on. He waited, beginning to wonder if there was any point, if he was simply wasting time. But he remembered the twitching curtain and that bright, knowing eye and schooled himself to patience. By now Lineham had visited three houses on the far side of Mrs May's and was approaching this one.

'Anything?' asked Thanet.

Lineham shook his head. 'No answer at two of them, the other saw nothing, heard nothing.' He nodded at the door. 'What gives?' he added, lowering his voice.

'Old lady being cautious.'

The eye reappeared at the crack. 'What are you whispering about, on my doorstep?'

There was a rattle as the chain was released, and the door swung open.

Mrs May's neighbour was small and thin to the point of emaciation. She was supporting herself on an aluminium walking frame. She held out Thanet's card. 'What do you want?'

He took it from her. 'Thank you. We were wondering if by any chance you might have noticed any visitors at Mrs May's house, next door, the night before last.'

'The night before last . . .' She thought for a moment, then said, 'Chris came round, knocked on her door. But he couldn't get an answer, went away again.' The sharp old eyes said, *And we both know why, don't we*? 'Came round last night, too, but that time she let him in. Two nights running, miracles will never cease. Sometimes he don't come near her for months.'

'He hasn't got a key?'

'Why should he? Got a house of his own now, I hear.'

'What time was this?'

'Look, it's all right for you, with coats on, but I'll freeze to death if I stand here much longer. You better come in.'

They followed her painfully slow progress along the hall into the sitting room, where she shuffled to an upright armchair in front of the gas fire and subsided into it with a sigh of relief. 'That's better.' The large marmalade cat on the hearth glanced sleepily up at her as she spread a blanket knitted in brightly coloured patchwork squares over her knees. She looked at Thanet expectantly. 'What were you saying?'

'I was wondering if you could remember what time it was that you heard Chris knocking on his mother's door, the night before last.'

'Just before the nine o'clock news,' she said promptly.

'You're sure of that?'

'My joints might be a bit creaky, but I've still got all me marbles, you know.' And she tapped her head, as if to demonstrate the soundness of her brain. 'I've got arthritis, see, and once an hour I makes meself get up and walk around a bit. Otherwise I'd seize up altogether. And I always takes my little stroll around the room just before nine o'clock because I likes to sit down after, and watch the news. And one of the things I always does is take a look out of the window. That's when I saw Chris.'

'You're sure it was him?'

'Dead sure. I've lived in this house for forty years, haven't I? Known him since the day he was born. Known the lot of them.'

'Have you indeed?'

Thanet's tone had betrayed his interest and she gave a high-pitched cackle of laughter and rocked a little, hugging herself with glee. 'I have. If you want to know all about them next door you've come to the right place.'

FOURTEEN

Thanet glanced at Lineham, who unobtrusively took out his notebook.

'So, Mrs . . .'

'Sparrow,' she said, with so broad a smile that her false teeth slipped. She pushed them back in impatiently, in a gesture that was clearly habitual.

Thanet looked at the small, bent figure with its little beak of a nose, twig-like limbs and tiny claws of hands and wondered if the name had always suited her as well as it did now. He smiled back.

'So, Mrs Sparrow, you're saying that you've lived next door to Mrs May ever since her first marriage?'

The cat stood up, stretched and looked at its mistress, and she patted her lap. It jumped up, turning round and round several times before finally settling down with its front paws neatly tucked under. She began to stroke it and it started to purr.

She nodded. 'Seen her husbands come and go, haven't I? And a rotten picker she was, too. Bad apples, both of them, not like my Bert. Mind, I'm not saying they had much of a bargain, either. Though to be fair, her and Fred, her first, didn't have much of a chance, really. Not much more than kids, either of them, and to be lumbered with twins before they'd been married five minutes . . .'

'She didn't keep both babies, though, did she?'

'No. That sister of hers, that Mavis, adopted one of them. Insisted on taking her pick, though, so Lena was left with the sickly one, Steve. I tell you, the first time I laid eyes on him I never thought he'd make it. Puny little thing he was, never stopped crying. He used to go on and on and on, you could hear it right through the wall. Really got on our nerves it did. We had to change our bedroom in the end, sleep at the back.

Wasn't surprising Fred up and went. Well, I mean, youngsters like that haven't got the patience, have they? I mean, they want to be out having a good time, and a baby soon puts a stop to all that, don't it? And, like I said, Steve was enough to get on anyone's nerves . . .'

'How old was he when his father left?'

'Three or four months. Something like that. But Lena wasn't on her own for long. Fred had only been gone a couple of months when Stan moved in.'

'How did she meet him?'

'At the pub, I s'pose. A couple of weeks after Fred went she came to me and said she was desperate to earn a bit of money and she'd heard there was this job at the pub, lunchtimes. Would I look after Steve for her, for a couple of hours each day? I had a cleaning job at the time, but I was home by half past eleven and I was always here midday because Bert used to come home for a bit of dinner, so I said yes. Well, I felt sorry for her . . . Anyway, it wasn't long before Stan was coming home with her and before we knew where we were he'd moved in. Never took to him meself.'

'Why was that?'

Mrs Sparrow shifted uncomfortably in her chair. 'Great big bear of a man, he was. Couldn't understand what Lena saw in him. Still, there's no accounting for taste . . .'

'He made you nervous?'

'You could say that . . . Well, to tell you the truth, I didn't like the way he treated the baby . . . He couldn't stand the sight of it, if you ask me. They was always asking me if I would babysit for them, and some of the things I saw . . . Well, I mean, I know Steve was enough to get anyone down, with that never-ending crying and that, but . . .'

'He used to ill-treat the child?'

Mrs Sparrow nodded, lips compressed. 'You ought to have seen the bruises that baby had on him, sometimes.'

'What was his mother's attitude to all this?'

Mrs Sparrow shrugged. 'I don't think she cared, really. I don't think she ever really took to him. Blamed him, I shouldn't wonder, for Fred leaving her.'

'Did you report this ill-treatment to the NSPCC?'

The old lady frowned, looked guilty. 'Not to begin with. I kept hoping Stan would move out, or things would improve, as Steve got older and didn't cry so much.'

'But you did later?'

'Well, Stan and Lena got married, and first Chris then Frank came along, and I kept on hoping that with other kids . . . But things didn't get better, they got worse.'

'In what way?'

'Well, Steve was the one they always picked on, both Lena and Stan. He just couldn't do anything right. For instance, the number of times I've seen that kid walking round with his left hand tied behind his back . . .'

'Why? Because he was naturally left-handed, you mean?'

'Yes. I used to say to Lena, what does it matter whether he does things with his right hand or his left, but she wouldn't listen. "It's all wrong," she'd say. Or, "Stan says we've got to get him out of the habit somehow." But to tell you the truth, I think it was just that they had to have something to pick on, as far as Steve was concerned. I mean, I didn't particularly like him, always whining he was, but then that wasn't surprising, was it, in the circumstances?'

'So what happened, in the end, to make you report them?'

'Well, like I said, Steve used to aggravate Stan that bad . . . One day, when Steve was about four, it was summer, I remember, and I was hanging the washing out in the back garden. There's a high fence that separates us, and I could hear the kids playing next door. Then suddenly I hears Stan's voice. "Steve!" he shouts, in that great roaring voice of his, "what the hell do you think you're doing?"

'Well, I was curious to know what Steve had been up to, so I put down the clothes basket and went over to the fence. There was an old box beside it and I stood on that and looked over. I got there just in time to see Stan give Steve a great clout on the side of the head, and then pick him up off the floor and throw him, yes, throw him away from him, towards the back of the house. Steve's head went crack against the kitchen windowsill, and as he fell his foot got caught in one of them little concrete squares they put around drains ... The ambulance came, that time, and carted him off to hospital. He had a broken leg and concussion, and when I heard Stan and Lena was putting it about that Steve had had an accident by falling off a swing I decided that enough was enough. I put on my hat and coat and went straight off to the hospital. Told them what I'd seen. After that they had the social worker in keeping an eye on Steve. There was talk about putting him into care, but that didn't come off. Stan knew he had to toe the line, or there'd be trouble.'

'Did they know who'd given them away?'

Mrs Sparrow grimaced. 'Stan saw me looking over the garden fence, didn't he, so he didn't take long to put two and two together. Came round here breathing threats, but my Bert soon told him where to get off. "You lay a finger on her and I'll get the police round," he said. "And you're in enough trouble over Steve, already." '

'So that was that? When Steve came home there were no more problems?'

'I wouldn't say that. Six months later Stan upped and went, and Lena always blamed me for that. Said Stan couldn't stand having the social services breathing down his neck all the time, and it was all my fault he'd gone. I was an interfering busybody and if I'd kept my mouth shut everything would have been all right. "Yes," I said, "for everyone but Steve. What about him? You can't just stand by and see a kid being knocked about like that." '

'What did she say?'

'Nothing. Just gave me a look as if to say, "Why not? It didn't worry me." '

'So what happened after her husband left? How did she treat Steve then?'

'Well, at least she didn't knock him about, I'll grant her that. Stan was the one who did that. But she still used to pick on him something terrible. Not that we was ever on what you might call visiting terms, after that bust-up over reporting them to the hospital. But living next door you can't help hearing sometimes, can you? I mean, in the summer the windows are open, and sometimes you're in the garden . . . Nothing he ever did was right. It's not surprising he turned out like he did.'

'What do you mean?'

'Well, he got into this way of needling people, if you see what I mean. Like as if he'd said to himself, nothing I can say or do is going to make people like me, so I might as well give them a good reason.'

'He used to behave like that with his brothers?'

'Oh yes. Especially with Chris. Chris was his mum's favourite, see, and it was as plain as the nose on your face that Steve was jealous. Not surprising, really. Used to make me sick to see the difference in the way those kids were treated.'

'What about Frank?'

'He was sort of pig in the middle. He wasn't favoured in the same way as Chris, but he wasn't picked on, like Steve.'

'And Geoff?'

'Who? Oh, that twin of Steve's . . . Haven't set eyes on him for years. Mavis went up in the world like a sky-rocket, by all accounts, and he's much too posh for the likes of the Orchard Estate.' The twisted hands were stil rhythmically stroking the cat and for a few moments there was silence while they all thought over what she had been saying. Then she sighed. 'And now look what's happened. Poor Steve. Went a bit too far, this time, I daresay.'

'So it doesn't surprise you, that it came to this in the end?'

'Not really. Can't help feeling sorry for him, though. He never really had a chance to make the best of himself.'

The cat raised its head sharply, there was a knock at the door, and Mrs Sparrow looked at the clock. 'That'll be Janet, my home help. D'you think you could let her in?'

Lineham stood up. 'Sure.'

The girl who followed Lineham into the sitting room was a surprise to Thanet. She couldn't have been more than eighteen and was wearing jeans and a boxy nineteen-forties-style fur jacket. Her hair was brilliantly streaked in fluorescent colours, orange, green and yellow.

'Hullo Janet, love,' said Mrs Sparrow, her face lighting up with pleasure.

'Got visitors today, have we?' said Janet teasingly.

'We're just going,' said Thanet.

'Would you like a cuppa, before you go?' said Mrs Sparrow. 'Janet's just going to make me one.'

'Sure, no trouble,' said Janet. 'Won't take a tick.'

Thanet declined, politely, and they left.

'Life is full of surprises, isn't it?' said Thanet as they got into the car.

'Janet, you mean? Seemed a nice girl.'

Thanet shook his head in self-disgust. 'You'd think we'd have learned by now that you can't judge by appearances. If I'd seen her in the street . . .'

Lineham grinned. 'Wait till Bridget starts dyeing her hair orange.'

The radio crackled. There was a message for Thanet. Someone had come into the police station asking to see the officer in charge of the murder investigation. He was refusing to talk to anyone else.

'We'll be there in ten minutes,' said Thanet.

FIFTEEN

Back at the station Thanet went straight to the enquiry desk.

'This man who's asking to see me. Do we know what it's all about?'

'Not really, sir. He wouldn't say. Just said he had some information about the murder and asked for the officer in charge. I told him you were out and I wasn't sure when you'd be back, but he said he'd wait. I gave him a cup of tea and put him in interview room four.'

'What's his name?'

'Bennet, sir.' The station officer glanced at the Occurrence book. 'Lives in Pearson Road, number 15.'

'A crank, d'you think?'

'I wouldn't say so, sir. Very sensible sort of chap. Well, you'll see for yourself.'

Mr Bennet was in his early seventies, tall, thin and mournful. Everything about him seemed to droop – hair, moustache, the pouches under his eyes, the corners of his mouth. He was neatly but shabbily dressed in an old fawn raincoat and a brown suit which, judging by the frayed cuffs, had seen better days. The collar of his white shirt was creased and slightly grubby. A widower finding it difficult to cope on his own?

Introductions over, Thanet sat down. 'I understand you have some information for us?'

Bennet nodded. 'I hope I'm not wasting your time . . .'

Thanet gave a reassuring smile. 'I can't tell until I've heard what you've got to say, can I? But in any case, we much prefer members of the public to come to us if anything is bothering them . . .'

'On the television the other night . . . It said you were trying to trace a jacket . . .'

So whatever the information was, it concerned Hines's case,

not his. Thanet was disappointed. He glanced at Lineham who, as he expected, was looking interested. Although the sergeant had been taken off the Coddington murder, he had worked on it long enough to want to know the outcome.

'That's right.'

'It was very unusual, it said. Grey leather, with a red dragon on the back.'

'Yes. You've seen someone wearing it?'

Bennet nodded. 'Boy across the street. Well, a youth, really.'

'He lives across the street from you, you mean?'

'Yes.'

'So you know his name.'

'Kevin Quarry.'

'You noticed him wearing the jacket before the television appeal?'

'Oh no. No. I saw him wearing it this morning, for the first time.'

'I see . . . Well, we're really most grateful to you for coming in . . .'

After getting all the relevant details Thanet thanked Mr Bennet for the information then rang Hines, who listened in silence, grunted and then rang off without a word of thanks.

'What did he say?' said Lineham.

'Not a lot,' said Thanet, non-committally.

'Probably furious that the information came to us, first.'

The telephone rang. It was one of the men who had been checking up on cars seen in the vicinity of Steve's flat, the night of the murder. One of them, apparently, had belonged to Ivor Howells.

'What time was this?'

'Between 8.45 and 9 p.m., sir.'

'Good. Well done,' said Thanet. He put the phone down and told Lineham.

'So,' said the sergeant. 'I bet what happened was that when he got home he managed to get out of Sharon that Steve had been round to see her, and he decided he'd teach Steve a lesson once and for all.'

'Maybe. But the question is, what happened when he got there? Did he manage to see Steve? If Frank's story is true, at half past eight Steve wasn't answering his door, and we have no idea as yet whether he was already dead or had simply slipped out for a while.'

'Perhaps we'll know more after talking to Carpenter, sir.'

'Quite.' Thanet sighed. 'Though I have a sneaky feeling we're not going to come away from the hospital with a nice cut and dried solution. Have they rung yet, by the way?'

'No, sir. Any minute now, I should think. It's twenty past eleven, surely the doctor should have finished his rounds by now.'

Thanet shrugged. 'Anyway, I think Howells has got some explaining to do, in view of the fact that we now have proof that he lied to us. But I think we'll wait to see him again until after we've talked to Carpenter.'

Just before twelve the hospital rang through to say that Carpenter was now fit for a brief interview.

He was in a small side-ward, up and dressed and sitting in an armchair beside the bed. Head bowed, hands clasped loosely in his lap, he seemed to have shrunk since Thanet last saw him. When Thanet entered the room he slowly raised his head and gazed at him without recognition. Thanet experienced a painful shaft of empathy. If it had been Joan who had been killed in that accident, Sprig who had just died after being kept alive for a year or more on life support machines . . . Mentally, he shook himself. He couldn't allow himself to think that way.

'Good morning, Mr Carpenter.'

Formalities over, Thanet and Lineham drew up two of the stools provided for visitors and sat down.

'Now then, Mr Carpenter, I suppose you can guess why we're here.'

Carpenter gazed at him blankly, without response.

'We'd like to talk to you about the night before last. Tuesday night.'

Carpenter frowned, blinked.

'Do you remember anything about that night?'

'No. I . . .' Carpenter's voice trailed away. It was hoarse with disuse, and he cleared his throat, shook his head. 'No,' he said again.

Thanet sighed inwardly. This was going to be difficult. It was his duty to try to activate those memories, but he was well aware that by doing so he would also have to tear down the barrier with which Carpenter had anaesthetised himself against the pain of remembering. Nevertheless, a man had been killed, and the loss of one human life does not justify the unlawful taking of another.

'We found you sitting in your car, just before midnight, in Hamilton Road. You had been drinking heavily.'

Carpenter frowned again, trying to relate this information to himself. 'Hamilton Road . . .' he murmured.

Thanet saw his expression change, his features slacken in shock then begin to harden, settle into grim lines of mingled anger and despair.

'I see you have recalled what Hamilton Road means to you. It was where Steven Long lived.'

Carpenter's lips tightened at the mention of Long's name. For a moment he was silent, then he said slowly, 'Did you say "lived"?'

'Yes. He was killed, in his flat, on Tuesday night.'

For several moments Carpenter stared blankly at Thanet, and then gradually, painfully, his features began to change. A spark of animation appeared first in his eyes and then a slow tide of colour began to creep up his neck and suffuse his face. He licked his lips, as if his mouth had suddenly gone dry.

It was almost like watching a dead man come back to life, thought Thanet.

'So,' Carpenter murmured at last, in a tone of wonder, 'I did it after all.' His voice strengthened, and he made no attempt to hide the triumph in it. 'I actually did it!'

132

'Did what?' Thanet knew what the man was going to say, of course, but he felt none of the usual rush of relief at a confession.

'Killed him, of course.' Carpenter had straightened up and his whole demeanour had changed. He was no longer vanquished but a conqueror.

'Perhaps you'd better tell us about it.'

Something in Thanet's tone must have betrayed his scepticism because Carpenter looked at him sharply and said, 'Well, aren't you going to caution me?'

Thanet doubted if there was any point, at this stage, but he decided to play it by the book. He nodded at Lineham, who duly delivered the familiar words.

Carpenter was watching Thanet's face. 'You don't believe me, do you?'

'I'm not sure what to believe at present, Mr Carpenter. One moment you're saying you don't remember a thing about Tuesday night, the next you're saying you killed a man.'

'I didn't remember at first, no,' said Carpenter. He leant forward in his chair, eager to convince Thanet of the validity of what he was saying. 'But that was because I've been ill. Then, when you mentioned Hamilton Road, I suddenly remembered . . . It all came back to me . . .'

'What, exactly, did you remember?'

'Driving to Hamilton Road. Sitting in the car in front of that Gothic monstrosity where Long lives – *lived* – having a drink to bolster my courage . . . I am not by nature a violent man, Inspector.'

And with any luck, thought Thanet, that nature might have saved you. 'What time was this?'

Carpenter frowned. 'I'm not sure . . . Late afternoon, I think.'

'You can't be a little more precise?'

Carpenter hesitated. 'Somewhere between six and half past?'

Thanet noted the question in his voice. 'But you can't be certain?'

133

Carpenter shook his head.

He was beginning to sweat, Thanet noticed. Was he really fit for questioning, after all? Perhaps it would be best to leave it for the moment, come back later, tomorrow, perhaps. In the circumstances it seemed positively inhuman to press the man like this. But if Carpenter really had killed Long, it was grossly unfair to all the other people involved, to have to go on feeling themselves under suspicion, if by a further few minutes' conversation the truth might emerge.

'Never mind,' said Thanet gently. 'Tell us what you did when you got there.'

'I . . . I sat in the car for a minute or two.' Carpenter took a handkerchief from his pocket and passed it over his forehead, then gave a wry smile. 'I was trying to pluck up the courage to go up and tackle Long, I think.'

'And then?'

'I went up to his flat, knocked at the door.'

'And?'

'He opened it.' Carpenter suddenly began to talk very fast, the sweat beginning to trickle down his forehead and drip into his eyes. He brushed it away impatiently with the back of one hand. 'I was wearing a hat which I'd pulled well down to shadow my face. He'd seen me at the inquest and I didn't want him to recognise me. I thought he might not let me in. I said I'd heard he was a very good mechanic, specialised in solving difficult problems, and I wondered if he'd be prepared to take a look at my car . . .' The words were tumbling out now, becoming almost incoherent, Carpenter's breath coming in irregular, panting gasps.

Thanet rose and pressed the buzzer, and almost at once a nurse came into the room. She took one look at the patient and reached for Carpenter's pulse.

'We'll go,' said Thanet. And he hustled Lineham out of the room.

'Just when we were on the point of getting a full confession!' said Lineham in disgust, when they were in the corridor.

'Yes, well there are certain limits beyond which I'm not prepared to go,' said Thanet.

'Oh I'm not saying we should have gone on, sir. Just that it was so frustrating to have to stop just there.'

'Couldn't be helped.'

Lineham glanced sharply at Thanet. 'You don't believe he did it, do you, sir?'

'I honestly don't know. Do you?'

They walked in silence for a moment, oblivious of the busy life of the hospital teeming around them.

'I'm not sure either,' said Lineham at last. 'He did admit to it, and on the face of it he does seem the obvious choice . . .'

'But?'

'Well, at the end when he was speaking so fast . . . In a way you felt you had to believe him, he was giving us so much detail, but I don't know . . .'

'You didn't feel he was telling the truth?'

Lineham hesitated. 'I think he was telling us what he *believed* to be the truth, and at the time yes, I did believe him, but thinking about it now, I'm not convinced it was what really happened.'

'That's what I thought. I'm not sure if, in fact, what he was doing was describing a scene which he had enacted so often in fantasy that, when he heard Long really had been murdered, it became for him the reality. That's why yes, it was frustrating to have to stop at that point. If he'd been able to go on for just a few more minutes and describe the actual murder, we'd have known if it really was the truth or not.'

'So you still think it could be?'

'Well, as you say, he is the obvious choice, the man with the most powerful motive of all . . . And we have to face the fact that it often is the obvious suspect who turns out to be the murderer.'

Lineham paused in the act of opening the car door. 'Well, I hope that in this case it doesn't.' He got into the car and slammed the door, hard.

Thanet got in beside him. 'Mike, don't tell me that that

135

heart of stone is softening at last, and you're actually sorry for the man?"

'Knock it off, sir. Don't try and tell me you don't feel exactly the same, because I wouldn't believe you.'

'You're quite right, Mike, and I apologise. I do feel exactly the same. Nevertheless, we have to face the fact that he might well turn out to be our man, in the end.'

'I know. In that case the only consolation would be that he wouldn't get much of a sentence, in the circumstances. Might even get a suspended.'

'Possibly.'

'So, what now, sir? Are we going to see Howells?'

'Yes, but I think we'll take a breather first, get a bite to eat.'

'How about the Cow and Mistletoe, sir?'

'Down on the river, isn't it? I've passed it but I've never actually been in.'

'I go there quite a bit. The food's good and it's very quiet at lunchtimes. Gets a bit crowded in the evenings, though.'

Thanet buckled his seat belt. 'Lead me to it,' he said.

SIXTEEN

The Cow and Mistletoe was everything Lineham had promised, quiet and unpretentious. While they waited for the food to arrive, the sergeant went off to check Howells's whereabouts.

'He rang in this morning to say he was sick,' Lineham reported when he came back, 'so he's probably at home. D'you want him brought in for questioning?'

'No, we'll go to the flat. With any luck we might find Sharon there, too. Kill two birds with one stone. This looks good.'

The food had arrived and Thanet tucked in to a generous slice of succulent cold beef and a baked potato, garnished with a salad which was more adventurous than usual, while Lineham enjoyed a home-made leek and potato soup and a ploughman's lunch of hot, crusty French bread and well-matured cheddar. The beer was good, too, and the two men left feeling well-fortified against the cold.

'Shouldn't think the temperature's risen above freezing all day,' said Thanet, turning up his collar and pausing to admire the inn-sign, which depicted a rather endearing cross-eyed cow standing under a huge branch of mistletoe growing from the fork of an apple tree.

'I rather like this weather,' said Lineham, gazing at the river sparkling in the sunlight. 'Just the day for a good, brisk walk along the towpath. That's how I discovered this place.'

'Not much chance of that today, Mike. Come on, let's see if Howells is at home.'

Sharon answered the door.

'Good afternoon, Mrs Long. Is Mr Howells in?'

'Who is it, Shar?' Howells loomed up behind her. 'Oh, it's you again.'

'I'm afraid so. Could we have a word?'

Howells stepped reluctantly back and putting an arm around Sharon's shoulders led the way into a depressing sitting room. All along the outer wall the ceiling was blotched and stained with damp, and in one corner it sagged dangerously. In many places the peeling wallpaper had been torn away, revealing irregular areas of crumbling grey plaster, and the battered furniture looked as though it had passed through countless salerooms.

In all this drabness Sharon looked as out of place as a fairy in a pigsty. She was wearing a spotless long-sleeved white blouse with frills at neck and wrist and a bright red corduroy skirt gathered in to a wide belt which emphasised her tiny waist. Her spun-gold hair seemed to halo her head with light. It was easy to see why Steve had been so reluctant to let her go, why Howells had been determined to hang on to his prize.

He was still standing with his arm possessively around her shoulders.

'What do you want?'

'Perhaps we could sit down . . .'

Howells gave a grudging nod.

'I'm glad to see you're feeling better, Mr Howells,' said Thanet pleasantly, when they were all seated.

Howells frowned. 'Feeling . . .?'

'We understood you'd reported sick, this morning.'

'Ah, yeah . . . I was feeling a bit off, wasn't I, Shar? Had a bit of a temperature, so I thought it would be stupid, like, to go and work outside all day in this cold.'

Thanet's guess was that Howells had simply wished to spend the day with Sharon, fearing, perhaps, that if he left her too long under her mother's influence she might not want to come back to him. Thanet couldn't really see Mrs Pinfold approving of her daughter's latest boyfriend, and who could blame her?

'And I hope you're feeling a little better today too, Mrs Long.'

Once again Thanet noticed her fondness for jewellery. Presents from Steve? he wondered.

138

Sharon bit her lip, nodded. 'It was going to . . . to identify him, that . . .'

'I do understand,' said Thanet, gently. Anticipating that Howells's reaction to being confronted with a lie might be somewhat disruptive to the interview, he had already decided to tackle Sharon first.

'My sergeant has a few points to raise with you. Do you feel up to answering some questions?'

Sharon glanced at Howells, who shrugged. 'Yes,' she said softly. Then, 'Yes,' she repeated, more emphatically. 'Of course. If it'll help.'

Thanet glanced at Lineham. *Take over, then.*

'The first question we have to ask you, of course, Mrs Long, is whether your husband had any enemies.'

'Enemies.' She gave an uncomfortable little laugh and her eyes flickered in Howells's direction. *His biggest enemy is sitting right beside me.* 'No,' she said. 'Not what you'd call enemies.'

'What do you mean, exactly?' said Lineham.

'Well . . . Steve wasn't very easy to get along with. He . . . he tended to put people's backs up. But not to that extent. Not so they'd want to *kill* him.'

'There was that bloke who . . .' Howells snapped his fingers. 'Hey, that could be it!' he said excitedly. 'You know, Shar, the bloke whose wife was killed in that accident.'

'Mr Carpenter, you mean?'

'That's it, Carpenter. I heard on the radio his daughter died, on Tuesday . . . And on Tuesday night Steve was killed . . . Yeah, that's *it*, it must be.' He turned back to Thanet. 'There's your answer.'

He leaned back in his chair with the air of a man who has satisfactorily disposed of a knotty problem and gave Thanet a smug grin. *It's easy when you know how.*

'One of many possible answers, Mr Howells.'

'Oh come on, Inspector.' Howells leaned forward in his eagerness to make his point. 'It's obvious, isn't it? I remember now, Carpenter actually threatened to kill Steve, didn't he,

Shar, after the court case when Steve got off with a suspended sentence . . .'

'We are aware of all this, Mr Howells,' said Thanet. 'And believe me, we're bearing it in mind. But we can't afford to neglect other possibilities.' He ignored Howells's derisive snort and turned to Sharon, his voice softening. 'So you can't make any other suggestions as to who might have wanted to kill your husband?'

She shook her head. 'Not want to *kill* him,' she repeated.

Thanet nodded and sat back.

Lineham took over again. 'Right. Well, the next thing we want to ask you is whether or not you know if your husband came by car, when he visited you after work on Tuesday.'

'Well, I didn't actually see the car, of course, but I should think so, because he was here by about twenty to six and he'd have been much later if he'd had to walk or catch a bus.'

'But you've no idea if it was his own or if he got a lift.'

'No. But it would be unusual for him to beg a lift. If there was anything wrong with his car, he could usually put it right pretty quick. And it's only a few months since he was allowed to start driving again, after that disqualification. He loves . . . used to love driving. He'd never let anyone else drive him if there was any chance of doing it himself.'

'But you don't actually *know* how he got here on Tuesday?'

She shook her head.

Lineham reached into his pocket. 'Perhaps you could now take a look at this photograph.'

He handed it over and she took it by the corner, gingerly, looking apprehensive.

'Oh, you needn't worry,' said Lineham. 'It's nothing distressing. Just a picture of the top of the sideboard, in your husband's flat.' He leaned forward, pointed. 'What we're interested in is this clean, circular patch in the dust. Could you tell us what usually stood there?'

'That's easy enough. A big round ashtray Geoff gave Steve. He brought it back from a holiday in . . . Italy, I think it was.'

'What was it made of?'

'A pinkish marble.'

'Heavy?'

'Oh yes, ver– ' She broke off abruptly and her eyes dilated. 'Are you saying . . . D'you mean . . .' She gave the photograph a dazed look, her face crumpled and she began to cry, turning her head into Howells's chest.

He folded his arms around her protectively and murmured into her ear, glowering at Lineham across the candyfloss curls. *Now look what you've done.*

Lineham raised his eyebrows at Thanet and gave a helpless shrug.

Thanet shook his head. *Not your fault. The question had to be asked.*

'I didn't mean to distress you, Mrs Long,' said Lineham.

'Rubbish,' snarled Howells. 'You couldn't care less, as long as you get what you want.'

'We have a job to do, Mr Howells,' said Thanet. 'And, believe it or not, we don't like upsetting innocent people unnecessarily.'

'Then you shouldn't choose the bloody job in the first place!'

'Someone has to do it. Just as someone has to repair the roads . . . Anyway, we're getting off the point. The point is, that we have only one or two more questions to ask Mrs Long, then she could go and lie down, if she wishes. Perhaps you could make her a cup of tea . . .'

Howells was not deceived, and Thanet had not expected him to be. The message was clear. *We want you out of the room for a few minutes.* He hesitated then eased away from Sharon, put his forefinger under her chin and tilted up her head so that he could see her face. Taking out a grubby handkerchief he gently wiped the tears from beneath her eyes. 'Would you prefer me to stay, Shar? I will if you want me to.' He pressed the handkerchief into her hand.

She blew her nose, sniffed, shook her head. 'I'm OK.'

'You'd like a cuppa?'

She essayed a smile. 'Yeah, I would. Ta.'

He went out, leaving the door ajar, and without a word Lineham got up and closed it.

Thanet leaned forward, lowering his voice. 'Now then, Mrs Long, I'll make this as quick as possible. First, can you remember exactly what time Mr Howells got back here on Tuesday night, after helping his friend to move the furniture?'

She hesitated and a faint colour crept into her pale cheeks. 'About half past eight, I think.'

She was a bad liar, thought Thanet. No doubt Howells had put her up to this.

'But I couldn't be sure,' she added quickly. 'I was washing my hair, you see . . .'

Thanet nodded. He had no intention of putting any pressure on her at this stage. She was in too fragile a state. Later on, if the point became crucial, yes. 'There's just one other matter, then. When your husband came here on Tuesday, did he by any chance bring you a present?'

She stared at him. 'How did you . . .?'

'A rather expensive present, perhaps?'

She bit her lip, glanced uneasily towards the door and nodded. 'A gold bracelet. Steve was ever so upset, because I didn't want to take it, in fact I refused. I knew Ivor would be mad, if I accepted it . . .'

'So what happened to it?'

'Steve wouldn't take it back. Said he'd bought it for me and I was going to keep it. He tried to persuade me to put it on, but when I wouldn't he just put it down on the table and left it there, when he went.'

'So where is it?'

'I'll get it.' She hurried from the room.

It was a heavy gold link bracelet, with a tiny gold padlock and safety chain.

'What shall I do with it?' she said despairingly. 'I don't want to keep it, it would always remind me of what happened to Steve that night.'

'May I make a suggestion?'

She nodded, eagerly, and he explained the trick that Steve

had pulled on Frank over the television set. She was clearly upset at the news that Frank had lost his job as a result.

'It was his wife's idea that your husband might have done it in order to have some spare cash with which to buy you a present. What I would suggest is that you give the bracelet to Frank, so that he can sell it and give the money back to the man your husband defrauded.'

'I will.' She shook her head in despair. 'Oh Steve . . .'

'Shar?' called Howells.

Quickly she snatched up the bracelet.

Howells came in. 'I've put your tea on the table by the bed.'

'I'll go and fetch it,' she said, rising. 'I'm all right, now.'

'I think it would be best if you did lie down for a while, Mrs Long. I want to talk to Mr Howells for a few minutes.'

She hesitated, nodded. 'All right.' She left, the clenched fist holding the bracelet concealed in the folds of her skirt.

'My turn for a grilling, eh, Inspector?' said Howells, sitting down and folding his arms belligerently across his chest. Now that Sharon had left the room he was allowing his animosity free rein.

'Your word, not mine,' said Thanet. 'But the matter is fairly simple. We just want to know why you lied about your movements on Tuesday night.'

Howells tensed, and Thanet was reminded of his first impression of the man. He looked feral, dangerous.

'What do you mean?'

'Well, according to what you told us yesterday, on Tuesday evening you went straight from work to help a friend who was moving house. You then came directly home, arriving here at about eight thirty. You had supper and then you and Mrs Long went out for a drink with some friends, returning here at around eleven fifteen.'

'So?'

'If all this is true, perhaps you would explain how your car came to be parked in Hamilton Road – *Hamilton Road*, Mr Howells, where Steven Long lived – between eight forty-five and nine o'clock that evening?'

143

Howells's eyes glittered like cut jet. 'You have to be joking.'

'Far from it, Mr Howells. On the contrary, I'm very serious.'

Howells lifted his hands in apparent incomprehension. 'It's obvious. Someone has made a mistake.'

Thanet shook his head. 'No mistake.'

'But it must be. Or they're lying.'

'To what purpose?'

'Well, to land me in it, obviously.'

'And who do you suggest "they" are?'

'Search me.'

'So you absolutely deny being anywhere near Hamilton Road on Tuesday night.'

Howells folded his arms. 'Absolutely.'

As they walked down the interminable flights of stairs Lineham said, 'You're not going to let him get away with it?'

Thanet shrugged. 'Depends on whether we eventually decide it's important or not. I certainly don't intend pulling him in at this stage. We'll leave him to stew for a while.'

'I must say I wouldn't like to have him for my enemy on a dark night.'

'Dangerous, I agree.'

'But did he do it? That's the question.'

'Patience, Mike. One thing's certain, if he did, we'll get him, in the end.' Thanet wished that he felt as positive as he sounded.

In the car a message came over the radio: Chief Inspector Hines was at the station, waiting to see Thanet.

'Did he say why?'

'No, sir. But they've picked up the boy with the jacket. He's in one of our interview rooms.'

'And Mr Hines?'

'In the canteen, with the rest of his team. Said they might as well grab some food while they could.'

'Tell him I'll be with him shortly.'

Thanet glanced at Lineham. 'Hear that? Better put your foot down, Mike. We've a treat in store.'

'That,' said Lineham, 'is a matter of opinion.'

At this hour in the afternoon the canteen was deserted except for Hines and his team, DS Draycott and DCs Roper and Flint. An aura of celebration surrounded them.

'Good grief, sir, he's actually smiling,' whispered Lineham as he and Thanet approached the table.

It was true. With a broad grin on his face Hines looked positively unfamiliar. He was a mountain of a man, tall and grossly overweight, with a thick neck, balding head and small, piggy eyes sunk in folds of flesh.

'Ah, Thanet,' he said. 'Our TV appeal paid off, then.'

'He's confessed?'

'Not yet,' said Hines. He glanced around at his men and winked. 'But he will. Any minute now. We're just leaving him to sweat it out for a while.'

'Good . . . You wanted to see me, sir?'

'Just wondered how your own case is going.'

'Slowly.'

'Ah.' Hines leaned back, tucking his thumbs into the armholes of his waistcoat, which strained across his huge belly in a series of horizontal creases. 'You know your trouble, don't you, Thanet?' He glanced around at his men, to make sure he had their attention. 'You're too soft.'

He curled his meaty hand into a fist and thumped the table. 'Punch, that's what you need, punch – metaphorically speaking, of course.' He waited for the dutiful little ripple of laughter from his team. 'Go in there and let them have it, I say. It's the only way.'

That is a matter of opinion, you great fat insensitive oaf. But Thanet had no intention of allowing himself to be drawn into an undignified argument in front of junior officers. 'We can't all work in the same way.'

Hines sat forward. 'Tell you what, Thanet, chummy's just

about ready to cough now, by my reckoning. Why don't you come down and see how it's done, eh?'

Thanet sensed rather than saw Lineham tense beside him and flashed him a warning glance. He knew that Hines was deliberately trying to needle him and had no intention of giving him the satisfaction of seeing that he had succeeded. It was obvious that the chief inspector was still smarting from having to return Lineham before he was ready to do so.

'I've got rather a lot on my plate at the moment, sir. Some other time, perhaps.'

He turned away and was startled when Hines, moving surprisingly fast for such a heavy man, was at his side in a flash, grasping him by the arm and hustling him towards the door. 'Oh come on, Thanet. This shouldn't take too long.'

Unthinkable that he should allow himself to become involved in a brawl with a superior. Short of tearing his arm out of Hines's pincer-like grip or shoving him away with his left hand, Thanet had no option but to comply. He clamped down on the anger surging through him, took a deep breath and glanced over his shoulder at Lineham. 'Mr Hines seems rather keen to have my company, Sergeant,' he said with an attempt at lightness. 'Looks as though you'll have to carry on without me for a while.'

'Right, sir,' said Lineham in a strangled voice, his face wooden. The two DCs studiously avoided looking at Thanet, embarrassed no doubt by their chief's boorish behaviour, but Hines's sergeant was watching with something approaching satisfaction. Perhaps he was enjoying the spectacle of someone other than himself suffering humiliation at the hands of his superior.

Hines snapped, 'You too, Draycott.'

Half-way down the stairs, satisfied that Thanet had resigned himself to accompanying him, Hines released Thanet's arm. 'This character fits to a tee the description of the chap seen in the pub on Sunday with Marge Jackson – medium height, slight build, brown hair . . .'

A description which could fit a large proportion of the adult male population of the British Isles, thought Thanet.

'But he's denying the whole thing, of course. Claims he found the jacket in a rubbish skip, yesterday. Some story, eh? Who'd chuck an expensive jacket like that away?'

A murderer trying to get rid of a piece of highly incriminating evidence? thought Thanet. Was Hines really so stupid as not to have thought of this, or had he simply fallen into the all-too-common trap of refusing to consider any explanation which did not fit in with his current theory?

'What's his name?'

'Quarry.' Hines gave a great bark of laughter. 'Rather appropriate in the circumstances, don't you think?'

'How old?'

'Nineteen. Here we are.' Hines flung open the door of the interview room so hard that it crashed against the wall behind and rebounded.

The boy slumped at the table leapt up as if at a signal. 'I didn't do it!' he shouted. 'I don't know nothing about it!'

He had a bad case of acne, Thanet noticed.

'Oh dear, oh dear, oh dear,' said Hines, advancing towards the table. 'We are getting upset, aren't we? Now I wonder why that is. Could it be guilt, I ask myself?' He thrust his face to within inches of the boy's and bellowed, 'Could it?'

'No! No! I told you, I don't know nothing about it!'

'Sit down,' snarled Hines. And when the boy didn't respond, 'Sit!' as if he were talking to a disobedient dog. Putting his hand on the boy's shoulder he shoved him down into a sitting position with such force that the chair almost overturned.

'Now listen to me, *Mr* Quarry, let's get one thing clear. You're not leaving this police station until we've got the truth out of you. If it takes all day and all night, we'll do it, d'you hear me?'

'But . . .'

'Do you?' bawled Hines.

'Yes, but . . .'

147

Hines turned on his heel and stalked out, nodding to Draycott. *Take over.*

It was obvious to Thanet that they were playing the bad-cop-good-cop routine. Theoretically Quarry, having been frightened out of his wits by Hines, would now respond all the more quickly to an apparently sympathetic Draycott. This had never been Thanet's favourite *modus operandi* and it had little appeal for him even though he knew that it was often highly effective. He followed Hines out of the room.

'He'll crack soon now,' said Hines, nodding with satisfaction. 'Getting really twitchy, isn't he?'

But for the wrong reason? wondered Thanet. Was it anger, not panic, which had caused Quarry's outburst? If so, the boy might well be innocent and Hines doomed to disappointment. Thanet felt no shame at the glow of satisfaction which this prospect afforded him.

'What, exactly, did he say about the jacket?'

'Like I said, he claims to have found it in a skip in Masters Road yesterday morning, along with a number of other saleable items.'

'What, for example?'

Hines shrugged. 'Kid's tricycle, some seat cushions, some old saucepans, a shoebox of cutlery, an old gas cooker, and an assortment of old clothes – a couple of suits, half a dozen dresses, an anorak, a few jumpers . . . I've got the complete list somewhere. Someone was moving, I reckon, and had been having a good clear out.'

'He's still got all these items at home?'

Hines gave a sarcastic smile. 'Of course, Thanet. All lined up for my inspection, just to back up his story.'

'What does he claim he did with them, then?'

'Borrowed a van, took them round to a pal of his who runs a junk stall and travels all over the south-east. Different market each day, you know the sort of thing. Quarry claims it's a regular arrangement and they split the proceeds.'

'And what does the pal say?'

'Sold the lot, of course, what did you expect him to say?

Always back each other up, don't they, these scavengers . . .'

'But Quarry kept the jacket because, presumably, he fancied it?'

'That's the story.'

'So, assuming that forensic come up with evidence which proves the jacket to be the one worn by the murderer of Marjorie Jackson . . .'

'They'd better!' said Hines. 'Because, get this, Quarry says he didn't wear the jacket until this morning because he wanted to clean it up.'

'Ah. So you could have a problem there. But assuming they do manage to link it with the murder, you have two possibilities. One, that Quarry has owned the jacket all along, and is telling a pack of lies, or two, the real owner saw the television appeal on Tuesday evening, decided it would be wise to get rid of it, and dumped it in the skip later on that same day, or during the night.'

Hines gave Thanet a basilisk stare. 'The trouble with you, Thanet, is you've got such a convoluted mind you can't see the truth when it's staring you in the face.' And swinging around he barged back into the interview room again, slamming the door in Thanet's face.

Thanet stood staring after him for a moment or two. How, he wondered, did anyone like Hines ever manage to reach his present rank? It was enough to destroy one's belief in the efficacy of the promotion system. Fortunately, Hines was the exception rather than the rule. The answer, he supposed, was that no filtering system is completely foolproof.

Lineham looked up and grinned as Thanet entered the office. 'Have a good time, sir?'

Thanet gave a non-committal grunt, determined not to encourage Lineham in criticism of Hines, who was, after all, their superior officer. 'Enlightening, perhaps . . . Anything come in?'

'Nothing much. We've had several phone calls from people who saw the lad wearing that jacket this morning. What's his story?'

Thanet told him.

'Makes sense to me,' said Lineham. 'It's a very striking design, that, with the red dragon on the grey background. Surely, if he'd owned it for some time, someone would have seen him wearing it before today.'

'Unless he'd just bought it, say on Saturday, the day before Mrs Jackson was killed.'

'Then surely someone in the shop which sold it to him would have recognised it and come forward.'

'You're assuming it was a local shop, Mike, and it might not have been. The TV appeal didn't go out nationwide, only on TVS.'

'Anyway, there'd still have been several days since for him to have been seen wearing it – it's two days, now, since the appeal went out. He obviously didn't see that himself, or he wouldn't have dared wear the jacket today. And it's interesting that it's only this morning, when he claims to have worn it for the first time, that Mr Bennet spotted him wearing it. Sounds to me as though his story could be true.'

'I'm afraid Mr Hines wouldn't agree with you. Anyway, Mike, intriguing though the problem might be, I think we're letting ourselves get too bogged down in all this. It's not our case, after all . . . What else has come in today?'

Lineham riffled through the pile of reports on his desk. 'Let me see . . . It's mostly negative stuff, I'm afraid. We can't find anyone willing to swear either that they did or did not see lights in Steve's flat during the early part of the evening of the murder. So we don't know yet if Steve left these on while he went to see Chris May and still wasn't back by the time Frank arrived at half past eight, or if he switched them off while he was out and put them on again when he got back, which would have meant that he was in when Frank arrived. Though even if he was, he could still have been dead by then, of course.'

'Hmm. Have they finished checking over Steve's car yet?'

'Yes. And I asked. There was nothing mechanically wrong with it. So there wouldn't seem to be any reason why he couldn't have used it to go and see Chris.'

'But if he did, why didn't he park it outside the house?'

'Quite. Anyway, Frank was pretty positive that it was in the car park at the back of the house in Hamilton Road, at eight thirty.'

'So we have to assume either that Steve got a lift to Chris May's house, which seems unlikely, or that for some reason of his own he parked around the corner, which seems improbable.' Thanet sighed. 'Ah well, perhaps we'll see daylight in time.' He took out his pipe, peered into it, blew through it and began to fill it with tobacco. 'Anything else?'

'The chap Steve cheated over the TV seems to be in the clear. He and his wife spent the evening in Tunbridge Wells, and they were over there by six thirty. It was his son-in-law's birthday and they all went out for a meal – confirmed by the restaurant owner. Oh, and you'll be pleased to hear there's no whisper of a pregnant woman being seen in the vicinity of Hamilton Road that evening, so Frank's wife seems to be out of the running.'

'Good.'

'Apart from that it's just a lot of vague stuff about cars, nothing of any use.'

Thanet glanced at his watch. 'Then we might as well go and see Chris May again. He should be getting home from school soon.'

'If what Mrs Sparrow said is true, then he'd have had plenty of time to stop off at Steve's flat, either on the way to his mother's house or on the way back.'

'I know. And he certainly gave us the impression that he spent some time with his mother, wouldn't you agree?'

'Definitely.'

Dusk was falling by the time they drew up in front of the Mays' house in Merridew Road and lights had been switched on in many of the houses, but number 26 was in darkness, the garage doors closed.

'No one home yet, by the look of it,' said Lineham. 'Shall I go and knock?'

151

'Might as well.'

But as they had expected, there was no reply.

'I suppose we should have made sure he was going to be here,' said Thanet. 'For all we know he could have stayed at school for some extra-mural activity, or even gone out for the evening. We'll give him half an hour or so, then go.'

But ten minutes later a red Metro came up behind them and turned into the Mays' drive. The Mays got out, and Clare May walked around to stand beside her husband as the two policemen approached. The top of her head barely reached his shoulder. She was wearing a red knitted scarf and bobble hat and with her hair in a long plait she looked more like a schoolgirl than a married woman.

'Sorry to trouble you again, Mr May, but could we have another word?'

'Yes, of course.'

He turned and led the way in, switching lights on as he went.

In the hall, his wife unwound her scarf and pulled off the hat. 'Did you want to talk to me, Inspector?'

'No.'

'It's just that there's always such a lot to do, when I get home from work.'

'Do, please, carry on.'

She gave him a quick, nervous smile, shrugged out of her coat and hung it in the cupboard under the stairs. Then she disappeared into the kitchen, closing the door behind her.

May, meanwhile, had shed coat and briefcase and gone ahead of them into the sitting room. Thanet gave the mural a lingering glance before following. May was drawing the handsome cream linen curtains.

'Please, sit down,' he said, taking up a stance in front of the empty fireplace.

Thanet shook his head. He had no desire to have May towering over him while they talked. 'Why did you give us the impression that you spent some time with your mother on Tuesday night, Mr May?'

'Oh, did I? I'm sorry, I didn't mean to mislead you . . . What I actually said, if you remember, was that I went to see my mother.'

'But you did not, in fact, see her.'

'No.' May stepped sideways and sank into an armchair, hands loosely clasped across his stomach, the epitome of a reasonable man whose behaviour has been misinterpreted. 'I knocked at her door, but couldn't get an answer.'

'And that was at what time?'

'Around nine, I should think. It usually takes about half an hour.'

'To get to your mother's house, from here?'

'Yes . . .' May glanced from Thanet's face to Lineham's, then back again, giving a little laugh of comprehension. 'I walked, Inspector. And that's how long it takes. About half an hour.'

'You didn't tell us this last night. We assumed you'd gone by car.'

May gave an eloquent shrug. *I'm not responsible for your assumptions.*

'Your wife can confirm this?'

'Certainly.' May waved his hand in the direction of the kitchen. 'Ask her, by all means. And I can give you the names of one or two people I met between Merridew Road and the main road.'

'You went and returned by the same route?'

'No. I prefer never to do that. I don't like covering the same ground twice.'

'Perhaps, then, you could tell us briefly the route you took, both ways.'

May reeled off a list of street names.

Thanet listened carefully and when May had finished said, 'Your route back would take you to within a few minutes' walk of Steve's flat.'

'True. And to be frank with you, Inspector, that is why I didn't tell you last night that I had walked, not gone by car, and why, admittedly, I deliberately misled you into thinking

I'd spent some time with my mother. It was stupid of me, I can see that now. It's just that I thought it would ... stir things up, unnecessarily. I had nothing whatsoever to do with Steve's death and I didn't want to get involved, if I could possibly avoid it.'

'But you already were involved, to a degree.'

'What do you mean?'

The relaxed pose had gradually disappeared and by now May was sitting upright, bony knees clamped together, fingers hooked over the arms of the chair.

As May's attitude had slid to one end of the scale, Thanet's had tipped over towards the other. Now he sat down on the settee and relaxed into it.

'Well, the night Steve was killed, you saw him.'

'Not by choice,' said May, tightly.

'Maybe. But you saw him, nevertheless. What is more, it might interest you to know that you are, so far as we know, the last person in the family to see him alive.'

May ran his tongue around his lips, a darting little snake that would no doubt have liked to shoot venom into Thanet if it could. But he was managing to keep his wits about him.

'In the family, you say ... So someone else saw him after me?'

'Your neighbours saw him leave.'

May relaxed a little, closing his eyes in relief.

'Not that that really makes much difference, of course,' said Thanet. 'The fact remains that on the night he was killed you had every reason to be furiously angry with Steve – when you refused to let him in he made yet another embarrassing scene, causing you further humiliation in front of your neighbours ... It wouldn't surprise me at all if you decided to follow him home, have it out with him on his own ground, away from here, where there would be no possibility of still more embarrassment.'

'No! My wife will tell you. I didn't. We ... I stayed here, and we had supper together.'

154

'And after supper you walked over to the Orchard Estate, to see your mother.'

'That's right.'

May was sweating now, and Thanet was becoming more and more convinced that the man was hiding something.

'You were still feeling pretty upset, I imagine.'

May made a pretence at nonchalance. 'A bit, I suppose.'

'You thought the fresh air might clear your head, calm you down, I daresay?'

'Yes, I did.'

'And you had absolutely no intention of going to see Steve.'

'None.' May was beginning to relax.

It was the right moment to attack. 'So what made you change your mind?' said Thanet softly.

May stared at him blankly for a moment before fear began to tighten the flesh over the prominent cheekbones, curl the long, bony fingers.

Thanet could almost hear him thinking. *How much does he know?*

'I – I don't know what you mean,' he said at last, hoarsely. He cleared his throat.

'Look, Mr May. You tell us that after leaving here at eight thirty, you walked to the Orchard Estate, which takes about half an hour. We have, in fact, an independent witness who confirms that you arrived there just before nine, and that after finding your mother apparently out, you left. But you didn't arrive home until a quarter to ten. Perhaps you wouldn't mind explaining why a walk which took you half an hour one way, took you three-quarters of an hour the other.'

'I explained to you. I came back by a different route. It takes longer.'

'I'm a native of Sturrenden, Mr May, and I really cannot believe that it would have taken you a whole fifteen minutes more to walk home by the route you gave us. But no matter. We can easily check. We'll get someone to walk it, in the morning.'

May stared at Thanet, his gaze fixed and unseeing. Clearly,

he was thinking furiously, trying to reach some kind of a decision. Then he lifted his hands in a little gesture of surrender and said wearily, 'Oh, what's the point? I can see you'll only go on and on till you find out, in the end . . . Yes, I did go to Steve's flat, on the way back. As you say, I decided it couldn't go on . . . All those hideous scenes . . . I decided to have it out with him, once and for all . . . But when I got there, he was out.' May leaned forward in his chair, desperate, now, to convince Thanet that he was telling the truth. 'I knocked on the door, but there was no reply . . . I knew the lights were on, I'd noticed as I came up the drive . . . But *there was no reply*, I swear it. If Steve was in there, he wasn't answering the door.'

'What time was this?'

'About twenty, twenty-five past nine. Something like that, it must have been.'

'So what did you do?'

'Knocked again, waited, hung about for a few minutes, in case he'd just slipped out to a neighbour's . . . After a while I decided he must either be out or wasn't going to answer for some reason of his own. But since . . . Well, I've been wondering . . . Do you think he was already dead?'

Thanet did not answer the question. 'Did you see anyone, while you were there?'

May shook his head. 'No. And I swear, that really is the truth.'

'You've already lied to us not once, but twice. Give me one good reason why I should believe you this time?'

Outside, Lineham said, 'Do you think he was telling the truth, sir?'

Thanet shrugged. 'Your guess is as good as mine.'

EIGHTEEN

It was after midnight when Thanet got home. As he turned into the driveway he could see that the sitting room was in darkness. Not surprisingly, Joan must have gone to bed. This would be the third night running that he had returned to the sleeping silence of his home, and he experienced an uprush of resentment against the work which was keeping him from his wife and children.

After leaving Chris May, he and Lineham had gone back to the office and spent the rest of the day catching up on paperwork and, when that was finished, going right through the entire accumulation of reports on the Steven Long case. This was an exercise which, though tedious, frequently proved invaluable. It was so easy to get so bogged down in detail that you lost an overall view of the case, ignored crucial areas of investigation and, occasionally, became so obsessed by one particular aspect of a case that objectivity was lost. But today the task had proved relatively fruitless. Apart from giving Thanet a clearer picture of the overall shape of Steve's life, they had found no glaring omissions, no unexpected revelations, no coalescing of hitherto apparently unrelated facts to produce a new vision of the truth.

So Thanet was feeling tired, tired and dispirited, and what he needed above all was the company of his wife.

He had thought he was past hunger and thirst, but as usual the light and the electric fire had been left on in the kitchen and there was a note propped against a thermos flask on the table:

> Darling,
> Tea in flask, lager in fridge, lasagne in
> oven. If u can't face latter, please remove
> plate and turn off oven.
> XXXXXXXX
> J.

He stared at the note for a moment, his mind almost incapable of choice. Tea in flask, lager in fridge . . . No, not lager. What he needed was something hot. Tea, then. He unscrewed the flask, poured himself a cup and sipped. The hot liquid slipped down to his empty stomach and gave him a comforting glow. He began to feel that perhaps he could eat something after all. *Lasagne in oven.* Lasagne. He hadn't had lasagne for ages and it certainly sounded more interesting than bangers and chips or even roast meat and two veg. He picked up the oven cloth, opened the oven door, removed the plate and uncovered it. A savoury aroma ascended to his nostrils. Ah, yes . . .

He was about half-way through the meal when he heard someone on the stairs. His heart lifted.

'Joan?'

A moment later she came into the kitchen, blinking a little in the bright light and tying the sash of her cornflower-blue dressing gown.

'I hope I didn't wake you.'

She shook her head. 'I'd only just switched out the light, when you got home. I took some work to bed with me, and that's always fatal. My mind starts going round and round . . . After I heard you come in, I lay there for a few minutes telling myself I really ought to go to sleep, I'd be tired in the morning, and then I thought oh, what's the point? I'll go and talk to Luke . . . I wasn't sure if you'd feel like eating that or not.'

'When I got home, I didn't, but when I took it out of the oven . . .'

Joan laughed. 'Sprig'll be pleased.'

'She made it?'

'I had to give her something to do, she was driving me mad . . . She's all tensed up about Saturday and there was absolutely nothing else she could do, as far as the competition was concerned. After she finished her homework she was wandering around like a lost sheep. So I said, why not try something new for a change, something completely fresh?'

'Delicious,' said Thanet, finishing the last forkful.

'Good. I wasn't sure if you'd like it.'

'Why?' he said suspiciously. Then he grinned. 'What was in it? Hemlock?'

Joan smiled back. 'Deadly Nightshade, as a matter of fact . . . Actually, it was a vegetarian dish . . .'

'Veget . . .' Thanet looked at his empty plate in pretended horror.

Joan rested her chin on her folded hands and gave him a cat-like grin. 'It was delicious, wasn't it? I told Sprig I didn't think you'd be too pleased, but she just said you were an old stick-in-the-mud and it would do your taste buds good to be shaken up . . . Oh, by the way, talking of taste buds . . . I have a bit of news for you.'

'Oh?' With relief Thanet abandoned his pose of dismay. The lasagne really had been very good, meat or no meat. 'What?'

'You remember you were saying how much more cheerful Doc Mallard has been lately?'

'Yes . . . Don't tell me! You've seen him with a woman!'

Joan nodded, eyes dancing.

'Well?' said Thanet impatiently.

'I had lunch in town today and on the way back to the office I was just passing the Black Swan when the door opened and out he came, with this woman.'

'What was she like?'

'Gorgeous! Oh, not in the glamorous sense, but sweet and gentle, just what he needs.'

'How old?'

'Early fifties, I should say. A little roly-poly type with a lovely smile and the bluest eyes you ever saw. Her name's Helen Fields.'

'He introduced you?'

'Why not? We practically bumped into each other. He was so sweet – went all pink and bashful . . . Anyway, you might meet her yourself soon. He was asking after the children, and I told him about the competition on Saturday. He asked her if she'd like to go along, and she seemed quite keen.'

'Good.' Thanet leaned back, smiling. 'That's terrific. I suspected that might be it . . .' His hand had strayed to his pocket and came out holding his pipe. He looked at it regretfully. 'I don't suppose I've got time for this. We really ought to go to bed.'

'You go ahead and smoke. I feel quite wide awake, I told you. Anyway, it's nice to be able to sit and talk in peace. We hardly ever seem to get the chance these days . . . I think I'll make a fresh pot of tea. Want some?'

Thanet was already filling his pipe. 'Please.'

Joan's company, the food, this late-night intimacy, had generated a warm glow deep within him and he felt that he would be prepared to sit up all night basking in this pleasant, undemanding domesticity. He watched his wife fondly as she moved about the routine task of making a pot of tea, and thought that it was moments such as this that cemented their marriage. The physical side was important, of course, and he knew how fortunate they were that their lovemaking had become more and more satisfying over the years, but it was the pleasure they found in each other's company that was the bedrock of their relationship. He couldn't understand people who were happily married jeopardising something so precious for a few cheap thrills. What fleeting excitement, what temporary massaging of one's ego could possibly replace the knowledge that one is known through and through and loved despite all one's faults and foibles?

As for Joan . . . They'd had their ups and downs, of course, and there had been times when he had felt perilously close to losing her, but he was a lucky man, and he knew it.

She dropped a kiss on the top of his head as she put a fresh cup of tea in front of him. Then she sat down opposite him.

'Luke, I was thinking.'

'Mmm?'

'About this video business, with Ben. All right, maybe he did get involved thoughtlessly, because he didn't realise the seriousness of what he was doing, but the fact remains that we can't possibly keep him under supervision all the time. Even if we managed to arrange something for the interval between school ending and our coming home, there are still weekends . . . Of course, I'd like to think that now we've talked to him we could trust him not to do it again, and leave it at that. In fact, I think we probably could. I honestly don't believe he would get hooked on such stuff. But we have to accept that at that age it's very important to be one of the crowd and the temptation to join in just because everyone else is doing so is very strong.'

'So? What are you suggesting?'

'Well, I know we've always held out against getting a video, for various reasons, but now they've become a fact of life for so many people . . . To be honest, I've been wondering if it wouldn't be sensible to get one of our own.'

Thanet grimaced. 'I feel as though we're almost being blackmailed into this.'

'Oh darling, I don't think that's true. I honestly don't believe Ben is that devious.'

'No, I know . . . But all the same, that's how I feel . . . . But I agree, the one advantage of having one of our own would be that we'd have control over what he watches – but even so, it wouldn't be total control. There'd still be nothing to stop him seeing all sorts of pernicious rubbish in other people's houses.'

'I think we could get around that by laying down conditions from the start.'

'You mean, by saying we'll get one so long as it's on the clear understanding that under no circumstances, unless he has our express permission, would he watch videos hired by anyone else?'

'Something like that, yes. I think it would work. I think he's basically trustworthy, and I think also that he'd be so delighted we've given in, he'd agree to anything.'

'What about when the novelty wears off?'

'I think we'd have to make it clear that if we find he's broken the agreement, the machine would go straight back to the shop. We'd hire it, not buy it, of course, for that reason.'

161

'And what then? What if we get it, he goes back on his word, and we get rid of the thing? We'd be back where we started – worse off, really, because Ben would then feel he's got nothing to lose and the reins would be well and truly off.'

'One step at a time, darling. I think we'd have to deal with that situation if it arose. But I honestly don't think it would. Besides, we have to trust him, and I think he'd appreciate being shown that we do.'

Thanet lifted his hands in surrender. 'All right, we'll give it a try. I agree, it might work.'

Joan smiled. 'I'll tell them tomorrow.' She sat back, satisfied. 'Now, tell me how the case is going.'

She listened intently as he talked, chin on hand, grey eyes solemn. He had always shared his work with her, right from the beginning. He had seen so many policemen's marriages break up because of irregular hours and broken promises that he had been determined to ensure that exclusion from his work did not erect yet one more, unnecessary barrier between them. When Joan had finally taken the decision to train as a probation officer his resolve had faltered, for the probation service and the police frequently find themselves diametrically opposed. But he had decided to continue and Joan, he knew, had appreciated this demonstration of trust. He himself had certainly never had cause to regret it.

Now and again she interrupted to ask for clarification or amplification, and when he had finished she sat back, looking thoughtful.

'Sounds to me as though Steve was hell-bent on disaster.'

'I know.'

'It's as if he were impelled to behave so badly that even the people he was closest to would turn against him – Frank, Chris, even his wife, who according to that funny little woman, Mrs . . .'

'Mrs Bence. Dara.' Just the memory of her was enough to make him smile.

'That's right, Dara.'

'You'd have enjoyed her, love. In fact, you must meet her. I'm sure she'd be pleased. I told her I'd like to go back, some time, and hear all about her days in the circus, and she was tickled pink. You could come with me.'

'I'd love to . . . But, as I was saying, according to her, he even treated his wife so badly that in the end she left him, and it really does sound, from his behaviour since, that he was still very much in love with her . . . It's the classic rejection syndrome, I suppose. He grew up thinking he was unlovable and had to keep on behaving in such a way as to make people reject him, just to see if they would. Then, when they did, he'd say to himself, "There you are, I knew they would, in the end." '

'There speaks the probation officer,' said Thanet with a grin. 'All the same, I agree with you. But I have the impression that since Sharon left, this process was accelerated. His behaviour became more and more outrageous, impossible, almost as though . . .'

'What?'

'I'm not sure. Almost as though he was trying to precipitate some kind of crisis, I suppose.'

'And look where it got him,' said Joan sadly. 'He didn't have much of a life, did he? His mother sounds awful.'

'She is.'

'And I suppose the fact that his twin did so much better than he . . . It does sound so unfair, doesn't it? What's the twin like?'

'All right. Can't say I really took to him. But he seems to be the only person Steve didn't manage to alienate. I suspect that's because Geoff, the twin, felt distinctly guilty that Steve was so much worse off than he, and was prepared to make considerable allowances for him. And I think he appreciated the misery Steve had suffered as a child, at the hands of his mother and step-father. He got quite hot under the collar at one point, when he touched on this, in passing.'

'Were they close, d'you think?'

'I don't think so, no.'

'Strange, isn't it? I thought twins were supposed to have this tremendous empathy.'

'Not necessarily, apparently. Doc Mallard gave me a book about it.' Thanet reached for his briefcase, delved inside.

'*Monozygotic twins, brought up together and brought up apart,*' read Joan. 'Hmm. Sounds fascinating. I'd like to read it, after you, if you don't mind.'

'Sure . . .' said Thanet abstractedly. His eyes were glazed and he was frowning.

Joan, recognising the signs, said nothing, continued to leaf through the book, and for a few minutes there was silence in the room but for the faint hum of the refrigerator and the soft flutter of pages turning.

At last Thanet stirred, as if coming out of a long sleep. 'You know . . .' he said slowly.

Joan laid the book gently on the table. 'What?'

'It's only just occurred to me . . . thinking of Steve and the way he's behaving to the people around him . . . What he's been doing, really, consciously or unconsciously, is systematically destroying what matters most to them.'

Joan stared at Thanet, assessing what he had just said. 'Yes,' she said, finally. 'I see what you mean. The most important thing for Frank was security for his wife and the baby, in other words the job he had taken so long to find. And Steve went out of his way to make sure Frank lost it.'

'Yes. And as far as Chris is concerned, well, I suppose that what really matters to him is reputation, respectability. He's managed to get himself a decent education, escape from his background, and then along comes Steve and proceeds not only to humiliate him at school, in front of his pupils, but at home, in front of neighbours . . . Then, going outside the family, the same principle applies to our other two suspects, Carpenter and Howells.'

'He was obviously determined to take Sharon away from Ivor Howells. But Mr Carpenter is different, surely, in that you couldn't say the car accident was intentional, could you? That isn't what you're suggesting, is it?'

'Oh no. But the end result is the same. Carpenter lost what he obviously valued most in the world, his wife and his daughter.'

Joan shivered. 'It's almost as though he – Steve – had some sort of destructive power, which reached out to the people around him . . . I don't know whether to feel sorry for him or appalled by him.'

'Does one necessarily preclude the other?'

'I suppose not.' Joan glanced at the clock. 'Look at the time! Come on, darling, we'd better go to bed, or neither of us'll be fit for work in the morning.'

Reluctantly, Thanet allowed himself to be persuaded up the stairs. He took Mallard's book with him. After such a long day he should be only too eager to get a decent night's rest, but after the discussion with Joan his mind was fully alert and he knew that there was no point in trying to get to sleep just yet. He would only lie there in the darkness, tossing and turning. He would try to read himself into oblivion.

For an hour or more he attempted to do just that, but he had chosen the wrong bedside reading. The book was, as Joan had predicted, fascinating, and confirmed what Mallard had told him. Steve and Geoff were typical in that the most common reason for the separation of twins was the mother's inadequacy, and it was usually the mother's sister or the grandmother who took one of them, a temporary arrangement often becoming a permanent one. The mother often kept the weaker, lighter-born twin, and the home was often poorer, both economically and psychologically. As a result, this twin would often be more neurotic than the one brought up probably as an only child in better circumstances. The first-born twin tended to be heavier and often one of the twins would be left-handed. Thanet found himself constantly relating what he was reading to Steve and Geoff and eventually he decided that the only way he was going to get to sleep was by switching off the light and hoping that he would eventually wind down.

Joan was fast asleep and for a while he tried to empty his

165

mind completely and match the rhythm of his breathing to hers. But it was no good, he simply couldn't do it. In the end he gave up, eased his aching back into a more comfortable position and allowed his thoughts to roam at random.

With his late-night reading fresh in his mind he continued to think for a while about the twins. It was interesting that Geoff was the one person in the family who didn't seem to have washed his hands of Steve – quite the contrary, in fact. Thanet thought of the two birthday cards on Steve's mantelpiece, one from Sharon and one from Geoff, and wondered if Geoff's tender conscience as far as Steve was concerned might even have prompted him to take his twin a present when he visited him on Sunday evening. Steve had seemed depressed, he said, and this wasn't surprising, Thanet thought, in view of what they now knew. The unpleasant scene at Howells's flat, followed by the disastrous incident at the Mays' house, would be enough to depress anyone, let alone someone in such a vulnerable state as Steve. The former, no doubt, had sparked off the drinking which had led to the latter, a chain reaction which had finally culminated in Chris May refusing even to let Steve into the house, when he later came around to apologise on Tuesday. Over the last few days of his life doors were constantly being slammed in Steve's face, it seemed, and apart from Sharon, who was dominated by Howells, Geoff was the one person who had remained sympathetic to him. Guilt, perhaps, as Thanet had suggested to Joan, at having had by far the best of the bargain? Or perhaps because Geoff had not been as close to Steve as the others, nor had his life been disrupted by him.

Thanet lay for a while thinking of those others. Frank, Chris, and Carpenter all admitted going to Steve's flat the night he was killed. Howells had been there too, Thanet was certain of it, despite his having denied it. And always the same story – lights on, no answer to their knock. If only forensic could have come up with some nice, clear, prints, some shred of useful evidence. If only they could have found that ashtray . . .

166

Thanet turned over, restlessly, and Joan stirred in her sleep, murmuring. He lay quite still until her breathing had resumed its steady rhythm.

Where could that ashtray be? At the bottom of the river, probably, or dumped somewhere, like that jacket young Quarry had picked up. Hines had all the luck. Although Thanet was convinced the youth was innocent of Marjorie Jackson's murder, that jacket would, sooner or later, get Hines his man.

Thanet's eyes snapped open in shock as a truly incredible idea winged its way into his restless mind. What if . . .?

Suddenly, it was impossible to lie still a moment longer. Mind racing, he slid quietly out of bed, reached for his dressing gown and slipped out of the room.

In the kitchen he went to lean against the sink, gazing out of the darkened window. Was it possible?

He sat down and, elbows on table, head in hands, began to think.

NINETEEN

Thanet often found that an idea which in the middle of the night had appeared to be a stroke of genius proved in the cold light of morning to be as full of holes as a colander. Not so this time. The moment he opened his eyes his new-found solution to the Steven Long case blossomed in his consciousness, flawless as a rose in high summer.

He couldn't wait to put it to the test. Despite his relatively sleepless night he felt fresh and alert, buoyed up by elation, and he threw back the bedclothes and hurried to the bathroom.

When he went down to breakfast Joan was alone in the kitchen, drinking coffee. She raised her eyebrows as he came in, whistling. 'You sound cheerful this morning.'

Thanet gave her a beaming smile. 'I think I just might have solved the case.'

'Really?' She leant across, put a congratulatory hand on his arm. 'Darling, that's terrific!'

'Well, don't let's get too excited, just in case I'm wrong. There are various things I'll need to confirm, before I'm sure.'

'So who . . .?'

'Sorry, love. I daren't give hostages to fortune. Ask me again tonight.'

'Daddy! You're up early!' Usually Bridget was down before him in the morning.

He smiled up at her as she came to kiss his cheek. 'Some of us have work to do.'

'You won't have to work tomorrow, Dad, will you?'

He put on a blank expression. 'Tomorrow? What's happening tomorrow?'

'Daddy! It's the comp . . .' She saw his face and stopped. 'Oh, really!'

He got up. 'Don't worry, poppet. Wild horses wouldn't

keep me away from the Black Swan tomorrow morning. Your mother and I will be sitting there beaming rays of encouragement and moral support in your direction. None of the other parents will be able to compete, will they, darling?'

Joan laughed. 'Of course not.'

At the office Lineham was sitting hunched at his desk, staring dejectedly at a single sheet of paper. Thanet's stomach clenched as he realised what must have happened. The sergeant had failed to get through to the Selection Board.

There was no point in avoiding the issue. 'It's come, then.'

Lineham nodded speechlessly.

'And no luck?'

A shake of the head.

Thanet crossed and put his hand on Lineham's shoulder. 'I'm sorry, Mike, I really am. But you mustn't be too disheartened. Only a third of those who passed the exams would have got through, you know that.'

'Some consolation! That still leaves me in the two-thirds who'll never make it. I suppose I was a fool to think I could.'

'Oh, come on, Mike. Cheer up. Maybe next time . . .'

Lineham shook his head. 'Oh no, there won't be a next time, I can assure you of that.'

'Why not? The trouble is, Mike, that this has come at a bad time for you, just after Louise has had the baby and you're both tired and on edge from lack of sleep.' *Not to mention worried sick that your mother is going to come and live practically next door and start causing trouble right, left and centre.* 'Just look at you! Bags under the eyes, pasty as an uncooked doughnut . . . In another month or two you'll feel quite differently about it, you'll see.'

Lineham shook his head again, vehemently. 'No, I've learned my lesson, believe me.'

It was, Thanet knew, the right decision. If Lineham hadn't even managed to get as far as the Selection Board, there was little chance that he would ever get through the even more rigorous Promotion Board. He felt desperately sorry for the sergeant and angry with Louise who was, he was sure, responsible for this fiasco. He wondered how she would react, when she heard.

'Have you told Louise yet?'

A despondent shake of the head. 'No.'

Thanet gestured towards the phone. 'I should get it over with.'

Tactfully, he withdrew while his sergeant made the call.

'Meanwhile,' he said when he went back into the office, deliberately ignoring Lineham's set face, 'I've got to admit that from a purely selfish point of view it's a relief that I'm not going to lose the best sergeant I've ever had. I didn't say this before, Mike, for obvious reasons, but I was really dreading having to get used to working with someone else. At the beginning of this case, when you were over at Coddington, I felt as though I was working with my hands tied behind my back.'

Thanet was not normally given to making sentimental speeches, but it was the best he could do, to restore just a little the sergeant's battered ego. And it had, in fact, helped, by the look of it. Lineham was looking marginally less gloomy.

'And talking of the case . . .' Thanet went on.

'What?' For the first time this morning Lineham looked at him properly, took in Thanet's air of suppressed excitement. 'Don't tell me you've cracked it?'

Thanet held up crossed fingers. 'With any luck.'

Thanet had anticipated a look of eager enquiry, but instead Lineham merely looked depressed again.

'What's the matter, Mike?'

'I suppose that that alone should have told me I was aiming too high.'

'What?'

'The fact that I've never yet got there before you.'

'You almost have, on several occasions.'

'Precisely. Almost, but not quite. The story of my life.'

Thanet could see that if he didn't do something fairly drastic the sergeant would allow himself to sink into a slough of self-pity which would help no one, least of all himself.

170

'Mike,' he said sharply. 'No one could be sorrier than I am that you've had this disappointment, but I would remind you that we have got work to do.'

Briefly, Lineham compressed his lips and looked hurt, then he shook his head as if to clear it of the preoccupations of the last half an hour and muttered, 'Sorry, sir . . . You were saying you think you might have cracked it.'

'I was.'

'Well?'

'Well what?'

'Aren't you going to enlighten me?'

The sergeant was beginning to look more his usual self, Thanet was pleased to see.

'Not yet, I'm afraid. No, don't groan, Mike. You'll hear soon enough. In fact, I can't wait to hear what you think . . .'

'But sir . . .'

Thanet shook his head. 'No, Mike. I want your opinion, but I'm not saying another word until I've confirmed one or two points. So come on, the quicker we get through them the sooner you'll hear what I've come up with.'

Lineham gave a resigned shrug.

'Now, first of all, can you tell me what happened about the lad CI Hines brought in for questioning? Did he get a confession?'

'No. He had to let him go. Wasn't too pleased, I gather.' Lineham grinned at the understatement. 'But the word is he's still swearing he'll get him, sooner or later. He's taken away a whole lot of his clothes, for analysis.'

'And the jacket? Did forensic come up with anything to link it definitely with the murder of Mrs Jackson?'

'I don't know, sir. But what's this got to do with Steven Long?'

Thanet waved a hand. 'Patience, Mike. All in good time. Find out for me, will you?'

While Lineham made the phone call Thanet reread the PM report, nodding with satisfaction. Yes, it was as he thought . . .

Lineham put the phone down. 'Yes, sir. A couple of hairs, caught around the left-hand cuff button, and traces of her face powder in the crease of the cuff opening.'

'Good. Excellent. Right, now I'd like you to go and have a word with Mrs Bence. This is important, which is why I want you to go yourself. If you remember, she saw Steve going out as she came in, around a quarter to seven on the night he was killed. Ask her if Steve was carrying anything.'

'What, for example?'

Thanet shook his head. 'I don't want ideas put into her head. Just say "anything".'

'Right.' Lineham hesitated. 'What are you going to be doing, sir?'

'Don't worry, Mike, I'm not going to get up to anything dramatic, like making an arrest, while you're out of the way. I told you, there are various things I've got to check. With any luck, by the time you get back, I'll be finished. What's more, I wouldn't mind betting that by then you'll have worked it out for yourself.'

'Fat chance of that,' grumbled Lineham, as he left.

As soon as he had gone Thanet consulted his list of queries, then reached for the telephone. First, he rang Sturrenden General Hospital. This piece of information was really crucial to the case he had built up and his stomach churned with anxiety while he was passed from one department to another. At last he found the right person and put his question. Again, there was a long wait, and he found he was gripping the receiver so tightly his fingers were aching. Deliberately, consciously, he relaxed. *Please let them come up with the right answer.*

'Hullo?'

'Yes?' Thanet's voice was hoarse with tension.

'Sorry I took so long. The records took a bit of finding.'

'But you've got them?'

'Yes. Shall I read what they say?'

'Please.'

He listened, holding his breath. Then relief flooded through him. 'Could you repeat that?'

Again, he listened. No, there had been no mistake. 'Thank you,' he said. 'Thank you very much indeed.'

'Not at all,' said the voice, bewildered. 'Only too pleased to help.'

Thanet replaced the receiver and sat staring into space. He would have liked to get up and dance for joy. Instead, he looked up the number of the hairdressing salon where Caroline Gilbert worked, the girl Geoff had taken out on the night of the murder.

'Miss Gilbert?'

'Yes.' The voice was fresh and young.

'We've not actually met, but my name is Thanet, Detective Inspector Thanet of Sturrenden CID. I'm in charge of the enquiry into the death of Mr Steven Long. There are one or two questions I'd like to put to you, if I may.'

'I told the other policeman, there was no way Geoff could have been involved. He . . .'

'No, you misunderstand me. I wanted to ask you about Sunday.'

'Sunday?' Caroline Gilbert sounded bewildered.

'Yes. I understand you went out with Mr Geoffrey Hunt on Sunday evening, as well as on Tuesday?'

'Well . . . Yes, I did. As a matter of fact, Sunday was my first date with him.'

'Would you mind telling me what you did?'

'Well . . . I don't see why not . . . Geoff picked me up at my place. We were going out for a drink. He hadn't told me before, but it was his birthday, and when I got into the car he said he hoped I wouldn't mind if he just dropped a present in at his twin brother's place in Hamilton Road. He had the parcel ready in the car with him, gift-wrapped.'

Thanet's scalp prickled with excitement.

'Did he tell you what the present was?'

'Well, I said it was an exciting-looking parcel, and he said it was a leather jacket he'd bought when he was on holiday in Wales. He'd got it for himself, really, but it was new, he'd only worn it once. His brother happened to see it and really went

173

overboard for it, so Geoff decided to give it to him for his birthday.'

'Did you see his brother open the parcel?'

'No. I didn't go up to the flat with Geoff. He said he wouldn't be long, and he wasn't.'

Thanet put his last question to her and rang off, well satisfied.

When Lineham arrived back, he was out of breath.

'I didn't tell you to *run* all the way there and back, Mike.'

Lineham shook his head and collapsed into his chair, panting. 'It suddenly dawned on me, sir.'

'Told you it would,' said Thanet smugly.

'Oh no, not our case, not who killed Steven Long . . . The other one.'

'Mrs Jackson, you mean.'

Lineham nodded 'That's why you were on about the jacket. It was Steve's jacket, wasn't it? It was Steve who killed her. I've been working it all out, on the way back.'

'I'm ninety-nine per cent certain of it. I gather you hit the jackpot with Mrs Bence. What did she say?'

'Steve was carrying a plastic bag. Blue. It was pretty full, bulging, in fact, so much so that the top edges didn't meet. A pretty sharp old bird, isn't she?'

'What did she see?'

'Enough. She's prepared to swear that the top item in Steve's carrier was made of grey leather.'

Thanet nodded with satisfaction. 'You'll be interested to hear that I rang Miss Gilbert while you were out.' Thanet repeated the gist of the conversation.

'So Hunt bought the jacket in Wales!' said Lineham. 'Of course. The red dragon . . .'

'Precisely.'

'That just about wraps it up then, doesn't it?' said Lineham excitedly. 'It all fits. On Sunday evening, his birthday, Steve goes around to see Sharon, is thrown out by Howells, and told in no uncertain terms never to show his face there again. He feels fed up, and decides to console himself with a few drinks.

He has too many and ends up feeling very sorry for himself, so he decides to go to Chris's house, as it's usually to Chris he turns for sympathy. But the Mays have guests and Steve doesn't exactly endear himself to them by being sick all over their carpet, so Chris throws him out.

'Steve goes home, and hasn't been there long when Geoff arrives, plus present, the nice new grey leather jacket with a red dragon on the back that Steve had fancied so much when he saw Geoff wearing it. Quite likely, Steve asks Geoff if they could go for a jar together, to celebrate their birthday, but Geoff has got himself a new girl and doesn't want Steve along, playing gooseberry, especially as Steve is still sozzled and might not make too good an impression.

'So, when Geoff has gone, Steve is all alone again. He can't stand it. It's his birthday, he should be out there enjoying himself. So he puts on his new jacket and drives out to the Fox and Hounds at Coddington, hoping perhaps to pick someone up. He does. Marge Jackson. He's too drunk to see past the make-up and they go off in the car together.' Lineham paused.

'I don't suppose we'll ever know, now, what went wrong, why he shoved her out of the car, but my guess is that at that point he may have had no idea she was so badly injured and so he would have got the shock of his life when some time on Monday, either on the radio or TV, he hears she's dead and the police are treating the case as murder.

'So on Monday night he stays holed up indoors, frantically trying to work out if there was anything to connect him with Marge's death. He may or may not have wondered if anyone had noticed the jacket, while he was with her. It is pretty striking, after all.

'Anyway, by Tuesday he was beginning to feel a bit safer, so after work he went to see Sharon, taking her a present, the gold bracelet he might well have intended giving her on Sunday, if Howells had been out. But Sharon refused to let him stay more than a few minutes and he went straight home afterwards, arriving in time to see the TVS news on *Coast to Coast*. There, to his horror, he sees an item about the murder of Marge Jackson, describing his jacket and saying the police want to interview its owner. He decides there's only one thing to do, dump it, and that's precisely what he does, in the skip where Quarry found it.'

'And then?'

'He's still feeling a bit shaken, so he decides he'll go and try to make it up with Chris, apologise for Sunday night. But Chris refuses to let him in, so . . .'

'So?'

'So he went home and got himself killed,' finished Lineham lamely. He sighed, shook his head. 'That's where we come unstuck, isn't it?' He thought for a moment and added, a wide grin spreading across his face, 'I'll tell you what though, sir.'

'What?'

'Chief Inspector Hines won't half be mad, that we got there first.'

'True,' said Thanet. The thought afforded him considerable satisfaction.

'He'll say that the moment we realised there was a possible connection between the two cases, we ought to have been in touch with him.'

'But it's all happened so quickly, hasn't it, Mike? All we were doing was going quietly along pursuing our own enquiries when, bingo! Suddenly it dawned on us . . .'

'That we'd solved his case for him!' finished Lineham solemnly.

'Exactly. Now, no one could blame us for that, could they?'

'Certainly not, sir.'

The two men grinned at each other.

'All the same,' said Thanet, 'I'd hate to go to him too soon and have him prove that all this is merely a product of my "convoluted mind", as he put it. There's just one more piece of evidence I'd like to have, first.'

'What's that, sir?'

'We ought to talk to Geoff Hunt again, make sure we haven't jumped to conclusions about the jacket.'

'Mr Hines'll say we ought to inform him now, and let him talk to Mr Hunt.'

Thanet's eyes opened wide in mock innocence. 'But we're merely being conscientious and checking our facts before laying them in front of Chief Inspector Hines. I'm sure he wouldn't want us to present him with a lot of half-baked notions, now would he?'

Lineham grinned. 'Certainly not, sir. We're going now?'

'Shortly. I've made an appointment for eleven thirty. But before we do, there's something you ought to know.'

As he talked, Thanet was gratified to see Lineham's eyes stretch wide, his mouth drop open in astonishment.

TWENTY

Geoffrey Hunt's arrangements for his move were obviously running smoothly. A furniture van painted with the sign R. W. BECKETT, AUCTIONEER AND VALUER stood in the drive, and as Thanet and Lineham parked beside it two men carrying a large wardrobe almost as easily as if it were an empty cardboard box emerged from the open front door. The van was already half-full.

Hunt was in the hall, talking to a third man.

'I'm afraid we haven't come at a very convenient time,' said Thanet.

Hunt waved a hand. 'Not to worry. It's all under control. Everything's labelled. We'll go into the sitting room, we won't be disturbed in there. I'll see you later, then,' he said to the foreman.

The big room looked like a saleroom itself. Furniture and rolls of carpet were piled up all around the edges and apart from a small area in front of the hearth most of the floorspace was taken up with packing cases, cardboard boxes and the thousand and one small objects considered by the civilised world to be an essential part of everyday life. It was obvious that in order to simplify today's operation Hunt had gathered together in here most of the stuff he had decided to keep.

'Sorry about the chaos,' he said, 'but it can't be helped.'

There was only one armchair free of clutter, the one nearest the fireplace, and Hunt quickly disentangled two small upright chairs from the nearest pile and set them down in the little island of clear space. 'The best I can do, I'm afraid,' he said.

'Thank you, sir.'

They all sat down, Hunt perching on the arm of the easy chair. A hint that he couldn't spare much time? wondered

Thanet. Or a desire not to have the two policemen looming over him?

Hunt looked at him expectantly. 'How can I help you?'

He looked tired, Thanet thought. There were hollows in the thin cheeks, as if the flesh had melted away, and his eyes seemed to have sunk back into the dark shadows of the eye-sockets.

'I can see you're very busy, so I'll come straight to the point. When we last saw you, you told us that on Sunday evening you went to see your brother Steven, to wish him a happy birthday. We know that you took him a card, because we saw it on the mantelpiece in the flat, but we understand you also took him a present. Could you describe that present to us, please?'

Silence. Hunt stared at Thanet, the tiny movements in the muscles of his jaw betraying the fact that he was clenching and unclenching his teeth. It was clear that he not only appreciated the significance of the jacket, but that he had not been prepared for this particular line of questioning. He was now torn between veracity, which would brand Steve as a murderer, and denial, which might well lead to even more trouble for himself, if it could be proved that he was lying.

The instinct for self-preservation won.

'It was a jacket,' he said reluctantly, at last.

Thanet, fully aware of the power of silence, said nothing, waited.

Hunt shifted uncomfortably on his perch. 'I bought it when I was on holiday in Wales. I only wore it once, and Steve saw it, took a real fancy to it.' He shrugged. 'So I decided to give it to him for his birthday.'

'He was pleased with it?'

Geoffrey Hunt attempted a smile. 'Delighted.'

'Could you give us a more detailed description, please?'

A small pause. 'It . . .' Hunt cleared his throat. 'Er . . . it was a leather jacket.'

'Colour?' put in Thanet sharply.

Hunt blinked. 'Er . . . grey. Yes, grey.'

'Plain grey?'

'Yes.'

'All over?'

Another silence. Then Hunt jumped up, began blindly to blunder his way through the jumble of furniture and household objects towards the patio doors. Lineham half-rose, but Thanet put out a hand, shook his head.

When he reached the tall expanse of glass Hunt stopped and shoved his hands into his pockets in a gesture of anger and frustration. 'Oh, what's the point of trying to cover up any longer?' he burst out. 'It's obvious, from the questions you're asking, that you know, anyway. And Steve's dead, the truth can't hurt him now.'

Hunt swung around to face Thanet across the cluttered room. 'Yes, it did have the design of a dragon's head, in red, on the back. And the very fact that I am aware of the importance of this information does show that yes, I did see the TV appeal on Tuesday and recognise the description and yes, I did go straight round to warn Steve not to wear the jacket again and that therefore yes, I suppose I am guilty of obstructing the police in the course of their duty, or whatever you call it . . .'

'Thank you,' said Thanet. 'And now, perhaps we could discuss this a little more calmly. Come and sit down.'

Hunt threaded his way back and flopped down into the armchair. 'In a way I'm glad it's out,' he said. 'It's been an awful strain, wondering if you'd find out.'

'Tell us exactly what happened on Tuesday.'

'Yes . . . Well . . .' Hunt passed a hand over his forehead, rubbed his eyes and shook his head, as if to clear it. 'Like I said, I saw the TV appeal. There was no mistaking the jacket, they'd even done a drawing of it and you'd have recognised it anywhere. Anyway, it was the first item on *Coast to Coast*, and I didn't wait to see any more. I went straight round to see Steve.'

'Arriving at his flat at about a quarter past six?'

'Something like that, yes.'

Thanet sensed Lineham shift beside him. The sergeant was

obviously thinking the same thing. Nowhere, in any of the reports, had there been any mention of a Scimitar parked in Hamilton Road. And such a distinctive car would surely not have escaped notice.

'You went by car?'

'Yes, sure,' said Hunt impatiently. 'How else would I have got there so fast?'

'Where did you park?'

'In the driveway of a friend of mine, in Beech Avenue.'

'Why not in Hamilton Road?'

'Various reasons. For one thing it's often impossible to find a parking space, there're so many flats, and for another I don't like leaving the Scimitar there. Some vandal snapped off the aerial when I parked there a few months ago, so ever since I've left it around the corner in Beech Avenue.'

'Your friend's name and address?'

Hunt told him, and Lineham wrote it down.

'Right, so you arrived at Steve's flat at about a quarter past six. He was in?'

'Yes.'

'What was he doing?'

'Watching TV.'

'He'd seen the appeal himself?'

'Oh no. No. I asked him if he had, but he didn't know what I was talking about. He'd only just got in, he said, and he'd missed the beginning of the programme.'

'So what did he say, when you told him about it?'

'At first he pretended he didn't know what I was talking about, but I said, "Oh come off it, Steve. There's no need to put it on with me. If you'd seen the drawing of the jacket – *your* jacket, which *I* gave you – you'd know there's no point in trying to pull the wool over my eyes." '

'What did he say?'

'He got very upset. Said he hadn't known she was dead, not until the next day, the Monday, when he heard it on the radio . . .'

Hunt was very pale now, and starting to sweat.

181

'Did you believe him?'

'Yes.' Hunt's voice had the ring of conviction in it. 'He told me all about it. He said he'd picked this woman up and they'd quarrelled, and he'd . . . he'd made her get out of the car. He said she must have tripped and fallen, banged her head on something. She had very high heels on, he said. It was the only explanation he could think of, for what happened later. After he put her out of the car he didn't look back, and of course it was pitch dark, anyway . . .'

'He didn't tell you he'd almost strangled her, first?'

'No! I don't believe that!'

'Post-mortems do not lie, Mr Hunt.'

'I . . . I didn't know that. But if it's true, then there must have been a very good reason . . .'

'Have you any idea what it was?'

Hunt shook his head.

'So after he'd told you all this, what did you do?'

'I advised him to go to the police, of course. I said they – you'd – only find out in the end. He told me he'd picked her up in a pub, and it had been crowded. He'd been wearing the jacket and it's very striking. It was pretty obvious to me that someone would have been bound to notice it, quite a lot of people, probably. I told him it would be far better to own up himself, first, than wait until he was caught. All he had to do was tell the truth, and he'd come out of it far better in the end.'

'Did he agree?'

'Yes. He said he could see my point. There were a few things he wanted to do first, then he'd go down to the police station and give himself up. I had a date, as you know, but I offered to cancel it, stay with him, but he said no, he'd prefer to do it alone.'

'Then you left?'

Hunt nodded, then buried his head in his hands. 'I should have stayed,' he said. 'If I had, then Steve would still be alive.'

'Isn't he?' said Thanet softly.

Hunt became quite still and for a long moment there was

182

silence. Outside, in the hall, one of the removal men could be heard shouting instructions, his voice unnaturally loud. Then, slowly, Hunt raised his head.

'What do you mean?' he said. 'What are you talking about?'

'I think you know very well what I'm talking about, Mr Long.'

Thanet glanced at Lineham and nodded.

Lineham stood up. 'Steven Long, you are not obliged to say anything unless you wish to do so but what you say may be put into writing and given in evidence.'

The man was chalk-white, but still in control of himself. He attempted a smile. 'I think you're becoming a little confused, Inspector, unless that was a slip of the tongue, just now. I'm Geoffrey Hunt, remember.'

'No slip of the tongue, Mr Long.'

'This is preposterous! And would you mind telling me what I'm supposed to have done?'

'Why, murdered your brother Geoffrey, of course.'

Steven Long stared at Thanet with such intensity that his thoughts were almost audible. *How much does he know? How much of this is guesswork?*

He gave a strange little gurgle of laughter, quickly choked off, as if a tiny bubble of hysteria had escaped against his will. 'You're out of your mind,' he said. 'Crazy.'

'Am I?' Thanet gave him a long, assessing look, then smiled. 'It must have seemed the perfect answer, the perfect way out of all your problems: get rid of the one person who knew you owned the jacket; ensure that if by any chance we, the police, did manage to trace it to Steve, then Steve would be conveniently dead; and, best of all, step into Geoff's shoes, inheriting his money, his new job – which you were sure you'd be able to cope with – his new life, waving goodbye to all your own problems for ever. Truly a stroke of genius.'

'No! No, I . . .'

'All you had to do,' Thanet went on, implacably, 'was kill your twin brother.'

'I'm not listening to any more of this crazy nonsense!' said Long, erupting out of his chair. 'I'm going to . . .'

'What?' interrupted Thanet. 'Ring the police? Complain to my superiors? Is there really any point? You'll only be putting off the evil hour. Because sooner or later you'd still have to face it all, wouldn't you?' Thanet paused. 'Aren't you in the least interested to hear what went wrong with your beautiful plan, Mr Long?' He folded his arms and sat back in his chair. *If you're prepared to listen, then I'm prepared to tell you.* Long, he was sure, would find the lure irresistible.

He was right. Long hesitated for a moment and then gave an exaggeratedly nonchalant shrug. 'My beautiful plan, as you call it, Inspector, does not exist. But I am interested in the twisted "logic" which has led you to make such wild accusations.' He sat down, crossing his legs and folding his arms in deliberate imitation of Thanet. 'So go ahead. Let's hear this *beautiful* theory of yours.'

Thanet noted the echoed mockery and reminded himself to be careful. Whatever else he was, Steven Long was no fool. At the same time Thanet was, he realised, enjoying himself. He relished a worthy adversary and besides, this was in many ways a unique encounter. In his work Thanet frequently found that during the course of an investigation he came to know the murder victim very well. Never before, however, had he actually met him, in the flesh.

'Well, you'll realise, of course, that we've spent a considerable amount of time talking to the other members of your family, and gradually a picture of you began to emerge. We learned, amongst other things, that you were very good at impersonating Geoff, "taking him off", as Debbie put it. We also learned that as a child you were naturally left-handed – and I had noticed, when we first interviewed you, that it was with your left hand that you grabbed for something you knocked off the table by the door there. We learnt that your case was typical in that when twins are separated, it is usually the mother who keeps the weaker, lighter-born twin, and that that difference in weight usually persists into adulthood – and I had noticed, when I first met you, that your clothes were rather loose. At the time I assumed that you had recently lost weight, perhaps through grief over the death of your adoptive mother, but later I began to wonder . . .'

Steve waved a dismissive hand. 'There's nothing in all this. It's all guesswork. Admit it, Inspector, you're just clutching at straws.'

'I haven't finished yet. Far from it. Now we come to the discrepancies . . .'

He paused, but Steve said nothing.

'There were several of these. One was to do with "Geoff's" attitude to your separation from your wife. He was the only person in the family who told us that Steve hadn't really been too upset by that separation, and had no interest in getting her

185

back. Everyone else told us a very different story. Steve, they said, had been pretty shattered by Sharon's departure and was still making a determined effort to get her back – to the extent of going to see her regularly and even giving her expensive presents. Of course, this discrepancy wasn't necessarily significant. As Debbie said, Steve might not have wanted to lose face in front of Geoff, and might have put on a show of not caring, so that Geoff could genuinely have believed that Steve hadn't wanted to get Sharon back . . . But I don't think that was so, was it, Mr Long? I think you couldn't bear to reveal to someone as impersonal as the police what Steve's feelings towards his wife really were – because they were your feelings, and to you they were private, not to be bandied about in front of a lot of unfeeling coppers . . .'

Steve had again folded his arms in apparent insouciance, but Thanet could tell that his muscles were rigid. The fingers of his visible hand were white with tension, hooked deeply into the flesh of his upper arm. Briefly, Thanet experienced a twinge of pity for the man. There was no doubt that Steve still cared deeply for his wife, and the loss of her must have been the one great sacrifice he had had to make in the course of action he had chosen to take.

'Another thing that puzzled us was why Steve had apparently not driven to Chris's house, when he went to see him on the evening of the murder. We were pretty sure that his car had been in working order, and everyone agreed that Steve wasn't the man to leave his car at home without a very good reason, so we were bound to ask ourselves, what could that good reason have been? I'll tell you the answer we came up with in a moment, when I get on to events on the night of the murder. But meanwhile, this was something that nagged away at us – like the anonymous phone call.'

'What anonymous phone call?' said Steve, sullenly.

Thanet sighed. 'If you must persist in this charade . . . At ten twenty-five on Tuesday night we had an anonymous phone call, informing us that there had been a murder at number 3 Hamilton Road. It was a man's voice – your voice, Mr Long.'

'Nonsense. I was here, with Caroline.'

'Not at ten twenty-five, you weren't. I checked. Oh, you were both here in the house, all right, but for approximately five minutes, at that time, she was in the bathroom. You had plenty of time to make that call.'

'Speculation again.'

'Maybe. But it all fits, doesn't it?'

Now that they were no longer talking about Sharon, Steve seemed more relaxed, and he shook his head in apparent disbelief.

'The point was, Mr Long, as we later realised, that it was essential that "Steve's" body be discovered while you still apparently had an alibi. You simply couldn't risk it not being found for perhaps a day or two. So you made quite sure, by informing us yourself. You wanted to make absolutely certain that you, as Geoff, would not be suspected of the murder. You had already gone to elaborate lengths to ensure this, earlier on in the evening . . . But I'll come back to that later.

'So, our investigation progressed. There certainly wasn't a lack of suspects. You've always had a knack of stirring people up, and just lately you seemed to have excelled yourself. And there was one person outside your family on whose life you had a disastrous effect.'

Long's eyebrows rose in polite enquiry. He seemed fully in control of himself again now.

'Mr Carpenter,' said Thanet. 'Ah yes, I see you recognise the name. Were you aware that his daughter's life support machine was switched off on Tuesday? You wouldn't have realised, but he spent most of Tuesday evening sitting outside your flat in his car, trying to get up the courage to kill you.'

For the first time emotion flickered across Long's face, so fleeting that Thanet almost wondered if he had imagined it. What had it been? Remorse? Fear? Regret? Or had it been triumph, elation? Thanet wondered if he had perhaps been indiscreet in telling Long about Carpenter, thus handing him a defensive weapon. But no. Thanet was certain that his case was watertight and that despite Long's apparent coolness sooner or later the man was going to have to admit it.

'But despite a plethora of suspects, except for Carpenter I just couldn't bring myself to believe that any of them had hated you enough to kill you. The one person who had apparently had no motive and who appeared as white as the driven snow, was Geoff. Now this might sound very strange to you, Mr Long, but that very fact made me look at him more closely. It is, occasionally, the most unlikely person of all who turns out to have committed a murder. But in this case everyone seemed to agree that Geoff had no possible motive. They thought he probably felt very guilty at having had so much the best of the bargain, and they all agreed that you, Mr Long, were bitterly jealous of him, even though you tried to cover up the fact by making jokes about it.'

For the second time Thanet had caught Steve on the raw. Again so briefly that if Thanet had not been watching closely he might have thought that he had imagined it, a fierce flash of emotion sparked in the navy-blue eyes, like phosphorescence in a midnight sea. Then it was gone.

'If you've nothing better to do than listen to a lot of gossip . . .'

Thanet ignored him. 'And I couldn't help thinking, now if it had been the other way around, if I had been investigating Geoff's murder, not Steve's, I could have understood it . . . I mean, it must have been truly galling for you, all those years, to see your twin getting so much more than you – not only materially, but in the way of affection, love . . . So that whereas Geoff would have had nothing to gain by killing Steve, this certainly wasn't true the other way around. Except that at that point there seemed to be no precipitating factor, no reason why Steve should suddenly have decided to kill his brother, after all these years . . .'

'But there had, of course, been a precipitating factor, though I didn't realise it at the time – the murder of Mrs Jackson and the subsequent publicity over the very unusual jacket her companion had been wearing the night she was

188

killed – the very distinctive, expensive jacket which Geoff had given you for your birthday.

'And so we come to Tuesday night, the night of Geoff's murder. By this time you were in a very precarious state of mind. You'd heard about Mrs Jackson's death, and you were naturally frightened that the police would catch up with you. You knew that Frank was likely to be on your tail the minute he found out about the fast one you'd pulled on him over the fake television deal. Chris had thrown you out on Sunday night and told you not to come back. And, worst of all, you'd just been finally rejected by Sharon, despite the gold bracelet you'd risked so much to give her.

'So, when Geoff arrived with the news of the television appeal over the jacket, you must have been feeling pretty desperate, and this was the last straw, especially when he insisted that you give yourself up. You argued, you lost your temper, you grabbed the ashtray which, ironically, Geoff himself had given you, and . . .' Thanet mimed the blow to the back of Geoff's head.

'Now you had to decide what to do. And this was the point at which the solution came to you. Why not change places with Geoff, leave all your problems behind you and grab the opportunity of starting a new life, in infinitely better circumstances? But first, you had to make sure that Geoff would not be suspected of killing Steve. You therefore had to appear as Steve to someone who knew him well, and at the same time provide Geoff with an alibi. You knew he had a date, he'd told you so, and you also knew he'd been out with the girl only once, for a couple of hours. Presumably he'd also told you where she lived. You were pretty confident you could pull it off, so you began by adding a touch of authenticity to the body by changing shoes with Geoff. You couldn't risk anyone who knew you noticing that those scruffy plimsolls you always wore had disappeared. Incidentally, it was lucky for you that Chris didn't notice you *weren't* wearing them when you called on him. Then you stuffed the coat Geoff had been wearing into a large plastic bag, together with the ashtray and the

189

incriminating jacket, and wearing your usual blue anorak you drove in Geoff's car to Chris's house. You had to leave the Scimitar out of sight, of course, which is why the neighbours reported you as leaving on foot. You left Chris at a quarter past seven and you then changed into Geoff's coat, and on the way to Caroline's house buried your own anorak, the leather jacket and possibly the ashtray in a rubbish skip. You knew that the police would work out that there simply wouldn't have been time for you to get home and for Geoff to kill you and get back to Caroline's house by half past seven. Geoff would therefore be in the clear and you'd be home and dry. All in all, it was a most ingenious plan, and it almost worked.'

Thanet paused and almost at once Long began a slow hand-clap. 'Bravo, Inspector. Bravo. You've missed your vocation. You ought to write detective stories.'

'You like my reconstruction, Mr Long?'

'Fascinating. There's only one thing wrong with it, of course. It's not true. Oh, I'll grant you that it has elements of truth, which is what makes it sound so plausible, but in essence it's a story, ingenious but with no foundation in reality. I am Geoffrey Hunt and nothing you can say or do will change that fact.'

'Won't it?' said Thanet softly.

'No. There's no way you can prove otherwise.'

'I'm afraid there's something you've forgotten, Mr Long.'

'Oh?' There was an edge of uneasiness in the monosyllable.

'Do you remember, when you were a child, you had to go into hospital?'

Long frowned. 'How can I, Inspector?' he said irritably. 'I haven't been into hospital in my entire life.'

'It was after an unfortunate incident with your step-father, in the garden. You were four years old at the time. You suffered concussion and a broken leg, and you were in hospital for some time.'

'What are you trying to say?'

'I'm saying that I've checked, and the hospital still have the X-rays they took at the time. The nature of that fracture was such that it would most certainly show up in an autopsy, many years later. The post-mortem on your brother's body showed no such fracture. The leg bones were intact, had never been broken . . .'

Something was happening to Long's face. The light of combat in the eyes was fading, the hard, fierce lines of cheek and jaw slackening as the inescapable truth of what Thanet was saying sank in.

'I presume that you would be willing to undergo some X-rays, Mr Long?'

Steve buried his face in his hands.

Silence.

Thanet and Lineham exchanged triumphant glances.

Then Long stirred, sagged back in his chair and gave a long, defeated sigh. 'OK, you win. I'd better make a statement.'

Astonishing, thought Thanet. Already Long's accent had reverted to the slurred glottal stop, the Kentish vowel sounds.

'In that case, I think we'll transfer ourselves to the police station.'

Long heaved himself wearily to his feet. 'OK.' His face hardened. 'But you might as well get one thing clear from the start, Inspector. This isn't going to be a confession. I may have changed places with Geoff, but I didn't kill him.'

TWENTY-TWO

'Chief Inspector Hines, please.'

'One moment, sir.'

Thanet gripped the receiver tightly. *Let him be out.*

Etiquette demanded he make this call, but Thanet wanted to take Steven Long's statement himself.

'Sorry, he's slipped out for a bite to eat, sir. Can I take a message?'

Relief. 'Just tell him I rang, and I'll try again later.'

'Right, sir.'

Thanet returned to the interview room. Long was insisting on making a statement about Marge Jackson's death before talking about the switch with Geoff. He wanted, he said, to get it over with. Thanet and Lineham had already arranged that, providing DCI Hines was not available, Lineham would begin the questioning.

After Geoff's birthday visit on Sunday evening, Steve had roamed restlessly around the flat for a while, drinking some cans of beer he had picked up on the way back from Chris's house. He was feeling very depressed, all the more so because earlier on his hopes had been high. Encouraged by the birthday card Sharon had sent him and knowing that Howells often played rugby on Sunday afternoons, he had counted on finding Sharon alone, and had taken along not only the birthday cake but the gold bracelet in the hope of softening her attitude towards him. Instead, he had been forced to leave, disappointed and humiliated.

After attempting to console himself with a succession of double whiskies he had gone to Chris and his wife for comfort, but once again things had gone wrong and he had succeeded only in antagonising them and being told not to come back.

By this time he had been desperate for company and

although in the normal way of things he wouldn't have been particularly pleased to see Geoff, he had appreciated the fact that his twin had remembered his birthday ('Not that he could very well have forgotten it, it was his, too') and had been disappointed at Geoff's refusal to go out for a drink with him, because of the date with Caroline.

So when Geoff left he had felt abandoned by the world. There was no one he wanted to see, except Sharon, and no one, apparently, who wanted to see him. And it was his birthday. So in the end, he had decided to go and see if he could pick up a girl.

He had tried several pubs without luck before ending up in Coddington, where he had struck lucky ('if you could call it that, she was forty, if she was a day') with Marge Jackson. By this time he was past caring what the woman was like. All he wanted was some warmth, some closeness, however artificial, to another human being. So when Marge suggested leaving he had agreed readily enough.

They had driven to a quiet place she knew, a layby off the minor road which runs through Coddington Woods. And it was there that horror struck.

It had been obvious for some minutes that Steve was approaching the part of the tale he dreaded telling. His speech had become more hesitant, his face the colour of tallow.

Until now Lineham had had to do little more than make encouraging noises.

'We were kissing, see, and, you know, getting down to it, when . . .' Steve broke off, shook his head in disgust, his face contorted.

'When what?' said Lineham.

Thanet wondered what on earth was coming. Surely Steve wasn't so innocent that any sexual ploy used by a prostitute would produce this degree of revulsion?

A complex succession of emotions chased each other across Steve's face – puzzlement, confusion, bewilderment. 'I still don't know why it got to me like that. I . . .' Steve gulped, tried again. 'One of my cuff buttons had caught in her hair and suddenly . . . suddenly it all came off, and she was . . . she was bald.'

So Marge Jackson had been wearing a wig, thought Thanet. Comprehension flooded in. Lena May, Steve's mother, also habitually wore wigs. What if she, too, suffered from partial or total hair loss? If so, there had perhaps been some traumatic incident in the past when Steve, as a child, had witnessed his mother's 'hair' come off, an incident which, though long forgotten, could have triggered off Steve's exaggerated response in the car that night.

Thanet glanced at Lineham, but the sergeant was showing no reaction. He had no doubt known about Mrs Jackson's baldness all along, but had no reason to mention it to Thanet.

'I'm still not really sure what happened next,' said Long. 'One minute there we were, getting down to it, like I said, and the next . . . It was just like if a bomb had exploded nearby.'

'Try to take it step by step,' said Lineham. 'Her wig came off, then . . .?'

'I jerked away from her and she must have realised why. I suppose her vanity was hurt or something because suddenly she just threw herself at me, screeching and swearing and hammering away at my chest with clenched fists.' Steve shook his head. 'Ever since I heard the news on the radio I've tried and tried to remember exactly what happened next, but it's just a blur. That noise she was making . . . It went through my head like an electric drill and I just wanted to shut her up, to stop her. I think I managed to get hold of both her wrists with one hand, while I tried to put the other over her mouth, but I couldn't because she kept twisting her head from side to side. So I transferred my grip to her throat, just for a few seconds, to cut off the air. But I knew I couldn't keep it up, it would be dangerous, so, very quick, before she knew what was happening, I reached across, threw open her door and shoved her out. Then I chucked her . . . her wig after her and drove off, fast. I didn't wait to see if she was all right, I just wanted shot of her. I suppose I should have checked she was OK, but all I could think of was getting away. I didn't mean to kill her, I swear I didn't.'

'Nevertheless, she fractured her skull and lay there all night, unconscious. She was still alive, just, when they found her next morning but she was dead on arrival at the hospital.'

'Oh God . . . If . . . Do you think, if I'd waited, taken her to hospital straightaway . . .?'

Lineham consulted Thanet with a glance.

Thanet shook his head. 'We don't know. All we know is that she is dead, and from what you say it would seem likely that you were responsible.'

'But I told you, I didn't mean to . . .'

'Intentions have very little to do with it at this stage, I'm afraid. Anyway, as I've already explained to you, we don't know a great deal about the case. Detective Chief Inspector Hines is in charge of it and I've no doubt he'll be along to see you as soon as I can get in touch with him. Meanwhile, my prime concern is the death of your brother. So if you don't mind I'd like to move on, now, to Tuesday evening.'

It seemed that Thanet's theory as to what happened on the night of Geoff's murder was substantially correct – with the crucial difference that, according to Steve, he was innocent of Geoff's murder.

Geoff had arrived at Steve's flat between a quarter and twenty past six. *Coast to Coast* was on TVS.

'*Did you see the beginning of the programme?*'

'*No, I've only just got in. Why?*'

'*What the hell have you been up to, Steve? That woman who was murdered in Coddington on Sunday . . .*'

'*What about her? What're you talking about?*'

'*Oh come off it, Steve, there's no point in trying to pull the wool over my eyes. Look, a man was seen with her, and there was a description of the jacket he was wearing – a grey leather jacket with a red dragon on the back . . . How many grey leather jackets with red dragons on the back d'you think there are around here?*'

'*Oh God . . .*'

'There was a sketch, too. Every five-year-old in the area would recognise that jacket if he saw it now. Where is it?'

'Oh, God. Look, Geoff, she wasn't dead when I left her, I swear . . .'

'Never mind that for the moment. I said, where's the jacket now?'

'On the back seat of the car.'

'If anyone should see it . . . Go and get it. This second. Then we'll decide what to do.'

Leaving the door to the flat ajar Steve had hurried off downstairs and along the passage to the back door. The car was parked at the back of the house and this was the quickest way to get to it. There was an outside light, but the bulb must have gone because it didn't come on when Steve depressed the switch and it took him a moment or two to adjust to the darkness.

He picked his way cautiously across to his car, and then, in his haste to open the door, dropped his keys. It had been raining earlier and there was a puddle alongside the driving door, so he had to grope about gingerly in the water and then dry the keys before finding the right one by touch and inserting it in the lock. Then he had grabbed the jacket, bundled it up under his arm and hurried back upstairs. He had seen no one, either on the way down or on the way back, though he thought that as he came in through the back door he had heard the front door close. He had been away perhaps five minutes, in all.

By now Thanet had guessed what was coming.

'As I came up the stairs I noticed my door was open wider than I'd left it. I thought the draught coming up the stairs must have done it. Until I went inside . . .

'I couldn't see Geoff at first and I thought he must've gone into the kitchen. I walked a few paces into the room and then I noticed the ashtray on the floor . . .'

'Where was it, exactly?'

'Half-way between the back of the settee and the door, and a bit to the right.'

Thanet nodded. 'Go on.'

196

'It usually stood on the sideboard. It was a present from Geoff, he'd brought it back from Italy . . . I couldn't think how it'd got on the floor, but naturally I picked it up – well, you would, wouldn't you? And then I saw there was blood on it, and on the carpet, too, underneath. It didn't register at first, what it was, but the second it clicked, I went further into the room, looking around, and . . . and there was Geoff, lying face down on the rug in front of the settee. Well, you didn't have to be a genius to see what had happened . . . I went and felt for a pulse, but there wasn't one and when I half-rolled him over and saw his eyes open like that, staring . . . Well, it was obvious he was dead.

'I just sort of collapsed into a chair and stared at him. I couldn't believe it. I'd only been away a few minutes and . . . Then it dawned on me. *Whoever had killed Geoff must have thought it was me.* After all, here he was, alone in my flat, looking just like me . . . It wouldn't have occurred to the man who killed him that it could be anyone but me. So someone out there wanted me dead, and when they found out it was Geoff who had been killed, they'd probably have another go.

'That was when I had this brilliant idea. Geoff was dead now, nothing would bring him back. Why not change places? Like you said, it seemed a stroke of genius. I was really browned off with my life, everything seemed to have been going wrong lately, and if I stepped into Geoff's shoes, I'd be able to make a fresh start. In fact, I'd be sitting pretty. Geoff's mum was dead, and I knew Geoff was moving to Staffs next week, for his new job with Scimitar. I was pretty confident I could step into his shoes, for a while, anyway. If it turned out the job was beyond me, too bad. They could fire me if they wanted to, and no one'd still be any the wiser I wasn't really Geoff. And in the meantime I thought if I lay low for a few days, kept away from his old friends on the excuse I was too busy packing and so on, no one need ever know. I'd get out of the mess I was in, over that woman on Sunday night, and also, which seemed just as important, I'd fool the character who'd done Geoff in into thinking I was dead . . . I must've sat there for a good ten minutes, working it all out, trying to think of all the snags. And in the end I thought, I'll give it a go. What have I got to lose?'

A flicker of pain crossed Steve's face at this point and Thanet knew he was thinking about Sharon.

'And I'd have everything to gain. By now I knew exactly what I was going to do, and I got on with it. I swapped my own stuff for Geoff's, keys, wallet and so on, and changed shoes with him. We've always taken the same size, and like you said, I was afraid someone might notice if he wasn't wearing my plimsolls. I never wore anything else. Then I . . . Well, you've already worked it all out, haven't you? It was just like you said, back at the house. I did wonder whether to leave that bloody jacket in the flat, and let them work out that Steve was the man they wanted in connection with Marge Jackson's death, but somehow I couldn't. Although I wasn't going to be Steve any more, I didn't want Steve blamed for a murder he hadn't done. So I decided to dump it. The ashtray was another problem. I didn't dare leave it there, because I'd got some of the blood on my fingers, and I was afraid the police would be able to tell I'd handled it after I'd apparently been killed. So I decided to dump that, too. Apart from that . . . well, like I said, you had it all worked out.'

And Steve looked at Thanet with grudging admiration.

'You were taking a bit of a risk going out with Caroline. Weren't you afraid she'd realise you weren't Geoff?'

'I had to do it. I needed that alibi. And Geoff had only been out with her once. I thought I could pull it off, and I did.'

'How did you know where she lived?'

'A bit of luck. She lives next door to a girl we both fancied at one time, and when Geoff came round on Sunday, he just happened to mention it, as a bit of a coincidence.'

'How did you know he had a date with her last night?'

'I didn't. I was just banking on it. I could tell, on Sunday night, that Geoff was pretty taken with her, and knowing he was moving in a week or so, I guessed he'd have arranged to see her again soon. If not, I thought I could always spin her some tale of not being able to wait so long before seeing her again. As I say, I was pretty sure I could pull it off.'

There was a knock at the door. Detective Chief Inspector Hines was on the phone.

Thanet and Lineham exchanged glances. *Now for it.*

'All right, Sergeant, we'll take a short break. Arrange for Mr Long to have a cup of tea or coffee, will you?'

Thanet went up to his office to take the call. He didn't want any distractions.

'Thanet here.'

'Hines. You rang earlier.'

'Yes. Things have been moving rather fast here, sir, and, well, I thought you'd like to know we've got your man.'

'What d'you mean, got my man?'

'The man who killed Mrs Jackson, sir.'

'He turned himself in, you mean?'

'Not exactly. But he is definitely the man you're after.'

'What the hell are you talking about, Thanet? You're surely not trying to tell me *you've* arrested him?'

'Well . . . Not exactly, sir. But we have cautioned him and brought him in.'

'You've WHAT?'

Thanet winced and held the receiver away from his ear as Hines started bellowing down the phone.

'What the devil d'you think you're playing at, Thanet? How DARE you interfere in my case like this?'

'Well, it wasn't exactly your case, sir. You see . . .'

'What d'you mean, "not my case"?'

'Well, we were . . .'

'I don't know what you're babbling about, Thanet, but get one thing straight. I'm going to have your guts for garters. I'll be right over.'

And the phone was slammed down. Thanet grinned at it and gave it a pat, as if it were a particularly obedient dog.

Lineham put his head around the door.

'What did he say, sir?'

'He wasn't exactly over the moon, Mike. Come on, let's go

199

back down to Long. As soon as Mr Hines gets here, we're not going to get a look in.'

Long was sunk in gloom, tea untouched.

'Detective Chief Inspector Hines will be here shortly, Mr Long. But before he arrives, just tell me this. Give me one good reason why I should believe your story that someone else killed Geoff while you were out of the room, and that the idea of changing places only occurred to you *after* he was dead?'

'Because it's true! I swear it is!'

'Maybe, but there's no way of proving it, is there?'

'There's no way of proving I did kill him, either.'

'True. At present, anyway. So what it's going to come down to is whether the jury would believe your version or mine. What do you think, Mr Long? Do you think they'll take the word of a man who, on his own admission, half-strangled a woman and then drove off, leaving her to die, and a couple of days later seized the opportunity of stepping into his dead brother's wealthy shoes and deceiving everyone – wife, family and police alike – into thinking that he himself was dead?'

Long stared up at Thanet, obviously assessing the truth of what he had just said, and then slumped back in his chair, as if acknowledging defeat.

'As a matter of interest,' he said, 'would it have been more sensible to have left the ashtray where it was?'

His tone was casual. Too casual?

Two could play at that game. Careful not to betray his quickened interest, Thanet shrugged. 'Difficult to tell. I can quite see why you decided to take it away with you. On the other hand, we might have found one or two nice clear prints which could have led us straight to the murderer. So on balance, I'd say that looking at it from your point of view, at the time it was obviously sensible to remove the ashtray, but that now you've been found out, if you could wave a wand and magically whisk it back from wherever it is, you would be wise to do so. But as that's impossible, I think it's a waste of time talking about it. I think you'd be wiser to concentrate on . . .'

'But it's not,' interrupted Long.

'Not what?' said Thanet, innocently.

'Not impossible.'

Thanet pretended enlightenment. 'Are you saying you didn't actually dump the ashtray in that skip, along with the jacket and your anorak?'

'That's right.' There was a hint of triumph in Long's voice now, and the beginning of a smile in his eyes.

'So . . .?'

'I just couldn't make up my mind, see, whether it would be better to get rid of it or not. So I hid it where I thought it would be least likely to be found.'

'In one of the packing cases full of china, I bet,' said Lineham.

Long looked crestfallen. 'How did you . . .?'

Thanet grinned. 'You can't do this job for long without getting rather good at that kind of guess. Which packing case?'

'The one marked "FRAGILE. HANDLE WITH CARE".'

'Keys?' said Thanet, holding out his hand. By now the men from the auctioneers would have finished, the house would be locked up.

Long handed them over and Thanet gave them to Lineham, taking him into the corridor outside. 'Get Carson on to it right away. Tell him – no, on second thoughts, I'd prefer you to do it yourself. You know what we're looking for. As soon as you find it, take it personally to forensic and stress the urgency. I'll give them a ring myself, in the meantime. In view of this rather tricky situation with Hines, it would help if we could get our own case cleared up quickly.'

'Like, yesterday,' said Lineham with a grin.

'Quite.'

'You think Long's telling the truth, then?'

In the distance there was a sudden commotion. Hines's voice could clearly be heard demanding to know where Thanet was.

'Not now, Mike.' Thanet gave Lineham an encouraging little push on the arm. 'Off you go.'

Lineham resisted. 'You'll be needing some moral support.'

'Mike! I can handle it. Go on, hurry up, or you'll get tangled up with Mr Hines and you'll never get away.'

Lineham capitulated. 'I'll be as quick as I can.'

'Thanet!' Hines had spotted him, and such was his single-minded concentration on the object of his wrath that he passed Lineham without noticing him. He charged along the corridor like an angry bull, head down, feet pounding. Thanet could almost see the angry little puffs of hot breath issuing from his nostrils.

'Well?' he roared. 'This had better be good, Thanet, or . . .'

Thanet had no intention of enduring a flood of abuse from Hines out here, where every word would be public. During Hines's advance he had opened the door of an empty interview room and now he backed into it. Hines charged in behind him and Thanet shut the door.

'. . . or you'll be sorry you ever heard of Marge Jackson.'

'Won't you sit down, sir?' Thanet was all courtesy.

'No, I bloody well won't sit down. I don't want a chair, I want – I *demand* – an explanation.'

'And I'm quite happy to give you one. Please . . .' Thanet indicated the chair he had pulled out.

Hines glared at him suspiciously. 'Very well,' he said, sitting down with a thump and folding his arms belligerently. 'No one can say that I'm not a reasonable man. But, as I said, it had better be good.'

Thanet launched into his explanation of how he had come to suspect a possible connection between the two cases.

Hines listened intently, his little piggy eyes glittering with a dangerous light. At the end he grunted contemptuously. 'If that's the way you work, Thanet . . . A load of airy-fairy notions and half-baked guesswork . . . Anyway, that's beside the point. The point is that the second, *the very second* you suspected that your case might be impinging on mine, you should have informed me. As your superior officer, it should have been up to me to decide how to proceed.'

He stood up with a jerk that almost toppled his chair over

202

backwards. 'You haven't heard the last of this, by a long chalk. I shall seriously consider making a formal complaint. Now, where's Long? I think it's about time *I* had a word with him.'

'In interview room 3, sir.'

Hines opened the door, glanced along the corridor and bellowed, 'Draycott?'

The sergeant hurried towards them, almost at a run.

'We're going to interview the suspect,' said Hines. And with one last venomous glance at Thanet he and Draycott disappeared through the door of interview room 3.

Thanet took a deep sigh of relief and felt in his pocket for his pipe. He was sorry for Long. He wouldn't wish a long session with Hines on to his worst enemy. Then he hurried up the stairs to his office. With luck he could persuade Specks, in forensic, to rush through the tests on the ashtray. He sent up a fervent prayer that they would provide him with some good, sound evidence.

TWENTY-THREE

All six houses in Benenden Drive were individually designed, generously proportioned, and set in extensive wooded grounds of an acre or so.

'At least five bedrooms, wouldn't you say?' murmured Lineham as he swung into the gravelled drive of 'Smallwood' and parked neatly beside the porticoed front door.

'We're not estate agents, Mike.'

Manicured lawns stretched away on all sides, bordered by well-tended flowerbeds, and at the far end of the garden beneath a stand of deciduous trees a man was busy raking up fallen leaves and piling them into a wheelbarrow.

'Full-time gardener too, by the look of it,' added Lineham, undeterred by Thanet's mild rebuke.

Thanet did not reply. He had been notified that morning that Harry Carpenter was insisting that he was well enough to go home and that the hospital intended to discharge him. Thanet imagined him now, drifting like an aimless ghost through the empty rooms of the big house which he and his wife must have bought – perhaps even planned and built – with such pride. Carpenter was a self-made man, and this spacious neo-Georgian house would have been for them a symbol of all that he had achieved. Thanet shook his head sadly as he and Lineham climbed the short flight of steps between the white pillars.

The door was opened by a dowdy middle-aged woman wearing an old-fashioned crossover apron and carrying a duster. She looked worried.

'May we speak to Mr Carpenter, please?'

'Who shall I say?'

Thanet introduced himself and presented his identification card, which she studied carefully before handing it back.

'You can't be too careful, these days.'

'Quite right,' said Thanet as she stepped back and gestured them in. 'How is Mr Carpenter?'

She hesitated.

'It's all right. We do know what's been happening to him, and that he only got back from hospital this morning.'

She shook her head, her mouth turned down, and with a glance at the door on the left drew them away to the far side of the hall. 'To tell you the truth I'm ever so worried about him,' she said in a low voice. 'Ever since he got back he's been sitting in there not saying a word. He didn't so much as touch his lunch . . .'

'You've been with him long?'

'About eighteen months.'

'Since before the accident, then.'

'Yes.' She shook her head again, mournfully. 'You'd hardly believe this is the same house. When I first came there was people in and out all day long – Mrs Carpenter knew loads of people, and Chrissie's friends were forever coming and going. There'd be a dinner party at least once a week and always people here for lunch and tea on Sundays . . .' She sighed. 'It was a lot of work, but I enjoyed it. But now . . . Ever since Mrs Carpenter died . . . And then Chrissie, on Tuesday, poor little scrap . . . The place is like a morgue.' She clapped her hand to her mouth. 'Oh, I'm sorry. I didn't mean . . . Anyway, the point is, I've never seen Mr Carpenter quite as bad as this.'

'You really are worried about him, aren't you?'

'Well, before Chrissie died he never lost hope. He kept on saying he believed she'd get better, that he had to believe it, or go mad. He did everything a human being could do, in the circumstances. He got one of them coma kits, so as to see how to go about it, and he'd sit up hour after hour in the evenings, trying to put together the things he thought were most likely to get through to Chrissie – the voices of her friends, the whinny of her pony and the sounds of him feeding, trotting, being groomed . . . oh, all sorts of things, I can't tell you. And he'd spend hours at the hospital every day, talking to her, playing her all the tapes . . .' The woman was almost in tears

205

by now. She took out a handkerchief and blew her nose. 'If there was any justice in the world,' she said, 'Mr Carpenter would have been rewarded for all that effort, all that faith, and Chrissie would be home and running about by now . . .'

'You were obviously very fond of the family.'

'Oh I was. I am. They're really nice people. I've worked for a lot of families, and I know what employers can be like. But the Carpenters – they were always so kind, so appreciative . . . You don't find many like that around these days, I can tell you.'

Especially self-made men, who've probably had to claw and struggle their way up, thought Thanet. Carpenter, then, was that rare creature, a man with sufficient determination to get to the top and the ability to retain his humility when he got there. It seemed unfair that the personal hell he had had to endure for the last year should have been his reward.

'It's so unfair,' said the housekeeper, echoing his thoughts. She glanced at the door across the hall again. 'To be honest, the state he's in, I'm surprised they let him come home from the hospital. I don't think he's safe to be left alone, I really don't.'

'You don't live in?'

'Yes, we do. Ron – that's my husband, he's the gardener – and me've got a self-contained flat in the house, but that's not the point. I can't keep an eye on him all the time – what about at night? He's alone for hours then. He could do anything.'

'You mean, commit suicide?'

She nodded, lips compressed.

'You really think it's a serious possibility?'

'You'll see for yourself . . . I'm very relieved you've come, I can tell you.'

The poor woman wouldn't be so relieved when she knew why, thought Thanet as she led them across to the door she had been looking at, and knocked. 'Mr Carpenter?'

No reply.

She tried again. 'Someone to see you, Mr Carpenter.'

This time there was a faint response and she opened the door, ushered them in.

The room was obviously Carpenter's study. It was luxuriously furnished – Persian rug on the parquet floor, heavy velvet curtains, antique mahogany kneehole desk, opulent swivel desk chair, floor-to-ceiling bookshelves laden with leather-bound volumes, a set of Jorrocks hunting prints. For Carpenter, dust and ashes all, now, thought Thanet.

A coal fire burned in the hearth and before it, slumped in a green leather wing chair, was Carpenter. Had he chosen this room because it held the fewest memories of his wife and daughter? Thanet wondered.

'Good afternoon, Mr Carpenter.'

'So you've come at last.' The man's speech was slow, almost slurred, as if he had just woken from a long sleep. 'Thank you, Mrs Epps.' And he nodded, dismissing her.

Thanet waited until the door had closed behind her, then said, 'You've been expecting us?'

'I knew you'd get around to it, sooner or later, when you'd eliminated all the other possibilities.' He paused. 'You didn't believe me yesterday, did you?'

'We weren't sure what to believe. You were very . . . confused.'

'I know.' Carpenter eased himself up a little straighter in his chair. 'Well, I'm not confused now – not, at least, over the part that matters. Do sit down, Inspector . . . Thanet, was it?'

'That's right. And this is Detective Sergeant Lineham.'

When they were seated, Thanet said, 'Are you saying that what you told us last time wasn't true?'

'To be honest, I'm not sure exactly what I did tell you, last time. Tuesday was still a blur in my mind, then. I wasn't even sure if I had killed him, until you told me he was dead. But when you did . . . Well, I was suddenly certain, then, that I had. But I couldn't remember the details, so I just told you what I thought must have happened, as I'd imagined it happening,

207

over and over again, while I was waiting for it to be time for me to go and see him, on Tuesday.'

It looked as though they needn't have bothered to rush through the tests on the ashtray after all, Thanet thought. Carpenter was obviously bent on making a full confession. A clear set of prints had in fact confirmed what Thanet suspected – that it had been Carpenter, the most likely suspect of all, who had delivered that fatal blow to Geoff's head, thinking him to be Steve.

'One moment, Mr Carpenter. In view of your confusion yesterday, I think it would be advisable to caution you again.' Thanet glanced at Lineham and nodded.

But Carpenter was waving his hand dismissively. 'You needn't bother. I remember it quite clearly, and in any case it doesn't matter. I'm not going to deny anything, now or later. I killed Long, it's as simple as that. And I can't pretend I'm anything but glad.'

Thanet wondered what Carpenter's reaction would be, when he discovered that he had murdered the wrong man.

'Do you want to tell us about it?'

Carpenter nodded. 'It'll make it more real. Until today it's all been so . . . fragmented, in my mind. At times I've even wondered if it was all a dream . . .'

'But you don't think so any longer?'

'No. When I woke up this morning, I had a clear memory of what had happened, for the first time.'

There was little that was new in Carpenter's story. Thanet had already worked most of it out for himself.

Carpenter had arrived in Hamilton Road at around a quarter past six. He thought that Long would probably be home from work by then. He knew where Long lived, even knew which was his flat, because at one point during the long months of waiting for Chrissie to regain consciousness he had gone to Hamilton Road with the intention of venting his anger and grief upon the man responsible for her condition. But Long had been out, Carpenter had come away unsatisfied, and the impulse which had driven him there had not returned

– until Tuesday, after Chrissie's death. On that occasion his purpose had been much more deadly. Quite simply, he had been bent on murder.

'I'm sorry, may I interrupt for a moment, there?' said Thanet.

'Of course.'

'How, exactly, did you intend to kill Mr Long?'

'You may not believe this, Inspector, but I really hadn't thought. I suppose I imagined I was going to choke the life out of him with my bare hands, or something like that . . . Sounds crazy, doesn't it? The truth is, I *was* crazy, I suppose. I was just in a daze of grief and misery. When I got home from the hospital after my daughter . . . When I got home from the hospital I took a couple of Valium . . .'

'What time was that?' said Thanet, sharply.

Carpenter frowned. 'I'm not sure. Mid-afternoon, I suppose. Why?'

'When we picked you up you'd obviously been drinking heavily. Whisky. Did you have anything to drink before you went to Hamilton Road?'

'I'd certainly had a few, I admit.'

'A few? What time did you start drinking, do you remember?'

Carpenter frowned.

'Around five, I should think.'

'Thank you. Go on . . . You were saying that you got there at around a quarter past six.'

'Somewhere around then.'

He had just pulled up when in the light from the street-lamp he saw Long come running along the pavement and turn in to the driveway of number 3. Because of the combined effect of tranquillisers and alcohol his reaction was slow. Long had disappeared into the house before Carpenter had really registered who it was.

Thanet and Lineham exchanged glances. *That was Geoff. Steve was already home.*

Carpenter had taken one final long slug of whisky before

209

getting out of the car and entering the house. As he came into the hall a door slammed at the back of the house, but he had paid no attention and had made his way up the stairs to Long's flat. The door was ajar and Long was sitting on the settee, with his back to him. As Carpenter pushed the door open with his elbow Long turned his head, revealing himself in profile, and said, 'You really are a bloody fool, you know.' The words were a match to gunpowder. All Carpenter's despair, suppressed by force of will throughout the long months of hope of Chrissie's eventual recovery, erupted now in an explosion of anger against the man he saw as the murderer of his wife and child. With just enough sense left to realise that in his condition he was no match for a much younger and presumably fitter man, he had looked around wildly for a weapon. The ashtray had been to hand and he had grasped it, staggered forward the necessary couple of paces and brought it down on Long's head with all the strength he could muster. Long had toppled forward and sprawled on the hearthrug. Carpenter had not waited to check that he was dead. Having done what he had set out to do, all he wanted now was to get away. Dropping the ashtray he had retreated back down the stairs and returned to his car.

His story told, Carpenter lifted his hands and dropped them in his lap with a gesture of finality. 'And that's it, Inspector. After that, I can remember practically nothing.'

But it wasn't quite as simple as that, thought Thanet. Now they were coming to the really difficult part.

'When you went into the room and the man said, "You really are a bloody fool, you know," you assumed he was talking to you, personally?'

'Yes, I did . . . Oh . . .' Carpenter broke off and stared at Thanet, obviously taking his point. 'I suppose he couldn't have been. He didn't actually turn his head far enough around to see who I was.'

'Quite.'

'I was pretty drunk, of course, and it simply didn't occur to

210

me that he could have been addressing someone else. There was no one else in the room.'

'But the door was open, you remember. Didn't that strike you as odd on a cold November evening?'

Carpenter shook his head. 'I can't say it did. I'm sorry, Inspector, but I really wasn't thinking logically . . . You're implying, of course, that he was expecting someone.'

'Expecting someone *back*, actually.'

Thanet's tone must have conveyed to Carpenter something of his reluctance to proceed beyond this point, because Carpenter looked at him sharply and said, 'You're working up to telling me something, aren't you, Inspector. What?'

'I'm sorry, Mr Carpenter. There's no way I can diminish the pain I'm going to cause you, when I tell you . . . He was expecting his *twin* back.'

'His . . . twin?'

Carpenter's face went blank as he stared at Thanet and realised the implication of what Thanet had just said.

'Oh, my God,' he whispered at last. 'You're not trying to say . . .'

'I'm afraid so. You killed the wrong man.'

TWENTY-FOUR

Thanet put an arm around Bridget's shoulders and gave her a brief hug. 'Good luck, then.'

The South-East regional heats of the Junior Chef of the Year competition were about to get under way.

The Fletcher Hall at the Black Swan, Sturrenden's premier venue for wedding receptions, Ladies' Nights and the glossier public functions, had been transformed for the occasion into something resembling the Domestic Science room of a well-equipped comprehensive school: gleaming electric cookers (by courtesy of the South-East Electricity Board), each with its surrounding island of work surfaces and basic cooking equipment, were spaced out along one side. Chairs for the audience waited expectantly, with reserved notices for the judges in the front row. It was now half past nine and doors would open to the public at ten thirty. The competitors had all arrived and were left to unpack their ingredients and equipment. Pairs of anxious parents were drifting towards the door, the Thanets among them. Ben was not there, having been picked for the school football team for the first time, to play in an away match.

'She looks quite cheerful, don't you think?' said Thanet, with one last backward glance over his shoulder.

Joan took his arm and smiled. 'If practice makes perfect, she should be able to get through the whole thing blind-folded.'

'She's never done it with an audience before, though. It's quite different.'

'She'll be all right.' Joan gave Thanet's arm a little shake. 'Don't worry, darling. I think you're more nervous than she is.'

'And you, of course, couldn't care less.'

She grinned back at him. 'I just hide it better, that's all.'

'What on earth are we going to do for the next hour? It's too early for coffee.'

'It's a beautiful morning. Let's walk down to the river.'

'Why not?'

It was still too early for the Saturday morning crowds to have arrived and they both enjoyed the novel experience of a leisurely stroll along Sturrenden's picturesque High Street. At the bottom, near the river, it widens out into a broad, cobbled area called Market Square, and it was in a tranquil little Victorian cul-de-sac nearby that the Linehams lived.

'Oh, by the way,' said Joan, glancing in that direction. 'I forgot to tell you. I ran into Louise yesterday afternoon and they've got a reprieve.'

'You mean, Mrs Lineham didn't get the house?'

'That's right. Apparently the vendor had agreed that Mrs Lineham could have it provided no one came along with the ready money before the negotiations were too far advanced. Mrs Lineham, of course, has to wait to sell her own house. Anyway, she was unlucky. Some people who've been living abroad turned up, cash in hand, so to speak. So that was that.'

'What a relief, eh? Perhaps it'll compensate a bit for the disappointment over the promotion.'

They strolled in silence for a few minutes and then Joan said, 'You didn't have a chance to tell me properly what Superintendent Parker said, about Mr Hines's complaint.'

After Carpenter's arrest yesterday, there had been much to do. Thanet had managed to get home to supper and tell Joan the gist of what had happened, but it had been difficult with the children about, and she had long been in bed and asleep when he eventually got home in the early hours. He had been determined to clear up as much of the paperwork as possible in order to be free this morning.

'Ah, yes. Well, it was most impressive, really. I'm still not sure how he did it, but he somehow managed to reprimand me and compliment me at the same time. And he persuaded Hines to let the matter drop. Reading between the lines I got the impression that he'd hinted that it was Hines who'd come off worst if he pursued the matter – be made to look a bit of a fool. And of course Hines wouldn't enjoy that one little bit.'

'Odious man,' said Joan, with feeling.

'Not my favourite policeman, I agree.'

They had reached the bridge now and they descended the long flight of stone steps to the paved walkway along the river bank. It was another perfect late autumn day: bright sunshine, cloudless sky and crisp, cool air still tinged with a breath of early-morning frost. There was no wind, and the bare branches of the cherry trees hung in motionless contemplation of their mirror-images in the water below. A pair of swans and a gaggle of assorted ducks converged on the Thanets, eyeing them hopefully.

'We should have brought some bread,' said Joan.

'We didn't know we'd be coming down to the river, did we?'

'Luke, last night, after you'd gone back to work, I was thinking about the case . . . How did Steve react, when he knew his plan had failed? Was he angry?'

'Strangely enough, no. Initially I think he felt defeated, fed up, and then he was, well, just resigned, I suppose. It was as if, all along, he never really believed he could pull it off.'

'That fits. Nothing's ever gone right for him, has it? By now it would be surprising if he didn't automatically expect things to go wrong. What about his family? How did they feel, when they heard the news?'

Thanet grimaced. 'I don't think they knew what they felt, especially as they heard at the same time that he was under arrest for the murder of Marge Jackson. To be honest, I think his mother and two brothers would have been relieved if he'd stayed "dead". I don't think any of them cares tuppence about him. Sharon, of course, is a different matter. I think she's genuinely fond of him, but finds it impossible to cope with him.' Thanet shook his head. 'It's difficult to tell how she feels. I don't think she really knows, herself. Relieved . . . Appalled . . . Sorry for him . . . Of course, as far as he's concerned, the one good thing about having been found out is that, theoretically at least, he now has a chance of edging his way back into her life.'

'I still find it difficult to believe that she identified the body as Steve, when it was Geoff. Oh I know you'll say they were identical twins, but even so . . . her *husband* . . . And she still insisted that it was Steve, even after you'd put to her the possibility that it might be Geoff.'

'Yes, but you've got to remember that people in that particular situation don't look very carefully. They are in a highly emotional state, and they see what they *expect* to see. They *expect* the dead body to look different from the live person they knew. And in this instance, Sharon had been told that her husband had been found dead in his flat, therefore she *expected* to see Steve's body in the mortuary. So she did. Why on earth should she think it was his twin brother? Even after I suggested the possibility, it would have seemed a very bizarre notion to her.'

'Yes, I see what you mean . . .'

They walked in silence for a minute or two and then Joan said, 'What I don't see, though, is how you made the connection between the two cases.'

'Ah, now that's much more difficult to explain. But I'll try. You remember the night we sat up late, talking? Well, afterwards, I found it impossible to get to sleep, so for a while I read that book Doc Mallard lent me. Then I just lay there, thinking – trying to relate what I'd been reading to Steve and Geoff, and going over everything that had happened during the day. And suddenly it all just . . . coalesced.'

'But how? Why?'

'It was simply a matter of a lot of apparently unrelated little facts coming together and making sense. As I say, I'd been thinking of Geoff and Steve, and how Geoff was the only person in the family who had even bothered to send Steve a birthday card. And I suppose it crossed my mind to wonder if he'd given him a present, too. Then I was thinking about the murder weapon, the ashtray, and wondering where it was, thinking it had probably been dumped somewhere, like the jacket in Hines's case. And I thought about the jacket itself, with that very unusual design on the back, the red dragon, and suddenly I remembered that when I'd gone to Geoff's house, in amongst all the stuff he was in the process of packing, I'd seen two brand-new Welsh blankets, still in their polythene bags. I recognised them because of the distinctive pattern that's woven into them – if you remember, your mother brought one back when she went to Wales on holiday last year. And suddenly I thought, of course! The red dragon – the national emblem of Wales! What if the jacket had been bought in Wales? What if Geoff had bought it, at the same time as the blankets, and had given it to Steve, as a birthday present? *What if Steve was the murderer of Mrs Jackson?*

'It seemed such a wild idea that at first I didn't know whether to take it seriously, but the more I thought about it, the more I came to believe it could, just possibly, be true.' Thanet grinned. 'I didn't tell you, but I sat up half the night, in the kitchen, thinking about it. Because once I'd decided it could be true I started to work out how it might affect our investigation, and I realised at once that it could provide a missing link. Up until then we could see no reason why Geoff should have murdered Steve, or vice versa. But now, if Geoff had given that jacket to Steve, and had seen the television appeal, if that was why he went to see Steve early on Tuesday evening – to persuade him to give himself up . . . If Steve had refused, then lost his temper, killed him and then changed places with him, to save his own skin . . .'

'An awful lot of "ifs".'

'I know. That's why I didn't want to tell you who I thought the murderer was, yesterday morning. I wanted to check one or two things first – whether or not Geoff had in fact given Steve the jacket, and whether or not that leg injury which Steve had had as a child was the kind to show up in an adult. If so, I knew I had him. The body which was supposed to be Steve's had no such injury. But the more I thought about it, the more convinced I became that I was right, and Steve had

216

taken Geoff's place. There were various things which backed up the idea.'

Briefly, Thanet explained about Steve's left-handedness, about the weight difference, and about Steve's reputed ability to mimic Geoff. 'Debbie, Frank May's wife, had told me that Steve had made them laugh by "taking Geoff off".'

'Ah, I did wonder,' said Joan. 'I must admit I thought it a bit unlikely that Steve, who'd had to leave school at sixteen, would be able to imitate convincingly the vocabulary and speech patterns of a graduate.' She spotted a crust of bread lying on the grass, a leftover from the previous day's largesse. She stooped to pick it up, then broke it into several pieces and tossed it into the ever-hopeful little flotilla of ducks which had been cruising along, keeping pace with them. For a few moments there was flapping, squawking bedlam.

'Pity we haven't got any more,' she said.

'Do you think ducks like lemon flummery?' said Thanet. 'We could always pop down after the competition's over.'

They both laughed. 'I'm not sure Sprig would appreciate that,' said Joan. 'And talking about the competition, what's the time?'

Thanet consulted his watch. 'Ten o'clock. Better be getting back.'

They turned, unconsciously speeding up a little.

'No,' said Thanet, picking up the thread of their coversation again. 'I think – well, in fact I know – that you're underestimating Steve. The IQ of twins is very similar, and the findings in the book were quite positive. There might be some personality differences owing to dissimilar environmental influences, but there was still an astonishing resemblance between identical twins brought up apart, in terms of voice, habits, mannerisms . . . I'm not saying it would have been easy for Steve to step into Geoff's shoes, but he had a better chance of succeeding than most, especially as the adoptive mother was dead. He had a lot to lose if he was found out, remember, and I should think the thought of a murder

217

charge would be enough to make anyone give the performance of his life . . .

'No, I think the impersonation was feasible, but a strain. It was interesting how quickly he reverted to his own accent once he knew that I could actually *prove* he was Steve. Where I went wrong was in jumping to the conclusion that if Steve had taken Geoff's place, then he was also the one who killed him.'

Joan frowned. 'He may not have actually killed Geoff, but he was still to a large degree responsible for his death, wasn't he?'

'What do you mean?'

'Well, if Steve hadn't been involved in the death of Marge Jackson, and Geoff hadn't seen the TV appeal and gone along to warn him that the police were looking for him, Geoff would still be alive today.'

'True . . . However sorry you feel for Steve because of his rotten childhood, there's no denying that he has, as you once said yourself, a kind of destructive power. Look at all the people whose lives he's damaged . . .'

Joan nodded. 'And the ones who have actually *died*, because of him. Mrs Carpenter, her daughter, Mrs Jackson, Geoff . . . It's terrifying, really. Perhaps it's as well society is going to be protected from him, for a while, at least. How long will he get, d'you think?'

'Difficult to tell.'

'I suppose he'll plead not guilty to the murder of Mrs Jackson and get away with manslaughter?'

'Probably.'

'So, seven years, perhaps?'

'Something like that, I should think. With possibly another twelve months on top, for obstructing the police – in deliberately misleading us over the identity of the body and then compounding the deception by pretending to be his brother . . .'

'What about poor Mr Carpenter?'

'That's a bit tricky. The trouble is that however many excuses you might make for him, the fact remains that he went

218

to Steve's flat with murder in his heart and actually killed someone. That it happened not to be the person he thought it was probably won't make a scrap of difference. Premeditated murder is premeditated murder.'

'Quite. I suppose the only way he could hope to get away with less than a life sentence would be by pleading diminished responsibility.'

'Yes. His counsel might well pull it off. He'd emphasise the long strain Carpenter had suffered . . .'

'The shock of Chrissie's death, that day . . .'

'And he'd stress the fact that although Carpenter freely admits he intended killing Steve, he didn't actually equip himself to do so – he didn't take a gun or any other weapon with him. So the defence could argue that the threats were really empty ones and Carpenter hadn't really intended to do more than have a stand-up fight.'

'There's the drink and drugs angle, too,' said Joan. 'Everyone knows by now that a combination of tranquillisers and spirits is disastrous, and that self-control is diminished to the point of non-existence.'

'On the other hand, it won't help Carpenter that all the while he thought it was Steve he had killed he showed no remorse whatsoever.'

'How did he react, when he found he'd killed the wrong man?'

'He was absolutely shattered. Appalled that he'd killed an innocent bystander . . .'

'And furious that Steve had escaped, after all?'

'No, I don't think so. I think that by then the first flush of his anger against Steve after Chrissie's death had worn off. I certainly don't think that at that point he would have been prepared to go off and kill Steve in cold blood . . . That was why the fact that he'd killed someone else by mistake was so horrifying to him. He's not by nature a violent man. His counsel will stress this fact, and rely upon it becoming apparent during the course of the trial . . . I should think Carpenter will probably end up with five or six years.'

'You liked him, didn't you?'

'Yes, I did. And I couldn't help feeling sorry for him. I suppose I couldn't help identifying with him, in a way, wondering how I would have felt, if it had been you who had been killed, Sprig who had died that day . . . I'd like to think that under no circumstances would I ever commit murder, but the fact is that we can never tell how we would react, in extremity. Most of us are never pushed beyond our limit of tolerance . . .'

Joan shivered. 'Thank God.'

They had almost reached the hotel now. A steady trickle of people was flowing through the doors of the Fletcher Hall, which had an entrance on the street. Joan pressed Thanet's arm. 'Look, there's Doctor Mallard and Mrs Field.'

The new, benevolent Doc Mallard had spotted them and raised a hand in greeting. The Thanets joined him and Luke was duly introduced to the woman who had wrought this wondrous change in his old friend. She seemed, as Joan had said, absolutely right for him, a plump, smiling little woman with calm, kind eyes as blue as forget-me-nots and laughter lines around eyes and mouth. She was neatly dressed in navy blue coat and flowered silk scarf. Thanet thoroughly approved and greeted her warmly. He was amused to see that the little doctor was blushing.

'Kind of you to come,' said Thanet.

'Oh, not at all. Fly the flag for Bridget and all that. And Helen's very interested in cooking, aren't you?'

'Very.'

'Writes cookery books, as a matter of fact,' said Mallard, with shy pride.

'Oh, *that* Helen Fields!' said Joan. 'Bridget would be fascinated. She'd really love to meet you.'

'And I'd be delighted to meet her. I'm always interested in young people who are keen on cooking.'

'Keen isn't the word,' said Thanet. 'The amount of practice she's done for this competition . . .'

Chatting, they moved into the hall and seated themselves

where they would have a good view of what Bridget was doing without being disconcertingly close.

At ten thirty sharp the competition got under way. The proceedings were briefly explained to the audience. There were ten competitors, of ages ranging from nine to sixteen. Each had brought his own utensils and ingredients, had decorated his own table, and would have an hour and a half to prepare two dishes, a main course and a pudding. Presentation was important, but taste would be the main decider. The judges were a cookery writer, the owner of a famous London restaurant, and the editor of *Food and Wine* magazine. The winner and the runner-up would go on to the National Finals in London, in April.

Time flew. The contestants settled down to concentrated activity, apparently oblivious of the audience. Delicious smells filled the air, mouths salivated. At last it was over and the judges moved from table to table as the youngsters stood by, ready to answer questions on their handiwork. The Thanets strained to hear as Bridget, two bright spots of colour burning in her cheeks, responded to the enquiries put to her.

Finally, the judges retired to the far end of the room to confer. Tension mounted as the young cooks and their anxious parents awaited the verdict. Thanet's mouth was dry and he and Joan exchanged supportive glances. At last the announcer approached the microphone, accompanied by the chairman of the judges. A cathedral hush immediately fell upon the room.

After the usual inordinately long preamble about the high quality of the food produced by the contestants and a string of compliments on their talent and originality, the judge at last raised the piece of paper upon which every eye had been riveted.

'I shall announce the results in reverse order. The runner-up is fifteen-year-old Karen Cunningham of Benenden, for her Smoked Haddock with Cream and Egg Sauce, and Hazelnut Roll.'

Applause. Karen came forward, obviously delighted to have won through to the finals.

221

There was an electric silence as the remaining nine contestants stood rigid with hope and fear and their parents agonised with them. Thanet felt sick.

'And now the result you are all waiting for . . .'

Come on, come *on*, urged Thanet silently.

'The winner, for her Pork Chops with Mint, which she tells us is an old recipe published in the *Daily News* in the excellent series that appeared during the winter of 1928–9, and for her Lemon Flummery, exquisitely decorated with the white horse of Kent, is thirteen-year-old Bridget Thanet of Sturrenden.'

Thanet felt as though he would explode with relief, delight and pride as Bridget stepped forward, eyes shining. No achievement of his own had ever affected him quite so profoundly. He and Joan clutched at each other's hands and exchanged exuberant smiles before turning to receive congratulations from Doc Mallard and Mrs Field.

Released by the judges at last, Bridget pushed her way through the crowd towards them, acknowledging the compliments showered upon her from all sides.

Thanet put an arm around Joan as they smiled down into their daughter's radiant face, and they all linked hands.

It was a moment of pure joy.